Scott Palter, Mike Rohde and Markus Baur

Deaths on the Nile
The Reich Without Hitler Book 2

ISBN: 978-1-938339-47-9
By Scott Palter with Mike Rohde and Markus Baur
Major Content Assistance from: Markus Baur, Marco Pertoni, Mike Rohde
Content Assistance: Jason Long
Soviet, Israeli, Zionist and Russian content assistance: Igor Bunimovich
German and Nazi background for initial ATL creation: Erik Fischer
Coming up with Coxita's full Catalan name plus a bit of Mexico City geography: Kier Salmon
Other Assistance: Fred McCann, Duane Oldsen, Don Hoban, Richard Moncure, Tony Zbaraschuk

Editing: Richard Moncure
Layout and Cover: Sam Pray
All errors remain mine: Scott Palter
Capitalizations and terms: German and English have different conventions for what nouns to capitalize when. We have mostly German and English speaking POV characters and have tried to be faithful to the two grammatical traditions depending on whether we are seeing the world through German or Anglophone eyes. We have tried to do the same with pounds versus kilograms, the two systems of temperature and miles versus kilometers. I am sure I slipped up multiple someplaces but that is the logic.

Isaac v Isaak: Same man but Isaac Cohen is for obvious reasons Isaak Schwabe. Which is used is a matter of social context.

Fan Group: The Reich Without Hitler at groups.io

Facebook Fan Group: The Falcons of Malta. (Yes, in Book 1 it says the Facebook Group is The Reich Without Hitler. Facebook canceled that group for violating community standards, reinstated it after I explained that we were not Nazi groupies, and then canceled it again without explaining why or answering any of my requests to discuss the matter. The magic word Hitler was enough. Hence the great renaming.)

The fan groups have general WW2 material, some in-greater-depth discussion of this ATL, and advance chapters on the next book in production, which will be Volume 3: *Jerusalem of Gold*. I plan to have that book out for first quarter of 2020. I planned to have this book, #2, out early December of 2018 and will be at least nine months late. I am optimistic on how fast I can write books this long with this much complex plot and characterization.

Historical notes – In the first volume, *Falcons of Malta*, the historic July 19th promotion list has moved up to June 22nd. The original date was misstated in Book 1: The Falcons of Malta as July 17th.

Soviet moves into Romania and the Baltic states are also somewhat altered.

In this book, it will be revealed that an order regarding airships was in fact not carried out.

I screwed up Jodl's rank in Book 1. In OTL he didn't become a Colonel General until 1944. So he should have been a General from the promotion list we moved up from the historic July 19th to June 22nd.

CET = Central European Time, which is summer time in this season. Time zones and when/if various places have daylight time were researched, but the results are often contradictory. We did our best, but your mileage may vary.

Chapter 1

0700 local time; 0600 CET
28 August 1940
Harbor, Tobruk, Libya

Hauptsturmführer Jochen Peiper stood on the dock watching his vehicles being unloaded. The Libyan heat was oppressive, and the ever-present flies were an even worse affliction. He was not inclined to complain about either. It had been a most strange, stressful two months. As Himmler's adjutant, he should have been liquidated during the coup. His patron, Reichsführer Himmler, had been shot out of hand; and his official family had died with him. Peiper had not been with the boss or at SS HQ that crazy night. He'd been on a three-day leave with his wife. The Gestapo had still found him by midday of the rebellion, which is how Peiper saw what had happened. Heydrich and Göring had allied with the Army to assassinate the Führer and elevate themselves.

Peiper kept that opinion to himself. He'd been in the death cells twice over a ten-day period. There had been lists. He was marked for death, removed to the detention cells, returned to the death cells, and then sent home. Arriving home, he had to first comfort his hysterical wife Sigi. He'd been gone with no word. Her best friend Hedwig, Himmler's mistress, had been arrested. Sigi had been terrified. Fortunately, her other dear friend, Lina Heydrich, had gotten Hedwig released. Peiper was unsure if that fairy godmother had also preserved his own life. There was no polite way to ask, so he just sent her a thank-you note on general principles.

He'd no sooner seen to that when a messenger arrived for him. He was to report to Oberführer Felix Steiner for combat duty. Combat duty? Peiper had served honorably with LAH during the French campaign, but why now and why Steiner? Peiper had never really been given detailed answers to either question. Heydrich now ruled the SS (and rumor said all of Germany with Göring just a figurehead). Peiper knew he should be thinking of him as Reichsführer Heydrich, but that would take getting used to. Reichsführer Heydrich, however, was giving him a chance at redemption. Because of Peiper's small combat history? Because Lina Heydrich wished it? No way to know. Steiner was no help. He was forming an ad hoc division of some new militia called the NL. His recruits were middle-aged SA men, mid-teenage HJ, and a bunch of semi-foreigners from the Baltic who claimed German nationality although many could barely speak the language.

This light Panzer Grenadier division, whatever that was, seemed to consist of a French brigade no one had seen, that was already in Libya, and various field-expedient units. The Army was 'contributing' the 288th Sonderverband, men combed from all over the Army for desert and similar-terrain experience. Felix Steiner had been an Army officer. He fully expected these 'terrain experts' to turn out to be the sweepings of every guardhouse in the German Army. Given a choice, a commander sent warm bodies, not his best. The only way to get quality was to send your own teams to root people out, something the Army would never allow. Steiner also expected this unit to be late. The second major formation, the 361st Panzer Grenadier regiment, was being created by recruiting out of the French and Polish POW camps for Volksdeutsche, Alsatians, and similar Aryan elements. For cadres this unit would get Aryans from the French Foreign Legion returned to their proper home in the Reich. Steiner felt they would be lucky to get a battalion this way, but needs must. That left making bricks without straw. The NL recruits were a mix of SA and HJ. The SA were mostly WW1 vets who hadn't seem a crew served-weapon since the Freikorps had been disbanded in the early 20's. His HJ were kids who knew nothing beyond marching and saluting. They needed exercises at every level from squad upwards to regiment. Instead they were being formed into ad hoc units of roughly company size, and told to train themselves while in transit. Nominally these companies were to be assembled into the 200th and 255th Light Afrika motorized regiments. Regiments? Right now they were company-sized march units scattered everywhere from Austria to Libya. Steiner felt this would only end poorly. Peiper agreed.

Steiner saw Peiper as a combat veteran. Peiper was also Waffen SS, the same service as Steiner. Steiner had been candid that he was surprised to see Peiper still alive, but glad to get him. Right now the 'division' was being formed around a shell left over from the demobilized Army 197th Infantry Division. Enough men had been kept with the colors to form the core of a division HQ and administrative services. Steiner had a few officers out raiding the overmanned rear area establishments of SS and Air Force for paymasters, engineers, bakers, butchers, and all the other specialties needed to make the administrative services work. He was getting transfers from the Navy to begin forming his artillery units. That left the 347th regiment. It had three real battalions. One each of Latvians, Lithuanians, and Estonians. Steiner spoke not a word of their languages, but their field officers all spoke German. Real soldiers and formed units, but how eager would they be to fight for Germany? This unit was already deployed to Libya. Time would tell if it was worth the bother.

The Afrika Division was supposed to have a Panzer reconnaissance battalion, the 580th. Someday it would. Right now it had a company of fifteen French AMR 35's. Also a Mercedes touring car with two radios as Peiper's command vehicle, and a dozen motorcycles for dispatch riders. The French had called the AMR a cavalry tank. Peiper thought armored reconnaissance vehicle was more accurate. He'd been promised one of the command variants, the one with actual radios, eventually. Peiper wasn't holding his breath. He had had nine days to train his HJ's till they could sort of drive their vehicles. They managed this mostly on roads in daylight. He had no support services. For now he had written orders to report to 7th Panzer Division, where something called KG Strauss would see to his needs. The vehicles had already shown themselves to be mechanically cranky, so he hoped those services included skilled mechanics. In the meantime, he'd sent his least clueless HJ to the harbormaster's office with instructions to find out where this KG Strauss was - and hopefully to get a guide. The port was a madhouse. Peiper had little doubt he could get lost, and first impressions mattered. The death cells still lurked if he got a bad report.

0800 local time; 0700 CET
28 August 1940
Camp Gorlov/advance camp KG Strauss
Southeast of Tobruk, Libya

Oberst Gunter Strauss was tired. He'd spent two whirlwind days on Sicily, plus the bumpy flights back and forth. He'd had to throw Heydrich's name around a lot to get passage plus the use of a car in Sicily. He hoped this wouldn't get back to Berlin. However, it had been necessary. Now he was in a staff meeting. Given that the KG ran more along the lines of a freikorps or a mercenary band from bygone centuries, it was less a formalized staff meeting than a gathering of his main deputies. Major Ivan Gorlov, originally of Baron Wrangel's White Army and now his advance force commander, was the nominal host. Major by the grace of Rommel's whimsy Isaak Schwabe, Gorlov's civilian boss and patron at the Ploeisti oil fields, had by now gained entrée into the inner circle. Majors Adolph Wrede and Gregor Voss were both still back with the main body at Bari. That left Hauptmann Joey Bats, mechanical wizard and full time hustler, plus the Romeo and Juliet pair, Major by the grace of chaotic misunderstandings Klaus Steiner and Leutnant by elevation in Libya Greta Schwabe, although for all practical purposes it was Greta Steiner by now whatever the formalities said. Greta had found the jewel-encrusted statues and was the only person who recalled the two nondescript British officers whose luggage the birds had been in. Including Greta without Klaus wouldn't work; and besides, she told him everything anyway.

The meeting room was a decrepit one-room wooden shack with a rickety table, a few mismatched ancient chairs, and an electric light that sometimes worked. The windows lacked actual glass. Instead, they had fine-mesh wire that allowed for what little breeze there was while keeping out some of the endless swarms of flying insects. None of these Europeans was enjoying the climate or fauna of their African 'vacation', but this was war. You went where you were ordered, and hoped to survive. So far they were all still alive, but the war showed no sign of ending soon.

"They never arrived in Sicily per the paper work." Strauss was disgusted by this turn of events. He had hoped to reacquire the prisoners, and 'persuade' them to supply details of the history and origins of these golden falcons. "Our records show them taking off, but nothing shows them checked-in on landing. Not on that flight. Not on any flight." Gunter paused again to catch his breath. This heat was going to take time to get used to. "It is obvious what happened. Whoever patted them down missed some coins, or gold, or wads of bank notes. Someone got well paid to let them vanish. Probably several someones. Gerbini was full-on chaos. No one was precisely making prisoner check-in a command priority.   However, without telling the Reichsführer what happened, we are at a dead end … "

"And if we tell Berlin, they will take all the loot." Joey was a courtesy Volksdeutsche. In fact he was an Italian-American semi-gangster from Brooklyn. "So we wing it. Find a fence in Egypt, and just sell it based on gold and jewels. Yeah, we get screwed on the real value, but we still get a major haul. There's got to be a story that makes it valuable beyond the basic components - but we don't know it, so let it be. We'll still get enough. In wartime chaos, moveable wealth goes at a premium. Egypt will be full of guys looking for wealth that fits into a carry bag. That's the way it would be if someone invaded New York." Joey had been more a vehicle mechanic for gangsters than a hood himself, but he knew the logic patterns. When things went bad, you couldn't go on the lam with real estate or businesses. You needed cash, or the sort-of-near-cash that gold and jewels were.

Deaths on the Nile

Greta was hesitant to speak up. The last time she had taken an initiative, she had gotten her parents and siblings murdered back in Romania. She was aware that her being a 'Leutnant ' was just a way of formalizing that her orders were to be obeyed for some reason beyond her being the Leutnant turned Major's woman. She was his mistress and the HQ cook. So far all being an officer had done, was ratify her recruitment of an actual cook because she was pathetic in a kitchen. She carefully phrased her comment as a diffident question, "Uncle Isaak, don't we have a relative in Egypt who could help?"

Isaak shook his head. He would love to have beaten his niece for opening this can of worms. However, her boyfriend could execute him out of hand and no one would care. Klaus was too unworldly to understand this. Strauss was not unworldly, and Heydrich even less so. Steiner was a lucky totem for them both; and his niece completed the propaganda package of the German Romeo and Juliet off to subdue King Tut. Fortune smiles on the clueless. "He's a fourth cousin by marriage. In Transylvania he was Hymie. He was a fence, a counterfeiter, a swindler; and he escaped one step ahead of the prison gates. He's been a few places since, but now claims to be a Canadian, Henry Morgan. Runs an 'import/export' business in Alexandria." Isaak paused for Gunter and Joey's peals of laughter. They understood the phrase, as meaning a fence who would buy or sell anything. Just the man to find a buyer. Just the man to try to swindle them out of the proceeds. Both had dealt with the type in their earlier lives. Both felt that between the power of their uniforms and the number of guns they had under their command, they could keep a fence honest enough on one deal. Besides, no one had a better answer. It neatly put the problem off till after the conquest of Egypt.

0900 local time; 0800 CET
28 August 1940
British military HQ, Cairo

The discussion had been going on since just after an early breakfast. It was not going well. General Archibald Wavell knew he was handing Major General Richard O'Connor, the commander of the Western Desert Force, a sticky wicket. O'Connor's position near Mersa Matrah was fortified. It was no Maginot Line, but it was a strong position. He had two good professional divisions, 7th Armored and 4th Indian, with brigade and smaller forces amounting to a third division. He lacked the heavy guns and support forces that would go with a standard corps, but Britain was overstretched in this second summer of a war undertaken from Chamberlain's fatal promise to Poland. A promise the British were years from having mobilized the force to properly honor. Haig had an army group in 1916 while Britain fielded whole additional armies in Egypt, Iraq, Salonika, and East Africa. Now, 1940, senior generals argued about battalions and batteries, about allotments of machine-gun ammunition. Other than rations and gasoline, the Empire was short of everything in this vast theater that stretched from Basra to Nairobi.

"I know you are promising me 6th Australian Division, even if it is incomplete. Doesn't matter. My southern flank is open to the desert. The Axis doesn't have to directly attack me. Just swing wide. They have the forces to do it. The Italian 10th Army may have lacked the trucks before the German reinforcements, but they are getting Panzers, whole divisions of them. RAF hasn't got the strength to contest the skies, but their photo recon lads are getting through. Paying a hell of a price, but we have the pictures. You've seen them. Let me pull back to Alamein. That line has a southern anchor, the Depression. We'll still be massively outnumbered, but our people know how to do a trench fight. We can form two more divisions between what got off Malta, and Winston finally allowing us to recruit Palestinian Jews without having to find matching Arabs. The Nazis hate Jews. The Jews will fight." O'Connor paused for breath, for a hope his commander would see reason.

"London insists. No retreats. Morale, the opinion of the US and the neutrals. The usual." Wavell didn't like defending London's decisions. He didn't like a lot of things, but would do his duty to King and Empire. "Best I can let you do is set the staff work for a run back to Alamein once it looks dark enough. Have to be nighttime or sand-storm. They will dominate the skies same as Malta. We finally have enough planes but they are all back home. We're supposed to start getting fresh squadrons ferried across Africa. This Gaullist thing in Chad should help. We have to buy time. As is, expect your officers to have to do extra work on morale. Fleet's leaving. The cripples already passed through the Canal, bound for Durban or Singapore. The rest follow over the next few days. They'll be taking the bulk of the port people with them. Technicians, headquarters, etc. The submarines and a destroyer squadron stay. Winston wanted more but War Cabinet seems to be growing a spine after Malta. Cunningham's death is a cudgel with which to beat his British lion act."

O'Connor's head snapped up at this. "So the Navy's pulling its dependents out? What about ours? We've got troops with family here. We've got retirees. Who else goes?"

"I have been forbidden an official evacuation. It is all being done word of mouth by us, RAF, Colonial Office, the usual dog's breakfast of agencies. Out by train to Palestine and then bus across to Baghdad. Train through Syria and Turkey is deemed 'unwise'; and I'm inclined to agree. The French authorities are being correct with us, but they will never forgive the attack on their fleet. We wouldn't if it were reversed."

"And from Baghdad?"

"Iraq is deemed safe." The two generals traded wry looks at that fancy. Nothing was safe at the moment this side of Nairobi or Karachi. "There's still civilian sea traffic out from Basra to India. The prices have gone through the roof but ... " Left unsaid was that military necessity would be invoked on ship captains who proved 'uncooperative'. No British would willingly be abandoned. What was to be done about other Empire peoples such as Sikhs and Chinese, was left unspoken. The two generals went back to arguing exact deployments, down to where to place armored-car forward scouts. They both knew they were probably arranging deck chairs on the Titanic, but one kept calm and carried on. What else was there to do?

0945 hours CET
28 August 1940
Bari, Italy

The command staff of the 25th Panzer Regiment was stuffed into a warehouse near the harbor. The port was a madhouse as thousands of troops arrived at the port in preparation for the Italian navy to escort them to Africa.

Oberst Karl Rothenburg was reading a report of timetables for when his regiment would arrive. Currently the three battalions and its 265 Panzers were on freight trains between here and Milan. 265 in theory. Many of the original AFV's were still down for maintenance; substitutes were, supposedly, coming from hither and yon.

Movement was being done, in theory, by companies. The result was the long line of trains making its way down the Italian peninsula, plus strays listed as arriving on other trains headed for Naples. When, if ever, these would reunite with the division was yet another mystery.

Once in the port of Bari, the Panzer companies were being loaded onto ships as they arrived. *What a beschissenes Schlamassel*, Rothenburg thought. A delay of another two weeks would have made this much more manageable. Instead, units were arriving out of order, and they wouldn't be able to reform the regiment until they got to Libya. Orders from Berlin were clear: speed was absolutely critical. Military Police, railroad troops, and even SS officers were rounding up stray troops and funneling them south.

It occurred to Rothenburg that the 7th Panzer Division was again living up to its nickname, 'the Ghost Division'. During the invasion of Belgium and France, Rommel had ruthlessly pushed the men and vehicles of the division, sometimes covering up to 250 kilometers in 24 hours. Oberkommando des Heeres, the high command, often had no clue where the division was at times. The Allies were equally clueless, as several times the division overran units whose enemy officers were shocked to discover Panzers in their rear area. Their commander, General Rommel, was at heart a storm officer who relied on his own battle instincts and a belief in rapid action. Currently Rothenburg only had firm locations and arrival times for perhaps half of his regiment, and division staff was equally confused.

His Ia, the operations officer, interrupted the Oberst's thoughts. "Major Sieckenius has arrived, Herr Oberst."

'Thank God!, thought Rothenburg. Sieckenius was the first of his battalion commanders to arrive. Sieckenius in his black panzer-troop uniform made his way around tables crowded by soldiers of the regimental staff.

The two Panzer officers exchanged military courtesies and then Rothenburg got to the heart of the matter. "What shape are your Panzers in?"

The fighting in France and Belgium had been hard, and the driving in many ways worse. The division had left a trail of broken-down Panzers between their end point, Cherbourg, and the jump-off point in Germany hundreds of kilometers behind. Broken-down Panzers had to be recovered, and far too many sent back to the factory for overhaul of the engines, suspensions, transmissions, or sometimes all three. By the armistice, the division was little more than a shell with so many vehicles of all kinds out of action. It was also moving in good part on 'liberated' trucks, often fueled by 'liberated' petrol.

Sieckenius shrugged helplessly at the question. "I can take you to the railyard to see for yourself. In theory my companies are at full strength … "

"But … "

"But … the Panzers handed off to us from other units to make good our losses really could use depot time. I am certain no one intentionally gave us bad vehicles, but after the French campaign everyone needs rest and recovery. Only replacement tanks from the factories are in top shape."

None of this was a surprise to Rothenburg. He had detailed reports, but hearing first hand was best. He still wished that it had been possible to stay back at their temporary base along the Somme rather than be here. Maybe he could have better handled the situation. General Rommel had been racing from one brush fire to the next, Romania, Malta, and now Libya. All the time he had been constantly taking officers and men from the division to make his various Kampfgruppen function. As a result, it had forced the regiment and brigade commanders to take on more of the administrative duties.

"I do have one bit of good news; I can confirm that all of the Pz-I's are gone. Returned to the factory to be remade into tank destroyers. It's just the Pz-II's, IV's and Czech 38T's."

The Third Reich's first tank for mass production, the Mark I, was little more than a training toy, armed with two machine-guns and laughable armor. They had to use the little 6-ton panzers at times against British and French tanks four times larger, and armed with real guns. Some mornings Rothenburg wondered how did the Allies manage to bungle the French campaign so completely? Back to business … "That's good to hear, very good. Three types of tanks will be easier to maintain than four. Someone is starting to pay attention in Berlin. How are the new men settling in?"

"Those from our home garrison are settling in well, as to be expected. I put them together with some from the other companies, to form the new fourth company. The drafts from the Panzer Troop Schools at Wünsdorf and Munster have brought us to full strength. We will have to just see how trained they really are."

Again, no shocks or surprises here. Rothenburg wished hopelessly for more time. The Oberst had no expectation that Rommel would be any less energetic in Africa, and there would be little time to really shake down the regiment as a single entity.   You fight with the tool you had, not the one you wished for. "Good report, Major. Areas have been set aside for your men and vehicles. Loading instructions will be ready shortly."

Next stop, Libya, then Egypt, and then who knows where? Rothenburg made a note to look again for a tourist guide book on Palestine to go with the ones he had already acquired for Egypt and Cairo. He had his orderly out looking for ones on Alexandria and Suez.

1700 local time; 1000 CET
28 August 1940
Harbor, Batavia (21st century Jakarta), Java, Dutch East Indies

Sukarno rejoiced in his good fortune. He had been exiled by the Dutch to a remote town as punishment for nationalist agitation. The security services had wished to impose further punishments to crimp his activities there, most of which amounted to pin-pricks like a touring nationalist children's theater troupe. Sukarno's attorneys had appealed this, necessitating his temporary residence in the colonial capital of Batavia for the duration of the appeal process. The result was preordained, but Europeans took great delight in following 'procedures' and 'due process'. Two interlinked sets of shadow plays on the power realities.

The Japanese squadron had arrived some hours earlier. After a brief discussion with the Dutch Governor General, the Japanese ultimatum had been accepted as the Dutch had no serious way to fight Japan. To 'protect the East Indies from German aggression', the Japanese 16th Division was to be allowed to occupy key points in Java. Other units of the Japanese 14th Area Army were to do the same in Sumatra and Borneo. The Dutch and Japanese agreed to make a joint request that Australia send militia units to defend the outlying islands such as Bali, Timor, Celebes, and New Guinea. The polite words hid nothing, but allowed the Dutch and their British protectors to save face. The oil, tin, and rice would henceforth go to Japan, to be paid for in IOU's denominated in yen. The realignment of powers following the Nazi-Soviet alliance had left Japan adrift diplomatically. This was Japan's answer to that situation, as seen through the lens of their seemingly endless China War.

The Dutch exile government was in London. Communication was spotty, as the direct lines through the Mediterranean were interdicted by the war. The British resident minister, the representative of the real power guaranteeing the nominal Dutch empire, had counseled against resistance. Britain's fleet had suffered reverses off Malta and was not available for a new war with Japan. Britain's armies and air forces were even more overstretched at this stage of the war. Rape was inevitable, so best submit to minimize the damage and loss of prestige among the natives.

All of this had leaked to the nationalists. The idiot whites ignored that servants had ears, minds, memories. Sukarno resolved to appeal directly to the new masters. The power game now had new players. Full independence would not come from the inevitable Japanese economic exploitation, but even a realignment of power in the interior provinces would advance the nationalist cause. Let the Dutch rule the cities, mines, and plantations … for now. Power came from the countryside and out of the barrel of a gun. Buy time for the nationalists to acquire strongholds. Unlike most Dutch, Sukarno spoke fluent Japanese. Most people preferred to do business in their own tongue. It was a start, or the chance of a start. Now he must somehow arrange a meeting …

1020 CET

28 August 1940
Gerbini Airfield complex, Sicily

Former Major Maurice was back from Malta, even if his machine-gun battalion was not. General Jodl needed him for a new training effort. As one of the deemed heroes of Malta, Jodl had had his command expanded by Heydrich and Halder to a two-regiment, six-battalion force. It was now the Kampfgruppe Jodl Special Artillery Force. A fresh wave of SA, HJ, and Baltic Germans was being sent to man the heavier weapons that had been abandoned for the Malta operations, including the near worthless 50-mm mortars. Maurice was now a full Oberst, in command of this second regiment. The SA had found a Freikorps veteran to command the Malta regiment, which would be shipped to Libya. Maurice was being given a real training cycle for his new troops. They would catch up after the fall of Egypt and be available for the Palestine campaign, so he had one hundred days, or a bit less as most of the troops were in transit but not yet arrived. Now he was here to argue about the obvious. "General, why those 50-mm pieces of shit? Can't you get us more of the French 60-mm? Find some other fools on garrison duty to take the 50-mm!"

Jodl agreed. He also knew the limits of his current powers. "Train on the 50-mm. For now, it was all I could do to get full battalion kit on the four weapons we had. As things develop and my relationships with General von Manstein and Deputy Chancellor Heydrich firm up, I may be able to get the equipment changed on deployment. The French are producing the 60-mm again. So is Romania."

"Deputy Chancellor? When was this announcement?"

"No public announcement yet. It will probably be stage-managed during the victory celebrations in Berlin when the Blue Max is brought back. The eyes-only announcement came over the teletype along with a flood of post-Malta redeployment orders. Schellenberg brought a written precis for me and Keller. It had all the correct signatures and official seals, so it is real. Seems none of the other three regard it as their job to pay attention to day-to-day governance. Almost as if they see Reichsführer Heydrich as their minion. A feeling he encourages. Three men concerned with their titles and personal rewards, who simply found the day-to-day grind of ruling to be demeaning, to be beneath them. Think of it as if the Reichsführer is Chancellor in the sense Bismarck was, but instead of one Kaiser we have a committee of three as head of state. Of course only one of the three does the head of state job in public. The Army sits in the shadows, a ruler whose rulership is known only to the elect among Germany's senior leaders. One of whom is now you, as I'm on the list being kept in the know and you are my number two. Welcome to the ruling class." Jodl paused. This discussion had turned in a dangerous direction. His absolution from prior sin was both tentative and quite reversible. "I will try to work though the hierarchies to get the 50-mm relegated to the new border divisions we are forming in the East. Trench units, like from the second half of the Great War. Units of lesser manpower and limited mobility, suitable for holding a certain number of kilometers of trenches and blockhouses. This will free up production for the 60-mm, whose superiority we will validate on campaign."

Oberst Maurice adjusted his new headgear, this baseball cap. A few dozen had been hastily made at Gerbini. He saluted and left to do the impossible ... again. At least the cap was lighter on the head than a steel helmet. This mattered in the Sicilian sun.

1100 British Double Summer Time/ 1100 Central European Time
28 August 1940
A rundown hotel near Westminster, London

Kim Philby's handler was furious. Kim was over 15 hours late to a meeting. Kim was too exhausted to care. He'd been up since before dawn the day before, as Britain dealt with a day without a government. Winston had resigned over removing the Fleet from Alexandria. Had done another of his British lion no-retreats tirades. Had refused to accept that the War Cabinet overruling him was not an 'issue of confidence'. So he quit three times, and the third time they let him go and ordered the Fleet to depart. As a face-saver, the submarines and half a dozen destroyers were left to die.

It had rapidly gone downhill from there. The War Cabinet wanted Halifax. The problem was that he was Lord Halifax, and as a "matter of principle" felt the PM had to sit in Commons. Halifax used that excuse. May even have been sincere. May have just not wanted the poisoned chalice – being the PM who would inherit the mess of a war he never believed in. Much of a day had been wasted on one appeal after another to duty to King and Country, with Halifax rejecting them all. This seemed to leave Eden or perhaps Lloyd George. Labor had qualms about both, and differing Tory factions disliked each. In a large sense, the war ran on autopilot until Atlee for Labor, and the Crown through minions, banged enough heads to get a somewhat chastened Churchill to again take office, but as first among equals. His days as El Supremo were over. His next resignation would be the last.

The handler was more concerned about some thing or other involving the East Indies, of all places. Philby said he'd do some digging, but odds said that whatever had happened out there at the edge of the world had been put aside in the battles over who sat in which chair at the next cabinet meeting. Philby asked his handler why Moscow Centre gave a damn about a bunch of Dutch islands? The handler was clueless. Moscow made demands of its espionage assets. It never explained.

Chapter 2

1200 hours CET
28 August 1940
Heydrich's office, SS HQ, Prinz-Albrecht-Straße, Berlin, Germany

Deputy Chancellor and Reichsführer SS Heydrich was curious when his chief subordinate Schellenberg requested an hour for a private liaison conference on an unspecified topic. He valued the man's creativity and zeal. What specific project had come to fruition? A special project he had apparently done without exactly getting prior permission. Heydrich chuckled to himself. Forgiveness was often easier than permission.

Schellenberg had the intercom turned off and the door safely closed. He then went into his portfolio and spread out paper money on Heydrich's desk. US currency in denominations of $1, $2, $5, $10, and $20. Heydrich examined them carefully. They looked genuine. They felt genuine. The obvious questions were, how and where? "Operation Andreas? Sturmbannführer Naujocks was liquidated during the purge." Both men knew that. while the charge against Naujocks was treason, the truth was that he was disliked. There was a needed quota of sacrificial goats, and his death helped fill a predetermined allocation of traitors to be unmasked, thus allowing deserving protégés promotions in rank and titles.

Operation Andreas was a plan SS HQ launched at the start of the war, to flood the United Kingdom with counterfeit bank notes and try to disrupt the British economy. Like many plans in the Third Reich, it went through fits and starts as Hitler or one of his inner circle would change their minds. A great deal of effort had been put into the plan to exactly copy the British currency - the rag paper was custom made, with specially chemically-treated water to match water in the UK, and a unit specializing in cryptography broke the British serial-number system. Heydrich had been a key backer of the program, but as one of the rulers of the Reich he simply didn't have the time to do anything about the project, and thought it abandoned.

"Yes, Reichsführer. While Naujocks was a "traitor", there was no reason to dispose of his staff; so I sent them to Ravensbrück and assigned them to the forgery unit." Both men understood this as meaning the staff had simply not been designated for liquidation before quotas had been filled. "One of the currency forgers was ambitious, and decided to make a try at US currency. That got back to me and so I ordered the currency project restored. I had the special paper and ink made to order for US currency. The unit was moved to a new camp building, separate from the general forgery shop. We've run these through various Swiss banks without complaint. There is, of course, the problem with the same serial numbers repeating endlessly, but I have found a solution via the Hoover agency."
Heydrich was intrigued. Finance was always an issue, especially on orders of finished goods and minerals from Sweden, Switzerland, Turkey, and the like. "Go on."
"We gave the Americans a group of extraterritorial warehouses and docks at Danzig. However, we have restricted their ability to spend money beyond this guarded zone. We were worried about a dual-

currency situation promoting black marketeering and other vices. That's still a problem, but we can minimize it by our usual methods. Currently they exchange the dollars for marks. The rate of exchange is fixed by us and is – shall we say – less than market rate. This in turn limits the desire of ship crews to spend money, and of American relatives of Europeans to send dollars. I propose we cease doing so. Let the dollars circulate freely at whatever rate the traffic will bear. Indeed, I further suggest we tell their American cousins that they can send dollars via some form of safe packet or money order system. The Poles and Jews may get dollars they can use to improve their standard of living. We allow Hoover's people to bring over banknotes which get mixed in with ours, and thus slide past the banks when we deposit them to our national accounts in Zurich and Geneva. It will, of course, also provide a guide on how badly we have depreciated our own currency and how civilians rate our chances of final victory.

Heydrich was decisive on one change. "SS accounts, not national."

Schellenberg was content. Operation Bernhard was now official. It was best to have a new name, to avoid confusion with the old operation and the unfortunate end of its predecessor. His next steps would be fix the serial number issue, restarting work on British pound notes in various low denominations, and then initiating work on Soviet ruble notes. Fiat money was just paper, after all. It had value based on states and armies.

1400 local time; 1300 CET
28 August 1940
Camp Gorlov, near Tobruk, Libya

Peiper found the installation. The gate guards seemed almost indifferent to his travel orders. They called HQ, and Major Gorlov appeared and welcomed Peiper in. Being welcomed by an obviously Slavic officer was for Peiper a shock. Meeting the rest of the command group was even more of one. Major Schwabe and Hauptmann Bats had virtually ignored him, the latter focusing on his vehicles. Bats started cursing in a strange mix of English, German, Italian, and something Peiper could almost swear was Yiddish. Had ordered one of Peiper's drivers to move the vehicle to a repair bay with a pit. Bats had then ignored his rank to drop down into the pit like a mere technician. Apparently, the defects in the vehicle's suspension were both obvious and, to Bats, alarming. Fortunately, Peiper had brought along the French technical specifications and maintenance manuals. Bats didn't read French, but Schwabe did. Schwabe also spoke proper civilized German. He was obviously an educated man. He also seemed able to channel Bats away from his nonstop complaining.

Peiper was served a decent lunch with the command staff. The cooking was some weird blend of European and Asian. Spicy but quite tasty. Far better than one should expect from a field unit in Africa. The new cook was some Indian with British connections, whom the unit had commandeered in Malta. Strange war. Schwabe explained over the meal that Bats proposed a wholesale rebuild of the suspension and certain other features. He also claimed to be able to install radios. Bats would have to absent himself for a week to get the parts made in Naples. He was also going to be recruiting more mechanics. Peiper asked how could new parts be acquired outside channels this way. When the table stopped laughing, he was informed that this unit was the Reichsführer's pets. A quick telegram from German port HQ in Naples to Berlin should produce the proper authorizations. Peiper mentioned that his wife was socially friendly with Frau Heydrich. The unit commander, Oberst Strauss, had Peiper dictate a brief telegram to his wife that would also be sent by Bats from Naples. Strauss seemed to Peiper to be an opportunist, but one who could advance Peiper's prospects. Perhaps this would work out after all. Peiper had been an ambitious young man before his near-death experiences.

1440 local time; 1340 CET
28 August 1940
Camp Gorlov, near Tobruk, Libya

Mary the cook cleared the lunch dishes with the aid of her two oldest children. She had been born Hindu, and named Madhubala, in Bengal. She had taken up with the aging British corporal as a way of helping ease her father's crushing debt burden. Her family had no money for a dowry, so marriage wasn't an option. Her Mom had died some years back, but her grandmother and two aunts had convinced her father that selling her as a concubine to the Irishman would mean more money over a few years for the family than what the pimp from Calcutta was offering. She had kept the soldier's house, laundered his clothes, and warmed his bed through to and past retirement. She had also given him three half-caste children. He gave her some cash, all of which went to her family.

He never formally married her, but allowed her to take his name, becoming Mary Collins. It hadn't been love or any silliness like these Westerners professed to believe. It was simply a comfortable, working household. She had of course taken his faith, becoming Mary the Catholic instead of Madhubala the Hindu. For Mary it was just new rituals to learn, the same way she had learned his language and style of cooking, had learned how to properly iron and starch his uniform. The gods had a million names and many times that number of avatars. Even the new Christian God had three selves, a divine virginal mother who had also borne her earthly husband other children, plus an endless multitude of saints and angels. Mary focused on ritual and holidays. Theology was for priests.

Her soldier was now a prisoner of the Italians. He had retired with her to Malta and been recalled to the colors during the last days before the conquest. That left herself and the children near-destitute on Malta. Then this female officer, Naiomi Saxon, found her running a roadside tea stand outside the Grand Harbor ruins. Mary found the idea of armed females strange, and female officers stranger still. She thought it was a German thing – except it turns out the Germans don't do this either. Some weird Jewish tribe called Revisionists. Mary thought they would ask her to convert again, but her new master, this Frau Greta, said no. They all say Fräulein, but she was the Major's wife – so shouldn't it be *Frau*? Whatever. Mary was now part of this unit. They let her bring her children. Mary really didn't care which empire won this war. Her children would not go hungry. It was a pity she could no longer send money home for now. Sooner or later the war would take her to a city where there would be a moneylender who could see to the informal transfers. It had worked that way on Malta.

0600 hours CET
29 August 1940
Ft-Lamy, Chad (now Gaullist)

Philippe Francois Marie Leclerc de Hauteclocque had left de Gaulle in London as Major de Hauteclocque. That had been an instant promotion by what was in fact a rebel movement funded by the British. By rights he was a cavalry captain and staff officer. Here in Chad, he had decided he was Brigadier General Leclerc. The "Leclerc" was an easy decision. Hopefully it protected his wife and family back in France from adverse effects of newspapers mentioning his name. The general's rank was dictated by circumstances. Or circumstances as seen sitting here in Africa, as opposed to theoretical discussions in London.

Chad had come out for de Gaulle. Much of the rest of Equatorial Africa was likely to follow, but the authorities in Gabon and Cameroun were still loyal to Vichy. The educated blacks were Gaullist, especially those of the civil service. The problem was that the bulk of the rest of the civilized classes were neutral in favor of the winner. The whites and Arabs would prefer not to be forced to make a decision, but if pushed most preferred Vichy. A provisional major did not look like a serious personage, especially when not backed by reinforcements of troops or planes or much of anything. The British had little to send from Nigeria. Besides, British troops would not be well received after the attack on the French Fleet at Oran.

So Leclerc announced that he had arrived with the Second Free French Division. A Second implies that there is a First someplace. A general is a serious personage. In the meantime, he would organize what mobile forces he had into a new unit that he proclaimed as the March (provisional) Regiment of Chad. In fact, it was a company of black colonial troops and a few hundred volunteers, mostly various sorts of refugees from Hitler. His local confederates said they could mobilize about another thousand tribal levies. These would be untrained men with a few retired colonial NCO's for stiffening. Some would be armed with black-powder muskets, and most of the rest would have hunting rifles of some sort. It didn't matter. It was a new regiment joining a whole division.   He would work magic until he was actually reinforced ... if he was ever reinforced. Napoleon had said the moral was to the physical as three was to one. Vichy's firm adherents were older men set in their ways. Leclerc proposed to move quickly on Cameroun before they recovered their mental equilibrium.

0800 hours local; 0700 hours CET
29 August 1940
Camp Gorlov, Tobruk, Italian Libya

Lieutenant Colonel "Oberstleutnant" John Marco Karoly Riva Di Salo had arrived a few hours earlier. Now he was taking the handover of his 'battalion'. Battalion? There had been a hundred and two original "Italian" volunteers, mostly Jews or part-Jews. One was somehow still in Bari, transferred out as too young. Di Salo didn't think he would miss a small eleven-year-old female with no special skills. That had left a hundred and one who had dropped on Luqa. Over a third were casualties – they had died, or were no longer with the unit from wounds. Some of those might return eventually, but not in time for this campaign. For untrained, mostly underage children, they had been fearless. Eight survivors had been given German decorations, starting at the revived Blue Max and descending from there to mere Iron Crosses second class. The surviving heroes were on a lengthy propaganda tour. This left him fifty-five 'veterans' arrayed before him in two ranks. They seemed not really trained in either common military formations, or even how to stand at attention in the proper manner. Oh well, every enterprise begins somewhere.

Di Salo had arrived with a small entourage. There was his Catalan ex-commissar mistress, war booty from his service in Spain. There were half a dozen Spanish Nationalist NCO's he had picked up as personal retainers during the mixed-division period. Yet Rome had made clear he was a battalion commander. He had been gifted with half a company, but it was to be quickly built into a battalion in fact as opposed to just name. The German publicity offensive after Malta had exalted the courage of the Italian volunteer heroes of Luqa, and of the march to the Grand Harbor under Rommel. The Italian and broader European publics thought this was a picked force of officer cadets, of *arditi*, rather than a self-selected band of disobedient youngsters who had used chaos and luck to hitch a ride with Strauss and Steiner's NL company. Indeed, the propaganda painted Steiner's Jewish Betar as Aryan Saxons from Romania. Di Salo was still laughing to himself at that fantasy. Strauss had explained reality in brutal detail when he had arrived before dawn.

The easy part for Italy was to create an actual battalion of arditi. The 592nd would be formed in Tuscany from good fascists bulked up by Hungarian 'volunteers'. That unit would be directly attached to 7th Panzer Division with a large propaganda unit to extol its exploits. However, the new unit commander did not want the Malta veterans. Hence this second 'battalion'. Di Salo had been a hero of the Spanish War against the Reds. He'd gone back to London after that service. In many ways he was as much English as Italian. The British were his mother's people. He'd been schooled there, had achieved success in finance in the City of London. His Spanish service was an adventure that had turned into a three-year crusade. Finance had been a mere profession for him. War had turned out to be his true calling. He'd made a unit out of mixes of Italians, Spanish, Catholic volunteers from elsewhere, and captured Red prisoners.

He thought Italy had been on the wrong side in European affairs, that it should have stayed allied to the West. Il Duce decided otherwise. Di Salo had seen the handwriting on the wall. He and his 'household' had left London during the Dunkirk days, headed for Italy by way of Iberia. Once home, he and his father had worked their social network to find him a suitable command. Which led to him standing here looking at fifty-five raw recruits who thought they were veterans. Mentally he shrugged. He'd started with worse when the Arrow mixed units were created. Had led his men to victory on the Ebro. One of the spoils of that victory, ex-company-commissar Coxita Arcau LaTorre, had occupied his bed and made his coffee ever since. He smiled to himself, recalling their first meeting where he had been forced to dispute ownership of her with a platoon of drunken Moroccans. Good warriors, but no sense of discipline.

He'd been promised a free hand with his unit. He'd even been allowed to name it. It was now the *Flechas di Malta* Battalion. Viva Christo, Rey! He nodded to his veteran sergeants and corporals. Time for them to get to work. His job would be finding more men and equipment.

1100 hours CET
29 August 1940
Chancellery, Berlin

Getting Führer Göring to schedule work before lunch was normally impossible. The Führer preferred his office work for afternoons, leaving him free for his head of state duties at evening events and rallies. This was an emergency. Deputy Chancellor Heydrich had called the meeting on receipt of a long telegraph message from the Moscow Embassy. He started the meeting with the key point. The Soviets had canceled the September peace conference at Brest.

The two generals at the table, War Minister Generaloberst Beck and Head of the General Staff Halder, were nonplussed. Their redeployment of the Wehrmacht to the East was still not complete. Germany had been defenseless in the East when the attack on France had begun in May. It was no longer defenseless, but still had only seventy Italo-German divisions stretched from the Baltic to Romania. There were twenty-five more Romanian ones of uncertain quality, and two halfway-decent Slovak ones. No serious person counted the Hungarian Army at this time. It was a nominal ally under Italian command, but its loyalties were quite suspect after the mini-war earlier this year. Too much of the German depot supply of munitions and other war materiel was also still west of the Rhine, a legacy of the victorious French campaign. The projected East Wall was still a set of pretty engineering plans. At best there were limited disconnected trenches, except in East Prussia where there were out-of-date fortifications from back in the Kaiser's time. Halder did the speaking for the Army side of the table. He asked what the Soviets were demanding?

Heydrich's answer startled the other three. "That's the funny part. Nothing. They have given us Finland as a good-will gesture. They won't evacuate their base at Hanko, but accept that the Finns are now part of our New Europe. They've asked that we limit our garrisons to two corps, and prefer we send mostly Swedes. Yes, that means they are conceding Sweden as well. They want to discuss bases for themselves at the Turkish Straits and on the Bulgarian Black Sea coast, but offer to let us occupy both nations pending this basing agreement. They are also offering to move forward and revise a bit upwards their promised deliveries of oil and grain. The only thing they are asking right now is a joint friendship declaration pending the negotiation of a ten-year non-aggression pact between themselves and Europe. So the question is, what's the catch?"

It took an hour of discussion for the four rulers to jointly decide to accept the Soviet offer, but upgrade the alert status of the forces in the East. None of them could find a plausible reason for Stalin's 'generosity'. Before Heydrich could begin a progress report on the deployment of the Afrika Korps and Second Air Fleet to Libya, Göring announced he was leaving. He'd helped see to the emergency, but felt he had a full calendar that precluded dealing with day-to-day trivia. The generals in turn reduced the discussion of the projected Egyptian campaign to a five-minute summary before telling Heydrich to send the formal report to their staff officers for review. With the Eastern situation in crisis, they felt they had no time to waste on a secondary theater. Heydrich tried to involve them in the French situation, where a colonial crisis was developing in Africa. Beck rudely replied that Heydrich could handle such minutia himself. Use the Foreign Ministry and OKW as needed, and just keep OKH and the War Ministry advised of what had been decided. Unless these decisions involved troop or supply movements, it was a waste of their valuable time. Heydrich bade them a courteous farewell and went back to SS Headquarters on Prinz-Albrecht-Straße. He was not even mildly surprised at their lack of interest in anything outside their narrow sphere.

1200 hours CET
29 August 1940
Franz-Josefs-Bahnhof, Vienna, Austria/Greater German Reich

Colonel Kevin Duffy was finding being a prisoner of war a trifle unreal. He'd been flown off to Sicily with the retired brigadier, whose name he now knew as Alistare-Smythe. He still hadn't learned the man's Christian name or history. However, his web of social connections seemed absurdly large.

Alistare-Smythe had name-dropped enough with Rommel to get them assigned a driver to see to their needs on Malta. Duffy and the brigadier's Chinese servant, who turned out to speak excellent upper-class English, had been driven back to Duffy's quarters – where, under his supervision, the servant had packed up his belongings for travel. Duffy hadn't brought much to Malta and had acquired only a few odd items since, but as he had no idea what awaited him in captivity it was best to gather everything. The stranger part had been that he was allowed to withdraw funds from a Maltese bank against a check on his London bank. A check that couldn't possibly clear until war's end. The bank manager protested, but would not directly say no to a German Hauptmann willing to provide a written order to show to the bank's auditors and the Italian occupation authorities.

On arrival at Gerbini, instead of the military police taking charge of them, they were welcomed by a Luftwaffe Major, a relative of some friend of Alistare-Smythe's from Berlin. They all had dinner at a nice restaurant in the vicinity, and then were given lodgings at the transit officers' facility on base, almost as if they were guests instead of prisoners. The next morning another German officer had taken charge of them. This one was an army officer from a mountain division, being sent on home leave to recuperate from a minor wound in the Malta fighting. The man had served as their minder as far as Vienna. Now they were taking their leave after a quick lunch. The two British officers, in uniform but with transit paperwork to show to various police, and their two servants plus luggage, had booked a first-class compartment to Berlin where they would be 'staying with friends'. The station police had found the paperwork amusing, but as Austrians were prepared to believe all sorts of pig-headed idiocy from Prussians. Duffy had given the brigadier his 'word of honor' that he would not try 'anything silly'. After seeing the letters the general had posted, Duffy was more than willing to do so. Sent out by regular German post to the British legation in Zurich, the old man had written notes taking full responsibility for the surrender of Malta to the War Ministry, seven undersecretaries, and nine members of parliament including two ex-ministers and the Tory chief whip. Whoever Alistare-Smythe was, he seemed to know important people all over. Clearly this was a man to earn the good opinion of. Besides, staying at a mansion in Berlin sounded ever more agreeable than in some fortress castle under guard.

1600 hours CET
29 August 1940
Hotel du Parc, Vichy, Unoccupied France

The cabinet meeting had been highly acrimonious. The Marshal and his immediate circle were obdurate. Petain's version of collaboration was minimal collaboration at maximal price to Germany. Fine in theory. Insane after Oran and now Chad. Left to itself, all of Equatorial Africa would fall to Britain, using de Gaulle as a cat's-paw. Indeed, there were rumors of a British expedition to Dakar. If West Africa fell as well, Britain could make peace with Germany, trading the Arab Empire she couldn't hold for a formerly-French African Empire she could more easily defend. This would be an Anglo-German peace at French expense. The key had been the two service ministers, Weygand for the Army as Defense Minister and Darlan for the Fleet. Even the Marshal would not defy a united military.

Pierre Laval had gotten Petain's consent to negotiate a new agreement with the Germans. Petain was head of state, but whether he was also head of government was still fluid. Laval, Weygand, and Darlan had the authority to make whatever concessions necessary to get Germany to allow rearmament in Africa. Laval saw this as an opening wedge. The Germans would, of course, want things. But as long as he could show progress in defending the Empire, he was now confident he could leverage a closer alliance. If the British or Americans wanted French neutrality, let them make offers. Until then, Laval's strategy for France would be to make the best deal possible with reality. That reality seemed to be Reichsführer Heydrich. Perhaps four ruled, but so far only Heydrich seemed to pay attention to other nations.

1900 hours CET
29 August 1940
Conference room, SS Headquarters, Prinz-Albrecht-Straße, Berlin, Germany

Recently-promoted Generalmajor Theodor Busse sat silently in the room, letting his patron and superior General von Manstein give the presentation to Deputy Chancellor and Reichsführer Heydrich and his chief aide Schellenberg. The command situation was tricky by conventional army standards. Heydrich was one of four rulers – and in theory the lowest-ranking one. Yet the other three, including Führer Göring and War Minister Beck, had ignored invitations to the briefing. They and OKH commander Generaloberst Halder had refused all contact with the Southern Campaign. Strange, as it was the only active war the ground forces had.

Equally unusual, von Manstein was both head of OKW, and thus Busse's boss, and the field commander of a subordinate corps reporting to Busse as Deputy Head of OKW. Heydrich seemed to have his own quite strange ideas on proper organization.

Reichsführer Heydrich let von Manstein, assisted by his new OKW liaison officer Major von

Stauffenberg, finish. He wanted to be sure he had all his facts before replying. "So let me sum up. You have 80% of your corps-level troops. Enough for combat, but not for perfect function. Hausser's SS division is 75% or so in Libya and ready for action. He is somewhat short of field artillery, and missing a good number of his AFV's, but he's got an oversized functional combat division. Rommel is a little less complete, say 70%. General Steiner's Afrika Division effectively isn't there. You've got stray bits and pieces plus one regiment of Balts who will be complete in another week or so. Strauss has two companies being upgraded to battalions. You have five of your nine 88mm battalions, the miracle weapon we are counting on against the British heavy tanks. Ramcke is back on Malta doing a full rebuild. He has one of Jodl's regiments, and the other is just being formed in Sicily. The Air Force has 8th Air Corps, the ground support specialists, in Libya, but nothing else so far. The Italian motorization and armor upgrade is a work in progress, but the deputy Rome assigned to actually command the Prince's nominal army, this General Carlo Geloso, seems a competent professional. You are asking for another month for deployment?"

General von Manstein knew this was not what his ruler wanted to hear. However, he was a trained general staff professional, not some lackey as Keitel had been. "You want victories. I understand the delays are annoying, but in a month I can have Hausser, Rommel, and the corps troops relatively complete. Air Force General Keller says he can have the bulk of 2nd Air Fleet in Libya by then. Steiner's division won't be ready, but he'll have a brigade-sized battle group to command."

Heydrich was aware that the two iron rules of bureaucratic work were that nothing gets done on time and nothing gets finished on budget. He also knew that, absent constant pushback from the top, the delays never cease and the cost overruns escalate endlessly. "Two weeks and you send light forces forward. Rommel with whatever of his 7th Panzer Division has arrived. Strauss's two battalions or however many men he has. Two of the 88mm battalions. Whatever of Steiner's troops have arrived, and the reconnaissance and motorcycle troops from Hausser. You give Rommel saddle orders to swing out into the desert beyond the British flank, brush aside their light forces, and see what develops." Heydrich was aware this was too vague for a formal operations order. That is what one had staff Generals for. The important part was to force action at some point. Two weeks might turn into three, but at least it wouldn't be one month turning into a whole season.

Von Manstein wanted to grimace. He was visualizing a real terrain map, and reviewing second- and third-order moves and counters. A German move in divisional strength would have to provoke a British reply. A reply in almost certainly corps strength, which would require an Axis counter of similar strength.

He and Heydrich both knew what a wild card Rommel was. Given saddle orders, he would be even more impossible to control than usual. The man was a storm officer at heart. Staff logic didn't appeal to him. Boring things like logistics and the other preparatory work needed for an army-level offensive in a major theater, were matters Rommel chose to ignore, to leave to others to handle. "A suggestion, Reichsführer. Add Hausser's anti-tank battalions and two battalions of heavy guns from my corps troops, to the two battalions of 88mm multipurpose guns. Put the six battalions of guns under Jodl's command. This would provide a mature, adult presence to offset Rommel's impetuosity."

Heydrich smiled and nodded yes. Von Manstein knew he couldn't relieve Rommel. Heydrich had made that clear when he first gave von Manstein command of the Afrika Korps. Having an older, wiser head along to keep Rommel somewhat in check satisfied both men. Jodl had rank on Rommel, for however little that was worth with such a prima donna. Besides, Heydrich remembered that they had managed to work well together at Gerbini during the Malta campaign.

0600 hours
30 August 1940 (2300 hours, 29 August CET)
Chinese Eastern Railway (6 kilometers beyond the frontier in the direction of Harbin), Manchuria

The Red Army colonel had initially been elated. The thirty-minute saturation bombardment had caught the Japanese by surprise. The razvedrota had secured the crossing points behind heavy direct fire from cannons and machine-guns. The heavy howitzers had plastered targets starting 300 meters back and extending out to three kilometers. There had been more than enough prewar commercial traffic for GRU's agents to have had plausible cover to have pinpointed all likely targets with exact ranges.

His regiment of T-28 tanks, with a small battalion of the superheavy KV's as a late add-on, had easily breached the border defenses and been advancing on both sides of the railroad in the face of only very minor opposition. He had been told that most of what he would be facing for the first day or two would be Manchurian and Mongol puppet forces with low morale and little training. He was a young man in his late 20's. He had been a major fourteen months ago. Between the purges and the rapid expansion of Soviet forces, promotions had come swiftly for many young men such as himself. Command of a tank regiment with an attached infantry battalion was a huge increase in responsibilities. He coped by relying on his briefings, and strictly following orders. The orders had stressed that for an operational maneuver group such as this, momentum mattered more than casualties.

Now he had encountered artillery fire. Heavy cannons had taken out five of his KV tanks by direct fire. It would take a mighty weapon to penetrate their armor. From his briefings he remembered that Japanese had a 15cm cannon, the type 89. It was probably a battery of those. He pulled back his tanks, deploying his accompanying infantry battalion to flush out the guns. It was almost dawn. The Japanese would be backlit by the rising sun, while his soldiers would be stalking forward in the shadows. That should work. If not, he would just take his losses and charge the battery. Losses were less important than gaining ground before the Japanese could bring up reserves. The Soviet state produced more tanks than anyone in the world, and his KV's were the best heavy tanks on the planet. Someday he would command a regiment made up solely of these behemoths, or perhaps a brigade if he performed well. The Red Army was on the march and he was its vanguard.

0300 hours CET
30 August 1940
Praha Hlavni Nadrazi (Prague Main Railroad Station)
Protectorate of Bohemia-Moravia (modern Czech Republic)

Colonel Duffy was finding Gestapo custody considerably less comfortable than his first class compartment on the Vienna-Prague express had been. Three Gestapo agents in their signature black leather trenchcoats had been waiting for them on the platform when the train arrived from Vienna. Alistare-Smythe saw them and walked right up to them. This nonplussed them. They found his documents equally bewildering. It was a set of Wehrmacht travel orders directing Alistare-Smythe, as senior officer, to move a POW party of four, specified by name and including Alistare-Smythe himself, to a particular Berlin address which was labeled the place of internment. There was even a helpful phone number at the War Ministry to call to confirm the documents. Also, a list of personal references who could confirm that Alistare-Smythe was in fact the man in question. Ten references, including their ranks, titles, and prewar contact information. Other persons noted as approving this arrangement included General Rommel and two senior Luftwaffe officers in Sicily.

The Gestapo found this absurd. Alistare-Smythe's German was excellent. He pointed out that one couldn't be a spy in full British uniform. Prisoners are required to follow lawful orders, and there was nothing unlawful in sending them to Berlin. The senior Gestapo officer tried to trip Alistare-Smythe up, badgering him on why this address in Berlin. Alistare-Smythe's cheerful answer was that this was reciprocal hospitality. He was to be the guest of an aristocrat he had entertained several times, for multiweek vacations on Malta in years past. Alistare-Smythe apologized for one of his servants not being in uniform, but pleaded exigencies of war. British resistance on Malta had collapsed too quickly for him to change, but both were retired military. Senior officers were entitled to having their batmen along to see to them. Surely it was obvious that Alistare-Smythe had too much luggage to carry by himself at his age.

The policemen were curious as to why so much luggage? Alistare-Smythe's reply was, why so little? He'd given his hunting shotgun to General Rommel on the surrender of Malta. It was in the propaganda film. Surely their agency could find a copy to confirm this. He had left his golf clubs, tennis racket, and other sports equipment with the general's staff for their use on Malta or after that in Libya. It was only hospitable. Gentlemen needed their leisure activities. He had left his riding horse and tack with the Italian command, as Malta was to become Italian. In reverse, he'd had to take his formal clothing. His hosts would expect him to dress for dinner.

The Gestapo operatives were most curious as to how he knew General Rommel and his command were going to Libya. Alistare-Smythe had laughed at them. Asked if they could read a map? One takes Malta to secure the sea route to Libya so one can conquer Egypt. Told them this was not a military secret, just common sense. Assured them that Germany had excellent staff officers who could read maps.

Both servants spoke excellent German, and provided Duffy with a running translation. Each had identified himself to the Gestapo by name, rank, and serial number. The Sikh had been Indian Army and was uniformed as such. The Chinese was in civilian attire but claimed to have been Hong Kong special police, which he asserted was a paramilitary unit. Now the four of them and the juniormost Gestapo agent, detailed as a minder, were waiting for the War Ministry morning shift to come on duty so the papers could be confirmed. The Gestapo office at the rail station had unpleasant older chairs and was a bit stuffy. However, the real inconvenience was the Ersatz coffee they were served. It was bitter brown water. Duffy hoped his Red Cross parcels would catch up with him. The beverage was vile. He looked forward to getting back to real coffee and proper tea.

0630 hours CET
30 August 1940
KG Strauss encampment, Bari, Italy

Major Gregor Voss stood at the head of the three companies he was leading to Libya. Two were Romanian Betar forwarded after his pal Gunter had already left for Malta. Someone back in Romania seem to have decided that if this unit had taken one company of Betar Revisionist Zionist Militia, it really meant they wanted all of them. Or at least an excuse could be made. A sufficiently plausible justification to dump piles of unwanted Jews on someone somewhere outside Romania.

The third company was a product of Gunter's little Hungarian adventure. He had left an NL garrison behind in one otherwise insignificant railway town, while transiting that chaos-plagued land. The new Italian-installed regime had brought quiet to Budapest and a few major cities. Also to the Carpathian frontier districts. Those were now occupied by mixed corps, each centered on an Italian alpine or cavalry division. The Germans had in turn secured the main roads, the railways, the Danube and the budding oil district in Hungary's west near Nagykanizsa. Gunter's Magyars from Ploiesti were by now part of this presence. They differed from the rest of the German presence in speaking Magyar. This had led to the other German garrisons seeing them as a convenient receptacle to dump refugees fleeing the depredations of the lunatic Arrow Cross fanatics. The Arrow Cross's protector, SS General Gestapo Müller, was gone. His successor, SS Gruppenführer Kaltenbrunner, was slowly trying to create order out of the prior armed anarchy; but the focus was on districts deemed vital to the Reich economy, not on the rural interior per se. The garrison was deluged with refugees, and decided to solve the problem by shipping them off to their former parent unit, which was in Bari, not in Taranto as they had thought. Gregor had had to go to Taranto each time to sign for the new group and guide them back. It was getting both familiar and annoying.

Either way, the encampment was stuck with these people. Gregor had sensibly conscripted the military-age males and started drilling them. When the demand from Bari Transit Command came for a new contingent for Libya, he just added the best of the Magyars to the two Betar companies to reach the required head count. He then added himself and his 'nephew' Hans. He was tired of being mayor of an encampment of civilians whose only daily activity was running a bar and brothel for Adolph and Wanda. He chuckled to himself. For Wanda. The Polack witch ran the place, and led Adolph around by the little head. The rest of the encampment pretty much ran itself. The Jewish Council of Elders Gunter had set up before he left, had simply expanded itself to be a more generalized Elders Council. They interfaced well with higher administration. They included enough former Habsburg or Romanov field officers to serve as their messengers. Gregor wanted more to life, a more active role to justify his Major's rank. Time to rejoin the active part of the unit, and the real war. In the meantime, he stood at proper attention for the farewell photos that were being taken.

....

Oriana was helping the part-Jewish photographer who was taking the portrait photos of the departing group. Aunt Wanda had detailed her to help because she had the neatest handwriting for the notes to accompany each photo. The bar would get the best prints, for the wall to show off their brave fighters. The relatives of the departing warriors would get the other prints to remember their absent men by.

Oriana was also assisting the photographer in various technical aspects of setting up the shots. He had promised to start teaching her his craft. She found photography fascinating. She already had a little notebook and had started a journal. Aunt Wanda had been a wonderful teacher, but Oriana still saw herself as a more intellectual, creative person than the very salt-of-the-earth Wanda. Oriana's world was expanding rapidly, and she was eagerly drinking in all the new vistas. She still wanted to experience war but Aunt Wanda had said she wasn't ready yet. Let their lads fight one more battle, while Oriana matured a bit more. She'd go with a later contingent and be there for the fights in Palestine and Iraq. Oriana wanted to be there for Egypt. Right now her Italian friends were in Libya, but Egypt was where the next fight would be. Oriana was still too small to properly use a rifle, but she had learned pistol and shotgun. Maybe if she learned photography too, there would be a place for her. Wars had stories, and the stories needed pictures.

1400 hours CET
30 August 1940
Camp Palestine #6, near Cracow, Poland

Company Political Officer Menachem Begin stood at attention with his new unit. Given Betar's favored status with the Nazi authorities, the movement had been swamped with volunteers. Original Revisionists were being used as political cadre in the Bolshevik Red Army manner, to instill proper values. Begin had been Betar national commander first in Czechoslovakia and then in Poland. As such he should have merited higher office. However, he and his mates had decamped from Warsaw to Vilna to avoid the Nazis in 1939. They had only come back to Poland in the tail end of the Baltic refugee tsunami, by which time the upper ranks had been filled by others.

Begin was still less than sure that working with the Nazis was the lesser evil to staying in Lithuania and dealing with the NKVD. The decision to leave had been collective. He'd been outvoted. He still thought that too much of it had been illogical, a human herd instinct. So many people left that everyone else just went with them, Jew and gentile both. The fiction was that the Reich Germans were evacuating the Baltic Germans. The Soviets were not fooled, but there had been orders from Moscow to allow this. Begin was sure that the NKVD and GRU had added their own agents to the migration. That was the Gestapo's problem, not his.

What was important was that the Germans were in fact arming Jews to evict the British from Palestine. They didn't bother telling lies that they would make Palestine independent. Their promise was that the Jews could go home and live in their lands in dignity. Could go home as conquerors with rifles in their hands. It was less than Zionism had hoped for, and far more than anyone else was offering. For now it would do. He was uniformed and armed, under the blue and white flag of Zion. He had a unit of recruits to indoctrinate. Others would teach them military skills. He would teach them to be Revisionists, and patriots of the Israel they would create.

....

Adolph Eichmann kept a proper mask on his face as the new Governor General of Poland, Gestapo Müller, droned onwards. Week by week Eichmann found his job more disgusting. To be a National Socialist was to be an anti-Semite … or at least it had been, under the old Führer and Reichsführer. Now he was the mayor of a vast and ever-growing Jewish city. Berlin assured him he was doing vital work. In point of fact, the damned Yids near to ran themselves. They would form new camps with his office just rubber-stamping the forms. One of Speer's minions would assign each new camp a German industrial partner, and work would begin. The fucking Yids were outproducing facilities in the Reich, much less what could be gotten from camps of lazy, hostile Poles.

Berlin had just ordered up a thousand of his Betar for service in Africa. Müller was here giving them a rousing speech as a sendoff. Enough of the Yids spoke enough German so they could sort-of follow. If not, their political officers would explain it in simple terms later. The thousand were Latvian and Lithuanian Hebrews who had come out of the resettlement as formed units. It made pragmatic sense to use these vermin to further Germany's interests, but it still made Eichmann feel dirty. His usual remedy had involved Jewish virgins, but that was getting stale. He thought the next time he'd try a filthy, rebellious Pole instead.   Maybe a convent girl. Fomenting incidents between the Yids and Polacks always amused him. Having his Jewish troops march into a convent and arrest two girls would maybe restore his humors. It was a pleasant daydream.

2300 hours local, 30 August [Manchuria]
1800 hours Moscow Time, 30 August [Moscow]
1600 hours, 30 August [CET]
The Kremlin, Moscow

Lavrentiy Beria was enjoying watching the Boss blast the army fools making their report on the first day of battle against the Japanese. The idiots had overpromised what they could accomplish, even with total surprise. He'd told Stalin that, while the invasion was still in the planning stage. The KV tanks had been fierce in battle but proved mechanically unreliable. Twice as many were down for technical problems as had been lost in combat. The cooperation between the army branches had also been suboptimal, and the coordination with the Air Force worse still. The Japanese Army had been overmatched, but even fiercer than the Finns. Their planes had run circles around the Red Air Force. Net, what the Soviet forces had were two fingers into Manchuria down the two branches of the Chinese Eastern Railroad. Twenty kilometers from the west and seven from the east on a line roughly 1800 kilometers long. This would be a long, slow campaign. The key was that it be victorious. It would need Red cavalry moved over the Amur. It would need a cavalry-mechanized thrust from Mongolia. Bringing in the pro-Soviet warlord of Sinkiang, Chiang's Nationalists, and the often disobedient Chinese Bolsheviks in Yen'an would also be necessary. Relations at the moment were better with Chiang, but all things were possible given time and support by the Boss. The Nazis may have conquered Europe. The

Soviets would conquer Asia, thereby sharpening the Red Army for its final battle to Sovietize Europe. Europe was the world's industrial heartland. So far Soviet efforts there had been less than successful. Finland, eastern Poland, and the Romanian borderlands – all had been less than optimal campaigns. Spain had been a clear defeat. Hence the tactical alliance with Berlin. They would be comrades … for now. The ultimate goal remained the same: world conquest.

0500 hours local; 0400 hours CET
31 August 1940
El Alamein position west of Alexandria, Egypt

Dawn was still a few minutes away, but Colonel Garth Mason had been up for hours and already on his second cup of coffee. Wavell's staff had greeted his arrival in Alexandria by immediately laying claim to him. They were forming three new divisions, and Coldstream Guards veteran colonels were not easy to come by. He'd been posted to command a brigade in the new 6th Commando Division. Brigade? Division? What a laugh. There had been eight nominal battalions of 'special troops' on Malta. Most had arrived in Egypt with strengths in the low hundreds of men, and no kit beyond some officers' side-arms. Fleming's battalion had come out overstrength from accumulated stragglers. Mason had been de facto part of it, arriving on the same armed merchant ship. The former Fleming battalion was now a new brigade. Mason's brigade had gotten three units with a combined strength just short of nine hundred men. He was gifted with the southern third of 6th Division's sector, while the Fleming Brothers' Brigade got the northern part, and a third brigade lay between them. On paper Mason's brigade should have totaled four thousand three hundred, plus another eighteen hundred missing brigade headquarters and support forces. The headquarters in fact was himself, three middle-aged temporary lieutenants, and a dozen part-British servants.

The ever resourceful Money-Penny had somehow found Mason twelve hundred 'recruits'. Warm bodies, was closer to reality. They were male, over puberty and under retirement age. Few were even nominally British. It didn't matter. They mostly understood enough English to do general labor, and the rest understood a bit of French or Arabic. Command had gifted Mason with six newly-minted engineering officers. They ranged from a retired French engineering officer from the Great War, to a Coptic building contractor. All were captains now by temporary wartime commission.

The master plan called for a defense line running some thirty-four miles from the Mediterranean Sea to the Quattara Depression, a geological feature supposedly impassible to vehicles. The 7th Division, being formed out of the evacuated remains of the Malta garrison, was digging the first stretch anchored to the coast. The 8th Division, being formed out of two brigades of Palestinian Jewish militia, had the southern end that fronted the Depression. The 6th Commando Division had the center of the line in the vicinity of Ruweisat Ridge, a low stone formation that offered good observation for miles to the west across the flatlands. Mason's brigade was digging out perpendicular to the ridge, and from there south to the linkup with the Jews.

The master plan was, to say the very least, lacking in fine detail. Everyone was working with maps from the land-registry offices. That was where the engineer 'captains' came in. The aged Frenchman provided the details of where to place trenches, bunkers, wire, minefields, firing positions for the guns they didn't have yet. The other five supervised work gangs doing the actual digging.

The supply situation was strange. There seemed to be an endless supply of barbed wire, tools, cement, telephone line, and rifles. There were ample machine-guns – but only if you counted obsolete models back to Maxim guns. Artillery was in such short supply that ancient muzzle-loaders were allocated as giant shotguns. Timber had always been a shortage item in Egypt back to Pharaoh's day, and the Alamein line lacked priority on what little there was. Autos were plentiful, trucks were scarce, and armored fighting vehicles nonexistent.

Mason saw the entire process as the forlorn hope it was. He still regarded it as worlds more realistic than the epic cock-up that had been Malta. O'Connor, with the Western Desert force, would fall back on Alamein in good time, even if he got a bit banged up in the process. This would give Wavell seven divisions to hold thirty-four miles of trench. A British army should be able to give a good account of itself in that kind of fight, more so if the five reserve divisions in Palestine were brought forward in support. They would be outnumbered and badly outgunned, but British troops on the defensive were hard to pry out of fixed positions. Such had been Mason's experience in the First War.

0930 hours CET
31 August 1940
Himmler's old office, SS Headquarters, Prinz-Albrecht-Straße, Berlin, Germany

Swedish Foreign Minister Christian Gunter had flown to Berlin last night, in response to a German diplomatic note demanding a meeting about an unnamed 'emergency situation'. The Swedish military had quietly been placed on alert against the possible German ultimatum. So far it had all been introductions and pleasantries by Reichsführer-SS Heydrich and his aide, Oberführer Schellenberg. Now lesser minions were putting up a map of the eastern Baltic, centered on Sweden and Finland. Gunter was a realist. Germany was about to make demands.

Heydrich was quite expert at reading faces. "Be at ease. We have demands, but none will quite violate your precious neutrality. Neutrality against the British Empire, to be precise. You are at peace with them, and at peace you remain. Your merchant ships outside the Baltic will continue to serve the British. We seek no bases and don't desire to place large numbers of troops on Swedish soil. Our demands relate to Finland."

"Finland?" Gunter was not prepared for this issue. He also hadn't missed the caveat of 'large numbers'. Even tiny numbers would enrage the British and be quite unwelcome to Swedish opinion, especially on the left among the Social Democrats.

"We have reached certain agreements with Moscow as regards Finland and Sweden. Both are now regarded as within the German sphere of influence. Stalin will retain his Finnish base guarding Leningrad, nominally from the British but in fact from us. You will provide nine divisions, including two corps headquarters, to occupy Finland. Nominally you will be defending Finnish neutrality. In fact, you will be there to aid the Finns should the Soviets attack again."

Gunter thought fast. His nation had been dealt away to Germany like the door prize at a bar. "We lack the strength to guarantee Finland from the Russians."

"Germany and Italy will stand as guarantors to both of your nations. We will send a combined military mission of fifteen thousand men to Finland, and two thousand to Sweden. Think of these as a mixture of liaison expeditors and technical experts. Four of your nine divisions will be active forces. So will one corps headquarters. The balance will be cadre units, but with full equipment sets. Easier to ferry men on mobilization that way. Finnish Marshal Mannerheim will be theater commander, but with a German deputy and a German chief of staff."

"Does this commit us to marching at your side against the Soviets?"

"Yes and no. If you are not attacked, no. Even if we are, you preserve your neutrality. However, if Stalin moves west, both of you will be targets. At least that's our best guess. In that case, you are allied to us for the duration, not just till the Soviets are repulsed from Finland."

Gunter had been prepared for worse. He hoped he could justify all of this to the British ambassador. "Are you asking for National Socialists in Sweden's government?"

Heydrich smiled. "No. I'm stuck with Quisling in Norway. As long as you are sensible, Germany is content to let Sweden preserve its domestic independence. Our demands regarding Swedish National Socialists are simple, and should be relatively painless for you. Unless the Swedish Party violates the domestic peace in your nation, you don't ban the party. We'll provide a few subsidies so they can maintain a newspaper and do a few rallies. We may also use them to recruit a few Swedes for our SS. I doubt many will choose to enlist, but a token Swedish legion fits our racial ideology. That's a public thing. In private, I accept that Swedish opinion runs far more to social democracy than national socialism. You are still fellow Aryans. That's enough for me. The other three rulers won't notice you either way."

Gunter felt he had to point out certain realities. "We barely have five divisions now. So I can announce your numbers, but it will take the better part of a year to fully realize this program. And two thousand Italo-Germans will end our neutrality as far as the British are concerned."

Heydrich took his time replying, letting the silence hang to discomfort the Swede. "You are acting as if this is a negotiation. It isn't. I said I wanted to avoid another Norway. However, at the end of things, that is the other alternative. You can blow up the iron mines. I can repair them in a year and can make up the shortfall from Stalin. It will cost Germany other concessions, but, with the Soviets tied up in an Asian War, we've got at least a two-year respite from any serious threat by them. So, I'm not changing this demand. You will take the two thousand. Explain it domestically, and in London, as you choose. Plead *force majeure*. Whatever. The smartest move is to not make a big deal out of it. We aren't sending all of them at once. We aren't sending formed units. It will be a few dozens of our men here and there, mostly on military bases and at ministries. I can instruct them to be on best behavior, but this is going to happen. If done quietly, your public won't grasp the full numbers. As for you needing a year, the first hundred German Army staff officers will arrive in a week. Convince them. I don't involve myself in such details. However, you will move a brigade in the next two weeks. You will send a divisional general and a corps commander. Our Führer, Italian Air Marshal Balbo, your two generals, and Mannerheim, will review the brigade in a march-by in Helsinki. It will get a full propaganda workup throughout Europe. Nod that you have heard me." Heydrich waited for the reluctant nod. "See. That wasn't so difficult. You Swedes are adults and fellow Aryans. Let us do this with at least a modicum of civility. It is better for everyone."

Gunter nodded. So far this was better than he had any right to hope for. There had to be a catch. Heydrich let him absorb all this, and then raised the difficult issue. Sweden had some fifty thousand Norwegian refugees, mostly young men of military age. Germany wanted these refugees, and any refugee Danes of military age, shipped to Finland and mobilized. At first these were to be labor units, but over time some would transition to Norwegian or Danish battalions under Swedish command. Gunter argued, for form's sake, but again eventually gave Germany what it wished. The final German demands were trivial. Germany wanted to set up a Swedish-language radio station as part of their new Europa network. They also had demands as regards making German a mandatory second language for Swedish secondary education. Both nations had bureaucrats that could quibble over the details. The final point passed almost unnoticed: Germany would be paying for Swedish iron ore and other goods in dollars, starting in a few months. It seemed the Germans were accumulating dollars via the Hoover Agency activities. Gunter saw no difficulty in taking US currency. After the war, it could easily be redeemed for gold. Dollars were the safest currency in the world. The US was rich and at peace.

1400 hours local time; 1300 hours CET
31 August 1940
The desert east of the international frontier between Italian Libya and British Egypt, southwest of the British fortified camp at Bagush

Peiper had had misgivings on this excursion from the beginning. His armored reconnaissance vehicles were back at Camp Gorlov awaiting the promised new parts. He had been sent off with his motorcyclists under the command of this hero, Major Steiner. Steiner had two platoons of his own in Type 82 Kübelwagen, plus a battery of captured British 81mm mortars in vans the Kübelwagen towed. Steiner admitted his troops had no training on these weapons. A few had a bit of experience serving Italian 45mm mortars, the Brixia Model 35, in the fighting on Malta. "A bit" had turned out to be a few hours of using such weapons supporting Rommel. A dozen of his people had gotten sent as reinforcements to Rommel, and were the only ones who had even that much familiarity with any mortars, much less with the new British ones.

Strauss wanted Steiner's people to fire off some rounds and get used to servicing the weapons. As no practice rounds had been sent, Strauss as commander had deemed it prudent to fire at an enemy. The British had a thin screen of armored cars forward of their position. The 'plan' was an exercise in desert navigation, fire a dozen rounds from each weapon, and perhaps pick up a prisoner or two. Peiper had been asked if he wanted to go along. To refuse would seem the act of a coward, so here he was.

Desert navigation seemed impossible. There were essentially no terrain features inland to steer by. This Major Steiner seemed unperturbed, but Peiper was getting seriously nervous. Oberst Strauss was a veteran of the Great War, as was Major Schwabe.   Major Gorlov was a decorated combat veteran from the Russian Civil War, and an aristocrat to boot. This Major Steiner had the two Iron Crosses, but had the affect of a clueless juvenile. He also couldn't possibly be as young as he looked. Veteran officers seemed to accept him as a field officer, and veteran troops reacted to him as though he were a respected combat leader. The SS officer kept seeing a short young man with a breaking voice. It made him nervous, and Peiper was not a good actor. Knowing that his discomfort was showing, made the Hauptsturmführer more uncomfortable still.

....

Major Klaus Steiner was happy to be given something to do. He had a compass and a vague map to guide himself by. He had a manual on land navigation he had studied with his Greta the night before. It seemed simply enough in theory. You marked directions and time. The time would be multiplied by approximate speed, and this should produce a rough location. From anyplace, the coast with its highway was always north. How lost could he get? Klaus had managed on Malta with no maps at all, only a vague clue as to where he was starting from, and woods to block sight lines.

Peiper seemed nervous. This disconcerted Klaus. The SS man was an experienced officer. What did he know that Klaus didn't? Klaus was tempted to ask him, but felt awkward querying a lesser rank from another service who was both older and more knowledgeable as a commander. Klaus was only a few months removed from being a rear rank HJ. The HJ had taught the superiority of the Aryan German race, with the SS as the pinnacle of that racial hierarchy. The Hauptsturmführer was formally his junior, a Hauptmann to Klaus's Major. Peiper was an elite Waffen SS officer, the elite of the elite. He had been in real combat in a real war against the French. This man had been a special assistant to the former Reichsführer-SS Himmler. Himmler was a traitor, but he'd still been the founder of that exalted institution. Peiper was things, had done things, beyond Klaus's capacities.

Klaus needed his status as a hero officer. His Greta depended on him. Klaus knew his brilliant reputation from Malta was a fraud, a set of lucky accident. He knew that he'd only seen skirmishes, not real battles. Everyone said that the new campaign would be against the best the British had, would be a real battle with tanks and artillery. Peiper clearly was finding fault with him, even if he didn't say anything. Klaus could read it on his face, in his gestures. Klaus told himself he must be stronger, braver, more decisive. He must earn this man's respect.

The combined force had found the British. They were several kilometers distant to the east. Ineffective fire had been exchanged, but neither side showed any inclination to close the range. The mortar crews proved they could service their pieces. They showed no talent at estimating ranges, or any form of accuracy. Klaus foresaw the need to get a few SA or Stahlhelm trainers. He knew he had a long way to go to be worthy of his promotion to Major. The two paramilitary services had men who had been gunners in the First War.

As the crews were breaking down the mortars for transport, the sentries reported the arrival of three Arabs on donkeys. Klaus had brought along Mary's thirteen-year-old son Bain in part because he spoke a bit of their language. The briefing had passed along Italian reports of desert Arabs wandering in the area, around and between the armies. They were bandits and thieves.

Bain's dialect was different enough from these three that communication was slow and hesitant. It took twenty minutes to arrive at the point. They had two British captives they wished to sell to him. They wanted a dozen rifles and ammunition. Bain countered by offering two. Thirty more minutes of bargaining was needed to reach a final price of four. Klaus had let Bain do the bargaining. He had no idea of how to haggle this way. Yet he felt this had lost him status with Peiper, that the experienced officer would have taken charge.

The Arabs called out, and seven of their fellows led in two white men in British uniform with hands tied and lead ropes around their necks. Apparently one of the new Arabs was the leader. He rejected the agreed price, and wanted to bargain again. Seemed quite arrogant about it. Klaus felt he could not let this go unpunished. He had Bain tell the man that he could take the four rifles or the price would drop, not rise. The Arab kept arguing. He also spoke too fast for Bain to follow. Bain had to keep asking him to slow down and repeat himself. Finally the new Arab leader became angry enough to raise a knife to one captive's throat. Threatened to kill the man unless the price was raised. He wanted five rifles for each.

Klaus had had enough. The Führer Göring had decreed proper treatment for British prisoners. If Germans were ordered to do this, then surely the same applied to barbarous Arabs. This was feeling like Romania and the mob. He unholstered his pistol and shot the man. Clearly this had surprised him. The Arab's eyes got huge just before the bullet went into his thigh. He fell over from that.

Two other Arabs went for their weapons, but Klaus's Betar were prepared. They gunned the two down, while keeping weapons leveled against the others. Bain quickly cut the bonds of the two prisoners. Turned out they were South African Dutch. What they spoke wasn't German but it was a cousin, especially if spoken slowly and using simple words.

One of the Dutchmen, or Boers as they called themselves, walked over to the wounded Arab, took the knife from his hands and cut the man's throat after first spitting in his face. He was screaming something about a third prisoner this man and his band had apparently first mistreated and then killed. Klaus sent out two of his Betar with one prisoner and a donkey. In ten or so minutes they came back with the dead third man tied down to the donkey.

That left the matter of the Arab prisoners. Klaus could feel Peiper's eyes on him, weighing and judging. He chose one Arab who seemed scarcely more than a boy. Had him stripped of his boots and tied onto another donkey. There seemed no need for the rest. One Arab and the two Boers would have whatever little information there was to be gathered. With Peiper watching, Klaus ordered his troops to kill the rest. Peiper seemed to nod approval. Klaus spent the time returning to base, weighing the lesson this SS officer had given him. Klaus knew he had so much to learn to be a proper German field officer.

1800 hours CET
31 August 1940
Conference Room, SS Headquarters, Prinz-Albrecht-Straße, Berlin, Germany

The French delegation of three (Laval, Darlan, and Weygand) had made their presentation. Their African Empire was in danger of falling to the British via their cat's-paw de Gaulle. France would need restrictions lifted on troop strength in the Empire. They would need to restart arms production. They would need at least cadres back from the German prisoner camps.

Heydrich let them finish. He allowed a silence of nearly a minute for the proper dramatic effect. "I'll let you bring back to active duty two surrendered divisions. General Busse of OKW proposes 15th Motorized Division under your General Juin, followed by the 1st Moroccan Division under whoever you choose. They both did well against us, and thus should do equally so against the British and Gaullists. We are also prepared to let you recruit eighteen battalions of airborne soldiers out of young French, Polish, and Walloon prisoners in combination with young men from the Occupied Zone that you will call to the colors early. They will go through our training center in battalion increments. They are more deployable as battalion-sized battle groups, but net that's two divisions. If you wish to form the brigade and division organizations for these airborne battalions, we will aid that. We will allow production of arms and munitions, including German designs, with an equal sharing of the results. We will provide some help on airlift for these deployments." Heydrich paused again to let them absorb this. They were men of the world. They knew that things had prices. "You will also remobilize from the prisoners ten divisions, three corps headquarters, and Ninth Army headquarters, all with proper support units. This formation will be placed under German command for the defense of Europe in the east."

Laval was allowed by the two military men to speak for France. "So you wish us as formal belligerents and allies?"

"Not exactly; and not yet. That would give the British the excuse to swallow your entire Empire, seize your merchant marine, et cetera. Your actions against the British will be defensive and reactive. You will tell your own public and the world such, starting with the Americans. You will ask the American government for permission to recruit new Lafayette Escadrilles and a Lafayette Legion. The Americans have fond memories of you from their Revolution, from that idiot statue you sent to New York, from the last war. Let us use these fantasies to our mutual benefit. You will try to involve Roosevelt in convoying reinforcements to Indochina. Perhaps he will be stupid enough to oblige. Either way, we do useful propaganda. Your Ninth Army will be part of a European non-aggression alliance between the New Europe and Stalin. You helped defend Warsaw from the Red Army in 1921. You are just doing so again. You will also ostentatiously protect some Poles in that army's zone from the evil Germans. Perhaps you will offer unhappy Poles a settlement area in West Africa?"

"So we will be invading the Soviets?"

"No. There is a mutual nonaggression pact under negotiation. France will sign third, after Germany and Italy but ahead of the rest of Europe. I know your national pride would prefer second place. That's something to work for, but at the moment you are third. I also have another offer for you to take back to the Marshal and the cabinet at Vichy. For each new army you form in the East, I'll allow one ministry back in Paris and return one arrondissement to French policing. As a gesture of good faith, I'll give you a ministry now. Which do you want, war or navy?"

It took the two squabbling General officers twenty minutes to take the colonial ministry as a compromise. Heydrich saved his last point till they were ready to leave. Germany would be making changes in primary and secondary education in the Occupied Zone. German was now the designated second language. Some other cultural matters were also being harmonized across Europe. There was to be a conference in October in Berlin. Please be sure the relevant ministries had delegations ready, and empowered to sign agreements.

2300 hours CET
31 August 1940
Skies over Europe

The RNZAF Vickers Wellington IC was lost. It had separated from its squadron over an hour ago. It had lost navigation lock over eastern Belgium. By flying time, it was now over Germany somewhere. It was also nowhere near its primary target of Berlin; and while it could intermittently see a river that probably was the Rhine, it was clueless as to where on the river it was, making finding its secondary target of Aachen unlikely. Right now there was a city somewhat lit up, a lake, and a fuel gauge that was nearing bingo. The lead pilot and bombardier agreed that they would write this up as Aachen. They aimed near the river, trying for a warehouse district. Clouds interfered with observation, but the mission report would state that they destroyed docks and six warehouses.

....

The Zurich, Switzerland, fire department spent an hour putting out a fire in an elementary school. Their national government would lodge protests with both combatants, who would in turn blame each other. The rest of the squadron managed to bomb random points in Germany between Magdeburg and Essen. In all the two squadrons flying this night managed to kill a cow, two dogs, a herd of deer, and an aging spinster. Five buildings sustained damage, and two small forest fires were started. At this stage of the war British Bomber Command was an annoyance, whatever lies the mission reports told.

Chapter 3

0640 hours Mongolian Time, 1 September 1940
2340 hours CET, 31 August, 1940
Road south from Ulaanbaator, Mongolia

Recently promoted Major General Lev Donatov was supervising the start of the march of his Second Far Eastern Cavalry Corps to a projected linkup in two or three weeks with the Chinese Soviet forces in Yan'an. The vanguard was a motorcycle battalion followed by a Siberian cavalry division. This was followed by a battalion each of light tanks, multipurpose 76mm guns, engineers, and NKVD. Then came a Mongolian cavalry division with the corps support troops bringing up the rear. All told he commanded some twenty thousand men, including a parachute battalion that would be flying in later today. That battalion would secure Yan'an and see to certain command arrangements that had been decreed from Moscow. A police general and NKVD company would land with them. General Donatov was quite happy to not be involved in all that. These Chinese had tens of thousands of men, maybe more. If their commanders did not take well to being relieved, this could all get very messy. Moscow tended not to accept explanations for failure.

2300 hours California time, 31 August 1940
0800 hours CET, 1 September 1940
SOCAL docks, Los Angeles harbor

The SOCAL tanker was burning at its dock in Los Angeles harbor. It had been doing so for hours and would probably continue to do so for at least another day. Harry Bridges, head of the West Coast dockworkers and senior official in the Congress of Industrial Organizations, was watching from a safe distance. He was sure the Party's illegal section had done this. He'd received no official notice of this. A prominent above-ground union official such as himself needed to be kept carefully segregated from what the illegals and their activist allies did. Bridges was followed day and night by Hoover's FBI. His current minders were some ten yards away, and making no attempt to hide their presence. By both physical type and clothing they were as easy to distinguish as Nazi SS. They were tall, well built, well if cheaply dressed, and of old American stock. Few immigrants, still fewer ethnics, and certainly no non-whites.

Formally, Bridges had never been a Party member. That too was part of his camouflage. The masquerade necessary to burrow into the capitalist beast was part of the class war. The Workers' State had gone to open war with the reactionary Japanese militarists. The Japanese military was supplied by oil, gasoline, steel, scrap, and other things that passed through the Pacific ports whose docks Bridges mostly controlled. There had been no courier from Moscow alerting him to this change in the world order. It was safer that way. Bridges had eyes and could see the obvious.

Hoover could also see the same game board. So Bridges would not demand his men boycott shipments to Japan. He would agitate against the Japanese, but his formal actions would all be within the bounds of lawful labor strife as currently practiced in the US. He could pass the word to go work-to-rule on any dock that dealt with the enemies of the Soviet Union. His war would be slowdowns, ceaseless wildcat strikes over any grievance however petty, and support from the top for any union local who boycotted on their own. He could use these tactics to paralyze most shipments to Japan ... unless the capitalists used the National Guard. Even then, he could probably bring the docks to a virtual standstill for a period of months. As a devout Soviet patriot, Bridges knew his duty to the World Revolution.

> 1300 hours CET
> 1 September 1940
> Schellenberg's office (formerly Himmler's), SS HQ, Prinz-Albrecht-Straße, Berlin, Germany

Berlin's oppressive summer heat had been broken this morning by a heavy rainstorm, a possible harbinger of autumn. Now the returning heat was turning the morning's deluge into even higher humidity than Berlin's summer norm. Major Graf Claus von Stauffenberg, OKW liaison to von Manstein's Afrika Korps, was in the lair of the Army's SS enemies. He had been summoned to a conference with Oberführer Schellenberg, Vice-Chancellor Heydrich's #2. Claus felt it a sad situation when the Army was at the beck and call of a glorified police clerk.

Schellenberg had received him in the vast office that had belonged to the deceased traitor Himmler. Von Stauffenberg found this peculiar. Why did the junior have the much larger, more prestigious office?

Schellenberg was not telepathic. However, this was not the first 'visitor' to experience this disjunction. "Reichsführer-SS Heydrich chose to keep his own office. He was making a point. Think. It should be obvious." Schellenberg gave the Graf a chance, but no light of recognition dawned. "My boss doesn't need a big office to show his importance. He could receive visitors in a broom closet for all it matters. On a day-to-day level, he rules Germany. The power speaks for itself. You were there for the prior conference. His three co-rulers simply refuse to sully their hands with the day-to-day grind. Führer Göring does the traditional duties as chief of state. Speeches, rallies, banquets. Think of him as Kaiser. To the public he is the face of the State, the regime, and the Party. That role interests him and he's quite good at it. He's equally adept with aristocracy in formal settings and with the masses at rallies in beer gardens. That leaves the two generals, whose interest in anything beyond the institutional independence of the Army and the social perquisites of their class is nil. We have one active campaign, and they cannot even be bothered with THAT."

Von Stauffenberg tried to defend the two generals and the officer corps. Schellenberg let him talk himself out, saying nothing beyond a sardonic expression. When Claus finally ran out of words, the Oberführer quietly asked, "Are you done?"

Von Stauffenberg nodded, curious at what came next. "The officer corps made its choices. They think we National Socialists are a collection of gutter-trash gangsters." Schellenberg shrugged. "So what? We can debate fine points of etiquette after the final victory. Right now we need to defeat the British and prepare for the Soviets. We hope Stalin won't attack us, but look what he did in Manchuria. If them, why not us when he thinks he can win? Any pact with Communism is always tactical and transitory. Their allegiance to Marxism is religious. Stalin and Lenin are gods that walk. Trotsky is Satan. Silly people with an absurd set of theories, but they have a huge army and vast resources. So you gentlemen of the Army must work with the gangsters who can deliver the masses. It's been the same bargain back to 1932, even before we took formal power. Hence it is best you and I get better acquainted. We will be working together frequently. Besides, there are a few things that need settling at our level." Von Stauffenberg looked attentive as Schellenberg went on. "First is your resistance contacts."

Von Stauffenberg needed iron discipline not to twitch in his chair at this. Was he being threatened? "Relax. We know you have refused to join. Besides, they are harmless enough. So far … But there are limits. I have been tasked to use you as a liaison to them, to remind them that there are boundaries that should not be crossed. We know names, we know details. We will tolerate their gatherings and musings, but if it goes operational there will be consequences. Those consequences will include entire families. Rank and connections won't protect people. Tell them to look at Adenauer's circle for where the bright lines are that will force the Gestapo to act. We have no wish for a Stalinist state. It stifles thought and would weaken Germany. At heart, despite our differences, we are all German patriots."

Von Stauffenberg nodded acceptance. This whole meeting was distasteful, but so far not dishonorable. Schellenberg went on, "Now some of your circle will find these limits frustrating. We have a proposition for them, and you are to be the messenger. Palestine is to be partitioned on conquest. Germany will get the port of Haifa, the pipeline to the Kirkuk oil fields, and the adjacent territories in Galilee. That's where we will dump the Grmanized Jews and part-Jews. Italy gets the rest of Palestine, but for their own reasons they are creating a Papal state with Jerusalem, Nazareth, Bethlehem, Hebron, and the adjacent counties. His Holiness will need cadres to police and administer these lands. The Hospitallers, the Knights of St John of Malta, will be revived as a working aristocratic order to do this. We have obtained a Papal bull, secret for now, allowing a companion revival of the Teutonic Order. You have the contacts among the Catholic aristocracy to begin recruitment."

"So you seek to subvert the Vatican?"

Schellenberg gave Claus a most patronizing look. "Subvert? By openly negotiating to recreate the Teutonic Order? By asking you to recruit oppositional Catholics who will honor their oaths to the Pope and Church? You aren't that stupid and neither are we. We seek to establish a German link between this new Papal Kingdom of Jerusalem and our colonies-to-be in the Near East. Cultural and blood ties. No subversion. No espionage. The thousand-year Reich will have its source of petroleum in the region. Linkages of family, of language, of culture will ease the inevitable frictions over the decades. In reverse, a bolthole for well-born Catholics who find the Movement abhorrent will minimize discord here. Learn to think long-term. Your class and mine don't like each other. Why not reduce the strife?"

The Graf sat sipping his coffee, trying to find some way that this was insulting to his class and church. The National Socialist was content to let him puzzle it through. Schellenberg knew the key was von Stauffenberg's willing cooperation, and that required that he examine the proposal carefully. As there were no hidden traps, letting Claus figure this out himself was just another step in the process.

1800 hours local time; 1700 hours CET
1 September 1940
6th Commando Division sector of El Alamein lines, Egypt

The screaming session had been going on since a dawn breakfast. The colonel from Wavell's HQ engineering section hated everything Fleming's brigade engineering officer was doing. They had argued theory. They had debated their prior CV's. By now they were questioning each other's paternity and membership in the human species.

"This is NOT what our plans call for. You are one brigade in a larger force. It simply won't do to create your own whimsical defense plans." The colonel had started choleric. By this time he was near apoplectic. He had the fine-bred face planes of a British squire, and the fine bloodshot lines around the nose and eyes of a career alcoholic.

"I was trained by Germans. They are better at this than you idiot Brits are. We showed you that in Palestine for years in the Great War. You had numbers, firepower, everything. We held you back for three years. Held you back with troops as untrained as most of these are." The brigade engineer was an ex-Ottoman, and had been a soldier of fortune in China for over a decade after Ataturk's victory. He was a slender Eurasian man with almost effeminate features. However, he had strong hands and sharp eyes, even though well into middle age. "You've never faced an enemy with air superiority. You need positions you can camouflage from above. You need multiple firing positions for every heavy weapon. You need strong positions for those near-useless antitank rifles of yours to survive long enough. You'll have to be within 100 meters to take out a German tank, and even then you'll need to knock a track off. Pity you didn't steal some French 75's. Those could work at maybe 300 meters." The Eurasian paused. He seemed to debate going over (yet again) what was obvious to him. He even gave an almost Gallic shrug before continuing. "It is all meaningless anyway. You have no plans for passage of the lines when your professionals get blown out of Mersa Matruh. You refuse to admit that you will get blown out of these lines, and so have no plan for a retreat to the Nile or Suez. You remind me of the Young Turk leadership in the Great War. Each major retreat was unthinkable because of morale, because of internal politics, because the results were too awful to contemplate. So we barely managed each time, and fell apart the last time, retiring on Damascus and Beirut. Fell apart and the war was lost. So was the Caliphate." The HQ officer was now screaming at the top of his lungs. The smaller man ignored it and plowed on. "A real army prepares for the worst, whether it is palatable to seniors or not. You are a farce, a paper tiger. You will lose your Empire in this region from blockheaded arrogance. Egypt can at best be a delaying action for you. Plan for it and you may save Palestine. You would then have a chance to hold Iraq, to keep Iran's oil as well. MY front will hold if you let me do it my way. If not, please write my discharge so I may quit Egypt. I'm only fighting beside you because however poorly you do so, you rule Egypt. My second wife's family has property here. I'll risk my life to save those estates. If you make it hopeless, then let me leave; and we'll see if she values her marriage vows over her family ties."

Fleming cut in yet again, tried to defuse this. He hadn't a clue as to who was right. He was trusting Money-Penny, who had found him this man. Commander Ian Fleming preferred running the headquarters of his new brigade to managing on a day-to-day basis. He and his brother Peter were official heroes of the Maltese debacle. Peter was a Grenadier Guards officer originally. So Ian made him his number two, allowing him active command of what had been a large battalion on Malta and was now a five-battalion brigade in Egypt. Using Money-Penny as a recruiting officer, he had three oversize infantry battalions, a heavy weapons battalion, a large labor battalion, an ample sized headquarters command, and Money-Penny's personal company. Officially they were the brigade's grenadier company. Lieutenant Commander James Money-Penny still thought like the soldier of fortune he had been. He referred to these men alternately as his villains, or just his gang. They seemed a nasty lot, but Ian had learned to depend on Money-Penny's judgment in these matters.

Peter knew how to actually train and command soldiers. The Eurasian civil engineer James had found knew trenches and construction, apparently from prior service with both the Ottoman and postwar Kemalist Turks, followed by some Chinese adventures involving various warlords. He was ignoring the plans provided by higher headquarters. Peter assured him the man knew his job. Convincing the higher muckety-mucks back in Cairo was Ian's job. Ian was a wizard at the sort of elite networking, that made the Empire work in spite of London and the Ambassador in Cairo.

Money-Penny had gotten his recruits via field-expedient use of his contacts to get the recruits' families passage. To India, to Ceylon, to Java, to where ever Money-Penny could find ships leaving Suez for. The accommodations were less than perfect, often jammed in with cargo on vessels who did not normally carry passengers. How Money-Penny was paying for all this was something Fleming chose not to know. Odds said it involved black marketeering, currency manipulations, and a host of illegalities. Money-Penny seemed to have neither scruples nor limits. He also seemed to know similarly bent operators all over the British sphere of influence. Fleming was sure James was forging his name on all sorts of questionable documents. It was worth it. Ian had seen the other two brigade sectors of his division and the frontages of the other two divisions. Only the Palestinian Jews had done as well, and no one else had done better. The fate of Egypt would turn on this line. He had been sending private reports back to Churchill outside the chain of command. Churchill was far from his only patron in London, but he was the highest placed … for now. Fleming had kept contact with half a dozen other senior Tory and Liberal office holders and power brokers. It was a game he well knew how to play. Those connections had led to his current rank and position.

0700 hours
2 September 1940 local time
2300 hours, 1 September CET
Yan'an, Chinese People's Democratic Republic

Yan'an was hot and dusty. This was nothing unusual for late summer in that region. Wang Ming didn't care. The wind could have been blowing straight out of Hell with temperatures to melt steel, and he would still have been in ecstasy. He'd won. The Soviet Union had entered the anti-Japanese War. They had dispatched a parachute battalion here. A large cavalry corps was coming. Also arriving had been minders from Moscow with peremptory orders. Mao and his clique were removed from power. Loaded onto planes and packed off to Moscow for 'consultations'. Wang's clique was back in power, his line validated. A new Chinese People's Democratic Republic was decreed. No more of Mao's peasant deviationism. This would be an exemplary proletarian state, advancing to the better future under the Lenin-Stalin Red Banner.

Wang had been forced to keep Deng Xiaoping and a large group of second-level cadres on. He could live with that. The key was establishing a rail link, paralleled by an all-weather modernized road, back to the Soviet railhead in Mongolia. Connections over which could flow the bounty of a modern industrial society, that would enable Democratic China to have a modernized Red Army, industry and an urban proletariat. He was Moscow-trained, and Moscow's line was the road to revolutionary utopia. Mao had been grinding him into dust before this gift from Stalin. Now sanity had returned. Internationalism as guided by Moscow was the only correct line to take. Stalin's will was law to any good Communist. Stalin's wisdom is like a lighthouse showing the right way to Communism to all humankind !

0600 hours local; 0400 hours CET
2 September 1940
Beirut Harbor, Lebanon, French Syrian Mandate

The nine French warships, led by the battleship *Lorraine*, had reached the harbor from Alexandria just before dawn broke. The French authorities were surprised to see them. This squadron had been in British captivity since the armistice with Germany. Now the British had returned the vessels. The RN had said this was a matter of honor. It seemed to be a confused tale involving homage by the surviving senior officers of the British Mediterranean Fleet to their fallen comrade, the late Andrew Cunningham. The guns on these ships were still inoperable, and their fuel bunkers were so near to empty that *Lorraine* arrived towing one destroyer where the margin had been cut too fine.

The ships were packed with 'French' refugees. Many lacked French passports, but thanks to the Alliance Française were culturally French. French had been made into one of Alexandria's major languages, and many residents were fluent in the tongue. The admiral's staff had seen how broadly the British had applied the concept of "imperial subject" in their successive evacuations of Malta and Alexandria. They made the decision to do the same here, and let Vichy sort the mess out later. The odds said there wouldn't be a second chance to leave the city. The rail line still ran through Palestine to Syria … for now. The Germans were coming, and would bomb it.

It was all of a piece with other intelligence. The British were evacuating the Eastern Basin of the Mediterranean. British and allied merchant shipping, including much of the Greek merchant marine, were all heading to Suez and through there to the wider oceans where Britannia still ruled the waves.

The British were also evacuating their civilians from the Balkans and Cyprus.

The naval attaches had been alerted by their usual local helpers when the tugs were sent out to help the war fleet in. They were grouped at the sea wall by alliances. The Germans, Italians, Soviets, Romanians, and the other lesser Axis allies occupied one section. The British, their lesser helpers such as the Greeks, the Japanese and the nominally neutral Americans, were a good hundred meters off in a similar pack. In between were the neutrals such as the Turks and Spanish. The French authorities had already sent a coded radio message to Vichy. All would send ciphered telegrams to their respective capitals. These would be varying mixes of observation and speculation. The core common content was that the Axis was on the march, and the British were not sanguine about stopping them.

0800 hours local; 0700 hours CET
2 September 1940
Three thousands meters altitude on a holding pattern a kilometer out to sea from the British base camp at Mesa Matruh

Hauptmann Bruno Dilley was leading his squadron in an oblong racetrack pattern off the coast. Their mission was 'targets of opportunity'. Mostly that meant waiting for the British flak guns to fire on the other bombers, and then doing dive-bomb attacks on the exposed anti-aircraft positions. His planes had taken off just after dawn for the morning sortie. They followed the coast here, and the daily dance began.

Bruno was aware that much of the squadron saw him as a vain fashionplate, obsessed with his good looks and silk scarves like some companion of the Red Baron in the Great War. He just felt they were jealous of his Aryan manly physique and chiseled features. What did his personal affectation, projecting an image of a hero airman, matter? He was a good commander and an excellent pilot.

He'd been happy when the posting in Sardinia had ended. Anti-ship patrol meant tricky long-distance missions involving navigation over water. Seas lacked geographic features for reference. It was so easy to get lost, and when you did there was no place for an emergency landing. His wing had managed. They had sunk a British carrier, the *Argus*. The fools at higher staff dismissed the feat, saying it was a training ship. Training ships stayed home to train. The British had sent it into battle and his guys had sunk it. Mission accomplished. The ground crews had painted a white carrier outline where an air-air kill credit would go.

Still, he'd rather bomb ground targets. They didn't zig-zag. Made aim easier. Ju-87's were designed for this. Bruno might affect the fashions of a fighter ace, but he was a dive-bomber expert, proud of his hard-won skills.

Two squadrons of He-111's passed over the British positions. The AAA started to fire, exposing themselves. The damned Limeys were getting better at camouflage day by day, but firing revealed the location of any weapon. He chose one battery, alerted his companions to follow him, and began his attack.

0900 Hours CET

2 September 1940

SS HQ, Prinz-Albrecht-Straße, Berlin, Germany

Over the last few months, many changes had been made in the headquarters of the SS. Now that the repairs were done, walls were being knocked down and new space created. Reichsführer SS Heydrich needed an ever-growing staff, and that staff needed work space. One of the first fruits of those efforts was a waiting area that had been set up so those needing to see the Reichsführer SS or one of his aides had a place to wait. In the just finished but well-appointed waiting room, Hauptmann Schmidt of the Luftwaffe found himself sitting on a comfortable couch. With a brief glance around the room, Schmidt observed other officers from various branches of the Wehrmacht, SS, and civilians. All waiting their turn to speak with the key power in Germany. Attempts to get a meeting with the Führer, even by those of cabinet rank, were met with refusal. Similarly, the two main generals didn't see people except when they chose to summon them.

***

Once Schmidt's letter of introduction made it past the gate-keepers, he was hurried into a meeting with Oberführer Schellenberg, Heydrich's personal aide. As his name was called, several more senior offers frowned at a mere Hauptmann getting a meeting so quickly. Some of those took note of Schmidt's face. A man that could so quickly gain access to one so close to Heydrich, was a man to remember.

Schellenberg waved Schmidt to a seat after the required military courtesies were exchanged. The two men had meet very briefly on Malta, after Schellenberg arrived to make a review of the situation and inform Ramcke of his promotion. "From Generalleutnant Ramcke's letter, you have not only his promised after-action report from the invasion of Malta, but you are available to answer any questions that might arise."

A brief nod, followed by a folder with many typed pages and several maps. "I can provide an executive summary … "

"Please, let's get to the heart of the matter."

Generalleutnant Ramcke had been most clear on what to say, and in particular that there was to be no attempt at sugar-coating things. "We were lucky."

Taken aback at those words, Schellenberg wasn't quite speechless, "Care to elaborate?" It was VERY rare that people in Schmidt's chair were this honest this soon in the process.

"The report goes on at length, but the key thing that won the day was that the enemy had a near-hopeless situation with our control of the skies, and too few troops versus so many of ours. Despite those advantages, defeat was a very real possibility for us." Before Schellenberg could try to pry more details out of him, Schmidt raised a hand to forestall the question, "I know you want specifics, but first it must be clear in your mind it could have gone another way. The paradrops had failed to take any airfield, only the NL glider attack succeed. If that had failed, the entire operation might have collapsed."

"Very well. Your point has been made. What caused the initial paratrooper attacks to fail?" So began a more in-depth review of the chaos that was the conquest of Malta. The poor coordination and not enough transports were already well known, so Schmidt didn't belabor those points. The details left were the paratroopers missing their drop zones, being scattered all over the island; with some, it was now clear, ending up drowning in the Mediterranean. A worse problem was the firepower of the paratroopers who did land at least near their targets. Most of the *Fallschirmjägers'* weapons were dropped, not with them, but in separate weapons containers.   Many MG-34 machine-guns and 98K carbines hadn't been found immediately, some not even until the next morning – forcing the troopers to fight with pistols; or, if they were lucky, MP-38 submachine-guns; or; if very unlucky, knives. The failure to locate the containers with the radios was quickly passed over. Ramcke had already made Berlin aware of THAT problem.

As always, when saying there is a problem, it is good form to give a possible solution.   Schellenberg politely asked, "What does the Generalleutnant suggest to resolve this in future airborne missions?"

"We need a weapon that can be dropped with the paratroopers themselves. Also, carrying multiple weapons, both rifles and submachine-guns at the same time, is a problem. If at all possible, a weapon combining the *capability* of the two types would both simplify the logistics and increase overall firepower."

Schellenberg finished his own notes while glancing through the formal report from General Ramcke. Trying to figure out how to condense this into reasonable length for Heydrich. "Thank you, Hauptmann Schmidt, I will be sure the Reichsführer SS gets the information. You need an all-purpose battle rifle capable of being dropped as part of the Fallschirmjäger's personal kit ... which will limit weight and length." Schellenberg made a note to himself to involve the Waffen SS in this project. They, also, needed weapons that they could get without having to fight the Army for them. The SS in Africa were mostly using captured Czech weapons as it was.

0930 hours CET
2 September 1940
Living quarters, Reich Chancellery, Berlin

Führer Herman Göring was lingering over his morning coffee. His wife, and their mutual 'best friend' Olga, were asleep back in the bedroom. Normally he would have been as well. They had not gotten to bed until almost dawn, after an all-night reception for party officials from Berlin and Brandenburg. Carousing with the cadres was one of his important functions, as both chief of state and head of the Party. Hitler had maintained a social distance with their predecessors. Göring preferred a different approach. A leader should be socially accessible. The drinking, the singing, the coarse jokes were all part of forming a bond with the minions he relied upon to rule his state. Including wives and girlfriends was part of the process. The hens would cluck together while the men clustered around him, laughing at his jokes. They would also beg favors. Favors that would interfere with Heydrich's well-run machinery of governance.

Heydrich! The man was an enigma to Göring. He maintained no social circle beyond occasional early morning rides with Admiral Canaris, the head of Abwehr. Other than Schellenberg (who seemed to be Heydrich's shadow or alter ego), Heydrich had protégés, tools in human form, rather than an entourage of eager sycophants.   The man seemed to live for work, and thrive on the boring bureaucratic drivel that made the mechanisms of state function.

The 'system' was Heydrich's office forwarding endless decrees and directives for the Führer to sign, and Göring sending requests for special treatment for a parade of self-seekers in the Movement, the aristocracy, and the other circles of power. Nine times out of ten, Göring's 'request' simply happened. The tenth would get a counter-memo explaining the problems something would cause, usually accompanied by another sweetener Göring could dispense instead. So far there had been two dozen times Göring had insisted – and every time Heydrich had not protested further. So Göring was still in charge, still the Führer … or was he? Were these instances of subordination, just another device by that blond devil Heydrich to keep Göring toiling away on the external formalities of power, while Heydrich really ruled? Göring sipped his cooling coffee and brooded. The infuriating part was, that there was simply no way to tell what the reality was. They jointly ruled, while actually conferring very little and almost never debating policy or even personnel.

Göring had seen seven years of Hitler's way – a solar system of senior people orbiting the Boss, all backstabbing each other while empire-building. He, Goebbels, Himmler, Bormann, Schacht, Hess, were the inner circle with eight or ten others dancing further out. All maneuvered shamelessly against each other, often resulting in nothing getting done for long periods of time. Other times, the successive contradictory Hitler-decrees produced endless waste and chaos. This new age was something else, but Göring couldn't find a name for it, didn't know a template to fit it into.

The truly funny part was that the two senior generals had isolated themselves from real day-to-day power. Their obsession with operational trivia filled their days, while Heydrich drew more and more power away from them. Away from them, but to where instead? Were Beck and Halder a Hindenburg-Ludendorff pair? Was he a mere front for Heydrich, or was Heydrich the tireless prop to his, Göring's, throne? The coffee was by now cold and getting colder. The answer still eluded him.

Chapter 4

1400 hours local; 1300 hours CET
2 September 1940
Headquarters Italo-German Panzer Army, Tobruk, Libya

General Carlo Geloso, de facto commander in place of the absent Prince Umberto, had let his sort-of subordinate, General von Manstein, commander of the German Afrika Korps, finish his presentation. Germany was the decisive partner in the Axis, but with Italy shouldering the main load here in Libya. So command was more a collegial exercise than staff manuals would dictate. Those were his clear instructions from Prince Umberto, and Geloso would execute his orders even when he found them unpleasant.

Present were all three of his Italian corps commanders, plus von Manstein with two of his German divisional commanders. SS General Steiner was absent, as was the bulk of his Afrika division. The eventual arrival of either was a matter of conjecture. Also present was General Jodl; although precisely in what capacity remained unclear. None of his corps was in Libya, nor was it expected anytime soon. Both air forces had junior generals present in a liaison capacity. Geloso made sure he had everyone's attention, and gave a simple answer to von Manstein – "No."

Von Manstein was nonplussed. He didn't like Heydrich's orders for sending Rommel on what amounted to a raid, but recognized that they were orders, not an opening in a negotiation. "Which part are you rejecting, sir?" Could this Italian not see who held the power here?

"All of it except the date. The order is absurd. I am sure your Reichsführer does not understand why. That's not his place. Government makes demands, and we military professionals must make reality conform. We have four corps here. Comprising nine Italian and two German divisions, plus considerable support troops. The British have a large corps with two further corps in reserves. So we attack on the required date, and General Rommel is placed in the ordered position, but everything else changes. Currently the British are in an entrenched position centered on Mersa Matruh and Bagush. We have advance posts some kilometers away at Sidi Barrini, with our main forces still back in Libya. We will not advance one German division against a corps. We will advance the entire army. Two Italian corps will advance first, fixing the British position frontally. They will move up the coast road in one column, with a second swinging onto the low plateau to confront the southern end of the Mersa Matruh position. General von Manstein, you will advance with the entire German force, not just Generalmajor Rommel's division. Your line of advance will be the high plateau south of the British entrenchments. Your advance will be spearheaded by the First Libyan Division and this provisional brigade of Oberst Strauss. The Libyans are experts on this terrain and born to the climate. Your Germans are neither. Your Oberst Strauss will set up an advance base for your corps. I am told he has a vehicle repair unit, and enough infantry to guard your corps trains and support elements. Generalmajor Rommel will be in your lead, to proceed further to develop the British position at Bagush.

General Jodl's forces will follow to mask this position, while Seventh Panzer swings eastwards beyond and tries to find a route north to the coast to complete the encirclement. General Messe's Italian mobile corps will deploy south of you, covering the desert flank. I will order its further advance, based on the British response to our advance. General Hausser's SS division will remain in army reserve, to exploit once the British flee. Which they will eventually do. They have a corps digging a line at Alamein. It is where they should be defending. We are lucky they are being fools and making a stand where they are. Questions?"

Rommel jumped up first before anyone else could speak. "I have orders from Berlin for a turning movement to exploit as I see fit. Those are my orders. Specified as saddle orders, which means I am given a force and an objective, then left to accomplish this in a manner I find appropriate. I will appeal any change to Berlin."

Geloso coolly looked Rommel up and down, letting him stand there in silence. "I'm perfectly willing to send my plan to Berlin first. Do you want the professional risk that General Busse will agree with me? That your rulers will?" He let the pause hang. "There are three professional British divisions in that fortified camp. They are acclimated to the heat, to the terrain, to the local diseases. You have a division of conscripts. They did good service in France … or so I am assured. That was against French conscripts with low morale. You were Reichswehr. You commanded professionals. You know the difference in quality. Even their privates are multiyear veterans. Their battalions have years of working together in harmony. This is not a semi-trained mass of Frogs who before call-up in 1939 had never met each other, much less trained together. The French system was absurd. British regimental soldiering is outdated, but it is sound military sociology. You fight for men you know, men you have trained beside. Keep thinking Reichswehr. The British tactics aren't as good as those of your interwar Germans, and their field officers are outmoded, but company and below they are the equals of your interwar force. Their second-line troops are a glorified militia, but they are digging positions back at Alamein, or on guard duty in the Egyptian cities. So you will make your raid in the manner of motorized light cavalry. It will do little harm, and might panic their higher command. Motorized armies need supply lines. They burn fuel and ammo. You are aiming for their one highway back to their depots in Alexandria, Cairo, and Suez."

While Rommel stood there thinking, Geloso turned to Jodl. "Can you run a division? You are an artilleryman and a staff officer. This is actual field command." Jodl looked determined, not apprehensive, which to Geloso settled that issue. "Von Manstein, can you handle this corps?" Von Manstein simply laughed at him. Command was to him a family tradition. These were clear orders with recognizable objectives. Not exactly the way Berlin had phrased things, but in no ways contradicting Heydrich. Von Manstein could justify this. That left Hausser, clearly unhappy at his role. "Alright, General Hausser, please state your objections."

"My division is as good as General Rommel's."

"I quite agree. Berlin Command made Rommel the advance guard. A command in Berlin headed by your service, the SS, not the Army. So feel free to protest there. However, an exploitation force is needed. One German division exists only in bits and pieces. That leaves two. Your Reichsführer specified one as this flanking force. Myself, I'd have used Messe and my Libyans. Troops acclimated to the theater and capable of navigating these waste lands. Berlin wanted the glory for a German force. They chose Rommel. I need a good mobile division to exploit. The big danger in this battle is not that we lose. Almost no way that can happen. We have numbers, firepower, and complete air superiority. The quite possible bad result is we inflict only a bloody nose followed by the British corps getting away intact back to their fortified position at Alamein. Our losses are less relevant than whether we bag any – or all – of these divisions. You Germans have far more experience at successful mobile battle than my Italians." Left unsaid, was that the German vehicles and equipment were also much more modern. This was starting to be addressed with the new production cartels, but those changes would not arrive in time for the Egyptian Campaign. "This sort of fluid warfare is what the Reichswehr trained for. I will make clear to Berlin that this is your main goal. You and Rommel. Jodl doesn't have real mobile troops and cannot be expected to keep up. Messe will cooperate as he can, but I will rely on you. Rommel will have position but be spread out. You will have the mass for a good clean punch." Geloso gave the subordinates a full minute to absorb all this, then dismissed them. Undoubtably they would complain to Berlin. So what? *This* plan had a good chance of working. If Rome wanted a diplomat, they should have chosen someone else.

2100 hours CET
2 September 1940
Commandant's Office, Pawiak Prison, Warsaw, General Government (Occupied Poland)

SS Gruppenführer Theodor Eicke was never a man of calm temperament. His demotion from combat division commander to police functionary, was not calculated to bring out his better side. Eicke had been forced to see his Death's Head division stripped of its heavy weapons, and near to half its men, by officers acting on behalf of that Reichswehr renegade Hausser. Hausser had only become National Socialist by decree when the Stahlhelm had been forcibly amalgamated with the SA. Eicke had been a Movement purist, a True Believer, back to the glory days of the early 1920's. Now here was Heydrich, a late joiner as well, demoting him over a petty matter of shooting a few British swine. Dietrich's LAH had done the same, and he was rewarded with the expansion of his regiment into a full guards division. It was all personalities and factionalism. Eicke had been a favorite of Himmler's, and now he was being punished for his loyalties to the SS's creator. Supposedly Himmler had turned on Hitler. Eicke didn't believe it for a minute. Göring and Heydrich were the plotters, the traitors. They were in league with the reactionaries of the officer corps against the true National Socialists such as himself.

The Death's Head division was now a field security corps of four regiments. The ranks had been built up with part-Germans from Poland and the Baltic States, instead of good Reichs Germans from the camp guards corps. The guards were Eicke's former command, and its cadres were loyal to him. So of course he was denied them.

Eicke himself reported to Gestapo Müller as head of the General Government. Müller ruled from Crakow. Eicke was left to serve in Warsaw. Even there he was not head of all police. The Polish Blue

Police had a separate chain of command, under Müller. The Jewish labor camps were under this clown Eichmann, on direct report to Heydrich. Eicke and the Polish Blues had been forced to cooperate, ghettoizing Warsaw's Jews, after which Eichmann took charge of them. Camps for Poles, such as Auschwitz, were still another bureaucracy reporting back to Berlin via the offices he, Eicke, had created for Himmler in the mid 30's.

This left Eicke running what amounted to a set of facilities-guards on depots, headquarters, rail yards, and the like. Almost as if he were back to his work as a security officer for I.G. Farben in the 1920's. Eicke could not accept that this was the end of his career, rotting away in a second-rank garrison town while dealing with minor pilferage and disciplinary issues. There was a Polish resistance. Not much direct activity, but everyone was sure the Polish exile government in London still ran a vast network. Eicke decided his mission would be to penetrate this apparatus. He would start with a campaign against the usual suspects among the Polish criminal class and black marketeers. He knew the game. You catch small fish. You punish some and flip others. Over a period of months, you build up a network of informers. He would find a way to prove his utility to Heydrich, while undermining Müller.

2200 hours CET
2 September 1940
Fortress of Metz, formerly French Lorraine, currently under German occupation and in some senses re-annexed to Germany

Newly promoted General de Division Alphonse Pierre Juin had had an eventful day. He had been released from officer's prison camp, with travel orders to Metz. The city had been a fortified French garrison town back to 1648, with a small sojourn as a fortress city under the Kaiser Reich. It was then returned to France at the end of World War 1. Now it was in the Occupied Zone. There were decrees re-annexing it to Germany, but no formal peace with France confirming this. There were both German and French civil administrations, but the French one was in place, with the Germans relying on the French to facilitate their wishes.

His arrival had further confused the situation. There was a German commandant who had greeted him at the train station this morning with a band and honor guard. A German band playing "La Marseillaise" was strange enough. Still more bizarre, he was not under this German's command. Juin had spent the day with his Minister of War, General Weygand, and the head of the German General Staff, General Halder. Juin was to command the French forces at Metz. The Germans would provide administrative support, but his orders would come from Weygand through the War Ministry at Vichy. The two national commanders were ordered to collaborate. Disputes would be referred to the two War Ministries to sort out.

The concept was to recreate his 15th Motorized Division, which he had led against the Germans before being compelled to surrender in the Lille pocket in early June. Some of his men had escaped by sea, and were thus lost to him – they were with other units serving Vichy, or demobilized. Either way Vichy wanted men returned from German captivity used, not their mobilization pool depleted.

Most of this shortfall was being gathered from various German prison camps. There was a team of officers out rounding up young, fit men with combat-arms training. A second wave was being recruited by three French-speaking Polish officers out of a different set of internment facilities that had Polish POW's. Weygand was utilizing the French civil administration, which remained in the Occupied Zone, to mobilize some eight thousand young men between fifteen and eighteen who would be put through recruit training here at Metz. These newly mobilized men would be field replacements for his division, and the Moroccan one that would in due course follow.

Nominally this would recreate his original 15th Division, plus a flow of march battalions to follow as replacements. In practice, something altogether different was being formed. The Trans-Saharan wastelands could only be transited in battalion-sized increments. At German instigation, his original force was being reorganized into a series of all-arms battalion-size battle groups. Each would have, in addition to the normal men and weapons of a battalion of infantry or artillery, a few armored vehicles, some antiaircraft artillery, some engineers, a few motorcycle troops as scouts, and enough support troops to be able to operate independently. Regimental and divisional headquarters were again to be configured into battalion-size formations. The first regiment headquarters would follow after the second battalion. After the fourth, a second regiment would come. After the sixth, he would arrive with the divisional headquarters. Weygand would in the meantime create, out of captured personnel, a Metz headquarters that would assume his command here when he departed.

The day had been very profitably spent, with the two French generals taking the German concept apart and reworking it in a manner more suitable for Frenchmen. They grasped the essence. The battalions would move separately, and must be able to fight individually without any support from higher forces. The entire interwar French doctrine had been top-down and very centralized. Now they were being forced into the reverse. The Germans saw this as a better way to fight. The French accepted that geography dictated such a solution. Having arrived in the Sahel, these battalions had missions ranging from recovering Chad, to defending Dakar –with a probable need to by that time retake Cameroun.

Juin was left to ponder the deeper levels at work here, levels that were never stated but were obvious to any intelligent officer of his rank. The British had attacked the French Fleet. London had used de Gaulle to poach Chad, and would try to take away the rest of France's African Empire. France would resist this. Obviously this meant alliance of a sort with their German occupiers. Yet this subtext was never directly addressed. His was the first of two oversized divisions to form here for African service. There was side-talk of an entire French army to be recreated in Poland. Yet no mention of France being at war with either the British Empire or the Soviet Union. Nominally this was all minor fiddling with the armistice terms. Minor? This was an alliance – yet the German flag still flew over Paris.

Juin could see Vichy's predicament. He could operate in this fog of concealed truths. He greatly wished he had been granted an hour alone with Weygand. This had not happened. So Juin would await a courier from the Ministry, nominally on some administrative matter, for a full verbal briefing. Best to have nothing in writing. The Germans would of course find ways to copy all his documents.

They would probably bug his office and quarters. So best to set up a riding stable, to make a daily ride part of his normal schedule. That way a confidential discussion was possible when this person appeared. France was slowly rising from the ashes, moving past the disaster of May and June. He would be a part of that rebirth. This filled him with quiet joy.

> 1000 hours, 3 September 1940 local time
> 0300 hours, 3 September CET
> Executive residence, Chongqing, Nationalist China

It had taken two days of meetings with his father, Nationalist China's Supreme Leader, and the Soviet envoys from Comrade Stalin, but Chiang Ching-Kuo was back in favor. The Nationalist KMT desperately needed a strong ally. If this meant that the regime returned to its original radical roots, the Generalissimo was prepared to sacrifice the big money interests centered on his wife's circle. This meant in turn allowing the more than half-Bolshevik Chiang Ching-Kuo back into the center of power.

Chiang's son had always seen Leninism as a means to advance China's national goals rather than an end in itself. However, Stalin had shown what Leninism could do to make an advanced military power out of a poor peasant state. Stalin had exiled Mao and his clique back to the Soviet Union. The Communist regional regime would now work at Soviet orders against the Japanese instead of against the KMT. New equipment would be sent, both to rehabilitate the KMT's German-trained regular divisions and to form two new four-division strike armies. Chiang Ching-Kuo would be given cadres and equipment to field a four-division Blue Army, dubbed the New First Army. After this was done, a second Strike Army of four Red divisions would be formed under his old friend from university in Moscow, Deng Xiaoping. This New Second Army would fight alongside the New First as twin spearheads, one on each side of the Yangtse River as the Chinese forces pushed the Japanese back step by step to Shanghai.

As a way to show his fidelity to Moscow, and to whittle down Madame Chiang's power base, it had been agreed to turn against the missionaries. The missions were to be closed. The foreign clergy would be expelled through Shanghai, Burma or Indochina. The native clergy and parishioners would recant – or be severely dealt with. There was no room in the New China for these carriers of foreign loyalties. Chiang Ching-Kuo had no doubt his father would try to waffle, keeping the benefits of the Moscow connection while not fully cutting his ties with the Western Devils. This was the Middle Kingdom. Nothing happened quickly or in a straight line. The key was the formal decrees. China had begun her journey towards the end of her century-long time of troubles.

> 0430 hours local; 0330 hours CET
> 3 September 1940
> Coffee bar, Ismailia Square (modern Tahrir Square), Cairo, British Egyptian Protectorate

Lieutenant Anwar Sadat was listening to his military academy classmate Lieutenant Gamal Abdul Nasser expound to a small audience on world events and pan-Arabism. Most of those listening were junior military officers or low-level bureaucrats. They were of a generation not prepared to blindly accept subservience to the British. This had resulted in Sadat, Nasser, and a group of like-minded officers being posted to obscure garrison towns in Upper Egypt. Days such as today, when military business necessitated a visit to Cairo-based ministries, allowed a bit of informal politicking without quite exciting the security services enough to lead to disciplinary charges. Besides, the core of what Gamal was saying was obvious to anyone. The Italians and Germans were coming. The British expected to be defeated. The fleet was gone from Alexandria. Gone south from Suez to parts unknown, but far from Egypt. After a century and a half, the Eastern Basin was no longer a British lake.

The fleet had taken off the shore establishment, naval retirees, civilian tradesmen who did RN business, and many others. Every week saw more British and other Westerners depart Egypt as well. There was no formal announcement of evacuation. Indeed, the papers denied any such thing was happening. Lies. Each family that left dismissed servants, put villas up for rent or sale, bought travel supplies. Servants and tradesmen had eyes, had ears; and told their tales to family and friends. The same was happening among sections of Egypt's Europeanized rich, especially the Copts. Anyone paying attention could see the manifestations. Real estate prices in Cairo and Alexandria were dropping steadily. Large tracts of agricultural land were suddenly on the market, but only for cash sale. The banks were running short of British and US banknotes in the larger denominations. Gold was going for a premium on the market. After over half a century, the British Raj might be coming to an end. This could leave an opening for a New Egypt, one that could deal with Italy on a more equal basis. Or it could just be swapping one overlord for another, the way Ottomans had given way to the Albanian dynasty and that had become a front for British proconsuls. Gamal thought he had answers. Sadat had questions, and was content to keep his opinions to himself.

0700 hours local; 0600 CET
3 September 1940
Camp Gorlov, near Tobruk, Italian Libya

Oberst Gunter Strauss was discovering the 'joys' of higher command. He'd been a glorified watchman for oil facilities in Romania. He'd taken a company into battle for the Malta operation, a role well within his prior service in the Baltic and afterwards with the SA. By the time the Malta force had been augmented to battalion strength, he'd had a real general there to supervise him. Ramcke hadn't interfered much, but he was there, a command presence.

Now Gunter was running Brigade Strauss. In theory, it had two battalions; but Steiner's force was still only a company, and the attached Italians were more of an overstrength platoon. Their commander, di Salo, was someplace getting them enough men and arms for a proper battalion, but that was for sometime in the indeterminate future. Gregor's ship, with three reinforcement companies, would land later today. The problems were what else was coming.

He'd been informed, by Schellenberg's office in Berlin, that Führer Göring had decided that the unit with the hero Steiner was to be reinforced. Arriving tomorrow was a composite volunteer battalion from the SS LAH, the personal guards of the Führer. As augmentation to this motorized infantry unit, the Luftwaffe had added a battery each of 88mm and 20mm antiaircraft guns. The Hessian SA was sending an armored car company. The Army was roped into providing a battery of captured French

75's.

This was now a real brigade. Gunter had no idea of how one ran one. In his war years, one didn't meet anyone higher than the battalion commander. Fortunately Greta's Uncle Isaak was versed in these things. Isaak was dragooned into being the chief of staff. That still left the question of what to do with his brigade.

The original warning order from von Manstein's corps headquarters had Strauss leading his two battalions out under Jodl as part of a makeshift division. The revised order, over the signature of this Italian army commander Geloso, had the brigade in reserve adjacent to but not *under* the command of SS General Hausser. This order referred to the force as a reconnaissance unit, probably based on the inclusion of Peiper's detachment. Or perhaps it was because Steiner's men now had vehicles, were motorized. Either way, Gunter would have to beg or borrow vehicles for Gregor's reinforcement companies. The brigade was tasked to move out with the Italian vanguard on the 10th. It was to 'create the German advanced base' for the army offensive. Gunter had not a clue as to what this meant. Time to send Major Schwabe and a few bottles of captured British whiskey to von Manstein's headquarters to get more exact instructions, and perhaps the necessary trucks.

Isaak Schwabe had been spending most of his time training Klaus' mortar crews. Steiner had remembered that his mistress's uncle had been an artillery officer who had commanded a battalion of field guns by the end of the Great War. No need to send for SA instructors.

If Isaak was to be chief of staff or deputy commander or whatever it was called at brigade level, then Gregor would inherit Ivan Gorlov's original job running the camp near Tobruk, leaving Gorlov to set up the new camp. Gorlov had been a field officer and was a combat veteran at battalion command. He'd even run a brigade for a few weeks at one point out on the steppe. Better to have him up near the action. Gregor's limited mobility wouldn't matter as much running a base camp. He'd be pissed at being made into a rear area swine, but Gunter could live with the bad temper. Gregor would flare when provoked, but adjusted fast. He didn't nurse petty grievances the way Adolph did.

1030 hours CET
3 September 1940
Villa Savorgnan di Brazza, Rome, Italy

Rome was past the true peak summer heat of August, but autumn had not yet begun to stir. The old palace chosen for this meeting had nineteenth-century furniture in seventeenth-century architecture. A few modern fans were doing little to reduce the cloying humid air coming up off the Tiber, and the heat of the day had yet to peak.

Prince Umberto was worried over the request by General Wolff for this meeting with Italy's two rulers. So far, the new European order of affairs outlined in Berlin two months prior had worked well for Italy. The new regime had a brilliant victory at Malta to trumpet to the Italian people. The naval battle had been unfortunate, but it was easy to disguise this from the public. The newspapers all had front-page pictures of damaged British warships exiting Suez for points south, followed by newer photos of Alexandria harbor empty of British warships. The Axis air fleets largely ruled the skies over Egypt, so there was a daily tide of new photos, some of which were passed to the press to create a favorable public opinion for the war. After the Alpine debacle against France and the years of bloodbath on the Isonzo in the Great War, the Italian public was not predisposed to see war as a glorious assertion of national greatness. The Italian flag over Malta was the first step in changing this predisposition.

The Prince had chosen General Geloso for command of the Italo-German Panzer Army in North Africa. Geloso had seemed the best choice, the foremost general in his age class. Yet now this chosen man had begun his tenure by countermanding a warplan from Berlin, from Heydrich personally. SS General Wolff had assured the Prince and Marshal Balbo that he was a liaison officer, a facilitator, not a minder. Now he was insisting on this meeting. The request was politely worded, but the demand beneath the diplomatic pleasantries was obvious.

Wolff arrived punctually. He seemed in good spirits. Perhaps that was a sign that his instructions were not dire. Still, the Prince was shocked when Wolff told the servants who had started with coffee service, with basic hospitality, to wait. That he had discussions that could not keep until after. "The Reichsführer reviewed your general's alterations to his plan, and wanted his answer conveyed to you both with extreme urgency. His answer is yes."

The Prince and the Marshal both knew how to keep their faces blank in public settings. However, Wolff was also expert at reading body language; he could pick up the tells, as both men ever so slightly relaxed. "He wanted me to be sure to convey to you that he regards your choice of Geloso as brilliant. His plan is by far better than what was drafted in Berlin. Indeed, there has been a much less pleasant message dispatched to General von Manstein as to how a proper commander interprets his superior's wishes. Von Manstein had at one point in the 1930's been on a career track to Halder's job. If he wants to rise that high, my boss has warned him to do better next time. Much better. Geloso is being held up to von Manstein as someone to emulate."

The three then relaxed to pleasantries for half an hour of coffee ritual and minor business before Wolff asked that the room be cleared. "One last matter. Il Duce. The Reichsführer would like assurances that his security detail knows its function, that the great man must be given his rest and not allowed to embark on travels." Wolff paused to see that he had the full attention of the two Italians. "Berlin suggests that perhaps Mussolini be allowed occasional radio broadcasts. Prerecorded of course. Let your people hear his voice, but with you two carefully guiding the words."

Balbo nodded. This would need thought. Berlin was taking an interest in purely Italian matters now. It was a dangerous precedent being set.

1350 hours CET
3 September 1940

War Ministry, Berlin

War Minister and Generaloberst Beck had originally felt Heydrich's plan to add a French army to his order of battle, to be the sort of absurdity one would expect from giving a cashiered naval Leutnant a senior post in government. Beck could not allow himself to see that he and Halder had brought this on themselves by refusing to deal with the French situation. The two senior Army officers had simply gotten used to Heydrich dealing with all the messy issues of day-to-day governance.

Beck had been dismissive of Heydrich's choice of the French 9th Army and its commander General André Corap for this project. Ninth Army had been the first unit to collapse along the Meuse in May, and Corap had been the man who was responsible for that debacle.

After a morning spent with Corap and his senior command staff, Beck now had a very different view of what had occurred. Instead of meeting an aged imbecile, which was how the French had portrayed Corap in their initial postmortems at Vichy, the man in Beck's office had been a lively man in his 60's. A bit of an older man's belly, but still a vital presence making his report. His prior record included key staff jobs in the Great War, and many brilliant combat exploits in colonial service in Morocco. What was more important was his lucid explanation of his army's failure. Corap had begun with the numerous faults of French interwar training, and the mobilization system. It had simply not created an army capable of maneuver warfare. He then went into the unforced errors made by senior French command on communications (lack thereof, to be more precise) – they refused to use radio for fear of interception, while choosing locations for higher headquarters without regard to available phone exchanges. The supreme headquarters fed through one rural exchange, that was not manned in the evening because the Army had not bothered to take over manning from the civilian phone service. And deployment. The deployment plan gave 9th Army, a formation mostly of second- and third-line divisions, a mission that required a major advance to contact followed by entrenchment while in contact with the enemy. Movement was only allowed at night for fear of air attack, yet too many armies were slated to move forward on too few roads. His army had been shorted on roads and trucks because, *ex cathedra*, an attack through the Ardennes was dismissed. Despite the German advance through the Ardennes creating the greatest traffic jam in European history, and being recorded by Allied reconnaissance planes, no one saw fit to alert Ninth Army.

Corap and his staff were scathing on their own errors in getting settled in in time. They had totally mishandled their cavalry/motorized screening force, and failed to properly supervise the emplacement of their regiments and battalions. Too much confidence was placed in newly-mobilized division and corps headquarters, instead of 9th Army command sending liaison officers to make sure orders were implemented fully and on a timely basis.

However, the after-action reports savaged them to protect the reputation of Second Army commander General Huntziger, a man with prominent sponsors in the senior officer corps. That Army had been in the same positions from mobilization until Guderian's attack. Yet it came apart the same way as Corap's, despite being given massive allocations of reserves.

Corap's staff people had been clear: think of 9th Army as a typical French Army of the second half of the Great War. Its divisions could hold a certain length of trench. The officers had provided estimates of how many kilometers of front a division could hold, with that frontage broken into a series of battalion strongpoints, each with 75mm guns that could be used in an anti-armor role. The divisions also needed to be reorganized. The battalions in the strongpoints could be reduced in strength. The number of machine-guns and mortars mattered more than the number of riflemen. This had been the French, and eventually German, pattern after Verdun. However, Corap's staff now proposed a change from the French 1917 model of a lesser number of attack or storm divisions. They proposed instead an echeloned series of smaller units of reserves, in the manner of the original WW1 storm units. These would be younger men kept in good physical condition. Their scheme was a company of such attack reserves per regiment, a battalion per division, and a brigade per corps. The brigades should have some armored vehicles. These could be obsolete types. The troops needed to see vehicles, even ancient Renault 17's, to feel that command cared if they lived or died. The other two major changes were plentiful telephone connections, with specialist troops to maintain the network, and on-call artillery support. Such barrages were the core of interwar French doctrine. It was all based on Petain's counterattacks at Verdun and after. Again, it was what the troops expected. Corap stressed that changing these mentalities in his rank and file would take years, if indeed it could be done at all.

There was more, but Beck was sure he could leave the details in the hands of OKH's expert staff officers. The main point was that French units could form solid blocks that German reserves could maneuver off of or behind. The Reichswehr had trained for maneuver warfare. Beck felt comfortable with these French allies, more so than he did with the Italians. Malta aside, what of consequence had the Italian Army ever done? Let them prove themselves in Egypt, and he would consider accepting Italians as anything beyond helpless cannon fodder. If they could beat the British, good soldiers Beck had spent most of his Great War service fighting, that would prove something.

1700 hours British Double Summer Time and CET
3 September 1940
A seedy hotel near Westminster, London

For once Kim Philby arrived early for a meeting with his Soviet handler. Which turned out not to matter, because this rare time the Comintern illegal operative had been late. There had been two air-raid scares that day in London. One was a drill, but announced to the wardens as real, with sirens blasting. The other came on the heels of the all-clear. It took the better part of an hour for the misidentification of a squadron of Coastal Command bombers, being ferried south from Scotland to patrol the Bay of Biscay, to be corrected. Radar kept showing planes, and Fighter Command kept failing to intercept owing to heavy cloud cover. Philby used the extra 95 minutes of otherwise wasted time to get mildly drunk on a pint of aged Scotch whiskey.

Kim had had a most trying two days. The Japanese were attempting to revive their former British alliance. The Cabinet was dubious, in part because Churchill argued in favor. The Americans had gotten wind of the discussions and were vigorously opposing everything. The normally ill-bred American ambassador, the Irishman Kennedy, had been even less proper than usual. The man was pro-Axis, anti-

British, and socially over his head. That he was an Irish Catholic former stock-swindler and bootlegger, was just an added touch of social inappropriateness. Yet America was offering nothing in terms of aid, pleading their neutrality laws, public opinion, the coming November election.

The British Empire would need the US in the long term, but right now it was Japan that was offering aid. Even if the formal alliance was not resurrected in deference to US opinion, Japan could offer protection to British Far Eastern possessions, allowing their garrisons to be drawn down for use in the Middle East. The Japanese had advised that Britain strengthen her forces in Hong Kong and Shanghai, but otherwise Japan could protect British interests. Japan would need every battalion and squadron of aircraft for this Sino-Soviet War, but could offer sizable naval forces for use in the Indian Ocean. As proof of good intentions, the Japanese were offering a battle squadron to sail to Aden and be placed under British command. Also a large submarine force. The British would have to allocate the merchant shipping to supply this force. Japan was deficient in merchant ships, dependent on Dutch and US ships to supply their Home Islands. A battle fleet had ceased to be a major need, beyond a fleet-in-being sufficient to defeat the small Soviet squadron in Vladivostok. This would all have been very tempting, if anything with Churchill's approval was not suspect from contagion with him.

His handler took in all that news but seemed less than really interested. Philby had long ago learned that predicting Moscow's interests was a fruitless game. He still took guesses for his own amusement. His guess was a good source in Tokyo.

What Moscow Centre wanted was details on the projected expedition to Dakar. Were the rumors that the War Cabinet had added more British army formations true? Also they had word that the ground forces commander, General Irwin, had been injured in an automotive mishap. Who was this General Montgomery who had replaced him?

2100 hours, 3 September 1940 Eastern Daylight Time
0300 hours, 4 September 1940 CET
White House, Washington DC

The District of Columbia was built in a badly-filled-in tidal swamp along the Potomac River. Before air conditioning, it had been nearly unlivable in the summer months. For this among many reasons, US government had mostly ceased to function during those months, except in wartime. Then came the New Deal, and the vast expansion of government activity. This had changed the city into a twelve-month-a-year operation. Pity there was no way to relocate to someplace with a better climate, but the US was extremely emotionally invested in their traditional constitutional order. The more the modern world forced changes, the more the public clung to their myths and familiar symbolisms.

Harry Hopkins was wishing for the thousandth time that FDR had not broken with Farley. Farley had done the political nuts-and-bolts work for the first two terms. FDR had dangled the presidency in front of the man, then pulled a bait and switch without bothering to do the personal politicking to smooth over the hurt feelings. Exit Farley, leaving Hopkins with still more work, as FDR simply didn't do details.

The latest example had happened yesterday. Franklin had done a deal for British colonial bases. Originally it was to have been a swap for old destroyers in the reserve fleet. The British had been sure they needed more escort vessels for the U-boat war … which had all but vanished in the past few months. The only two areas of major U-boat activity currently were the Mediterranean, and the Central Atlantic off the Azores, shading south to Dakar. Instead the pressing need was for bombers. So by executive order, the US had swapped existing bombers and near-term production, for the needed advance bases located in the South Pacific, Caribbean, and Western Atlantic.

The President had then departed last night for a late summer rest at his Hyde Park estate. Congress and the press were in an uproar that the agreement had stripped the US of desperately needed aircraft. It was impolitic to admit that these were largely obsolescent and obsolete designs, traded for extremely useful real estate. That would have opened the door to why the US had inferior planes. Congress would not accept that their own penny-pinching and anti-militarism had stalled developments.

In the midst of that rolling public relations debacle, came this Soviet war. The Communist Party's activist wing was running wild with street riots and sabotage against economic links with the Japanese militarists. The public face of the Party was organizing a recruiting drive, based on the veterans of the two International Brigades that had fought in Spain. Eleanor had abandoned prudence to address an emergency 'aid to China' rally in Madison Square Garden last night. The Neutrality Acts were being openly flouted, with organized convoys of internationalist volunteers boarding trains for Mexico City. Trotsky, still recovering from a nearly successful Stalinist assassination attempt, had blessed this, as had outgoing Mexican president Cardenas. Moscow had also thrown in their support, most unusual in any case that their demon Trotsky supported. Hoover and the *Chicago Tribune* were going wild in response.

So Hopkins had not been at all surprised when his Comintern liaison officer had requested an immediate meeting. She was a still-somewhat-attractive graduate of a prestigious eastern women's school and had a master's from a second such, with impeccable New England social connections. Nominally she was a political operative for a Prisoners' Aid Committee spun off from the American Civil Liberties Union. The excuse for this meeting was the pending execution date of some poor black sharecropper in Georgia. The man's trial had been a farce, but Dixie did not regard justice for the colored as especially important.

She and Hopkins had established a backstory for Hoover. The G-man had her pegged as an ex-mistress and occasional lover. Her youthful blond good looks had faded some years back in her late thirties, but an intellectual such as Hopkins might well prefer brains and breeding to nubile beauty. So there she sat in her sensible shoes and plain if well-made dress, trying to put a good face on the Party's latest reversal of policy. They had gone from militant anti-fascism, to justifying a de facto alliance with Hitler against 'the plutocrats war', to this new crusade against reactionary Japanese militarism. Yet somehow they were still allied to Hitler. Or if not fully allied, at least de facto cooperation. "We had to save China. Chiang may be linked to reactionary and feudalist elements, but he originally was allied with the forces of progress. The West was doing nothing."

Hopkins wearily shook his head. He'd dealt with politicians and their selfserving lies far too long to be conned this easily. "Save the propaganda speeches for Eleanor. I'm not a starry-eyed dreamer. I'm the one who has to keep Hoover from forcing Franklin to outlaw the Party and all its front groups. In case your masters haven't noticed, we are knee-deep in an election campaign, one we could lose. Third term is new. Intervention is unpopular. Our tilt towards the British rubs too many people wrong. It is necessary, but could cost Franklin another term. Now you've just flouted the Neutrality Act. No one will believe the fig leaf that these Internationals are off to join an Aztec force of Mexican-led Latinos to do 'humanitarian work' in liberated China. Could you have been any more transparent? No one will swallow that."

She had in fact raised this exact line of debate with *her* handler. There was no time to consult Moscow, so they had to improvise. Hopefully Centre would approve. "You can make it believable. Tell the *Chicago Tribune* that the US remains neutral in word and deed. Internationalists can leave for Mexico and follow their conscience, join the Aztec Force. Anglophiles can go to Canada and do the same. Those enamored of the French can form a Lafayette Legion via Lisbon. The Italians can sail for Lisbon too, as Garibaldi volunteers. You can let whatever few fans Hitler has sail for Danzig under a von Steuben banner. You tell the Isolationists that you are ridding the US of interventionists, sending them off to their true homelands so the real patriotic America can remain pure in its continental fortress."

Hopkins let her expound on in this vein for maybe ten minutes. She often came prepared this way. Best to let it run its course. He was mentally weighing the second- and third-order ramifications. It was novel. It was dangerous. He thought he might be able to sell this. The hardcore types like the *Tribune* would never buy this, but they hated FDR with such a fiery passion that they were not worth seriously wooing. By the time she finished her justifications and diversions, he was ready to begin serious bargaining on how many Party front groups she was willing to rally to this new program.

1030 hours local; 0330 hours CET
4 September, 1940
Governor General's mansion, Batavia/Jakarta, Netherlands East Indies/Indonesia

The disturbances of the previous night had burned themselves out by dawn. Sukarno was on the balcony, addressing a crowd of Javan nationalists which his minions estimated at over one hundred thousand people. The Dutch authorities were arguing that, at most, only seventy thousand people were overflowing the square.

This was the climax of two days of clashes with the Dutch as the nationalists tried to march their followers from the countryside into the city. There had been scattered battles, massive pogroms against the local Chinese, and many thousands of people dead (mostly Indonesian and Chinese, but more than a few Europeans and Eurasians). However, not one Japanese had been as much as accosted – much less assaulted. Japanese houses and business had been surrounded by honor guards of nationalist youth, with clear instructions to kill anyone who threatened or even inconvenienced any Japanese. Sukarno's deputies had rigidly enforced this. The nationalists sought friendship with Japan. Their disputes were with the colonial order. Japanese persons and Japan's economic interests were sacrosanct.

The cadres had begun the marches armed only with clubs and *golok* harvesting knives. Enough of them now had rifles taken from colonial soldiers, and pistols seized from the police. They also had a few thousand heads mounted on pikes in place of flags. The heads were a mix of races, ages, and genders. The governor-general was livid. Sukarno was exultant. The heads, the pall of smoke, the still raging fires in Chinatown, were all marks that the nationalist movement had come of age. The Japanese had recognized their power, and were prepared to negotiate for a guarantee of future peace. The dominion of the white race was beginning to ebb.

0600 hours CET
4 September 1940
German Army Terminal, Port of Naples, Italy

It would not be dawn yet for some minutes. Sturmbannführer Karl Siegel, Schellenberg's trouble shooter for the Mediterranean Theater, was used to insanely long hours. He made up for this by naps on planes as he shuttled about from Italy to Sicily to Malta to Libya and back, seeing to his master's business as Schellenberg saw to that of his patron, Reichsführer Heydrich. Karl had advanced himself by raw intelligence, plus a bottomless capacity for work. He knew he lacked charisma and family connections. So he compensated with drive.

He was accompanied for today by his new helper, an 18-year-old former HJ, named Johann Schmidt. Schmidt was an American-born youth whose parents had returned to the Reich in 1937. The lad's German still needed polish, but his American English was supposedly perfect. As Siegel was meeting with Hauptmann Joe Bats of the NL, it was best to have a translator to his native American dialect. Notes from Malta had pegged Bats's German as pathetic.

Bats had been early, and was waiting when Siegel and Schmidt had arrived at the commandant's office. Siegel was pleased to discover that Bats's German was actually somewhat intelligible, if he spoke slowly and stuck to a simplified vocabulary. It turned out that American had dialects. Schmidt, who introduced himself to Bats as John Smith, spoke standard American. Bats spoke a regional dialect called Brooklynese.

Berlin had been alerted that Bats was on a high-priority mission for Oberst Strauss, and would need someone to 'expedite the paperwork'. Siegel had been detailed, but not given any specifics as to precisely what he was supposed to accomplish. Bats was not one to waste time with pleasantries. He got to the point, switching to American when the initial explanation began to get complex. "It's two things. I ordered a bunch of parts on rush from shops I know here in Naples. Need formal purchase orders for the factory bosses and some idea of how many vehicles we are working with. Oh yes, and you'll need to pay cash. I got prices based on that."

"Vehicles?" Siegel was finding that dealing with this unit seemed to involve facts that were never in his briefings.

"You sent us this guy Peiper. Got these French armored cars. Suspension sucks. No radios. A bunch of other little things. It's a two-day rebuild once I get the parts. Problem is, Peiper hasn't a clue as to how many more of the AMR-35's are coming, so I don't know how deep a parts inventory to buy. Oh, and if you're buying more of these things, send a factory guy down to us and we'll go over the specs to have them built right in the first place. Whoever approved this design was a penny-pinching moron. You don't go cheap on heavy-bodied types like this. Just gets you a pile of immobile hulks sitting at the side of a road or the middle of a field, waiting on the repair truck. The trick isn't how many you have. It's how many are functional after a few days of rough use. Truck drivers, armored car drivers, for all I know tank drivers – all of a type. They push what they're driving past any limits you tell them, then sit having a cigarette, bitching on how long the service truck takes to arrive. So you build to survive mistreatment."

Siegel heard the translation and paused. This was a supposed street mechanic, but he was talking like a senior factory design engineer, a man with degrees. "We were not aware you had such credentials."

"No piece of paper from some college, but I've taken enough courses. I also have the experience. You work on enough different types and you have a brain, you learn. I know my stuff."

Siegel knew of no agreed procedure to order material outside channels from Italian manufacturers. He also was sure that the Reichsführer would not accept that answer. He had purchase orders typed by the commandant's staff, for enough parts to cover Peiper's current vehicles. Berlin was telegraphed, asking how many more were in transit. He gave the commandant's aide written orders to up the parts-quantities, in multiples based on how many more AMR's were coming. Siegel's letter of authority with Heydrich's signature, seemed able to move mountains in the military bureaucracy.

Siegel also had kept in mind that the NL Hauptmann had said, "Two things." Parts was first, so he asked Bats what was next.

Bats had a list. "Did a bit of recruiting. We need more mechanics. I recruited a few on Malta, but this is turning into a serious business. I knew a lot of guys I'd worked with here in Naples, and they knew people. Mechanics, welders, metal workers. I've got sixty-two guys who need travel orders to be flown out with me to Libya. I need a second round of travel orders for their families to the camp. It is in Bari, right, not Taranto like we thought?"

People, Siegel could deal with. He just needed a justification. "Why more people? Why outside of channels?"

"I've seen that wilderness you're sending the war to. No way anyone's going to walk much of anyplace, so we need trucks; and trucks break. I've seen all different types of trucks there already, and we'll steal more different ones from the British. Which means hand-crafting parts far too often. Hence the metal workers. You need welders for battle damage and field modifications. And however many guys you have, you'll need more in Iraq. Been going over how that all works, with Isaak and Peter. Pipes will need fitting. Motors will need work. A fleet of vehicles will need maintaining. So I've been promising that once we take the oil fields, everyone can start their own shops, hire a bunch of locals as general labor, and all be bosses."

Siegel panicked. The goal of the oil was supposed to be a state secret. "Why are you telling people this?"

"No one told me not to. Egypt goes to Italy. The oil goes to Germany, and we all work for Germany. NL's German, right? That's the gang I'm signing people up for. People I deal with don't like the Rome government much. Some think Naples should be its own kingdom. Some are refugees. I don't deal with political types. Just skilled tradesmen looking to get ahead in life. Same as me. This whole oilfield thing sounds like an opportunity for a young guy like me. You need the oil and don't like living with a bunch of wogs and whatever. Keep your race pure or something like that?"

Siegel chuckled despite himself. This Bats had the core of the race theory even if his approach was backwards. However, he needed a minder. Siegel decided he could do without 'John Smith', who could be his eyes and ears with the NL unit. Smith was now to magically at once become an NL Leutnant instead of an HJ Rottenführer. He was fairly sure he had the authority for the promotion, and absolutely certain Berlin wouldn't care either way. He had the travel orders prepared. He made sure that Obergruppenführer Wolff in Rome was sent copies of everything, in case difficulties arose with the Italian authorities. Siegel frankly doubted the less-than-well-organized Italians would even notice any of this.

1100 hours local; 1000 CET
4 September 1940
Camp Gorlov, Libya

SS Sturmbannführer Wilhelm Mohnke was pissed off. He had been in a foul temper ever since his former patron Brigadeführer Sepp Dietrich had exiled him to North Africa. Why was everyone so upset at a few dozen dead British? The prisoners had been inconvenient. Since when did the Waffen SS make war by the rules of the gentlemen of the General Staff? The National Socialist Revolution was supposed to do away with such reactionary drivel.

Mohnke had been swiftly educated that Himmler's Waffen SS no longer existed. Heydrich's learned how to take orders. If this meant that some former SS officers merited summary execution ... Heydrich was not someone inclined to be squeamish. The prohibition on dead prisoners was for reasons of state, not Christian morality. Anything in British uniform was to be treated with fire tongs, even Niggers and Wogs, even Kikes. The next unfortunate incident would produce a dead Mohnke. No court of inquiry. Just two pills behind the ear delivered by some minion of Schellenberg's. That swine had certainly proved talented at landing on his feet. He was Himmler's loyal henchman, and then under twelve hours later was Heydrich's number two, making up lists of Himmler loyalists to be sent to the wall.

Mohnke had delegated to his number two getting the men and equipment unloaded in the chaos of the port. What else were second-in-command's for? He had gotten himself driven out to meet his new commander. It had taken all his rigid discipline not to go into drooling shock at what he found. The flies were everywhere, clouds of the foul creatures. The heat was appalling, and not even yet near its zenith. But the truly disgusting aspect of the situation, were his fellow officers. An obvious Yid, and a foreign one at that. A Slav. A short boy with a Major's rank tabs, and, somehow, the Iron Cross First Class. A middleaged defective with an artificial foot and a cane. Even the one true Aryan was so overmuscled as to seem a circus freak. This Strauss had shaken his hand with a paw so large as to seem more suitable for a bear. "Welcome Sturmbannführer. How was the voyage?"

Wilhelm kept his composure by an act of pure will, as befit a *Reichsdeutschen*. "The idiot Italians got me here. I suppose I should be grateful they are capable of that much competence."

Strauss frowned. "I don't care if you like Italians, or indeed any of the other types you will find here. But save those comments for home leave among friends. The Reich has decreed we are here. Our unit's patron, the Reichsführer, decided for reasons of state he has not regarded me as needing to know, that non-Germans will serve among us, that we will serve under Italian command and alongside Italians. The Falcons of Malta Battalion was instrumental in our victory, so the Reichsführer's wisdom was affirmed. The unit previously won mention in *Wehrmachtbericht* for exemplary service in Romania and Hungary. Now if you cannot cope with this, just speak out. I'll relieve you. You can see if General Hausser needs a spare battalion commander. Or you can scurry back to garrison duty in Berlin. I could care less. The extra battalion you bring will prove useful. I have no need for you. Major Gorlov here has command experience at both battalion and brigade. Major Schwabe also has battalion command experience. Your promotion to that level is quite recent. Your experience is as a company officer." Strauss had been speaking in a conversational tone. He now switched to a drill sergeant's scream. "ARE WE CLEAR?"

Mohnke came to rigid attention with his eyes fixed a few centimeters over the head of his screaming giant troll of a commander, while he bellowed back variants of no sir, yes sir, till the screaming session slowly tapered off. All the while he cursed his luck and wondered how he would survive this African 'vacation'.

1200 hours CET
4 September 1940
Wanda's Happy Time Bar and Brothel, German cantonment, Bari, Italy

The cantonment area was vast and poorly marked. Even with a supposed map, the three SS 'minders' had to repeatedly ask for directions. The base was a chaotic hive of men. Large numbers jogged around doing tasks, but most just lolled in whatever shade their tents gave from the stifling midday heat.

Clara Fischer was amazed that her journey had led her here. Since her arrest (or 'being taken into protective custody' as her SS jailers preferred to call it), she had been nearly a week managing a brood of youngsters and her emotionally-shattered brother through a succession of railway cars, waiting areas, and overnight holding cells as they were shipped south through the overworked new Euro rail cartel. Why? Guards don't tell prisoners why. Just another disaster in her interactions with the Nazi beasts. Why had they been added to a second traveling group straight out of Ravensbrück? Whores? Some of these young women looked awfully young, but Clara was aware of street realities. She had too much self-respect to be a whore, but felt only pity and class solidarity for those who had made the other choice … or more often, in her experience, been driven to it by parents and boyfriends.

Her entire adult life had been one long tragic farce. In 1933 she had been a student teacher, a *Praktikantenlehrer*, about to embark on doing her small part to make a better world by teaching working-class children their letters and numbers. The Party had warned that this Hitler was a demon, but Clara had been Communist in a utopian, religious sense. Her parents were Communist. Her whole family and neighborhood were. Communism was a heaven on Earth, a paradise for the working classes. No more bosses, no more rich, bread and shelter for all. Everyone labored for the common good, and no one starved in the gutter. The Party youth league ideals had led her to teacher training. She was the first in her extended family to have gotten any sort of higher education, any professional certificate.

Hitler became Chancellor in January of '33. There are farcical elections and an Enabling Act. She's fired and black listed. She was Aryan enough, but no Communist would be allowed to pollute young German minds. So a trained teacher is reduced to being a cleaning lady at one of Solingen's many industrial plants. Clara had never been one of the more obvious militants from the Red Front street battles. Thus she was spared the attentions of the new Gestapo. Her neighborhood police made sure that she knew she was watched, was under suspicion. Suspicion of what? Her only sins against the new regime were those of solidarity. Comrades would vanish. Into the underground, into exile, into the regime's camps. Neighborhood activists such as herself would take in abandoned children. That's what class solidarity meant to Clara. She would skip a meal when necessary to keep a child fed. She took a second job. The older children took what work they were able to, to supplement her meager pay; and other party members would lend a hand when they could.

Seven years had put working calluses on her hands and knees, had trained her to keep her eyes lowered and her mouth firmly shut. Her poor brother had tried to do the same, but his boyhood friendships kept coming back to bite him. Too many of those friends were illegals on the run, or old-line militants of the Rotfront. When the police couldn't find them, poor Carl would be summoned for another beating to 'loosen his tongue'. How do you beat the truth out of a man who knows nothing? He'd been the last three years in Dachau, over refusing to give up hiding places he didn't know concerning people he often hadn't seen since 1934. Her laughing brother had been reduced to the frightened mouse of a man now beside her. At least he helped with the children.

Clara had spent the days of travel trying to decide which supposed sin had exiled her. She was totally unprepared for the answer. Wanda! Her old neighbor and sometime employer. Clara and the older ones had sometimes made extra money tending Wanda's still or doing deliveries of her bottled lightning. What was Wanda doing here, clearly in charge?

Wanda's man Adolph came out and signed for the prisoners. Clara was amazed to see SS women salute Adolph. Then she noticed the rank tabs on his collar. Adolph an officer?

Wanda detailed the Ravensbrück girls to some middle-aged lady who answered to the name of Gretchen. Wanda led Clara, Carl and the flock of kids through the tap room to a kitchen area. She ordered someone to feed the youngsters. Their ears perked up at a mention of food, more so when the food proved to be pastries with real sugar. Wanda led Clara and Carl to a rough but sturdy table. She introduced a well-dressed young man, Paul Schwabe, sat the two Fischers down to some real coffee with more of the baked goods. "Glad to see you survived the trip, dear. Did they tell you that you weren't in trouble, as they had been ordered to do?"

Clara wanted to explode. Wanted to but didn't. Wanda the Polack bootlegger seemed to be a power now. Clara had no fight left in her. Her goal was survival. "They may have said something, but why would I believe Nazi police?" Clara knew Adolph was a Nazi, but he'd never been rude or violent about their political differences. Besides, Clara had grown good at reading situations these past years. Adolph might be an officer, but Wanda was clearly dominant. It had been that way all the years she'd known the two.

Wanda spent a few minutes making sympathetic noises, and then got to the point. "I've got a new job for you. You and your orphanage get to spend a Hauptmann's pay. All you have to do is teach him proper German."

"All? I've never put myself on the street before. Besides, I'm facing up to thirty. Why not someone younger, prettier, more his class?"

"His class?" Wanda and this Paul found that amusing. "He's a working man Gunter recruited. Skilled mechanic. This Mr. Joey Bats is an Italian from New York City, only knows pidgin street German apparently. Orders came from Berlin, from the Reichsführer-SS's office, to find him a language tutor. You don't have to make him polite company. He merely has to be able to make reports to senior officers in intelligible German. Can you teach basic grammar and vocabulary to a bright man in his twenties? As for the rest … you are better off fucking him, making his coffee and being his woman, but that's your choice. I'm promising room and board as a teacher. He can provide far more to a mistress."

Clara thought fast. On an officer's pay, there were things she could get for the children, ways to better educate them. She wasn't a prude. There had been lovers before. But she'd never been a mercenary bitch like some girls she'd known. Even some Party comrades had used sex to snag the guy with a bigger wallet, instead of the nicest guy or the best-looking. "Can I meet him first?"

"That happens either way. Tomorrow you are shipping out for North Africa. You'll meet him there." Wanda saw the terrified look on Clara's face. "Gunter's the boss man there. A full Oberst now. If you say no, his fists will back it up. Just give it a real try. Your life back home was killing you. You were working yourself to an early grave. This will be better. Just be a little flexible."

Clara was left brooding, sipping her coffee while Paul motioned her brother to follow him. Carl went, terrified about what would come next. He was afraid of more beatings like at Dachau. This was a new camp and he didn't know the rules. Paul had to enlighten him – this was a military unit, but it ran like a private company. Carl was now a new worker, an apprentice to this Paul. They did metal and building work of various kinds. Paul got him a beer and quizzed Carl on his skills. Told him the key was to do what you were told, but never bluff on what you knew. If Carl didn't know, ask a supervisor. That's how you learn. There were punishments for fucking up, but these involved more work at things like burning latrine barrels, rather than insane exercise routines with beatings when you collapsed. Carl started to cry. He was to be a working man again. He wasn't a prisoner anymore. All he had to do was work. Carl had worked all his life. A boss that fed you beer was better than any he had ever had before. He vowed to find a way to recover some of his manhood, to be able in some way to protect his poor sister. He then laughed to himself. Nothing short of a pagan god could protect someone from Gunter. Even the old pre-Dachau Carl would have known better.

1500 hours CET
4 September 1940
Schellenberg's office (originally Himmler's), SS HQ, Prinz-Albrecht-Straße, Berlin, Germany

The aged German Monsignor was a long-habituated denizen of the corridors of power, first as a liaison between the German hierarchy and the Catholic Center Party of Weimar Days, and currently as a special assistant to the Papal Nuncio. He was a frequent negotiator for the Vatican with the SS. All parties found discussions on this level more rewarding than the Nuncio attempting to do serious business with head of state Göring. The Nuncio was often a guest at various functions the Führer graced with his presence. There was a good personal relationship between them, but never any attempt at serious negotiation.

Today's meeting was on the ever-vexing problem of the Polish clergy. Week by week, the occupation forces were sweeping up church people. So far, senior clergy were exempt. The SS was starting at the bottom – parish priests, monks, nuns, lay servants of the church, young people who had expressed a vocation and were in training. This would provoke a revolt if not dealt with. A revolt that could only fail, and possibly could lead to the Church being abolished in Poland.

Schellenberg heard the complaints, and again offered the same answers. "The issue is their politics, their loyalty, not their faith. Assign new people from Spain. It is overflowing with clergy. Bring them from Portugal. Use the refugee Lithuanians. But the entire Polish hierarchy is linked to their exile government in London. They nurture the parallel underground state these London Poles have blessed us with. Don't bother denying it. Neither of us is talking in public. So let us deal in facts."

"How am I to run Polish parishes with Spanish priests?"

"Your problem, not mine. Will you order your priests to obey, to render unto Caesar?" He waited for the sad shake of the churchman's head. They both knew such an order would not be obeyed. "So accept reality. However, I'll make you a counteroffer. Let the parishioners leave with the priests. Vichy will need settlers in West Africa. You can set up a new Poland there. We'll fill in the vacated land with other people willing to bend the knee."

The prelate filed this away for future reference, but for now it was stalemate. Time to raise the other issue. "Euthanasia. Your police general Eicke in Warsaw has revived the program. We will be forced to make a public condemnation … "

Now it was Schellenberg's turn to shake his head. "The idiot acted without orders. I'll summon him to Berlin and give him a proper dressing-down." Schellenberg kept to himself that he'd ask the Boss to let him simply disappear Eicke. Take him down in the cellar, put a bullet or two behind his ear, and appoint a new commander. "Give him a noodle", in SS parlance. Eicke was an old Himmler loyalist and an impossible person. Yet Heydrich had kept him on. There must be reasons. Reasons above Schellenberg's pay grade, beyond the need-to-know of the second in command of the entire SS apparatus? So, best to say nothing to the Nuncio's man about that part. Never show weakness. "I cannot bring the dead to life, but how about this: send us Spanish clergy for a few of the Polish monasteries we cleaned out. I'll let you set up church homes for all these unfortunates. Surely you can get your American bishops to send food to support religious orders."

"Why monks and not nuns?"

"Either or both. We don't care. I'll even let you keep some Poles on, as long as the abbots and prioresses are Spanish. They will still have to avoid resistance activities, but surely your Spanish can watch their fellows?"

The monsignor saw an opening here. He let the discussion wind down. This must be reported to Rome. There were religious Poles to protect, good works to do and souls to be saved. Schellenberg was always very careful with his words. He said unfortunates, not *Catholic* unfortunates. He was dangling bait. The Church could acquire a new social mission and a permanent presence in what had once been Poland. Souls could be saved via conversions.

2000 hours Central Daylight Time, 4 September 1940
0400 CET, 5 September 1940
Soldier Field, Chicago

The roar of the crowd in Soldier Field swelled to an oceanic roar as Charles Lindbergh, the legendary aviator Lucky Lindy, took the stage. There were a hundred and fifty thousand souls packed into the stadium, with at least two hundred thousand more in the spillover crowd clogging every street and lot for blocks around, listening from loudspeakers strung up to every light pole. Millions more were in the radio audience.

The America First Committee had been formally unveiled earlier in the day by the nominal founders, a set of blue bloods at Yale Law School. Gerald Ford, absent on duty with Hoover's European

Relief program, had sent a fulsome telegram of support. Wendell Willkie, the Republican Presidential nominee, shrugged and grimaced. The high-born law students at Yale and their Ivy League friends who would come aboard, like Joe Kennedy's brat Jack at Harvard, were fluff for the picture magazines. What was happening in Chicago was what mattered.

The *Chicago Tribune* hated FDR with a fiery passion. The *Trib* was backed by a coalition of big Midwest money. Money that had organized all this on a day's notice, including a nationwide radio hookup with over a hundred major papers and magazines up in the press boxes to trumpet the event. A cabal that could tell both members of the Republican ticket to bark like trained seals. His potential Vice President, Senator McNary, had done just that forty minutes ago. Barked for his supper and would now be thrown some half-rancid fish in the form of campaign cash and jobs for relatives. Charlie was clean as politicians ran, but that much financial power could turn men's heads. Besides, they were only steering him someplace he felt comfortable to go. McNary was an old progressive and a sincere isolationist of the Fortress America mold.

Willkie himself didn't hate the New Deal or FDR. He just felt Franklin had been pushed by his wife and a circle of White House radicals to positions not suitable for America. Socialism was for Europe, same as Bolshevism and Fascism. And yet, here was Lindy going into his oration against the Bombers for Bases Deal, and already he'd gotten to the Jews. Not with the fire of a Hitler, but there it was. Warning the Jews not to push America into England's war. Lindbergh was honest in his accusations. The Jews were pushing, but so were the others he named – the old East Coast elites, Wall Street, the perpetual anti-fascists on the Left still whining about Spain.   Lindbergh's warnings were sharp. Warmonger Jews, Wall Street Jews, Red Jews. Hell, Willkie knew enough US Poles as hopped to fight the Nazis as the Jews were.

Willkie was due on when Lindbergh was done. He could support much of what the man said. The bases were useful, but not at the price of gutting our air forces. Both men could support a Fortress America, well armed to keep the Old World's wars at bay. They could both see merit in this new rumor out of DC to let the war hawks leave and go fight for whoever they chose. Willkie wasn't socially fond of the Jews, but his circle included a few decent ones. Maybe over time he could moderate Lindy on all this. Maybe. Willkie was aware he was lying to himself, but didn't see a way out. Running for President had seemed a good idea at the time. Keep the party out of the hands of the paleolithic heartland isolationists like Taft, who would gladly have cut New York off and floated it out into the Atlantic. Come to office after Franklin, and curb the New Deal's excesses without returning to the errors of the Roaring 20's. That was then. This was now. He was committed. The crowd roared again as Lindy pounded on his theme about dual loyalties, about a foreign people who never really wanted to be true Americans. Shit!

1130 hours local time; 0430 hours CET
5 September 1940
Gates of the Imperial Palace, Tokyo

Very recently promoted Field Marshal Tomoyuki Yamashita marveled at the workings of fate. He'd been exiled to command of the Fourth Infantry Division in Manchuria because of his unfashionable views as regards the China War, relations with the Anglo powers, and Army politics. Now the Soviets had attacked, retroactively validating much of what his Imperial Way colleagues had advocated. Yamashita has been too busy to gloat. His division was blocking the western arm of the Chinese Eastern Railway, locked in blood-drenched combat with vastly superior Soviet forces backed by endless numbers of tanks and seemingly infinite artillery and air support. All that was left to do was trade blood for time. Yamashita had lost over half his division in four days of furious round-the-clock action. Yamashita did the only things that were possible. Suicide infiltration platoons sent into the Soviet rear to create chaos. Frantic digging of company and battalion strongpoints, each of which was then defended to the death. The junior officers under his command were ready to die for the Emperor. Yamashita just placed them in the best places to kill while they sacrificed themselves.

Then suddenly he had been pulled out, ordered back to Tokyo. He had considered ritual suicide. He had been forcibly restrained from such action. Yamashita just saw that as one more indignity inflicted by Tojo's dominant Control Group on him as a defeated follower of Imperial Way/Strike North. Yet his arrival in Tokyo at dawn had been a shock. The city reeked of high explosive smells. There were Imperial Guards and Kenpeitai all over, guarding installations that had clearly seen recent damage.

His minders now asserted they were not, in fact, his jailors. He was given a fresh uniform and a chance to properly bathe, and then ushered into the Imperial Presence. The Son of Heaven had been cryptic. Yamashita was now the sword of the empire and a field marshal. His command was the Kwantung Army in Manchuria. His duty was to lose slowly. Losses didn't matter, time did. The Empire must mobilize against this new threat. The survival of the Yamato race was at stake. The Throne expected to lose Manchuria, but every day this could be delayed was a victory. Japan was now in alliance again with the British. The ill-advised Strike South to the East Indies was being ignored, but would not be allowed to go further.

With this, Yamashita was ushered out of the Imperial presence to a cabinet meeting.   His guards now became talkative. Elements in the Navy had not reacted well to the changes. The Army had been forced to occupy naval bases to 'enforce the Imperial Will'. The new Navy minister was a septuagenarian relative of the Emperor's recalled from retirement and promoted three grades at the Imperial hand. Tojo was Army Minister. Many dozens of senior military officers in both services had been invited by the Kenpeitai to rejoin their ancestors. A massive Communist spy ring centered on the Nazi German embassy had been uncovered. Reservists were being recalled to the colors. Divisions would be formed of surplus naval personnel, as the Soviets lacked a major fleet to fight. The entire air strength of the Navy would be fed into the Manchurian meat grinder. For now, the new theater commander must meet the cabinet so that his extraordinary powers in Manchuria and North China could be properly defined. Holding the Chinese conquests was no longer a priority. The issue was, would the Imperial state survive in the Home Islands? If possible in Korea and Taiwan as well, but anything beyond that might not prove possible. Yamashita reflected on these days of wonder. If the game was to die in your tracks, it was a game his poor outgunned army could play. It emphasized courage and basic military skills which they had, instead of equipment, which they lacked.

0800 hours local time; 0700 hours CET
5 September 1940
Italo-German Panzer Army HQ outside Derna, Italian colony of Libya

Oberst Gunter Strauss was not used to being included in such rarefied circles. The corps commanders conference had been yesterday. Today's meeting was for the German commanders: von Manstein as head of Afrika Korps, Hausser as commander of SS Reich Panzer Grenadier Division, Rommel as commander of 7th Panzer Division, Major von Stauffenberg from OKW in Berlin, the former deputy head of OKW Jodl as the man in charge of a special-purpose division cobbled together from spare units and reassigned ones, and then himself. Himself who had been a Leutnant by self-promotion two and a half months previously. Two aristocratic von's, four general officers, and him. This was not his world ... except now it was, and he'd best adjust fast.

The meeting room was stifling hot. Whoever had done construction, had done an abysmal job on locating and installing fine-mesh window screens compared to Gorlov's efforts. The hot air was full of the perpetual flies of Libya. Still, the lighting was good, the wall maps were excellent, and the chairs comfortable. The coffee wasn't up to what his headquarters had, but then he and his boys were living on captured British stocks from Malta. Fräulein Greta had done good work 'liberating' food stocks from British dumps, while he and the guys were preoccupied with saleable loot like unit flags and British pistols. The garrison people rotating into Malta, and now the rear area clowns flooding into Libya, all wanted to impress the folks back home with trophies.

Gunter had been trying to tune out the running fight between Rommel, and essentially everyone else, on the order of march. Rommel was the spearhead. He wanted to march first and then drive around the British. The Italian general's plan was for him to follow Strauss and something called First Libyan. Then the bits and pieces from Jodl and SS General Steiner, followed by the corps troops, and finally Hausser. If Gunter thought platoons instead of big units he could mostly follow. Rommel was a storm officer and simply didn't think in traditional terms. Strauss had made sergeant in a storm battalion, and sympathized. What's worse, he saw too large a role being assigned to his supposed brigade. This led to certain conclusions. Gunter raised his hand, asking von Manstein's permission to speak. The aristocratic General ignored him for almost ten minutes before allowing this. Finally, he deigned to notice that a mere Oberst was alive. The general's tone made clear his lack of interest in anything a militia Oberst might say. "Yes Oberst Strauss. What could you possibly have to add to this?" Von Manstein's staff had included this brigade commander as a courtesy, but never expected the uncouth fool would show such idiot bad manners as to actually speak.

Without thought Gunter was out of his chair and at the position of attention. This was reflex to him. It was the tone of voice and the rank of the speaker, rather than the words, that provoked the instant snap to attention. Someone of von Manstein's rank noticing he was alive in that manner of speech, triggered a parade-ground reflex that required this reaction. Reflex he would have to work on modifying ... sometime in the future. Now was now. "Herr General Corps Commander, your organization chart has a bunch of battalions being allocated from Herr General Hausser's SS division to Herr General Rommel's Seventh Panzer. Three reconnaissance battalions, two motorcycle battalions, and three anti-tank battalions.   7th Panzer already has one of each of these. Added all together, that's an eleven-battalion force. My brigade is quite small, but until today was nominally attached to 7th Panzer." Gunter could see the seniors losing patience, but knew he needed to make his points in the proper order. "Without violating what the Army Commander ordered, surely Herr General Rommel could lead these eleven battalions up with his former attached brigade. He lets his Ia, Oberst von Thoma, bring up the balance of the division in the proper place in the line of march. In the meantime, Herr General Rommel's advance force keeps sliding south and then east as the First Libyan Division deploys. Herr General Rommel is never out all alone in case something goes wrong, but he is already in position to be turned loose should the battle develop into a mobile phase. Herr General Rommel's training was as a mountain Jäger. His specialty is fast forces and fluid situations. I had such commands at much lower level in the Great War, and was trained in the thought patterns."

Von Manstein stared hard at Strauss and considered the possibly sensible proposition. He had been given a précis of this militia fool's service, but hadn't paid much attention. All he recalled was "jumped-up SA thug". The bored tone switched to a senior officer's command voice. "You don't have any real officer training, do you, NL Oberst Strauss?"

"No, Herr Corps Commander General. It is been all field promotions from recruit to here. Riga and Michael in the last War. Iron Division in the Baltic. SA. NL. But I've watched Leutnant's and Hauptmann's work around the official orders to get something done. Herr General Rommel wants to be up front. He is quick to seize initiative, but good at what he does. I saw it on Malta. This sort of agrees with the big plan and lets us all get back to our units, to start getting ready to move in a few days. No complicated plan survives contact with the enemy anyway. We'll start this and then the British will do something that makes no sense. After that it is all improvisation anyway." Von Manstein had to use his careful breeding not to laugh at this impolitic truth, 'quick to seize initiative'. Rommel was a prima donna, headstrong and never followed orders when his own battle sense conflicted. A wonderful feature in a storm Major. Less so in the divisional General spearheading an army.

Rommel started to interject ,and got glared down by von Manstein. Von Manstein was recalling the briefing on the vastly-oversized monster that Heydrich had made of Hausser's 'division'. Division? It was a corps in all but name, and overstrength for that. Von Manstein's voice went to a field command tone. Harsh and assured. "You, Oberst Strauss, how many real battalions does your so-called brigade have?"

"Two, Herr Corps Commander von Manstein. The rest is make-believe."

Von Manstein thought for a moment. He knew what size force he could justify as a brigade. Thirteen battalions was an overstrength division, not a brigade. Six battalions was the maximum, and this Strauss already had two. "General Rommel, pick four battalions as this advance force. Only one can be Panzers. You assign them to Oberst Strauss's command. If you choose, you may, as his superior officer, march with him in a supervisory capacity given his level of training; and take command of the four added battalions back under your personal direction, should circumstances dictate when you are in contact with the British. The four, but not the original two – who have their own mission dictated by Army Command."

Rommel started to argue, and von Manstein just raised a hand. "This is not a negotiation. Four battalions. Write them down before leaving this room, or I choose them. The rest of you know what the plan calls for. Dismissed." Von Manstein resolved to send a staff officer along to observe this Strauss in action. The man might prove useful.

1400 hours CET
5 September 1940
Conference Room of SS Headquarters, Prinz-Albrecht-Straße, Berlin

With Defense Production Minister Todt conducting an inspection of Hungary and Romania following the recent fighting, Deputy Four Year Plan Administrator (and SS Standartenführer by the grace of Heydrich) Albert Speer found himself chairing a meeting on electric power – or, to be more precise, lack thereof. Total war was complicated even for an ace bureaucrat such as Speer. Every decision had endless contradictory ripple effects. Plus, Speer was never certain his reprieve from the death cells was not revocable. The old Heydrich may have been his friend. This new Reichsführer SS had subordinates, minions but not friends.

As was normal, General der Infantry Thomas of the Heer, Air Marshal Wolfram von Richthofen of the Luftwaffe and Vice Admiral Werner Fuchs of the Kriegsmarine represented their three services. Von Richthofen made clear he also represented the new Führer Göring personally. Thomas found it hard to do the same as regards Generals Beck and Halder, as all were aware that Heydrich had moved Thomas out from under them with Göring's blessings. Thomas was now part of OKW, nominally Führer Göring's planning staff. None of the assembled worthies were in any doubt whose plans OKW did, not after Malta.

Fuchs during the first few meetings had sulked. His service had been effectively castrated. In the last few meetings he had begun to exhibit signs of life. Fuchs had focused on tactical objectives for his service. If the campaign was to be in the Mediterranean, small ships would be needed, more so as no one in Berlin trusted the Italian Navy. Getting funding for improved diesel engines for U-Boats and small surface ships had been his achievable goal. Getting interim funding for now, for improved U-Boat designs on the basis of long-term strategic needs, was Fuch's hoped -for second victory. So far progress on that had been quite provisional. The Navy felt that Germany would need progress in these areas if Britain declined to make peace after Iraq fell. Heydrich, speaking through OKW, had disagreed, preferring further advances in Arabia and Africa should Iraq not be the key to peace. Either way, Germany's leaders weren't interested in a battle fleet. Work on *Bismarck* and *Tirpitz* was put aside. Cheaper weapons like destroyers and U-Boats were possible to get funded, if assembled in Trieste for ease of deployment. Speer had been working on plans to send pre-fabricated sections of U-Boats and destroyers for final assembly by Cantieri Riuniti dell'Adriatico (CRDA) (United Shipbuilders of the Adriatic).

Von Richthofen spent a great deal of his time at these meetings sparring with Thomas over resources – with Todt (or in this case, Speer) casting the deciding vote while Fuchs either kept quiet or offered suggestions from the sides. Indeed, Fuchs had used these bureaucratic battles to get the AAA defense of the key ports handed to his service. After all, with the battle fleet not needed, they had surplus gunnery officers and technicians.

This meeting's current argument was over electrical power. Any type of production needed electrical power at some point during the manufacturing process, and most likely at multiple points. The worst hog in terms of need for electrical power was the chemical industry, which needed it for the manufacture of artificial nitrates, and the synthetic oil programs. As those programs ramped up, energy demand would get even higher for the chemical industry and for the war economy as a whole.

Dr. Richard Fischer the *Reichslastverteiler* (Load Administrator) head of the Reichsstelle für die Elektrizitätswirtschaft (Central Office of Electrical Supply) was tasked with attempting to meet these various and never-ending demands for electricity. He was at this meeting to explain why he couldn't.

"Gentlemen, with the summer months over, our supply of hydro-power is going to begin to drop – and with it, what little safety margin we have in the power grid." Fischer wasn't going to attempt to sugar-coat the bitter pill he was handing these men to swallow. "Soon we will have to start to make choices as to what facility does and does not get power."

Von Richthofen shrugged. "Take it from the civilians."

On his side of the table, Thomas smiled. Having been involved in the war economy for roughly the past decade, he knew that von Richthofen's suggestion wasn't practical. But he let the good doctor explain the facts of life.

"Air Marshal, the load on the grid from houses and public buildings is just over 6% of the grid's demands. We have plans in place to do rolling blackouts, but that simply will not cover emergencies such as one of the major plants going down or transmission lines being disrupted."

The Luftwaffe officer was an engineer himself, and tended to view problems as a question of application of resources. "What about the occupied nations … "

"I am sorry, Marshal, but each nation's grid tends to be a self-contained unit. It's really not possible to take capacity from, say, the Netherlands or France."

Not wanting the meeting to bog down, Speer tapped the table. "Marshal, I believe the good doctor has a suggestion." Speer's face was an easy read to those familiar with him. He had briefed Heydrich and already had his backing. So they looked impatiently to Fischer for a miracle.

Doctor Fischer frowned. He wanted to have some magical solution to the problem, but there wasn't one. If this displeased Speer and therefore Heydrich … his will was in order; and besides, he was safer being shot for saying no, than telling lies to the Reichsführer-SS. At least the truth would save his family and co-workers from execution. "We are adding primary capacity at roughly 5% per year, but growth in demand continues to outstrip supply. The electrical parts manufacturers AEG, Siemens, and Brown-Boveri are working as hard as they can with current resources; and we are keeping old plants running past shut-down dates, but there isn't any magical pill to this problem. I need a priority list from you gentlemen, as to what keeps going when we can no longer meet demand."

The uniformed officers were not pleased to hear this, but Fuchs and Thomas had been expecting it. Von Richthofen still wanted to find a solution. His service desperately needed more aluminum, and producing it required gobs of electric power. "No way to increase production of plants faster?"

Thomas chuckled, "It's the old story, my dear Marshal, to build A means taking resources from B. What Luftwaffe project gets short-changed to allow for Siemens to build more generators?" Thinking it over, Thomas laughed again, "We are robbing Peter to pay Paul, and have been for some time. So, short of Professor Diebner's project turning up wonders, we are limited to coal-fired plants."

Everyone was confused at the apparent non sequitur. Thomas caught himself and clarified. "A physicist, in charge of the Uranium Project. That is under Army control."

Speer vaguely recalled the project. It wasn't very large, "They are investigating the potential of atomic fission for military applications." The other two nodded uncertainly. Von Richthofen made a mental note to have Göring's staff chase this down The Führer didn't do detail work, but some good young men had been seconded from the Air Ministry to the Chancellery staff. They had some technical knowledge, blazing ambition, and the energy of youth. Ah, to again be that young and clueless.

"Not having much to show for it either," grumbled Thomas. But seeing the continued baffled looks, he elaborated: "One of the possibilities is for creating some type of power plant using splitting of atoms , instead of coal. You would have to talk to Professor Diebner or perhaps Doktor Heisenberg for more details."

Dr. Fischer interjected, "Replacing coal could save energy, as a lot of coal is such poor quality that having to haul it any distance makes it uneconomical as a power source."

Speer saw it as saving manpower and railway capacity. Everything was in short supply, and anything you gave less to managed to screw up the things you were trying to prioritize. He morbidly recalled being in an Air Force supply bunker a few months ago waiting to be liquidated. Dealing with endless shortages as a senior official, was far better than awaiting liquidation as a minor architect whose patron had just died.

Speer made a note. "Perhaps it's time for an update on their efforts. In the meantime, as to Doctor Fischer's problem. Berlin … " An obvious place marker to the rest, for his patron Heydrich " … has dictated that we consider long-term implications. So I want you three to evaluate programs in terms of where you can come up with resource cuts." Then, turning back to Dr. Fisher: "Draw up various program scenarios for expansion of the grid, depending on different levels of additional resources. Also start to look into the lack of integration with the rest of Europe. If electrical power is a bottle-neck on production, then we should address that sooner rather than later."

2000 hours Eastern Daylight time, 5 September 1940
0400 hours CET, 6 September 1940
Yankee Stadium, Bronx, New York

The stadium was packed to the rafters for the America First Rally. It had been booked on roughly a day's notice. As in most major cities, money can move mountains. Permits had been expedited, fire marshals paid off to ignore limits on occupancy, and massive publicity used to assemble the crowd. Of course, the publicity had also assembled the mob outside attempting to storm the gates and occupy the stage. There was a deafening roar outside, as the mass of leftists and Jews fought the mostly Irish NYC police, aided by 'loyal Irish volunteers' recruited out of parish churches by the promise of a good night's pay in cash – plus an opportunity to stick it to the British.

Lucky Lindy had never been a coward. Cowards don't fly the Atlantic solo. If the mob made it to the speaker's platform, he would go down fighting. Father Coughlin was warming up the crowd. Lindy found the level of Jew- and banker-baiting unseemly, but this was a crusade to save his beloved nation, not a lady's garden party. Lindy wasn't socially fond of the Hebrews, but his real objection was their dual loyalties, prioritizing their European brethren over their supposed nation. Coughlin seemed to physically loathe the Jews. They were all communist bankers ready to impoverish decent Christians. Lindy knew the origins of the Depression were far more complex than gutter theories of Jewish cabals. Lindbergh was also aware that Willkie was, at best, a fair-weather friend. At heart he was as Anglophile and internationalist as that fiend Roosevelt. Lindy had heard some of the Irish followers of Coughlin refer to the president as *Roosenfelt*. Absurd. The man was a Hudson Valley Dutch patrician, a follower of that idiot Wilson, not some half-assimilated refugee from a Ukrainian shtetl.

Lindbergh was also aware that Roosevelt had traded near-useless planes for air bases. That part was fine. He'd never admit it in public, but the planes were worthless, years behind what was needed. The problem was that Franklin knew nothing of aviation technology. He'd be likely to bargain away good planes, planes that could sink invading fleets, next. Lindy was prepared to make multiple pacts with demons, if that was the price of saving America from this nest of traitors and idiots.

1200 hours local time; 0500 hours CET
6 September, 1940
Just south of the middle Yalu, Japanese-occupied Korea

Provisional Second Lieutenant Takagi Magao examined the hill path cautiously. He had been 'graduated' ahead of schedule from Changchan Military Academy by the outbreak of the war. Now here he was, commanding a platoon of Manchurian police plus a dozen Korean volunteer scouts against the red guerrillas of the Northeast Anti-Japanese United Army. There had been reports of Soviet air drops into the hills south of the river last night. Soviet regulars? Chinese or Korean partisans returned from training in the Soviet Union? Spies? Saboteurs? Supplies? For all Lieutenant Takagi knew, this was fantasy from overexcited local peasants.

The various Japanese forces had been waging a large 'anti-bandit' campaign in these steep hills for the better part of a year. The mixed Chinese and Korean force had proven to be formidable foes. Takagi had hoped the war would have brought him service with the Imperial Japanese forces. Instead here he was chasing political rural bandits. Rationally he understood the need. The rear had to be kept clear so the Emperor's forces could be supplied from the Home Islands. As a Korean-born subject of the Son of Heaven, his language skills would be put to best use here instead of directly at the front.

One of the scouts, a teenage volunteer, was running back. They had found two poorly-buried parachutes. So the reports were real. Time to chase Reds. The lieutenant got his men moving, heading deeper into the trackless mountain wilds of far northern Korea.

0800 hours local; 0700 hours CET
6 September 1940
HQ Western Desert Force, Mersa Matruh, Egypt

Major General Richard O'Connor had his staff up before dawn. He had small scout groups out. The RN had landed small scouting parties where they could monitor the coast road. The armored cars prowled the desert interior ahead of his lines. All three sets of reports told the same story. The enemy army was stirring. The few photo recon flights that survived to return home confirmed this. The encampments were full of the sort of last-minute activity that foretold a major movement. Units were being prepped for combat.

He faced a strong Italo-German army. To oppose it he had a weak Empire corps. The first brigade of the partially trained 6th Australian Division had arrived, as had two South African armored car regiments. All that he could expect to follow was another brigade of Australians, plus the divisional support units. The deployments had to be done under cover of darkness. Axis planes ruled the coast highway from dawn to dusk.

O'Connor didn't blame Wavell. London had its head so far up its ass, it needed a glass stomach. He was the one left with the sticky wicket. He had two brigades up front in the Mersa Matruh fortified area, including the Charon Cross strongpoint. He had light forces forward from the sea to the northern fringes of the deep desert. He had an entrenched camp at Bagush for the rest, not the Maginot Line. When the Australians all arrived, he would have four divisions with the artillery firepower of three and a half. The Axis force looked to be between four and six corps. Granted that most of that was Italian, who had not exactly shone with glory in the Alps against the French back in June. The Germans weren't yet acclimated to the weather, the sand, the dust, the local diseases. However, it was still a fully mechanized army. It was still backed by a huge air armada that totally ruled the skies.

The only edge he had was the training level of his core units, especially the Indians and the armor. These were professionals, not conscripts and recalled reservists. That in turn provided the core of an idea. His men had the skills to fight at night. The enemy air force was helpless in the dark. The coast road would not allow the whole enemy force to deploy at once, and the plateaus were terrain his men knew far better than these invaders. An attack force on the lower plateau south of the Charing Cross strongpoint … of two Indian brigades backed by the Matilda's of the heavy brigade, used in an army support role with companies or platoons supporting Indian battalions, had possibilities. It meant trusting his captains and majors to improvise. Perhaps it would work. If it didn't, the repulse might provide the justification for a retreat on Alamein – where his force should have been in the first place.

1030 hours local; 0930 hours CET
6 September 1940
Camp Gorlov, outside Tobruk, Italian colony of Libya

Joey Bats was in shock. He had never in his mind joined an army. He saw what he had done in Naples as having joined a gangland crew of the kind he knew from Brooklyn. Gunter was the capo and dealt with the big bosses. This fit Joey's sense of his place in the universe. He was no one's pantywaist, but he'd never been a seriously violent man in a street sense. The bosses were stone killers with quick brains, people like Gunter. Gunter was unusual only in having huge physical strength as well. Usually the muscle guys had a rock to hold their ears apart. Gunter was scary smart, as well as strong enough to break a guy like Joey in two.

The idea that the big bosses like this guy Heydrich, were assigning him a girlfriend just didn't fit Joey's concept of how real life worked. A big shot giving him use of a joy girl for a night or two was within Joey's frame of reference. That wasn't what was happening. This Clara was to be his sort of wife as well as his language teacher. Wife? She was a personal friend of Gunter's. The huge guy saw himself as her protector. Joey was to treat her right or else.

Joey had sort of envied Klaus having Greta to do the mattress polka with. Same for the Betar boyfriends of the Betar girls. Joey had not been tempted by them. He had nothing against Jew broads … in New York. Armed Jewish warrior women from Romania were a turnoff to him. Joey liked to see himself as a hepcat, but he was still quite traditional on sex roles, even if he just saw it as not being some European weirdo.

Joey had seen to those needs on his trip back to Italy. He'd been prepared to do without till Egypt. This Alexandria was supposed to be a big city. Joey had planned on seeing if he could get lucky there. Now he was being offered the sort of every night Klaus got. Sounded good but … but wife! When his dad had pushed the idea on him on the boat over from the States, Joey had laughed it off. Now he wasn't laughing. If he told this lady no, he'd need a reason that didn't lead to Gunter punching his lights out. Shit!

1200 hours local; 1100 hours CET
6 September 1940
Meeting Room, Headquarters Strauss Brigade, Camp Gorlov, Italian Colony of Libya

Major Klaus Steiner was fiercely concentrating as Gunter and the other seniors broke down the results of the von Manstein meeting for the brigade.   Klaus understood that he was a hero officer. He had no problem with the hero part. So far physical courage under fire had not been a problem for him. The problem was the officer part. He had never really been in command of anything in Romania or Hungary. On Malta, his 'command' was normally leading a counterattack platoon in skirmishes, while first Gunter Strauss and then General Ramcke had been in actual command of the airfield. His one foray at 'independent command' had been leading such a platoon, plus an attached mountain company that he hadn't even realized was his to command until halfway through the fighting. Even then, Gunter had recalled him before he did something stupid at Hal Far.

Now he was being gifted with two more Jewish companies, plus Peiper's light armored contingent. He was the lead element in the order of march, whatever that meant. His battalion was to advance directly behind the Libyan division. He was to 'coordinate' with them on this. He would then entrench at the to-be-built new German base camp, wherever that was.

He had four manuals. He and Greta were puzzling them out. They covered some things. They presumed prior knowledge on a million other things. What he needed was a 'battalion command for morons' manual, but such a title wasn't on the list. He'd asked for ten official tomes, based on Isaak's advice. He'd gotten four. What he was missing was a few pages of basics. Hopefully Uncle Isaak could write one up.

Then two thoughts occurred to him. Peter, now Hauptmann Peter, had run work gangs for his father. That was sort of command experience. Plus Naiomi had had some sort of officer training in Betar. Between the two as tutors, perhaps he could fake commanding a battalion in battle. He couldn't allow himself to fail. Greta was his princess and needed his protection. All he could do, was his best. So he just trusted to hope and his Reichsdeutsche bloodlines. German Aryans were all supposed to be natural warriors under National Socialism. Part of him was aware of just how silly this line of thought was, but it beat crying and gibbering like a circus monkey.

1200 hours CET
6 September 1940
Conference Room, Reichschancellery, Berlin

The meeting was officially that of the four who governed. As usual, the Führer and Chancellor sent a secretary to represent him. Following the norms, that secretary had no instructions from his boss concerning anything on the agenda. Such was how an emerging superpower ran its war.

Most of the list of action items was approved somewhat pro forma. Each ruler had staff to predigest most potential choices, and often to work out bargains where possible. No one except Heydrich trusted his minions enough to allow them the power to make binding decisions. That left the two difficult discussions.

The first was an evolving and escalating Gestapo investigation of misappropriation of supplies, black marketeering, and general financial malfeasance in the officer corps. The investigation had started with OKW, been extended to the occupation commands in the West, and was now beginning to tap at the doors of the War Ministry. Generaloberst and War Minister Beck wanted this stopped now. "Heydrich, don't recite legalities at me. You only follow those that suit you, anyway. You are doing this to undermine us. I want it stopped."

Heydrich was his normal sardonic self. "I want to avoid another November of 1918. The corruptions of your class brought down the Reich. I won't permit you to do so again. But I have a proposal for you. Have the Chain Dogs take over the investigation. You can handle the mess with quiet transfers, if you will publicly disgrace a few cases for propaganda."

Generaloberst Halder, head of the Army General Staff and thus of OKH, saw a possible bargain here. "How many sacrificial goats?"

"How corrupt will you allow the headquarters class to be? The fewer obvious cases of misbehavior, the fewer examples that need to be made. Every NCO and officer who abuses access to luxury goods like coffee and gasoline, who is clearly living beyond his salary, has neighbors. Friends. In-laws. Servants. People see, they feel aggrieved, they gossip. Our regime doesn't need this. So I can live with ... say, one a quarter thrown to the wolves, and none of those unfortunates being from the military aristocracy, if it is a joint Gestapo and Chain Dog investigation."

Beck wanted to laugh in the Nazi swine's face. "That way you have full files to use against everyone, as and when you wish."

"Of course. So discipline your class. Keep the sins minor, less even than venal. Small things don't get noticed outside your social circles. They can be written off as class privilege, as a reward to a warrior caste. I'm purging the upper echelons of the Party and the civilian bureaucracies with a harder hand. The public sees and approves. Why do you think each Gauleiter's hanging is a public event?"

Halder had thought Heydrich did it because he was a bloodthirsty barbarian. He would deal with Beck's ire later. "Approved. Now: what is this about army units?"

"I asked for a particular mountain division, so I could get its commander. I still want General Dietl. However, I don't need mountain troops per se. According to your staff Obersts, mountain units are specialist experts. I don't need the expertise. I'll give it back for your 22nd Airborne Division, whose specialty I *will* need. I'm also asking you to form a new division. Why is that a problem?"

Beck accepted the trade. It actually made sense. This cashiered naval Leutnant never ceased surprising him. He had promised Dietl, but never intended to honor it. He enjoyed putting Heydrich in his place. Let him have to beg Göring. "What's this about a new division?"

"It is General Jodl's concept. We wanted the mountain division for its light, air-transportable equipment. Jodl sensibly pointed out that one could generate the equipment set without the specialist manpower, and create an air landing division. Now I could do this from the Waffen SS, from the NL, even from the SA. If I needed first rate manpower, I could ask Führer Göring to make one from the Luftwaffe. I'm trying to honor the concept of our bargain that the bulk of the ground forces remain Army. My minions don't understand why your staffs were so difficult about this. We are talking second line manpower. Older reservists or Volksdeutsche or Balts. I'll even take Czechs. It's the equipment set. They fly to an airfield the paratroops or glider forces take, entrench, and then hold till the mechanized forces arrive."

Beck wanted to argue. He would detest free money if it came from Heydrich. Halder wanted to get back to his office, and voted with Heydrich to approve the formation of the 91st Airlanding Division, which was to be ready for deployment in the south by March 1st of next year.

1300 hours CET
6 September 1940
Stendal, Germany, Garrison of 7th Flieger-Division

Recently promoted Sous-Lieutenant Marcel Bigeard was glad to be out of captivity. He had volunteered for this new parachute service to accomplish that feat. He could see where his service in the Corps Franc had fitted him for these new forces. He welcomed the physical challenge of parachute training.

His problem was getting such training from the hated Boche. He was born on the borders of the old Kaiserreich in Lorraine. These Germans were to him the perpetual foe. His recruiting officer did not disagree. He merely offered logic, Cartesian as well as patriotic. The Nazis held Paris. France was helpless to fight the Germans at the moment. All such a further war would accomplish, was the occupation of the Unoccupied Zone and the extinction of the French Republic. National suicide was hardly a wise course.

In the meantime, the enemy was Britain. It was the British who had pushed poor France into this war. Then when serious fighting began, the British ran away to their island, leaving the French army behind to die. When France had been forced to an armistice, the British had treacherously attacked the French fleet at anchor. Now they were stealing France's Empire in Africa, using this General de Gaulle as a cat's-paw.

Bigeard's training contingent would form the 6th Colonial Parachute Battalion. All in all, the French were forming eighteen such battalions for African service. First France would fight the British. Then they would extract themselves from Germany's death grip. Germany had managed this from Napoleon's grasp. Nothing lasts forever. Bigeard didn't like the chain of reasoning, but he accepted it. He had faith in Marshal Petain and General Weygand. These men were patriots, not tricksy political scum like Laval. If they could do these things with honor, Bigeard could do the same.

1800 hours local; 1700 hours CET
6 September 1940
Camp Gorlov, Italian Colony of Libya

Joey Bats had never been shy around women. He'd always hung with older guys because of his mechanical abilities. So when his balls dropped at twelve, he went out on Saturday nights with guys in their late teens and twenties he worked with, not the local kid pack. He'd taken his share of serious teasing in the beginning for his youth and short stature (he'd never been tall, and his growth spurt had been late). He'd dealt with it. He did a man's work and earned a man's pay. He could hold a drink, and when necessary take a punch. The good-time girls they would buy drinks for, dance with and try to get in the pants of, were looking for a guy who could dress sharp and pay to take them someplace nice. These were Depression years. He was an earner and a lot of guys weren't.   His mates could drop the right names to get into the best clubs, to get into the hottest scenes. Being connected meant you had such entrée.

Now he was sitting at the office table with a jug of wine and a pot of coffee. Across from him was this Clara Fischer. She didn't look half bad (or as old as he had feared). However, she was not shooting come-hither looks. It was more like the wary glances a passerby gives a vicious guard dog. What the fuck?

Clara was looking Joey over. She didn't mind the ground-in dirt and grease on his hands. She was working class, and such decoration was normal in guys who worked with machines. He was a little short, but he had a pleasant face. The problem was, she'd never been a whore and wasn't really sure she wanted to start now. "Talk to me in German. I need to see how well you can speak, to design a lesson plan."

Joey went near bug-eyed. "Huh?"

"You seem as unsure about the mistress part as I am, so let's focus on teacher. Berlin wants your German improved. Do you plan on telling the Reichsführer SS that you refuse?" She gave a mordant laugh, thinking of what would follow telling the top thug no.

This was not a boy/girl script Joey knew. "Look, I didn't say no. But this is kind of sudden. Gunter tells me I'm acquiring a wife, a live-in lady. My old man had been on my ass about marrying, but I sort of expected I would get to choose … "

"And your choice didn't include a German Communist cleaning lady with thirteen kids and a very damaged brother. You Americans! You think everything is a Hollywood movie. The Gestapo shipped me to you because our mutual friend Wanda the bootlegger thought it made sense. On one level it does. On a Hauptmann's pay I could better bring up my kids … "

Joey was now in shock. Thirteen kids! How old was this bimbo? "Pardon me, but thirteen? How young did you start?"

Clara showed her weariness. "Foster kids. Their parents would vanish. Dead, in jail, gone underground, fled to Moscow. One never knew, and one didn't ask. We surviving neighborhood activists would make sure they all had homes, had meals. The Party was a family. We take care of our own."

"Party? Reds I knew were Puritan weirdos."

Clara finally found humor in the absurdity of this all. Besides, his German wasn't any worse than the kids of Polish miners. Ruhr was full of them, and she'd been trained to handle bad grammar and strange pronunciations. She stopped Joey and ran him back through how to correctly say she was a Puritanical political killjoy, as opposed to a member of a vanished English religion sect. He had a poor tongue but a good ear. More tools she could use on the lessons. She mentally nodded to herself. She'd made her decision. If she changed her mind, Gunter could get her out of this later. He could break this man in two without using more than one of his well-muscled arms.

Clara stood up. She knew how to strike a pose to sexually display herself. Never having been a street girl was different than not knowing the sidewalk dance. She enjoyed watching the reaction she was getting. The young man flushed, his breath subtly quickened, and a bulge started in the right place. OK. The equipment worked.

"I can satisfy a man. None of my past lovers complained about the physical side. It is healthy exercise, and we Germans pride ourselves on physical fitness." She walked over, a street corner strut, and caressed his face. "Can you satisfy a woman? Really pleasure, not just service her like a bull does a cow?"

Joey was trying to bluster, and lacked the German for it. Switched into a mix of Italian and English, none of which Clara knew a word of. "Don't worry lover, I'll teach you those words too, not just how to give a technical report." By now her hands had found his belt buckle, were helping him out of his pants and underwear. She got her hands on his engorged phallus, stroked twice and then gave a savage twist. Joey yelped in frustration and pain. "But let's get a few things clear. You beat me and I'll have Gunter knock your teeth out. I'll be faithful to you. You're a man, which means left to yourself you'd fuck a dog or a melon after a few drinks. Now you will exercise some judgment. Bring home diseases or lice, I'll take you in my mouth and gnaw off your favorite parts. So use care or use condoms. You have bastards and I'll raise them, but I get a say if we take the bitch into our household." She had gone back to caressing. Joey was slowly losing his ability to formulate words. She knew that male state. "Nod yes and we'll work out the details in the morning." Joey was nodding like a child being told there would be a meal all of sugar desserts. Clara pushed him back in the chair, mounted him and set out to show German racial superiority in this Olympic event.

2300 hours CET
6 September 1940
An aristocratic general's mansion, Charlottenburg, Berlin, Capital of the Reich

The bid had been set at 6 diamonds, doubled and vulnerable. Colonel Kevin Duffy was dummy and thus free to stand and move about. By house rules, that meant he saw to beverages. The servants were mostly all in the bomb shelter out back. The RAF 'visit' to Berlin was in its second hour. There were never many planes, and they never seemed to hit anything of note. As the Luftwaffe general he partnered with at tennis assured him, he and the household he was guesting at were in more danger from fragments of flak shells than from British bombs. The Nazi Party insisted all those guns be fired so that the morale of Berlin's people would be kept up. The general thought it was both idiotic, and typical of the new Gauleiter. The man should give more time to making beds squeak with his receptionist, and cease pretending he was competent to do anything more. Just tell the public the truth about what damaged what, and like good German subordinates they would accept and obey. Duffy kept to himself the retort that if Berliners had been so good at obeying what their betters decreed, why had there been so many Communists, Socialists, and Nazis there?

Duffy found this all a most strange sort of captivity. Clothes had been borrowed for him from serving officers of roughly his size and build. He now had tennis whites, golf outfits; he could dress for dinner or to attend opera. His days were given to gentleman's sports – golf, riding, tennis, swimming, boating, shooting. Here he was a prisoner in the Reich doing competitive shooting. Even that was less bizarre than a morning ride where his party had come upon a party centered on the head of the Abwehr, Admiral Canaris, and the head of the SS, Reichsführer Heydrich. He had been formally introduced to both. Cards had been exchanged, and the Admiral had invited him to a dinner he was giving in a few weeks. The Brigadier's social contacts seemed bottomless. He and the Admiral had mutual friends. Had broken bread in Sicily back before this war.

Kevin's German was still marginal, but improving day by day. He could now bid bridge hands and take drink orders in a social setting. He had learned how to clearly say 'I have little German. Please speak slowly and use small words', with what many Berliners told him was a rustic East Prussian accent. The mansion's owner was Count and General. His extended family was from that province. He was on active service, as were two sons. A third son had been crippled in a training accident and was on a ministry staff in Brussels. The count's granduncle, the retired general, was not recalled to active duty, and thus presided over the mansion and a floating population of relatives, servants, and hangers on. Which now included the Brigadier's party of four.

The Brigadier's two servants had objected to using the air raid shelter. They felt as retired military they had as much right to show courage as the older men, who refused to let these silly British pinprick raids interrupt their evening socializing. The problem was that all the male servants were also retired military who had followed their local nobleman into the army and back out the other side. The younger ones were all on active service, so that most of these men were well past retirement age. They would joke they had been called back to the count's colors for duration.

The wives, widows, and spinsters were also of either of the military aristocracy or their hereditary retainers. They too felt they had the courage of their class. A compromise was reached. To get the children into the shelter, all the women and servants went as well. Duffy laughed to himself. All turned out to be many. The teens were all HJ or BDM, and refused. They and a few of the adults colonized the air raid precaution service in this precinct, and served as unofficial helpers on two ack-ack guns. Twelve-year-old girls helping to load a gun whose fire director was an eighty-year-old retired artillery sergeant, was not what the RAF lads up there in the clouds thought they were fighting. Modern war was strange that way.

Still stranger were the interrogations. Duffy expected to be confronted on knowledge he had of supreme command in London. He was months out of date, but it still might be of value. No one cared about that. He'd been quizzed incessantly about his Great War service. When he'd asked why, the answer was that this was important socially. One couldn't bring him to party X where Widow Y was, if he had served in a particular corps for Third Ypres as she had lost her husband and two sons there. That was a memory she didn't wish to revisit. However, Widow Z's husband never came back from Fourth Ypres. Missing presumed dead. She found reminisces of anyone on either side of those days, a way to anchor her memories of him. Indeed, one of his bridge partners – a one-armed, one-legged retired major – had sought him out as his CV spread around. Turned out they had fought at quite close quarters during the Cambrai Campaign. That was where the then-Hauptmann had lost the leg below the knee. Those six days of nonstop combat were the high point of his life. He couldn't find a German of his class he hadn't bored to death with his war stories. Now Duffy could hear them all and tell his own.

The brigadier was being quizzed far more closely. This seemed absurd. The man was a retired fossil. Alistare-Smythe had been quite clear on the why's. Preliminary peace discussions had begun in Lisbon. Maybe. At issue were the bona fides of the alleged crown representatives. The brigadier was scathing, about what an idiot the Nazi ex-Foreign Minister von Ribbentrop had been. As ambassador to London he had fallen in with a set of aristocrats and industrialists who were fawningly pro-Nazi. Saw Hitler as a bulwark against the trade unions, the Labor Party, the Bolsheviks, and, to a large extent, the 20th century. Von Ribbentrop confused the social standing of these fools with their utter lack of political power. They might just have enough clout to get the local council to fix a pothole in a road, but scarcely anything more. The brigadier saw himself as providing the education a proper ambassador would have on who was who and what was what in the factions of the Tories, National Liberals, Liberals, and the more patriotic cliques in Labor. It was easy to say you had the power to oust Churchill and do a deal. It was even possible to do. Churchill had few personal adherents, and many of those who had opted for him in May had done so only because they disliked other possibilities more intensely. That said, the obvious replacements for Churchill – Eden, Lloyd George, Halifax, Atlee, Bevin – all had enemies as well. Britain needed peace. Someday London would see this. However, if some clique had fouled the pool by promising the Axis peace, and then failing to bring the War Cabinet and parliament along, this would be bad for the Empire. Told Duffy that, by all means, report everything you saw me do once we are repatriated. Let higher-ups decide what was treason. Just for now understand the game.

Chapter 5

0800 hours local; 0700 hours CET
7 September 1940
Vicinity of Mersa Matruh, Egypt

Haptsturmführer Max Seela was yet again wondering at the workings of fate. His division, Eicke's Death's Head, had been demoted to a field security force. No one knew why, but the betting was, it was because Eicke had been Himmler's man. Stood to reason he would be out of favor with the new Reichsführer. But then why not cashier the General, instead of demoting the division? It had then been combed over by officers from Hausser's Reich Division, and SS Headquarters in Berlin, for 'volunteers' for transfer to the Reich Division for unspecified 'overseas service'. His pioneer battalion was transferred over as a unit, and the men in the unit had been asked to 'volunteer' to stay with the colors. "Volunteer". They were in formation at the position of attention in front of a Brigadeführer. The order was that those not wishing to volunteer should fall out to the rear. Of course no one moved. Who wants to appear the coward in front of his friends? So here he was in this oven-hot land of rocks and sand.

The SS Engineering officer had been sent forward by his division commander, General Hausser. A ragtag militia unit, the Strauss Brigade, was tasked with establishing the advance base camp for the German contingent of the Italo-German Panzer Army. Militia, but the official heroes of Malta. Propaganda was making much of how their National Socialist loyalty could more than compensate for lack of formal training. Less than a month ago this NL force had been two battalions (or a company, depending on who you asked). Neither Generals Hausser nor von Manstein had a clue as to whether this Oberst Strauss had an engineering staff. So the SS Hauptführer had been ordered to liaise with Strauss. In plainer terms, to provide such expert advice.

Major Klaus Steiner asserted that the British were mostly some 60 kilometers east of here, in a fortified camp that prisoners said was called the Bagush Box. Up here was a screen of British armored cars. Signals intercept said they were South Africans. This Steiner had provided a prisoner from these units confirming this. To drive them off Oberst Strauss had taken the field himself with an SS light armored company, an SA company of armored cars, a battery of old French 75's from the Army and another of Luftwaffe 88's. Combining this with two companies of some Jewish militia from Romania, he had established a forward position. A communications truck was calling down JU-87's and Me-110's who were arriving in groups of half a dozen and loitering till assigned targets. Some ex-Habsburg artillery officer, a Major Schwabe, was directing the guns. Three South African armored cars were burning a thousand meters out or so, and the rest were prudently scurrying out of range. The Hauptsturmführer was an SS officer, a member of an elite. He was surprised this rag-tag bunch could fight this well. Rumor with his division was that Oberst Strauss's brigade was a joke, some special project of the Reichsführer. Perhaps laughter was not in order. There was even a good SS officer, Hauptsturmführer Peiper, commanding the light armor.

A column detached itself from the main force and tore off into the desert. Eight motorcyles with sidecars, and four of the new Kübelwagen. The engineer was in a sidecar, holding on for dear life. His cyclist seemed fearless, but less than totally in control of his machine. The ex-HJ seemed to be maybe 15, and had a look on his face of pure glee as he sent the bike flying over small gullies, and sprinted ahead of the pack to recon forward before looping back. Young men and loud, fast machines seemed a marriage made in some obscure corner of Hell, which was what the morning sun felt like.

For three hours they dodged across the plateau. It wasn't some flat pan of sand the way the picture books said. It was a wild mix of pebbles, scrub, rock, gullies and gentle rises. The SS officer could see nothing to guide by, yet suddenly the party was stopping at a small flat spot in the middle of nowhere. The two officers, Major Steiner and Hauptmann Schwabe, were out of their vehicles walking the ground. Schwabe was probing the sand and dirt with a long metal stick with a sharp end. He looked nothing like the older artillery Major, but had called the man 'father'. His German was poor but understandable. Strange people whose children look nothing like them, but then to Seela's eye, this whole expedition was unusual. This seemed nothing like a proper survey, but neither other officer had asked for his expert advice. The engineer went over to stand with them. Perhaps physical proximity would remind them why he was along. They nodded, but continued to ignore him.

The tall Hauptmann did most of the talking. "Klaus, this place should do. It is flat enough for parking. Surface is hard enough that the heavy stuff shouldn't bog down badly. Are you sure on the distances?" Peter caught the Hauptsturmführer's expression. "I've been bossing work crews since I was fourteen. I've done oil wells, pipelines, roads, parking areas, small buildings, whatever was needed to make a spread-out oil field run. This place is not ideal, but we can make it do – to improve it, I'd like a lot of heavy equipment we don't have, and my old labor crew from Romania. I might as well ask the British to sail home because it is inconvenient for them to be here opposing us. Life is what it is and you deal with it. You are the official expert. Have you seen a better location?" The SS officer shook his head. He was lost. He was also not about to ask to be allowed to wander around a wilderness for hours, looking for perfection while dreading a probable British counterstroke.

Klaus saw the Hauptsturmführer's nonverbal response. "I'm sure as I need to be, on this location. Twenty kilometers from the British artillery per your father. Gunter said less, but he's not a gunner. Ten kilometers for that Italian division to deploy in. I've done enough desert navigation so I'm probably within three or four kilometers of where I think we are. Mark it and let's get out of here. The planes are keeping the British away … for now. Remember Malta. These Brits are slow off the mark, but tough once they start reacting."

Peter's shrug said he had his own ideas of who was a hard guy, and so far the British didn't rate it. But Father said otherwise, and Isaak had never been wrong yet. Peter started hammering three large crosses into the ground.

The SS officer had never seen a position marked like this, and asked. He was quite unsure that this child Major had a firm grip on where he was, where the British were, or much else. The Major smiled and said most people didn't disturb graves. Asked the engineer if he had a better answer. The big push was a few days off. These might hold up. For sure the British would be back to investigate. If worse came to worst, the Major felt he could find the place again if he weren't dodging South Africans. The formally-trained engineer was nonplussed but went along. Asked if he could ride back in one of the larger vehicles. The two other officers laughed but made it happen.

1000 hours CET
7 September 1940
Air Ministry, Berlin

Air Marshal Wolfram von Richthofen was not amazed that his service head, Führer Göring, had deputized him for this meeting. Reichsmarshall Göring didn't do mornings, and where at all possible didn't do meetings. Deputy Chancellor Heydrich and his lapdog Schellenberg had something that supposedly couldn't keep, and about which they refused to provide an agenda memo.

Heydrich dispensed with the usual coffee service and pleasantries. He asked that the room be cleared, but his minion Schellenberg remained seated as the other Luftwaffe personnel exited. Even at the Air Ministry, Führer Göring's lair, Heydrich was acting as if he were in charge. Von Richthofen thought this rude but sadly typical. Heydrich waited till the door was firmly shut and began, "We have a major policy issue here and need to reach a decision jointly with you as representative of the Luftwaffe. We have uncovered a significant piece of fraud on the part of some officers of your service, and a major contractor."

Von Richthofen knew of the Gestapo's crusade against corruption at senior levels. The SS seemed to be executing a Kreisleiter every few days, and more than one Gauleiter a month. The Heer had yet to allow any of its people to be actually killed, but many were under various levels of investigation or custody. "What's the problem? We'll convene a court-martial and put them through the wringer."

Schellenberg gave him a sardonic look. "That's the problem. The fraud is real, but they may deserve medals for initiative, for creatively working towards the Führer."

Von Richthofen looked at this toady of Heydrich's strangely. "How can fraud be meritorious?"

Heydrich answered. "Remember back in the early spring we ordered the Zeppelin program shut down, and the working machine broken up for its raw materials?" Von Richthofen nodded warily. Heydrich actually smiled. "Well, they didn't. Faked the paperwork, kept the project alive, and even paid them under the designation of some secret rocket program. With this new French campaign in Africa, we now have use for the damned things."

Von Richthofen thought for a few seconds. "I can recall us using earlier ones for resupply to our East African colony in the Great War."

Heydrich was glad the air marshal was getting the point. "Yes. We can use them now to resupply the French, and later when we make our own campaign towards the Congo mineral deposits."

"Then what is it you want of the air force?"

"If we send the Gestapo to arrest these fools, it will panic the whole program. I need you to call the people in – your officers, and the senior people from the contractors. Threaten them with the Gestapo, then say they can redeem themselves by spinning the whole program back up quickly. Demote someone as a warning. The officers cannot all be indispensable. Transfer the demoted one to someplace unpleasant. You must have some bases that rate as punishment tours. Every service does. Then send a team of your accounting people to make sure no one can run this sort of a scam again. This time it proved useful. Normally it would just be more fraud and waste, something we have far too much of."

"When do you need the airships operational?"

"Yesterday. Which is of course impossible. Send someone good you trust, to write us both a report on what capacities will be available when. Then get your service's gossip net going on how you personally saved all these people from the Gestapo. Make clear that you won't be inclined to work this magic again, so, if someone is going to disobey orders this blatantly, they damned better be right. Working towards the Führer is the equivalent of saddle orders. The results validate the latitude taken. This is extreme disobedience, so the gains must justify it. Also, please find out what this silly rocket program is and why we are wasting resources on it. We wage war on Earth, not the Moon in some Jules Verne or H.G. Wells fantastic novel."

Once rid of the two SS officials, the air marshal made his first priority getting his senior accounting staff in. This fraud should have been caught internally, regardless of whether outsiders were informed or not. The Luftwaffe needed an accounting system that couldn't be gamed this easily. He was also curious what this rocket program was. It sounded like waste, but Heydrich wasn't an engineer.

1200 hours CET
7 September 1940
Comando Supremo delle Forze Armate dello Stato (COMANDO SUPREMO), Palazzo Vidoni-Caffarelli, Corso Vittorio Emanuele II, Rome

Prince Umberto of Savoy and Air Marshal Balbo didn't enjoy getting yet another request from SS General Wolff for an expedited meeting. Wolff had assured them both that he was a facilitator, not a minder, but kept making these requests. Peremptory requests, however politely they were worded. The subject was blandly listed as armaments. They waited to hear what fresh indignity awaited Italy.

As was typical on such occasions, the better part of an hour was wasted on coffee service and pleasantries before any real business got done. This was after all Italy, not barely-civilized Berlin. Wolff was unusual for an SS general. He had manners and knew how to make the proper small talk. He also could gauge when the Italians were ready to discuss serious things. "The Reichsführer would like to have a discussion about tanks and planes. We have been sending you fifty first-rate tanks a month, Panzer III's and IV's. Also a hundred each of our bombers and the Me-109 fighters. We know that delivery has gone smoothly. We have met any requests on technical assistance and spare parts. Berlin wants to know how you propose to use these, especially the tanks. We have starved our own forces of these models so our Italian allies can have proper armored vehicles. Your staff people have been quite evasive on how and where these will be employed."

The two Italians had wondered about this. Their reports from Libya had the assembled German forces with a weird mix of older German models, Czech designs, and booty AFV's from everyone Germany had overrun. Only the SS division was getting the modern tanks, roughly a battalion a month. Umberto was the commander-in-chief and answered. "We are working up new battalions with these. They will transition south late this year, and early next year when we bring on a new armored division and a companion mechanized one."

Wolff took that in. "So they will miss the campaign in Egypt, and probably Palestine as well." He seemed to be weighing his words carefully. "We'll have to jointly decide if they are best employed then in Trans-Jordan or Sudan. I'd guess Sudan, and on from there to Kenya."

Balbo was curious. "You really think Egypt will fall so quickly?" Italian intelligence rated the British Nile Army as of similar size to their own Libyan forces; to which would have to be added, of course, the British garrison troops in Egypt and the British-trained Egyptian Army.

Wolff was at his affable best. "Abwehr was right about the British weakness in Malta. We think they are right again in Egypt. Next to no air force, limited artillery, and under four trained divisions. Your general would have to be incompetent on a French scale to not have you in Cairo for Christmas. Oh, by the way, we're getting feelers from the Egyptian monarch. We keep directing them back to you. Have your embassies in Lisbon and Madrid contact ours, and we'll arrange meetings. We ask that you do the same as regards Iraq."

Balbo knew this was somewhat impolite, but Wolff seemed never to mind such probes. "We are grateful for the weapons. Why are you living up to your promises?" Balbo had unsuccessfully pushed Italy to get licenses to make German equipment for years. He'd been roadblocked by Italian vested interests, but also by pig-headed German refusals. Now licenses were suddenly available on commercially sensible terms, as were direct shipments of German aviation engines for Italy's aircraft manufactures. Balbo wished to learn the logic behind these changes.

Wolff gave him a level look and a pleasant smile. His specialty was public relations in various forms. "The Reichsführer is a man of his word. He honors promises and expects others to do the same. The deep strategy isn't very complex. You are providing most of the men for this war. Most of the blood spilled will be Italian. It would be natural for your troops to see their German allies with better arms, and feel angry at the blood they are spending fighting with obsolete junk. Being able to show off your new tanks and planes voids this dispute before it gets started. In reverse, we need to sell our public that Italy is a serious military power. Most Germans have done military service. They need to see photos of victorious Italians with good German arms. This shows them you are worthy allies, not like the idiots the Kaiser yoked us with. Italian troops who win victories beside us, and have acquired a huge empire. Worthy comrades of a Greater Germany. We used to have a union of two leaders, a personal relationship. The Reichsführer wishes this to be an alliance of entire Völker. This will take years, but this is a crucial first step."

Balbo knew how to keep his face a mask. He and the Prince would have much to discuss. He promised Wolff that his air force staff would provide the proper details on where the German planes were being posted. Another half hour of small talk saw the German on his way. The two Italian rulers had much to ponder. They had been politely asked to start a propaganda campaign of their own. They decided to lead this off with a radio speech by Il Duce. Balbo foresaw that getting Benito Mussolini to accept a speech anyone else wrote, was going to be one of the labors of Hercules. Yet the damned Germans were right. To many Italians, Germany was just an extra-large-sized version of their traditional Austrian foes. It would take the magic of their leader's oratory to begin to change this.

1400 hours local; 1300 hours CET
7 September 1940
Joey's expanded auto repair workshop, Camp Gorlov, Italian Colony of Libya

Joey had woken up satisfied with the bargain he'd made. He'd never had his ashes hauled more expertly in his young life, even by pros. What he was unprepared for started with being handed his morning coffee straight out of bed. Clara's 13 kids included many old enough for chores. His uniform was cleaned and lightly ironed, neatly folded across a camp chair. The heavy stains would need an industrial cleaning, but it no longer stank of sweat and machine-oil. His work boots were clean. Not polished. Polish was silly for a working mechanic. Clean was nice. Something he himself never made time for, but nice.

Breakfast was the same food the mess hall was serving, but it was brought to him. Clara had somehow commandeered a folding table to serve from. Thirteen kids, Joey, Clara, and her brother sat down for a quick 'family' breakfast. Joey was sure he wouldn't remember half the names, but it felt homey. Sort of nice.

Clara spent most of breakfast reviewing a 'lesson plan' with a girl who looked barely thirteen. The younger lady was in charge of the 'littles' while the rest worked. As Joey got up to leave for work, her brother Carl fell in behind him. So did Clara and seven teens and tweens of both sexes. Joey started with a 'What the Fuck?' but Clara, clearly in charge, just motioned him to keep going. Weird.

Joey did as he was told. There was a new gang at work. Peter's brother Paul had brought them from the camp in the same ship that had taken Clara to Libya. Joey and Paul did a quick meeting, reviewing the morning's work. When work crews started to be formed to do it, Clara's kids were all lined up, waiting to be given assignments. Joey shot her another 'what gives?' look. "Apprentices, dear. They can fetch and carry. Tools always need putting back. The boys need to learn a trade. The girls might find this a good trade as well. If not, they are extra hands. Besides, women have better fine-finger dexterity than men anyway. You guys supply the raw power. We supply the finesse." Joey had only seen one lady mechanic in his life. She was female by anatomy, but a bull dyke who dressed, acted, and cursed like a guy, with muscles to match. These girls looked like girls. But extra hands were extra hands. He'd argue it later in bed. He laughed. She'd have to teach him the words to argue with.

Clara stood a bit apart from Joey as he worked. He couldn't figure out what she was doing, until he got hung up trying to explain to someone with no Italian, Yiddish, or English what he wanted done. He knew the words in those three but not in German or this guy's native Magyar. Clara inserted herself into the conversation, helping each of the two men to master the words needed. It took four such situations before Joey realized what was happening. She was teaching him German. His head whipped around. She laughed, nodded, and blew him a kiss. "Yes my man, this is language lessons. Later I'll go speak to Gunter. I hope either you are well paid or the unit has funds. We need roughly a dozen books from a store I know of back home. Pictorial and technical dictionaries. Right now I'm teaching you the simplified German words for things. We need these books to have you learn the correct nomenclature. My training didn't include that jargon. For right now don't worry about pronunciation or grammar. That comes later, when your vocabulary will be bigger."

The day had gotten weirder from there. Midmorning, the three young girls had vanished. They came back with coffee and snacks for everyone. Now they were setting up for lunch. No more time wasted going to and from the cook tent. Joey was no fool. He could see where Gunter had played him, but damn, this was just better living. This wasn't marriage as he understood it from Brooklyn. Maybe it wasn't what such a union was like in Germany either. It sure as Hell wasn't how it went in Naples. So call it marriage NL-style. He and Clara as a second Klaus and Greta. Joey Bats was liking this. A lot.

1700 hours local; 1600 hours CET
7 September 1940
HQ shack, Camp Gorlov, Italian Colony of Libya

Oberst Gunter Strauss was still coming to terms with what was to him his exalted rank, one beyond his Leutnant's dreams of someday making Hauptmann and commanding his own company. He'd been a Leutnant by field promotion in the Iron Division, and again in the SA. Now he was a brigade commander and host to a 'commander's conference' with two real generals, the German Erwin Rommel of 7th Panzer Division and the Italian Pietro Maletti of the 1st Libyan Division. The three were supposedly working out how the 'van of the army', which was the three of them, would 'advance to contact'. Gunter hadn't a clue, and just was waiting for the two generals to tell him what needed to be done. Right now they were having tea with a light spread of finger food that Mary the Cook and her kids had set out. There was also a good bottle of Italian brandy, should things proceed in that direction later. Gunter had two of the Italian volunteers from the Malta operation on hand for translating, although Maletti had solved that problem by bringing along a *capitano* who spoke decent German. He also had Ivan Gorlov sitting in. Major Ivan had once commanded a brigade of White cavalry on the Ukrainian steppes. He was Gunter's designated number two in case of big technical military terms beyond Gunter's understanding.

The two generals had spent half an hour fencing with each other, trying to get a feel for the man behind the rank and title. Rommel seemed to have reached some sort of a decision, and laid a map on the table. "The plan is that you march your Libyans first, with Strauss and my advance guard following. Can we all agree this is absurd?" The Italian said nothing, but motioned with his hands for the German to continue. "I have four battalions of veteran mobile troops, including a Panzer battalion. Five battalions, as I will 'borrow' the SS that Mohnke brought."

He looked over at Gunter to see if there would be an argument. Gunter's quick, "Yes, Herr General," was the only possible reply. This violated von Manstein's orders, but Rommel was a General and a Blue Max wearer.

Rommel caught his thought. "Rethink it, Oberst. Von Manstein said I couldn't steal the SS for my march around the British. He never said I couldn't command them here." Rommel regarded that as settled, and turned matters back to Maletti. "Let me lead with the five German battalions and one of yours. We'll drive in the British outposts and armored car screen. You follow behind. The battalion you gave me, sets up an outpost line that you dig in behind with your division. You park your administrative services with Oberst Strauss here. He can build that base the higher commanders want, including a headquarters for you. He'll be under your command as a reserve force with his remaining overstrength battalion. Oh, and he also has some excellent mechanics for the inevitable vehicle problems. As you arrive to dig in, I'll slide south, but without the Italian battalion on outpost duty, and without the SS battalion. They move back to the HQ area as your divisional reserve. Oberst Strauss here has some French light tanks and an armored car company. Add them to the SS unit, and you have a strong counterattack reserve. I'll be guarding the inland flank against a British sweep out of the high plateau."

Maletti looked over the map. He had Gunter mark the forward base position that Klaus and Peter had surveyed. "Sounds good. Except if the British get active as we are getting into position. My division is small, more the size of a large brigade. Good lads. Well trained, and they know this sort of terrain. But what we have are two large brigades facing a British corps. The British have this large entrenched camp, and higher command's plan presumes they will sit in it. What if they don't? Then we have two commands mixed together and two divisional Generals, neither totally in command. What then?"

"Daytime is easy, so let's presume it is night. Any unit who sees a general obeys him. You and I will have radios I presume?" Maletti nodded. Italy's problems didn't extend to lack of radios at the level of division headquarters. "Oberst Strauss, you have your Malta Italians here?" It was Gunter's turn to nod. "Find me two dozen more officer cadets, and equip them with motorcycles please. They can be couriers between the units." Rommel then proceeded to give an accounting of their predecessors' bravery on the march to the Grand Harbor.

Maletti took this all in. "Colonello Strauss, I'll be sending my chief engineering officer to you tomorrow to review what is to be built, where and in what order. Do you have problems being under the command of an Italian?"

Gunter didn't see Italian when he looked at Maletti. He saw a species called 'General'. "No Herr General. The best liaison would be with my Major Schwabe. He handled major construction at the Ploiesti oil fields. He's also an artillery veteran."

After this, brandy was served; and in under an hour both walking gods had departed. Gunter sent a runner for Clara. He had a more urgent task for her than continuing to teach Joey German. There were a few dozen Italian lads who needed a crash course in military terms.

0200 hours Indian Time, 8 September 1940
 2130 hours CET, 7 September 1940
Bose's residence, Elgin Road, Calcutta, Bengal, British Indian Raj

Subhas Chandra Bose had reached a decision. He had been a loyal member of the Congress Party for long enough. Gandhi and Nehru had thwarted him at every turn. The news of Sukarno's unfolding revolution in Java had reached Bengal. His Forward (or Left) bloc in Congress would follow him. Gandhi's strength was the Hindi-speaking plains of India's north. Bose's was regionalized in Bengal and the south. The two separate cultures had been amalgamated by the British into the Raj.

Bose had been contacted by the German Abwehr. They were offering him escape through Afghanistan to Germany. He took the small sums they offered, but had no intention of following their direction. Bose had been given quite a bit more money by agents of the Comintern. Money and the use of their cadres within the Indian left and labor movements. They promised more money and arms, through China and into Assam, over time. Bose would believe that when it happened. His time was now.

There was no question of immediate revolution. The army, police, and civil service would stay loyal to their salt … for now. Which meant a war of guerrilla, of assassins in the manner the genius Michael Collins had used against the British two decades ago. Bose knew many who joined him would be *dacoits*, bandits whose main wish was for loot and the thrill of action. So be it. They would fight. They wouldn't take orders easily, but for now he needed the illusion of revolutionary ferment while he built his political base, subverted the Raj and Congress. For every youth who would throw a bomb or use a revolver, he needed a hundred who would act as eyes and ears, who would provide a sleeping mat to a stranger with a code word, who would carry papers down the rail line to another town without reading them. He could never beat the British in the field. Collins in Ireland had proven that such a conventional victory was unnecessary. All that was needed, was to make continuing the Raj expensive and unpleasant for long enough.

He was enough of an adult to be aware that the Bolsheviks were trying to use him. The pattern was there before with Chiang, with Ataturk, with others. It didn't matter. Each battle in its own time. The die was cast. He had never felt so alive as this moment. He escaped from his house to begin his life underground, away from his current house arrest. India would be free!

0500 hours local; 0400 hours CET
8 September 1940
Western Desert Force HQ, Bagush Box, Egypt

General Richard O'Connor's staff had spent most of the night preparing this briefing on yesterday's victorious repulse of an attack by General Rommel's 7th Panzer Division. The few recovered prisoners had been from components of some augmenting force to that formidable unit. Rommel had been beefed up by volunteers from the SS, SA, Luftwaffe antiaircraft arm, and the Nibelungen Legion, the heroes of Malta. There was even a battalion of elite Italian arditi. Yet his screening units had beaten off this force. The furthest penetrating spearhead had been pushed back by a sortie of cruiser tanks from his own 7th Armored Division, the Desert Rats. Scouts reported that the Germans had left three metal crosses, but no graves had been discovered. This seemed strange, but first reports were often garbled in O'Connor's experience. He dispatched a staff lieutenant to drive back to this spot and see what was so special about either the place or the three pieces of scrap metal.

In the meantime O'Connor put his staff to work. His men had proven they could handle more than their own numbers of the best the Germans had. Perhaps the disaster in France was a matter of how dissolute the French were, rather than a mark of Nazi excellence in war. He had two divisions of well-trained professionals, 4th Indian and 7th Armored. The 4th was the first and best contingent of the Indian Army, long-service volunteers with splendid records in many of Britain's wars of the last century. The 7th had begun life as the Mobile Division of the Egyptian garrison. Even with wartime dilution, it was the best British unit of division size, fully acclimated and well versed in the terrain of the Western Desert.

The Axis plan seemed to be an army-sized push straight at him. They probably expected their bombers to do all the work. Massed bombers as flying artillery could be deadly. Bombers were near useless at night. So O'Connor would start with a plan to use two Indian brigades backed by the two South African armored car regiments and the Matilda heavy tanks of the Desert Rats, in a surprise night assault on the head of the advancing army as it came up. He would keep the cruiser tanks in reserve awaiting developments. Perhaps he would disconcert the enemy, halt the advance before it got rolling. Either way, maybe Wavell would see the approaching disaster, buck London, and let him fall back on Alamein. O'Connor knew he was clutching at straws. Best that could be done was what he would do. There would be time later to fall on his sword.

0700 local time; 0600 CET
8 September 1940
Camp Gorlov, Italian Colony of Libya

Fräulein Greta had discovered the true secret of command. Find good subordinates and delegate. Between the cook Mary Collins and her second-in-command Naiomi Saxon, things would happen when Greta gave instructions. She was even losing her shyness on ordering older people around. Klaus now had a thousand or more people who jumped to it when he spoke. Mary and Naimoi would find a solution to the tons of stolen British supplies that the unit did not have spare trucks to haul. It would probably involve some version of holding onto the camp with a small remainder force till trucks could be found. The army was moving out to have some big fight. Greta was hazy about where. Mostly, "where" didn't matter to her. They would beat up the British and eventually the war would settle down someplace else. She could then have Klaus badger Joey and plead with Oberst Gunter for trucks. The Oberst had grown accustomed to real coffee, meals with real meat, and the rest of the luxuries she and her girls had 'liberated on Malta'.

She laughed to herself that she had not regarded having Klaus do this, as a difficulty. She had been somewhat frightened at originally becoming his mistress. She had been warned by her aunt and the rest of the elders to expect ill treatment. That was a woman's lot, and she would have to learn to endure. She chuckled again. It just wasn't like that. To Klaus she wasn't some slave kept for sex and morning coffee. She was his Princess. He was in hopeless romantic love. She had grown fond of him in return, but saw herself as simply more practical about her needs, her family's needs. They needed a protector, and a Major with an Iron Cross could cast a protective shadow sufficient for this unit. Klaus was a favorite of both Oberst Gunter and the head of the SS. Truly fearsome patrons. The world didn't like Jews, and such guardian angels were needed.

Young men were easy to lead around. The key was sex. Lots and lots of sex. There was never such a thing as too much for an eighteen-year-old guy it seemed. Her aunt's instructions had provided the initial moves for her. Naiomi and the ladies had added varieties to experiment with. Klaus had never met a sexual possibility with her he wasn't enthusiastic about. She'd even grown to enjoy it. Not with his fierce addiction, but she had taught him how to pleasure her. Having never been with another man, she was not sure if he was especially skillful. However, he was certainly energetic. Their tent at night was noisy enough to get laughs from those near them, but then she and Klaus would laugh at the noise from Naiomi's girls and their boyfriends in the adjacent tents. This being on campaign was a fun adventure, as long as no one was currently shooting at them.

This left Greta free for her current chore. Her uncle had been one of the Elders who had essentially ordered her into Klaus's bed. Now she had an order for him. Klaus needed a quick guide to how to run a battalion. He'd never really run a whole company at once, and battalion was beyond him. The few manuals they had were only a bit helpful. Her uncle had at one point in the last war commanded a battalion of guns. What does a battalion commander do? Simple sentences that she could drill Klaus on, till he was sure enough of them to manage in the midst of battle chaos – like his march to relieve Jung's embattled airborne forces on Malta. Greta loved the role reversal. Now she could give orders to her uncle. And he would obey.

1300 hours CET
8 September 1940
HQ Sicherheitsdienst in Prinz-Albrecht-Straße, Berlin

Heisenberg again ...

Heydrich noted his next appointment was with Speer, his old friend Dr. Heisenberg of the Uranium Project, and Sturmbannführer Walther Schieber. The latter had been a member of the SS since 1933, and had been involved with various industrial items, mostly in chemistry. With the change in management and Heydrich's growing role in the management of Germany, Schieber had been tapped to Heydrich's staff as an industrial expert.

Heisenberg had been selected by his nominal superior as being the most well-known of Germany's physicists, and thus best able to see about getting more resources for the Uranium Project. Heisenberg gave a presentation on the state of the project and what they hoped to achieve. When done, Heydrich just raised an eyebrow for a moment. "Well, if Porsche's tanks didn't prove that Germans are the supreme toymakers of the world, then your project does. You have perhaps 70 scientists and engineers working in a vague direction on what might, could perhaps one day, produce a weapon of vast destructive power – but you don't know when you will be done or how much more resources will be needed. Beyond 'more', that is. Have I left anything out?"

While Heydrich had a smile, it was anything but friendly. The temperature in the room seemed suddenly to drop to an Arctic chill. Heisenberg wondered suddenly if his boss Diebner had sent him here on the off chance that Heydrich would have someone from the project shot, and didn't want himself to be the messenger with bad news. Heisenberg decided that now wouldn't be a good time to mention that his early critical-mass calculations suggested a rather large device was needed to produce an explosion. At the same time, he *was* the winner of the Nobel Prize in 1932.

Still, he had to move with great delicacy here. This might be their first face-to-face meeting, but Nobel Laureate and Reichsführer knew each other quite well. Those 'Deutsche Physik' idiots in the Reichserziehungsministerium – the REM – and their toadies in the universities had tried to bring Heisenberg to heel with accusations that he was a traitor to the Aryan Race, a 'white Jew' who backed Jew physics instead of proper Aryan science. Heydrich's own office within the SS had investigated him, but he had triumphed – after three years they had not only cleared him, but all three academic investigators had switched to support him scientifically and personally.

Himmler – by weird coincidence the SS-head's father had been a rector-colleague of Heisenberg's grandfather – had made the final decision that his brilliance was too valuable to the Reich, for him to be driven into exile by a cabal of third-rate failed academics. "No, Reichsführer-SS, you have summed things up very well. All I will say is that research goes at its own pace. It's not like building a rifle. We are discovering as we go. If you want useful results, my team must be left to do our work in a proper scientific manner."

"In peacetime I could accept that from a Nobel Laureate. But not now. This is a war for national survival, Herr Doktor. My only thought is, what best serves the Reich? My predecessor may have been in grievous error on a number of issues, but he was correct that we need your mind. With or without his direction, that would have been my finding also. So this decision will not be made from animus over you or your academic infighting four years ago.

"The Reich's resources are not limitless, and there are many projects demanding resources. Speer brought this project to my attention because of the massive long-term electrical power crises the Reich faces. I ask you: can this project be a solution to that particular problem? I don't care about possible utopian wonder-weapons. We can destroy cities easily enough. Just ask the Poles and Hungarians. I *do* care about power plants to run the factories. We can deal with fanciful H. G. Wells super weapons or pure science when peace comes, and we need government projects to prevent a return to mass unemployment. Your pure research cannot be more useless than the endless municipal building projects the Gauleiters so love."

Not waiting a second, "Yes Reichsführer-SS, this project can one day provide an alternate power source."

" 'One day' does no good. What day? Justify the existence of your project. How long till you have a prototype?"

Heisenberg thought fast. He was sure he could make something that produced fission, and thus heat and thus some electricity, within a year. So he said eighteen months because reward went to those who succeeded early rather than late.

Pleased at a straightforward answer, Heydrich nodded towards Schieber. "I want an updated feasibility study, Sturmbannführer, for this Uranium Project. Consolidate the other similar projects into this one." Then Heydrich waved them out, seemingly ending the meeting. Just as the minute-taker was about to clean up, Heisenberg spoke his mind. If Heydrich's only goal truly was the triumph of the Reich, then perhaps it would be possible to undo some of the damage caused by the criminal REM and that buffoon Deutsche Physik movement – declaring certain modern theoretical physics to be mostly 'Jew science', driving too many of the brightest minds in the physics community out of Germany. That, and the REM stymied selection and education of new students. Nothing could be done about those who had already fled to the United Kingdom and United States, but something could be done about the future. "There is one more thing that is needed. We need people; and not just numbers, but the correct types of people. Too many men who should be working as interns and the like, so that one day they will be the next generation of physicists, are instead toting rifles or driving trucks."

"I will see what can be done, but you aren't going to get a limitless supply of deferments for the universities. Show me verifiable progress in six months, and I'll get you some. Finish in a year instead of eighteen months, and we can talk more." Heydrich knew the game. The man was reputed to have a huge ego; but if he promised 18 months, he could be pushed for 12 months, and would perhaps produce in 15 months with a few excuses and the offering up of a few rivals as scapegoats.

Deciding it was now or never to double down, Heisenberg drew himself up to his full height. "And I want those fools in the REM to have no involvement in the selection of students or educators involved in this project."

Heydrich was openly surprised at the pushback from Heisenberg. He well remembered the hell the man had gone through in the late 30's over 'Jew Science'. He would have expected him to keep a low profile out of self-preservation, but instead this Nobel winner had the ego to take on the whole Ministry. Perhaps he could deliver results as well as international prizes. Heydrich took his time, fixing the scientist in a withering glare. Clearly Heisenberg wanted to expand on his victory from back then, and push his tormentors back even more. Ego was a tool Heydrich knew how to manipulate. "I will do this for you, Herr Doktor. I will give you the freedom you ask for, and if you succeed we will have a talk on the structure of the REM – but if you fail … "

Heydrich left the possibilities hanging, unspoken.

If nothing else, Heisenberg was supremely confident of his own abilities and that of other German physicists: "We will deliver atomic power for the Reich."

Heydrich held up his hand to signal the good doctor was not to leave yet. He finished his notes and spoke. "You can recruit 50 now. I get a working demonstration plant in fifteen months." It was a flat statement, not a subject to debate. Heisenberg bowed his head and left. *Fifty good assistants, for 3 months off the project.* He'd bring it in ahead of schedule and ask for 500 more.

2000 hours local, 8 September 1940
0300 hours CET, 9 September 1940
El Zocolo, Federal District, Mexico

The first battalion of US Internationals had led the parade. They were a mix of veterans of the anti-fascist struggle in Spain and eager young volunteers. They were followed by battalions from Cuba and Guatemala, and Spanish Republican refugees. There were platoons and companies from everywhere in the Americas, and a full regiment of eager Mexican Marxists. What they lacked in parade-ground polish, they more than made up for in revolutionary zeal.

Mexican President Cardenas had proudly stood on the podium beside the famous leader of the Cuban Revolutionary Communist Union, Blas Roca Calderio, and the Soviet ambassador. The speeches were brief if fiery. The high point was the famous American singer Paul Robeson leading the crowd in singing the Internationale in Spanish, followed by a medley of various war songs of the Spanish struggle against fascism. The plaza and parade route were festooned with Soviet banners and flags of the Spanish Republic. The entire Aztec Force was a Comintern project, with Moscow directing every party in the Western Hemisphere on participation.

The Aztec Force would leave by rail the next morning for Vera Cruz, where Mexican and Soviet ships waited to carry them to Riga, to the start of their journey to join the war of liberation in Manchuria and China. Safe passage through the war zone had been arranged. The British sensibly chose not to add the Soviet Union to their formal enemies just yet. London accepted Moscow as a de facto almost-belligerent on the Nazi side, as the US was doing the same on the British side. Germany allowed passage of Soviet ships into and out of the Baltic as and when the Soviets wished. That was just how the de facto alliance played out. The German war machine ran on Soviet petroleum from Baku. Their factories needed minerals from Stalin as well. This had been true since the original pact the prior year.

Stalin's Red Army was on the march to liberate the East, and all true revolutionaries must rally to the Red Banner. Nominally these were humanitarian volunteers for the new Manchurian People's State. As the speeches made clear, they were successors of the legendary International Brigades, the shock troops of the Iberian war.

....

The fourteen-year-old Alexander Ruz was in ecstasy. He had run off to enlist, following his more-accomplished older brother Ramon. He'd used his mother's name on the enlistment form to buy him time against his father tracking him down, dragging him 'home'. How could he stay behind as a mere schoolboy while Ramon went off to do great deeds? Ramon had made him a runner, had arranged for him to carry the company's banner in the great parade. A few more days and he'd be safely at sea, beyond the reach of his father's influence.

....

Trotsky smiled to himself. He had stayed away from the ceremonies. That was a Stalinist enterprise, and he would not have been welcome. Trotsky was sure this would fail. Stalin had bungled China before. Trotsky felt he would do so again. Stalin had always been a second-rater, to Trotsky. The man was only fit for clerical activities like Party Secretary. Trotsky grudgingly conceded to himself that Stalin had proven a formidable factional plotter, but his collectivization had been a disaster; and his alliance with the Nazis could only end badly.

Mexico was a safe refuge. Trotsky's former refuges were mostly under German occupation. Even Turkey seemed to be in the process of acquiring Soviet bases at the Straits, and an Axis 'military mission'. The British were respecting the tattered remains of Turkish neutrality ... for now. Trotsky needed the new developments to finish manifesting themselves. He still saw himself as a world revolutionary figure. He just needed to choose the proper moment.

For now, those preparations consisted of sending a party of 'emissaries' to young Chiang. The man had been friendly to Trotsky's point of view while still in the Soviet Union. He had been forced to recant, to swear allegiance to the Georgian monster. Trotsky was not asking that this change, at least not yet. For now he was sending two dozen people to assist Chiang's Blue forces, the National Army of the KMT. A mix of medical people and more practical technicians. Trotsky didn't have money to send, or masses of arms. For now all he could do was send a message of greetings. One to be delivered privately. No papers that could fall into unfriendly hands. Just two dozen useful people, with the implied promise of more. For now Blue and Red were united. They had been before, and fallen out before. Trotsky was placing a small bet that this might happen again. There was a small trade from Mexico to Hong Kong. Small ships no one paid any attention to carried this trade. One had a first officer who had sympathies Trotsky would exploit. Step by step ...

0900 hours CET
9 September 1940
War Ministry, Berlin

War Minister Generaloberst Beck and OKH head Generaloberst Halder had just finished a formal OKW briefing on the new offensive in Egypt. Beck had been sarcastic and hostile to the briefer. Halder felt somewhat ashamed at this behavior. The Oberst doing the presentation was a competent general staff officer, and was doing a standard by-the-book recital. He refused to defend himself against the War Minister. Every swipe was answered with proper deference of junior to senior.

Further, there was nothing especially wrong with the plan. It was a textbook solution to the problem of attacking a fortified camp, given the force ratios and geography. Allowance was made for the inferior equipment of the Italians. Halder would have preferred a German army commander, but, given the disparity of forces, it was reasonable for an Italian to have the assignment. His attaches in Rome spoke well of this Italian general.

What was really troubling was that a major theater of war was now the bureaucratic property of Heydrich and the SS. The Heer had allowed this. Each decision leading here had seemed sensible. Every decision the army had made 1932-1935 had also seemed logical at that time. The end result, had been Hitler as their master instead of their political figurehead. Halder was worried he saw the same pattern developing. He was even more disturbed that neither Göring nor Beck seemed to care. Each was preoccupied with their own petty, narrow games. Halder supposed he could strengthen the Army's position by forming his own links directly with Heydrich. He caught himself and laughed bitterly. Heydrich was Stalin. The three who should ally against him simply weren't motivated enough to keep a united front. Yet if he, Halder, broke with Beck … would this not shatter the Army's unity?

Malta had given Heydrich prestige among the field-grade officers. A victory in Egypt would do so to an even greater extent. So should the Army wish for a defeat? The best hope was a quick peace with the British.

0930 hours CET
9 September 1940
Heydrich's Office, SS Headquarters, Prinz-Albrecht-Straße, Berlin

Schellenberg had been notified that a special representative of the NKVD chief Beria was arriving by air from Moscow. The notice came from air traffic control. The Soviet Embassy in Berlin had said nothing. Perhaps they didn't know. The SS could make no sense of the internal politics of the Soviet regime. An honor guard of the Begleit Battalion Reichsführer-SS, reconstituted since the coup with Heydrich loyalists instead of Himmler's, was awaiting this minion at the airport, along with Schellenberg himself. The representative, a senior commissar named Ivan Serov, was traveling with only a small entourage. These were packed into a convoy of Mercedes limousines shepherded by a large motorcycle escort. Traffic police sealed intersections to allow rapid passage. This arrival was given all the pomp and circumstance of a full state visit. Heydrich had felt it was better to err on this side of too much protocol rather than too little. The time to settle accounts with the Bolsheviks remained in the future.

Heydrich found the man an otherwise unremarkable Slav. However, the commissar carried documents claiming to speak with his master's voice. The truly funny part was that it took over thirty minutes to get this special envoy to spit out what he wanted. Apparently, the regime he represented had doctrinal problems with the request. Interesting. "We wish to have sent to us the Spanish Republican forces. Many are in camps in Unoccupied France, and the rest are in Spain. We expect you to arrange this."

Typical of the Soviets. A demand instead of a request. Still, every bargaining session begins somewhere. "Possible in theory. They are useless to our new Europa. However, there are practical details. Our rail system is overstressed. So is our food supply. We will need some material aid to make this happen." Serov nodded. "There is also the issue of dependents. You wish the working-age men and women. We'll send you all of these. We will also send the useless mouths – the crippled, the children, et cetera. And so the accounts balance, we wish the Volksdeutsche you promised us. I doubt you have enough Germans to balance what we are sending, so even the accounts with Poles, Ukrainians, or kulaks. Roughly similar numbers of healthy adults and dependents as we are sending you."

Serov was not exactly prepared for this, but gave a provisional 'yes' subject to Moscow's approval. He then got to the second demand – large numbers of Communist cadres from Germany, from France, from Europa in general. Moscow wished those as well.

Heydrich found the idea of ridding his camps of incorrigible prisoners amusing, but knew better than to show it. He instead made a long debate over the value of skilled industrial workers, compared to the unlettered peasants he would take in exchange. Serov was curious why Germany wanted more Poles. The Poles hated both Communists and Nazis. Heydrich replied that they were fond of the French, and Vichy would need settlers in Africa.

The meeting then devolved into the perpetual squabbles over late deliveries by Germany of arms and machine tools, versus delays by the Soviets on shipments of minerals and food. The endless impasse would be kicked back to lesser people on both sides, who would continue the bureaucratic trench warfare. This took up the time till lunch. The Russian didn't seem to care about the food, but found the French brandy congenial. As soon as the meal was concluded, he demanded to be taken back to his airport to start the return. Heydrich was able to offer a farewell present. Nearly a thousand German Communists out of the Berlin-area prisons. They would be shipped at once as a gesture of good faith.

He had a feeling this had more to do with losses in Manchuria than to an in-gathering of the Marxist flock to its New Rome. He'd ordered up a staff appreciation from OKW when Stalin had begun this campaign. Until 1938 there had been German cadres training Chiang's Chinese. They had had extensive experience fighting the Japanese. Their verdict was unanimous. These Asiatics were not especially good as offensive troops. Sloppy staff work, not enough heavy weapons, an almost complete absence of initiative at the lower command levels. However, they were demons on the defensive. They dug in fast, and would die in their tracks if ordered to. Some sort of religious cult centered on their Emperor.

After he had bid his 'guest' farewell, he left a note for Schellenberg to set up an appointment with the Ukrainian exile leader Bandera. Certain possibilities were beginning to present themselves.

1500 hours CET
9 September 1940
Dockside headquarters of the Hoover Relief Commission, American extraterritorial zone, Danzig

Special Representative Gerald Ford had not been looking forward to this appointment. Juggling the twin relief efforts for the Jews and Poles was trying enough. The two nationalities hated each other, and the Germans despised them both. There were a few sensible people like Commandant Eichmann, but mostly it was endless backbiting. Almost like dealing with Southerners and blacks back home.

Working with the actual US zone was easier. The US Marine Force guarding the enclave was nominally the 2nd battalion of the 6th Marine Regiment. In fact, what came over was only half the strength of a proper battalion. The Marines were rapidly expanding back home, and simply didn't prioritize this mission. Such administrative sloth was typical of Roosevelt's minions. Grand announcements in the press and then half-assed follow through. The Marine colonel in command solved this by recruiting locally. He'd signed up every volunteer who presented himself and shown a knowledge of even a few dozen words of English. The 'battalion' now had twelve companies. No new heavy weapons, but more than enough men to keep order as a gendarmerie. Even obsolete rifles, hunting shotguns, and pistols were enough to combat pilferage and break up the endless fights between Jewish, Polish, and Balt workers. Turned out the Marine cadres had had decades of experience solving the language problems in various Carib garrisons.

The German response to discovering he had representatives from the Polish exile government, had been 'interesting'. Nominally these were two Polish-Americans, a former Indiana State Senator from East Chicago and a thirty-year veteran National Guard colonel from outside Pittsburgh. It took the Gestapo under a week to figure out that they were the liaisons from the London Polish Government and Polish Home Army, respectively. What surprised Ford was the reaction of Heydrich's point man. He slapped down the local Gestapo head and the German Army commandant. It took one phone call to Berlin to bring both to heel. Heydrich's man was a former resident of Milwaukee who had been active in the brewery trade. From his years in the US, it was obvious that the man had operated all through Prohibition, only returning to Germany in 1932. The brewer didn't even pretend this was a matter of patriotism. There had been some outstanding warrants necessitating a quick departure. The SS officer had introduced himself to the two Poles, laid down some ground rules, and allowed them to go about their business. Ford had asked why. The answer surprised him – Berlin expected such a subterfuge. Felt that two known personages would be less trouble than searching for their replacements.

The SS officer and the former Indiana politician had jointly come to Ford with this problem. There was a new Catholic relief program for unfortunates being started. The first location was to be a currently closed nunnery outside Warsaw. Warsaw meant dealing with Police General Eicke. Eicke was a most unpleasant individual. He opened the meeting having a tantrum at the entire project. "These are useless eaters. Better to liquidate them. This is the second time we have been blocked by the damned Papists!"

The German clergyman also at the meeting started to reply, but was motioned to silence by the former adult-beverage businessman. "We can call Berlin if you want to disturb the Reichsführer." He said this in a pleasant tone. His expression was predatory mixed with mocking. Eicke opened and closed his mouth a few times. No actual words came out, but rather a low sound almost like a dog growling. The clergyman smiled but said nothing.

The Pole took this as his cue. "We know it will take maybe 10 weeks for the Church's new food drive to result in cargo dockside. I have orders to make do, and deduct this from Polish stocks here. I'm asking you, Director Ford, to allow some of this to come from Jewish stocks as well."

Gerald Ford thought 10 weeks was optimistic, extremely so. He had no doubt food could be bought in a few days, but organizing ships took longer; and nationwide efforts took more time than spot purchases near the docks in Brooklyn. Ford was not a rabid anti-Catholic like many of his class and religion. He merely found the Church of Rome distasteful and reactionary. His people were Episcopalian, the religion of the Midwest Upper Middle Class. Catholic neighborhoods were where the saloons were. So he was not inclined to do any favors for a Catholic quarrel with the SS. "Jewish food stays Jewish, unless I receive a cable from the Jewish Joint Distribution Committee in New York." Ford had no doubt that the New York Catholic Archdiocese could twist the right arms. Let them do so. His organization under Herbert Hoover was neutral. Neutral as they all devoutly hoped America would stay. Europe's tribal conflicts were not worth the blood of a single American boy.

2000 hours local; 1900 hours CET
9 September 1940
Camp Gorlov, Italian Colony of Libya

Erwin Rommel had 'improved' on his orders from von Manstein. He had been told four battalions. He had improved this to four Kampfgruppen. He'd brought along a company each of engineers, 88mm antiaircraft, artillery, and 37mm antitank guns. He'd also rebuilt his two shattered companies from the original Malta force, into a small headquarters guard via drafts on his line battalions. He then indented higher command for replacements for his 'missing men'. Then there were the two weapons companies he'd acquired on Malta and managed to neglect to return.

He could see von Manstein's assigned watchdog was taking notes. He'd gotten the man's name but had paid no attention. Like most military aristocrats, von Manstein's headquarters 'family' included minor relations of his via all four of his parents and his wife. The young Leutnant was a von something or other. To Rommel such minders were simply part of the furniture. Rommel would willingly take the reprimand later, in return for having the extra combat power up front where he needed it.

Rommel wasn't a staff officer. His battle sense was intuitive, rather than the product of years of doctrinal training. His gut was telling him this plan was going to go badly wrong. Rommel remembered Arras all too well. It was the only time he'd ever been near to defeat in battle. The British did things that made no sense from a General Staff point of view. But they were hard fighters, and those big, slow, heavy tanks were frightening. So he'd eat the reprimand, even a formal, written one forwarded back to Berlin.

He was pleased to see that Strauss had his brigade in hand. He knew the man lacked the administrative training to make a formation this size ready for a movement order. Rommel was pleased to see that Strauss had handled this by finding subordinates with the proper experience. That was how Rommel did things. He let his Ia (chief of staff and operations officer), Oberst von Thoma, run his division. The commander was needed up at the sharp edge. By the time information reached a headquarters, it was often out of date and frequently garbled in the retelling. You had to be up with the lead platoons and companies. Opportunities were fleeting. He'd breached the Meuse this way.

The part that truly amazed Rommel was the technician Bats. He was roaming back into the tracks of Rommel's arriving column, rescuing broken-down vehicles. This American seemed even to have recruited some young girls for his operation. They were out with lanterns, waving different vehicles into the proper parking areas. The girls were being bombarded with ribald comments from his men. These were no blushing schoolgirls. They gave back as much bravado as they were subjected to, while doing their jobs competently. Strauss was a subordinate worth keeping. How he had gotten German girls into a combat zone was a mystery. When Rommel asked later, he found the answer perplexing – this was another special project of the Reichsführer. Heydrich's influence was everywhere.

Bats had done another miracle, 'finding' two dozen motorcycles for his new ranks of officer cadets. Rommel smiled to himself. Likely Bats had stolen the vehicles. A very enterprising fellow to have along. The new dispatch riders had been eager to meet their general. Some of them looked a bit young. The young are often the bravest. They lack the knowledge to be properly terrified. Tomorrow at dawn they set off. His Italians were supposed to start before dawn to arrive on time here, but either way Rommel wasn't waiting for a missing battalion.

Rommel's last task for the night was an inspection of Mohnke's SS battalion. The men seemed good. Their morale was high. The same could not be said of their commander. He seemed out of sorts and quite distracted. Rommel made a mental note that he might have to relieve the man. Strauss had mentioned that he had an experienced SS officer with Steiner if needs be.

0500 hours local; 0400 hours CET
10 September 1940
Camp Gorlov, Italian Libya

Leutnant John Smith finished his last radio message back to Rome for his boss. He then retransmitted a copy to Berlin for the attention of Special Deputy to the Reichsführer Schellenberg. He signed all those as Johann Schmidt. Serving with Bats and Strauss, his American name was just fine. Smith thought of himself as John, not Johann. He only had a few minutes to break down the equipment and get it on the truck. The one-time pads he kept in a briefcase chained to his wrist. If he lost these, he'd been told he'd be shot. He believed it.

Everyone and everything was leaving this camp, except for a small guard on the reserve food stores. Rommel's new plan had scrambled the old concept of leaving a proper garrison behind. Smith was learning the iron law of armies: by the time you have mastered the plan, it has already been modified. Rommel was determined to bull right through the British outposts, dragging both forces behind him, whatever the rest of the army did.

He'd never really seen himself as a soldier back in Oregon. He took comfort that at least he wasn't fighting Americans. He had nothing against these British, but from grade school he had learned that they were the hereditary enemy of America.

0600 hours local; 0500 hours CET
10 September 1940
6,000 meters over Alexandria Harbor, Egypt

The Ju-86 had taken off in the dark. The flight plan had them over Alexandria at first light. They were running a few minutes late. The harbor was still deserted. They would take a few photos to confirm this to the various higher commands, but this was old news. So was the chaotic hive of activity in the city. It was the main forward supply base for the British. Most of the truck traffic was at night. Daytime, the Axis air forces had made the coast road too expensive to use. However, Alexandria worked every hour of the day. The second stop would be the British defensive position being constructed at the chokepoint around El Alamein. Each Ju-86 sortie brought back photos of more entrenchments, and work on what were obviously minefields.

Tomorrow's sortie would be Cairo, where the main British air bases were. Agent reports were consistent. The British were not yet reinforcing with large numbers of modern aircraft. The four-time-a-week Ju-86 recon flights confirmed this. The arrival of Hurricanes or Spitfires would be a major change in the correlation of forces. So far these superior British planes had only been seen over the Channel and the adjacent French coast. They were nasty opponents, as the surviving Luftwaffe fighter pilots who faced them could attest. The easy-kill days had ended at Dunkirk. The RAF with modern planes was a worthy foe, the first Germany had faced.

Against modern fighters the Ju-86 was helpless. Its one defense was to stay higher than the interceptors could reach. To date these recon sorties had been milk runs. When they ceased to be, higher command would have learned something important. The crew understood the logic, but preferred that the knowledge was not bought with their lives. Far better another boring day.

0900 hours local; 0800 hours CET
10 September 1940
Camp Gorlov, Libya

Army Oberleutnant Ernst von Kleist-Konitz was sipping a mess kit cup of coffee, watching the forces of what he thought of as Kampfgruppe Rommel roll out of the cantonment and down the coast road. He was waiting for his dispatch rider to return from von Manstein's headquarters. The rider attached to him, had taken the motorcycle which was to be his transportation forward.

Ernst had refused recuperation leave for his wound from the French campaign. He was 23 and, in his mind, indestructible. The wound would heal just fine as a supernumerary on von Manstein's staff, as well it would wasting time in Berlin or on the family estates in Pomerania. There was a war on, and this was the only active theater. Ernst wanted to be doing things, not getting fluttering eyelashes from young Aryan maidens. Women bored him. When it was time to perpetuate the family name, his mother would present him with a brood mare from a proper family. His brothers already had male offspring, so his would just be spares anyway.

Von Manstein's staff had offered him a car and driver. Ernst instead requested a motorcycle dispatch rider, along with a machine with a sidecar, for them to use as his transportation. The official reasoning was that he could better communicate via such a courier. The truth was that at 23 he thought motorcycles were fascinating. He planned to have his rider teach him the use of the vehicle. After that they could alternate who drove. This was in some ways a breach of class decorum, but it fit the populist ethos of a National Socialist people's state.

His family despised the Nazis as trash. This was true of most of the aristocracy. But Germany was at war. His class were the arms-bearers of the nation. So it was his duty to serve, and be seen to do so. The Junker class had duties as well as privileges.

Ernst's message to von Manstein had dwelled on General Rommel, not Oberst Strauss. He'd been assigned to observe Strauss. He was using the initiative expected of someone with his lineage, to focus on the more important matter of Rommel's conduct. It was clear Rommel was exceeding his orders. Ernst felt it best that higher command be aware of this. Rommel had hidden nothing from him. It was clear that Rommel regarded orders as suggestions. Typical of a mountain Jäger with the Blue Max. Success justified deviation from instructions, in all cases, to such storm officers. Von Kleist-Konitz decided that observations on Rommel's developing battle were of more interest to corps headquarters, than the details of how Strauss ran his brigade – which so far had consisted of letting his chief subordinates command their respective units. Ernst had grown up around senior officers, and thought this traditional and sensible. It was Rommel's actions he found worrisome. The man seemed to have no consciousness of how his unit fit into higher command's scheme of maneuver. This could be dangerous. Even a young Oberleutnant could see this. Or at least a junior officer descended from generals and senior Obersts.

1300 hours local; 1200 hours CET
10 September 1940
South of Sidi Barrani, Egypt

Rommel knew he was supposed to halt here for the day. It was an order he never had any intention of obeying. The Axis covering force, a mixed battlegroup of German reconnaissance troops from his division and Italian mobile troops, had spent the morning chasing back the British screening force of similarly-equipped troops. Supported by relays of Ju-87's and Me-110's, it had been a one-sided if lively affair. Half a dozen wrecked vehicles of all three nationalities dotted the landscape. A few dozen Empire prisoners, most wounded, sat quietly under Italian guard. Reports said they were a mixed lot of British, South Africans, Rhodesians, and New Zealanders. They seemed a collection of fit young men in good spirits.   Rommel could not understand why Italy, a nation noted for making fast, high-quality automobiles and motorcycles, had managed not to field either armored cars or motorcycles. He simply instructed this von Kleist-Konitz, as his assigned minder, to query higher commands on why such could not be provided to the Italians. The truck-mounted Italians had fought quite well. Better than the attached Germans, despite the Italians having inferior equipment.

Rommel's own spearhead from 7th Panzer Division was with him. It was a mixed battlegroup, centered on a battalion of motorcyclists and the one Panzer battalion von Manstein had allowed him, plus a company each of motorized engineers and the ever-so-useful multipurpose 88mm guns. Sadly, the eight-eight's were towed by halftracks. He had strongly suggested after the French campaign that some way be found to put this weapon on its own carrier. A turret would be nice but was not a necessity. The key was not needing the time to go into battery. At some point those huge British heavy tanks would appear, and only the eight eight's could cope with them.

He wrote a quick note to corps headquarters asserting that the fluid combat situation made a halt impossible. This he sent directly rather than through von Kleist-Konitz. It would take the dispatch rider hours to reach von Manstein's location, by which time countermanding orders would obviously be out of date. Rommel sent radio messages back urging his follow-on troops to push forward fast while he himself chased the retreating British back towards their lair at Bagush.

1600 hours local; 1500 hours CET
10 September 1940
Track on the lower plateau, in the Brigade Strauss column

Abdul Collins was a most happy young man. As a war captive he had expected ill treatment, possibly torture. The best he thought he could hope for was life as a slave servant of the infidels. Instead the young man who had interrogated him, had claimed him as a prize of war. His mother was a clan head in this camp of soldiers. Abdul discovered he had been adopted rather than possessed. His new clan worked him hard; but he ate with the free men and was treated as a clan member, not an outcaste enemy. The British prisoner was sent away. Abdul had food and a bed roll.

He found the clan name 'Collins' hard to pronounce. The Collins clan was allied to the great chiefs. His new foster mother gave her loyalty to the Major's wife, Greta. This meant Abdul was allied to half the fighting men. The fighting men seemed to include some women. Abdul thought this strange until he saw the women handle machine-guns. He'd been taught that Christian women were shameless. Women who could fire machine-guns and small cannons could be as shameless as they wished. This was a powerful warband, and Abdul was now part of it. He'd been given a rifle and two dozen bullets.

Now they were off to Egypt. There would be a few battles, and then cities to plunder. Perhaps Abdul would find a concubine in the loot of this vast city, Alexandria, which was their destination. His people had fantasized about plundering cities. It was all brags. These Germans were mighty. Better to be with the conquerors than the vanquished.

1800 hours local; 1700 hours CET
10 September 1940
Approaching the position marked with the three crosses (no longer actually there), southeast of Mersa Matruh, Egypt

Major Klaus Steiner had a water-soaked cloth across his nose and mouth. He had learned about vehicle columns in this idiot wilderness, through all the patrols Gunter had made him lead. The machines kicked up clouds of pebbles, dust, and sand. Klaus's battalion was behind the five Rommel was leading and ahead of the rest of Strauss's brigade. In violation of corps orders, the Italian First Libyan Division trailed him instead of the reverse. Rommel, as ever, did things his own way.

Besides, it sort of made sense. Peter and Uncle Isaak had to begin construction of the base before the Libyan artillery and support services arrived. As is, they'd only have a few hours to do so. The van of the Libyans were right behind Greta and brigade headquarters at the rear of the road column.

....

General O'Connor had been amazed that the enemy forces were coming straight at him with no halt for regrouping. What would have been a 3-4 day movement exercise for British troops, they were attempting in one day. Nothing for it but to order the attack now. The moon was up. Not yet full, but past quarter. The Axis warplanes were gone. They left in good time to land in daylight, and dusk was less than a quarter-hour away. His screening forces were backpedaling fast.

General Beresford-Peirse of 4th Indian Division would command his two Indian brigades and the heavy brigade of the 7th Armored Division. The enemy would be blinded by the dust cloud they had created. The balance of the two divisions, including all the cruiser tanks with Selby Force added, would be the follow-on strike force, probably to be released just before dawn in the event the night's fighting was successful. O'Connor would keep the British 16th Brigade as his personal reserve. Another brigade's worth of bits and pieces, plus a newly arrived brigade from 6th Australian Division, would hold the camp. The garrisons at Mersa Matruh had been thinned out to two brigades.

The plan relied on the professionalism of the Empire troops to handle a night-meeting engagement. Night fighting meant a swirl of company and battalion dogfights. It might work. Sitting and waiting to be pulverized, was a sure route to destruction. O'Connor elected to roll the dice, and sent a message to Wavell advising him of what was to follow.

....

Generale di Divisione Pietro Maletti had been notified by his lead battalion that Rommel had blown past the agreed halt points. He was not especially surprised. The German was self-impressed in the extreme. He was relying on his past exploits as a guide. Maletti expected that Rommel would find the British a tougher nut to crack than French reservists, inept Romanians, or exhausted and mal-deployed 1917 Italians.

He had his staff notify Army Headquarters that he would follow closely behind Rommel, aiming his deployment at the supposed advance base of Strauss's brigade. The Germans would not have had time to construct this position. However, it would have armored vehicles, guns. and a firm location on the maps of higher headquarters. It would all work out … unless the British attacked tonight. If they did, he preferred to be concentrated rather than spread out in a linear deployment.

1900 hours local; 1800 hours CET
10 September 1940

On the plateau below Mersa Matruh, Egypt

The Italian Milmart multipurpose artillery unit was lost. The battery of 76/40 mm gun trucks had been added late to 1st Libyan Division. There had been some confusion over whether that division was to be on the coast road or the plateau. These weapons were designated coast artillery and thus needed for the coast. When First Libyan was settled as advancing on the plateau, the guns had been left there, their mission shifting to more generalized artillery support. The weapons were in fact multipurpose, suitable as coast defense, anti-tank, or field artillery.

There had been artillery and machine-gun fire, followed by tank noises, and then several dozen German motorcyclists retreating. The German officer had said there was a British brigade with Panzers about five minutes behind them. The battery commander knew his gun trucks couldn't outrun tanks the way motorcyclists could. So he'd turned inland, hoping the British would pass north of him. Vehicle noises seemed to indicate this had worked. Now what?

Before the Italian officer could formulate a plan they heard another motorcycle out in the dark. The brief flashes of moonlight made it impossible to see, but the noise was getting quickly closer. The rider was clearly all but flying over the broken terrain. There was no way the driver could know where they were but he made right for them. The rider proved to be a young Italian. Claimed a rank of volunteer officer cadet. He was in German Luftwaffe uniform, but the boy was definitely Italian. It was obvious from his speech. An educated youth, probably from Tuscany. He claimed to be part of an Arditi unit. Said he was Fascist Militia, the same as the gun trucks were.

The officer cadet confirmed there was a British breakthrough north and south of here. His general was coming north with a regiment, including a tank battalion. The battery commander gratefully followed behind the motorcycle towards someone in authority. The route was almost due east, which seemed to be away from battle and movement noise. Further away from those damned British heavy tanks.

1930 hours local; 1830 hours CET
10 September 1940
Scene of the three metal crosses from the recon excursion, southwest of Bagush Box, Egypt; and southeast of the British Charing Cross fighting position

Two of the crosses were missing and the third was knocked down, but Klaus had found the place again. Found it in the gathering darkness. Oberst Gunter Strauss was amazed. He'd sent the boy out in the desert to toughen him up. He hadn't expected the land navigation manual to actually teach him anything. Gunter thought for a few seconds, and chuckled softly. He was aware of Greta's teaching methods. He reflected on what lengths the 18-year-old Gunter would have gone to, if it had meant getting his rocks off regularly.

The Oberst left the actual construction project to those that knew such things. He had Isaak, Peter, the SS engineering officer (back on semi-permanent loan), and three Italian engineering officers from

General Maletti. Instead Gunter focused on defensive preparations. He pulled Isaak off building-work to place the Army 75mm battery for best effect if British tanks came calling. The massive Matilda's were a definite problem. Gunter had worked up a plan with Isaak and Peter for fighting positions geared to all-round defense, with a central citadel bunker to hold the priceless falcons and bags of gold. He had left Gregor and a reinforced platoon guarding the precious treasure. Gregor knew what they were guarding. The rankers just thought it was some secret gear in crates.

There was no way most of this construction would be finished by dawn, but the work was in capable hands. So Gunter saw to placing the heavy weapons. Once he had personally sited each crew and gotten them started on digging in, he'd gone off to set up his outpost line. Gunter would command this personally. He simply didn't trust anyone else. The two generals had all these grand plans. In Gunter's opinion, the enemy gets a vote. He remembered the British from 1918. Stubborn bastards and hard fighters. Gunter didn't want to get caught out, the way the British he had attacked during the Michael Offensive had been.

....

Clara watched a squad of machine-gunners setting up their Spandau 08/15's near the designated repair area. Joey, Paul, and the mechanical staff were all busy getting everything set up, plus the usual emergency repairs. That left Clara with nothing to do. This wasn't the time for language lessons anyway. The littles and their minder were back at Camp Gorlov with the guard force, holding down the real estate and thus preventing other units from looting the many tons of stolen British supplies.

Clara was not raised to prize idleness. After bouncing around through clouds of sand and dust, the machine-guns would be filthy. She had never been a street fighter for the Red Front, but everyone had helped clean the weapons stashes. She found a barrel of the proper machine oil, some relatively clean wiping cloths, and started barking orders. The crews knew her as an officer's woman. Not exactly an officer, but what ranker wants an officer's lady as an enemy? She started teaching the guys proper cleaning technique. Klaus walked by, saw what she was doing, and started sending her more crews for 'instruction'.

1945 hours local; 1845 hours CET
10 September, 1940
Plateau north-by-north-east of the three cross camp

SS Sturmbannführer Mohnke was bouncing over the Marmarican plain in a Kübelwagen. He was at the head of the column of trucks that carried his battalion from LAH. The SS officer was worried. He was the tail end of Rommel's Kampfgruppe, so it was not difficult to follow the vehicle tracks and cloud of dust even in the poor light of a barely-more-than-quarter moon, when that moon could be seen past the heavy cloud cover. However, if anything broke that chain of vehicle tracks, he was truly lost. His compass had him heading north by northeast on the lower plateau inland from the first escarpment, in the middle of some forgotten wilderness. Ahead, he could see flashes of light from cannon fire. The British were advancing in force. How many? Heading where? Mohnke had no clue. The German signals traffic was confused and mostly coded. How was he to decipher codes in a moving vehicle?

What traffic was in the clear, had British infantry in trucks and columns of heavy tanks. The same nasty ones from France. Mohnke's battalion had no artillery, had no anti-tank weapons of any sort. For reasons no one could quite explain, it had been raised as pure infantry without the usual heavy-weapons support a battalion would have. There were tanks in front of him, Czech T-38T's from 7th Panzer. There were eight eight's as well, being dragged by halftracks. Rommel even had a section of the pathetic three-seven antitank guns, the ones that had proven useless at Arras back in May.

Supposedly there were two platoons of German motorcycle infantry screening his right flank. He could hear intermittent machine-gun fire vaguely in that direction. Sounded like MG-34's and British Bren guns. Bren guns were a sound he knew well, as his own troops were equipped with Czech ZB-30's, a quite similar weapon. He was tempted to turn his troops eastwards to confront what was coming but, if he broke contact with Rommel, odds were he would not find the main body before dawn.

A minute later the problem settled itself. Tank noises to the east followed by the sight of Matilda tanks, slow and deadly. German trucks exploded after being wrecked by cannon and machine-gun fire. The vehicles scattered in every direction except east, while the lumbering monsters picked them off. Behind the tanks trotted a skirmish line of brown-skinned men in British Army tin hats.

The Matilda's were deadly, but amazingly slow. His boys tried to make a fight of it. (LAH was always more a parade-ground unit than an elite combat formation.) Its specialty was men who looked like Movement recruiting posters. They were tall, well-muscled, athletic. More often than German norms, they were fair-haired and light-eyed. They tried to swarm the slow moving AFV's, going for mines under the tracks or grenades into the hatches. The British infantry supporting the tanks were professionals. They picked his men off faster than they could inflict serious damage on the Matilda's. Those not crushed by the treads were bayoneted by the South Asians. A few of his machine-gunners got their weapons into action. They gunned down a few dozen Indians, but it was too little too late. The only thing that prevented a total massacre was that the trucks could outrun the Matilda's.

Mohnke told his driver to flee. The attempt to do so got his vehicle raked with machine-gun fire. The dying driver missed a gully, and the broken Kübelwagen fell over on its side. Mohnke passed out.

When he came to, he had been pulled from the wreck. His arm felt broken. His spine felt as if on fire from shooting pain. He was seated and barely keeping his head up. He was also a prisoner, one of many. When he'd killed his inconvenient prisoners back a few months ago, it had seemed natural. True warriors don't let themselves be taken. He hadn't exactly allowed himself to be taken captive now, but it had happened. He found himself hoping the British were better at respecting the rules of war than he had been.

2000 hours local; 1900 hours CET
10 September 1940
6 kilometers north-north-west of Rommel

General Maletti was not a trusting soul. He had his doubts about both this General Rommel and the British. So he had advanced with a mixed *raggruppamento* of a battalion each of artillery and motorized Libyan native infantry, to which he had sensibly added a company each of tankettes, anti-tank guns, and small trucks with open tops and mounting heavy weapons. These armed trucks were a sort of reconnaissance force. The artillery and antitank guns would provide some protection against tanks, and the infantry would keep the gunners alive long enough to do so. He wasn't sure the tankettes would do anything useful against the much larger British machines, but had brought a few along hoping he'd find a use for them. If nothing else, they would probably be of use for scouting. He wished yet again that Italy had some real tanks, or even assault guns. He had heard the Germans were providing some, but had yet to see one.

When he'd seen German motorcyclists approaching, he had sensibly gone out of road column into a defensive alignment. The guns were set up on a north-south axis, with the infantry grouped in defensive positions around the guns.

The senior German motorcyclist was a young SS Untersturmführer. The officer was lightly wounded and covered in dust. He gave a good report of British heavy tanks in pursuit, with strong infantry support. The motorcycle platoons had been slowing these down by repeatedly forcing the truck-mounted infantry to deploy under machine-gun fire, while sensibly keeping out of the way of the ever-so-slow Matilda's. Maletti had a junior officer with him to translate. The preparation had been proven worthwhile. He told the SS man to fall back through his position and rest. The German answered with one simple word, "Nein". Maletti gave him an inquisitive look, so he went on. "The Waffen SS is an elite service. To retreat until now was sensible. To keep running while mere colonials stand and fight is an insult to our service, to our Aryan blood. We will stay and fight. Where do you wish to post us, Herr General?" Maletti thought the junior officer to be arrogant, rude, and very typically German. He had his men placed on the southern flank, as that was the one he most feared being turned. Signals traffic had more British in that direction.

2015 hours local; 1915 CET
10 September 1940
North of the overrun SS battalion and southwest of Maletti's position

Erwin Rommel was surveying the landscape. This rocky plateau was nothing like what he had known in Europe. Equally, it was nothing like the sand seas he'd been told North Africa consisted of. He chuckled to himself. That was the problem with making war via tourist guidebooks. They worked quite well for Belgium and France, but not for these colonial lands. Still, he'd been told by his staff that once past the chokepoint to the east at Alamein, there was terrain he'd understand. Lowland farms, broad rivers, cities built mostly on a European plan. He expected to take several of those, starting with Cairo.

The SS trucks had overtaken his column some minutes ago. He'd gained most of a company from that lost unit. They seemed decent young men. Pity they were wasted on that bastard new service, instead of being properly enlisted in the Army. He'd fought beside Death's Head and LAH in the West.

Neither had impressed him. Inept officers and poor training. This idiot Mohnke seemed cut from that mold.

Rommel spent a few tens of seconds considering reversing course to salvage the SS officer's disaster. As he did so, new fire erupted to his northwest. This now made a nearly 300 degree arc of combat, leaving out only a wedge to the southwest. No, better to stick with his plan. He bellowed out the order to continue north. He did change the order of march to put this new Italian battery upfront with his own eight eight battery. If he ran into those British infantry tanks, best have his only suitable weapons where he would need them.

2030 hours local; 1930 hours CET
10 September, 1940
4th Indian Division advanced headquarters, 15 miles southwest of the Bagush Box

Major General Noel Beresford-Peirse, General Officer Commanding, was getting more and more frustrated by the signals traffic. His superior, General O'Connor, saw what was happening as a battle. Beresford saw it as a raid. In a battle, he would have been allowed to deploy his artillery and division trains forward to support the advance.

He'd been allowed a mostly free hand in planning the operation. He had taken two brigades of his infantry, six battalions of Indian Army troops and two British battalions. He'd split these into three columns, each commanded by one of his brigade commanders. The remaining infantry had been left in Bagush under his artillery commander. The northern and central columns were each assigned three Indian battalions and a battalion of Matilda army support tanks. This was the entire strength of 7th Armored Division's heavy brigade ... but not the brigade commander or staff. He'd then assigned the two battalion commanders as tank advisers to the respective brigades, breaking up their battalions into companies under the various infantry battalion commanders. Beresford hoped that this firm subordination to experienced infantry officers, would cure the tankers of their willful refusal to actually coordinate with the infantry they were supposed to be supporting. The after-action reporting from Arras had been extremely critical of these defects.

The southern column was a makeshift brigade of two battalions of British infantry and two understrength South African armored car regiments. This force had a specific target, the barren flatland where a prior Panzer advance had left three absurd metal crosses. Corps command saw this as important. Beresford for the life of him couldn't see why, but felt that this unit should be able to do the job. Except it now appeared to be lost. Scouts had the Germans back in that place, but no British column. The column claimed to have arrived in the proper place, but found neither Rhodesian scouts nor foes.

The two northern brigades both were reporting victories. Each claimed to have destroyed a brigade or more of Germans. That part was good. Beresford decided the only solution to the southern problem, was to motor up to the central group and assess the situation. If the victory was as great as claimed, he could detach a force to rendezvous with the scouts. Corps headquarters was getting decidedly forceful on this matter, and he had nothing good to report. This business of so many levels of command having radios was wonderful for artillery coordination. (Beresford had previously been the divisional artillery head.) Unfortunately, the radios also meant that higher commanders, or probably their staffs, could meddle in things best left to commanders on the spot. However, he couldn't make that argument without actually being on the spot himself. His driver had brought his Rolls around. Seemed like a good night for a drive.

2040 hours local; 1940 hours CET
10 September 1940
Three Crosses position south south east of Rommel

Gunter Strauss was glad he had taken personal command of the forward pickets. The fools had been letting the British scouts far too close to the main position. The British were using a Canadian version of Dodge small truck, armed with machine-guns, as scout vehicles. When pressed they simply drove away. Unless discouraged by heavy weapons fire, they would then return. His boys were not trained in this sort of dancing brawl, but proved fast learners under his tongue-lashings.

....

Peter Schwabe regarded his Hauptmann's rank as an amusing family joke. He'd been a crew boss in the oil fields since not long after his balls dropped. With his size and as pappa Isaac's son, he had quickly made roughnecks acknowledge his authority. He'd posted himself on the north side of the perimeter. Gunter was handling the east and southeast. North was where radio traffic said the nearest large British units were.

He'd laughed at the fleeing trucks full of SS men, all with tales of huge British hordes on their heels. The SS were physically large enough, but men who ran away from a fight didn't impress him. They were so terrified they hadn't even bothered to slow up nearing the brigade's positions. Peter had had to use his quite loud voice to avoid his own nervous little virgins opening fire before they were sure what they were shooting at. The twits couldn't tell German trucks from British tanks. He'd added swats with his large fists to make the point. The SS cowards he'd directed to Peiper. They were his service. Let him gentle down the silly gang of schoolgirls.

2100 hours local; 2000 hours CET
10 September 1940
1st Libyan position on the first plateau

General Maletti was amazed that the idiot British had not brought up artillery. All his position was being hit with was mortar fire. Maybe a dozen tubes, and no serious effort at spotting or adjusting fall. Now the British infantry was coming on, supported by well-sited machine-guns and led by two dozen of their monster tanks.

Under his orders his gunners had held their fire until the armored vehicles were a hundred meters out. His old pre-WW1 Austrian 77mm cannons were obsolete pieces of junk. Poor Italy simply hadn't spent the money to equip his men better. Instead, fortunes had been wasted on a useless navy.

Typical.

His machine-gunners and mortar men had forced the enemy infantry to ground. At close range the guns were at least doing some damage to the clanking metal elephants. Two were stopped with damage and a third was on fire. The screams of the crew being burned alive inside rose above the battle's din. The rest kept coming, destroying five guns and creating a huge mess before inexplicably retreating. While they rampaged around, his men had pushed vehicle mines under the tracks of two more, rendering them unable to move. The crews had bailed out and surrendered. His men were trained in how to treat white men. There was no gunning down of the stranded Britishers.

Maletti had toured his battle line. The arrogant SS officer was dead. One of the stray mortar rounds had found him. Battle was like that. Several of his men had left position, been among the ones who had swarmed the Matilda's with mines and grenades. Maletti decided that he'd credit the officer with their actions, put him in for the military cross for valor – posthumous, of course. If Italy were to be yoked to these German bastards, best to be courteous.

2120 hours local: 1920 hours CET
10 September 1940
Von Manstein's command vehicle, 60 kilometers back in an endless traffic jam

Erich von Manstein ignored the lack of progress of his stalled command vehicle. A mass vehicle movement on unfamiliar terrain in intermittent moonlight, was by definition going to be a stop-and-go nightmare. Instead he focused on the precis of the signals traffic. The Libyan Division and Rommel were engaged. Rommel had as usual ignored orders and commandeered the SS motorized battalion, which he had proceeded to lose. Typical. The man was simply sloppy in his command style. Von Manstein would file a protest with Berlin, but didn't expect anything to come of it.

More interesting was that Strauss was reporting only very light contact. This could mean the British were bypassing him. However, that only made sense if the British were aware that Strauss's 'brigade' was a collection of half-trained militia reinforced by small propaganda components from the other services. It was doubtful that British intelligence was that good. Propaganda from the Malta operation had labeled Strauss's command an elite unit of Volksdeutsche that had prior victories against the Soviets in Romania. No, the next British blow would be on Strauss. He had that Oberst radioed to be on alert, to expect a British attack in brigade or larger strength backed by tanks. Von Manstein also had his operations officer draft an order to General Hausser, to forward a Kampfgruppe to Strauss as quickly as the traffic situation permitted.

The final signal was a missive to Luftwaffe General Keller's advance headquarters, requesting a maximum effort at first light. The British had come out from their fortifications, and thus from under the protection of the anti-aircraft guns. That meant columns of vehicles in plain sight at daybreak. Which needed Me-110's to strafe and Ju-87's to dive-bomb.

The report to Berlin was left till real information had been assembled. However, a warning message was sent that the first battles had begun. As a courtesy the message was copied to SS General Wolff in Rome and Italian Comando Supremo. Von Manstein presumed that the Italians would have sent their own messages to Rome, but it never hurt to be courteous.

2130 hours local: 2030 hours CET
10 September 1940
HQ Western Desert Force, Bagush Box

General O'Connor again had cause to wonder if the British Army promoted people on the basis of anything beyond bloodlines and ingrained stupidity. He appoints a man divisional commander of a serious attack. The man leaves his headquarters for a moonlight drive to survey one of his three brigades, without leaving a firm operational plan with his staff. The fool gets ambushed by remnants of the German motorcycle infantry screen. In the meantime, the Rhodesian scouting force locates the missing division strike force which had somehow arrived southwest of its attack point. That brigadier radios Division for instructions. Should he retrace his steps to his original jump off line northeast of his current location, or just attack from where he is? The idiots at 4th Indian Division are now dithering, losing precious minutes of darkness before dawn and hostile air attack. His staff has to intervene and state the obvious. Attack from where you are instead of wasting time. Where did London find these twits?

2200 hours local; 2100 hours CET
10 September 1940
In the rear of the forces assaulting General Maletti on the lower plateau

Erwin Rommel was in his element. His Panzer battalion had destroyed large numbers of British supply trucks. He had captured hundreds of British and Indian personnel. The Libyan Division had the British attack force fixed in place. As a guard against them reversing course, he'd posted this Italian truck gun battery and the company-sized Waffen SS motorized infantry force he had 'acquired'. For now, he was pushing back up the path towards Bagush, running down more enemies. This felt like France.

2220 hours local; 2120 CET
10 September 1940
Three Crosses camp, southwest defense sector

Company commander Jochen Peiper had been gifted with the LAH fugitives. He had initially been elated. This was his old unit from France. He felt honored to command them. That feeling had lasted less than two minutes after the shaken LAH men had descended from their trucks. Mary Collins and her people had quickly gotten a refreshment line up. Hot coffee and little buns with canned meat, and some silly nut mix the British seemed to have had tons of in depot. The nuts had come both in bagged form mixed with other edibles, and as a spread. All could be folded with slices of the tinned meat inside dough and quick-cooked. As the 'bully beef' tasted and chewed like rubber, Mary found that adding one or both of the nut foods made it less disgusting to eat and equally nutritious for soldiers doing heavy labor. Infantry had always been loaded up like mules, back to the days of the Roman general Marius. Mary didn't know Romans. She knew her Irish corporal, whose field kit often weighed near as much as he did. She'd been a soldier's 'lady' since her early teens. Whenever the gods that wore shoulder boards allowed, give the men caffeine and calories.

Peiper's original men were a mix of middle-aged SA and middle-teen HJ. An SS NCO made a crack about grandpas and infants. The SA men were mostly WW1 vets, usually combat branches. Most had served in the Freikorps, and all in the political street battles of the late Weimar period. None were willing to take shit from cowards who had run away from the British. Since arriving in North Africa, Peiper's unit had spent most days out on patrol with the Malta hero Steiner's elite warriors. They had skirmished with the British and never run away. Words were exchanged.

Peiper had come running out, bellowing at everyone to shut up. He had a proper command voice. He also had visions of the death cells, with no reprieve from Lina Heydrich this time. He shouted down almost every fool. German military men know that tone, and when it is linked with an officer's uniform it almost always works. Almost. One LAH fool chose to make a crack about how this must be soft duty, as the grandpas had hauled around subhuman field whores. Enough of the rest of the LAH started to laugh.

Mary's German was perfunctory at best. She heard 'whore'. That word she had learned in many languages over her life. The word didn't bother her. She'd been a concubine, not a whore. Besides, in this unit, she had armed protectors with rank. Let the fools laugh. They couldn't touch her body or the bodies of her children. Even when reduced to beggary on Malta, she had set up a tea stand, not sold her body. She was quite willing to be a concubine again, but knew whore was beneath her. She was proud of this, and nothing a bunch of cowards who had fled from the Indian Army could change that. She thought it amusing that she was on the other side from 'her people', but war was funny that way. After all, think of how India had ended up British, with India's warriors fighting for their white masters.

Kali is a fickle goddess with a nasty sense of humor. Within hearing range, Clara was leading two squads with their newly clean machine-guns out to the perimeter where they could test-fire their results. She expected problems, as some of the kids had been less thorough on the cleaning than her instructions had told them was necessary. She was trained as a teacher. She saw this as a learning technique. Same as letting a child make a mistake with fractions at a blackboard, after which you went over the correct method again. Her teacher's school professors said people learned better this way.

Clara had spent seven years eating insults from any Nazi clod with a uniform. There was no choice. Resistance would just lead to her being raped and jailed, to 'her' kids being homeless again. That had supposedly ended by becoming Joey's woman, by joining this gang of fascist killers. Clara turned, MP 34 in hand, and marched up to the SS NCO. She asked one word, "Whore?"

The idiot tried to bluster, called her a cheap slut and loudly inquired, "How much for me and my buddies? A mark each?" He followed this up with the start of a nervous laugh.

It was only the start of the laugh because she swung the machine pistol at him, smashing in half his front teeth. She followed up jamming the barrel into the back of his mouth, forcing him to his knees to avoid having his throat ripped out.

Two of his friends started forward to help him. They froze in place as seven machine-guns, a mix of MG-34's and MG 08/15's, trained on them. The bearers all looked eager to test out their weapons.

Clara leaned forward and spat into the fool's face. "Suck on it, faggot. Lick that barrel hard or I'll let it come in your mouth. Want to bet whether I can manage single shot, or just blow twenty rounds through your empty skull?" As he frantically tried to comply, she kept him at it while he first pissed and then shat himself. Laughing loudly, she pulled the barrel out, and gave him a good football kick in his testicles. He fell over shrieking, cupping his crushed manhood. She then turned on the others asking, "Anyone else want a session with the slut?" As they all shrank back, she sweetly asked where her five marks for doing him and his buddies was. One of Mary's kids came forward with a camp-made baseball hat, into which all the SS men dropped bills and coins. When this was done, Clara turned her voice back to classic schoolteacher tone: "We don't have whores in this unit. We don't have sluts like your League of Soldier's Mattresses that your Movement trains. We have fellow soldiers, some of them officers. The ones that want boyfriends already have them. The rest don't bed down with cowards just because you have good bodies. Learn how to fight like men, and maybe you'll eventually get a woman … after the grandpas and infants who are battle-tested comrades. You insects probably became headquarters guards because you lacked the balls to mix it up with real men like the Red Front. The SA may have been swine, but they fought like men. Worthy opponents."

With that she turned sweetly and led her trainee machine-gunners away while bellowing out her song in a perfect alto,
"Wacht auf, Verammte dieser Erde
Die stets man noch zum Hungren zwingt!
Das Recht, wie Glut im Kraterherde,
Nun mit Macht zum Durchbruch dringt.
Keinen Tisch macht mit den Bedrängern!
Heer der Sklaven, wache auf!
Ein Nichts zu sein, tragt es nicht langer,
Alles zu werden strömt zuhauf!

Volker, hört die Signale!
Auf zum lezten Gefecht!
Die Internationale
erkämpft das Menschenrecht!"

2230 hours local; 2130 hours CET

10 September 1940
Western Desert Force HQ, Bagush Box

Major General O'Connor had to work hard to keep himself from relieving the division commander and all three brigadiers in this night's operation. The southern brigade was 'reorganizing', but had yet to move. The center brigade had dispatched a party to retrieve their divisional commander, but he had not yet turned up. In the meantime, the brigadier had remained in place except for sending a battalion north to investigate a report of a Panzer division. If it truly was a Panzer division, it would make a quick snack of a motorized infantry battalion with a few Matilda's. If it was a light raiding force, there was no way infantry in trucks could catch it. Plus, trying to do so would just separate the trucks from the slow tanks.

The northern brigadier, however, earned top prize. He claimed to have been stopped by an Italo-German corps with heavy artillery support. He alleged there was a German Panzer division marauding in his rear. His solution was to send his Matilda's, with no supports, off to fight the division while he awaited 'reinforcements'. He was asserting that he needed the cruiser tank brigade, a second brigade of infantry, sappers, and the full artillery of 4th Indian to defeat this 'corps'. So he wanted a fresh ad hoc division that would have to fight through a Panzer division to reach him, and could not see the contradictions in any of his actions and requests.

O'Connor would have liked to relieve all four of them. It would feel so good. However, the problem was, who on Earth to replace them with who might do better? If his infantry generals couldn't master combined arms, why should the generals from the tank division do any better? And these were the two best divisions left to the British Empire! O'Connor silently bemoaned the two decades after 1918, which Britain had spent swearing it would never again do mass warfare against a serious enemy. The army had mentally retreated to a late-Victorian mindset. That was what the nation had wanted. Pity world events had not cooperated.

2300 hours local; 2200 hours CET
10 September 1940
Blocking position covering Rommel's rear, lower plateau

The Italian gun truck battery commander had tried to take under his command the SS infantry left him by this German general, Rommel. They clearly understood his schoolboy German. They refused to be commanded by an Italian. They said no most unpleasantly. Instead of properly deploying in support of guns, they clustered around their trucks, smoking cigarettes and chatting amongst themselves. Master race? That was a laugh. Cowards, and poorly-disciplined ones at that.

The limited moonlight was getting obscured once again. Mostly it was cloud cover, but enough of the problem was dust clouds from the vehicles that had gone past. Yet he was hearing noise. Vehicle noise, approaching slowly from the west. Sounded like heavy vehicles, which meant those damned British tanks. He shouted out "Action Front!" in both Italian and German. His gunners responded well. The German scum mostly got back in their trucks and drove away. Ten trotted up to him, led by an Oberschützen. The boy's cheeks lacked any hint of a beard, but he seemed 1.8 meters tall with the muscles of a heavy laborer. He was carrying a Czech ZB-53 machine-gun as if it weighed nothing. His mates had ammo boxes and mines. The young man came to attention, gave a good fascist salute, and called out, "Where do you want us, sir?" in passable Italian. At the Italian major's surprised look, he answered the implied question. "Tyrolian. My mother's an Italian from Bolzano." The major returned the salute, and posted the Germans at the center of the position. The boy was clearly in the wrong military service. He obviously had inherited his good features from his mother's bloodlines.

2315 hours local; 2215 hours CET
10 September 1940
Southwest perimeter, 3 crosses position

Clara Fischer was doing a third round of instruction on why getting dust and sand out of machine-guns is necessary, not military busywork, when she began to hear vehicle noises out in the gloom. Tanks? Armored cars? Trucks? Clara was sure she didn't know. She sent runners for Peiper, Klaus, and Gunter with the news, and started pulling her guys back. Their machine-guns wouldn't be of much good against what was coming. Time to find someone with cannons.

2330 hours local; 2230 hours CET
10 September 1940
Italian gun truck position

The Italian major shook his head trying to clear it. Fighting these British was something like hunting elephants, which he had done on campaign in Ethiopia. The damned British heavy tanks were large like elephants, hard to cleanly kill like elephants, and even slower than the damned beasts. Four were burning. Two more were disabled in other ways. One of his guns was a crumpled, burning mass of wreckage. The other three were all being worked with short crews from wounds and deaths. Still, dozens more of these prehistoric metal monsters were lumbering out of the dark at him.

It was past time to leave. His trucks were fast enough to outrun these Britishers. It was also impossible to flee. Six of the Germans were down. They had been shot up attacking the tanks with mines and grenades. These SS were fearless. They had shoved mines under tracks, heaved themselves onto tank decks to try to pry open hatches to fire inside and drop grenades. The last four wounded ones were helping to man his guns.

How as an Italian, a fascist, an officer, could he show cowardice in front of these men? Logic said he should. Honor wasn't allowing him to. He more than half-realized he was signing his death warrant. "Action Front!" He would die a proper death of a patriot. Besides, the targets were so slow they were almost impossible to miss. At 300 meters they would materialize out of the darkness. They showed no tactics, no unit cohesion. They just advanced. Iron beasts manned by faceless goblins.

2340 hours local; 2240 hours CET
10 September 1940

Peiper's position in Three Crosses camp, southwest quadrant, 100 meters northeast of where Clara heard the noises

Hauptsturmführer Jochen Peiper had not yet mentally recovered from watching a 'German' officer's woman leading a machine-gun detachment while singing the "Internationale" at the top of her lungs. Did he report this to Berlin? Take direct action himself? This lunatic Red woman was supposedly here on the Reichsführer-SS's personal orders. She was personal friends with the brigade commander, Strauss. Was this SA and NL officer a Communist as well? This Leutnant Johann Schmidt was the personal representative of SS Headquarters. Report this to him? Report what, exactly? That the woman was a Communist? Surely the Gestapo already knew this. What action or inaction avoided the death cells? This time there might be no reprieve.

And now the witch was back with an absurd story of a major British attack shaping up from the southwest. The British were east of them. Surely? Maybe? She was badgering him for where to set up her machine-guns. She'd scribbled a note on a piece of paper and sent one of her boys off with it. As he started to trot, she screamed at him to run faster or she'd shoot his legs out from under him and send someone else. The lad had sped away as if he had been transformed into winged Mercury. Who was this demoness?

Peiper sent one of his motorcyclists out to see if there was anything to this story of British hordes. In the meantime, he tried to improvise a battle position against a possibly imaginary attacking British brigade.

2345 hours local; 2245 hours CET
10 September 1940
Italian gun position on lower plateau east of 1st Libyan Division position, and west of Rommel's main forces

Erwin Rommel was back from his romp against the British rear areas. He'd been alerted by the fleeing SS men. He planned to gift these cowardly clowns on Hausser at the earliest opportunity. Let the SS deal with their own training and disciplinary problems. If they called these sad excuses for soldiers elite guards, the entire service was hopeless.

Rommel's driver and adjutant had 'interpreted' the general's orders. The general had ordered a fast return to the Italian gun position. Instead he was sensibly driven about two hundred meters to the right rear of that cauldron of fire. As the Mercedes touring car coasted to a halt, the junior officer handed the general his binoculars to observe. Generals are supposed to observe and command, not engage at close quarters like an expendable Leutnant .

What Rommel saw amazed him. Multiple dozens of British tanks burning or wrecked. Three of those Italian gun trucks reduced to scrap iron. Stray SS men dead on the battlefield. From their location, they had died attacking these huge vehicles with hand weapons. Perhaps the whole service was not lacking in military virtue after all.

The last gun, was continuing to fire with a mixed Italo-German crew. Two British tanks were slowly moving forward at them. The cab of the truck was shot off, but the gun continued to fire. Rommel watched transfixed.

....

The major could barely focus his bloodshot eyes. It was down to himself and the damned Tyrolian. He would die fighting beside the hereditary Austrian enemy, sending shells into the hereditary British ally. Italy had fought beside Britain, back to the Crimea almost a century ago. Three shells left. The two of them put one into a British tank at under 100 meters. The shell blew the turret off. That left one last Matilda, boring in straight for them firing its machine-gun. Why not use the cannon? Perhaps the Brit was low on ammo just as he was. "Action Front!"

He and the Austrian put the next-to-last shell into the British tank at 50 meters. It blew in the front. The machine-gun stopped, but the engine growled as it shifted to a lower gear. Whoever was still driving the beast, aimed to crush him. The major looked over at the Austrian, but he was dead. This was it. Last man, last shell. Didn't matter. He was bleeding out too fast to do anything more. He loaded the shell himself, and fired one last time as he faded away to join his Austrian comrade. In Hell? In Valhalla? He'd know soon enough. He'd done his duty.

....

Erwin Rommel watched in amazement as the last shell slammed home. This time the turret blew off the Matilda. The chassis slid forward ever so slowly on inertia the final 10 meters to slam into the remains of the truck body, knocking it over. The dead gun crew members went flying. The gun's barrel was tangled in the wreckage of the English vehicle.

Histories spoke of fights to the death, of the Spartans at the Hot Gates, of the French Foreign Legion at Camerone. This action on a nameless speck of rocky plateau in Egypt deserved to be included among them. Rommel got three juniors collecting soldiers' identifications. When this action was over, he had requests for decorations to write. He idly wondered if an entire unit could be awarded the Blue Max? Definitely one for the legends.

2350 hours local; 2250 hours CET
10 September 1940
British central brigade position

Major General Noel Beresford-Peirse regarded his near-death experience as one of the prices of command. He'd been under fire as a junior officer in the Great War. He was a professional solider. It was part of the everyday life in his trade.

It was the ineptitude of his current juniors that enraged him. After reading the signals traffic from his northern brigade, he had relieved its commander. The dismissed fool had allowed the tanks and infantry to become separated. He now had major enemy forces in his front and rear. The new orders to the former senior battalion commander, were to get his troops back on trucks and break out southwest. After getting free, he was to move east to the current position of center brigade, the place divisional command now was.

He berated the brigadier present with him, for marking time and sending a battalion off on a wild goose chase. Said-battalion was now getting attacked by a mixed German force of tanks, infantry, and artillery. Disengage and return here at once.

The 'discussions' with corps HQ were 'frosty'. Beresford wanted his artillery. He wanted the cruiser tanks he had been promised. Corps wanted a clearer picture of the situation. Beresford seemed unable to make the staff twits at Bagush comprehend that night raids such as this are messy and confusing. In the heated back and forth, neither commander had time to wonder where the southern brigade was.

2400 hours local; 2300 hours CET
10 September 1940
Peiper's position, Three Crosses camp

The HJ motorcyclist was back. The boy was 15. His knowledge of war was skirmishes these past few weeks. He'd seen a lot of British out there in the darkness. Armored cars, men in trucks, men on foot. He had not seen tanks or cannons. Yes, he was sure. Peiper was aware that *sure* and *right* were not the same thing. He radioed this to headquarters and sent two messengers. He used HJ motorcyclists. He wanted his veteran SA men, and was sad to think it, but didn't trust his SS refugees.

The insane bitch's boyfriend had arrived with 'friends'. He had some fancy-looking shotgun. His associates from the motor pool had a mix of MG-34's and captured British Bren guns. He also had truckloads of ammunition and grenades. The new arrivals looked like the crew of a pirate ship. They were eclectically dressed in pieces of uniform, workmen's clothing, and whatever else struck their fancy. They also set up with weapons as if they knew how to use them.

The last addition was the cook. She had left earlier and was now back. She had a truck filled with urns of hot coffee, and hot buns with nuts. His guys never had to leave their positions. She had two kids of her own, and some armed Arab boy, as runners. His guys took this efficient organization as a sign that everything was going according to plan. Just as she and her kids were finishing up, Major Isaak arrived leading the seven five battery and the two-centimeter AAA guns. Peiper did a double-take at the latter. There were no planes to shoot at night. Then he realized that the same shells could hurt armored cars and kill men. He trotted over to confer with his superior. Peiper felt happy that someone else was now in charge.

0015 hours local; 2315 CET
11 September / 10 September
Hausser's headquarters vehicle, stuck in a traffic jam well to the rear

Division commander Paul Hausser had not been surprised at the senseless order from von Manstein. Rommel had made a mess, and now Hausser's oversized SS division would of course bail the Army out. Hausser had arranged his order of march with just such a contingency in mind. He started with Hauptsturmführer Fritz Klingenberg. The officer had distinguished himself in the Western Campaign. Reichsführer Heydrich had given Hausser authority to make promotions to NL rank. So Klingenberg was made a *Titularrang* ("provisional") Oberst of the NL. This gave him rank on the division's company and battalion commanders. Hausser and the new Oberst had chosen for this battlegroup a reconnaissance battalion; a company each of Panzer II's and Czech T-38-T's; two companies of motorized infantry; an anti-tank battalion; a battery each of 10.5 cm and eight eight mm guns; and a pioneer company. This was designated the division 'fast group'.

Von Manstein's request triggered the release of this unit. It was to pull out of the stopped line of vehicles and make for a probably-besieged brigade camp. Hausser had an approximate compass heading and distance. He and Klingenberg trusted neither, but felt that a force this size could shoot or maneuver itself out of whatever it bumped into.

....
Titularrang-Oberst Klingenberg regarded his temporary rank as a joke among gentlemen. What mattered, was being given an independent command with loose enough orders for him to assert that absolutely anything was within the scope of his instructions. He looked forward to beating the British like a drum.

0020 hours local; 2320 hours CET
11 September/10 September 1940
Peiper's position, Three Crosses camp

Major Isaak Schwabe of the NL was in his mind back to the Great War when he was Isaac Cohen and a Honved officer. Being a gunnery officer for the Kaiser und König often meant being a rally point when the front dissolved in front of you. He was commanding better equipment than he had in those four years of brain-dead slaughter. The terrain was easier to cope with. Dealing with the prospect of being overrun by vastly superior enemy forces … that felt normal.

Peiper had a few good SA NCO's who had been through the mill. After Isaak gave them their orders, they turned his general battle concept into specific machine-gun emplacements. They were making a 200 degree arc of overlapping fire lanes for the various machine-guns and Bren guns. The force was short of line infantry as supports, but Isaak had faced similar situations scores of times. This was easier. More than enough automatic weapons, plentiful ammunition, and gunners who weren't looking over their shoulders waiting to see when the next panic to the rear was starting so they wouldn't get left behind. SA, HJ, NL, repair guys, even the crazy Communist schoolteacher Gunter had imported for Joey. These were people prepared to fight and die. The SA and HJ were drowning out her red songs with the "Horst-Wessel-Lied". None of those men or boys would run away while a woman kept fighting.

He pulled the machine-guns and gunners off the motorcycle sidecars to beef up the line. He sent the trucks and motorcycles to the rear with Mary and her food truck. All the vehicles would do here was attract lead and otherwise get in the way. Isaak didn't plan on retreating. This makeshift unit would fall apart if asked to move. He'd seen it happen in Poland and Galicia. You stood your ground and let the tide flow around you. Live or die, it was the smart bet.

That left his two gun batteries, Peiper and his armored cars and SS men. Peiper had seemed as eager as a lost puppy dog to find someone else to take responsibility. Isaak knew of the man mostly third-hand. His detachment patrolled with Klaus, and Greta kept her uncle up to date. Klaus thought Peiper an experienced junior officer from an elite service. Klaus was clueless, but tended to get broad strokes right. So he gifted Peiper with the SS refugee infantry. They were his service. Hopefully they would find courage in being commanded by one of their own. Forty-six SS riflemen, five more with Czech versions of a Bren gun. Five of the French 'light tanks'. Isaak laughed to himself. They were machine-gun-armed even if moved on tracks. Mobile machine-gun emplacements.

His orders to Peiper were simple. Ignore the armored cars or any tanks if they appeared. Those were for the guns to handle. His job was counterattack reserve. Fifty-one men and five vehicles, so assign ten men to each as infantry supports. If the British breached the perimeter anyplace, he counterattacks. If the British came around the rear, the open one-hundred-and-sixty degrees, he was to stop them. Do not split his force up. Move as a unit. Hit hard, and then, when the job was done, pull back to reserve with the survivors.

....

Peiper had been terrified. Now he was mentally on firm ground. The Major had given him clear orders, not bottomless problems. He took a few seconds to address the SS men. Told them he was LAH himself, had served with them in France. Dropped some officers' names. Then he reviewed the orders with them. Appealed to their racial pride. Couldn't they fight better than a gypsy crew of Jews and castoffs? Were they not the elite of the German nation? He got their blood up. They had been proud of their unit, of their bloodlines, of their National Socialist zeal. This was an SS officer, a former adjutant of the original Reichsführer. It would be an honor to serve beside him, to – if needs must – die beside him. They responded to the end of his speech by shouting, "Heil Göring!" in unison.

Peiper posted two vehicle and squad groups watching the rear, with the other three bunched tightly beside him. He was betting all their lives that it would be action front, not action rear. Peiper didn't fear death in battle, the way he was afraid of the death cells. He was an Aryan warrior, and this would be a worthy death!

0025 hours local; 2325 hours CET
11 September / 10 September 1940
Center of the Three Crosses position, roughly 400 meters east north east of Peiper

National hero Major Klaus was leading a column of a dozen Kübelwagen towards where he thought Peiper might be. The British were supposed to be attacking. So said both radio and messengers. No one had given him orders, but heroes don't need orders. Of course, somehow Oberst Gunter hadn't seen things that way on Malta when Klaus had gone off on his own to attack the British airfield at Hal Far. The post-action reports had sort of said he might have taken that airfield if allowed to continue. 'Sort of', because no two reports agreed on much of anything.

Klaus did know that he was expected to use initiative and intelligence. He had mortars. Uncle Isaak had shown the crews how to fire them. No one had exactly trained Klaus in what were worthwhile targets. Klaus decided the solution was to bring the tubes to the artillery officer.

The night was dark, with intermittent flashes of moonlight. There were more frequent flashes of weapons fire to his southwest. Most were a bit distant. A bit was much closer. He'd seen muzzle flashes fairly close up. One round had sliced off the bill of his cherished baseball cap. These British must be early arrivals. Scouts? Skirmishers? There was some technical term from his instruction manuals. For now, he just used the Bren gun in a center mount on his vehicle to hammer the space the flashes had come from. His lads were doing the same. Klaus was abstractly aware that this meant they were slinging hot metal around his unit's own positions. That didn't seem right, but neither did not firing back. Klaus made a mental note to ask Gunter what the proper answer was. Gunter was an experienced front fighter.

Klaus chuckled softly to himself. A year earlier he had imagined that he might be afraid in battle. Turned out he wasn't. He was aware he could die, could be horribly maimed. He'd seen enough of it on Malta. That didn't really concern him when the bullets were flying. What terrified him was fucking up. Did this make him a hero? A fool? Both?

Klaus decided that such deep thoughts were for someone older than his 18 years. His schoolmates wouldn't be called up for the Army for a year or so. Then they would endure recruit barracks, screaming training Feldwebels, and all the rest. Klaus was getting his chance to die a few years early. He also had his bedroll occupied by a bouncy girl friend who brought him coffee in the morning. If he ever met his old classmates or the boys from his HJ unit, Klaus thought he would love comparing notes. Dead was dead, maimed was maimed. Major or recruit private, the metal shredded flesh the same way. At least he Klaus wouldn't die a virgin. He laughed at the callow child he'd been less than three months earlier. Two new muzzle flashes, real close. One round singed his hair going by. Klaus returned fire. He was a hero.

0030 hours local; 2330 hours CET
11 September / 10 September 1940
Central headquarters area with the five falcons and the unit treasury, Three Crosses Camp

Major Gregor left the rest of what was happening to the other officers. His mission was simple. Defend the loot. He had two squads of machine-gunners with the old 08/15's he remembered from the Real War. Problem was that he was defending a tent, not a bunker.

Leutnant Greta had appeared with Naiomi and her girls. Gregor thought that he had no need of a bunch of hysterical females. However, they didn't seem frightened. One of the Yid bitches, a large-boned plain girl with Gefreiter's insignia seemed to be in charge. Girl was already larger than Gregor. Looked like the type who'd go to fat with middle-age and a couple of kids. Her voice was shrill but loud, very loud. She had everyone running around. She even started giving orders to poor Hans. These Hebrews had no concept of rank or discipline.

They were hauling wooden crates over. Rations, building supplies, spare parts from the vehicle repair bays. Piling them three deep, three high in a line. A line that stretched 15 meters in a roughly straight direction, then did ninety degree turns. The light came on in Gregor's head. She was building him a fighting position. Others were coming in now, hauling freight dollies piled high with ammo boxes for his machine-guns, boxes of grenades, ammunition for the MP-38's these girls all carried, medical supplies.

He saw one of the Jews he didn't recognize using big lanterns. Must be one of the Malta crew, as he knew the faces from Bari. A truck came up, was directed around back. The cook was back with her kids and the Arab boy. Abdug, Abraham, something like that. She started getting the truck unloaded. Big urns of coffee. Big jugs of water and wine. Someone drove the truck off, with the motorcycles following.

Gregor walked up to the girl. If she was in charge, he needed directions, and rank be damned. She saluted him and asked if he had suggestions to make for improvements? He thought fast. Said keep extending to behind the tent, and then finish the box off. She nodded, and called out orders in Yiddish. Gregor knew a bit of street Yiddish. Enough to ask directions, order coffee, things like that. Serving with the Kaiser, he'd learned a hundred fast words of maybe twenty tongues. The big girl clearly also spoke German. He asked her where she got the idea. The answer amazed him. She had been a university student in history. Some fight the British had with African savages. Greatest number of their highest decoration in one fight. She didn't remember the name, but the concept stuck in her mind. Medal was their version of the Blue Max. A Victoria something-or-other.

Gregor sent out a half dozen of his boys to see if they could find more machine-guns and maybe one of those British anti-tank rifles the Malta group had 'liberated'. Crates wouldn't stop bullets like sandbags, but they were the best he was getting tonight. He had a position to defend and troops to do it. He laughed at the thought of commanding Yids, women, and some Sand Niggers in battle. A part of him wanted to be offended. The Movement were supposed to clean up Germany of all these foreign elements. Well, this rocky plateau wasn't Germany. He'd command monkeys and dogs if it advanced his mission. With his handicaps, he couldn't maneuver anymore. This collection of halftrained fools would come apart even on a simple set of moves, anyway. So it was stand and die. He started singing the national anthem and was amazed at how many of his 'troops' knew enough to fake it. Heil Hitler, Heil Göring, and Hoch Der Kaiser. He'd learned this game well enough on both fronts in the Kaiser War.

0040 hours local; 2340 hour CET
11 September / 10 September 1940
Rear of Peiper's position

So much for expecting action front. What seemed like a battalion of British infantry backed by a platoon of armored cars had come around to the rear. Peiper had faced his men about and had at them, with the Major's German guns firing over his head at the British vehicles. It was a swirling mass of close combat, with three British Roll Royce armored cars on fire and one of his rendered immobile and smoldering. Then suddenly a mass of new vehicles arrived, firing into the British rear. The enemy broke and leapfrogged back, covered by machine-guns and what were probably two mortars.

The new arrivals were Klaus Steiner, bringing up their own mortars. The hero Major barely noticed Peiper, going into immediate conference with his sort-of father-in-law, the other older Major. This gave Peiper time to take stock. He had taken 4 dead and 10 wounded. The LAH men weren't cowards after all. Given a coherent mission and led by someone they had faith in, they had fought off maybe 12 times their own number. It made Peiper proud.

The ill-dressed mechanics were swarming his smoldering vehicle. The whole thing looked as though it could blow at any second, but it didn't stop them. In two minutes they had the fire out. The boss, this Hauptmann Bats, trotted over with his woman. Bats started to give a long, technical description in hard-to-understand and near-childish German. His woman talked over him. Made him slow down. Corrected his words till they made sense. Kept telling him no one needed all the fine details. What could the damaged cavalry tank do? Answer was, it couldn't move. For now the turret worked, but one more good pounding would end that. However, the machine-guns were operative. So think of it as an armored pillbox, and site the gun for a line of fire that would be of use when the turret failed. Peiper thought it was a strange sort of teamwork on a battlefield, but it was getting him some use out of the partial wreck.

Jochen took stock of the situation. He'd lost 14 men repulsing one attack. Three more and he'd be out of men. It occurred to him that the camp had not been entrenched. The general orders stressed that they were a rear-area service position, and that no British attack was expected. It hadn't occurred to him to question these orders. Then again, he'd only served in combat for six weeks before this. Surely his superiors here knew better. Then again, this being a militia unit, perhaps they didn't. Food for thought.

....

Isaak was grateful to Klaus for the mortars, more so for the rescue. The question was, now what? Gunter refused to leave the position he was in. Claimed there were other British forces to the east. Isaak didn't like the position he had, didn't know how many British he was fighting, and was reasonably certain his 'unit' would fall apart if he tried to move it.

It felt like Galicia in '16 during the Brusilov Offensive. The reminder of how much worse that had been cheered him up a bit. Stray mortar rounds were nothing compared to Czarist field guns. The men he had under him, even the Nazi swine with Peiper, were more reliable than the Slavic Landwehr conscripts he'd had guarding his two batteries then. He'd been leaking runners every hour of that four-day debacle. If more refugees from overrun units hadn't kept appearing out of the chaos, he'd have been lost on the first day. His supposed commander had eaten his pistol. He'd been the over-educated scion of a noble Hungarian family. Isaak was sure he'd been an excellent courtier at some higher headquarters. Commanding a line artillery battalion was beyond him. Forced to make decisions, all he'd wanted to do was run. Isaak had found him a horse and said leave. The dolt was too afraid to do that either. Something about family honor. Good thing he hadn't. The horse made good eating till a German corps had restored the line.

Klaus had wanted to stay. Isaak overruled him. Sent him with his cars and the wounded to the rear.

Someone had to clear out their camp. There were British loose there. As he left, the mortars stopped firing. New attack, or were the British shifting their positions? He'd find out soon enough.

0045 hours local; 2345 hours CET
11 September / 10 September 1940
Headquarters area, Three Crosses Camp

Gregor was aware he should have gotten his people started digging in earlier. He'd gotten out of the old habits after so many years of just street fights, and then more years of peace. The British were coming at his position out of the dark. It wasn't pitch-black but between clouds, dust, and gunsmoke there wasn't much light. He was under fire from what seemed to be four machine-guns, and a few hundred men were working their way in on him in rushes.

The crates were slowing bullets as much as stopping them. He'd had to go up and down the firing line smacking his gunners to wait for targets, to squeeze short bursts. He laughed to himself. They were as green as he'd been at Ypres, going in with the barely trained youth volunteers in 1914. Everyone remembered the dead schoolboys, but there had been more working-class lads like himself, all patriotic and every bit as good a German as the fancy-pants ones. The old training cadre they had, had taught them how to fight like it was the Old Kaiser's French war. Big thick lines and charge. British had shot the shit out of them. The British regulars fired so fast that it seemed as if every man had his own machine-gun.

The only one who didn't need training was the Arab boy, Abduh. He treated each round as if it cost a hundred marks. Took his time, made sure he had a target, and drilled them right in their chests. The idiot could barely speak German, and didn't know from personal cleanliness. Worse that way than a Pole. But he followed simple instructions and knew his marksmanship. Gregor guessed that made him worth feeding.

Suddenly there was a scream of grenades! Gregor threw himself flat, pulling Hans down. Out of the corner of his eye, he saw a large figure jumping down over both grenades, then getting blown a meter up by the twin blasts. The Arab cried out that he had shot one of the throwers. Two machine-gunners both claimed the other. He looked to see who the fool hero had been. Have to thank him for saving Hans and himself. Correction, thank her. Only she was past hearing it. It was the big girl who would now never go to fat. She was stone dead, her body a mass of butchered meat. Asked one of the others what her name was. Esther. Now he had a name for the grave marker. He yelled at his idiots for letting the two Brits get this close.

Firing died down. The British were pulling off. Vehicles were coming, firing into the retreating Brits. Klaus was back. Gregor felt stupid reporting to a child, but Gunter had established the order of rank. Among the Majors, Gregor was last. Only absent Adolph ranked lower. Klaus took the report and got back on the radio. Was pulling Peter and most of the northern guard in. Asked Gunter to do the same. Gunter refused. Gregor knew what a mule the man could be. He directed the cook to find pallets for the wounded. Gregor felt the British would be back.

0050 hours local; 2350 hours CET
11 September / 10 September, 1940
Headquarters Western Desert Group, Bagush Box

Major General O'Connor was again wishing he could shoot every officer he had over the rank of major. The brigadier sent to attack the camp of some ill-organized militia had been given two first-rate British infantry battalions and two regiments of South African armored cars who had some experience in skirmishing. First he gets lost. Next he mishandles his attack. This in turn provokes a mutiny from the two South African commanders. They are claiming the idiot tried to use machine-gun firing armored cars as infantry tanks. They obeyed. Once. They refused pointblank to repeat this. Instead they invoked the right of Commonwealth commanders to refer orders to their home government. ANZAC's insisted on this from memories of Gallipoli in the First War. Others said 'me too'. Which was sort of workable for the Australians and New Zealanders, each of whom had sent a corps headquarters so one was dealing with fellow professionals. South Africa had sent two armored car regiments. Nearest South African general was up on the Somali border north of Mombasa. It was even worse with the Rhodies. They had sent a few platoons of home-made armored cars, and their nearest senior commander was home in Salisbury. Which was why they were left on permanent outpost duty, thank you very much.

So a man with four battalion-sized units cannot fight a militia, and is about to lose two of those units to de facto mutiny. O'Connor had tried reasoning with both South African lieutenant colonels. Tried despite his being sure they were right and the brigadier was wrong. Their vehicles simply couldn't survive closing with good artillery. There was dispute on the size of the guns they were facing, but any field gun could punch holes in an armored car. What was the idiot brigadier thinking?

Even then he wasn't the worst idiot commander this night. Beresford had clearly ordered the northern brigade to break out south WEST. The new idiot decided on his own to go south EAST as this was the shortest route to his supports. Yes. It was. It also put him in the easiest position against which the German Panzer division that had savaged the unsupported tanks, could intercede. Unsupported, in violation of clear orders the relieved brigade commander had been given.

The Panzer division had intercepted the move, as could have been predicted. Brigade was now mostly pocketed and screaming for help.   The only possible help was the center brigade, which was in turn being menaced from the north by other elements of the same Panzer division. What an utter balls-up. Nothing for it but to order the south brigade to reinforce the center.

Easy to get the two armored car units to drive away. They were refusing brigade orders anyway. Extracting the infantry might prove interesting, in several nasty senses of 'interesting'. When this was over, O'Connor promised himself a full purge. He doubted Wavell would back him, but the thought gave him a happy glow.

0100 hours local; 2400 hours CET
11 September / 10 September 1940
One kilometer north of headquarters tent, Three Crosses position

Hauptmann Peter thought Klaus's order absurd. Pull back the bulk of his force where, precisely? To do what, precisely? Drive in trucks to Gregor before finding out where the British were? Peter had been getting evening lessons from Pappa Isaac and Uncle Ivan. This went against everything they had taught.

Thinking the orders stupid, wasn't the same as not following them. Both elders had preached the same thing. Obey till it is proven wrong. In battle, the side run by a debating society lost. When in doubt, do something.

He had given hasty instructions to the two platoons he was leaving behind. Don't get overrun. Radio when the British hit you, then dance out of the way. He was leaving them with two machine-guns. He was taking the Boys antitank rifles and the eight eight gun section. So they were to treat all engine noises as tanks until proven otherwise. Observe, report, stay alive.

The main group in their trucks and motorcycles hadn't gotten fifty meters when there were suddenly large numbers of engine noises to their south and southeast. Both were coming for him, which made no sense. The camp was in the opposite direction. But it was happening. Dozens of armored cars were bearing down out of the dark. Peter got everyone out of the vehicles. Ordered the two guns to deploy. He trusted the crews knew how to do it, because he didn't. The Luftwaffe Leutnant saluted and started barking technical orders to his crews. Peter had been around big equipment since before he was ten. Each type had their own jargon. Peter knew better than to think he spoke 'gunner', so he focused on deploying the Boys rifles. His gunners weren't good enough for direct hits at over a hundred meters. The volley caused the armored cars coming straight at him to sheer off to the east. Peter ran up and down the line, swatting machine-gunners who were wasting ammo shooting at the retreating British. He let the Boys fire one more volley and stopped them. No need reducing the ammunition supply. They hadn't hit anything in two tries. Or at least Peter couldn't see any cars that had stopped or caught fire.

He radioed Gunter and then Pappa. The armored cars were going away. Peter hadn't a clue as to what that meant in terms of a battle. He was content to let the adults puzzle it out. He'd seen bar fights that showed more organization than this shambling dance in the dark.

0115 hours local; 0015 hours CET
12 September, 1940
Central Brigade Forward Headquarters

General Beresford had by now relieved a second brigadier. His southern brigade had already seen the mutiny and departure of the two South African armored car regiments. That left the 'brigade' with two battalions of motorized infantry. The supposed commander now admitted he had lost control over both of these. He sort of had an idea where they were, but neither was with him and the support element. He was southwest of the German position. He had one battalion attacking the rear of the first German redoubt. The second was inside the German camp … someplace. Not inside the wire, as it seems the Germans had neglected to wire the position. But clearly inside the perimeter. In turn, that battalion commander had split his companies. He had a confused, less than coherent account of where anyone was; and which made no sense in terms of the reports of the other infantry battalion commander, brigade HQ, or the two departing units of South Africans. Indeed, if all these reports were added together, the German brigade was the size of a corps, which the Rhodesian recon screen asserted it clearly was not.

Beresford and Corps HQ were inclined to believe the Rhodies, as so far they had been the only ones who knew where they were, much less anything else.

Beresford clearly was in a tight spot. He needed his artillery. He needed the brigade of cruiser tanks, and another infantry brigade, as supports to salvage a draw from a looming disaster. Corps was seeing this as good money after bad. Dawn would come in a bit over four hours, and waves of hostile warbirds would be right behind the early light.

0120 hours local; 0020 hours CET
12 September 1940
Southwest bastion of Three Crosses Camp

Peiper kept waiting for the next serious British push. He refused to believe the report that the mass of armored cars had driven away. He was trading shots at a distance with a large number of British infantry. He was hearing the sound of large numbers of vehicles to the British rear which would be north north west of him. Major Schwabe had deployed a section of 75mm French guns to backstop his position, and rearranged his own lines to give Peiper a screen of machine-gunners. He left placing them to Peiper. Peiper in turn had detailed one of his SA Scharführers to get the fire lanes properly set. He kept his SS together with his surviving 'cavalry tanks' as a counterattack reserve. The last British attack had come close to carrying. It was his job to make sure the next one failed as well. He couldn't explain the delay.

0125 hours local; 0025 hours CET
12 September 1940
HQ Bastion, Camp Three Crosses

The British were pulling off. Gregor had enough combat experience to feel it. The machine-guns were still firing, but it was covering fire. If he'd had even one veteran company, he could give them a further bloody nose. He knew it, and knew he didn't have a squad he'd trust maneuvering against good troops in the dark. Another time, he'd give the British the whipping they deserved.

Klaus was off with his Kübelwagen, sweeping the space between Gregor and Isaak. There was limited firing, but even that was dying down. The camp was returning to sleep, as it were. Gregor instead oversaw policing up the position. Part of that was stacking the dead for burial. He saw Naiomi and two of the other original Romanian Betar girls come up to Esther's body and cut bloody strips off her blouse. Weird fucking Yids. He'd served with a few and had buried a couple. He asked, expecting some bizarre religious ritual. Answer shocked him. Esther was dead. The meat was just meat. Bury it anywhere that was convenient. The cloth with Esther's blood was going to Palestine. Esther would be buried in their Homeland of Zion. She died for her country. There would be a military graveyard to honor the fallen. Jabotinsky, who Gregor gathered was their Führer, would return from exile in the US to dedicate the cemetery.

Gregor felt he'd have to think about this. These were Yids pretending to be Europeans. They had their own soil; they would redeem it with their own blood. Like a real people. Which begged the question about what Germany got out of all this. Girls said Germany wanted the oil. The pipeline ran through Jewish land to a Jewish port. The new Israel would guard these for Germany, same as the new Slovakia ruled some patches of dirt for the Reich. Jews had been part of other people's empires before. Persia, Syria, Egypt, Rome, Turkey, Britain … why not Germany? Did he doubt Germany would win this war?

0145 hours local; 0045 hours CET
12 September 1940
British Theater HQ, Cairo

General Archibald Wavell had a decision to make. The problem, of course, was that he didn't like any of the options. O'Connor's offensive had failed, even as a spoiling attack. Indeed, it seemed quite possible that the three brigades sent forward might all be lost. O'Connor's solutions, however, seemed worse than the mere loss of an irreplaceable division. He was taking 7th Armored Division headquarters with its support forces and cruiser tank brigade, adding to it the artillery and the balance of the infantry from 4th Indian Division and a motorized infantry brigade, the 16th. He had wanted to add the Australian brigade, but they had refused the order. Their answer was "Gallipoli", followed by a demand to consult First Australian Corps Headquarters back in Palestine. The Australians would defend the camp, while their own support forces and the elements of their second brigade motored back to Alamein.

O'Connor was using the mess as an excuse to get what he had wanted all along. He had ordered the evacuation of the two reinforced brigades from the Mersa Matruh position back to Bagush. He was alerting his corps-level support elements to follow the Australians back. He was arguing that daylight losses from air attack, would be less severe than waiting to be overrun by multiple panzer divisions plus the corps that was now asserted to be at the fortified German base camp on the plateau.

O'Connor also had left Bagush to 'go in' with 7th Armored. On the surface it was sensible. You don't untangle two divisions without a higher commander present to bang heads. This also put O'Connor beyond reach of anguished screams from London about 'no retreats'. London wanted to micromanage by teletype. O'Connor had precluded this. Which meant all of London's backbiting was going to hit Cairo like a ton of bricks as soon as anguished junior aides could wake the War Cabinet. Winston had not yet been to bed, and was bombarding Wavell with demands for information, insane schemes of maneuver, and not-so-thinly-veiled threats of dismissal. Wavell was quite ready to be given the sack. He saw that as a when, not an if. For the rest … he wearily shook his head and said a simple prayer. It was his duty to King and Country to be London's punching bag. Wavell would gladly take the blows, if the end result was a major reinforcement of modern fighters. They weren't coming anywhere near to soon enough, but even full generals could dream as little boys did of Christmas.

0200 hours local; 0100 hours CET
12 September 1940
Three Crosses Camp

The Italian motorcycle dispatch rider had arrived a few minutes ago. He was one of the teen-aged Malta veterans Rommel had taken as couriers. The message was to Gunter, as Brigade commander and as senior officer defending the position. Rommel described the fighting to the north. Asserted that he was engaged with two British divisions plus elements of a third. Ordered Gunter to form a battlegroup to move north to support him. Mission orders. Rommel didn't specify what was to be included in the Kampfgruppe, or its route north. Gunter as man on the spot would make those decisions, which he was now attempting to do. He'd assembled Isaak, Ivan, and Gregor for a council of war. Gunter didn't know the fancy words. He just saw it as a senior officers meeting.

The Italian described having to detour around a major British position, and then avoid retreating British vehicle columns near the camp. The boy's concept of locations and distances was vague and probably fanciful. Gunter distilled it down fast. 1st Libyan and Rommel's de facto brigade on the north. A few German recon and motorcycle troops southeast of them and northeast of the camp. Large numbers of British south and west of Rommel, north and west of the camp. How large? Camp had been hit by at least a brigade, so figure at least a division. The rest of von Manstein's German corps was west of everyone, but supposedly in motion east. East, aimed where? Real good question. Small British recon screen to the east of the camp. Hadn't attacked when the brigade did before, so maybe it wouldn't now. What was behind that screen? No way to know for three to four hours, till dawn was followed by a sky full of friendly planes with radios?

Gregor felt they had been lucky beating off the last British attack. Argued to send a minimal force, so as to preserve the camp and loot. Gunter's answer was simple. "What Rommel's first name?"

Gregor blinked, thinking fast, "Edo, Erwin … something with an E?"

Gunter fixed his old friend with a basilisk's stare. "No. It is Generalmajor Division Commander. This is not one of us having a discussion in the front line trench with some Leutnant or Hauptmann in command of our company whose farts we have smelled for the last month. A 'suggestion' from a General is an order." He caught Ivan's look. "Yes, this order contradicts von Manstein's order.   We'll send a radio message confirming what we are doing, but we will obey. The two people with the word

'General' in their name can sort out the pissing contest later. A General says we are needed for a major battle. We march. We make a mobile battalion. The SA boys in their Panhards. Peiper with what's left of his recon vehicles and those SS who turned up here. That Magyar company you brought over, Gregor. Klaus, you get your boys in the Kübelwagen and motorcycles. It is not much of a battalion, but it's the best we have. Isaak, you follow behind with the 75 battery, the two flak batteries, and one of the Betar companies in trucks as supports for the guns. I'll go with you to supervise, but you two worked together for enough years back in the oilfields. This is an approach to contact. We keep going till we find British. Then radio where we are, skirmish, and hope for the best."

Gunter could see Gregor was still uneasy. He nodded for the man to speak. "I understand why I'm being left behind. The foot, the leg, Hans. But you are leaving me with a company plus dribs and drabs of another. A bunch of mechanics, cooks; and the rest pretending to be infantry for a third. My biggest weapons will be some Boys antitank rifles. One serious push and we'll get overrun."

Gunter knew that. He also knew Gregor was still unused to this whole being an officer thing. Gunter had lost his virginity on command during a day of chaos at Luqa. "You pull everyone back to the one position and dig in. You send a radio message to von Manstein asking to have a mortar battery with illumination rounds and a few truckloads of wire forwarded as fast as possible. Radio traffic said there was an SS relief column on the road. So it is half a day of heroic last stand, and this SS Oberst arrives with a Kampfgruppe."

Gregor didn't like it. He hadn't liked a lot of things he'd been forced to do in the Great War and its aftermath. He started barking orders and left the meeting. Do his best and die if it all fucked up. That felt familiar. Galicia 1916. Vimy 1917. It all went to shit, and either the reliefs arrived in time or everybody died. Different banner, same Fatherland.

0230 hours local; 0130 hours CET
12 September 1940
5 kilometers south south west of prior battlefield of 1st Libyan Division

The rest of General Maletti's division had caught up with him. It was arrayed on an 8-kilometer arc to his south, more than half surrounding the main retreating British force. There were very few of those giant tanks left and the British were being careful where they deployed them. A second British brigade was in action off to the southeast, holding off Rommel. There was a third brigade coming up from the south, but it had not yet made its presence felt.

Maletti had had a brief conference with the German general. Rommel had congratulated him on the fine performance of 1st Libyan. He had been ecstatic about some 76mm gun truck battery that had by accident found itself with his force. Maletti had been wondering where that lost unit was. The German was boastful and arrogant, but otherwise treated Maletti as a valued colleague. Unusual for a German, in Maletti's experience. Rommel claimed his number 2, an Oberst von Thoma, would have the balance of his 7th Panzer Division up by first light. Hopefully it would complete the encirclement. However, night navigation was tricky, so Rommel was more sure *when* it would appear than where.

Maletti concurred. His Libyans were experienced professionals used to this terrain, not conscripts still getting settled in to the climate and geography. Maletti's biggest concern was British tanks. Rommel concurred, and radioed von Thoma to leave an 88mm battery with 1ˢᵗ Libyan when he arrived. Rommel had gone motoring off. Maletti sent his tankettes off to probe, covering his exposed southwest flank. These Indian soldiers were serious professionals, and it paid to be prudent.

0245 hours local; 0145 hours CET
12 September 1940
Headquarters area, Three Crosses Camp

Leutnant Greta Schwabe/Steiner was working on removing food stores from wooden packing crates so that others could shovel sand and dirt in as a pseudo-sandbag. Sand and dirt, but not rocks and pebbles which could serve as a secondary shrapnel source.

Greta was neither particularly athletic nor especially strong. She had been raised to be a wife and mother, not a woman who did manual labor. When a proper suitor did not materialize by the time she left school at 16, her father had taught her basic bookkeeping. She had worked since as a cashier or accounting clerk, depending on what work he could find her among his business contacts. So instead of digging graves or using a shovel to scoop dirt into crates, she did the sort of stockroom work that had been part of her stream of temporary jobs. It was mindless repetitive action, well within the physical capacities of a healthy teenager.

This left her mind free to roam, and the place it kept returning to was Esther. Greta had met Esther with Naiomi on the train from Ploeisti to Naples. She couldn't claim they were instant best friends. Esther was a few years older, far more educated and a fanatic Zionist. Yet for months they had all been daily companions. Now Esther was gone, never to return.

Until now the war part of this adventure hadn't exactly been real to Greta. She had seen people die on Malta. Had seen wounded, mangled bodies. But they were strangers. Greta was aware things were bad for the Jews. Always, and even more so now. Her parents and siblings had been executed for a crime Greta had committed. She had not taken the rules seriously enough. The Hungarian fascists had tried to do a pogrom in her train car, but Klaus and the Betar company had made short work of them. She's heard about what else had been happening in Hungary, in Romania. There were really bad stories circulating from German-occupied Poland.

Greta had allowed herself to remain apart from the blackness of the times. She'd been able to see herself as a movie heroine on an adventure. Klaus treated her like a princess, not a whore. The other Nazis treated her politely. The regime hated Jews, but that was abstract and elsewhere. The small parts of the Nazi state she interacted with actually were nicer to her, to her family, than the Romanians often were. No casual beatings. No death threats. But now Esther was dead. Dead, and this war was just really getting started. How many more dead till Palestine, till it ended?

The Betar's Revisionist Zionism had just been words to her. Yet Naiomi and the others were taking

Esther's blood to Palestine, to be buried in the new Israel. This meant so much to her girls. Greta simply couldn't wrap her head around a Jewish nation. All that Bible-times Jewish history meant nothing to her. Neither did Talmud or Torah, the way the observant Jews ordered their lives. To Greta, being a Jew was a mix of blood and holidays. She could describe the food for each holiday, how to prepare it, what special decoration the house needed. That was a Jewish home to her, not the droning voices on the radio reading the latest decrees being Jewish, speaking Yiddish. No, wait, Naiomi had said Yiddish was out too. A language of exile, whatever that meant. They were all to speak Hebrew. Why? No one *spoke* Hebrew. Hebrew was for prayer. Observant men would spend hours talking to God in Hebrew. Jewish women said a few simple Hebrew prayers each sabbath. A few prayers, but then you went back to speaking Yiddish. Even the zealots who debated Talmud did so in Yiddish. Greta hadn't come from a particularly religious family, but she'd had girlfriends who did. None of this made sense. A Jewish state? A Jewish Army? Here she was shooting at British. Might have killed one or two for all she knew. She had never known any Britishers personally. She'd been introduced to a few when her family had visited their wealthier relatives in Ploeisti. They seemed nice but kept their social distance. Didn't particularly like Jews … but who did? This was all so confusing. She worked on keeping a brave face as these emotions and thoughts washed over her. Her family needed her to maintain her position with Klaus, with the unit. There was no time for silly schoolgirl crying jags.

....
Gregor was taking this burden of command thing quite seriously. He had commanded a company for periods at the front. The army was always short of junior officers and he had been line infantry, not a stormtrooper like Gunter. His unit was perpetually understrength. What replacements they got were green kids fresh out of training barracks. Newly minted junior officers would arrive. Many died quickly. The more successful would get sifted out for some better assignment with a counterattack division, or later with the storm troops. So the same few officers would cycle back from hospital to his battalion or company till wounds or disease put them back in hospital, or shells put them in a hasty grave.

Gregor had been one of the few to serve all four years in the company, from First Ypres to the Final Retreat to home after the armistice. The 'battalion' he was commanding now was scarcely larger than the full-strength company he had marched with at the end of 1914, before the killing fields of Flanders. He may not have known how to be a Major. He knew how to be a small unit leader. He sent Hans to fetch Greta. When she came over, he seated her on a camp chair inside the headquarters tent, beyond prying eyes and open ears. He handed her a tin mess kit cup. Half and half, coffee and good captured brandy. The girl took a sip and near choked. Fancy little thing apparently wasn't used to drinking the way good German girls were. "Sip it if you have to girl, but you are drinking it and we're having a chat. You see it is real now. Esther. Battle. The war. I was younger than you when I first saw a field covered with dead men. Boys I'd gone through training with. Thank your Jew-God we don't do that way of fighting anymore. Line up in pretty rows and charge machine-guns." Gregor shook his head. What fools they had been, the aged veteran officers from the Kaiser's French War and the patriotic lads like himself that cheered and followed them like lambs to the slaughter. "If you need to cry, do it here and now, where no one can see. All they'll see, all they'll know, is commander's conference. The commanders seem to spend half their lives chatting with each other while the rankers sweat. No one will think twice about it. They'll just bitch. Troops need something to be indignant about."

Greta looked at him strangely. The man didn't like Jews and didn't care who knew it. Why was he helping her? "Sir, why? You don't like my kind. You don't like me. You don't like Klaus."

Gregor wearily shook his head. God, what he'd give to be that young and clueless again. Eighteen seemed back before the Stone Age, to his current middle-aged self. "Don't like Yids and won't bother to hide it. Why should I? I'm a German, and I don't even like all of them. Fuck the aristocrats and the Reds, screw anyone who puts on airs and wears a necktie to work. But we're at war. Units are different. A platoon is like a family. Company is like a clan. A battalion is a village. Think of it that way. You can hate your kin or not. Doesn't matter. Blood is blood. You'll spend your days among them. Hear their dumb jokes and dumber brags. Smell their farts, and swap things you can't stomach out of the rations. I don't smoke. One of the other guys in my company couldn't digest cheese. Some allergy thing to milk. We'd swap. So your all-lady platoon are a family. And one of them died. It hurts because it is your first. Won't be the last. When we finish working, you break out a big jug of brandy and call your girls over. You toast the big girl, tell stories about her, make stupid promises on how you'll make the fucking English pay a dozen times over. You all act brave to each other. You'll all know it is acting, but it helps. It's a ritual like your Friday nights, like Sunday sit-down dinner for normal folks." Greta gave Gregor a look. "Said I didn't like Jews. Never said I didn't know any. Had one in my first platoon. When we got leave together in '15, his folks had me to dinner. It was a short leave ticket, shorter because the trains were late getting us to the Rhine. So it was Friday night with his folks. Saturday night drinking at the beer hall and Sunday sit down with my Mom. She served pork roast. Only meat she could get. He ate it and never said a word. Sunday night we shipped out for Poland. Buried him in a nameless field southwest a bit of Warsaw. If there was a town nearby, no one told us. All we knew is we were east of Cracow. Saved his personal jewelry and a lock of his hair. Carried it fourteen months till the next leave ticket. Brought it to his folks and told them a fairy tale of how he died a hero with no pain. As if. Gut shot and spent three hours bleeding out, screaming and whimpering. We hadn't time to evacuate him to an aid station. Ivan was being energetic that week. One attack after another. Those Ivans are brainless but they have balls."

Gregor shut up. He'd said more than he meant to. Greta sat there silently sipping. When the liquid was half gone she thanked him. Asked if at the next quiet period she could bring Klaus by. Gregor knew things Klaus needed to learn. Gregor laughed, slapped her on the back and walked out. Told her to finish sipping the drink and catch her breath. Thought to himself he must be getting soft with old age, but damn – it was up to the veterans to teach the clueless young. He should have done that with the green-around-the-gills replacements they would get during the last war. Except then Gregor had been too stubborn sure of himself to waste his breath on new meat that hadn't proved itself yet. Besides, they mostly died before you really learned to remember their names anyway. So far this war wasn't anywhere near as bloody. Gregor kept waiting for it to be back to trenches and daily bombardments.

....

Greta sipped the coffee/brandy mix. She disliked the taste but was coming to appreciate the way it was dulling her senses, easing her pain. So this is why people drank? Then why did they also drink to celebrate? This being an adult thing was hard. First her aunt had to beat sense into her. Now it was a Nazi who would rather she just conveniently died, thereby ceasing to pollute his world. Gregor was a hardass Brownshirt son of a bitch, but Greta felt the truth in his words. He'd been through this all as a teen. Through worse. Been at it for four years and had the drive left to keep fighting after the war was lost with the Freikorps. She wondered who the next life lesson would come from. Hans the slow witted? Mary the Asian cook? Greta was sure it would be someone who would surprise her. She did get the essence of what Gregor had said. The Falcons of Malta Battalion was her second family. Each death in it was like losing a cousin. So they would all toast Cousin Esther the university Zionist. A Zionist whose bloody shirt would be buried outside Haifa. Greta wasn't sure she knew where Haifa was, but decided she had better learn. Whether she liked it or not, she was a German and a Zionist both. She was two things that could not mix. Life was like that, or at least it was to a Transylvanian Jewish girl in a Nazi Army in Egypt killing Englishmen to make the place Italian. She slugged the remains of her drink, gagged, nearly threw it all up, and trotted back to work with her ladies. She was their officer and they were her people, for better or worse. Sort of like getting married.

0300 hours local; 0200 hours CET
12 September 1940
British field hospital, central brigade area, 4th Indian Division

Wilhelm Mohnke had been moping outside the main hospital tent. His arm would heal eventually. His spine already felt a bit better. The British medical orderlies had quite professionally treated his scrapes and cuts. He was probably fit for duty, at least in the sense that if within his own lines and still having a unit, he would have retained command.

He had had a battalion. He had lost it. Stupidly. He could catalog everything he'd done wrong. If this were a training exercise, he could have written a brilliant critique of his failures and done better next time. This was real. He was a British prisoner. He would serve the rest of the war in some colonial prison camp. Mohnke was lost in his thoughts, which were mostly self-pity.

Mohnke had been abstractly aware of the tempo of activity, of truck traffic rising quickly. He didn't let any of it penetrate his gloom. However, he couldn't avoid the medical corporal who was tugging on his unbroken arm, trying to get his attention. He sort of remembered the young man trying to talk to him in German. Mohnke was retroactively aware he had ignored it. He looked up at the fellow. The German was decent, educated even. Mohnke drew the obvious conclusion, "Jew?"

The lad frowned. "Czech. British passport now." The orderly showed Mohnke the cross he was wearing around his neck. Man was apparently a Catholic. "You are needed in the radio tent, sir. NOW!"

Mohnke clumsily got to his feet. The tent was maybe twenty meters away. A squad was already taking it down, packing it up. The radio was on a folding table. Mohnke abstractly thought to himself that the British seemed to have a lot of useful equipment like this. Must be nice to go to war as part of a rich army. There was a British major waiting by the radio. He looked annoyed. "You took your bloody time getting here. Thought you SS were model Germans, precise and on time." The major was clearly annoyed with far more than Mohnke's punctuality. "We're pulling out here. Why isn't your concern.

Fortunes of war. Haven't the trucks or the time to move the hospital or the last loads of your men that we captured. I'm turning this all back to you as senior German officer on the spot. We've found a pair of frequencies your army is operating on. I'm giving you three minutes to notify whatever of your side is out there. First one, then the other. Just get on. Give your name, rank, and say the hospital has a big red cross and nothing but Germans. Oh, we have eight Italians as well. Almost the same thing. We were stuck with them last war. Now it is your turn."

Mohnke stood there speechless. The major slapped him to force him to concentrate. So he got on the first frequency. Proved to be the boy Major from his unit. Mohnke never got a chance to make the second announcement. He was shoved aside and fell on his ass. The radio was taken down, thrown into the back of a small truck along with the table, and off the last half-dozen British vehicles went. Mohnke was by now attentive enough to notice that they went in different directions. West, east, and northwest.

Seventeen minutes later Major Klaus Steiner arrived with his light forces. Mohnke was back in the fight. Ten minutes after that he was surprised to see General Rommel arrive from the north. The boy gave a good report. Not quite proper military etiquette, but he described where his superior's forces were, what they thought they were doing, where they thought the British were. Seemed there was a major British attack force to the east, spearheaded by armored cars and a lot of British tanks. Not the big monsters. The smaller faster ones. This was all backed by a lot of artillery support. Major Schwabe was claiming the British guns were firing blind. How did Schwabe know this? Four years war experience. Rommel congratulated Steiner and Mohnke. Told them to wait here on developments. Motored off to confer with Oberst Strauss. Steiner assigned Mohnke to assemble his still-fit men, and police up the area looking for abandoned British small arms to equip themselves with. The medical tent was left to Rommel's medical detachment. Plan was to wait till daylight and air support, before organizing an evacuation of the wounded.

Mohnke was now back in command of a short company of former prisoners. They were even finding a few weapons, most of them German, among the debris left behind. Mohnke was beginning to realize just how pitifully low his place in the universe was.

0330 hours local; 0230 hours CET
12 September 1940
4th Indian Division Headquarters, northwest of previous location which Rommel has by now occupied

Beresford regarded calling what he had here a 'divisional headquarters', as more than somewhat optimistic. He had the remains of his northern brigade and the bulk of his center brigade backpedaling on a 200-degree arc running northwest to east. He had an open left flank, and two semi-mutinous South African armored car units vaguely patrolling his right and right rear. His two southern infantry battalions and brigade headquarters were lost, collectively and separately. They couldn't seem to find each other or him. The positions they reported had them on top of each other, yet all denied they could hear each other firing. None seemed to have a clear concept of what they were firing at, beyond a belief they were facing overwhelming numbers and about to be overrun. Beresford was learning yet again why commanders hate night attacks, had done so back to the ancients.

Logic said send patrols of South Africans out to locate the strays. Given the bad blood between those five units, THAT was not happening. Yet if he did nothing, dawn would come before he could extricate his entire force east. They would be sitting ducks for air attack. Nothing for it but to go himself. Even the most dimwitted British officers would know a Rolls Royce coming could only mean a British senior officer.

0345 hours local; 0245 hours CET
12 September 1940
Brigade Strauss forward HQ, northeast of Camp Three Crosses

Erwin Rommel arrived at 'brigade headquarters' to find the commander absent elsewhere. Strauss had left the actual fighting to his two battalion commanders while he took personal charge of the screen of scouts, outposts, and fighting patrols. Rommel wanted to be upset. He was too honest with himself not to see shadows of his own actions on the Meuse and elsewhere in the West. He had won honors by his exploits. He had also effectively demoted himself to advance guard commander, letting his operations officer run the division. He had done the same today, leaving von Thoma effectively in command.

Strauss had been sending back a stream of prisoners, reports, even fairly detailed maps. British column seemed to be a medium tank brigade, a reconnaissance brigade, two infantry brigades, two artillery brigades, and support troops. Higher headquarters was called Western Desert Force. Under it were elements of 7th Armored and 4th Indian Division plus 16th Infantry Brigade, a battlegroup under someone called Selby or Shelby, and corps troops. The artillery was in battery and lightly guarded. The infantry seemed mostly on its trucks, stuck in road column. The tanks and reconnaissance vehicles were making frontal assaults in the manner of Napoleonic cavalry. The artillery was firing, but seemed not able to coordinate well enough to be 'supporting'.

Gorlov and Schwabe gave a joint report. Gorlov saw his duty as screening the guns. Schwabe had reinforced him with the 2 cm flak guns, as they were useless in a field artillery role. The screen was slowing down the British vehicle charges enough for the guns to kill them. This allowed step by step backpedaling. They were being driven back roughly a kilometer an hour. Both officers had prior war experience and saw this as normal. Galicia, Poland, Serbia, Transylvania, Ukraine, Kuban. Neither was a professional officer in the sense of war college or the like, but both were veterans with battalion and higher command experience.

What amazed Rommel was the 'staff'. The minder assigned him by von Manstein, Ernst von Kleist-Konitz. A Leutnant on convalescent leave and a dozen essentially civilian Jewish clerks from the camp in Bari. Von Kleist-Konitz he knew as a type. Hereditary general staff officer destined for big things. So he asked the chief clerk for his prior experience. Turned out the man had run a group of women's shoe stores in Bucharest. Told the general that office work was office work. At least military supplies didn't come in sizes and widths, didn't go in and out of fashion. Clerk then excused himself to see to a problem getting more shells up to the two firing batteries, each of which used different ammo.

Rommel had paid no attention to supply lines or indeed to the rest of his division. He had been living on captured British fuel for some hours. He had never bothered querying his subunits for ammo status.   It was just now occurring to him that there was more to this being a divisional commander than taking personal command of the tip of the spear. Food for thought.

....

Richard O'Connor was distracting himself from wanting to throttle subordinates, by mentally composing a new training manual for British armored divisions. The support group was too small and had no training in working with the tanks. The tanks brigades had no concept of combined arms cooperation. Every lesson that had been learned from Vimy Ridge to the Hundred Days, had been scrubbed from their minds. Officered out of the cavalry branch, they were maneuvered like squadrons of horse from the days before cavalry had become mounted rifles, when they expected to deliver attacks with sword and lance. Charges through German screens of light vehicles, heavy weapons, and infantry, did nothing except provide beautiful targets for the supporting German artillery.

In the meantime, his gunners were helpless in a fluid situation. Lacking the doctrine to keep forward observers up with the tanks, they were reduced to firing on map grids. Beyond wasting shells, anything they accomplished would be blind luck.

O'Connor had two hours to get the attack force, the bulk of Fourth Indian Division, out of this trap. So far the only contact was by one British armored car which had somehow punched through on its own. It had found 4th Indian field HQ but not the commander who was, once again, away trying to find missing or wayward subordinate units. This army simply couldn't fight a mobile battle. As is, he was getting pin-pricked to death by German forward recon patrols, who prowled in the wastes to both sides of his stalled advance. Which meant they were in position to call in air strikes at dawn. Time to be back at Alamein in fixed positions, which was all this army understood.

0400 hours local; 0300 hours CET
12 September 1940
Plateau south of Charing Cross position, north of Three Crosses Camp and west of where Rommel was meeting with Gorlov and Schwabe

General Beresford had found three missing companies of infantry and directed them on the proper compass headings north-north-east. He was trying to locate the rest of his lost lambs when he sighted two of what appeared to be Bedford OY trucks. Clearly these were British trucks, but the men clustered around them were taking a cigarette break. Pathetic. Stopping for personal time in the middle of a battle zone. What was their officer thinking?

He directed his driver to the two trucks, intending to give the lieutenant a piece of his mind. When they saw his limousine, the troops dropped their smokes and scrambled into an inspection line. They knew they were caught. He was almost seeing red as he stepped out of the Rolls. At which point, he and the sergeant in command noticed the cut of each other's uniforms. Too late. He was now a prisoner of the Seventh Panzer Division.

....

Major Klaus Steiner was chafing at being left guarding a hospital. He simply didn't see the sense in fighting around a medical installation where his unit would serve as a bullet magnet to further wound the already maimed.

So he pulled his combined unit 150 meters away to the southwest, where he had the tent in sight but would direct combat away from the tent with its clear red cross markings. He sent out motorcycle riders on sweeps while keeping his core in a lump around their vehicles. He chose not to entrench. If attacked, surely it made more sense to use speed and just move away. Klaus's experiences since Malta were skirmishes, not battle.

One of his riders returned with a contact report. The contact was clanking in behind him. Two Panzer II's and four 37mm anti-tank guns being towed by captured Polish trucks. They were Seventh Panzer, and quite lost. Mohnke suggested keeping them to avoid an overrun such as he had experienced. Klaus had more respect for the word General, plus he'd seen Rommel in action on Malta. One did not hold back his reinforcements. Not and expect to live through the follow-up encounter. Klaus detached two of his motorcyclists to guide the new folks to their General.

Peiper took Mohnke off before matters deteriorated. Snagged some tea from the hospital tent and sat his fellow SS officer down for a serious talking to. "You have to remember he's really that young. Also no formal military training. He's our superior officer, even when he fantasizes that moving a couple of hundred meters matters with modern weapons. If you hope to resurrect your career, stay on his good side. The Brigade commander and the Reichsführer have adopted him like a pet. Those 37's were useless. Everyone saw that in the West. Bounced off British tanks like pebbles from a kid's slingshot. You'll need French 75's or 105's. Not sure if the issue cannon company 75's will work. You speak to Major Schwabe. You pretend he's Volkdeutsche like his papers say. You ignore that he's a Yid. Berlin wants us to play pretend. Man knows his guns. Shot up some British armor for me earlier tonight."

Mohnke had his head down. He was acting the beaten man. "The report will never reach Berlin. All they will hear is that I lost a battalion to a British attack. I'm ruined."

Peiper considered slapping the man to get his attention. That would be a bit extreme to do to a fellow SS officer, even one who had clearly lost his balls. Instead he grabbed his undamaged arm, jerking him around to shout at him. "Get hold of yourself! You are an SS officer, not some effete subhuman. This is a warzone for the Reich, not some degenerate Weimar cabaret. I thought we had cleansed the Movement of this kind of unnatural behavior after the 1934 Blood Purge." Peiper paused to see Mohnke start to snap out of his funk, to remember he was an elite specimen of Aryan, not some multiracial transvestite degenerate from the dark days before the Movement had taken power. Peiper assumed a more comradely tone. "We have our own liaison officer. Reports go straight to Oberführer Schellenberg's desk, where they are hand-carried to the Reichsführer. Oberst Strauss and I will polish the report. You'll get a new battalion, better equipped than before.   The Reichsführer's pets don't have defeats. I have two dozen of what were once yours, to write commendations for. Recognition of their service under my command and Schwabe's. The propaganda people will feast on this. Your unfortunate engagement will get lost in the weeds. Handle yourself well over the next few days and we'll get you a Wehrmachtbericht for something. This is a matter of the Reichsführer's prestige. Can you manage this? Can you act like a proper graduate of the Junker Schools? If not, I'll take over the remnants of your battalion and ship you home in disgrace."

Mohnke looked up at Peiper. He had presumed Peiper would steal his command. It was the smart career move. Peiper read his face and replied to the unspoken question. "I'll get my own command raised to a Battalion before this is done. Have to get formally transferred to Strauss's Brigade. Strauss has me sending direct reports to Berlin as well. My wife is socially friendly with Frau Heydrich. Stick with us and we'll get you a career. But we start with how you lost your Battalion. I need the unvarnished truth so we don't make the same mistakes twice. It was lack of proper anti-tank guns and no scout element, right?" Mohnke sadly nodded his head, decided to entrust his professional future to Peiper, and began the story.

0445 hours local; 0345 hours CET
12 September 1940
Command vehicle Western Desert Group, southeast of Charing Cross position [now abandoned]

Dawn was a bit less than an hour away. Daylight meant air attack. Normally. However the last thirty minutes had seen the start of a khamseen, the fierce sand and dust storms that would spring up in this area from time to time. General O'Connor had a decision to make. Hopefully this would shield the Empire forces from the Axis warbirds. Hopefully. It would certainly impede such attacks. For as long as the storm lasted. Which could as likely be minutes as hours or days.

Two things were certain. His attack simply wasn't pushing the enemy back far enough fast enough to matter. Saving some of the lost men was better than losing them all. The signal he had sent was *sauve qui peut*, save what you can. All units were to head east, converging on his force and using the sand for cover. He had instructed his base area at Bagush to start broadcasting so as to provide a direction. He was having the Rhodesians east of the camp with its corps-sized garrison do the same. Everyone had been warned there was an active mobile corps there that had savaged a brigade-level assault earlier. The third aiming beacon was his own corps radio.

Not every vehicle had a radio. Not every one of those which did, would manage to use them as directional aids. Needs must. He had given the order. Breakout east by southeast. Good god what a balls-up!

0500 hours local; 0400 hours CET
12 September 1940
Three Crosses Camp

Titularrang-Oberst Klingenberg had gotten his column to the camp just ahead of this idiot sand storm. If the Reich was to be a world empire, its legions must learn to campaign in all climates, in all types of terrain. He accepted this in the abstract. He merely didn't wish it on himself now. He still had great deeds to accomplish, promotions and decorations to win.

He'd hoped for a chance to get a heads-up from the three Waffen SS officers supposedly at this barely constructed base. Two, Peiper and Mohnke, were absent to the north, undoubtably winning victories. That left Hauptsturmführer Max Seela, the engineering officer detailed here from Hausser's division, plus an NL 'major' who freely admitted his prior command experience ended at company command as an NCO under the Kaiser. He'd been SA but only a mid-rank NCO there. Major Gregor Voss was quite content to have Klingenberg in charge. Issue was, in charge of what?

The British attacks had ended hours ago. The few British scout cars to the east had seemed content to keep their distance. Voss had focused on entrenching, while seeing to the supply needs of the absent combat elements via truck convoys loosely guarded by some motorcycle troops.

The radio was near exploding with message traffic. Mostly in the clear because of time constraints and chaotic conditions. The British were apparently using the storm as cover for some type of disorganized mass breakout back to their own lines. Klingenberg knew better than to charge off into the teeth of this storm. For now he'd just see to refueling his vehicles. But let the storm just lift a bit, and many great things could be done. And he felt himself the man to do them.

0530 hours local; 0430 hours CET
12 September 1940
Hospital tent position

Klaus, and to a lesser extent Peiper, had by now some experience with these sand storms. You hunker down on the leeward side of a vehicle with a wet cloth over your face. You keep your breaths as shallow as possible to avoid breathing in too much of the sand, dust, and grit. You pray the storm isn't big enough, long enough to suffocate you or bury you alive. Mohnke was not experienced outside of camp, where there had been buildings or at least tents to hide in. His Battalion hadn't been sent on Strauss's desert missions. Besides, the man was barely functional and his Waffen SS ex-prisoners not much better.

The British were counterattacking out of the walls of flying dust. Or they were doing something. Truckloads of them would careen through the position at high speed. The drivers couldn't see. The trucks frequently lost traction. They were all headed more or less east, if east could be described as a hundred-and-twenty-degree arc around the true heading. If the combined German forces fired so much as a pistol at a truck, its occupants would spray fire in a three-hundred-and-sixty-degree arc.

Klaus and Peiper were being sensible about all this. Stay in the windbreak formed by their vehicles, parked cross-hatched in two lines running northeast to southwest. They'd deal with whatever British were still left once the storm broke. Mohnke, on the other hand, would lead parties out of the windbreak's relative safety, to brave the elements and battle truckloads of stalled or wrecked Indian Army men. The man seemed determined to win the Knight's Cross. He was coughing his lungs out so badly that he was bringing up blood, and still he kept at it. He was also killing off his own men, who were following him enthusiastically. Klaus decided he should be grateful the man was at least taking prisoners. Führer Göring had decreed such treatment even for the brown-skinned mercenaries the British had recruited in Asia. The Waffen SS had a bad reputation on prisoners, even white Nordic ones. Klaus had been warned by Strauss and Smith both. Told he would be held responsible if things were done in his presence, regardless of whether he had ordered it or not.

Suddenly there was a loud crash. Klaus forced himself to stand up and peer into the wind. A British truck had slammed into a parked French 'cavalry tank' at speed. Klaus led out a squad to take the survivors of the crash prisoner. The wounded who could walk were pointed at the hospital tent. The others were made as comfortable as they could be, which amounted mostly to providing water for a shirt over their faces as a breathing aid. He saw two walking wounded hobble towards the medical area, each holding up a more injured comrade on one side. They were mostly there when yet another truck growled into sight and ran them down. Mohnke led a squad out to deal with it. Klaus went back to hunkering down. Crazy land to fight over. Who would want it?

....
General Maletti had ordered his men to hunker down as soon as the wall of blowing sand hit. He and his Libyans knew the weather, the terrain, and how to survive both. The Germans intermingled with his troops mostly ignored the orders. Maletti had never believed this 'any order from a general' fantasy Rommel had given him. Germans! Hearts and heads of iron.

....
Ivan Gorlov had pulled his screen of fighting units back to Isaak's guns. The idea of fighting to the death against all odds had been burned out of him fighting the Reds in Ukraine. Higher orders were often absurd. You saved your men for another day, and if possible the equipment. When worse came to worst, you ran for it. At least the officers and key cadres did. The Reds would shoot all of them anyway. The helpless peasants in the ranks would just switch sides. More often than not his rankers had served in every army one time or another – Czarist, Kerensky, Constituent Assembly, White, Red, Green, Black. Flags came and went. The war goes on forever.

Isaak knew the game from the Habsburg side. Make a circle. Stand by your guns. Outrunning the Russians rarely worked. Having Ivan's troops fold in on his was second nature. The insane storm wasn't. He made a windbreak with the vehicles and rotated people on the guns. They couldn't last more than ten or fifteen minutes and still breathe. A few British tanks had rumbled up to try gun duels. These ended badly for the English. Vision was difficult in a tank normally, and near impossible in these conditions.

Suddenly a mass of vehicles appeared traveling in some approximation of eastwards. A few hit the German vehicle barrier, but most passed north of the circle. And ran into the huddled mass of British tanks. The combat that followed was more heard than seen. Four minutes of every weapons discharging at any target, real or imaginary, before quiet came. The flickering light of burning was vaguely seen through the clouds and the first vague lights of the coming dawn. Isaak was content to lob some eight eight shells in the right general direction and trust to fate. Two generated large secondary explosions, which was gratifying.

....

Erich von Manstein had ordered his units to hold in place pending a return to some level of visibility. Hausser's command reported compliance, as did the Corps troops. Von Thoma with the main element of Seventh Panzer admitted they had lost control of a number of subordinate units. Rommel's forward headquarters truck admitted they had lost track of their General. Typical of the man. The Luftwaffe agreed to hold flights until conditions improved. Their airfields were outside the storm, but there was no way to distinguish friend from foe in this mess.

0800 hours local; 0700 hours CET
12 September 1940
Comando Supremo, Palazzo Vidoni-Caffarelli, Corso Vittorio Emanuele II, Rome

Prince Umberto and de facto ruler Italo Balbo were having the ever-polite SS General Wolff to coffee. There had been a message from Berlin regarding the new fighting. The two Italians found this strange, as their own commanders in Libya had sent no report yet. Wolff had politely explained that the Deputy Chancellor's staff had their own liaison staff forward. The actual battle reports were still cryptic and confused. Mobile battle was frequently like that. However, General Rommel wished to give posthumous decoration to an Italian battery whose entire complement had died heroically at their guns repulsing many times their numbers of large heavy British tanks. He would write up individual decorations, but wanted to know if the revived Blue Max could be awarded to an entire unit as a permanent pennant – in the manner of traditional battle honors. These Militia artillerists had died in the manner of the Spartans at the Hot Gates. He was also asking that the unit be rebuilt and made part of his division. He was raving about the success of their Italian gun trucks.

Wolff was instructed to convey the issue for Italian input. Berlin saw the new decoration as one from the united Europe, which Heydrich was calling the European Union, and felt the decision should be jointly made. The two Italians were noncommittal on the decoration. The German obsession with these mystified them. They understood the propaganda aspects, but simply didn't see why it was worth the time of people at their level. If the Germans wanted a unit honor attached to the flag of the reconstituted unit, they had no objections in theory. The particular form of battle honor was strange but not a problem. Italy was getting the highest honor, not an inferior grade for lesser allies in the manner of a colonial force.

They found the European Union more worthy of their attention. What would this mean in terms of Italian sovereignty? Wolff was at his placating best. Europe had three powers. Germany, Italy, and Vichy would deal with each other as nations. A more formal structure was needed for the three powers to supervise everyone from Finland to Portugal to Turkey. The idea was a Union. Headquarters in Vienna, because it had so many underutilized government buildings. A German head. An Italian second. In time a French third. A League of Nations-type transnational staff to handle the production cartels, technical issues on such as safety standards for consumer goods, joint educational standards, and the like.

The Italians found the idea of Vienna repellent. They found Italy as deputy ruler of Europe fascinating. The idea of France being elevated was a dish of unique flavors to them. They didn't trust the French. They expected the French to try to usurp Italy's position as Europe's second power and the main colonial and naval member of the alliance. Plus, this was all happening with no notice as yet another strange diktat from Berlin.

Wolff had to keep gently reminding them that so far these were just proposals. Perhaps Italy would care to send a staff from the relevant ministries to Berlin to make sure the structures saw to Italy's interests as well as Germany's? The Italians kept the discussion at generalities. When Wolff took his leave, they spent the rest of the day discussing this together. If this could not be avoided, there were endless details that needed to be arranged to Italy's satisfaction. Heydrich was offering Italy a major hand in these decisions, but only at the price of accepting the basic concept. Could Italy avoid this? Should it be seen as trying to?

0900 hours local; 0800 hours CET
12 September 1940
Various places in the Western Desert

The khamseen had about blown itself out. These storms came and went with precious little warning. What remained was transient and localized, but visibility was still poor from the dust thrown off by thousands of vehicles and more thousands of exploding artillery rounds. General Maletti split his division in two. He left the bulk of it under his chief of staff to police up the battle area. Most of the enemy had fled, but enough men remained to be rounded up, enough equipment to salvage. He split off his original fast group plus the various stray Germans he had acquired, and started off for Rommel's last known position.

....

Oberst Wilhelm Josef Ritter von Thoma had wanted to command a Panzer Division since leading the ground component of the Condor Legion in Spain. Nominally he was Rommel's Ia, the operations officer. However, the higher levels of the Army officer corps was a small town gossip net for the military aristocracy. He'd been warned that Rommel left command to his Ia. Rommel was upfront somewhere doing something with his advance guard brigade or whatever he was calling it. No one knew where, and the supposed commander had not bothered to call in even a position reference. Fortunately, 1st Libyan Division and the advance camp command had both provided enough data to pinpoint the boss within a half dozen or so square kilometers.

Theoretically von Thoma was under orders from von Manstein to hold in place. Orders at his level of rank were an interpretive game, not a matter of blind obedience. As soon as the storm started to lift, von Thoma had Seventh Panzer subunits in motion. The trains were to rally on the advance camp, called Three Crosses on the staff maps for no reason anyone had told Seventh Panzer. A medical column with armed escort had been sent off to take charge of the captured British hospital with its recaptured German wounded. Some militia unit or other was there now

Von Thoma was in-gathering the rest of his combat elements, piece by piece, on a basic progress of northwest to southeast. He wouldn't find everyone. He expected to find most of his wayward lambs and lead them to refuel at this advance base. Von Manstein's staff had mentioned a large column of fuel trucks in progress there before the storm.

That left this British general, Beresford. Von Thoma felt badly for the man. He was a fellow professional done in by the strange nature of this theater of war. Motor vehicles, difficult navigation, and no fixed front lines would mean many people would get captured by accident as he had. There but for the grace of God might go any of us. Von Thoma got the man comfortably situated in his own headquarters, eating from his own mess. He'd try to have dinner with him to show honor and compassion, before shipping him on to some castle in Italy for confinement. The Rolls Royce he appropriated for himself. Rommel wasn't the type to use a limousine in a combat zone.

....
Klingenberg had been off like a shot once conditions improved. His fast group was fully motorized. He posted the reconnaissance battalion on his left in the direction the British were likely to be encountered. The rest of his force made up a second column to the right. The SA Major's forces had attacked the small British screen to the east of the camp, brushing it back to the southeast.

Klingenberg gave himself the objective of the British base camp at Bagush. His left was getting light contact from the stalled, disorganized British attack force. Klingenberg respected the British as foes, but felt they were slow in action. This sort of a war without front lines was perfect for an enterprising fellow such as himself.

....
Klaus had delegated the handover to the Seventh Panzer forces to Peiper. The SS Haptsturmführer had been through proper officer training. He knew how to do such things. Klaus got the rest of the unit in motion to where Rommel and Strauss were. Mohnke refused to surrender his command. Had a German medic give him a pain shot, plus a few ampules for 'later'. Klaus had never seen a man so driven. This must be what real officers behaved like. He filed the memory away for future reflection.

When he arrived at the guns, Rommel, Strauss, and Gorlov were all out leading different groups striking at the head and shaft of the stalled British. The British were trying to both defend and reverse direction at once, which for some reason was difficult for them. Klaus chalked that up as another manual to procure and have Greta help him master. Uncle Isaac took time from working his guns, to suggest that Klaus swing wide to the south and join up with some SS Standartenführer's column. Things were chaotic enough in this sector without trying to insert another battalion into action. Isaac knew Klaus's limits, and this sort of passage of the lines was well beyond him. Besides, the bulk of his unit was SS and SA. Isaac felt they would be more comfortable with their own then fighting beside Jews and Italians.

....
Peiper was at the tail end of Klaus's battalion. He was content to let the boy Major lead on. He'd come to respect the kid's combat instincts. Some people had them and some didn't. This boy from the Oder was one of those you followed. Promotions and decorations seemed to trail in his wake.

Mohnke had agreed with him, but the man almost seemed looking for a heroic grave. Peiper mentally shrugged. Mohnke would either snap out of it or buy a bullet. Either way, he'd do nasty things that could get sane people killed. Sane people like Peiper, who preferred life to glory right now.

Chapter 6

1200 hours local; 1100 hours CET
12 September 1940
Various places on the plateau east of the prior locations

Gunter Strauss was in his element.   This was Michael in 1918, mixed with the good times in Latvia in 1919. Open warfare with no fixed lines, where mobile elements like the ones he commanded could shoot up artillery and support units. The keys were artillery parks and headquarters. The big guns were the real killers on the battlefield. Taking them out with machine-guns and grenades cost ever so much less than counter-battery work. Headquarters were the nerve centers. Tommy Atkins was a tough fighter, but more ponderous than a German Fritz without clear lines of command. In small unit warfare British would defend well, but lacked the German skill in rapid warfare such as waged by storm units and motorized troops.

Right now his men were cleaning out the last holdouts of what had once been the headquarters of the British 16th Infantry Brigade. The document haul was fantastic. He'd already detailed off twenty of his men carrying British POW's to the rear. You packed them into captured trucks with German drivers, and followed the trucks with machine-gun-carrying autos. Prisoners who jumped off the trucks got shot up. It usually only took one or two to quiet the rest. The ones who really wanted to fight hadn't surrendered. Gunter wasn't stupid enough to chase small packs of fleeing enemies. Stick and run. Steal what equipment you can and torch the rest. Create chaos.

Gunter had thrown himself flat from the sound before he heard the shell explode. Old combat reflexes. Two British tanks firing at about 300 meters. Time to pull back again. The British never chased his pack of raiding wolves far. The ones who tried that in the beginning, tended not to come back. He always kept an overwatch reserve on these forays.

....

O'Connor was trying to bring order out of chaos. Mostly he was failing. The run-for-your-life orders had gotten under half his attack force out. They came out as platoons and companies with no higher organization. Many came out as lone vehicles. They plowed into the relief force and frequently tried to drive through, heading to the rear. Sometimes they were halted. Sometimes elements of the relief force bolted with them. He had to reverse this ponderous force while getting hammered from the front and jabbed from both sides. There was also a nasty dust cloud to his south, heading for his rear. If this was a race back to Bagush, he dare not lose it.

....

Klaus Steiner swept the horizons, looking for enemies as his command motored forward. The British were mostly to his left. The SS Brigade was supposed to be somewhere up ahead. He had his company with Kübelwagen in the lead. The SA company of Panhards were second, and the combined NL / SS unit under Peiper was bringing up the rear. He thanked the God whose existence the Party questioned, but whose Church his parents had dragged him to on occasional Sundays, for Joey's Naples trip and the resulting radios. He, Peiper, and the senior SA officer had send / receive sets. They could talk to each other. He could talk to some other senior officers, at least sometimes. It depended on range, which kept changing in a fast-moving situation.   But EVERY vehicle except the captured British ones had receivers, even the trucks. The unit could be made to maneuver by words sent as if by magic.

The original SA Sturmhauptführer had been invalided out with sandfly sickness. The Obersturmführer who succeeded him in command seemed ancient to Klaus. The man must have been at least sixty. He'd been a village blacksmith and was built like an anvil. A little less than medium height with massive muscles second only to Gunter's in the unit. He was not formally insubordinate to Klaus, but it was obvious he did not regard orders from a teenager as anything more than suggestions. This made things difficult, as his Panhard 178's had the only cannons along for this jaunt.

Klaus had quickly learned several things about this sort of warfare. No one could hit anything, firing while a vehicle was moving. Most found it hard enough to hit moving targets from a stable rest position. The second was that in the heat of the moment no one could identify vehicles worth a damn. Anything that was neither truck nor auto was a tank. Sometimes even those were confused with tanks. Everyone was obsessed with tanks. Klaus had been schooled by Gunter, Ivan, and Isaac that artillery was what killed you.

Right now he was facing half a dozen British tanks and a few more than that Bren gun carriers. The trick was to shoot the Bren gun vehicles and then scoot out of the way of the tanks. Enter Grandpa Lothar, the SA officer who wanted to shoot it out. Technical discussions of why his French 25mm shell wouldn't penetrate a British cruiser tank, except from the rear, bounced off his skull. He was an Aryan warrior and he had a cannon. He would fight, and no boy who never deserved his decorations would enforce such an order on him or his men.

So far the score was three Panhard's brewed up for zero British even disabled. Klaus was forced to again be a hero. He, Peiper, and Mohnke had chased off the Bren gun carriers and gotten in the rear of the tanks. Klaus had a Boys antitank rifle, 'liberated' from the earlier fights by the hospital tent. He had nine rounds. He thought he could make it work, but right now he was hiding beneath the wreck of his Kübelwagen. Machine-gun fire from a British tank had killed his driver and half destroyed the vehicle. It had also blown the remains of his precious lucky baseball cap off and cut three holes in the fabric of his blouse. All he'd lost of himself was skin.

The cruiser tank was closing in for the kill. Klaus let it come on while the near misses from the machine-gun kicked pebbles and sand in his face. He was abstractly aware his face was bleeding. What mattered that? He wanted a clear shot with this silly excuse for an anti-tank weapon. Suddenly the tank stopped. There was someone on its rear deck. Mohnke? How? Despite his wounds, there was the SS officer firing a pistol first at the head of the tank commander, then shooting through the open turret hatch and finally dropping a grenade down. The tank stopped moving. It was maybe 60 meters away. Klaus took his shot. Missed the front but clipped a track. Mohnke tried to drop another grenade but was shoved away, off the vehicle by a British crewman erupting out of the vehicle like an enraged bear. Klaus grabbed up a captured Bren gun and started shooting. He thought he'd hit the were-bear. The Britisher either fell or ducked back into his tank. It tried to move but the broken track made that ungainly and then impossible.

The tank was emitting smoke out of its viewport. However, someone inside was still keen to fire. Klaus rolled away as he saw the turret rotate towards his hiding place. A blast demolished the wrecked Kübelwagen. A side panel near to took his head off. It kissed him with its hot breath in passing. Before the tank could fire again, artillery shells started falling. Klaus crawled to the sidepanel and hid under it. He supposed he should have been afraid of dying. He could cope with that. He was a patriot and soldier doing his national and racial duty. But what would become of poor Greta? Of his unit? The rain of artillery shells continued.

1215 hours local; 1115 hours CET
12 September 1940
Advance headquarters, Italo-German Panzer Army, Sollum, formerly British and now Italian Egypt

General Carlo Geloso was composing his report for Rome. His German 'subordinates' had been remiss in making timely reports. He had made preparations to overcome this. He had liaison officers assigned to most German headquarters down to brigade or regimental level. Sadly, he had not included the silly militia brigade, which had ended up a key component of the fighting. He would remedy that immediately.

His army had won the battle. This was clear from the reports from his forward units outside the British fortress at Mersa Matruh. There were explosions as the British were dynamiting what could not be carried off. They would not destroy their own base camp unless they were retreating. As this position had not even been attacked, the retreat must have been caused by events further south on the plateau. The fragmentary reports from von Manstein's various units, plus 1st Libyan Division, painted a consistent picture. Thousands of prisoners taken. Hundreds of vehicles seized or destroyed. No artillery captured, which was strange. A good number of those nasty British heavy tanks out of action. The Seventh Panzer Division had even captured a divisional general. It was a victory. He would need a few days for a detailed picture, but Rome could be told of this triumph of Italian arms. How much of the deserved credit should go to the Germans, he would leave to higher authorities to debate. His account would be honest. The Libyan division had done quite well, but it was mostly a German victory. Rommel and this Oberst Strauss.

Now was the time to ask for more resources. He needed more sappers, to dismantle the British minefields and get the small port at Mersa Matruh back in operation. The bulk of the Italian army was in garrison back home. Surely half a dozen combat engineer battalions could be spared, for the only war Italy was fighting? Then again, he'd been making the same argument for weeks now – with no success.

1230 hours local; 1130 CET
12 September 1940

Plateau battlefield, KG Steiner

The British had left. Half a dozen more were prisoners, and the rest had withdrawn north and northeast. The artillery fire had ceased as suddenly as it started. Klaus found artillery on a battlefield mystifying. It would descend out of nothing, and vanish the same way. Seemed as if you never would know why. Had the batteries been forced to withdraw? Was ammunition low? He wearily shook his head. Adult life seemed to include a lot of mysteries.

An SS column had arrived. A mixed-arms Battalion Kampfgruppe escorting a supply convoy and a large medical detachment. It was searching for the SS fast group, and had stumbled into Klaus's engagement. Their arrival was heralded by a large dust cloud growing quickly nearer. Had this provoked the British retreat? Again, Klaus was sadly certain he would never know. Things just happened in battle. Hell, he was the hero of Malta because, lost in midair, he had followed a British plane with a burning engine to an airfield. At that point all Klaus had cared about was not ditching in water and drowning them all.

The medical detachment had a real doctor, not just a hospital orderly. The man tried to see to Klaus's wounds first. Klaus was a field officer and rank had its privileges. Klaus ordered him to see to the seriously wounded first, and rank be damned. Led the man over to the near-dead Mohnke. As the doctor worked on him, Klaus sent out parties to bring in the injured, even the British ones. Führer Göring had mandated good treatment to these foes. He also scribbled a fast note to be taken back with Mohnke, saying a commendation and write-up for an Iron Cross would follow. That way, if anything happened to both Klaus and Peiper, there would be a paper trail to start an inquiry. Mohnke might have fucked up his initial battle, but he had fought like a hero the next two times. Uncle Isaac had instilled in Klaus the need to reward people who did especially well. Said the rankers noticed this. Said it made for better morale under fire. That the natural tendency was for people to curl up at the bottom of trenches and pray they would live. They had to see that sticking their necks out was noticed and honored.

Klaus had no idea how advance medical detachments worked. The doctor seemed fast, appeared competent. He told Klaus that Mohnke would live. The available ambulances were filled with the most serious cases. The rest went into two trucks. Klaus detached a Kübelwagen and four motorcyclists as escorts. There were stray British all over the rear. Best to be careful.

With those duties taken care of, Klaus allowed himself to remember that he had to deal with his real problem. He motioned half a dozen of his 'old Malta hands' to follow him. Told them to grab MG-34's or Bren guns. They were clueless as to why, but used to obeying him. He marched himself up to where Grandpa was directing his men in salvaging ammo and useful parts from the five wrecked Panhards. Klaus drew himself up to his full, if short, height and told the old SA officer, "You and I need to have a talk. I gave you an order to avoid combat with the British tanks. You disobeyed. Five lost armored cars, plus our other losses because you don't know how to obey orders!" Klaus was aware he had stuttered a bit and his voice broke twice. This happened when he got angry. He was experienced enough to no longer be embarrassed. He was a hero officer, and his defects were just part of the baggage he carried in life.

The large bear of a man looked down his nose at Klaus and laughed at him. "Go away, you stupid child. Your protector Strauss isn't here to back up your let's-pretend officer's rank tabs. Do you take time out from fucking your Kike cunt to bare your ass to him, or is it that you just suck his cock? Stabschef SA Lutze ran your kind of faggot out of the SA when they bumped off that traitor Röhm and his gang of drag queens. Even those junkie degenerates didn't pollute their race with Jews. I'll be reporting on what your gang does, back to Lutze's office in Berlin. You'll be in Dachau for race defilement within a month you worthless little runt … "

Grandpa pulled up short in his rant. He was staring down the barrels of six light automatic weapons wielded by people who looked forward to an order to fire, to the SA officer making a move that would justify gunning him down. He started to bark orders to his guys to counter, but before they could scramble back to their Panhards, one of Klaus's guys loosed half a clip from his Bren gun. It was sprayed over everyone's heads, but not by much. The SA men froze in place. Message received.

Klaus was not quite pointing his own Bren gun at the man, but it wasn't far off a direct aim either. He simply shook his head and laughed at the man. "Everything that happens here is within the knowledge of the Reichsführer SS. He personally approved my promotions and decorations. Back when our new Führer Göring was Air Minister he famously said of his ministry 'I decide who is a Jew here'." Klaus had heard the tale from Strauss, who had gotten it from Schellenberg explaining the whole situation. "NL is the Reichsführer's creation. So is who we enlist, where we go, how we do it. We are his personal creation. Whereas you are just a pathetic old man in a service that was a fossilized shadow of its once great self until our Reichsführer chose to give you some life again. Your Lutze is just a lesser minion of our patron. Complain as you choose. But you'll do it elsewhere. You are relieved for insubordination." Klaus pointed at the next most senior SA junior officer, told him he was in charge. He was looking around for a motorcycle with sidecar, to dump this worthless clown back on Gunter, when the man exploded with rage.

"Fuck you, Jew-lover! Obergruppenführer Lutze is the man who gave me this command, and he's the only one who can take it away." The man was beyond reason with anger and disdain. He was nerving himself to charge the Bren gun. He respected the weapon, but not the man-child wielding it.

And Peiper came running over. Peiper was a trained officer, not a jumped-up HJ. As such, he had a trained command voice. He let out a bellow of, "Halt right there!" He threw himself between Klaus and the advancing SA officer. He may have lacked the physical strength to subdue the man. He straight-armed him to the chest, halting the rush and allowing the habit of obedience to overcome foaming rage. "This is mutiny, you fool. So far all you have been is relieved. Two more steps and you are dead. Get in the sidecar and go back to Strauss. Get briefed by an old SA comrade on why it wouldn't be healthy to be sending such messages to Berlin. Heydrich was accused of Jew blood, you may recall. Want to guess what happened to his accusers since he came to power?" He let the bear-sized man start to come to his senses, begin to realize just whose soup he was proposing to piss in. "Cross the Reichsführer at your peril. He is not a forgiving man. He rescued me from the death cells.

Thousands of others were simply liquidated. I'm still plugged into the SS gossip net. He's executing Gauleiters. What are you to him, except an inconvenient parcel of pork roast?" Peiper quickly barked an order. The dazed SA officer was sat down into a motorcycle sidecar and driven off by one of Peiper's young former HJ's.

Klaus told the remaining SA they were under Peiper's command until further instructions. He told Peiper that to even out the unit sizes, he would personally take Peiper's motorcyclists and half the SS infantry. Klaus wasn't sure putting all the armored vehicles under Peiper was the best possible choice. He was certain the newly promoted SA Sturmführer would swallow Peiper's orders better than Klaus's. He was even more sure Peiper would obey him. The man was used to being commanded by NL.

Klaus went to the next item on his checklist. It was time to get moving and get back in the war. Uncle Ivan had taught him this mental system. Arrange what needed to be done in order of importance. If you weren't sure, guess. There was never enough time in battle so be sure the most important things got done, even if it meant the bottom ones just never got dealt with. Which was part of why units in action degraded step by step to uselessness. Ivan had commanded a brigade for a while out on the steppe, fighting the damned Reds. He KNEW!
....
SS Doctor Ernst-Gunther Schenck would have preferred to have remained in the Dachau medical detachment, running his vast and varied herb garden. He had accepted his transfer to Hausser's division in Afrika because this was wartime, because the SS obeyed orders. They weren't a mutinous street gang like the SA had been.

He had silently taken in what had happened. None of this would ever be put by him into a written report. But the verbal accounts would spread throughout the Waffen SS division, back up to Uncle Paul Hausser and his staff. This NL brigade had insanely deep connections in Berlin. Handle them as if they were made of poison. Gossip about them reaching the wrong ears could be fatal.

1400 hours local; 1300 hours CET
12 September 1940
Von Manstein's command vehicle, still stalled in traffic but some kilometers to the east-south-east of the last time we were here

The battle situation was continuing to clarify. The British were clearly in retreat after losing last night's battle. Whether measured by prisoners taken or terrain seized, the results were clear if not yet completely tallied. Where the Corps's forces were was a bit more complex. Hausser's division was mostly enroute to the Three Crosses camp. He had the equivalent of a regimental Kampfgruppe there already. He had several mixed arms battalion Kampfgruppen covering supply convoys heading east, trying to find his fast group … which had vanished. It was somewhere east or northeast of the Three Crosses. Radio traffic confirmed this. Positions given were all relative to each other. The terrain seemed to have no features to serve as guides. Trailing in this Kampfgruppe's wake were Strauss's brigade, or at least most of it. Also Rommel's reinforced advance group and Maletti's fast group. The bulk of 1st Libyan was still cleaning up the battlefield, helped by stray elements from von Thoma and

Hausser. Von Thoma's main force had relieved Rommel and Strauss opposite the main British force. It was conducting a slow advance against what seemed to be a corps-sized force.

Elsewhere, the Mersa Matruh fortress was abandoned according to the Italians. They had gotten a foot path through the minefields, but estimated two days to clear the road and camp for vehicle convoys. This in turn meant that two British brigades had gotten away clean. The Bagush camp must still be garrisoned by someone. The Luftwaffe was reporting flak from there. Orders of magnitude less than before, but still worrisome. The road back from Bagush to Alexandria had been bumper-to-bumper traffic. The air units had had a field day bombing and strafing.

He instructed his Ia to have someone prepare a report for Geloso outlining all this, with a copy to Berlin. He chuckled to himself at that. Here he was a man of the military aristocracy, and his report would go neither to OKH nor the War Ministry. Instead it would go to Heydrich, in theory a glorified police clerk, and in practice the ruler of Germany. However, unlike his late unlamented predecessor Adolph the Deceased, this top dog let professionals do their work without constant micromanagement.

1500 Hours local; 1400 hours CET
12 September 1940
General O'Connor's command vehicle, east of the original battlefield and rapidly being pocketed from the south by the various Axis advance and fast elements

The situation was getting clearly out of hand. He'd saved a portion of 4th Indian, but was now at risk of losing the bulk of the Western Desert group. He had German light units to the north, and large German units to his south and perhaps southeast as well. He was being attacked by a corps-sized force in front. The two brigades coming out of Mersa Matruh were one long traffic jam leading back to Bagush. Their lead elements were in the camp refueling. The camp itself was in the process of trying to move itself back. Back to where? London was adamant that it could not retreat. Cairo was trying to split the difference, and directing him to an imaginary position at Fuka. He signaled receipt of message and instructed his staff to ignore it. He was quite prepared to be sacked, but he was going to save as many men as he could. If he couldn't hold a prepared position at Bagush, how on earth was he to create one on the bounce at Fuka?

As is, Bagush was shaping up as a first-class disaster. The nominal defenders were a brigade of 6th Australian Division, plus some pieces of a second brigade, that had been deploying before this was reversed by the Australian C-in-C back in Palestine. Both Australian generals, brigade and corps alike, were giving very equivocal answers on whether their troops would make any serious attempt to defend the camp. Yet it would be many hours before the two brigades withdrawing from Mersa Matruh would be untangled enough to assume the burden. Lovely.

The air situation was worse. The two enemy air forces had come out in strength. Turned the motorway and Barrel Track back to Alamein both into giant truck-wrecking yards. What remained of the RAF had come forth to battle. Came in the small numbers they had, flying planes mostly obsolescent and obsolete. The fighters had shown near-suicidal bravery trying to protect the poor lads on the highway. The end result was that fighter strength in Egypt was down to 3 Hurricanes, 5 Gladiators, and a lone Hawker Demon. This presumed those nine could be gotten back in flying shape by dawn. It didn't take a genius to surmise that by the end of tomorrow the probable strength of Fighter Command would be zero. Oh, they could try using Blenheim's as heavy fighters, but that was suicide.

The bombers had suffered heavy losses in order to drop bombs all over the plateau. O'Connor hoped they had killed some Germans. At least fourteen times they had hit British units instead. O'Connor appreciated the difficulty of distinguishing friend from foe in a confused battle of maneuver; that didn't help the situation. His men were now shooting at everything they saw in the sky. He had sadly been able to confirm three British planes shot down by his chaps. He was an experienced enough Army man to know that this meant more incidents had been hushed up at company and battalion levels.

This whole idea of fighting in front of the Alamein position was insane. He was getting his forces back there, and damn the consequences to his own career.

1700 hours local; 1600 hours CET
12 September 1940
In O'Connor's rear and half a kilometer south of the outer defenses of the Bagush Box

Klaus had caught up with the main SS force under Standartenführer Klingenberg. The superior officer had corrected Klaus and said he was an Oberst, which made no sense to Klaus as Oberst was an Army and NL rank, not SS. Klaus was quite sure, but not about to correct the man. It turned out that while Klingenberg and Peiper didn't personally know each other, they had mutual friends among the SS officer corps.

The Oberst outlined the battle plan. He was going to break into the British camp. He would take the former members of Mohnke's battalion back into his own force to give himself another company of infantry, even if it was pure infantry without the usual heavy weapons support. He wanted to take Peiper to command them. Peiper politely demurred. His original lads needed the commander they were familiar with. The SA men in the Panhards responded better to an SS commander than a somewhat youthful NL officer. Klingenberg didn't make an issue of it. Klaus filed this away for reflection. Officers could debate orders. It wasn't iron discipline as he'd learned it in the HJ.

The mission for Klaus and Peiper was to loop around the British position and cut the coast road. Interdict as best they could, but don't risk getting overrun. Interdiction by fire was better than nothing, and preserving the force for the pursuit was the highest priority. It was going to be a race to the British positions at Alamein. That was 130 kilometers away, a day's hard push. Klingenberg saw a chance to unravel the entire British position in Egypt. Klaus was awed to be deemed worthy to take part in this. As he took off with his guys, the Oberst beckoned Peiper back for a small chat. Told Klaus he'd send Peiper along soon.

....

Klingenberg waited till the callow youth with the Major's tabs had departed, then asked Peiper, "Can he actually do the job? I can give you written authority to relieve him."

Peiper smiled and shook his head. "He doesn't look old enough to command a machine-gun section, but I've seen him in action. He's a natural, with the devil's own luck. Oh yes, and a pet of the Reichsführer's. So save the note. He knows he lacks real training. He takes my advice well enough on the technical aspects. Think of me as his Ia. If the job can be done by a unit this small, we'll do it. Either way, it is my unit now and I'd rather stay with it."

"So you're leaving the SS?" Klingenberg couldn't believe anyone would do that.

"No. The NL as Heydrich has decreed it is an amalgam of new militia, SS, SA, Heer, and Luftwaffe. We all keep our service uniform and rank but work jointly. It *is* weird, but at least in this brigade it works. They were heroes on Malta and so far in Afrika. I'm betting they will also be heroes when we cross Suez into Asia."

Klingenberg felt he had wasted enough time on personnel matters. Peiper jumped into his touring car and had his driver floor it to catch up with his unit, with what he saw as his future destiny. As he did so, he was forced to a temporary halt. Klaus's detached mortars, the ones Peiper had last seen being added to his force back at the camp, had caught up. He left his car to take command of them. They knew him by face, and had no difficulty following behind him to their Major. Peiper decided it was a good omen.

1830 hours local; 1730 hours CET
12 September 1940
250 meters south of the Bagush-to-Alamein Barrel Track

Klaus had been told to choke off the coast road. No one had mentioned that there was a second road a bit inland. It seemed marked by metal barrels. Wall to wall flows of vehicles were attempting to drive east on this track. Klaus and his men were shooting them up. Many responded by fleeing in their vehicles towards the coast. Many others abandoned their shot-up trucks or autos and fled on foot.

Klaus reported the new situation to the Oberst. He also reported that he was starting to run low on ammunition, especially for the small cannons in the Panhards. Absent a supply convoy, Klaus would have to stop sometime soon and pull back. The Oberst heard him out, but made no promises. Peiper and the SA men promised to be more selective in their targeting, but they were still burning precious shells.

1930 hours local; 1830 hours CET
12 September 1940

General O'Connor's headquarters van, west south west of Bagush Box and by now loosely surrounded

The sun had just gone down. O'Connor's problems were if anything worse. The camp was under attack by what the senior Australian general present asserted was a Panzer division with support of corps-level artillery. O'Connor was extremely uncertain how whole reinforced Panzer divisions seemed to transport themselves around the battlefield as if by magic. London's intel was usually fairly accurate, and claimed only two Panzer divisions plus elements of a third. Yet he had one pressing him from the west, a second inside the camp wire, and supposedly the main vanguard of a third attacking the Barrel Track. London's 'man in Berlin' had been spot-on for Malta and after. Yet the armored car screen to the southwest reported what seemed to be a second Panzer corps reinforcing the original one at the camp where the assault had failed. A corps was at least two divisions. Two plus two makes four and three more makes seven, which is more than twice what was supposed to be present. It was also beyond what the Navy boffins asserted the Libyan ports could support, given the number of Italians and the huge combined Axis air strength.

London regarded Commonwealth divisions as if they were British, in adding up in-theater strengths. A different bureaucracy in London was solicitous of Commonwealth sovereignty, and granted their expeditionary forces rights of appeal on orders as if they were fully independent allies like the Belgians had been in Flanders. The Australian general was standing on this special status. Asserted he had been left to defend a large camp with a brigade against a division. Given no tanks and insufficient artillery to defeat a reinforced Panzer division. He refused to listen to a British version of 'reason'. He was pulling his people out. Informing O'Connor as a courtesy. The word Gallipoli came up repeatedly in the message exchange.

O'Connor was able to appeal to the man's sense of Empire loyalty and get him to promise to try to clear the Barrel Track on his way out. O'Connor was aware that the Australian probably said yes because given the positioning of his men, it was the best way out.

The Australian's usurpation of the chain of command settled other things. O'Connor messaged the camp HQ to order *sauve qui peut*. There was simply no longer a possibility of an organized evacuation. He separately notified the two brigades from Mersa Matruh that they were to proceed straight on to Alamein, even if it meant leaving the road to find a path. He begged Cairo to send forward tanker trucks to meet these two brigades, and coordinate link-up without involving him, as he might be out of radio contact.

Finally, he started rapidly reorienting his own force due east. With any luck he could pass south of the Panzer division attacking the Barrel Track, through its soft administrative rear areas. German tank strength must have some upper limit. If the tanks were at the road, perhaps all he faced would be service forces. Perhaps. Hopefully. This is what his planning was reduced to. What on Earth had London been thinking, leaving him this far forward for this long?

2000 hours local; 1900 hours CET

12 September 1940
Bagush Headquarters

'Oberst' Klingenberg had just watched the SS flag being run up the flagpole. This had, if anything, gone too easily. The outer perimeter collapsed as if made of wet cardboard. There had been a few sharp engagements with Australian troops. Tough fighters those. For the rest, it had been rounding up prisoners from British service and administrative troops. He'd captured several thousand of these and at least a division's worth of equipment. Despite last-minute British attempts at fire and demolition, he'd recovered enough supplies for a corps. Maybe for an army. He had also shot his bolt. The northern third of the camp, however, was still British and held in strength. Good troops that refused to be spooked by a few obsolete tanks and a handful of howitzers. He was up against at least a brigade, deployed by good professional officers who knew their business. Thankfully these British seemed most uninterested in pushing him back out. In turn he was content to let them leave at their own pace. For now.

He had radioed Rommel for support. Rommel, it turned out, had his own agenda and was dragging the Italian Maletti with him. Klingenberg was not surprised. Uncle Paul had warned him about Rommel's attitude problems with other people's agendas. Von Thoma and Hausser had been more accommodating, but both stressed they were at least a day out. So it was hang on and hope for the best. Klingenberg had faith in his men, more so in his own talents. The British as a whole hadn't impressed him as being quick off the mark.

2030 hours local; 1930 hours CET
12 September 1940
Kampfgruppe Steiner fighting position, south of the Barrel Track and two kilometers east of the Bagush Box

Major Klaus Steiner decided he owed Gregor a good bottle of something strong. Man had put together a small supply convoy for Klaus. A fuel truck, a truckload of machine-gun and Bren gun ammo. A second truck of generalized supplies including some boxes of illumination rounds for the mortars. Someone had been scavenging what the British had abandoned on their retreat after attacking the base. Even some urns of coffee and large jugs of mildly chlorinated water. Alas, no more cannon rounds. Also half a dozen motorcycles with light machine-gunners in the sidecar.

The Kampfgruppe needed it all. It was getting hammered by an organized attack force out of the Bagush camp. No artillery or tanks, thank God, but accurate mortar fire, good machine-gun covering fire, and well-trained infantry that came forward in rushes.

The long 'training sessions' with Greta and the manuals were paying off. The immediate rewards were obvious to any teenage male. That was for late night in their tent. Right now he was a Battalion commander, not a sex-obsessed manchild. The manuals were quite clear that mobile forces should use their mobility to avoid getting pinned down in close-in dismounted action. Klaus was not about to let these attackers get into range for grenades and a final rush. His orders specifically tasked him to avoid losing his unit, all three weak companies of it. So he was using mobility to keep leap-frogging back a few hundred meters. Half the force would move, get into position, and then cover the other half while it pulled back to join them.

The problem was the SA idiots. They would refuse to move at all if sent first, and hold their positions too long if left with the rear guard. Unless Klaus or Peiper personally kicked ass, no one else would move when the SA balked. It had become 'a matter of honor'. Peiper's cadres were SA also, and not willing to leave their fellow servicemen hanging. Klaus's Betar were not about to live down to being cowardly Jews in the eyes of these Brownshirts. He was taking avoidable losses to accomplish nothing but an extra few minutes delay. He made himself a promise. When this combat was over, he was sending to the rear every remaining SA officer and senior sergeant. If he had to cross-mix the vehicle crews between the Panhard units and Peiper's boys, so be it. If Gunter didn't like it … Klaus caught himself and laughed. The idea that he could stand chest to chest with Gunter like a schoolyard fight was laughable. He guessed he was starting to get comfortable with the idea of actually being a commander.

2130 hours local; 2030 hours CET
12 September 1940
O'Connor's command vehicle, some miles to the east of the last segment we visited them

The Australians claimed they had tried. They were patting themselves on the back for driving this Panzer division back a mile or so. Now they were veering off northeast of the Barrel Track. They felt they had done their duty and now must save themselves. The two brigades still at Bagush had blunted the attack of that Panzer division, but were starting to pull out. They said they would try to destroy stores and equipment that couldn't be moved. Their priority would be using night to get their units back to Alamein through the endless wrecked and abandoned vehicles on the coast road. They were not optimistic.

O'Connor had wasted forty minutes in a spitting fight with London as relayed through Cairo. The now-awakened War Cabinet could not grasp the speed of modern warfare. Their minds were still in 1917, when four miles was an excellent day's advance. Motorized units could move that far in ten minutes. He'd been cajoled with fancy words and threatened with the sack. Neither moved him an inch. If Cairo wanted to send a replacement forward, let them do so.

London's next ploy was to promote Creagh, GOC 7th Armored, to succeed him. Creagh's reply was priceless. He refused the new command unless formally ordered to take it. He also announced that he would do exactly the same thing. Sauve qui peut. Bagush was lost. Losing Western Desert Force as well was the same sort of half-measures blundering that had plagued Britain since Hitler's rise. Creagh's comments were NOT well received in London. O'Connor had been ordered to relieve him, which he refused to do until everyone was back behind the Alamein lines, after which he would accompany Creagh into ignominy and retirement.

The Force was facing probes from German mixed combat groups to their south and southeast.

Nothing for it but to push past the rear areas of the division the Australians had been fighting. O'Connor dreaded another night battle, with all the ensuing chaos; but needs must.

2300 hours local; 2200 hours CET
12 September 1940
Three Crosses Camp

Fräulein Greta was taking a break from the endless labor details Gregor kept everyone jumping with. He'd stood down the women about 20 minutes ago. Told them to take a light supper and a nap. He'd started rotating people this way a few hours back, and now it was their turn. So she and Naiomi had the Betar girls at a table sipping watered wine and trying to relax enough to fall asleep.

She only noticed Mary Collins come up because two of the girls turned their heads. Turning in her own chair, Greta saw the Asian woman waiting for permission to speak. Wondering what the problem was, Greta motioned for Mary to talk. "Frau Steiner, I would like to talk with you about what happens when the war ends."

Frau Steiner? "It is Fräulein Greta. Klaus and I aren't married."

The Asian woman gave a sad smile. "I'm Mary Collins, but my Irishman never formally married me. Concubine becomes wife in an everyday sense. Until your Major gets a formal wife, to me and the world you are Frau Steiner. It's the way the world works." She saw Greta's confusion, but kept talking. It was obvious Mary had rehearsed this speech and was trying to get it all out properly, that this was something quite important to her. "You hired me on Malta because your skills don't include cooking. Mine do. Your man is Catholic so your household will be Catholic, any children will be as well. I cooked for a Catholic man and raised our children in his Church. I learned Irish and British cooking styles. I can learn German cooking as well. Learn his holiday dishes, what Saint's Days he celebrates, his regional cooking styles. I am asking you to consider me remaining as your cook after the fighting ends. As long as my children are properly fed and clothed, I wouldn't need much in salary. Just a little pocket money plus something to send home to my father every month for his debts, for his old age. What are tiny sums to you, ease the life of a poor man in Bengal more than you will ever be aware. Poor means different things in Asia than Europe." Mary looked frightened, but also glad she had managed to get the entire speech out to an officer's lady. Mary's German language skills were still a work in progress.

Wife? In a strange sense Greta could cope with wife better than 'after the war'. She knew she was more than a mere whore. Wife? Mistress? The word concubine was strange to her outside of Bible stories, but maybe it fit. She'd ask her aunt when the civilians caught up with the unit in Egypt or Palestine. She and Klaus never spoke of 'after'. The war just was. They just were. You didn't think of someday when any day, any hour you could die or be sent to different places or ... or far too many things, most of them unpleasant to say the least. "I will ask my man." Mary stammered thanks and backed away quickly.

The Betar girls focused on a different matter. "Catholic?" Greta shrugged. She'd never asked and he never mentioned, yet somehow this Mary Collins knew. Naiomi as usual spoke for the platoon. "So you convert. So you baptize your children. Your blood is still Jewish, and so will theirs be."

Children! Greta knew how babies came, but at war you lived in the moment. Still, if she wasn't pregnant now, she would at some point be with child. Would Klaus still keep her? Why was life so complicated? Naiomi caught her confusion, and sent one of the ladies for brandy to get the quite startled Greta to sleep. Gregor had only allotted two hours for a nap. Best to make use of it.

 0015 hours local; 2315 hours CET
13 September / 12 September 1940
KG Steiner's position, 2 km south south west of the Barrel Track

In all his young life, Klaus had never heard this many vehicles at once. He couldn't exactly see them. The few illumination rounds he had risked, had been met with so much return fire that he didn't repeat the mistake. Still, he was able to confirm to Rommel and the other generals that the British Army was retiring south of him in a huge mass. His small force was a tiny German island in a sea of enemies. His possible salvation was that they were probably too preoccupied with retreat to waste the time exterminating an irritation as small as this Kampfgruppe.

The Panzer Army's advance had been more vehicles than this. Klaus was objectively aware of that; but he hadn't seen them all, or even most of them. Still less heard the growl of this many engines laboring at once.

He'd used the quiet time to load his wounded onto trucks. Klingenberg had taken a large medical complex in the British camp. Enough personnel had remained behind to see to the British wounded and sick. His couple of dozen injured men would get top notch care, or so he'd been told by radio. In reverse, a team of artillery and Luftwaffe forward observers had arrived to be in position for morning.

The observers were junior to him in rank, but five to ten years older. They regarded the situation as insane. There were still British up at the Barrel Track. There was a large organized British corps retreating roughly a kilometer to the south, being harried by Rommel's advance forces. This small battalion with nothing more in firepower than a few mortars was standing its ground. They politely asked the Major why. He was young. Perhaps he did not see the danger. They noticed the Iron Cross he wore, and feared he was a glory-hound chasing more decorations.

Klaus's answer wasn't at all about glory. It was duty. His superiors knew the situation and told him to remain. He told the forward observers they were free to leave. He offered written orders to the rear if that was what they wanted. He spoke loudly, telling his men he'd do the same for any of them who wanted to withdraw back to Bagush. He was staying. It was his duty to the Reich. There were perhaps a hundred men willing to be the third man who asked. There were twenty who would have been the second. No one was willing to be first. Klaus knew he would reflect on this someday, when things were calm again. He could ask Isaac and Ivan. Gunter still frightened him on these things. He had no idea that hundreds of men were looking on him as a heroic, noble figure. He was just Klaus, a young man who was no longer too poor to have coffee every morning. Seven years of the Third Reich had burned patriotism into even the least likely people.

0200 hours local; 0100 hours CET
13 September 1940
15 miles in advance of the El Alamein lines, along the coast highway

Lieutenant Commander James Money-Penny had wisely kept a party with the three needed languages monitoring signals traffic. He lacked the fine details of the evolving debacle. His men could only sample the message traffic, and then only copy down messages sent in clear. It didn't matter. The outline was clear. Half a division of Australians, plus minor bits of this and that, were going overland between the two roads … and running out of fuel.

He'd assembled a small relief column. Six fuel trucks and three wreckers. He didn't wait on permission. That wasn't his way. He simply informed the Fleming brothers, and left dealing with the office wallahs to them. Money-Penny had the social skills to do their work. It merely bored him, and he hated to be bored unless well paid to do so.

Getting onto the Australian command frequency was ever so easy. Establishing his bona fides was somewhat more difficult. Money-Penny was reduced to social name-dropping from prior excursions in the East Indies and New Guinea. Apparently one of the fifteen names he dropped registered with someone. He'd been met by a forward patrol, escorted to headquarters, and grilled on the name. Money-Penny's memory for people wasn't quite photographic, but it approached those levels. He could describe personal tic's, favorite cigar or whiskey, and taste in bints, on people he'd known for a few days a decade back if the man had seemed important.

The Australians were grateful for what Money-Penny was offering. Not just the fuel and mechanical help. The commando officer had dropped men with red blackout lanterns every few hundred yards, back to a small gap in the minefields in front of 6th Commando Division. No need to say the gap was there because Cairo had shorted the Commandos on mines. Things were in short supply, and the former regulars from Malta in the 7th Division that covered the coastal route were seen to first. As is, 6th was treated better than the two Jewish Brigades that made up the 8th Division. It wasn't even conscious with the staff types. They just saw to their own first and the Sheenies last. Their minds were still stuck in peacetime class prejudices. What a war!

0400 hours local; 0300 hours CET
13 September 1940
General O'Connor's command caravan, 25 miles west of the Alamein lines

The tap on his shoulder awakened him. General O'Connor had been dozing in the bouncing Leyland

Retriever that was his command vehicle. After nearly two days without anything more than cat-naps, bad coffee, and stay-awake pills, he would drift off whenever not needed to make decisions. Right now the decisions were being made by majors and captains. Between night-time darkness and exhaustion, all the decisions were being made at battalion level and below. No visibility, no terrain or tactical intelligence, and severely degraded reaction times as sleep-deprived troops struggled to cope with the tempo of round-the-clock action.

The situation hadn't changed since his eyes had betrayed him by closing some twenty minutes ago. The Australians had been sent help by some commando unit from 6th Division. He would have his aides track down this Money-Penny and give him a gallon of good Scotch for using initiative. He seemed the only one awake in the whole of Alamein Force. Cunningham had been brought up from Kenya to run this. Wavell had too much to do as a theater commander to also run a field corps. Kenya and its settlers were a backwater of the empire known mostly for wild parties and flagrant adultery. Both seemed to stem mostly from boredom. Cunningham was well regarded in Army circles, but he and his staff seemed to have imported Kenyan sloth with them. Not that Cairo needed much help in that direction.

O'Connor's staff wasn't really sure which division sector they were going to run into. Neither corps HQ nor any of the three divisions had come up with helpful replies. No one except this Money-Penny, who worked for some other naval type named Fleming, had done the obvious – sending out a patrol to establish contact. Cairo had been even more unhelpful. The key men all seemed to work banker's hours. The overnight staff seemed to be low-ranking Territorials who knew how to do nothing beyond making placating noises.

The Panzer division whose rear he was moving through seemed to have pulled in their supply trains to Bagush. The combat element seemed preoccupied with chasing the Australians. All Western Desert Force had to contend with was a reserve regiment centered on the vicinity of the Barrel Track. The other Panzer division was nipping at the heels of the two brigades from Mersa Matruh, both of whom were claiming their rear guards were hard pressed. That left the Panzer force to his south and southeast. O'Connor's right flank was skirmishing with them, but the main force seemed to be racing him to Alamein. It was a race he could not afford to lose.

0515 hours local; 0415 CET
13 September 1940
Kampfgruppe Strauss, half a kilometer from the advanced outposts of British 8th Division, Alamein Lines

Oberst Gunter Strauss wanted to be sure he understood precisely before he sent the radio signal. "Tell me again, guys. You're sure?"

The oldest of the Betar involved, a Leutnant of twenty-four, spoke for the platoon. "It was dark. They couldn't see our uniforms. You had us forward on scout, observing. The patrol was talking Yiddish. Litvak dialect, but Yiddish. I've got a Litvak aunt by marriage. I can sort of fake the dialect. I called out and said we went lost. Claimed I'd forgotten the password. They were a bit suspicious, but I claimed to be from a kibbutz in Galilee one of my uncles migrated to. He sent enough letters and pictures where I could describe it well enough. Seems the British recruited a division of Palestinian Jews. Guys out of the special Night Squads, Haganah and anyone who did military service in Europe. He warned me about the minefields but told me the landmarks for where they end. Gave me the challenge and password. I invited him to dinner at my uncle's when this is all over. Dawn's coming too soon to try it now. Wait till it gets dark tonight, and I'm pretty sure I can talk the unit through. No one can really see uniforms at night. If we leave the helmets off, or, still better, put on British tin hats. They're a different shape from German. We put our captured British trucks up front. Anyone calls out, we answer in Yiddish. Even you speak it enough, sir, to be some New York assimilated type who suddenly went Zionist."

Gunter spent a few minutes weighing his options. Then he left Ivan and Isaak in charge while he set off to find Rommel. Some stories you don't risk to wireless. Codes could be broken. This had to be face to face.

0600 hours local; 0500 hours CET
13 September 1940
Fleming Brigade position, El Alamein lines

Sergeant Billy Lincoln was in command of the section that had filled in trenches so the Australian column could drive through. The Australians had sent a large labor detail to help. The work had gone quickly. Billy was aware that digging the position back out would be far harder work … and probably without the Australian helpers.

He'd fought beside Australians for two years on the Western front. These young lads reminded him of their predecessors. Probably their fathers and uncles. Big, tough-looking country boys. From what they had told him then, even laborer's kids grew up fed plentiful meat back down under. As they were all British stock, it had to be diet. They had towered over the English in Billy's WW1 Pals battalion. It had given Billy food for thought. He'd considered emigrating, but never done it. It had always been one of those 'when I get married and settle down' kind of plans, and Billy had never married.

The whole arrival of this Auzzie force had been a shock and surprise. Shouldn't have been. People had field radios these days. Not like the First War, with motorcycle messengers and runners. By the time any serious message reached the front, odds were good it had already been countermanded twice.

Just like Money-Penny to have made this all work. Billy would never like the man. The lieutenant commander was far too much the gentleman, and Billy was proudly working-class. No, never like; but definitely trust and respect. Officers were a separate species, but Mr. James was a good one. Tough enough to face off against anyone, and smooth enough to work around the idiot staff drones. Christ, Haig's armies had spent four years learning their trade … and the damned gentleman officers seemed to have forgotten it all. This level of balls-up ineptitude took Billy back to his early days in France in

1915. His battalion had been among the first of the New Army formations deployed. That was before Haig had taken over from French. The British forces were strained to the breaking point staffing an army group, three armies and all the rest. The old sweats told Billy's lot that they arrived just in time for the staff swine running the show to reach total ineptitude. Young Billy had no standard to gauge this by, but it was one balls-up after another.

Bad as 1915 was, this seemed worse. Billy had cautioned his lads, keep extra rations in your kit. Double up on water bottles. If this all went to Hell, these could save your life. Billy had been under the hammer when Fifth Army fell apart spring of 1918. You could scrounge ammo on a retreat better than food or drinkable water. A man without water for more than a day was useless. Starving took longer to kill you, but by the second day of an empty belly it messed with your reflexes, even under fire. The young ones knew he'd been through the mill. He'd also gotten them off Malta alive. They listened.

0900 hours local; 0800 hours CET
13 September 1940
General O'Connor's command vehicle, 10 miles west-north-west of Colonel Mason's brigade position, center of Alamein lines

The general and his staff were hiding in a slit trench by the commander's caravan. The air attacks had been near nonstop since roughly an hour after an early dawn. The Western Desert Force was barely in contact with the forward British positions. The idiots there had made no preparations to clear lanes in minefields, prepare trenches to be crossed by vehicles. They seemed shocked to see British forces arriving.

O'Connor was aware that the British regular army had taken for the BEF everyone they regarded as competent. That had made easy sense. The real war was supposed to have been in Flanders and Picardy, same as the last time.

The secondary theater should have been officered from the Indian Army. O'Connor had been born in India of the higher levels of the British ruling caste. A good part of his interwar service life had been there. The Indian Army was full of first-rate officers. That Army had fought the bulk of Britain's imperial wars from Victoria's time onwards.

In the meantime, he was being worked over by German artillery, and in constant danger from German attacks on his southern flank. The German commander kept trying to sever the link to the Alamein lines. If this happened, the Western Desert Force would be lost today. Yet it was bloody hard to maneuver to counter, when every movement triggered more strafing and dive-bombing.

1000 hours local; 0900 hours CET
13 September 1940
Rommel's advance headquarters, 5 kilometers southeast of O'Connor's

The interruption had been most unwelcome. Rommel was concentrating on the progress of the battle. He was so close to severing the connection between this British corps and their entrenchments, he could all but taste it. Rommel felt he had a sixth sense about the flux of a battle. He'd relied on it for his exploits in Italy in the last war, in Belgium and France in this one. If the commander was up with the lead element, he could short-circuit the confusion and delays of battle. The air attacks were pinning the British in place. His lads had the link under fire. One more push, two at the worst, and he would be sitting astride their escape route.

He couldn't prevent them from moving north. There was next to nothing there, except the boy Steiner's Kampfgruppe. Right now that unit was doing miracles protecting the forward observers who were guiding down the air attacks, calling in what German artillery was within range.

Let the British move north in the dark. While they did, he'd breach their line here. The entrenched English were providing fire support for their nearly trapped comrades. And that was the key. There simply wasn't enough fire coming from the British lines. He should have been on the receiving end of army-, corps-, and division-level batteries. It wasn't happening. He was getting very light fire, and quite intermittently. There wasn't even enough mortar, heavy machine-gun, and sniper fire for a serious fortified zone. The intelligence was wrong. The British were much weaker than anticipated.

And yet Strauss was interrupting all the necessary preparations, all the needed time going forward to lead this or that company in person, with this preposterous tale of British Jews giving his Yids a route through the line, passwords, everything ... and all because some Leutnant could describe a communal agricultural settlement.

Rommel had been impressed with Strauss on Malta, and even more so here in Africa. Now he was bringing in this likely preposterous story. Rommel wanted to snap at the man, but kept control of himself. Everyone was running on too little sleep and at the ragged edge of dysfunctional, after this many continuous hours of combat and rapid maneuvering.

Besides, even if Strauss could trick his way through the British lines, then what? His slapped-together Brigade simply wasn't strong enough to win a battle on its own against an army-sized force. At a minimum, it would need Rommel's own force and the arriving fast group from Maletti's 1st Libyan. These could not be moved south in daylight without the British observing it, without them following behind at dusk and pocketing the advancing Italo-German forces. If all of both divisions were up, maybe. If Strauss's attack could go in at the same time as Rommel's own further north, perhaps ... No. Rommel's battle sense worked under his own eye and command, not by remote control to Strauss. The man and his unit weren't experienced enough to pull this off. Too bad.

He tried not to be too brusque with Strauss, tried not to let his own exhaustion get expressed as anger. He needed the man functional. Doing his job the way he had the previous night. Strauss had been brilliant. Had gotten more than Rommel would have believed possible out of his untrained troops.

Rommel focused on what Strauss had done right. That he had come to Rommel to review the situation instead of going off on his own. Reminded Strauss that the focal point was to be Rommel's own breach of the British lines here, rather than an unlikely trick to create a breach to the south. Ordered him to leave a reconnaissance screen behind, and bring his Brigade north. The Brigade wasn't good enough to be part of the main attack force. Seventh Panzer would do that work. Strauss would guard the left flank.

....

Gunter Strauss didn't take Rommel's disbelief personally. Isaak and Ivan did, but they came from different military traditions than Germany's. The general knew the big picture. Gunter didn't. He'd mention the situation in his after-action report, but if that report went up the chain through Rommel, he expected the paragraph to be edited out. Shit flowed downhill, not up the ladder.

1300 hours local; 1200 hours CET
13 September 1940
Headquarters Mason's Brigade of 6th Commando Division, 3 miles behind main line of resistance

Colonel Garth Mason was back at his headquarters after a tour of his 'front lines'. By the standards of proper positions from the last war, it was nothing more than some hasty trenches linking dugouts with machine-guns. His 'brigade' was closer to being a general labor regiment. The three battalion remnants from Malta were Winston's special troops – collections of refugees, adventurers, and misfits. The rest had barely had weapons training. They would dig, but Mason had doubts they would stand their ground in the event of a serious push.

O'Connor had left his troops forward at Bagush, to buy Mason the time to get this grab-bag of barely civilized men, few of whom were even formally subjects of the Empire, to dig a proper position. Now the remains of this powerful force were clustered in front of his positions.

For the second time this summer, Mason had run up against abysmal, complacent staff work. First Malta, and now Egypt. The problem, in his opinion, was too many Indian Army men. The whole force was a glorified cross between armed police and over-glamorized frontier guards. Chasing Pushtuns in the Hindu Kush, or cordoning off Gandhi's latest mass demonstration, simply was not preparation for serious warfare. Even the field officers had fought Johnny Turk in the Great War, not the Germans. Malta, Cairo, the entire Mediterranean Theater, simply had too many banker's-hours office wallahs who belonged back in some sleepy garrison in India, dreaming of polo matches and assignations on summer leave up at Simla.

Mason was aware that there were enough regulars in theater, but felt correctly that these were mostly second-raters and odd ducks. The best the service had to offer had been creamed off for the BEF, been sent off on the doomed crusade that ended at Dunkirk. That's why they had seized on a first-rate Guards officer like himself, had given him a brigade instead of a desk job on staff.

For a second he wondered yet again about his companion from Malta, Kevin Duffy. He was listed as taken prisoner on the Red Cross forms, but was not check-in at any of the senior officer's facilities. Swiss and Swedish Red Crosses were doing stand-ins for the British on this.

Reality intruded on the idle thoughts of Duffy. Cairo or 6th Division should have notified him last night that passage through his lines would be needed. Damned bad staff work to fail to advise him. Mason had used his status as a Guards officer to get more than his share of what landmines there were. Left the Yiddish to his south bare, but working the Old Boys network was what one did. His brigade was going to be adequately covered, if there was anything he could do about it.

Clearing vehicle lanes through these minefields couldn't easily be done under fire. So that froze Western Desert Force in place. Again Mason came back to the sloppy staff work.   Fleming's brigade had arranged passage for the Australians. Why not direct O'Connor's men there?

1600 hours local; 1500 hours CET
13 September 1940
KG Steiner position, astride the western face of the British pocket

Sometimes Klaus Steiner chuckled to himself at how much had changed in his life in a few months. He arrived in Berlin having never had a girlfriend. Not even an unreciprocated schoolboy crush. Now he had a wife in all but name. This occurred to him because he now regarded Ivan and Isaac as his in-law's, his uncles by marriage. As the British position slowly shrank and flattened, Major Ivan Gorlov had been detached with reinforcements for him. Klaus heard the radio message, and it registered in his mind as 'Uncle Ivan' was coming. Uncle, not Major.

Ivan arrived with a company of Betar and an alarm company of stray motorcyclists and armored cars Gunter had acquired. Klaus was quite happy to have an adult back in charge. He looked forward to Uncle Ivan critiquing his performance. He knew he had so much still to learn. About how to be an officer. About how to be of use in running the oil fields they would all take from the British. He couldn't take Greta home, so he would have to stay with her in Kirkuk, whatever that was besides an oil production facility. Klaus caught himself and chuckled again. He would be getting a job from his in-law's. How much more married can you get than that? He remembered table talk from his parents about how older boys, sons of their social circle, had 'married well', been taken into their in-law's firms or gotten jobs with companies their new in-law's had high position in. New books for Greta to teach him from. Besides, if the oil fields were to be owned by Germany, there should be places for real Germans like himself.

Peiper had been the third person at this family reunion. The SS officer seemed to be trying to ingratiate himself. Ivan had heard the joint report, made a quick response of things that could bear improvement, and sent Peiper off with his French cavalry tanks and Panhards to feel for how far north the British position ran. Made sure Peiper knew the recognition color with the air forces was now red. There had been bad incidents earlier in the day.

1800 hours local; 1700 hours CET
13 September 1940

North of the Cauldron position

"Damn all regular officers!" Lieutenant Commander James Money-Penny had had enough of higher-level buck passing. Western Desert Force was less than ten miles south of him. It was obvious, from where the enemy airplanes were attacking.

Mason hadn't done the needed work making a pathway, as he had with the Fleming Brothers. That was why Money-Penny had joined the RN. To avoid being forced to serve under a bunch of Colonel Blimp types like Mason.

Sun would be down in a few minutes. The very last planes, the tiny artillery spotter birds were turning away to Bagush. Money-Penny would push on south with his refilled fuel trucks and the last remaining wrecker vehicle, to guide the lads home. The higher officers were welcome to all die. It was the poor bloody infantry that deserved sympathy. Money-Penny laughed at himself. He broke out in patriotism at the damnedest times.

2000 hours local; 1900 hours CET
13 September 1940
Camp Three Crosses

His headquarters staff had just finished installing proper communications in this rudimentary advance base. Von Manstein now had teletype back to Berlin. The day had been one long set of tennis volleys back and forth to his perpetual bad boy, Erwin Rommel. Von Manstein had gone into this job knowing that Rommel was a cross he was fated to carry up the hill. Higher command had costs as well as prerogatives.

Rommel was simply incapable of grasping logistics. If he somehow managed his night-time breakthrough, he still had three weak brigades up against two British corps plus army-level assets. The campaign was over a month ahead of schedule, but a pause was needed. The supply depots, air bases, the whole paraphernalia of modern war. This wasn't the age of the Mongols where your ponies ate grass. Absent fuel, vehicles sit there. This battalion commander Steiner, whoever he was, had apparently shot all the ammunition for his French Panhard 178's. Supply officers were scouring records trying to find more this side of Marseilles. Von Manstein's corps had been assembled with stray bits of equipment from everywhere. Each weapon and vehicle had its own unique parts and munitions needs.

He had sent Rommel firm orders to cease pushing, and stop overrunning his halt lines. There is a point in every pursuit where the correlation of forces changes. Von Manstein felt that point had been passed at Bagush. He notified Berlin that if Rommel didn't listen, he would have to take more drastic measures. It was too late in the day to force a personal conference on the bad-boy Panzer general. So Berlin had all night to review his message and countermand it. If they didn't, von Manstein would treat that as tacit approval.

2100 hours local; 2000 hours CET

13 September 1940
General O'Connor's headquarters caravan, driving north by slightly northeast towards the transit point in Fleming's lines

Thank God for Lieutenant-Commander Money-Penny and his brigade of Naval Commandos, whatever on Earth those were. He had his staff people writing up a pages-long letter of commendation to be hand-delivered to the brigade commander, Commander Ian Fleming. A copy would go to Wavell's headquarters in Cairo, which hopefully would get this magician a mention in dispatches.

The problem was the operational balancing act. He doubted he could get everyone and everything through the exit gate by dawn. Pure military logic said, save the tanks and artillery. The guns of both divisions were mostly intact, as were what corps guns Western Desert Force had. The same could not be said of the armor. In rough terms he had begun this battle with two brigades of armor, one each heavy and medium. He was down to a platoon of heavies and a composite battalion of the medium cruiser tanks. This made them especially precious. But the funnel mouth through Fleming's lines was narrow. He could be reasonably sure he could get the entire force to close proximity to Fleming's positions. Navigating the narrows across Fleming's trenches was another story. Considerable elements would be stuck waiting their turn come daylight.

Generals are generals to make hard decisions. The tanks first, the artillery second, and everyone else takes their chances. He would leave a screen against the Germans. Infantry with Boys anti-tank rifles and the remaining armored cars. The bulk of the infantry could exit their trucks and just walk through the trench line. A man on foot could walk over a set of duck-boards from one side of a trench to the other. A platoon or company could jump in a trench and jump out on the far side. But these would be men with rifles. The crew-served weapons were a slower and harder portage, and the trucks of supply and other kit would be left to be sitting ducks for the air attacks. He'd hold off torching the trucks until the screening force was pushed back. Perhaps they would be lucky and there would be another sand storm. Fog was unlikely, and thunderstorms even more so. O'Connor was not an air expert, but knew the mass of warplanes needed sunshine to operate. Night and bad weather kept them on the ground.

0200 hours local; 0100 hours CET
14 September 1940
Colonel Mason's sector, 6th Commando Brigade positions, El Alamein lines

Having neglected to bring a staff section along, Rommel had commandeered Strauss's. Leutnant von Kleist-Konitz and his gang of Romanian Jewish clerks. Rommel was upfront with his break-through force, a composite Battalion of dismounted infantry and the Pioneer Company he had brought along. They had three pathways through the British minefields, and had captured half a kilometer of forward trenches. Rommel had not chosen to try his luck with the British positions on the small ridge. He'd aimed to its south. The defenders were clearly a second-rate force. They showed neither the will nor the ability to counterattack. There was a core that would defend strongly. These manned the blockhouses. The interval troops between, collapsed when hard pressed. Many simply surrendered to the first Germans they saw. Many more took to the rear.

The blockhouses were crude affairs by Great War standards. None were designed for all-round defense. So the standard drill worked. Get on top of them via the trenches to their sides. Then it was grenades through the firing slits, followed by using flamethrowers. Most surrendered at grenades. It would take into the morning hours for the Pioneers to get heavy-vehicle lanes through the mines. If only he had brought his entire engineer contingent up …

....

Mason had repeatedly warned division and corps that his troops lacked the training and morale for a serious fight. He'd not been precisely ignored so much as kept at bay with pleasantries. Even senior staff officers thought twice about directly telling a Guards officer with good London connections to just fuck off. In point of fact, his troops weren't even the lowest quality in the division. The third brigade hadn't had Money-Penny to line up 'recruits'. What GHQ had provided them was even more pathetic than the poor sods Mason had had to work with.

The normally dismissive and unresponsive office wallahs on division and corps staff also took seriously Mason's running commentary on the collapse of his lines. Yet again the social cachet of the Guards worked in his favor. Plus there was his hero status from Malta. His attack against the German paratroop elite at Hal Far had rated mention in dispatches. A man of his age and rank, taking a company-size forlorn hope attack in against greatly superior numbers, had generated serious talk of a decoration, perhaps of a knighthood.

So he'd been allocated reserves. Two battalions of Australians plus their brigadier. Mason found the Australian to be a sensible chap. The man insisted on keeping command of his fellow countrymen. The dominion saw itself as a nationality, not just transplanted Brits. Mason cheerfully allotted the new brigade the south half of his lines. The two new battalions weren't willing to make a night attack to recover the original trenches. Unfortunate but sensible. They started digging a new second line while sending forward fighting patrols to reconnoiter the situation … and hopefully extract some of the bypassed men. Mason said he'd support them from his ridge position. The bad night appeared to be the harbinger of a still more unpleasant day.

0900 hours local; 0800 hours CET
14 September 1940
Rommel's break-through, south of Ruweisat Ridge

The first vehicle lane was open. The British artillery fire was pathetic. It was intermittent, and clearly fired blind. Rommel had expected more from the army of a serious power. The English clearly had good observation positions on the ridge. It wasn't much of a height, but in the relatively flat lands here a good observation post should have been able to see for kilometers. So the British must be seriously short of artillery, or perhaps just short of shells. Either way, these units were nowhere near as good as the ones he had run into at Arras a few months back. Abwehr reports had said the BEF in the West was the best the British empire had, that these colonial garrisons were mostly second- and third-raters. Compliments to the spies.

He'd fed Strauss in with two of his battalions to guard his southern flank. Apparently, Rommel had broken in just north of a division seam. Strauss had been his usual energetic self. He led out patrols to develop the enemy positions. Was sending back good detailed maps and prisoners. Also a sad joke. The passwords had worked. Strauss had twice used them to pass through the Palestinian Jewish lines. He'd even tricked a company into letting his men into their positions. Had sent back two hundred prisoners from that action, plus an amazing haul of documents. Rommel decided that the next time Strauss came to him with something off-the-wall unbelievable, that he would pay Strauss more mind. This whole NL unit was proving its use.

The panting messenger came up to General Rommel with a note. General von Manstein had flown in. He was to return immediately for a liaison conference. Rommel wanted to start cursing like a recruit-barracks Feldwebel, but he simply wouldn't allow mere rankers to see his distemper. He stalled for twenty minutes by insisting that Major Gorlov be called forward to relieve him. The man supposedly had brigade command experience.

Rommel wanted to stall further. Strauss had found the seam between the Palestinians and the Australians. A battalion battle group based on the company of T-38's he had almost forward, would rupture the line. He was sure. He was even more sure one doesn't keep a Corps Commander waiting for hours. Once Ivan Gorlov arrived, Rommel spent three quick minutes giving him the plan of attack, and trotted back to this stupid meeting.

....

Erich von Manstein received his bad-boy General with a blank affect. He might have wanted to strangle the insubordinate son of bitch, but a proper aristocrat does not betray such emotions in public. He simply ordered Rommel to accompany him into the Storch for a short flight back to Bagush and a commander's conference with Hausser and von Thoma, who had both been ferried up by air in advance of their main forces.

Rommel tried to argue. "The line is ready to give. With air attacks to keep the Australians pinned, Major Gorlov and I will break the seam between the units. Then Maletti and I roll up their whole line while Oberst Strauss devours their Palestinian Jewish division. I've already instructed Gorlov. The attack goes in, in the next hour … "

"No it won't. I have sent my aide Claus von Stauffenberg forward to take command. I've promoted him to Brigadier … ". He saw Rommel's blank reaction. "NL is a new service. I've cleared with Berlin to create a rank parallel to Oberführer. Above Oberst and below Generalmajor." Von Manstein had in fact only sent Berlin a message informing them of this. He was presuming permission as inherent in his original mission orders. "This attack is over. You've completely outrun your supplies and reinforcements. If you break the British line – and I repeat the word *if* – then what? Two advance force Brigades and a ramshackle Brigade equivalent of Strauss's. Total of an understrength Division with under a Brigade's worth of artillery support. To defeat an Army? What is the ammunition status of your tanks, your guns?" He could see Rommel's face start to cloud. "You managed impossible feats against the French. These are British. You didn't make your magic work at Arras … " Rommel started to object. Von Manstein plowed over him. "Make all the excuses to yourself you want. You didn't. You were saved by their abysmal inter-arms coordination between their tanks and the supporting infantry, by the companion French attacks never getting really started. Now you have precisely two choices. You may return to Bagush with me as a Division commander, or as a prisoner under arrest. Choose!" The last word was near whispered, but the command bark was clear in the tone.

Rommel opened and closed his mouth twice. Then his shoulders sagged and he boarded the Storch, still a Division commander but no longer in command.

....

Von Stauffenberg expected to have to assert his new rank, and argue over whether such a thing as Brigadier existed. Gorlov, and then Strauss, made no objections. They were both quite sure they could split the British lines, but both were also dubious on what came next. Each had seen campaigns they'd been on make operational gains that led nowhere except to the exhaustion of the attacking force. Instead the three spent an hour devising how to dig in properly for the inevitable British counter-strokes. Requisitions went to the rear for wire, mortars with illumination rounds, and more trained engineers to relay the British mines someplace more useful than where they were currently placed.

1600 hours local; 1500 hours CET
14 September 1940
Prisoner cage, 20 kilometers to the rear of the new front line at Alamein

It was shaping up as another scorching summer day in the Western Desert. Strauss's brigade had come out of the lines around noon. The captured Empire prisoners had grouped themselves by nationality. British, Indian, Palestinian, and Australian all were clumps of listless sweating men. Major Ivan Gorlov had tasked himself with a job he'd performed often enough back in Russia. He was with two Betar men, a Leutnant and a Company Commissar. He was 'recruiting'.

Explaining what he intended to the guard commander was easy. The man was a Waffen SS Hauptsturmführer. He was seated on a captured British folding chair so as not to strain his wounded thigh. His guards were all walking wounded. As long as the prisoners kept fairly quiet, the guards were inclined to let them pant from the heat in peace. Dealing with the swarms of flies was bad enough.

Ivan came up to the wire with his two helpers. Tossed a few water jugs over the barrier. That rapidly got attention. Ivan's Yiddish was accented but serviceable. "Looking for Revisionists. I'll take General Zionists as well. Labor types, stay seated."

A few men piped up. "Looking for what, Nazi pig?" "Fuck off!"

"Recruits. We are going to take Palestine. Who wants to go home a conqueror?"

This got more interest. "Why Revisionists and General? Labor runs things."

"Not any more. Italians are getting most of Palestine. Germany gets Haifa and Galilee. We are

Betar. We'll be the army and police of the new empire. Jabotinsky will come back to run things. What the Germans want is the port and the pipeline. Rest doesn't mean shit to them."

By now a crowd of men were up against the wire. Ivan left it to the Commissar to screen the politics. Odds said a lot of Reds would suddenly convert. It had been that way in Russia as the fortunes of war swayed back and forth. For now he was recruiting laborers. A few would run back to the British. No matter. They'd just be swept up when the next German victory happened. Ivan knew they had almost broken the British this morning. It would have been like the 1919 advance on Moscow. Too far too fast. Had Denikin cleaned up his rear, chasing Makhno far enough West, he could have taken Moscow some months later. This German drive had the supplies. It was going to win. Ivan was happy for once to be on a winning side.

1400 hours EDT; 2000 hours CET
14 September 1940
White House, Washington DC

Harry Hopkins had just finished yet another frustrating campaign meeting with Franklin, and then a separate – thankfully briefer – one with Eleanor. Franklin was living in a fantasy world. He refused to be made to see that Farley had actually been a most useful minion. The man had done the endless handholding and petty deal-brokering necessary to keep the New Deal coalition together. It had been fracturing on its own since Franklin's disastrous 1938 moves on court-packing and party purge. Without Farley's daily labors of Hercules on repairs, it was now near collapse.

The Roosevelt Depression of 1938 had partially wiped out the New Deal enthusiasm of the first term. The ever more strident anti-capitalist rhetoric from the White House had thinned down a lot of Main Street support. Eleanor's left alliances and causes had alienated much of Dixie's ruling elite on race, and many big city machines on patronage control. Franklin's visible tilt to Britain in the European war was alienating the Irish and much of the Midwest. No one particularly liked the Nazis or Fascists. Many were adamant against sending millions of Americans to risk death for the British Empire in Europe's perpetual wars.

In the Willkie-Lindbergh-Coughlin triad, Franklin was faced with formidable opposition instead of the usual reactionary Republican hacks like Taft. Willkie could say 'me too' on most of the New Deal, other than the TVA, and promise to simply run the machine less corruptly. Lucky Lindy could beat the America First drum without being successfully called a traitor. He was a popular hero for his aviation exploits, and a tragic figure from the death of his kidnapped child. Coughlin could siphon off a lot of the populist anger against those whose profits in the 20's had bankrupted the nation. Hopkins had access to the real polling data, to thousands of local big shots who could take the temperature of their little piece of earth as alderman or judges or whatever. Outside the South, Willkie was ahead. Ahead enough to maybe win. This was going to be razor-close. It would need more than the same old tired rhetoric. Yet neither Roosevelt was of a mind to listen to reason. Each had their circle of sycophants and ideologues who preferred flattery and ideological purity to victory in November. The next weeks were going to be unpleasant, and potentially brutal in terms of sharp-elbows infighting. Hopkins found himself the advocate of the more conservative end of Franklin's base. These were not Harry Hopkins' natural allies, but needs must.

0800 hours local, 15 September
2300 hours CET, 14 September
#33 The Bund, British Consulate, International Settlements, Shanghai

The meeting had played out well. Wang Jingwei, President of the Reorganized Government of China, was enjoying the power reversal placed on Japan by their new Soviet War. Their own propaganda spoke of heroic defenses, valiant incursions behind Soviet lines, and new air aces. Vladivostok was blockaded and North Sakhalin seized. The maps told the tale. The Soviet lines inched towards Harbin in Manchuria.

Wang had 'defected' to the Japanese from Chiang as part of a long-game strategy. Placate the Japanese to end the war. A war that was tearing China to pieces. Regardless of who won month-to-month warfare between Chiang and the Japanese, the real winners were chaos, starvation, and, ultimately, the Communists. A China slagged down to semi-bandits hiding in the interior mountains was Mao's vision of the future.

The meeting had been in the British consulate because the two Anglo-Saxon powers had intervened on Wang's behalf. The main cause of this was the Christians. Chiang had turned on them, missionaries and converts alike. There had been mass jailing, selective murders, and quick expulsions through the lines. The missionary community as a bloc had vast power in the Anglo world, especially among the rich, powerful Americans. These had promised food, arms, and experts. That was for later, and would take time. What they offered now was money. Money that could buy food for the refugees, that would buy materials to build them new housing on the fringes of Shanghai and the other ocean and river ports. Dollars that meant contracts to local businesses; and jobs as guards, as construction labor. Contracts and jobs that would flow through his regime.

The Chinese business community had already been given cause to turn from Chiang. He was now in alliance with the Reds and the Soviets. The KMT had been left, right and something else entirely, at different phases over its decades of history. This was a renewed turn to the left. That threatened the business owners, great and small alike, with expropriation and murder. But those inputs were all negative and somewhat distant. The KMT and Communists both had activists and assassins in Japanese-occupied territory. They could kill anyone, but scarcely everyone. The Kenpeitai were too powerful. The dollars were a positive inducement. US money was widely accepted. The patronage effect was immediate. Most people were not political. Beyond a core patriotism, they gave no thought to anything beyond their own rice bowls.

There was also a second-order effect. If you had the merchants and manufacturers on your side, you didn't need the landlords. The French Revolution showed a pattern. Give land to the peasants, and they would fight to keep it. A fight that these Westerners had promised to aid. Back in the crisis years of the 20's, the British had a division in the treaty ports. The Americans had two brigades. Now it was down to battalions. Both were promising the equipment kit to rebuild their forces. Both were now rapidly recruiting locally – White Russians, Jews, refugees in general, Eurasians, and even westernized Chinese. Two Western divisions to play off against the now static, and due to shrink, Japanese invaders. Both were offering his forces money and arms in return for protecting the treaty ports and the Christians.

Like any good nationalist, Wang despised the whole treaty port system. But in the long term those could be dealt with in a generation or two, at China's convenience. The whole peace-faction program was based on buying time for China to reassert its natural superiority. All the advantages the others had could be negated, given time for China to industrialize, to educate itself in new technologies. China always won in the end. There were just too many Chinese and too much Chinese land. Thus the wisdom of Chinese history. Even the Mongols had passed in a few generations.

0900 hours local; 0700 hours CET
15 September 1940
Private residence, Jewish quarter of Baghdad

David Baghdadi saw himself as a prudent, careful man. His family had prospered in the Baghdad area back to Persian times, and perhaps earlier. They knew how to accommodate themselves to shifts in the winds … and the wind was shifting. The British had been defeated in France, Malta, and Egypt. Their fleet had left for the Indian Ocean. A wise man took precautions.

The Iraqi senior army officers of the Golden Square were pro-Italian and supporters of the Palestinian Arab Revolt. Neither group loved Jews. Why the British in their imitative idiocy had created an Iraqi Army in the pattern of their Indian and Egyptian ones, then allowed the officer corps to be dominated by ambitious Sunnis with their own agenda, remained a mystery. In Trans-Jordan the armed force was a small militarized police, officered by loyal Britons. Leave the external defense of Iraq to Britain as protecting power, and the army becomes small and manageable. Instead the army had delusions of grandeur. Its ruling higher-officer clique, the Golden Square, made and unmade governments like some US-protected banana republic. (David had relatives in Panama, and thus was current on such adventures.)

So the wise course of action was to cultivate protectors among the rich, well-connected Sunni Arabs of his acquaintance. The Nazis and Fascists would rule through those. The British did, often to their cost. These Sunnis had converted the new British-imposed monarchy into a regime both unstable and unpopular. Their reward to the British was to be anti-British. These same families had treated the Ottomans equally poorly. Such protection would probably be expensive. Better to lose some wealth than to lose it all, to lose the lives of his family as well. His first choice had not proved helpful. His next possibility was due for coffee in an hour.

1200 hours local, 1100 hours CET
15 September 1940

GHQ, Cairo

General O'Connor was amazed that he had not been relieved … exactly. He was still GOC Western Desert Force, as was Creagh of 7th Armored Division. They were each left with their staffs, aides, and batmen. The two commands merely had all their units stripped from them. 4th Indian Division was still in the line as a unit. The other brigades and battalions of Western Desert Force were being used independently, or parceled out to the three divisions of Alamein Force.

In two days, Cunningham had failed to restore the line. His attacks, in O'Connor's opinion, had been poorly prepared. Hammering at the Germans wouldn't work. As their army came up, they would just shuttle fresh forces into the salient so that the weary Indian, Australian, and British attackers also faced fresh defenders in ever-deeper entrenchments. Plus ever more artillery, pre-registered to cover likely channels of assault during the darkness.

Trying to break the nose of the salient was a fool's response. Aim for the south side of the penetration. Go west beyond the original lines and try to sever the cauldron at its base. Of course, all this presumed the original line was worth retaking. O'Connor couldn't particularly see why. A few square miles of wilderness had no special value. Colonel Mason had saved the key position on the ridge.

Of more importance was the reappearance of the few platoons of Rhodesian armored cars, last seen screening the Three Crosses Camp. Everyone had forgotten them. Sloppy staffwork, but they figured out on their own that withdrawal eastwards was the correct answer. In doing so they scooped up strays from the South Africans and British, so what returned was now a two-company battlegroup. The important part was where they reappeared *from*. They had gone across the Quattara Depression. Staff maps listed that as 'impassible'. It seemed the correct answer was 'difficult', at least for small forces of determined men with vehicles and winches. O'Connor was failing to get anyone on either Wavell's or Cunningham's staff to take any of this seriously.

Which returned again to just what his status was. Wavell's staff got quite evasive on the subject. This smelled like a London-induced fudge. London had wanted his head. Now, perhaps, a different set of factions were protecting him. More likely using him as a cudgel to beat Churchill and his gang. War Cabinet factionalism had been a constant drain on Britain's warfighting in the First War. It had created unending problems during rearmament, and so far in this war. Shouldn't victory matter more than which well-pampered ass sat in which seat at cabinet meetings?

1400 hours CET
15 September 1940
Schellenberg's Office, SS Headquarters, Prinz-Albrecht-Straße, Berlin

The initial 'liaison conferences' in North Africa having proved less than fruitful, von Manstein had adjourned the proceedings to Berlin, hoping to get higher authority to help him bring his wayward Division commander to heel. He'd asked for a meeting with Heydrich. That lord of creation turned out to have a full calendar. Something about a European Union. So Schellenberg had been deputized in his master's place. The 'voice of Heydrich' listened to a full report by von Manstein, seconded by his Berlin-based second-in-command at OKW, General Busse. Rommel was ordered to be silent and just listen. He was not graceful about it but was compliant … so far. Schellenberg took it all in, then spoke. "General Rommel, you have a wife, Lucia Maria. A son, Manfred, and an acknowledged daughter, Gertrud. We have had them brought to Berlin. They are waiting downstairs."

Schellenberg could see the shock on the three Generals' faces. The SS was threatening families? "If I wanted to make a threat, it wouldn't have been implied. We have let the Army use caste privilege to shield thieves and idiots. You all have heard the stories. You are welcome to think we are all street gangsters, but stop thinking we are stupid. Some of our low-level minions may be overmuscled thugs with badges. We at the leadership level are not." He could see the palpable relief behind the three iron masks. He had much practice at reading very minor body language cues in interviews. "You are also aware we have our own lines of communication through the headquarters of Divisional General Hausser and Brigade Oberst Strauss. You are both right and both wrong." Now he had the attention of all three. The Army action reports were nowhere near ready for final synthesized conclusions. "General Rommel would have broken their line. We would have gained a few more square kilometers before the inevitable stalemate. General Rommel, do you wish to be permanently relieved? I have written authority to do so." Schellenberg paused, but there was no response. "I thought not. You will join your family when this meeting is concluded. You will take a three-week vacation someplace nice in the Alps that your wife has chosen. She's down with our travel department. First class transport and hotels at Reich expense. You will unwind. You will then spend a week with your wife, but without your children, doing a propaganda tour. Speeches, galas for notables in selected cities, a few popular beer hall events. You will have a propaganda team to make the arrangements and write your brief speeches. This will culminate in a ceremony in Berlin where the Führer will decorate you with Oak Leaves for your Blue Max. You will be the first such recipient." He again paused for the broad smile on Rommel's face. "Now one more little thing. Your return to command of Seventh Panzer Division will require a written request for you from your commander, General Corps Commander von Manstein. If he takes you back, he will have in his desk a signed, undated relief order with two signatures – Herman Göring, Führer and Chancellor; Reinhard Heydrich, Reichsführer SS and Deputy Chancellor. Higher command admires your zeal and generalship. It does not intend to countenance any more insane risks or willful disobedience. The prestige of Germany requires an unbroken string of victories, one unpunctuated by a British success brought on by you pushing your luck past all bounds of sanity. Push comes to shove, the Reich needs von Manstein more than you. We can find you a nice training command here if you cannot grasp this." He waited three beats for a response. What he got was what he expected, dead silence. He spoke into his intercom. "Please accompany General Rommel to his wife." Two large SS officers entered the room. Rommel stood up, saluted, and left.

Schellenberg let Rommel's exit play out and then turned to the two Generals. "We are serious. He is a most useful tool, but tools must be chosen in regard to function. His disobedience got us to this Alamein line faster than planned for and with some notable victories. A breach of a fortified line is not a mobile battle in a desert. Trench warfare is something our public knows and fears. It brings back memories of the Kaiser's War and page-long lists of dead and missing in the papers. My master suggests keeping him, but that's your decision. He also suggests that the main breach be done by Hausser and Steiner. Steiner's Division should have enough elements by November to be worthy of including in the line of battle. Use those two. Keep Rommel and the Strauss brigade in reserve until mobile conditions return. Can you live with this, gentlemen?"

The two generals put aside the decision on Rommel for another day, and spent four hours reviewing what special reinforcements would be needed to do this positional battle. Rommel spent the time sitting in a First Class railway compartment with his family. His *Bursche* military orderly (what the English would call a "batman") had also been reunited with his own family, and was available on call from the Second Class carriage. Rommel was overjoyed to see his loved ones; but he regarded the implied threat to his family's survival as still on the table, whatever facile words the SS Oberführer had used. It gave even his huge ego pause for thought.

2000 hours British Double Summer Time and CET
15 September 1940
A third-tier gentleman's club in a non-posh section of London

The doorway lacked any markings. Ernie Bevin had needed a guide to walk him here from his cab. Said guide was a nondescript middle-aged man in an unremarkable grey suit. The man had introduced himself as a member of parliament. Bevin couldn't place him, but the Conservative Party had a legion of such people, middle class suburban and secondary-city types with non-Oxbridge accents and a good (but worn) grey suit. Labor had similar myriads of academics and shop stewards.

The interior of the club was shabbily decorated and poorly lit. Bevin was not an expert on such clubbiness. This was a thing for people of another class, the type who voted Conservative or Liberal. This room appeared to have not seen a refurbishment since Edward VII had still been a playboy prince back in the Gay 90's. Who were these drones? He'd only agreed to take this meeting at Atlee's insistence. Yet Clement had been vague in the extreme as to the who, what, and why.

Bevin found himself seated at a table with two more men. Also Conservative MP's. They looked like second cousins of the guide, down to similar grey suits. "May I ask what this is in reference to?"

Two of the grey-clad drones originally seated stayed silent. It appeared as if the guide were the spokesman. "Think of us as emissaries of the 1922 Committee. We wish to discuss certain changes in government, both people and policy."

The 1922 Committee? A self-created lobby of Tory backbenchers who made and unmade ministers. Why were they talking to him? Bevin was Labor and Trades Union Congress to the core. "What has this to do with me?" And why had Atlee, of all people, near-ordered him to take this meeting?

"Peace talks have begun in Lisbon. The War Cabinet as a body has not been informed. Certain key members have been, privately."

Good God! This was potentially treason. "May I presume Atlee was included and our supposed Prime Minister was not?'

"Precisely. Churchill will destroy this nation. He must go. The issue, of course, is his replacement."

"I cannot speak for Labor on this." Damn it! Atlee knew this decision would need the full meeting of Labor's leadership.

"You seem to misunderstand the situation. Mr. Atlee was approached with the general concept. We wish a National Government. As with MacDonald's government, we wish a Labor PM. It shows national unity better than a few Labor and Liberal token showpieces in a Tory cabinet. However, we do not wish Mr. Atlee. We wish you as Prime Minister."

"Me? Clement's the head of the party. You Tories cannot change that at your whim."

"We aren't. When Churchill became PM back in May, Chamberlain stayed on head of the Tory party. This would be the same. Winston is losing this war. Refuses all sensible proposals to retreat, won't allow peace talks, fights limiting our war expenditures to the financial resources of the Empire. We are already insolvent. He will convert that to open, public bankruptcy, chasing a mirage that the US will enter, that the Soviets will fall out with Hitler. It is absurd. We need a generation or two of peace to rebuild. We accept that we cannot rebuild under party government. Too much pain will mean perpetual defeat at the polls. It will need a national government and joint responsibility. Mr. Atlee has given us a set of Labor demands on social justice, starting with national health insurance. We've accepted those on a basis of implementing them step by step as funds become available. We've worked out controls so Labor will at all times know what the real financial situation is, so we cannot evade these promises. The problem remains the unions – which brings us to you. De facto, we have nationalized the economy for the duration. Management is to be a mix of private ownership and strong state supervision. This only works with labor peace, which you are the man to deliver. The TUC knows you. They trust you. We want labor issues handled in cabinet, not by strikes and the like. You will be the defender of the worker's interests. If you feel the working class is being abused, you can resign and bring us down."

"Clement's approved this?"

"In concept. We don't know precisely who he has approached or how much they have been told. As you yourself just said, that is internal Labor Party business. We have done soundings in our caucus. In broad generalities, there is enough buy-in. You want socialism. We don't. We agree to put that debate off till full recovery, which will take thirty or forty years of peace. You get a welfare state more to your liking, and a somewhat nationalized economy, with a large share of total income beyond needed investment going to the working classes and those poor unfortunates who cannot labor. We accept that many class privileges will shrink or vanish. You accept that what survives of the Empire won't just be given independence in a fit of universalist good feeling ... "

Bevin couldn't contain himself on this one. "India? Do you seriously mean to try to rule a subcontinent by force?"

"No. We will at the margins try to safeguard British commercial interests, but India will become independent. We propose to pack Winston off as Viceroy. Compared to his reactionary squawkings, whatever we offer from London will seem mild and civilized. India, Burma, probably Ceylon, are gone. The current Arab Empire will be lost as well, either by the sword or at the peace conference. That leaves the rest. We'll need it as export markets and raw material sources. If the British Empire is going to continue to be a world power facing a Nazi Europe, we need the extra heft. Otherwise what we buy isn't peace. It's a ten-years truce for Göring to build the fleet to invade us with. They are promising naval limitations. The last Führer's word was worthless. Probably this one's is as well."

Peace? "What terms are they offering?"

"Fairly mild, actually. They want some recompense for direct financial losses."

"Reparations?"

"Of a very specialized kind. They took losses in 1914 and 1939 when we seized their merchant marine. When we expropriated their holdings in the City. Those sort of very specific things. On the military side, they offer naval limitations which we can monitor in return for the exclusion of heavy bombers from these islands which *they* can monitor. We can build as many large planes as we wish in Canada, but none here, and no airfields big enough to take them. Beyond that, it is colonial issues. They aren't asking for anything they won't likely seize in the next year. But they make clear that the longer the war goes on, the more they will seize; and what they take they expect to keep."

Bevin had been thinking furiously. "I cannot commit without consultations."

"Of course. I presume you will want to get the program from Mr. Atlee, to sound out key Trades Union people. We only ask that you be discreet. Time is of the essence. We would prefer the transition is in place before this all leaks. Once it does, our members will be bombarded with offers of office from the likes of Lloyd George. Men are weak and often shortsighted. Better we hand them a plan for a yes or no vote with little time for thought. They are quite good at falling in line when pushed properly."

Yes, Bevin thought. They were well-trained sheep. The idea of himself as PM seemed absurd, but with Clement to back him and deal with the ideologues and the over-ambitious, it could be done. He owed it to his men to try.

1600 hours CDT; 2300 hours CET
15 September 1940
Chicago Board of Trade Building, 141 West Jackson Boulevard, Chicago

The skyscraper dominated the skyline of America's second city. The large banquet room was filled to capacity with what the press called the China Lobby. This was a weirdly interlocking set of squabbling religious sects with missionary pretensions, commercial interests linked to the Far East, fanatic anti-Communists, and the Luce periodical empire. They were a power in the land across party lines and regional allegiances. Even FDR had family links to the missionary community.

This day, the amorphous mass was flexing its muscles. It wanted support for the new Chinese government in Shanghai, and for Christ's servants in China. Eleanor had just spent an hour extolling her husband's commitment to the crusade. Now Willkie must perforce match or exceed it.

On one hand this was just pushing Willkie where he wished to go. While not as vocal about it, he was as much an internationalist as Franklin. More so in the Far East. The new alliance structure removed the danger of a US-Japanese War. The Navy's Plan Orange would continue to gather dust. This in turn would leave more strength to keep the Atlantic sea lanes open. The US Pacific Fleet had recently sent a major squadron to Norfolk, with more expected to follow. Doubtless the Atlantic fleet staff was giving Plan Black, the one for a sea war with Germany, a reworking as it became ever clearer that Germany meant Europe, which meant the French and Italian fleets.

But there was another hand. Eleanor had just promised an air contingent. An 'American Volunteer Group', a version of the Lafayette Escadrille for China. All volunteers, but the US would 'lend' the Chinese the planes and other supplies. Would 'lend' the British a division's kit to rebuild their China forces. Still more weapons would be 'lent' to the new Chinese forces. Lindy would have a fit at planes and pilots being stolen to fight someone else's war in Asia. Father Coughlin would scream about wasting the taxes of his hardscrabble flock on far shores for dubious purpose. Willkie's country club followers would bemoan deficits and high taxes.

All true, and none of it relevant. The key components of the China Lobby owned the national Republican Party and thus by extension him. If "Time" and "Life" magazines turned against him, his campaign was over. It had been so nice to once have had a soul, an independent conscience. A serious candidate could afford neither. Maybe he'd up Eleanor and offer an American training mission for this new Chinese Army. It would give some of the younger officers combat experience. Better they spent Asian blood learning the basics, rather than dead American conscripts.

0630 hours local; 16 September 1940
2330 hours CET; 15 September 1940
Comintern headquarters, Kunming, Yunnan, Republic of China/KMT

The promised arms had finally been delivered. They were a near-random mix of British, German, and Japanese rifles and light machine-guns; plus two quite ancient Italian mortars. The available ammunition was limited, and much of it of dubious quality. None of that mattered. There were arms for the three hundred-odd assembled men. They were predominantly Viets and southern Chinese, but included Laotians, Thais, Cambodians, border hill peoples both from the nearby hills and from as far away as the Assam-Tibet frontier, Eurasians … and even two Frenchwomen, of all things.

The leader had been serving the Comintern in China for the best part of a decade. Now he was tasked with returning home, with raising Indochina in revolt against its colonial masters. Nominally this action would lack support from both Moscow and Chiang. Both were hoping to maintain the friendly neutrality of the French viceroy in Hanoi. So the theory would be that this column was Vietnamese Nationalist, not Indochinese Communist. A fig leaf, but for now a necessary one if one were to expect more arms and money at intervals later. The man who had been born Nguyen Sinh Cung and as of yesterday had been Nguyen Ai Quoc, noted Communist international, was now just a humble Vietnamese patriot, Ho Chi Minh. An invented name was a blank slate on which to inscribe the future.

1100 hours CET

15 September 1940

A conference room, Gerbini aerodrome, Sicily

The summer heat had finally broken. The room was merely hot as opposed to ovenlike. Oberst Hans Maurice was surprised to see Generalleutnant Gerhardt Ramcke at a scheduled meeting with General Jodl. Maurice had met Ramcke on Malta. What had brought this paratroop officer to Kampfgruppe Jodl? Maurice was generally aware that what had been the Ramcke Brigade on Malta had been redesignated Second Fallschirmjäger Division. Precisely what that entailed Maurice didn't know. He'd been too busy whipping his new battalions into shape.

"Hans, our friend Gerhard has a problem. We have decided that you are the solution." Maurice looked puzzled. What precisely was Jodl saying?

Ramcke picked up the discussion from Jodl. "I've rebuilt my old brigade into a two-regiment division. Ministry has used Student's First Fallschirmjäger as a depot unit for me. The problem is the heavy weapons components. The battalions have been given machine-gun companies but no mortars. The weapons battalion of each regiment has more machine-guns, and a company each of those worthless 50mm mortars. So instead of four battalions I have six; but when it is all said and done, it's a light infantry force. It would be blown over by a 1918 British division with real artillery and armored cars. I need some sort of firepower for counterbattery and some antitank capability. That's where you come in."

Thinking furiously about how many men he was about to lose and what it would do to his training schedule, Maurice asked the obvious, "How many men? What weapons? It will ruin my training scheme but you seem to have priority." Shit. This was the chaos before the Malta drop all over again. Germany's forte was supposed to be planning …

"You have it backwards. Two battalion-sized Kampfgruppes. A true Artillery Regiment. You will of course command. You choose the men, the weapons and such. I will procure the needed gliders."

"I am SA and NL, not Luftwaffe."

"I was originally Navy. Then naval infantry, then Army, and finally Luftwaffe. We Germans need to be flexible. Keep your SA uniform. The whole theater is doing mixed units since Malta. General Felix Steiner's new Division is having all its artillery in Navy uniforms. The issue is the right weapons and the proper commander. You are the commander and you know the weapons."

Jodl chuckled. "It gets more complex than you've realized. Ramcke's six battalions and your two make eight. Which will be split into two battlegroups. He will take one and you the other. The mission is the bridge over the Suez Canal here." Jodl unrolled a map.

Maurice's head was reeling. "When?" He needed to know how long he had to make this abortion work.

"Sometime in November. You will be shifted to air bases in Africa in late October." Jodl looked to Ramcke, who took over the discussion. "This time we'll have enough trained pilots to actually find our target; and this time, no idiot night landings. We take off in the dark but we drop half an hour after dawn, when the pilots can see, when the pathfinder bombers can drop colored smoke bombs to mark the two drop zones."

"This is a lot to take in. Why me?"

"I saw you work on Malta. It was brief but you made a good impression. I don't trust relying on who Student or the Ministry would send me." Ramcke then recounted the sad history of the mutiny that had given him command. "So you see why I want to rely on comrades who have been through the same battle I have. We Malta hands need to stick together!"

Jodl got technical. Ramcke was content to let them argue weapons characteristics versus weights. He was out of his depth, and needed an expert. He also hoped to acquire a senior General as a patron, even if that officer was presently somewhat in disgrace.

1000 hours Eastern Daylight Time; 1600 hours CET
15 September 1940
Director's Office, FBI Headquarters, Department of Justice Building, 950 Pennsylvania Avenue NW, Washington DC

The Director had a decision to make. Given the political and media connections the Bureau possessed, J. Edgar Hoover was as aware as Harry Hopkins that the race had tightened, and probably more aware than Wendell Willkie was. Hoover did not especially like Franklin. He loathed his red dyke wife and the little pansy Hopkins who ran the machine. But they were a familiar thorn in his shoe. A modus vivendi existed between them. They didn't interfere with the Bureau, and he didn't turn his fabulous treasure trove of scandalous information against them. Hopkins had at least been careful with his Commie lover. Franklin and Eleanor both had numerous lovers. In her case lovers of both sexes. The Bureau had still pictures, movie footage, audio recordings, phone taps. Had this all and never used it.

Overthrow of a President could motivate the new President to remove the Director. Technically, any president had such power. Willkie was from a different wing of the Republicans than that ambitious little toad Dewey. Still, a presidential administration usually doled out the jobs between the different party wings. Dewey as Attorney General put him over the Bureau, over Hoover. The little bastard would seize the files in the blink of an eye.

So the one to be smeared was Willkie. The weapon would be the married mistress, Irita Van Doren. Just the sort of Manhattan literary parasite who wouldn't play well to the Babbits of small town America who were the Republican bedrock. The problem would be getting past the press blockade. Everyone who was anyone knew who the mistresses, gigolos, and lovers were. Everyone had them, and nothing was printed. He needed someone far enough outside the mainstream to break the wall of silence, but with enough of a following to matter.

Hoover decide to approach this from a different compass heading. There were half a dozen movie tattler gossip sheets which shared dirt with the LA office. If two or three were offered pictures, one would bite. The Bureau could then spread it. Willkie was for race equality. Enough Dixie papers would run with a story that he was a degenerate as well as a race traitor, as long as they could claim they were reporting a story already public.

No need to tell the Roosevelts. The one to relay with through-out, was Hopkins. The tool would be his Comintern courier. Give it a few weeks for the story to ripen. Pick the bitch up leaving the White House, on a material-witness warrant to compel appearance before a grand jury. Leave her inside for a few days, so Hopkins would have to call about it. Arrange a meeting and lay out how the administration owed him big.

Big enough to cover a new Bureau project. The FBI had done nothing to hinder people heading off to Mexico to join the Aztecs and fight in Manchuria. Indeed, his agents had 'aided' some people. Picked them up, driven them to El Paso and pushed them across the bridge. Communists, anarchists, race mixers, Jews, troublemakers. Let them fight for Stalin and never come home. Every sheriff in Dixie had half a dozen hard cases he'd be happy to unload.

0900 hours local; 0800 hours CET
16 September 1940
Joey's new workshop behind Axis Alamein lines

Getting the men and equipment up from the Three Crosses Camp had been a nightmare. One that Paul Schwabe had been forced to handle largely on his own. Papa Isaac and Brother Peter were off playing soldier. Uncle Ivan was as well, but he always wanted to return to being a soldier. Papa and Brother would rather have been back in equipment repair and use, the real family business before all this idiocy with Nazis, Soviets, and Africa.

Brother Luke was still back in Bari with mother and his sisters. His cousin Greta was back at the original Camp Gorlov, organizing the transport of the food stocks. The SS had gotten most of the loot from this new battle. Pity, but war was like that. Joey was out gathering loot in terms of fixable vehicles. He had 'liberated' dozens of trucks and autos, plus three Matilda tanks. Paul had grown up around machine workers all his life. He understood the lure of making workable the wrecks idiots could create from perfectly good metal constructs. Everyone had their reasons to be elsewhere, but that left him managing the truck convoy and the new base setup.

The SS engineering officer Seela and the three on-loan Italians were supervising the hundred-plus new Betar 'recruits' as construction labor. Three had already deserted. The SS had returned two dead bodies, so one was still at large. Uncle Ivan had sensibly tattooed the 'volunteers' with the word 'Betar' and the Afrika Korps palm tree. The SS had a battalion sweeping up stray British wandering the battlefield. They were ordered to check the left arm for the marking. Two fools had not believed this, and paid accordingly.

That left Gunter's gift to the repair shops, SA officer and former blacksmith Lothar Engels. The fool had gotten run out of Klaus's unit. Sent back to Gunter, the fool had refused to calm down, to 'face certain facts'. He and Gunter adjourned to the repair yard, to continue the discussion 'outside the boundaries of rank'. Gunter had taken the charge of the enraged Nazi, lifted him over his head and smashed him to the ground. When the fool refused to sensibly stay down, Gunter had simply cold-cocked him.

As is, the fool was lucky. Had the instructor in manners been his brother Peter, he'd have been dead. Peter had killed people in street fights back home. Peter didn't go looking for trouble. He also didn't back off from trouble that found him. He saw himself as the family's protector, especially mother and his sisters. People who harassed them in the streets were apt to be paid a visit by Peter and a few of his cronies from the roughneck crew Peter bossed for Papa. Work wasn't easy to find in those lean years in Romania. Papa paid well and treated laboring people decently. Said it was the way to get and keep good people. Papa's attorney had had to have words with the local police a few times over these 'fair fights'. Twice senior foreigners from the oil field management had had to intervene. The local tough guys, even the lunatics from the Iron Guard, had learned that this firm, this family, were out of bounds.

Lothar was a decent blacksmith and metal worker. The twin problems were his sour attitude and acid tongue. Paul was not as large as his huge brother Peter. He had a watchmaker's almost feminine hands and amazing eye-hand coordination, enabling him to do fine machining. However, he was still 1.9 meters tall and 120 kilos of young muscle. He had considered just beating the fool into sullen submission, but that wasn't the sort of workplace he wanted to run … unless there was no other choice. His way was to try talking, one more time. Thank God Papa had made him learn basic German and English back in Romania. Papa's excuse was that too many machine spec's were in those tongues. Explaining to a young lad why studying languages wasn't too girly needed finesse.

"Lothar. Shut down the forge and come here. We need to chat. Again." The extremely muscular old man put aside his tools, made sure his fire wasn't a hazard, and walked over. The man was a craftsman, even if he was a bull-headed Brownshirt asshole.

"What the *beschissenes Schlamassel* now?" Lothar paused. He wanted to call the boss-subhuman here a Kike Slavic animal, but was aware enough to know Kike and Slav were separate. "And which are you? Kike filth or filthy subhuman Slav?"

" 'What now' is your attitude and your mouth. As for which thing you dislike, Slav by birth, Hebrew by rearing and conversion. They don't do baptisms, but the equivalent." Paul assumed a fighter's stance. "Is this what you want, fool? To be beaten like a mad dog? We tried giving you away. SS won't take you. Army doesn't want you. There's an NL division forming up. Got some French and Balt units, but the core is Germans. SA and HJ, same as Peiper had. We've got feelers out to their General. You've got combat experience, but you were also relieved for insubordination after making as ass of yourself on the battlefield."

Lothar made a growling noise and rushed Paul. Paul straight-armed Lothar's charge, used his momentum as leverage against him, and flipped him over on his back. Knocked the wind out of the fool. Paul left him gasping on the ground. Eventually the old blacksmith caught his breath and levered himself up. Paul just shook his head. "Fool. I'm younger and stronger than you are. You got more strength in your arms but I have the reach. If you just want a ticket home, say so. We can arrange a trip back to Prinz-Albrecht-Straße where you can explain to the Reichsführer why he is mismanaging Germany."

Lothar shook his head a few times, trying to clear it. "So you Kikes bought Heydrich. He was always of tainted blood." Lothar caught himself. Reminding Heydrich of the accusations against him was the road to death, not vindication. "So tell me, Slav Yid, what are you subhumans doing in German uniform?"

"The Romanians hate us worse than you Germans do. We did essential work at the oil fields. Strauss recruited us with Heydrich's blessings. After the short Soviet war ended, the new SS master at Ploiesti wanted us out.   So we got sent here, to help capture new oil fields."

"There's oil here in Egypt?"

"No. Which is why Italy gets Egypt. The oil is someplace called Iraq, four or five conquests from now. Geography was never my best subject in school. I preferred learning in our machine shop. I apprenticed to every master craftsman we had. I have the eye and the hands for machining."

Lothar looked at this young giant strangely. He remembered some Karl May adventure novels that featured an Aryan hero and his Bedouin. "This where the Kurds come from?"

"Near there. Kurds are mountain folks. This is the plains beneath their mountains. Supposed to be hellish. Been told it hits 63 degrees in high summer. Imagine being in front of a forge's fires in that heat."

Lothar chuckled in spite of himself. "63? I used to bitch when it crept up near 40. Germany need the oil that badly?"

Paul smiled back. "Damned if I know. Ask the big bosses. Heydrich says so. Doesn't trust Stalin and doesn't want Germany depending on the Bolshies for keeping your planes flying and tanks running. So we take it, get it back to running, ship the oil back to Germany from some Jewish port called Haifa. That's the plan. As for Klaus fucking my cousin Greta, why shouldn't he? Your race laws don't apply here. Ask that engineer from the SS. This side of the water even the SS can fuck who they choose. Heydrich wants to keep the brats they spawn for Germany. Something about what the British did in India. Reichsführer thinks long-term. Gets the people you Nazis hate out of Europe, sets them up being useful to your Thousand Year Reich. That's how empires run. Could be a place for you if you could ever get a grip on your bullshit. Oil fields are always a kludge of machines. Mostly German, British, and American; but back home we had Italian, French, Belgian, Swedish and Swiss, and that only counts what I remember fast. There's always a need for fast spares and never enough of some damned part. Good metalworkers earned well. It is dirty, but men's work always is."

Lothar was confused. "Why do you damned Yids know so many state secrets?" He was thinking also, why the fuck was the young asshole telling him instead of just beating him into submission?

The younger man gave a weary shake of his head. "Awfully hard to recruit good people without some sort of story. You think Germany beating the British matters to most of us? Germany, Italy, Britain … it is all the same with us. Why should we give a shit beyond staying alive? Just avoiding being executed doesn't cut it for getting first rate technical labor. So we got a story where we matter, can have decent lives. Got it in bits and pieces through our minders and Berlin. I doubt we know 5% of it, but why would the high strategy matter to little people like us?" Paul gave Lothar a stare, shook his head sadly. "And that's why I'm explaining to you. My brother would just as soon twist your neck off, write it up as a shop-floor accident. No one will rat us out. My brother Peter was always a hothead. Ran rough crews with his fists and boots. I was the one doing the machining back in the shop for his roughnecks to install. I am short of first-rate metal workers. Who am I going to recruit out here? Another illiterate raghead like Abdul Collins?" Lothar looked at Paul blankly. "The Arab boy, works for the head cook Mary." Lothar nodded slowly. He vaguely remembered the sand nigger. "You do good work when you pay attention to anything besides your stupid grievances. Made it worth five minutes to try. Five but not thirty."

Lothar hated everything about this. But he'd still rather be an SA officer than a village blacksmith. Röhm had promised a revolution to guys like him. A revolution that had never happened because Röhm and his boys turned out to be pansy degenerates. "I've lost my command. What's my pay status?"

"Whatever it says it is for your rank. When we ever get a paymaster section, ask them. I'll tell the pay clerk what you'd get as a master craftsman by our scale. He'll pay you the higher. Meantime, doubt you need your pay anytime soon. Nowhere to spend it before we take the big cities. Gunter's asked Berlin for a paymaster." Paul had never learned military discipline. Oberst Strauss was a family friend, not a commanding officer. "The one we were expecting, Greta's father, got himself killed. His fool wife, Crazy Ruth, back-talked some SS officer. Bang, bang, too bad, so sad. Ruth's big mouth was a running family joke. We always said it would kill her. She's no loss. Pity she took her husband and kids with her, but that's war. He was a good bookkeeper. We've got dozens more at our base camp in Italy, but Berlin hasn't decided if they want to send their own guys or not. You need pocket money before it all gets worked out?"

Lothar saw red. "What interest?" Jews were always slick with money.

"No interest. We write it up as advance against pay and sort out the advances and the back sums you are owed. I'm sure there's someone doing the usual 6 marks next Monday for 5 marks today game. Every work crew I ever knew of had a few. But it is not a scam we run on our own. The words you need to learn are 'us' and 'them'. The oil fields are going to be a boom town from all that gas."

Lothar blinked. "Gas? Thought you said oil."

Paul had forgotten that ordinary people didn't know much about oil fields. "It all comes out together. Oil, gas, some more solid stuff you use to pave roads. It's complicated. Refinery work isn't my thing yet. More shit to learn, machines to fix. But there's no cheap, easy way to ship the gas back to Europe. So it usually mostly gets flared off. Joey and I have been talking. That's a shame. We get the gas into canisters, or better yet eventually its own pipeline. The gas burns. Fire means heat. Means steam and electricity. Be a boom of plants needing cheap power. Joey recruited a bunch of guys with that lure. Work with us through the conquest and start your own shop when we get demobilized. Get a bunch of locals for sweat labor. When the shooting ends, I'll catch a ship home to Romania. Got a whole bunch of our old guys I'll try recruiting."

"More Yids?"

"A few. Mostly Romanian Slavs, but there's Magyars, Serbs, Roma. Bit of this and that. Oilfield work is a gypsy kind of trade. A lot of guys drift from one field to the next. Labor need falls off once a field stops expanding. No more bonuses and overtime. Strangers get bounced so the bosses can bring in nephews and cousins. Way of the world. Worked with a black man from America for a while. He'd worked oil in the States, the islands to the south, Mexico, Venezuela, Borneo and Persia before ending up in Romania. Story was he had to leave Persia fast."

"Why?"

"Got caught in the wrong bed when her husband came home. Don't tell me that never happened in Germany."

Lothar thought for a moment. He still hated this all, but unless that new General took him he was out of options … for now. Meantime, working was better than getting beaten up by young men half his age. Lothar put out his hand and Paul took it. Paul knew he was buying a truce at best, but for now it was enough.

Chapter 7

1300 Hours CET
16 September 1940
Heereswaffenamt (Weapons Office), Jebensstraße corner Hertz Avenue, Berlin

The six-story building that housed the Army's weapon office had been a hive of constant activity almost from the moment that Hitler took over Germany. Waffenamt had coordinated the procurement of tens of billions of Reichsmarks of weapons, equipment, and munitions for the Wehrmacht. This process hadn't always gone smoothly. Once war began, the Army had cried out for ever more munitions and weapons. The crisis over munitions had driven the previous head of the Waffenamt, General der Artillerie Karl Becker, to suicide just before the invasion of Denmark back in April.

Poor Becker, thought General der Artillerie Emil Leeb, current head of the Waffenamt. *If he could only see where Germany was today*. Totally triumphant on the continent, and now driving across Africa. Still, there had been ample cause for the stress that finally caused Becker to end his life. When the Reich went to war in 1939 the army was just! Not! ready! The outside world only saw Germany going from triumph to triumph; people had no idea how hollow a shell the army really was, or what a disaster the procurement and production process was. Design and industrial expansion programs had been started not intending to be finished until 1942 or 43! Germany had been armed in breadth, not depth. There were never enough raw materials, enough money, enough manufacturing facilities, enough skilled labor, enough anything except competing bureaucratic empire-builders. The National Socialist state appeared from the outside as an invincible monolith working towards the Führer's will. The reality had been a set of squabbling satraps lurching from crisis to crisis. On top of that, the directives from the national leader had been like a weathervane, blowing in the breeze of whoever had his ear last.

Those problems had ended when Heydrich assumed power. The problem was now quite the reverse. All programs suddenly had to justify themselves. Waste, lies, and minor feathering of one's nest produced visits from the Gestapo. Army officers were spared the worst. Their civilian contractors frequently got to experience the joys of scientific interrogation, often followed by an appointment with the hangman or the headsman. Hitler had lived in a world of imagination, of the projection of his will on mundane matter. Heydrich and his henchmen such as Todt and Speer, were pure technocrats. Germany must henceforth cut its coat to fit its cloth. Resources were all finite and carefully guarded. Efficiency and combat power were now the rules of the weapons procurement process.

One of those programs was the source of today's meeting. The service rifle of the Army was the Mauser 98K, accurate, long ranged, rugged ... and first produced in 1898! A specification had been issued in 1938, 40 years after the Mauser first entered service, for a new service rifle. The new service rifle was to be capable of single-shot or fully automatic fire. Of course, the war started before that project, like so many others, could finish.

After Malta there had been a change in membership of the Reich Council on Armaments and Munitions. Von Richthofen was now Deputy Reich Minister of Aviation and Deputy Chief of the Luftwaffe. No one was fooled by this polite fiction of titles; von Richthofen was in total control of the Luftwaffe. The Malta triumph had deeply embarrassed Führer Göring with the poor showing of his service. The new head of the Luftwaffe had taken his mandate from Göring to clean up the service and run with it. Besides replacing himself on the council and as Generalluftzeugmeister (Luftwaffe Director-General of Equipment) with General Der Flieger Wilhelm Wimmer, there had been a general removal of deadwood and old Göring flunkies. Old comrades of Göring had been moved out of technical slots. A prime example was Erhard Milch, moved from Inspector General to a combat command. The lesser deadweights had been seconded to the Chancellery staff. The new Führer and Chancellor preferred not to do actual government business, so these clowns could do little harm there beyond consuming champagne and caviar at galas.

For Wimmer, his new appointment was life coming full circle; before Udet held the role of Generalluftzeugmeister it had been his. Along with Wimmer, General Thomas of the Army, Admiral Fuchs of the Navy, and Speer were here to get an update on the Maschinenkarabiner (Mkb) program launched in 1938 to replace the 98k. The invasion of Malta, it seemed, had sparked some renewed focus on the state of German small arms. Heydrich had talked to Todt, and the Minister for Armaments and Ammunition had set his four minions to look into matters. Malta had yet again shown the need for selective fire was far more important than accuracy at long ranges. Conscript armies did not produce masses of marksmen. The need was for heavy firepower at close-to-medium ranges.

"Gentlemen, Haenel is scheduled to do a live-fire demonstration later this year; Walther, it is not clear if their prototype will be able to make that date." As General Leeb explained, junior officers passed out information packets to the four that made up the Reich Council on armaments and munitions. Turning a page, "Mauser and Walther are working a parallel project for a semi-automatic rifle. It is not expected for either to have a prototype ready for first demonstration until next year."

At mention of having two weapons programs, the four men across from Leeb frowned almost in concert. A clear and (recently) ruthlessly-enforced mandate was to rationalize and consolidate research and production programs. The new mandate was currently playing hell with production, as lines were forced to shut down to convert over, but there would be major dividends later.

Noting the response, Leeb quickly explained, "There are problems with the Mkb program. An alternate possible source was thought prudent; the rifle grenade and other requirements are proving difficult to meet, and from the reports received from Poland and the West … "

There was a shuffling of papers by all in the meeting room. While Leeb continued to talk, Speer glanced through the reports. *Incredible, some of these actually date back to the early 1920's, right after the Great War!* In brief, the reports pointed out the same thing, anything above 400 meters for a service rifle was superfluous in terms of range for the vast majority of battles. What was needed was higher rates of fire, larger magazines, and faster-changing magazines.

The paratroopers had cried out to their parent organization, the Luftwaffe, to do something about the issue of small arms, and General Wimmer had listened, "General Leeb, the day of the bolt-action rifle is done. The Americans four years ago started to issue a new semi-automatic rifle … the … "

"The M-1 Garand, General Wimmer." Leeb helpfully supplied; and General Thomas added his own information, "The Italians have started production of the Armaguerra Model 1939, a 6-round semi-automatic rifle."

Then Speer: "The Soviets are working on a semi-automatic rifle, produced by an engineer named Tokarev; they used it against the Finns, but rumors suggest they are still trying to refine the design." By now everyone was used to him functioning as the funnel for SS requests and foreign intelligence findings.

"The Reich cannot be left behind, General Leeb." Thomas' statement left no room for debate. More and more, the Army was looking east with concern at the Soviet Union. The invasion of Japan's puppet state in Manchuria would provide only a temporary distraction. Stalin's Hitler Pact, and now the vast eastern campaign, had clearly shown that all dealings with Moscow were transactional and transitory. When Stalin saw advantage, he would strike West.

Previous to the meeting, Heydrich through Schellenberg had impressed on Speer and Todt the need for continued integration of Europe's economy and armaments industry. "If the new rifle programs are having trouble, perhaps additional sets of eyes are required. I suggest we add a replacement service rifle to the Europa Cartel system. The French and Italians have skilled small arms designers and manufacturers. So do the Belgians and Swiss."

It was difficult for the other members of the group to hold their tempers at this point. France had been a bitter enemy for decades, if not centuries, and Italy was viewed with contempt, but the directive from Prinz-Albrecht-Straße was logical when viewed dispassionately. The three uniformed officers silently nodded their agreement to one another. General Leeb, when the meeting was over, reissued the replacement service rifle specification – but it would also go to firms across Europe, not just to German ones.

The Luftwaffe general added that, as regards his service, the rifle-grenade capacity was expendable. Speer had been about to make the same statement as regards the Waffen SS, NL, and SA. He did get to add that a lighter cartridge was also acceptable for the services he directly represented. The important factors were ease of cleaning, simplicity of use, and firepower in the assault. For defense, the primary weapon would remain the machine-gun. As ever-greater numbers would be needed, the meeting turned to the projected simpler replacement, the MG-39.

1400 hours Central Daylight Time; 2000 hours CET
16 September 1940
Ft. Riley Kansas

Newly-promoted Brigadier General George Patton could have regarded being moved from commanding an Armored Brigade, to be the commander of a yet-to-be-formed Armored Cavalry Regiment, as a demotion. He never for a second thought of it that way. This was a combat command, the only one the US Army currently had.

In theory, this was a training and demonstration force for the new Christian Chinese Army. That was a polite fiction. He would teach their cadres via service alongside his troopers. What was better, for political reasons, his regiment would consist only of volunteers. No draftees whining to their mothers, Congressmen, and the press about hard-nosed discipline, severe training, or casualties.

Higher command had created the idea of armored cavalry as a light armored force, geared to rapid mobility in a combined-arms setting. Patton smiled to himself. Lot of swell-sounding words for the press release. Reality was something else. The US military had almost no armored fighting vehicles, and what they had was pathetic. M-1 and M-2 cavalry combat cars, and two variants of the M-2 light tank. The first real tank, the M-3 Stuart, was months away if everything went well, and nothing ever went that well on new weapons systems. General Marshall promised him a hundred of these models combined. Patton was more concerned with spare parts and trained mechanics. He doubted the order for a hundred would produce eighty vehicles, and would bet half of those would be nonfunctional repair-bay queens. That was how he would have responded to such an order if he were still commanding an armored brigade.

His former division commander, General Chaffee, wouldn't let him steal his former command's vehicles wholesale. Chaffee had allowed Patton to interview for volunteers, and had gifted him with eight totally obsolete M-1 armored cars. For the rest, he would use WW1 four-wheel-drive light trucks, touring cars, and whatever else the supply people could scrape up. DC wanted something that could be deployed fast, not a perfect unit for 1942.

Patton had a thought on how to get good men. He planned to field at least one battalion of colored troops. The Buffalo Soldier regiments always had career privates who could easily be made corporals, and corporals who were worthy of being sergeants. They were also less likely to have racial problems with English-speaking Chinese and Eurasians serving in their ranks. Plus Mrs. President was a big defender of the darkies. Having patrons at the top helped.

The unit had been promised test models of every tank, half-track, and armored car the Army put into prototype production. That was for later. For now he would fight battles along the banks of the Yangtse, as the legendary Ever Victorious Army had done almost a century ago under American commander Frederick Townsend Ward. And later, after Ward's death, under his successor Chinese Gordon. He'd have his staff people make up a comic book on this all, for the troops to read on the transports over.

His old friend Ike Eisenhower had served a few years in the Philippines. Knowing Ike, he'd made good connections. He'd asked Marshall if he could have Ike as a battalion commander. Marshall said Eisenhower would have to volunteer. Battalion was a step down for a lieutenant colonel, although not a big one. Patton had sent him a telegram that had led to a phone call. Ike would leave in a few days for Manila by air. The twin gifts offered were a promise that when the regiment was upgraded to a two-regiment brigade, Ike would get a regiment with a colonelcy and combat. Ike had been stuck in a training command in WW1, and had never lived down not being a combat officer. It had done much to stall his career.

Ike would raise a Philippine battalion with the promise of pay at US wages as if they were white men. MacArthur was commander-in-chief in the Philippines. He would scream, but Marshall now outranked him. Plus it would help the Philippine Army in the medium term. Blooded junior officers and NCO's would be worth their weight in gold.

1200 hours local; 1100 hours CET
17 September 1940
General Headquarters, Cairo

What a difference a day can make. The news came in on the teletype just after dinner yesterday, marked Top Secret. Winston was out, at long last. Replaced by Ernie Bevin of all people. The new War Cabinet was making fast decisions. So fast O'Connor's head was whirling.

Fifth Indian Division was to come north to Egypt as fast as First South African Division could replace it in Sudan. Second South African would be brought north to Kenya as replacement as quickly as it could be formed, but the whole movement starts now, not waiting for Second. Kenya would be left naked if needs be. If Egypt were lost, the new 8th Army (renamed from being Alamein Force) would retreat to Nigeria from Sudan if and as needs must.

The compromise on the Fleet was over. The submarines and the remaining destroyers were to leave within the next two weeks, after evacuating all but a remnant of the Cyprus garrison. A cobbled-together force from the Cyprus regiment would maintain order for now. London would try to magic together a joint Greco-Turkish occupation to replace this, but the understrength British brigade that made up the garrison was coming out to Alexandria, and as many Empire nationals as wished to leave would evacuate by boat to Haifa.

The Australian First Corps, with 2 Australian divisions and the British First Cavalry Division, were to be sent to the Alamein front. London was working on getting Canberra's permission so no more threats of mutiny. O'Connor with Western Desert Force was for Jerusalem. The WDF would be renamed British 9th Army. Headquarters 7th Armored Division would come over to Palestine with him. It was to be rebuilt as circumstances permitted. 7th would join Second New Zealand Corps with its single New Zealand Division, plus as much Jewish militia as could be mobilized for home defense. The simmering Arab revolt would be met with force. The day for kind words was over. The other half of his army was coming from India. Third Indian Corps with 10th Indian Division, followed by 8th. Also an Australian contingent once that Dominion agreed to it. The Indian troops would start to move now, but the command and organizational details would wait on the new Viceroy, Churchill, and the new C-in-C India, Claude Auchinleck, both en route via Africa.

Winston Churchill, the arch-opponent of Indian independence, would be a rude shock to the Indian political establishment. To make this happen, the guiding principle must have been the need to get him out of London. There was no way this strange new government would seem real with Winston on the floor of the House of Commons, waiting for a comeback. Lloyd George in that role was bad enough.

O'Connor was also warned that an Iraqi revolt was all too possible. His instructions were to stall for time, until he had at least one Indian division. Then he was to move, stripping the Iraqi military of its artillery, aircraft, and armored vehicles. If there was resistance, he could disband the Iraqi forces and recruit new levies. The same levies the British had abandoned to their fate in the 1930's when the idiots in the Foreign Ministry had taken the League Mandate seriously enough to offer something close to independence. The French had not been so stupid in Syria. Thank God London had seen the light before trying it in Palestine. No peace deal or partition would have survived ten minutes after British departure. The Arabs wanted the Jews dead, or at least gone, not some messy power and land sharing.

Now O'Connor had clear instructions. Save Iraqi oil and the sea connection to India. If possible save the Hashemite dynasty. If not possible, save the royal family. Both of these took hind place to not losing his army.

There was one sticky wicket. In the event of major retreats, priority was to evacuate British troops, officials, and nationals first. Other Empire peoples would come on a space-available basis … except the Palestinian Jews, who were not wanted elsewhere. No evacuation was to be permitted. If necessary, deadly force would be used. Hostages could be taken to assure obedience. Nasty. More so as Britain was using their men as both line troops in Egypt and as occupation troops in Palestine. O'Connor understood the imperial politics involved. If you evacuate them, you must bring them someplace; and no one wanted more Jews. The logic of empire was not for the squeamish.

1130 hours CET
17 September 1940
New Malpensa industrial park, vicinity of Milan, Italy

The ever-so-polite SS emissary Wolff had disrupted the government of Italy yet again. Had met the two rulers, himself and the Prince, three mornings ago with yet another poison pill from that fiend Heydrich. Germany was making a major research effort in something called nuclear physics. Led by the German Nobel laureate Heisenberg, they were going to use this magic of what until recently the Party had called Jewish Science, to bring cheap electric power to Europe.

Wolff had announced that this was to be focused on electric power generation. Italy's leading physicist, Professor Edoardo Amaldi from the Sapienza University in Rome, had been playing Army *tenente* in Libya. An S79 transport, from the squadron reserved for servicing senior government people, had quickly shuttled him home. Amaldi revealed what Wolff had significantly neglected to mention – that the same physics could also make hugely destructive bombs. The theory said these would be deadly enough that one bomb could kill Milan. Amaldi admitted this was all very speculative, so perhaps the Germans had simply declined to waste money chasing a possible mirage. As he put it, Heisenberg could well have induced Germany to spend a fortune chasing the cutting-edge-science version of the Philosopher's Stone or the Fountain of Youth. All anyone had to go on was a lot of complex mathematics, buttressed with theorizing. It was supposedly validated by one set of experiments by a couple of refugees. In the end it could all lead to nowhere, beyond a few Nobel prizes. Balbo admitted to himself that this could be true, but governments plan for worst case. There was no way Italy could allow itself to be excluded.

What's worse, Italy's best expert on this strange field, Enrico Fermi, had been chased to the US by Il Duce aping Hitler's Jew manias. Fermi had a Jewish wife. The bulk of the worldwide experts in this branch of knowledge seemed to be some combination of Jews, Magyars, and Marxists.

Heisenberg would do his work in Germany, but Heydrich proposed that a European companion project be set up in Italy. The polite wording was that Jews et cetera would find Italy more socially congenial than some German facility where they would be oppressed by the race laws and harassed by the local National Socialist Party militants.

Yes, Italy had long known how to have special rules for special people. Easy enough to pass the word to the right people – these few hundred (or few thousand, as the program grew) were to be treated like nobility, not commoners. It was a social and administrative matter. He had a hundred good subordinates who could smooth over such a situation, given clear authority from Rome and the ability to make a few very visible examples. Your Marxist half-Jew scientist really wasn't expecting to be invited to go hunting at the local baron's villa anyway.

Indeed, a very polite invitation to Fermi could be made. He might not come, but word of the offer would spread. Other lesser people, who lacked his tenured position at such a fine university as Columbia, might migrate back.

The big problem was the damned French. Turned out they had even better physicists than Germany. Wolff made clear that Italy's participation was voluntary. If they opted out, the institute would go in Lorraine near Metz; and the directorate would be Franco-German instead of Italian. He and the Prince were in agreement. Italy must not be cheated of this prize.

So a first class institute would be set up on Lake Garda at the Hotel Victoriale Deligo Italanini. It was near Salo, a luxury vacation district which should appeal to the senior researchers. This would show that CERN, Consiglio Europeo per la Ricera Nucleare, was considered a prestige project. The local heads of the Fascist party, and the local notables, were quite pleased with getting a new population of highly-paid year round residents.

That left de facto co-ruler Italo Balbo here at Malpensa. The facility was coming along nicely. The new Jewish and Magyar labor was working with speeds normally not seen on Italian projects. Balbo was now telling the project managers to adjust their plans for a large CERN installation. The thinking elite would go to Salo. The administrative backup, the technical shops and whatever else would be needed, would go here. You don't put a major facility in a vacation town. You set it near Italy's financial and industrial heart in Lombardy. His subordinates would oversee this, but the local grandees needed his presence to impress on them just how important Rome rated all of this. He had had to do the same when starting the whole Malpensa development project, including the huge airfield. He also reviewed the progress on the massive Malpensa railway loop project. Major industrial development needed rail transport with good links through Switzerland to Germany. The new cartel system depended on this.

2000 hours Central Daylight Time; 1200 hours CET
17 September 1940
Ft. Benning, Georgia

Thank God for long distance telephone calls. Temporary Captain Benjamin O. Davis, Jr. had been alerted by his Brigadier General father that George Patton was going to recruit a Buffalo battalion of colored troops for his China expeditionary force. Dad telegraphed him to get his ass from Tuskegee, where Junior was an ROTC instructor, to Ft. Benning to present himself as a candidate for executive officer of this battalion. It was a stretch for a young man only a temporary captain for a few days, but most such juniors did not have the only Negro general officer in US service as their father. A father who could work the Army version of the old boy network for all it was worth. The interwar Army officer corps was a small, very clubby institution. Who you knew and what strings you could pull, counted far more than notional fitness reports.

Junior had followed orders … up to a point. However, he had also been making phone calls on his own. He had the flying bug since going up with a barnstormer as a boy. The Air Corps had rejected him out of West Point, because that service was all white. At the height of the Depression, near to the entire officer corps was white; and white opinion intended to keep it that way.

That was then. This was now. Now was an election year. Franklin Roosevelt would need massive turnouts of black votes in Chicago, New York, and the other big Northern cities to win a historic third term. Blacks would need to be motivated. FDR also needed segregationist Dixie. So he would do nothing substantive about Jim Crow or lynchings or any of the real issues. Enter symbolism. Enough of the civil rights establishment were incrementalists. Through the Tuskegee faculty, Junior had introduction to A. Philip Randolph of the Brotherhood of Sleeping Car Porters. That man heard the young officer's excited proposal for a Colored Lafayette Escadrille to fight for Jesus in China. He in turn had immediate phone access to the First Lady, who championed the idea to her husband within an hour of being told the concept.

It fit FDR's political needs. It undercut a Republican campaign issue. It gave a symbolic victory to the civil liberties champions, while tacitly reminding Dixie voters that Republicans kept proposing anti-lynching bills that could use Federal power to kill Jim Crow. The temporary captain now had a telegram with the authority of the commander-in-chief to enlist black pilots and mechanics, to set up a flight training program at Tuskegee for reinforcements. The official line was to apply 'separate but equal' to the air. Claire Chennault, a retired Air Corps officer with Chinese connections, would create the white flying unit. Junior would create the Negro, starting with existing pilots who could be enlisted as specialists outside normal Army channels. The officer corps would bury the project if given a chance. An officer reporting directly to the White House could evade this gaming. There were enough Colored crop dusters, barn stormers, and private flyers for the opening round of enlistments. The key was moving fast before the bureaucracy could find reasons to shut this down. It was amazing what could be done in an election year when large blocs of votes were at stake.

0800 hours local, 18 September 1940
2400 hours CET, 17 September 1940
The Lodge, Deakin, Australian Capital Territory

"I've already rejected a National government. You know damned well my party leftwing won't stomach it." John Curtin, leader of the Australian Labor Party, was a fine judge of what the coalition of factions that made up his nominal party would and would not do. He and the Coalition PM, Pig Iron Bob Menzies, knew each other and somewhat respected each other's ability to 'play the game' as it were.

"So we phrase it differently. Advisory War Council or some such government speak. I'm PM on the strength of two independents who could bolt to you on a whim, and London knows it. They have made a most interesting set of offers, but insist that it be crossparty. Otherwise they correctly fear Australia can keep the goodies, while you declare on assuming office you aren't bound to the commitments."

"What now?" Curtin had let Menzies get away with committing conscript Australian Militia to policing duties on the Dutch outer islands such as Bali and Timor. The Labor left saw this as a backstab. The promise had been conscription only for home defense. "I cannot let Militia be sent further afield."

Menzies made placating noises. "The Militia's safe. Indeed, I may be able to get those withdrawn … mostly. It's a complicated deal. Defects first. London's reviving the old Japanese Alliance … "

"Shit! No! It is your damned Pig Iron shipment a thousand times worse." Menzies had the name from a labor dispute over shipping pig iron to Japan for their China War. The dock unions saw the Japanese as war criminal barbarians in China. The Communist cadres in those locals fanned the flames and produced a mess that would stain Menzies till the day he died. Curtin was not eager to be hung with the same.

Menzies shrugged. "They will do this with or without us. The two are jointly backing a new Chinese government in Shanghai. Chiang's gone Bolshie again. Thrown out the missionaries and their flocks. London and the Yanks back the god pilots. Who are starving. London is proposing that we feed them. We are awash in food, with no ships to send our wheat, meat, offal, and the rest to Europe. China will buy it all. Send junks to move the stuff. London guarantees payment."

Curtin's head came up like a shot. "How much food?"

"All of it. We will have to tin the meat, as no reefer ships come with the deal. Your ever so Red dock workers won't have to load that many Japanese ships. The part going to Japan will get crossloaded in China. But agriculture and mines. Whatever we can produce. London is willing to be a bit expansive on prices. Supposedly this is to cover bringing more expensive marginal production on board. In fact it's a sweetener, and a hedge against postwar inflation. We get paid in pounds. War's expensive. Postwar prices on British manufactures may be higher than prewar."

"Dock workers' wages?"

"How does a 15% raise on Australia signing the deal, and doubletime for overs sound?"

"Sounds like I'm being asked to swallow a lot of bitter medicine to get the sugar treat."

Pig Iron Bob had saved the tough stuff for now. "Our corps in Palestine is going to be ordered up to Egypt, ready or not. Our general will protest. We back London. We don't let our boys bear an inordinate share of the blood price of battle. No idiot Gallipoli. But they fight and bleed, same as our corps did on the Western front."

The prime minister paused for a sigh. He didn't like this bartering of blood, but needs must. "London thinks the next battle will go no worse than the last. Lose some men, lose some ground. They admit they expect to lose Egypt, but with a river as wide as the Nile as a fallback position they don't see how they can lose it quickly. Indeed, they think it will take the Huns the winter to crack the Alamein line. I would note they haven't been right yet in this war, but that might be unkind."

"So we now have three divisions to be hammered at the front."

"Five. They want 8th Infantry and 1st Armored sent to Palestine via Basra along with every tank, artillery piece, armored car, and plane in Australia. Even the ancient stuff and training pieces. All these get replaced out of future US and Canadian production, but in the interim the Militia becomes a force of riflemen in trucks. The two divisions sent to Palestine leave Australia untrained, and do their workups as Imperial garrisons. London claims no risk partially disarming the Militia, as invaders cannot march here. They have roped the Japanese and US fleets into their China combine. This makes us safe. Indeed, they are about to make us safer still. The Japanese are sending a destroyer squadron through the Panama Canal and leaving most of the rest of their Fleet with skeleton crews dockside at their home bases. RN officers will verify all of this with daily updates. The Americans have quietly agreed to match this. All their carriers, except the old *Langley*, go to the Atlantic plus most of their battleships. The Pacific starts edging closer to living up to its name. Mother Country protects us with brilliant diplomacy, whatever happens in Egypt or Palestine."

"Is this all?"

"Nope. Most of our Militia in the East Indies comes home. The officers and enough senior sergeants remain. The rank and file get replaced by refugees fleeing Egypt and elsewhere. We may have to teach these chaps English, but plenty of time in garrison."

"White Australia is not subject to negotiation." The unions were adamant on this, and Curtin agreed with them. Immigrants were simply cheap labor for strikebreaking.

"Not at issue. The refugees get Dutch quasi-citizenship good only for the East Indies. They get to bring their families. So most of our lads get to rotate home over the next year and half. The rest the year after, as we find sergeants and lieutenants out of the new chums. We show our gratitude on this by getting enough Militia to volunteer for two years in the Shanghai garrison. Enough to cadre a brigade made up of still more refugees, and probably some English-speaking Eurasians."

Curtin weighed this all. "Any more stink bombs?"

"No. We get fat and happy. Most of our conscripts come home fast, and the rest at fixed times. We pay in blood supporting Home Country colonialism over a bunch of wogs we wouldn't let leave ship in Sydney harbor for more than an overnight bar crawl. However, Labor publicly backs all this. Full vote in caucus so the next Labor government is bound. You sit in some National Council so your hands are as dirty as ours on implementation."

Neither man looked forward to selling this to their caucus, much less dealing with the press. Both would do it. It was sound patriotism and sound politics. Menzies was the political arm of the farmers and ranchers. They got their export market back. Curtin was the political front for the dock, mining, and manufacturing unions. This meant full employment and lots of overtime packets. Most important to both, it meant war happened someplace else where their voters didn't live.

1200 hours local; 1100 hours CET
18 September 1940
GHQ Cairo

General Wavell was beginning to find this Alamein fighting distinctly unpleasant. He had assigned the remains of 7th Armored Division to 4th Indian Division. The surplus brigade staffs were sent off to join their old commander in Palestine. London swore they would send drafts to reconstitute the division. They just wouldn't say when.

General Blamey with his headquarters of First Australian Corps had arrived from Palestine. First Cavalry Division would be up in the next few days. The two Australian divisions were frozen in place in Palestine, awaiting something complicated being negotiated with London. The new War Cabinet was being reticent on details, which probably meant the usual economic and diplomatic dodgy business was afoot.

He'd flipped the two Palestinian Brigades to 7th Division up towards the coast, with the arriving Cypriot garrison brigade as a stiffener. He'd commanded these Jews in Palestine. He'd made their old friend Ord Wingate a lieutenant colonel, and given him command of a raiding battalion to be formed out of the better-trained Jews who had once worked for him in Palestine. Command in Khartoum had a fit. Sudan Command had been using Wingate to build up for some guerrilla raid into Ethiopia. Local commanders saw such narrow tunnels. They didn't see the theater as a whole.

The Jews on the coast, meant both Malta garrison brigades could be sent to replace the Jews with the 8th Division in the south. At their core these had storied regular battalions. They should be able to whip their quite poorly trained fillers into some sort of shape. Good captains and good corporals can make even totally raw privates function.

The Australian Corps would be given the salient battle. 4th Indian, 1st Cavalry, 6th Australian, and the three independent brigades. Alamein Force would be renamed 13th Corps; he appointed General Godwin-Austin to command it. With Churchill gone the cloud over this man from Somaliland passed. Winston had demanded more blood from a lost cause. It was so good to have Winston out.

The problem was the salient fighting. He simply wasn't budging the enemy. By company and battalion his men were performing. By brigade and division they were being outgunned. Eighth Army, as the newly expanded Alamein forces were now named, couldn't afford to play Haig in Flanders. Attrition favored the enemy. Wavell wanted to break these attacks off and preserve his men for the next enemy offensive. London asked for one more try. One more it would be.

1300 hours local; 1200 hours CET
18 September 1940
French artillery positions in the rear of what had been Rommel's salient, Alamein lines

General Jodl's Kampfgruppe Jodl was still in transit. The Maltese unit would arrive over the next two weeks. Oberst Maurice's deletions, to make up two battalions for Ramcke's division, would take another month or two to be made good. The first of the four heavy-gun battalions, the 15 cm howitzers, would arrive the first week in October. When the other three would appear was still being described by OKW in vague terms. Jodl had previously run that headquarters. Such weasel words meant that likely these units only currently existed on paper.

He was in Egypt today to observe a French weapon, the 12 cm mortar, in action. The French brigade had a battalion of these as well as one of 15 cm guns. They used their more widely available seven five's as heavy infantry weapons instead of artillery. The deployment was a battery in each line battalion as anti-tank and general purpose artillery. Unlike the German eight eight's they could not do further service as flak.

This total air superiority was proving most interesting. The French guns had nothing to fear from British counter battery – British guns that fired, exposed themselves to circling aircraft. They were immediately bombed. Worse, their positions were relayed by radio to waiting Panzer Army artillery units. The British guns could not 'shoot and scoot'. Exposing themselves by moving during daylight was near-suicide. The trucks towing the guns would die, as would the trucks carrying the ammunition. The surviving British had learned to seek good overhead cover before dawn, and to remain there until dusk.

In reverse, the Störche and the Italian Breda Ba.88 Linces were up by dawn to direct the Panzer Army's artillery fires. It was almost like working on a range with spotters doing corrections. With the little coastal ports opening to lighter traffic, artillery munitions could be brought almost straight to the front in massive quantities. Gone were the days when batteries were rationed to a daily maximum of shells.

This was much better for the gunners than WW1. Given a few weeks for redeployment, Jodl had no doubt that his guns and the others working with him could crack any British position. The key wasn't week-long bombardments such as the British had used on the Somme and at Ypres. Bruchmüller had written the outlines for what Jodl was going to do, in 1917-1918 – hurricane bombardments and the forward observers. These days the forward detachments were not dependent on easily-cut phone lines and forever-late runners. They had pack radios.   Meanwhile, the 12 cm mortars were worthy of serious study. Mounted on a Panzer I, they could perhaps keep up with the spearheads.

1400 hours CET
18 September 1940
Prinz-Albrecht-Straße, Berlin, Germany

Schellenberg caught himself laughing at von Manstein's invention of the rank of Brigadier. Using the excuse of Schellenberg's own rank of Oberführer, he had conjured up a grade between Oberst and Generalmajor. It took just a flick of Schellenberg's pen to approve Stauffenberg for this rank, and approve the rank for the NL in general. That led to a consideration of promotions and awards for the Reichsführer's pets.

Strauss was favorably mentioned in all reports. So it was easy to make him a Brigadier, more so as the size of his unit was being increased again. His subordinates Gorlov, Schwabe, and Voss all were mentioned well, so they become Oberstleutnant's. Steiner was his usual self. Send a letter from the Reichsführer, but no promotion this time. Otherwise he would be a Generaloberst by the end of the campaign. Major was enough for an 18-year-old. Decorations? Strauss and Voss had both levels of Iron Cross from the Great War, but would have to start the ladder again at 2nd. Pity, but no one had been thinking of this unit being permanent back in the earlier battles. Give the four Iron Cross seconds, and start them up the ladder.

Peiper? Frau Heydrich had asked for an update on him. Husband of one of her friends. Good reports, so promote to Sturmbannführer. Check what decorations he had and give him the next one. Raise his unit to a full battalion, and formally make it part of Strauss's brigade.

Mohnke? Schellenberg was inclined to blame the initial disaster on Dietrich. He or some staff drone of his palmed off a battalion with no heavy weapons company, no anti-tank guns, nothing beyond infantry in trucks. Silly to waste a promotion on the man till it was clear if he'd recover from his wounds. Knight's Cross, and a note to LAH that the new volunteer battalion would have the full weapons suite, and to which was to be added a 75mm battery for anti-tank work. There were enough surplus guns from the spring campaign.

This led seamlessly to Hausser's division. A letter of commendation from the Reichsführer was in order. This Klingenberg who had taken the British fortified camp? Jump him two grades to Obersturmbannführer, and make his provisional unit official. It was now the fast regiment of SS Division Reich. The SS Personnel Office could fill in the missing pieces of the units his men had come from. Knight's Cross as well, and a letter from the Reichsführer.

All this was within his authority. He'd rubber-stamp the boss's signature. Heydrich had too much to do to deal with this trivia personally. More and more work got done this way.

1700 hours local; 1600 hours CET
18 September 1940
New Strauss Brigade base to the rear of Italian 61st Division Sirte, near the coast road and 20 kilometers to the west/behind the Alamein front

The air was deathly hot. Worse than a blacksmith's forge in high summer. Also quite dry, even this close to the sea. Company Commissar Menachem Begin was still getting accustomed to this strange land, after several days in a truck to reach this place. The welcome-in was by a Jewish Lieutenant Colonel in Yiddish. The German Brigadier in charge also said a few words of welcome, again in Yiddish. The Lieutenant Colonel was fluent. The Brigadier was not. Spoke street Yiddish with a New York accent. Didn't matter. The Nazi in charge spoke street Yiddish, did not look down his nose at a new battalion of Jews. Perhaps there was something to the Nazi promises about a new home in Palestine.

When the formation was dismissed, he'd asked around among the Betar officers and commissars. They were all convinced the promises were real. A Jewish home in Haifa, Galilee and up the pipeline. They would be part of the German Empire, yes. Why would real Germans, with their race obsessions, want to live in a furnace full of Arabs? There would be a few to boss the Jews who would rule the Arabs. Why else bring Jewish petroleum experts along?

The Oberstleutnant invited Begin to his tent. Had a glass of wine with him, and introduced his niece. The niece it turned out was a nominal Leutnant. The rank didn't matter. Her status as mistress to one of the chief German officers did. She spoke with his voice, with the voice of command. The Oberstleutnant had a task for Begin. The niece wanted a crash course in Revisionist Zionism. She was mixed in with Betar, but knew absolutely nothing beyond Zionism meant Jews go back home to Palestine. Oh, and she knew the name Jabotinsky. Niece seemed like a nice Jewish girl. Turned out to be politically clueless. Also extremely uninterested. She didn't care about the rights or wrongs of Zionism, or its various schools of thought. She just wanted to know the right things to say, to do, to believe. She actually cared, but it was all surface things. Her man was sure they were going to Zion, and it was to be their home. Begin resolved to make this young lady a special project. Politics worked by milking connections. She took her meals with the senior officers.

2300 hours local; 2200 CET
18 September 1940
Reserve position, Rommel's salient, Alamein lines

The man who pretended to be General Kellermann of Napoleonic fame tightened the chin strap of his helmet. The Australians and Indians had pushed in the nose of the salient. He was going in with the Legion battalion to restore the line. General de Lattre knew that leading an assault battalion was beneath his rank. He simply didn't care.

France had been ruined by chateau generals sitting comfortably tens of kilometers behind the front, issuing meaningless orders. Meaningless, because by the time they reached the real fighting men the orders were hours old and hopelessly out of date. He had a staff to do the administrative idiocy. His job was to manage a battle.

He'd made his dispositions in daylight. He knew the British had at least one more push in them. He'd spent the day supervising the work on the strongpoints, preregistering the artillery on the likely British staging areas and their probable attack lanes into his position. His bet had been on just this push at the nose. Their prior attacks had failed at the base of the salient and at its flanks. The nose was the next step. If there were to be more after that, it wouldn't be his problem. The plan was to relieve his men with Felix Steiner's regiment of Balts, plus an Italian division tomorrow.

It was time. The star shells went up to illuminate his move. The guns began their hammering at the preset locations, plus the one overrun strongpoint. The legionnaires formed up behind him. To a harsh cry of *Vive la Legion!*, *Vive la Republique!* they followed him at the trot. This was not going to end the way that putrid spring campaign had. France would avenge Oran.

0800 hours Eastern Daylight Time; 1400 hours CET
19 September 1940
White House, Washington DC

FDR was doing a whistle-stop tour of the Great Lakes states. He had at last begun to take seriously the threat from Willkie. Lindy was barnstorming the same states doing football stadium rallies. Each appearance provoked riots. The street brawls in turn showed Franklin as the candidate of the Jews and Reds. The non-Communist left was mostly interventionist, and the Communists were being fairly quiet this election cycle. Hopkins felt they simply found it hard to reconcile their Japanese War and Hitler Alliance with their prior Popular Front propaganda from the Spanish War. The true believers would follow the backflips decreed by Moscow. The much larger mass of fellow travelers found it difficult.

The US Navy, in the form of the Chief of Naval Operations Admiral Stark, had just presented Hopkins with a most complex fait accompli. The Japanese Navy was sending a task force through US waters. A light cruiser and eight destroyers would be stopping at Pearl Harbor en route to the Panama Canal.

For decades the Japanese Navy had been the main threat to the US … at least as far as the USN was concerned. The Japanese agreed to reduce their fleet to mostly unmanned ships at anchor. The US agreed to match this. Our carriers would go to the Atlantic to guard against the Nazis. The main battlefleet would go to Norfolk, from Pacific Fleet home base San Pedro.

Stark saw this in terms of the naval balance in the Pacific. The US was building the ships for a Two Ocean Navy, but they were years from being ready. This gave the US a maritime defense in the Atlantic without taking on risk in the Pacific. The Japanese had even agreed that the old obsolete carrier *Langley* would be left in the Pacific to ferry planes for the new US buildup in China.

Hopkins saw the politics. A more peaceful Pacific would be well regarded by the Isolationists. There had been arguments when the draft bill passed, on whether conscripts should be forced to serve in the various Pacific bastions. Many objected to sending them to the Philippines or Guam. Some objected to Hawaii as well. A few idiots had argued that Alaska really wasn't US soil. Now those garrisons could be left to regulars, because many fewer men would be needed. The same would be done in the new Pacific bases such as Rabaul and Guadalcanal. The Marines had been recruiting in the Danzig special zone. The US had gotten a string of bases from Britain and Australia as part of the Bombers for Bases Deal. The Commandant was sure he could recruit many more men for Pacific service if permitted. These could man that set of installations, providing a lifeline to Manila if this agreement with the Japanese unraveled. The State Department would whine about adherence to dead treaties, but the Secretary of State was a Dixie fossil with no political clout. Hopkins would rubber-stamp FDR's name to begin this. The draftees would stay in the forty-eight actual states, plus the Caribbean garrisons like Panama and Puerto Rico. FDR would be for continental defense, not a new AEF and foreign wars to serve foreign interests. Hopkins felt this was within his authority. If it wasn't, Franklin could fire him for all he cared. Hopkins saw himself as a man juggling knives in a vaudeville show. He'd signed up to help manage the New Deal, to bring social justice to the US. Now he was assistant president, doing all the things Franklin was too busy being a candidate to bother with. The strain was killing Hopkins, and he knew it. He was willing to die for his country if needs be, but he'd do the best job he could while he was still above ground.
 0830 hours local; 0500 CET
19 September 1940
A Congress Party safe house in New Delhi, India

The secret impending arrival of Churchill as the new viceroy had of course leaked. There was too much protocol and red tape involved in a twin handover of the viceroy's office and command of the Indian Army. Too many offices had to be given at least pieces of the news for a smooth transition. Offices that all had Indian staff, from senior administrators to clericals and trash collectors. It was less that Britain ruled India, than that the mostly-Indian pillars of the regime were headed by white Britishers. The machine was too big for a few hundred thousand white men to really run it on their own.

Nehru, the practical head of the party, was clear on what must be done. Congress could not allow Bose's national liberation war to eclipse them. So far, all that the 'war' had to show for itself was pinpricks. A few police commissioners shot, a handful of bombs in shops or cafés frequented by whites, several small riots. How insignificant these were across a sub-continent didn't matter. The politics of the deed would always attract a following. A following gained at the expense of Congress, from among its youth wing, its labor radicals.

The problem, as ever, was Gandhi. His militant pacifism meant the official Congress campaign must be presented as a species of noncooperation. This left Nehru walking the delicate line of encouraging more activist interpretations, while not quite leading to a breach with the irreplaceable Gandhi. So the banners would read 'Quit India!'. He, Gandhi, and the rest of the presidium would be imprisoned. Verbal messages would pass to the outside via attorneys and prison staff. The second and third echelons would know what to do. He had spent the day before briefing enough people who would each pass the word. No written directives. Just a perpetual war of flea bites against the British, till the police and army defected. It was time to leave to make the speech. Odds said he'd be arrested before he finished it. So be it. The die was cast.

0800 hours local; 0700 hours CET
19 September 1940
Forward Headquarters, 16th Australian Brigade, 400 yards beyond the nose of the Rommel salient, Alamein Lines

Command of an army was a serious full-time job. More so for a slapped-together force like the new British 8th Army. General Alan Cunningham, General Officer Commanding 8th Army, could think of dozens of more productive uses of his time than a verbal slagging match with a subordinate. Sadly that subordinate, the Australian General Blamey, was not just the commander of First Australian Corps. He was also commander of Australian forces in theater, with the right to protest any order back to his home government on the other side of the globe. Blamey was ready to fry a bevy of Cunningham's staff officers. Cunningham had come forward to try and placate the man.

"Those pipsqueaks called my lads cowards. Easy to say, hiding in a bombproof miles from the front lines. Get them up here, and they can go in with my troops the next time you order another useless push at a few square miles of worthless wilderness!"

Cunningham tried for measured tones. "I'm sure they didn't mean it the way it came out. Last night was a four-brigade assault. They simply expected better results out of two such fine divisions." There. That sounded right.

Blamey wasn't having it. "Brigades? Up front you fight as platoons and companies, not brigades. If any of them had any combat time in the last war, they'd know this. Two Indian brigades with a strength of two weak battalions. Two brigades of mine shot to shit. Four battalions bled out, and two more that had to consolidate down to two companies each. All this so that we proudly control one hundred and fifty yards of what this time yesterday was the French outpost line."

"French?" Was Blamey shell-shocked?

"The people we were fighting were a French brigade in German service. London sent us word of this months ago. Revenge for what our navy did at Oran, or somesuch. Whoever was fighting the unit is top notch. Pre-registered guns, excellent fire lanes for the machine-guns, counterattack forces at every level from company up. This could be the Western Front in 1917 if the trenches were better." Blamey paused for breath, to slowly shake his head in frustration. "They have total command of the air. They have more artillery. They have armor, and enough small unit coordination to use it during daylight with their infantry. They used three of the old Renault's from 1917 to throw us out of the one strongpoint we took. Give me one good reason to keep beating my men to death simply so you can tell London that you 'restored the line'?"

Cunningham didn't have a good answer, beyond Wavell's staff being on his neck. Half the brigades in this force were military units by courtesy only. They were beaten shells of old units, trying to make soldiers out of the riff-raff the recruiters had found in Egypt. Plus two Jewish brigades no one this side of London regarded as serious fighting men. The Jews had many reasons to hate the Nazis, but none to love the British. It took an hour of frigid dialog to arrive at the only mutually acceptable solution. The 6th Australian artillery and crew-served weapons would be left in the line. Their three infantry brigades would be swapped out for three British brigades. If blood was to be futilely spent, it would not be Australian.

1200 hours CET
19 September 1940
Wawel Castle, Cracow, General Government (formerly Poland)

Heinrich 'Gestapo' Müller would never have chosen this antique setting for his offices as Governor-General. He belonged in Warsaw. That corrupt idiot Frank had picked Cracow for idiot ideological reasons, and he was stuck with the decision.

In his current office there was no such thing as 'off-the-books-time', away from the scrutiny of subordinates and his security detail. This made appointments with Moscow's new controller 'difficult'. So when a female he didn't remember called his aide asking to be put on the appointment list, Müller took the appointment. He gave off to this staff that it was probably an old flame. He claimed to have had so many from his days in Munich that he could never remember all of their names.

The lady in question turned out to be a comely Franco-German ex-professor of Slavic languages who claimed to have been a cousin of an old girl friend. This lady he did remember, even if the supposed affair was pure fantasy. She ostensibly wanted his administrative backing to open a small institute in the vacated buildings of Cracow's famous seat of higher learning, the Jagiellonian University. The school had been closed by the Nazis in 1939 as part of a decapitation of Polish intellectual life.

The institute was in and of itself harmless. Its purpose would be to gather Polish, Ukrainian, and other cultural artifacts that would in time be rehoused at schools in Italy and France. The money behind her was supposedly Swiss. Her papers were seemingly authentic. Müller had had his security people vet her, alleging concern for his safety. The Gestapo could find no holes in the paper trail. Neither could the SD.

As his mistress, she rated travel passes, a gasoline ration, and an ID card telling any German or Polish official to contact Müller's office to 'resolve difficulties'. There would be staff gossip about all this, but he had had a known mistress in Berlin, so it fit his pattern.

For now, he was back to being just an intelligence source for Moscow. For now. The day of reckoning with the Nazis would come. When it did, the Governor-General would have his active duties to perform, facilitating the liberation march of the Red Army to the Oder and beyond.

1900 hours British double summer time and CET
19 September 1940
A small meeting room near the Houses of Parliament, Westminster, London

Being prime minister was still a new experience for Ernie Bevin. As an old Trades Union Council man, he found all the pomp and pageantry the civil service, and even worse the Tory backbenchers of the 1922 Committee of whose coup he was the nominal front man, inflicted on office-holding to be a total waste of time. This especially included the endless little chats diplomatic niceties inflicted on him. He had thought this request for a private cuppa tea with Maisky, the Soviet Ambassador, to be more of the same.

Bevin had been rudely shocked. So this was the source of Churchill's super-secret intelligence he would so proudly display to the War Cabinet. Stalin was betraying his ally. Today's papers were twenty pages of Axis orders of battle, defense production, reinforcement rates for the Egyptian Front, and much more. The verbal part had, if anything, been more intriguing. Moscow knew of the revived Anglo-Japanese alliance, of the proposed three-power intervention in China. Moscow accepted this. There would be war of a sort between Britain and the Soviet alliances in Asia. Moscow wanted this to be clear. China meant all of Asia, but not Africa, Europe, or the Atlantic. Moscow saw mutual interest in restraining the growth of Nazi Europe. Moscow asked for reassurances that Britain would stay in the fight. Bevin regarded this all as food for thought.

1900 hours Eastern Daylight Time, 19 September 1940
0100 hours CET, 20 September 1940
Briggs Field, Corktown, Detroit, Michigan

The latest outbreak of fighting was out in deep right field. There was almost a rhythm to it at this point. Attempts to storm the hotel the campaign was staying at. Daytime speeches conducted only with armed security, punctuated by hecklers, sign wavers, stink bombs, and the odd pistol shot. Today was relatively mild. No dead, and less than a dozen hospitalized.

The motorcade to the evening stadium rally was a running battle. The Auto Workers Union and

Communists were out in force, assuming there was much of a line between the two. Everyone knew the Union, from the Reuther brothers on down, was riddled with Party members. However, Detroit was also home to Father Coughlin's radio empire. Enough of his flock, aided by the same moneyed interests that had booked Soldier Field some weeks back, insured that the attendees could get through the riot to the stadium gates. These 'security people' tried to screen for 'trouble makers'. That provoked more fighting and was never 100%. The enemy included blonde, fair-eyed Nordics as well as the more swarthy elements.

Wendell Willkie would never be the dime-novel picture of a hero that Lindy was. That man had been near-shot two days back. His only response was to go off the lines of his speech to laugh at his attacker's poor marksmanship. He then resumed his oration against the enemies of all America, as the enraged crowd stomped the would-be assassin to death.

By now Willkie had his applause lines down. Promise everyone the New Deal without Franklin. A clean, Republican version of Big Government. Eliminate waste, fraud, and political graft; but never allow another Depression the way FDR had done in 1938. This enraged a good section of his own voters who still worshiped Hoover and Coolidge. Didn't matter. He had red meat for them on foreign and defense matters. Keep bringing up that the last Democrat, Wilson, had sworn in 1916 that he wouldn't send their boys to die in France. Wilson had lied, and FDR was lying as well.

What's worse was that the war wasn't even for Western Civilization. Göring hadn't tried to invade Britain. The only air battles were over the southern ports like Dover. Murrow and his crew were direct-broadcasting the night raids. All the Germans hit were ports and airfields. Clearly military targets. Meanwhile the British were bombing cities in Germany. American correspondents like Shirer were shown the damage, invited to take pictures and interview people. There was one funny human interest story of an anti-aircraft gun with a 12-year-old girl as a loader, and some half-blind great-grandfather as gun captain. It was hard to hate people like that, more so when they had faces that would blend into a crowd scene in half the towns in the US. A lot of Americans had some German blood.

Willkie was happy to leave the overt Jew-baiting to Lindy. He just kept hammering on about sending draftees to die in a second AEF. No draftees outside the Western Hemisphere. He had words with his speechwriters when they tried upping that. Alaska was US soil as far as Willkie was concerned. So was Puerto Rico and the Panama Canal. Hawaii? Willkie was content to let that one slide. The way things were going, Japan was no longer a threat. Let them all die killing Godless Bolshies.

He'd gotten over being queasy at how rabid on the Jewish Question many of his admirers were. Even Lindy was not proposing to harm the citizen Jews the way Europe did. Willkie felt he could make peace with the decent elements of America's Jews after the election. In the White House, he'd have a few to lunch, then sponsor some refugee children. There would have to be a one-time bill to expedite getting Europeans with US family out of danger. It would be a chance to look non-partisan and liberal after the European War ended. Then again, the war already had almost stopped. It had devolved into a war for who ruled which set of Arabs or blacks. The US simply had no business shedding one drop of blood for such squalid colonial bickering. At least in China the new volunteers would be fighting for

Jesus and modernism.

The right-field fight was over, but now something was starting up at the third base line. Willkie threw in his stock line that the tools of Britain might kill him, but nothing short of that would silence him. The crowd roared its approval.

1000 hours local; 0500 hours CET
20 September 1940
Batavia Harbor, Java, Japanese-Dutch-British East Indies

The twelve hundred young men were neatly lined up on the dock for boarding. Sukarno's Nationalist movement's youth wing had found the volunteers. They had no military skills. They couldn't even stand at attention properly, much less in formation. None of that mattered. They were teen-age day laborers. Dutch colonialism had brought modern medicine to Java. The plan had been to start at Java and spread to all the islands. Then came the Depression, and resources vanished. So Java was exploding with excess young men, but no jobs for them.

These teens could work from dawn to dusk in Manchuria, digging trenches, repairing roads, doing anything that strong backs and willing hands could do. Japan's Soviet War was not going well. Japan would need to entrench the rail line kilometer by kilometer back to Mukden from both directions, and then south to Port Arthur.

The families had been promised a one-for-one. A volunteer for labor service who probably wouldn't return, meant another son would be given work in the new nationalist security battalions. These security units were currently rounding up Communists. The Communists and nationalists had cooperated for decades. Now the nationalists backed Japan, while the Communists remained true to their man-gods in Moscow. So Sukarno shopped these saboteurs to the grateful Japanese. In the process, Sukarno was also liquidating what rivals he had in the nationalist movement, just as his new security units would use their official status to settle village quarrels and clan rivalries. The Japanese were indifferent to such details. The Dutch would intervene to save those with good connections to the colonial regime. Sukarno was content to let those be shipped off to Celebes, Bali, and Timor. Japan had given him rulership of whole districts on Java already, and were discussing the same for Sumatra. Step by step.

0700 hours local; 0600 hours CET
20 September 1940
GHQ, Cairo, Egypt

The three 'representatives of the War Cabinet' had arrived from London via Gibraltar late last night. Sensible people would have taken a day to recover from the uncomfortable journey via S 25 Sunderland Flying Boat. The three men saw time as pressing, wanted an immediate briefing.

Logically the conference should have been with Wavell as theater commander and Cunningham as

8th Army. Some staff johnnie had added O'Connor at 0140 local time. He'd barely had time for a shave and shower before a quick drive to the airstrip and a nightmare flight to Cairo. The enemy hadn't many night-flying aircraft up, so danger was miniscule. The ground forces, however, were so used to anything in the sky being hostile that they fired at aircraft noise on reflex by now. O'Connor's plane had been under British fire at least eight times before touchdown. On landing, there were clear shrapnel holes in the right wing and tail. He had already sensibly decided that he'd take the train back to Palestine when this dog and pony show was over.

Wavell and Cunningham had focused on the names, tried to find acquaintances in common, the usual social dance. O'Connor took a different approach. He asked after the men's prior service history in the Great War. To O'Connor that would determine what frames of reference they had, how to explain in terms they might understand. It wasn't their political affiliation that mattered. They were respectively a Tory squire, a Labor solicitor from the Midlands, and a National Liberal chartered accountant from Devon. What really mattered was they had been Territorial Army lieutenants and captains in '14. Staff majors and lieutenant colonels by the Hundred Days in '18. No one on Haig's staff. They had served their war as company commanders, then battal on. Transferred to staff by the end of '15. Been planners at brigade, division, corps for the rest of the war. Somme. Third and Fourth Ypres. Cambrai. Two had been part of the routed Fifth Army in the spring of '18. All of them had been part of the great victory, the Hundred Days. Meant they knew both trench and mobile war. Meant they knew what it was like to be under the hammer, instead of just the ones going over the top to try yet another suicidal Big Push.

When it was his turn to speak, he laid it out in simple clear terms. Five brigades of quite marginal troops, good for not much more than digging and first-line defense. Probably couldn't even organize serious counterattacks once the front line was breached. Two more brigades with good cadres, but a mass of reluctant newbies. Seven brigades of his old Western Desert Force that were good troops – but down to battalion strength. Twelve brigades of reserves coming up. There were eight good brigades on the line. On London's orders, 8th Army was beating these troops to death on idiot counterattacks. What would retaking the salient really accomplish? The whole force had essentially no air, next to no armor, and nowhere near enough artillery. If the counterattacks weren't stopped and Egypt substantially reinforced, when the line was finally breached the whole army would be bagged. When that happened, the whole region would be lost.

O'Connor had expected the Tory to do the talking. The London government was Tory, given their parliamentary majority. Instead it was the Liberal National, the numbers-cruncher from the West Country. He rounded on Wavell and Cunningham for why this had all not been made clear to London. Wanted casualty rates, artillery ammunition expenditures plotted against stocks ... just the sort of nuts and bolts a smart staff planner who had been through the mill would have asked in '17 or '18. When told that all of this was relayed to London daily, the Laborite solicitor took over. He wanted a volume with all the signals traffic. Sounded as if he was thinking it would make quite the charge sheet. He didn't threaten about heads rolling. Wasn't necessary. War Cabinet wasn't getting the proper information. Someone would pay.

The truly scary part was the firm assurance from all three that the real offensive shouldn't be expected before the end of October at the earliest. No they wouldn't put this in writing. Commanders were cautioned that they were to do the same. Verbal only. London had some scary good sources in Berlin. Sources that could give relatively complete orders of battle. How much more was London getting and not passing along? Food for thought.

0800 hours local; 0700 hours CET
20 September 1940
Brigade Strauss compound, rear of Alamein lines

Oberstleutnant Peter Sommer got out of the staff car not exactly knowing what to expect. As a half-Jewish officer in the German Army, what he was and wasn't allowed to do was complicated – and subject to revocation at whim by any politically conscious official who took a mind to do so. The Army had allowed him to be 'detached for overseas service' at the 'request' of the Reichsführer SS. Usually the officer corps protected their own. But was a half-Jew exactly 'one of their own'? Not this time.

His new orders were, shall one say, a trifle vague. He was to report to Brigadier Strauss as his Ia. When he'd asked his SS briefing officer what a Brigadier was, the answer had been an NL rank equal to Oberführer. So he was a senior Oberst or very junior General. Whoever this Gunter Strauss was, he ran a Brigade of NL and was in need of a proper staff officer. Sommer was an April graduate of the staff course, and for reasons of state a part-Jew was considered suitable for this post by the head of the SS and thus overall head of the Gestapo.

Stranger still was a cover letter he'd been given, stating that his ancestry was known to those at the highest levels of command. Anyone having a problem with dealing professionally with Oberstleutnant Sommer was to forward such complaints to the signatories below for further action. The letter was doubly signed, Herman Göring as Führer and Chancellor; and Reinhard Heydrich as Reichsführer SS and Deputy Head of the National Socialist Workers Party. Sommer had never heard of such a blanket grant of authority. He chuckled to himself. Even the most 110% Nazi might think twice about arousing the attention of these two senior officials. The Reich was on an efficiency campaign. There were new public executions weekly. The message seemed to be getting across. The Reich was at war, and what mattered was productivity and loyalty.

His new commander welcomed him in and gave him a quick capsule history of the unit. Light bulbs began to shine in Sommer's head. "Sir, so we have a mostly Jewish unit in German uniform by orders of the Reichsführer SS?"

"Probably why he wanted the staff officer to be someone who didn't loathe Yids. We already had an incident with an SA officer over that. We've got the man stashed in the metals shop till I can find General Steiner's headquarters to try a transfer. A duty that is now yours." The two men shared a laugh. Sommer was a Lower Saxon, and found having a Rhenish commander an easy situation. The two dialects weren't that far apart. Neither were the cities. His birthplace of Hildesheim and Strauss's home city of Solingen, were some 275 kilometers apart.

The welcome in from his 'staff' was more amusing. Leutnant von Kleist-Konitz was happy to have a proper superior. He was less happy at being told he'd been permanently assigned here as assistant Ia. Made clear that he was a combat officer, not a rear headquarters swine. The subtext said, he would use his family contacts to try to work for a transfer. Sommer had no problem with this. Young men from the military caste all knew the ladder of success. Combat commands and decorations. Let von Kleist-Konitz's high-ranking relatives work the favor bank at OKH and the War Ministry on his behalf. In the meantime, Sommer expected to use him as an 'eyes and ears' forward observer. The rest of the 'staff' seemed disappointed that the half-Jew spoke no Yiddish. That said, they all spoke adequate German. The only problem was that their procedures, while undoubtedly effective, were not Wehrmacht-standard. Sommer had no doubts as to his ability to retrain them.

....

Gregor Voss took the assignment of this new staff expert the same way he took his recent promotion. Both were marks that their patron in Berlin was always watching. Gregor had lived his whole life as one of the masses. He was just a good German who did his duty, went to the beer hall, and still showed up at work sober and punctual six days a week. The important people were an enemy, 'them'. Now here he was a field officer. In his head he was still the same Feldwebel he'd been. He was slowly accepting that the world no longer saw him that way. Gregor had thought this whole adventure was madness. Adolph and Wanda had talked him into saying yes to Gunter's telegram. Now he was a new man with a new place in the world.

The truly strange part was that this new higher status rubbed off on Hans. This Mary Collins had taken Hans under her wing. He ran messages, did deliveries the way he had for the grocery in Solingen. But he was no longer treated as a halfwit. He was the 'nephew' of an important man. Mary, Greta, Naiomi all treated him that way. The damned Arab boy even saluted Hans. If everything went the way Gunter and Isaac kept telling him it would, Hans would have a future even after Gregor passed on. The thought made him smile, and few things did.

1300 hours CET
20 September 1940
Polish offices, American Special Zone, Danzig

The exchange went exactly as planned. Police General Eicke arrived with six high-ranking prisoners for the two representatives of the London Poles. They had been knocked around a bit, but had no serious damage beyond a new tattoo. This was the arrangement. Exchanged personnel were marked with a red *GG*. They were to be exited on the next freighter out. If caught again on European territory, they would be hanged. The Polish Resistance had paid the price – four captured German officials were returned, plus two high-ranking cadres of the Polish Communist Party. The Nationalist Resistance were quite willing to shop Reds to the Germans. To true Poles, both were the enemy.

This whole process was the result of a visit Eicke had made to Berlin, to Prinz-Albrecht-Straße to be precise. The discussion was a trifle one-sided. The new Reichsführer had made clear that the next time Eicke was summoned to Berlin, it would be for a date with Frau Guillotine. Heydrich started with a simple fact for Eicke to bear in mind. The living could be easily made dead. Bringing corpses back to life was more than a trifle more difficult.

It was a whole new frame of reference for Eicke. His supposedly secret program to build an informer net, turned out to have been shopped to Berlin already. By subordinates? Rivals? The Poles? Schellenberg brushed aside the implied question when Eicke tried to raise it. Told Eicke bluntly that everyone reports on everyone. That said, the idea was good. Please continue with it, c/c'ing Berlin by confidential courier.

Learn to think of the entire Danzig arrangement from the proper prospective. Yes the Poles, Jews, defectives were in many ways useless eaters. Except the Reich wasn't feeding them. Their rich cousins in America were doing that. Germany actually made a 'profit'. There was an approved 'wastage' rate of 10%. This included not only staple foods, but also luxuries and medicines. The Reich was not rich in resources, compared to its current and future enemies. The Reich must be efficient and frugal. This was the only path to final victory.

Approach the Polish and Jewish Questions from that standpoint. The Poles would have a Resistance. They were as stubborn as the Irish that way. Plotting endlessly, and periodic rebellion, were national traditions. Better to have known representatives that could be talked to. The General Government was not going to be colonized anytime soon. Look at the annexed border regions. The Jews and Poles were cleaned out by the former Gauleiters. Yet it had proven impossible to find enough German colonists. The Volksdeutsche ingathered preferred to be industrial workers to becoming peasants. The Reich needed factory output more than what horse-drawn plows could bring forth from sandy eastern soils. So the new farmers were Balts. Germanizable, but not yet Germans.

Someday the war would end. Some Poles would remain and be Germanized. At the peace, the rest would be parceled out to America, Canada, England, and France. For now, keep them quiet and keep them producing.

Eichmann had his Jews producing. When the war ended Italy would get most of them. Germany would retain the best educated, the most productive, to work the new oil fields. Eicke was a hard man but blanched at the description of the summer heat in the new oil province. There would be some German overlords, such as the new Romeo and Juliet pair from Malta. Those two would be celebrity heroes, propaganda models of defenders of Germany's new riches. The girl would also have a huge brood of children. That could be publicized, to start to resurrect a fashion for large families. A continent-spanning Germany needed more Germans. This Volksdeutsche young lady from Romania would be a model New Aryan Woman.

Eicke had taken this all in. Perhaps nursing his loyalty to the dead Himmler was unwise. The new masters were offering him a career in this new eastern marchland. In the meantime, his slowly expanding cadre of informers had brought him some delicious news. This supposed mistress of Müller's was not just a cosmopolite intellectual. She had dangerous taste in friends. Communists. Communists who seemed to have connections back across the partition line to Moscow. This he wasn't telling Berlin yet. He'd need MUCH better proof. Patience. That was the key. Turning informers was ever so easy … if one knew how and had a bit of patience.

0900 hours Eastern Daylight Time; 1500 hours CET
20 September 1940
Bolling Field, Washington DC

"God damn all Nigger officers to Hell!" Retired Captain Claire Chennault was having a fit. Fortunately for him he was doing so in private. The public expression of his tantrum could ruin his plans to become a Colonel or perhaps a Brigadier General in the new American Volunteer Group. He'd been a mercenary adviser to Chiang's Air Force. The Generalissimo had been the darling of the China Lobby and the Missionaries. They had ignored Chiang's past left turns and current Soviet ties … until he'd turned on the missionaries. Now he was the exemplar of both Godless Bolshevism and the Yellow Peril. "Fuck the Holy Joes! Screw that rug-chewing Commie cunt of a First Lady. God Damn Frankie Cripple!" Chennault had been negotiating leaving his Chiang connections behind for the new Bible Thumper darling, Wang Jingwei. Then this mother-humping Nigger officer came out of nowhere with his 'Tuskeegee Airmen'. Suddenly there was competition for the role of Air Corps savior of the Far East. The best he'd been able to scrape together was that his project wasn't shelved altogether. The Volunteers were on, but at Army pay, not mercenary wages.

It was still a white man's world, especially among the service brass. His men would get P-40's. The Coon would have to make do with P-36's and Brewster Buffaloes. USN would ferry him. The Nigger would have to book tramp freighters. Chennault wasn't a young man. This was his last shot at Dame Fortune.

0730 hours local; 0630 hours CET
21 September 1940
GHQ, Nairobi, Kenya

The South Africans were still tidying up for final departure. They were off for Sudan, some by road march and the rest by ship through Mombasa. There was a Second Division of them forming back to home. It was expected real soon now.

Major General Arthur Percival, newly arrived, was taking up his duties as GOC Kenya. GOC? Of a few brigades of militarized African police and a militia of sorts from among the Kenyan settlers. The local settlers knew the bush and shooting. They had no concept of discipline, and little inclination to learn. Churchill's usual nostalgia for a bygone age had added half a dozen battalions of Ethiopian and Somali 'patriots', officered by the usual mix of soldiers of fortune, refugees, and wild-man volunteers from the Dominions. 'Patriots'! Glorified bandit gangs enlisted from the promise of regular wages plus loot. They could be used to harass the Italian rear, but wouldn't do standup fights. If the British position seemed to falter, likely as not they would shoot their officers and switch sides. At least his colonial black brigades were regulars. Percival had served with their fathers in Nigeria. They had the habit of discipline, and the skill of marksmanship.

As a trained staff officer he quite understood the gamble London was taking. Push came to shove, Kenya was expendable. All of East Africa was. Sudan wasn't, because the Army in Egypt was precious. Britain couldn't afford to throw away whole armies. Interwar penny-pinching on the military had left the Empire scrambling for resources. Pity the various cabinets had seen fit to not adjust Britain's overseas commitments to the small forces they were willing to fund.

1000 hours CET
21 September 1940
Forest bridle path outside Metz, Lorraine (claimed by both France and Germany)

It was a fine autumn day. Crisp but not cold. An excellent day for General Juin to go riding with the colonel courier up this morning by train from Vichy. The formal meeting in Juin's office on base had been nothing the Germans couldn't hear. The order was for shipping two battalions de marche south by rail to Toulon the following day. The War Ministry would try to make good deficiencies, drawing from the post-armistice stocks in North Africa, but the need was urgent. There was no way to hide a troop movement from German eyes.

The *why's* of the movement could best be done verbally. Hence the ride the two officers were taking now. "It is bad." The colonel worked directly under the Minister of War, General Weygand. "That traitor de Gaulle is making his move at West Africa." He held a hand up before Juin could reply. He was an excellent horseman. Truth be told, he didn't need the reins at all. He could certainly handle a riding horse on a path with one hand while the beast ambled along. "His agents have been contacting important people seeking support. Enough play both sides and reported the conversations. Our German friends confirmed this. Condor flights out of Brittany with French observers. It is funny. They don't expect us to take them on faith."

Lovely, Juin thought. Two larger powers using France as a cat's-paw. "Germany is aiding us?"

"Near to all their submarine fleet has been deployed to screen the routes south from Gibraltar to Dakar. They have allowed French volunteers to join the crews. They are being scrupulously honest. Frightening, in its own way."

"How is our brigade doing in Egypt?"

"Kicking the British in their gonads. The British are making a minor diplomatic fuss, but we keep replying with Chad, and now Congo and Cameroun. They are trying to steal our empire one piece at a time. Alliance with Germany may be poison in the long term, but for now our problem is Britain."

"So when do I leave?"

"With your fourth battalion. Say mid-October." The men resumed their ride, urging the horses to a moderately brisker pace. Juin was lost in thought. The colonel was content to let him puzzle the situation through. Weygand had tapped Juin as a man of whom great things might be expected. This rearranging of sides was a delicate process.

2300 hours British Double Summer Time and CET
21 September 1940
Labor Caucus Room, Westminster, London

Prime Minister Ernie Bevin knew he would expect crisis moments in Cabinet. He simply hadn't expected them this quickly. The heavily cyphered message from Cairo had exposed multiple interlocking cans of worms. So had the most unhelpful attitude of the Chief of the Imperial General Staff, General Sir John Dill. The man's pig-headed duplicity was a shock even to an old Labor stalwart such as Bevin, who held the ruling class in contempt.

Dill managed to simultaneously deny that Cairo had been ordered to keep making pointless attacks, and yet maintain that the 'suggestions' from Dill's staff had been the proper course of action. The same old high-born toff shit about maintaining morale by making the poor bloody infantry leave their trenches and attack, to 'keep a keen edge on their offensive spirit'. Bevin had known enough union lads who had paid the butcher bills in the last war. He was no pacifist, but lives were not to be wasted on medieval notions of warfare. The men would fight when they had to, but there was nothing glorious about it.

What was worse was the two-faced way the report on the strength (or lack thereof) in Egypt, in the theater in general, was handled. Dill waved away complaints about the air strength. He wanted to refight old battles about the RAF as a separate independent service. The Army felt that the Air Force lived in a fantasy universe about an independent air war. Which at vast expense was producing jack shit. Some captured brigadier was sending air raid reports from Berlin – with the full knowledge and backing of the Abwehr, who saw to their delivery at the British Embassy in Madrid. The bombers were doing just enough to be annoying. The Germans had made that point repeatedly in the Lisbon talks. Had sweetly asked if they should set the East End of London ablaze in a tit for tat?

Needless to say the Air Chief, Air Marshal Cyril Newall, was having none of this. Backed by the head of Bomber Command, Portal, he had resolutely defended strategic bombing, and pronounced direct support of the army useless. They even saw no use of air defense beyond the Home Islands. Idiots!

Bevin had won the vote to dismiss the two air generals. They were out, and Hugh Dowding of Fighter Command was in. The same had proven impossible over Dill. Oh, Bevin had the votes in Commons. The 1922 Committee could deliver that on their own. Good old Clem would help Bevin deliver a majority of Labor as well. On a raw vote they had sixty percent or more of Commons that would back pretty much anything. But the entire concept of National Government was to avoid such public splits.

The Liberals were hopelessly split. Two factions in theory, and three in practice. Combined they were only just over 10% of the voters in the last general election. So, at this moment, a remnant caucus with absurd pretensions. And yet ... and yet Liberal was a storied name in British politics. They were also the only name that could contest near every seat in Commons. They were left-enough to fight for working-class seats against Labor, and still conventional enough to fight the leafy suburbs against the Tories. Getting this three-headed monster to accept anything new was like herding cats. It could be done, but not quickly.

The Tory Party was easier and harder. As long as the 1922 Committee stayed loyal, the big names could be decapitated. The faceless grey men of the Tory benches were natural followers. They were not Big Capital. They were its servants. The country squire justices of the peace. The suburban solicitors, branch managers, spokespeople, and the like. They had next to no interest in policy – besides being against socialism and the income tax. Most would obey the whips out of habit, and the more ambitious could be bought off fairly cheaply with lesser offices, knighthoods, and small bits of patronage. Bevin had negotiated workplace disputes with these sort of men. He didn't like them, but quite understood them. The Names were the problem. They had been aced out of the PM's chair. Each saw himself as a potential successor, when the 1922 Committee came to their senses as it were. Each also wished to make sure that no blame attached to them for years of failed appeasement, for the string of truly dumb decisions that had led to a large fraction of the Empire being on the verge of being pissed away. Britain now had enough planes, tanks, field guns, trained men. All of this was in the UK, and while Winston was in charge these great Names had fought him hammer and tongs over NOT reinforcing Egypt. Dunkirk had panicked the lot of them. They wanted it all sitting in the Home Counties to defend London. Which is where it was. Leaving Egypt vulnerable. Now they wished to blame each other. To prepare briefs for the day when they leaked these polemics to rival newspapers in a bid for power.

Poor Clem had the reverse problem. Labor's factions cared only for ideology. There was a Jew-ridden Marxist wing up in arms over something or other involving China and Japan. Bevin had been in War Cabinet, but Winnie had been vague as hell on details. It hadn't seemed important then, only now the usual fellow travelers of Moscow were baying for blood. The 1922 Committee chaps had explained this in terms of China trade. The coastal parts of China were prosperous enough to import. The interior wasn't, and was most inconvenient to reach anyway. So, back the Japanese and this Wang chap to preserve markets. Bevin felt he'd won a few concessions on trade union rights in the key ports. Symbolic for now, but a start to build on. The semi-Bolshies wanted fraternal alliance with Stalin and Chiang. The same Chiang they had spent the better part of a decade wanting boycotted because he had broken with Moscow in the 20's. Most annoying.

What was worse was Morrison's old wing. They included many ex-Liberals, and were – to Bevin's mind – a collection of cranks and kooks. Vegetarians, legalists, internationalists, pacifists, single-issue fanatics of various stripes. The left side of smug British eccentricity. They didn't want an orderly expansion of the welfare state, geared to sound finances and the needs of this war. They wanted it all now. They wanted to argue every detail of every program. They wanted total moral purity in every British alliance and foreign association. These same idiots had argued for the League, and thus against Italy over Ethiopia. Which had lost Italy for the anti-German block. They then turned around and howled to save the Spanish Republic, while opposing rearmament. Right now they were baying at a point of the German proposed peace terms. The Huns had demanded all of Iraq. The representatives of the 1922 Committee had talked them mostly around to a partition of the place. Germany gets Kirkuk and that oil. Britain keeps Basra to protect the adjacent oil fields in Persia and Kuwait. Baghdad was still in dispute. The idiots wanted to argue Iraqi sovereignty. International law. Humanitarian rights for minorities. A thousand points of drivel. They could not be made to see that once the front collapsed in Egypt, Germany's price for peace would rise again.

In the meantime, getting a reinforcement convoy started for Egypt had to be the next order of business. RN was pleading that they first had to finish some Gaullist demonstration off West Africa. Bevin recalled Winnie being enamored with some plan or other in that direction. He asked for details. RN and Dill got into a tiff on who should provide them, and there the matter rested.

Chapter 8

0300 hours local; 0200 hours CET
22 September 1940
A back-stairs room in a fine Alexandria mansion

The mansion oozed respectable wealth. It was a dowry gift of the householder's father-in-law, a formerly great man fallen on hard times with the coming of the Depression. His high-social-status young daughter had thus been wed to a man a bit more than twice her age, whose wealth was vast but the sources of which did not bear close inspection. As arranged marriages went it had been successful. The father-in-law's debts were quietly bought up. Father of the bride was now a well-paid front man for his less reputable son-in-law. The daughter had produced heir, spare, and a few daughters. She lived well but quietly, devoting herself to her children and parents. She displayed herself on her husband's arm as, when, and where required. Otherwise they led essentially separate lives.

Lieutenant Commander James Money-Penny had known of this man prior to the war. Since his return from Malta he had become in many ways this man's minion, his expediter with the British military as it were. Money-Penny was wise enough to realize he was scarcely the only one. However, he was the one tasked with expediting this gentleman's departure from Alexandria as and when necessary. Right now he was trying to advance the day these services were rendered. "You and your money need to leave now. Line almost gave out as soon as Jerry made a serious push. Can't for the life of me see why they stopped. Word is that they wanted a sure thing, that they are trucking up supplies and the like. Jack-all we can do to stop them. Next big battle, the line goes and British Egypt goes with it. You must be aware. Your wife, kids, in-laws and your own mother, are all up in Beirut. You've got properties there. You've transferred a lot of wealth. I've helped facilitate it. Forms, official stamps, armed uniformed guards. Yet here you sit with that big yacht of yours in the harbor."

The big man had grown this wealthy by knowing how to work many angles, cut many dark but profitable corners. "There are still large sums to be made. More every day, as movable wealth gets converted into fixed assets by those who think their Italian connections are solid enough. Same in reverse, by those who see Java or Malaya as more secure places of abode. You will know when the line is on the verge of collapse. You get here with enough of your uniformed gang, your 'Villains'. You get myself, my gold, and my yacht to Beirut. I make you richer. That is the arrangement."

"You are presuming I can break free at just the right moment."

"I presume that if you cannot, others can. I pay well."

The discussion went on till dawn when they adjourned for coffee, still at stalemate. Money-Penny needed this cash flow to work his other magic for Fleming's brigade. The wheeler-dealer had an iron nerve for risks, and trusted his gut. He planned to leave at the last possible moment.

1000 hours CET
22 September 1940
Comando Supremo, Palazzo Vidoni, Corso Vittorio Emanuele II, Rome

The Prince having grown weary of dealing with SS General Wolff, Air Marshall Balbo took this meeting himself. Wolff wanted to discuss the nuts and bolts of Italian war propaganda. Strange thing to be a major matter of state.

Wolff had a few dozen examples of Italian articles, all from the new Egyptian front. His complaint, or to be more precise Berlin's, was that Italian censors were too liberal in letting the exact geography into the article. Berlin felt that this put pressure on local commanders to avoid allowing operational or tactical retreats, for fear of appearing to be 'defeated'. Blood was precious and should not be wasted. Best to focus on heroism, but avoid making keeping special worthless dirt a 'matter of honor'. Balbo agreed just to terminate the meeting. He then had his staff alert General Geloso to expect von Manstein to raise the issue with him.

1130 hours local; 1030 hours CET
22 September 1940
Bagush Box, now under Panzer Army ownership

The command conference had three senior generals (Geloso, von Manstein, and Messe) plus a veritable galaxy of translators, aides, and clericals. The wall map in what had once been O'Connor's office, showed the front line as an overlay of recon photos. The key issue at hand was Rommel's salient. Many issues were more important. None was as time-sensitive.

"Can any of you see any logic in the British behavior?" General Goloso was a very professional officer. The terrain in question appeared to have absolutely no military value. The adjacent ridge mattered. A few square kilometers of waterless wilderness simply didn't. He knew people who knew the key British commanders personally. These British generals were wasting valuable trained men on these nightly attacks. This wasn't a question of blooding green troops. This wasn't some historic town that had national emotional significance.

Von Manstein had actually seen stupider behavior. Then again, in his opinion virtually everyone on the planet was an idiot compared to his exalted self. His Kaiser's War experience had seen attacks endlessly repeated because no one wanted the blame of ordering them stopped. He'd missed First Ypres by his unit having been redeployed to East Prussia just in time. He had friends who had not been so fortunate. Many had died or been crippled, because of a similar refusal to believe that the next attack wouldn't fail the way the last eight had. "Forget why they are doing this. Why are we rising to the bait? I shut down General Rommel when he could probably have breached their lines. Breached, but little more. We need 5-6 weeks to resupply and redeploy. I propose we pull out today and be done with it. Yes, it a minor propaganda victory for the British. This isn't a war where neutral opinion matters. If our papers don't report the withdrawal, then it is as if it never happened. Let us save the shells and men for that late October push." He looked around the table to see two nods. He then unrolled a map on the conference table. It showed a two-corps push at the south end of the front. Messe's corps just south of the east-west ridge with the DAK extending the line south to up against the northern fringes of the Depression. Both of these behind the Italian XXIII Corps. He would let a pair of Italian divisions breach the lines of the 8th Division, which (based on prisoner interrogations) seemed to be mostly third-rate militia. Messe would exploit the breach. There were obvious east-west ridges that the British would redeploy on to face this. Messe would make the short swing to that east-west axis, with Steiner's division coming up behind to deploy on Messe's right while Hausser's oversize division followed on to keep extending ever eastwards until the British couldn't match the movement. Hausser's division was the size of a corps. It would have a number of modern tank battalions by then. Good upgunned Mark III's and IV's. Those would form the spearpoint to roll up the new British line, while Klingenberg's new fast regiment kept sweeping northeast to break the British lines of communication to Cairo. The British position would implode in a disorderly flight, or they would bag the entire British Army. Either was acceptable. Von Manstein saw the approving glances of the two Italians. He took this as proof that they appreciated his genius. He was not a good reader of minds or body language. They were both separately thinking, that any competent Capitano on his first staff course could have put this together, given terrain and relative size of forces deployed.

Messe was left to ask the obvious question. What about Rommel and Strauss? Did von Manstein think so little of Italian prowess, as to believe they needed German reserves to hold their line – as if they were Ottomans? Von Manstein found himself forced to explain that Rommel was in reserve as punishment. All three shook their heads at the petty personal politics of higher command.

No one was really that concerned with why Berlin took a special interest in Brigade Strauss. It had performed well, but was a minor unit in a large army. If Berlin wanted it near the coast so the men could go swimming, who cared?

1850 hours local; 1750 hours CET
22 September 1940
I Australian Corps forward HQ, northeast of Rommel's salient

The reports had at first not been believable. Blamey had sent multiple officers he trusted forward to observe and verify. The enemy was pulling out. They were shielding the movement with massed artillery fires, but the nose of the salient was vacated. British patrols had confirmed this. Even the boobytrapping wasn't all that severe.

From observation and noise reports, the rest would be vacant by morning. He had 'won'. The question, of course, was what now. He would have to occupy the vacated ground and dig in at least one of his newly-arrived British brigades. The same staff idiots who had asked for nightly attacks, were now making difficulties about the obvious urgent needs – mines, wire, timber to construct bombproofs. If these weren't available, why in the nine names of Hell had they been so keen to take these worthless acres back? More and more he was convinced that a Home Counties accent was a guide to who the idiots were.

1600 hours local; 2200 hours CET
22 September 1940
Apartment of a Revisionist sympathizer, Flatbush, Brooklyn

Ze'ev Jabotinsky felt himself lucky to be alive to take this meeting. His heart had almost given out on him in early August. To think, he had almost died just when such wondrous things were happening. His movement had found powerful friends. The first armed units of Betar were in Egypt, on the road to Palestine.

The Betar delegates from the Palestine Camps in Poland arrived with German diplomatic passports. Their Nazi minders accompanied them. He'd been allowed private meetings with his followers. The Germans were very businesslike with him. They were along to prove that the promises being made to him in Germany's name were genuine.

He was being offered the presidency of a Jewish state on both banks of the Jordan. Not all of Palestine. The Germans were concerned with the oil pipeline, not the rest. He was to get German north Palestine and the Italians were to get south Palestine. Europe's Jews would be sent home. As long as German wishes were respected, he and his party could rule as they chose. Rebellion would be dealt with by harsh measures. Ze'ev could visualize what the Nazi definition of harsh was.

The Germans were not sure if the Italians had contacted Ben Gurion. They really didn't care one way or the other. He and Ben Gurion had their differences, yet had come close to merging their movements back in 1935. There was still Western Union service to Palestine. Some of the stations were down from the war, and the rest outside the US were under British control. So it had to be some simple code. Send so and so to Istanbul to meet his cousin such and such. The Germans assured him they could get any cadre he named from the camps to Istanbul in four days' time.

This was not the future for the Jews he had dreamed of. But still, it was so much closer to that dream than anyone else was offering. There had been much worry on the fate of Europe's Jews, and now he would be their savior. The convoluted story of how Betar and the Nazis had become allies made little sense, but these were days of wonder.

0900 hours local; 0100 CET
23 September 1940
Soviet submarine Shch-117, East China Sea

The target had been a merchant ship. The positioning made its probable destination Shanghai. It had no escort. It wasn't zig-zagging, and was sailing with full running lights. Best guess made it eight kilotons, so the commander had fired two torpedoes. Somehow he'd managed to miss with one. The other hit the aft of the merchant ship, which broke apart. The aft went down at once. The rest took maybe 10 minutes to sink beneath the waves. The captain didn't think it was worth surfacing to move the process along faster by cannon fire.

....

The US radio intercept station in Shanghai picked up the distress signal from the SS *Wayne County* out of Seattle. The USN lacked China Station assets for a rescue. The Japanese out of Okinawa did not. Only six lives were lost, thanks to prompt Japanese response. US accusations against the Soviets were met with bland denials. The Soviets simply said the pirate submarines that had previously attacked shipping bound for Loyalist ports in Spain, must have relocated. As everyone knew those submarines were really Italian, Italy and Germany promptly denied blame. US opinion on this split by party lines. The insult to the flag would go on to be a campaign issue.

0700 hours local; 0600 hours CET
23 September 1940
Joey's office at the metal and vehicle repair depot, Strauss Brigade, behind the Italian lines at Alamein

Being summoned to the office meant trouble. Lothar was not looking for more trouble. Since his talking-to by Paul Schwabe, he'd done his work and kept his head down. He'd tried to find his guys for a beer once, and been warned off by Peiper. Shit! It had been getting lonely. Now some Army asshole wanted to see him. Another perfumed dandy with a staff stripe on his pants. Lothar still regretted Röhm's death. Despite having been a Strasser man, he'd hoped for much from the promised Second Revolution, where the fancy boys would all be bumped off.

Fancy boy ignored Lothar's salute and waved him to a chair. "I'd rather keep this informal, if you don't mind. I've been tasked with expediting your transfer to Steiner's division. His HQ is arriving today. Don't know if the General will be with them, but this isn't business at his level. I'll look up some junior serving under his Ia. If I am going to sell you, I need some questions answered."

Lothar tried to keep his big mouth shut. Intelligence lost to aggressiveness. "If this is man to man, then fuck you very much. I can march over there and ask for a place on my own."

The staff jerk actually laughed at Lothar. "Go ahead. Just makes one less thing on an endless to-do list for me. The line cadre of this division is mostly SA. The staff is holdovers from a Heer division that's been demobilized. They won't pay any attention to an aged SA veteran with bad-conduct marks."

"Bad conduct! The little pansy has less right to be a field officer than my dead hound back in Hesse. All he's good for is defiling his race with the Jew whore, and displaying his lack of manhood sucking off his commander. Are you another boy-lover, or just a damned part Kike!" Lothar knew he was burying himself. He was too enraged at the entire situation to fully care. He'd be mad at himself later … but that was later and this was now.

Sommer restrained himself. He'd been baited about his mother's race, and therefore his, far too often to be seen rising to the challenge. He just reached into the pile of papers on the desk in front of him and handed a copy of his 'reference letter' to this blockheaded country oaf. He let the man read it, watched the color drain from his face, and just asked in a polite, almost bored tone, "So shall I cut you travel orders to Prinz-Albrecht-Straße, or are you prepared to listen?"

Lothar took three deep, shuddering breaths and got control of himself. "Sorry, sir. I'll listen."

"Major Kike-lover, as you so sweetly labeled him, actually gave you a decent set of references. He said you did an excellent job training and motivating your men. They took good care of their vehicles and kit. They fought well. He found fault with you on two levels. The first was insubordination. He states that he doesn't see you having the same problems with an all-German unit. Peiper seconds him on this. Me, I'm not so sure after your behavior here, but we'll pass on that for the moment. He also had this made up for you." Sommer passed across a sheet of paper with a grid layout. It had charts of armor penetration for various German, French, and Italian fighting vehicles at various ranges. Again he let Lothar skim it. "Steiner said he will give you the benefit of the doubt, on not understanding that your pathetic cannon was essentially useless against the British cruiser tanks you tried to fight. Said with your personal physical strength, you'd have done better assaulting the road wheels with a sledgehammer. I'm not as sure as he is that you are not just an idiot with a large rock to hold his ears apart. But your two current supervisors, Schwabe and Bats, testify to your intelligence as regards machines and metal. So does how well you kept your vehicles running. You taught field maintenance to your unit quite well. Better than most that I have served with. As a nation, we have way too few Germans who are knowledgeable about driving or fixing vehicles of any sort. Now, are you willing to be adult enough to memorize this chart as regards armored cars? If you want that transfer, I'm going to quiz you myself before I carry the file over."

Lothar promised that by breakfast tomorrow he could recite the key lines to Herr Oberstleutnant's satisfaction. He wanted to be back to serving with his own. There was one thing the staff officer said, that he didn't like. That he couldn't promise armored cars. Lothar would go into the divisional replacement battalion, and be assigned wherever there was a need. Might be infantry or guns instead of vehicles. Lothar would take being in the field bakery if it got him out of here, but he'd grown to love those vehicles.
1300 hours local; 1200 hours CET
23 September 1940
German field hospital, Benghazi

The pain was so intense that Mohnke kept going in and out of consciousness. That was an improvement on how bad he had been doing a week earlier. He still couldn't quite grasp why he was still alive. He'd spent his last battle trying to commit an honorable suicide, to atone for pissing away his battalion in its first engagement. And had failed at even that.

Now he was fighting to stay awake despite the agonizing pain and stifling heat. He had visitors. Peiper and that silly boy Johann Schmidt. They were babbling incomprehensible drivel about a Knight's Cross. "I got decorated for letting my battalion get massacred?"

Mohnke expected Peiper to answer, but instead it was the barely-German Schmidt, the one that command called "Smith", from some Länder named Oregon. "Berlin managed to blame that on General Dietrich for not equipping you properly. The General blamed his staff, who are blaming each other and the Waffen SS Main Staff. My two bosses are chuckling over it. Expanding LAH from a regiment to a small division, plus expanding Reich from a division into whatever this new organization is. has them all in chaos. Not enough men, not enough equipment, OKH fighting them over any allotment of either. The official line is, you performed brilliantly but had been asked to make bricks without straw. Your rebuilt battalion will have a proper anti-tank company, probably French 75's as Oberstleutnant Schwabe used them effectively in that role. Also an oversize weapons company and a company of motorcycle infantry. By the time you are ready for field service, it should be here. Probably mostly class III or IV Volksdeutsche, but as long as they can speak enough German for basic commands, who cares?"

"You are a Leutnant by courtesy. How the fuck can you possibly know all this?"

"My boss has rank, and my messages go directly to Oberführer Schellenberg at Prinz-Albrecht-Straße. The SS gossip comes from my boss. He calls it 'keeping me current'. The new unit is via a set of teletype messages from HQ signed by the Reichsführer. Neither you nor your unit will be ready for the Battle for Egypt. So instead you will march through a bunch of Bible towns in Palestine."

"You are also getting the Knight's Cross." This was Peiper. As senior, he felt he had the right to convey the good tidings to a fellow LAH veteran. "Steiner and I put you up for it. Berlin approved. Brigadier Strauss will pin it on you when you return to duty. Which may be sooner than you think. All the Jews who got dumped on the unit's camp in Bari left us with surplus medical personnel. He's sending two specialists to review your case. We told him you would recover better adjacent to your headquarters where your second-in-command can give you daily briefings, even if only for a few minutes, till your strength comes back."

Was he hallucinating? Mohnke had had vivid nightmares from the morphine. He hoped this was real. It was beyond his wildest dreams of salvaging his career and honor. He would have to thank Major Steiner. The boy had done Mohnke better than he had any right to pray for, much less expect.

2200 hours British Double Summer Time and CET
23 September 1940
War Cabinet Room, King Charles Street, Westminster, London

It had been a bloody long session. Prime Minister Ernie Bevin was beginning to see some of the troubles Churchill, and before him Chamberlain, had faced. Getting anything done with either the full Cabinet or the smaller War Cabinet, was akin to pulling teeth minus the anesthetic. The Names maneuvered for advantage as if it were peacetime. They all saw themselves as selfless patriots. Bevin saw them as scheming prima donnas.

Cairo messaged that they had retaken the otherwise worthless salient. It took several hours of back and forth traffic to establish that, as this had happened in daytime, they hadn't exactly forced the enemy to do much of anything. For reasons of their own the Nazis had pulled out. Was this a response to the prior attacks? Dill proudly asserted yes, and the Names chose to back him.

Both then wanted to 'suggest' more attacks to make a salient of Britain's own. An 8th Army that was outnumbered and outgunned was to slug its way to victory by the valor of the Poor Bloody Infantry? On its face, this was so stupid as to beggar belief. Bevin wanted an end to stupid attacks, and to give Dill the sack. The fight took up most of the day. In the end Dill was out, with Lord Gort back in as Chief of the Imperial General Staff. Dill was to go to Shanghai to do bugger-all running the to-be-assembled China Force. He was going as a theater commander, despite his 'theater' having under a division between Hong Kong, Shanghai, and the lesser Treaty Ports.

He'd also managed to rid himself of one of the Names. He was able to force Lord Halifax to accept the role of floor leader in Lords, and a meaningless lesser cabinet office. Eden had tried to reclaim the Foreign Office, but the other Names had ganged up against him. The new Foreign Secretary, Rab Butler, at least was a peace advocate.

Both the War Cabinet and the larger full Cabinet were full of people who now saw this new 'victory' in Egypt, as a reason to try to avoid the harsh but essentially fair German terms. Even good old Clem went wobbly on this. The same Names that had resisted any reinforcement to Egypt, now were demanding to reinforce success. Dill, covering for his yet-to-arrive successor, admitted that a brigade of armor could be found between 1st and 2nd Armored Divisions. The support services from 7th Armored were still there. So it was one brigade as soon as the RN was finished at Dakar, with a second ten days later. These would be plugged into 7th Armored's structure, with one of the independent motorized brigades as a Support Group.

RN was extremely evasive about the first day's actions at Dakar. Bevin knew this tune. It meant things had gone poorly and the senior people were trying to find a scapegoat. Tomorrow Winston arrived in India. God only knew what mischief he'd bring.

1200 hours local; 0730 hours CET
24 September 1940
Viceroy's Residence, Rajpath, New Delhi, India

The endless ceremonial was over. Winston Churchill was now Viceroy, and Claude Auchinleck was now commander-in-chief of the Indian Army. The two were not by nature simpatico, but days of being cooped up in the same airplane while taking the roundabout route via central Africa to India, had led to a certain mutual understanding. Auchinleck did not exactly agree with what Churchill proposed to do, but, pending receipt of contrary orders from London, he would obey, which was what the general felt was the constitutionally proper response to the civil authority.

The fake Bodhisattva that was Gandhi, and his scheming henchman Nehru, had brought out mobs of protesters when the plane had landed at Bombay; and then the same all along the rail route to New Delhi. The police had kept these mobs in hand, but there were deaths, fires, riot. The Congress big men were in prison but obviously still communicating with the outside world. The Quit India campaign was a declaration to him, that even from a cell they ruled. Churchill had a program to prove they did not. His first move was this evening where he would host Mr. Jinnah and his chief associates from the All-India Muslim League. Congress's mistake was to presume that Britain had to give independence to India as a whole. They had conquered it piecemeal. They could withdraw from it the same way, if needs must.

1200 hours local; 1100 hours CET
24 September 1940
Joey's Repair Section, lunchtime serving tables area, Brigade Strauss, rear of Italian lines at Alamein

The girls who brought lunch had brought back visitors. The Major's woman Greta and the cook Mary, had driven over and asked if they could chat with Clara over lunch. Clara was wise enough to take the request for the command it was. Her girls had cleared a section of an eating table, and waited in silence in case Mama Clara had orders.

It took five minutes of the usual social pleasantries to arrive at the point. Mary had children who could benefit from education when not on duty as cook's helpers. What might induce Frau Bats to consider allowing her early-teen 'daughter', who did the daily lessons with the 'littles', to permit the three Collins youngsters to sit in? Perhaps occasionally Abdul as well.

Clara Fischer was not a person who shocked easily. 'Frau Bats' shocked her. She knew what she was with Joey and knew it was major steps up from street whore, but 'Frau'? Greta saw the confusion in the older German woman's face. "Do you prefer another form of address? I know my German is still less than perfect. We both are mistresses to officers. Field wives, as it were. Is Frau the wrong term?"

"My officer hasn't married me. No white dress and a church with the organ playing … "

"I thought Communists were atheists. Mary here was a soldier's concubine. She took his name. I've accepted that whatever I think of myself as, others see me as Frau Steiner."

Frau? "Isn't this all temporary?"

"Our lives are temporary. We could be blown to pieces by a bomb from the sky. Berlin could tire of whatever game it is playing with this unit and have the SS Division liquidate us all. The SS does such things. They murdered my parents and siblings over a postcard I sent." Greta paused to choke back a tear. "My own damned fault. That was months ago and I was so naive." She gave a shrug and a sigh. "High price that others had to pay for it, but it seems life is like that. It has neither justice nor mercy. We can all die or be discarded. But if we aren't, our war ends at the oil fields. My uncles and cousins and your Joey will be repairing those so the black gold can flow to Germany. Mary will cook. We all presumed you would teach school. Haven't a clue as to what I'm good for. Something will turn up."

Something will turn up? Clara looked at this 18-year-old who was somehow a power to be reckoned with in the world Wanda had dropped her into. This child was trying to cope with this new world while Clara was just sitting in shock, living in the momentum of day-to-day. If Clara was doomed to spend the rest of her life with these people, best to make friends. So she started that dance of social connection.

....

Greta struggled to keep the smile off her face. This older, better-educated German woman intimidated her. It was so hard to live up to her role as Mrs. Klaus. He was settling into the role of hero officer quite well, if Gunter and her uncle were to be believed. It was her job to be the 'wife' he deserved.

....

It had gone well, Mary thought to herself. With her corporal, she never had had to deal with officers' ladies. Those were a separate species, accorded deference but mostly avoided. The female gods that strutted were the companions of sergeants-major. For Mary, social alliances with these two were a terrifying step up, but she had forced herself to have the courage to try.

1700 hours local; 1600 hours CET
24 September 1940
8th Army Field HQ to the rear of Alamein lines

New Chief of the Imperial General Staff, same old brown stuff. One could hope that given time, the new CIGS, Lord Gort, would replace the staff idiots he inherited from General Dill. Given the widespread belief in the upper ranks of the officer corps that Gort had the brains of a grapefruit, Cunningham was not sure this would improve the situation.

"Suggestions" from the staff of the CIGS kept undermining the generally sensible orders from the War Cabinet. The War Cabinet ordered an end to attacks. The staff Johnnies ever so helpfully 'suggested' that the 'fighting edge be kept up by raids and heavy patrol actions.' And were demanding daily reports of these activities. Complaints were met with bland responses that these were just 'suggestions'. Cunningham and his boss Wavell knew the Army game of 'suggestions'. The next step would be replacing brigade and division commanders who failed to heed these 'suggestions' with others 'more keen'. War Cabinet would notice an Army or Theater commander being replaced. Lesser commanders and key staff officers, could over time all be relieved without the political masters quite taking notice.

The brigades full of new 'recruits' from Egypt, its expats and refugees, were useless for this. These men could dig and build, but were not able to do anything more in combat than defend the trenches and bombproofs they had labored on. The Indian Army battalions were superb professionals. They were also horridly understrength. What field soldiers India had to spare, were being siphoned off to Basra to deal with the unfolding Iraq mess. The entire theater was unraveling. The Australian government would have kittens at its men being wasted this way.

His British were easily good enough. Their field officers had all played this game, as lieutenants and captains in France and Flanders back in the last war. The problem was that raiding ate men. There were no new drafts of British coming anytime soon. That was why there were brigades full of barely trained laborers. No, he'd need his British for when the enemy Big Push came.

That left the Yids. Winston's stupidity in mobilizing them was obvious. The Palestinian Arabs were back to sniping and raiding. Iraq was aiding them and drifting into outright rebellion. There were rumbles even here in Egypt. But the Yids would fight. Hated the Nazis with cause. Wingate had trained a bunch of them in just this sort of patrolling 'little war'. These two brigades included men from his 'Special Night Squads'. Given some British cadres, these gentlemen could be a raiding battalion under Wingate's personal command. A start on creating one had begun already. The Zionist Agency could supply the recruits to replace these men in the two line brigades, to supply fresh drafts to replace losses. There would be an obvious quid pro quo. He would send a staff man he trusted to O'Connor. In turn, O'Connor would tell the Zionists that as long as these volunteers were forthcoming, the garrison command was prepared to quietly suspend the immigration limits. No vast convoys of ships and publicity but, if handled with discretion … No need to tell London. No paper trail. Perfectly deniable. Need to wisely use available resources etc.

1830 hours Eastern Daylight Time, 24 September 1940
0030 hours CET, 25 September, 1940
The White House, 1600 Pennsylvania Avenue, Washington DC

The big toothy smile never left his face. Franklin Delano Roosevelt prided himself on his charisma and affability. He was sure that if he set his mind to it, he could charm the scales off a snake. Plus he'd always been an advocate for the Navy, back to his days as Assistant Secretary of the Navy under Wilson. He'd gotten them the Two Ocean Navy Bill this summer. More money, planes, ships, men than they had ever dreamed of. Certainly more than they had even asked for.

Yet the Chief of Naval Operations, Admiral Stark, and his bureau chiefs had stood before him like wooden cigar store Indians. Every time he mentioned destroyers to the China Station, they had fought him. Destroyers were for the battle fleet. Escort operations and show the flag were wastes of time. A battlefleet to fight who? Where? The Japanese were breaking up their main force, with active assistance from the USN and RN. A destroyer squadron headed by a light cruiser off to aid the British, and more than half the rest stood down. The one battle was against these 'pirate submarines' off the Chinese coast.

Pirates? What stupid public relations. The damned Reds had every right to be pissed about how the 'pirate' tripe had been used as a fig leaf in the Spanish War, for what everyone knew were Italian subs. But taking that pique out on the US flag had real-world consequences. He had three Reds that he knew of in his inner circle. His new would-be Vice-President Wallace was their creature. Hoover was supplying him with all the stupid details. If there was a quiet way to do so, Franklin would have dumped the clown. Pity Hoover had held the evidence back until after the announcement. Hoover was a snake. The only thing keeping him vaguely loyal was his feud with Tom Dewey. Dewey was trying to steal Hoover's gangbuster laurels.

No one owned his estranged wife Eleanor. But her whole circle was full of Party members and fellow travelers. It amazed him that Eleanor had managed to avoid the formal, public taint. Hoover had certainly leaked enough hints.

Hopkins. Poor, overworked, never-healthy Harry. The man was a godsend. He'd been right about how much Farley was missed. Franklin never admitted errors in public. Didn't suit his image. Damn, but Farley was the man who had kept the city bosses, the county court house gangs, and all the other petty oligarchs of the Democratic Party on board. Hopkins was trying, but it was a man-killing kind of job, more so for Hopkins than Farley. Farley socially fit in with the hard-drinking local crooks. Hopkins was far too goody-two-shoes. Not so high-minded as to break it off with his Communist mistress, though. She was his courier to Moscow. That was why Harry was in the room for this. He'd call the maybe-ex-lover and pass along the demand to respect the US flag. Hoover kept FDR appraised of every meeting. The nasty little man was extremely competent that way. He may have been an odious toad, as well as one of *those* kind of pantywaists, but he did his job well. He ferreted out secrets and, as long as allowed to run his little empire, kept secret the secrets each President needed hidden.

Back to Stark. He'd given the man his say, and more. It was time for orders. The Asiatic Fleet was to sail for Shanghai. It was to be responsible for moving the American volunteers to China. No ifs, ands, or buts. Fifty-five destroyers from the reserve fleet were to be made ready for sea duty. Stark had whined these WW1 relics couldn't fight with the battle line. So be it. That meant they were available to convoy ships from the West Coast to China.

FDR had China connections back to his Delano ancestors and the old clipper ship tea trade. He wasn't letting Willkie steal this issue. Willkie himself wasn't a bad apple. He was a decent liberal at heart. Lindy was pro-Nazi scum. FDR loathed the Nazis. Adolph had been a gutter-scum populist, a European Huey Long, not a true progressive like Stalin or Mussolini. And the Nazis just overdid it on the Jews. The Hebrews were a nuisance and not really white men, but Franklin had known decent ones back to his old mentor Bernard Baruch. Didn't mean he was going to let the millions of European Jews come here. Wasn't going to let the smart ones overrun Harvard Yard, either. It was enough that he had forced the British to break the blockade so their own charities could feed them. He had Wallace out campaigning in corn and cheese country about how many millions of dollars they were getting from the European relief programs ... and not one cent of it out of their precious tax dollars.

USN was also to build escort vessels. Dedicated ones like the British *Flower*-class corvettes. FDR had full blueprints from the British. Handed them to CNO Stark and ordered him to let contracts for a few dozen as a trial order. FDR knew there wasn't a prayer in hell that the US Navy would build these ships. They had always had a severe case of not-made-here disease. But it would force them to come up with another design. Something that small shipyards could make. US still had large numbers of unemployed men, and little local shipyards too small even for regular-size fleet destroyers. Franklin saw all this war spending in political terms. He needed contracts let, and men to be hired, before election day.

0700 hours local; 0130 hours CET
25 September 1940
GHQ India, New Delhi, India

Dawn had been an hour and change ago. The Congress mobs had been rampaging all night, with the police needing army backup to maintain some level of order. Congress would not accept that anyone other than themselves could interact with the British. Churchill as Viceroy would not tolerate being dictated to. Congress had chosen rebellion instead of negotiation. The Muslim League last night, and a delegation of princes later today, were exercising their option to talk, to have their voice heard on the issues of independence and partition. General Claude Auchinleck was now addressing a joint meeting of senior British and Indian officers and other officials from the Army, police, and civil service, including the railways. He was relaying the message he and Churchill had refined on that endless flight from London. Britain would leave once the war ended. That was no longer subject to debate. The issue was how and on what terms. India had not been a whole when the British arrived. Thus the British were under no obligation to leave it as a unified state. One man, one vote clearly wasn't going to work. A block rural Hindu vote would just hand everything to Gandhi and Nehru. Mr. Jinnah had already made clear that this was not acceptable to the Muslims. He and Churchill jointly doubted that this was acceptable to the princes. Now it was *possible* that a unitary India could be created, with autonomy for Muslim areas, various princely states, the linguistic minorities, British interests in a few port cities, and the like.

The key was the attitude of four pillars. The army, the police, the civil service, and the railroads. They were what made India a nation instead of a geographic concept. They could truly say they stood above religion, caste, regional language, and the like. Right now, these pillars were all run by white Britishers. Come independence those would depart. Not all on the same day. A proper handover of responsibility might take a few years. But in the end Indian generals of the army and police, heads of the railroad, cabinet and bureau chiefs, were the pillars of a united India. Or they weren't, and the services would be divided. The viceroy wished these four new service castes to conduct their own internal discussions, and appoint committees to speak for them as collegial entities. The Viceroy and GHQ saw this as the correct form of democracy for India. The four pillars plus the princes and the chambers of commerce. Mr. Jinnah had accepted this for the purposes of negotiation. Congress could join the talks, but only on these terms. No, this was not a state secret. How would each pillar secretly contact its scattered members? The viceroy asked for discretion, but wished serious dialog. It was a new day for India.

0900 hours local; 0800 hours CET
25 September 1940
Brigade Strauss Headquarters, behind the Alamein lines

It could have been worse. Di Salo had put together a nominal battalion in under a month and actually gotten it to the 'front'. One company of Italian Jews or part-Jews eager to prove their loyalty … and to get their families removed from the 1938 Race Laws. A company of Young Fascists hypnotized by the glory of joining such a prestige unit. A company of Transylvanian Magyar refugees fleeing Romanian oppression, who wished full residence and work permits in Italy for themselves and their relatives. A company of Hungarian Horthyite exiles. The Young Fascists and Horthyites for infantry. The Transylvanians for a heavy weapons company. The Jews for an oversized headquarters and services battalion. There was a third infantry company in transit from Spain. Middle-class Catalans who had been conscripted for the Reds … against their will per their families, but then that was the line to take to get release from the prisoner camps. Their service would buy redemption for their families.

Also eventually to arrive was a second Horthyite company and a battery of the multipurpose 76mm guns that had done so well serving with Rommel. Equipment was proving to be a problem. Everything was in short supply, and despite his family's excellent web of connections, he was simply not able to jump enough lines. His infantry had motorcycles. Civilian ones of a variety of makes and models. His heavy weapons relied on being dragged in trailers behind touring cars and light civilian trucks. His mortars and machine-guns would have been considered obsolete by the end of the Great War. Even the uniforms were old and still stank of preservatives.

Thankfully, his officer cadets had again been heroes. A dozen more were up for various decorations thanks to their patron General Rommel, including four posthumous Knight's Crosses. He'd been given authority to make the survivors Second Lieutenants in the Fascist Militia. One of Marshal Balbo's aides had assured him personally that this unit was in favor at the highest levels of the state.

Strauss had a present for him as well. Three repaired British cruiser tanks as his personal reserve. This Hauptmann Bats seemed a true miracle-worker. Now Di Salo just needed a few weeks to train up his ragtag unit into something like a combat edge. He'd done the same with worse in Spain. So had his little dove Coxita.

....

A welcome lunch from the ladies. How disgustingly bourgeois. Fascist Jewish Nationalists, a colored cook somehow allowed to sit in with her employers, and the one Party comrade was ideologically unsound. Nothing Comrade Stalin did could be wrong. Even the disasters in Spain were the work of Francoite Wreckers undermining the Republic. Stalin's line had been correct on Germany — the Hitlerites would in due course lose their hold on the masses.

In the meantime she let these bitches try to make friends. Coxita may have sold herself to a class enemy but at least her man was rich and powerful, with an excellent body. If Soviet Russia could do a tactical alliance of convenience with the Nazis, then what Coxita had done was similarly valid. She could not allow herself to believe otherwise. In her own eyes, she was a valiant Joan of Arc of the permanent revolution.

....

No wonder we lost in Spain. If the Party had promoted the likes of this shallow, materialistic slut, it had lost its roots. Clara felt she could see through the façade of this Catalan ex-commissar bitch to the spoiled little daughter of privilege she was. Class origins could not be hidden. They had both whored themselves. Clara was clear-eyed on what she had done and why. *Her* man was proletariat to the core, even if the Nazis had given him officer's rank tabs. This silly cow had spread her legs for an aristocrat and financier. *Communist*? Clara kept the sarcastic laughter out of her voice, but she had made up her mind.

1700 hours local; 1600 hours CET
25 September 1940
Railway siding high in the Transylvanian Alps

It was starting to get chilly. Again. The same as the past two nights. Obersturmbannführer Hermann Fegelein had had enough of this discomfort. The Hungarians and Romanians seemed to delight in causing difficulties for each other on this rail line. It was a form of slow-motion warfare.

Fegelein had been a devout Himmler toady. This had gotten him command of the Death's Head Cavalry Regiment. Despite its fancy name, it was a field security unit, its ranks padded out with Polish and other East Volksdeutsche. It had been part of the Warsaw garrison until the brief Soviet War. The regiment had then been shuttled off to Romania to 'guard' the Ploiesti oil fields. Guard? The command there consisted of an SS Security division, a Luftwaffe flak division, his regiment, and some other miscellaneous troops. It was a corps-sized command, when all that was needed was a battalion of nightwatchmen. Beyond the usual petty pilferage and vandalism that any spread-out industrial enterprise attracts, the oil fields were not menaced in any way. The Romanians were more than content to avoid Soviet occupation by being subservient German lackeys. Romania's oil and food were sent on to the Reich by the Antonescu regime, less a certain amount of probably unavoidable theft and corruption. All ex-Ottoman lands seemed to have inherited a Turkish fondness for minor graft.

This left Fegelein free to keep recruiting. His regiment was on its way to becoming a brigade, even if the new Volksdeutsche were of extremely dubious Aryan ancestry. In Poland he recruited men who knew 500 words of German and could show at least a definite German grandparent. Here, he was swearing in men who knew 100 words of German and claimed a German traveling salesman may once have fucked their great-grandmother.

Berlin had proven indifferent to just how good the blood lines were. The recruiters checked for cut dicks. A full foreskin, enough German to be taught simple commands, and physical health were all he was required to demand. The new enlistees were learning basic German fast enough and their military skills almost as fast. They were extremely willing, and healthy as horses.

The lack of threat to the oil installations left time for the regiment to be assigned other security activities. One of these was Jew transport. Which left him here on this siding with six hundred forty-two Jewish oldsters and children. Two nights with no heat, no engine, no resupply of food or water, nothing. He'd sent men into the next town to telegraph his complaints. All he received in reply were excuses and evasions.

Why the damned Kikes needed guards was beyond the Obersturmbannführer. They never ran away. The locals would just kill them, if the weather and steep mountain trails adjacent to the tracks didn't. They were all happy to go to Italy. Berlin had deeded these useless eaters to the equally worthless comic-opera Italians.

Fegelein was not about to spend a third night on this siding. He got the Yids off the train, neatly lined up by the ditch that ran adjacent to the road that followed the rail line. He posted guards at each end of the line with rifles, and then led the rest of his men in with bayonets and rifle butts. Some of the children ran. His riflemen picked off most, but a few made it into the mountains where they would die. The old folks and most of the children just accepted their fate and waited quietly while the SS moved down the line methodically crushing skulls and slashing open organs. They mainly prayed in their revolting language to their invisible deity. They tried to shield the eyes of the terrorized children to what was happening. Disgusting. Real humans would have fought even if it was hopeless.

It took the better part of an hour to kill them all. Or at least enough of them. Many were still howling in pain or whimpering. A few doubtless faked death and would sneak off later. Screw them and fuck this worthless assignment. He got his men into column and started off for the mountain village with the telegraph office. It must have an inn and something strong to drink. He'd run out of palinka, the local rotgut brandy, the first night. He was unused to being without strong drink even for one night. It left him sweaty and achy, worse hour by hour.

1400 hours Eastern Daylight Time; 2000 hours CET
25 September 1940
Football Stadium, Morehouse College, Atlanta, Georgia

Not being a huge school, Morehouse lacked the huge stadium of a football powerhouse like Notre Dame. However, every square inch of the stands and field was jammed with people, with thousands more listening by the exits to hastily mounted loudspeakers. The Georgia rally for the Freedom Brigade was in full swing.

Patton had proposed a Negro battalion for his Sixth Armored Cavalry Regiment. That had lasted less than a day, as in the neighborhood of forty percent of the four historic black regiments attempted to volunteer. Chief of Staff General George Marshall refused to allow his regiments to be gutted. Each regiment was limited to supplying one hundred cadres, with the actual choices being by lottery. The First Lady had then taken charge. The active duty Army could not prevent retired members of the four regiments from enlisting, or bar the recruitment of men not yet drafted, particularly those under the nineteen years of age that was the minimum for conscription.

The intent had been to recruit seventeen- and eighteen-year-old's, who in peacetime had often been allowed to enlist. Intention vanished in a wave of popular enthusiasm. The Baby Buffaloes had coped with ceaseless lies by changing the standard to height, weight, and some vague growth of facial hair. Even that rule quickly became more a guideline than a rigid law.

Similarly, the battalion was now the Freedom Brigade of Patton's hastily renamed 6th Armored Cavalry Division. The crowd roared encouragement as each little farm town's party of young volunteers marched themselves to the podium to be sworn in. They were going to fight for Jesus in China and for liberty, for freedom. No white officers for them. General Davis, Senior would lead the brigade. Negro officers from the reserves, and young Negro college men from places such as Morehouse, would command. In Lincoln's war of freedom, the officers had learned with the men. It would be the same with the new legions of emancipation.

Reverend Martin Luther King, Senior of the Ebenezer Church preached the sermon and led the crowd in gospel song. He proudly said he would go as head chaplain. Accompanying him would be his eleven-year-old son Martin, Junior – who already felt a calling to the word of God.
....
Harry Hopkins had had his hands full with Eleanor's Freedom Crusade. He had managed to sell it to Dixie's governors and sheriffs as a safety valve. Let the dissatisfied go off to China. As his minions kept reminding the elected heads of Jim Crow Dixie, no one ever promised to bring these Freedom Negroes home.

0600 hours local; 0400 hours CET
26 September 1940
A sealed freight car somewhere east of Moscow

It was hot. The freight cars the Aztecs were transported in had poor air circulation. Their Soviet hosts provided not much food, too little water, dirty straw, and, to use as chamber-pots, barrels that had probably not been really cleaned since the days of the Czars.

The Aztecs had been herded off their ships in Riga in the middle of the night. Herded like cattle by loud-shouting police to the rail yards and bundled into freight cars. They were let out twice a day to stretch their legs and try to clean the barrels. The only joyful part of this had been a big parade in Moscow. The Aztecs had joined a long column of Spanish Republicans, German Communists, and others who paraded past Stalin and the other revolutionary Gods.

Alexander Ruz had carried the Cuban Party's banner at the head of their battalion. They were off to liberate China, and then all of Asia, from capitalism and exploitation. Two brigades of American volunteers would be following them, or so the political cadres informed them. At fourteen the fine points were beyond Alexander. So was the heavy hand of his father. No one could keep him from this great adventure now.

1400 hours local; 1500 hours CET
26 September 1940
Government House, Freetown, Sierra Leone

General Bernard Montgomery was proud of himself. The RN had made a total botch of the entire Dakar Expedition. Only to be expected. Now he would do this the right way. No half-thought-out attempts to get the Vichy garrison to defect. The day for that was over. The ones who would turn coat had done so already. Now the remaining fencesitters would need a bit of armed assistance. He had beefed up his Third Infantry Division for this expedition with a brigade of armored cars. It would take several days for all the equipment to be unloaded. Plenty of time for him to send London the list of what he'd need to do this all properly.

In the meantime, the big French general, de Gaulle, had successfully landed with his chaps and a brigade of Poles. Conakry had surrendered without a fight when faced with a large RN squadron. So part of the French Empire had been secured for the side, at the cost of no casualties whatsoever. Montgomery as ever was proud of himself.

1800 hours CET
26 September 1940
Heydrich's Office, Prinz-Albrecht-Straße, Berlin, Germany

"That idiot Fegelein did WHAT!" Reinhard Heydrich rarely lost his temper in public. His public persona did not allow for showing external things as changing him. He changed the universe. The universe bent to his will. However, the only audience here and now was his *eminence gris* Schellenberg, who would simply forget the emotional display ever occurred.

"I can send Obersturmbannführer Siegel to administer a noodle." A 9mm noodle behind the ear made most problems vanish. "The few survivors can be quietly deposited in Africa where no one will ever find them." The floating circus that was Strauss's unit served so many useful functions. Schellenberg was prepared to ignore how it had come into existence mostly by accident and whimsy. After Luqa, those things were not expedient to remember.

"No. We do this properly. A full court, then the death sentence. To be clear, the charge is not war crimes or any such silliness. The charge is usurpation of command prerogative. Get OKH to send an observer. Same for Waffen SS Main Office. Decisions on liquidation of prisoners are made in Berlin, not by some idiot field officer who feels burdened by cold weather on a railway siding in the mountains." Thus the wheels were set in motion on an alcoholic fool of an officer's demise.

1900 hours British Double Summer Time and CET
26 September 1940
War Cabinet Room, Westminster, London

"That idiot Montgomery did WHAT?" Ernie Bevin's contempt for the senior officers on His Majesty's Service went down to new, even more abysmal lows. "On whose authority did a division commander convert a demonstration against a port into a new theater for land warfare?"

There followed two hours of the two services blaming each other, while the exiting and entering CIGS each claimed lack of authority. It seemed that two generals-in-chief amounted to no one exactly in charge. Bevin made a mental note to start fishing for a successor to Gort when he got done purging the RN.

More bad news followed. General Weygand had been in Dakar. On hearing of de Gaulle's landings in Guinea on French territory, landings from British ships that just the day before had been attacking the French Navy, he had ordered the occupation of Gambia and the bombing of Freetown. Vichy was demanding answers on why they should not consider themselves at war with the British Empire, from Gibraltar to the Congo River?

1900 hours Eastern Daylight Time; 26 September , 1940
0100 hours CET; 27 September, 1940
White House, Washington DC

That idiot Hoover had truly stepped in it this time. His silly beggar's game of outing Willkie's mistress was palpably transparent. It of course never occurred to Mr. G Man that the Republicans would immediately counter with the obvious weapon, Vice-President-designate Wallace's 'Dear Guru' letters. Tainting a Democrat with Communism was easy, but just didn't move that much of the electorate. The Republicans had been crying wolf on that since the start of the New Deal. It felt old and flat by 1940.

The US was still in many ways a church-going country, regardless of how modern people were now. Their clergy couldn't deliver them to the polling place with the same regularity that was once the case twenty years ago. However, a President was expected to be a white Protestant of northern European, and preferably British, stock. He was expected to be nominally faithful to his wife, and at least go through the motions of being a Sunday Christian from some acceptable sect.

Willkie's sexual dalliance was titillating. It could perhaps have cost him the nomination, had it been made public months earlier. However, even church-going people knew men were men and some men strayed. Mistresses, call girls, cat-houses ... every major city had them, and many smaller ones did as well.

Weird Eastern or Asiatic mystery cults were something for Hollywood movies and dime novels, not a belief that serious men practiced. The idea that some flake who worshipped occult gods could be one heartbeat from the White House, just wouldn't fly. Wallace was toast as of early tomorrow AM when the *Chicago Tribune* broke the story. Hopkins had been given a courtesy warning by his Republican counterparts. All of a sudden, this was becoming an election Franklin could seriously lose.

1000 hours local; 0300 hours CET
27 September 1940
Ft. Santiago, Manila, Philippines

Douglas MacArthur was putting on a fine show. Ike knew Mac far too well. The old man had been seething at Ike's orders to create a Filipino volunteer battalion for China service. Had tried every roadblock he could think of, had subjected Ike to the sort of verbal tongue-lashing that Mac excelled at. Ike had served this man before. He knew how to just remain at attention and let the storm pass.

Ike had ironclad paperwork from the President of the US and Chief of Staff Marshall. He had the support of Philippine Commonwealth President Quezon, in large part because he had the active, vocal support of the Archbishop of Manila O'Doherty. The Vatican wanted the Catholics of China protected. The Commonwealth was overwhelmingly Catholic. A Vatican 'request' for something as harmless as raising volunteers, was not something to oppose in an electoral democracy.

Mac had stinted Ike on cadre. Ike didn't care. He had enough decent Philippine Scout sergeants. Manila University ROTC could provide the lieutenants. Ike's little black book of officers he'd served with could provide his two majors, who would have protégé lieutenants who wanted a fast ticket to captain. The recruiting had brought in too many men. War Department answer was to enlist them all, and worry about tables of organization later. He was also to get these men to China post haste. They could do basic and unit training in Shanghai. For now there was a need to show the flag beyond the understrength 4th Marine Regiment.

1000 hours CET
27 September 1940
Reichschancellery, Berlin, Germany

Führer Herman Göring did not like waking up much before noon on mornings after all-night galas. This time he instantly grasped why his personal staff had violated custom to awaken him early. His Luftwaffe was putting on a major operation late this afternoon and into the night. Could a Führer who was also Air Marshal leave such a stage to lesser beings? Also the Italian leader, Air Marshal Balbo, would be there. This was to be a European operation. The overwhelming portion of the planes would be German, but Italy and France had squadrons flying. There would be hastily repainted planes with the national colors of Slovakia, Hungary, and Romania as well. Air Marshal von Richthofen had done the staff work. The British had provided the pretext last night.

1100 hours CET
27 September, 1940
Heydrich's office, Prinz-Albrecht-Straße, Berlin, Germany

Air Marshal von Richthofen had just given his verbal report on the planned air force mission over London and the lessons expected to be learned from it, and presented the written version to Heydrich, who was sitting behind his desk.
"Thank you, Herr Marshal , please be seated." Heydrich pointed at one of the chairs. "Coffee?"
Von Richthofen remained at attention. "Herr Vice Chancellor, may I be allowed to add a few personal words, off the record?"

Heydrich favored the Luftwaffe Marshal with a wondering look – these kind of requests had become rare in the past few months. "Please, go ahead."

"Herr Vice Chancellor, you are a good pilot -– with a bit more experience you might even become an excellent one. But Germany has enough good pilots, it might even have enough excellent ones. But you are more than that, you are one of the very few truly indispensable men in Germany."

A look passed between the Air Marshal and the man they both knew was the day-to-day ruler of Europe. Just as von Richthofen was in fact the operational head of the Luftwaffe, whatever Göring's list of titles and offices said.

"I feel it is my duty to point this out to you. Your proposal to fly in this mission is completely irresponsible. The days of Kaisers and their chief office-holders leading cavalry charges in full armor are far in the past, and should remain so. Modern war is too vast an enterprise for such personal displays of valor. Remember Gustav Adolph throwing away Sweden's future at Lutzen. If you want to keep on flying, by all means do so – but do it in a multi -engine aircraft, together with a second pilot, and not in an active combat zone."

Dark clouds had collected on Heydrich's face ... he stared at von Richthofen, who kept his face properly blank while staying rigidly at attention.

Heydrich sighed. "Do sit down, Herr Marshal. It must have taken a lot of courage to say that."

"Yes, Herr Vice Chancellor."

"And you did the right thing, Herr Marshal, both with daring to tell me this, and with waiting for a moment when we are alone. I respect you for both, and I will think carefully about your suggestion. Will you take some coffee now? And I would like your comments on the recent Italian aircraft production numbers."

0600 hours British Double Summer Time and CET
28 September, 1940
War Cabinet Room, Westminster, London

The Germans had warned them time and again via the Lisbon talks that these RAF raids would provoke a countermeasure. The British government had not responded by abandoning them. There was a large belief in strategic bombing as a high-tech way to avoid another Western Front-type bloodbath. There was a perceived need to be seen hitting back after Dunkirk and Malta. There was a large amount of institutional inertia.

So Prime Minister Ernie Bevin was now facing his first severe cabinet crisis. The night of the 26th / 27th, Bomber Command had attacked a Renault plant on the outskirts of Paris. The French were asserting that they had instead bombed the Louvre. The neutral press had been shown the damages, allowed to take pictures. Much of the precious artwork had been spared, but only because the French had sensibly relocated it for the duration. Bevin hoped that was not a cover for the Huns having stolen these treasures. The same night, a raid on Berlin wiped out a children's home. Over one hundred dead little orphans, again with photo evidence from the neutrals.

At the Lisbon talks, the German and Italian representatives had announced that Europe's patience was at an end. They had then suspended talks for the day. Europe's patience? This European Community they were forming was beginning to acquire shape and substance.

The first news last night had been bad enough. Heavy dusk air raids on the East End. Large fires throughout the warehouse district, and scattered fires dozens of other places. Fighter Command was claiming a large score of German planes brought down, and various local authorities were confirming wrecked planes, dead and captured aircrew. The fighters landed at dusk. The bombers kept coming. Wave after wave. Guided no doubt by the dusk fires.

By now the entire East End was in flames. Thousands were dead, tens of thousands missing, and well over a hundred thousand rendered homeless. The fire brigades, the air raid wardens, all the emergency services were overwhelmed. Until now the air war had been little port towns in the south. This was London, the beating heart of the British Empire. Its government had totally failed to protect it. The few obsolete night-fighters had proven near to useless. Britain was at great expense fighting an imperial war for far-away colonies, but had not spent the money and effort to safeguard the core of Britain.

The Lisbon embassy had been awakened a bit after midnight and presented with an ultimatum. The powers of Europe proposed to hold London, and then the Midlands, hostage. They wanted the bombing of Europe stopped immediately and publicly. In return, no European bomber would enter British skies. Let this be a war of gentlemen, or choose barbarism. They made clear that they had more bombers and were prepared to use them. They had refrained because they saw this as a cabinet war, a dispute over imperial possessions. Did Europe need to try suicide for the second time in this century? The ultimatum was being broadcast in the various national languages over their new Radio Europa Cartel. The major neutrals had been informed, starting with the US and USSR. They would give the British Government the 28th to accept, or be responsible for the consequences.

The dispute in the War Cabinet was along generational lines. The Names from the 1930's tried to evade responsibility, to blame each other, to wish to explore 'alternatives'. Bevin and the 1922 Committee people weren't having it. Whether by accident or design, the Germans had struck at the class fissure. They had bombed working-class London, while leaving the middle-to-upper-class West End alone. Bevin was making his stand on this. These were Labor's people. He demanded an emergency session of Commons to support his decision to accept the proposal, and invited any Cabinet member uncomfortable with this to resign. He made clear this was a matter of Parliament's confidence in the prime minister's conduct in office, of the fate of the government. Two Liberals resigned. (The rump Liberal Party was long on fine principles. The rest could count. Bevin and the 1922 Committee had the votes.) The late afternoon session confirmed this by a tally of 412-118. The BBC announced the acceptance scant minutes later. The 'Europeans' had already been notified at the day's session in Lisbon. Radio Europa read translations of the British acceptance note within the hour. Europe was still at war, but it already felt somewhat less so.

0900 hours Eastern Daylight Time; 0300 hours CET
28 September 1940

Deaths on the Nile

White House, Washington DC

Edward R. Murrow's reports on the air raids against the British southern ports had been stirring interventionist sentiment for weeks. His report from a London hotel rooftop this past night had been earth-shattering. It polarized both sides of the intervention-versus-isolation dispute, while galvanizing the perceived need for continental defense. Lindy had already issued a statement on the lack of sufficient air defense for America's cities and coasts. FDR, campaigning in Ohio, had done one of his classic broad-stroke off-the-cuff remarks. He had declared the western half of the North Atlantic Ocean to be a US defense zone. The Navy was to institute continental defense patrols, whatever those were. Attacks on planes and shipping in that zone were forbidden.

Harry Hopkins was left to sort out the mess with the Navy and the newspapers. Had the US gone to war? If not, were only German warships excluded — but not British transiting to and from Canada and other British possessions? The Naval command was saying that to enforce this, they needed to massively draw down the Pacific Fleet beyond what had already been agreed to. Hopkins' ulcers were killing him, but there was no rest today.

0800 hours CET
28 September 1940
Military Headquarters complexes of OKH and OKW, at Zossen, 20 miles south of Berlin

General Beck, Minister of War for Germany, was on one of his rants. The subject of most such rants was Heydrich. "One of his thugs murders some Jews at a railway siding and now he is making a giant deal of a trial!   The SS have been murdering Jews and Poles since the war started!"

The last few months had taught Halder that the correct move was to let Beck wear himself out. Sooner or later the older general would have to take a break, and sometimes he paused to think. Most of the time Halder would have to guide his superior when the subject was Heydrich. To be fair, Beck's rant had a basis in fact. The SS had murdered a great many Poles and Jews. Himmler had fantasies about reshaping Poland's ethnic makeup. Since Heydrich took over the SS and joined the 'counter-coup', the number of murders had dropped in Poland, and the Americans were now feeding the ghettoes, most of Poland, and some new Catholic homes for unfortunates. A small surplus of food and medicine was even accruing to Germany.

There was something behind this move for a trial. Halder was certain of it. Heydrich had his own communication channels to the various SS and police minions of his ministry, that he could use for a warning. He could have just left this thug Fegelein face down in a shallow grave. A trial made it public, which meant a different audience. An audience that probably was supposed to include the Army, the other European police services, and the lesser European powers.

Once Beck calmed down, Halder would guide him to agreeing to send someone to Heydrich's show trial; and in the meantime, he would try to find what game Heydrich was really playing at. As a hedge against failing at this, he would discreetly have one of his aides take a verbal message to General Busse at OKW to send someone. Busse had enough officers from the hereditary military caste, many with legal training. The key was someone whose family connections would make the report credible. The important result was what the gossip net said, not what was on the formal documents.

1200 CET
28 September 1940
Louvre, Paris

Führer Herman Göring was back in his element. There had been a victory breakfast for senior air officers, presided over by the three leaders, at the municipal hall at Calais. Now the triumvirs were doing a joint wreath-laying at the Louvre, where they would each proclaim that the Louvre and Versailles were treasures of their joint European culture. Admiral Darlan had been elated to see a French naval honor guard there for the three to inspect. (Heydrich had seen to it.) The Führer had grown accustomed to his number 2 seeing to such details. Göring had played bountiful monarch, informing Darlan that the two treasures would henceforth be part of the Free Zone, with perpetual honor guards from the French military.

As a lover of fine art, Göring found his speech on France's contribution to the Christian West's grand culture an easy one to give. He held his tongue at the lies he had been given to utter on the fine air forces of his allies. The French had used an American bomber, the Martin 167 Maryland. Their Dewoitine D520 fighter was at best a decent competitor to the pre-war marks of the Me-109. The new Fw 190 would leave it in the dust. All the Italians could offer in terms of their own planes were two squadrons of CR-42 biplanes. The fighter squadron had escorted the bomber version for a symbolic tip and run raid over Dover. The real Italian contribution had been two squadrons of Ju 88 bombers escorted by two squadrons of Me 109 fighters. The Italian flyers were first-rate, but it was German mechanics who prepped these German-built planes for the mission.

There was a state banquet in Paris for the threesome. Then they would fly to Berlin to be on the reviewing stand for the mass funeral procession for the hundred or so dead Berlin orphans. Abandoned in life, these dead children were now national martyrs. Such is the way of empires.

0700 hours Hawaiian Time; 1700 hours CET
28 September 1940
Pearl Harbor Naval Base, Oahu, Hawaii

The full US base turned out in dress whites to welcome their Japanese visitors. Eight destroyers and a light cruiser of Vice Admiral Nagumo Chuichi's 'Special Mobile Force', were paying a call on the US Pacific Fleet. In addition to the naval brass, led by CNO Stark and Pacific Fleet Commander Richardson, there was a special present for Nagumo to review, the US 100th Infantry Battalion. This was a volunteer unit of American Japanese who had heeded FDR's offer to let those Americans with sympathies for the various belligerents go fight for their chosen side, but not try to drag the US into the conflict on any side. These 'Yankee Samurai' were awaiting transport to the Manchurian Front.

For decades, the US and Japanese navies had seen each other as certain enemies. Now they were slowly coming to terms with the concept that while still not friends, they would not be foes. The USN's Plan Orange was as dead as the dodo. The new active space for both fleets would be in the Atlantic. Again not exactly as friends, but definitely not as enemies.

0630 hours local; 0530 hours CET
29 September 1940
Reconnaissance Detachment HQ, Afrika Division, behind Hausser's division in Alamein lines to the south near the Depression

The so-called headquarters was a ramshackle shack that looked as if a small gust of wind would blow it over. Units on the move don't waste a lot of time building temporary structures. The logic was that it was better than a tent.

Lothar was giving what amounted to a lecture to a half-dozen junior officers. The so-called detachment was a company each of motorcyclists and armored cars. The cars were SdKfz 231's rather than Panhards, but Lothar would adapt. He was back serving with Germans, the way the original Führer would have had things run.

Peiper and Sommer had sold Lothar to the staff people at Afrika Division HQ as if he were a side of beef. They were upfront about his attitude problems, but stressed the value for a green unit of having an officer with combat experience in this theater and against this foe. So he was now a supernumerary deputy detachment commander. This meant he would probably end up an armored car officer. It also meant answering endless stupid questions from middle-aged SA officers who seemed unable to wrap their heads around mobile war. Lothar mentally shrugged. He'd teach as much as they let him. An hour in combat would teach the rest.

0700 hours CET
29 September 1940
Ministry of War, Berlin, Germany

Minister of War Generaloberst Beck had long been pondering where the initial putsch had gone wrong. He still felt the original conception had been correct. Use Göring as a Nazi symbol for a monarchist regency. The various royalist factions had been unable to agree on which royal would ultimately assume the throne. The Spaniard Franco had shown how it was possible to do monarchism without actually deciding who the monarch should be. As the crown was merely a symbol behind which the better elements of a nation could unite, the actual choice of the king-to-be could be sorted out later. Franco had not even made a clear choice between two rival lines of claimants. Franco had personal ties to one line, but the other brought with it an excellent militia.

When Nebe had returned with Heydrich instead of liquidating him, Beck had seen it as a minor error, easily corrected. And then it all came apart. Göring by upbringing should have been with them. His father had been a functionary of the Kaiser. Not of the military class but of the one beneath it, nobility of the robe instead of the sword. The father's type aped the true Junkers in everything. Hermann had been a cadet-school graduate and medal-winning officer. His nominal Nazi associations could be overlooked. By 1940 Göring was a lazy sybarite, unlikely to be any real trouble to a government of experts backed by the sword of the Army.

What stung worse was the betrayal by Halder. The man had done the same several times in the run-up to the war. Halder could see the evils of the Nazis, the dangers they posed to rule by the natural aristocrats. The nation needed a firm Prussian type of enlightened monarchy. Democracy led to socialism. Nazi or Communist, it was just two faces of the same gutter coin. The masses should be given firm orders the way it was done in the Army. Yet every time it came to a point of decision, Halder had refused to issue the coup orders. The man was exasperating.

Heydrich. The man had been run out of the Navy in a sexual scandal. Yet once part of the new regime, he had shown himself to be a quite pragmatic technocratic nationalist. Heydrich used the Nazi trappings to run what was a personal regime founded on efficiency. This attracted the younger members of the traditional service elites, civil as well as military. Serving Heydrich after Malta (and now the first North African battles), was a route to quick promotion, to decorations, to combat commands. On the civil side, the new cartels offered posts with power and high compensation to the hard chargers. Heydrich was not from the socialist wing of the Nazis, but neither did he treat private property as something of importance. To him everyone and everything was at the disposal of the state. It was Trotsky's War Communism run with Teutonic efficiency.

Beck caught himself. In all honesty he wished for a regime of the type Heydrich had created, which was functionally the antithesis of Hitler's regime of endless leader whims and frantic improvisations. And yet ... and yet it did all come down to breeding, to class. Such an enlightened royal autocracy needed to be run by the traditional service nobility of the Prussian state, such as had been cultivated back to the time of the Great Elector; aided by others who consciously schooled themselves in the ruling class mix of honor and duty. A Ludendorff or a Göring was acceptable. A young naval Leutnant who could despoil a decent girl with a promise of marriage, and then not honor it, was just the wrong sort of individual. How could anything good come from such poisonous roots?

The Generaloberst knew all the arguments against action. The Fatherland was still at war with the British Empire, a mighty force. The British had the US and Japan as de facto allies, making them potentially stronger still. The hold the Reich had on much of Europe was quite new. Chaos in Berlin could lose Germany all the advantages gained in the past year. The Soviet menace still existing. At any moment Stalin could move west, with millions of men and with tens of millions of internal Communists as devoted helpers. Looming over it all was the million men whom Heydrich had summoned out of nowhere to Berlin the last time. The masses were with the Nazis, not with the proper rulers. But if not now, when? Every month lost was another month for Heydrich to gain control of more of the levers of power, for Göring to acquire more of a mass following. The aristocracy had been handed a gift from heaven when Hitler conveniently died. Should they sit frozen waiting for yet another miracle of the

House of Brandenburg? No! Real men do not just sit in the dark muttering about how someday they would act.

Beck sighed. He saw that he had made his decision. All this was mere rationalization. He had kept the arch-plotter Carl Goerdeler on his ministry staff against such eventualities. He had kept the key military conspirators on the staff of the Replacement Army. Both groups had been politely pushing him to take action. Now he was ready. The coup plots of the late 30's had been to save Germany from the unwinnable wars Adolph the Idiot had risked by his brinksman's diplomacy. The threat now was quite the reverse. Another year, and there would be a victorious peace with the British. A hugely popular peace that would cement the Nazi hold on power. In peacetime the Nazis could afford to purge the officer corps the way Stalin had done. Without their hold on military command, the Old Order was doomed. Action must be taken. The die was cast. A Rubicon needed to be crossed.

1600 hours local; 1500 hours CET
29 September 1940
Brigade Strauss Compound, in rear of the lines of Italian XXI Corps at the northern end of the European Alamein lines facing 8th Palestine Division

The plane ride had been bumpy. Major Albert Witt had no idea if it had been especially so. He'd never flown before. Neither had his two sons, Arne and Uwe, who had accompanied him on this 'adventure'. It had all started with a Gestapo summons two weeks earlier to appear at Prinz-Albrecht-Straße at a particular day and time, presenting themselves at main reception with the written summons in question. As part-Jews living quietly in Berlin, this prospect had not seemed pleasant. And yet … it was a summons to appear. They had not been arrested and held to make sure of their obedience. They were being treated as in some sense citizens of the Reich. Which they had once been. All three had done military service, the two sons having been with the colors until expelled this past April.

At the designated hour, all three arrived, dressed in their best business suits. They had their personal documents with them … just in case. Reception checked those carefully, then led them upstairs to another waiting area where in due time they were ushered into the presence of an Oberführer named Schellenberg. The name meant nothing to Herr Witt. Being informed that this Schellenberg was first deputy to Reichsführer Heydrich was terrifying. What had his family done to merit such exalted attention?

All was quickly made clear. Schellenberg had queried his bureaucratic contacts at the Finance Ministry for a patriotic part-Jew who might be available for a mission of national importance. Germany was in the process of conquering a port facility in Egypt, specifically the city of Alexandria. It was necessary for this port complex to be quickly restored to efficient use after the repair of the inevitable British demolitions. A naval detachment was being created to handle the technical side of this, but there would be a financial aspect as well. Very large sums would have to be spent buying local labor, materials, and such. Absent financial controls, there would be theft, fraud, and waste. Albert Witt and his sons should consider themselves as conscripted by the Interior Ministry.

The manner of conscription was, from Witt's point of view, quite unexpected. His dismissal under the prior Aryanization decrees was rescinded. He was restored to his old bureaucratic rank, with the missing years listed as 'unpaid personal leave'. He was given a Major's rank in the NL, as a courtesy because he would be in a war zone. However, his own pay and pension rights would continue to be civil service. His sons were made Hauptmann in the NL, with a civil-service grade two degrees below his. Their mixed blood was waived away "in the interests of the Reich". Witt was now a direct report to this Schellenberg via a Leutnant Schmidt, whom he would meet in Africa.

The family threesome would be forwarded support staff from some camp in Italy. These support staff were alleged to be people with proper financial, administrative, and legal backgrounds. Oh, and this 'Advanced Party of the Interior Ministry' was also for some 'reason of state' to be the paymaster section of this nebulous Brigade Strauss. The eldest son was handed a traveling case, with binders inside with the pay tables for NL and attached services.

The more interesting part was the rest of the baggage. Three suitcases having in them a million British pounds, half a million US dollars, and three quarters of a million German marks. Witt and the sons had to sign for these amounts. Witt would have liked a chance to count the currency first, but wisely chose not to raise the issue with a man who could order his execution.

The final part of the instructions had, if anything, been even more bizarre. Witt had been handed a pre-written letter to his wife and his mother, and was forced to sign it at once. It notified them that he had been recalled to duty along with the sons. They were to expect SS 'helpers' tomorrow, to pack the house for shipment. The personal effects of the three men would be forwarded to them at a location that must remain undisclosed for reasons of state security. The women were to pack their own personal items for a rail journey they would be taking, to Italy. The furniture and the remaining possessions would be placed in storage pending a future date and location where a permanent residence would be found. Had this Schellenberg seemed a more sympathetic sort of man, Witt would have asked leave to add a few words in his own hand to the note, for the ladies' peace of mind. Even a few personal thoughts would have eased their burden. Pity, but even begging for this did not seem prudent under the circumstances.

The steamer trunks filled with currency had come with handcuffs to secure them to their owners. The three men had taken this precaution. The section of HJ's who had picked them up at the forward air strip had found the situation amusing, but nothing that teen-age male muscles couldn't cope with. Now they were in the command building, half drunk with fatigue and near bowled over by the intense heat. The General they would be working with looked like an advertisement for a body-building school. Senior officers were expected to be fit, but not circus freaks. Most confusing.

Strauss was glad to be finally getting a paymaster section. He saw the rest as Schellenberg's business. "Welcome to our little outpost of Greater Germany." He then shook hands all around.

The two sons had agreed to let their father do the talking. "Thank you, Brigadier Strauss. I take it the naval contingent and our support staff have not yet arrived?"

"Naval group lands at Benghazi tomorrow. They will be multiple days getting driven up here. Don't know how many yet, as they don't rate priority. The support staff made it onto a ship to Mersa Matruh. Last minute thing. Harbormaster's office in Bari had a missing military contingent, so we got a warm body order to fill out the load. About your women. The Italian railroads are in chaos, but at some point they'll arrive at Bari. My Major Wrede has orders to get them settled in."

"About this camp. How strict a regime?"

Gunter started laughing, then caught himself. He knew it wouldn't be funny from their side. "It's not a camp in the sense Dachau or Belsen is. It's a military encampment. Some of it is hasty-construction wooden buildings, and the rest is good-quality tents with wooden floors. Many of my people have family parked there. It's boring but safe, with decent food and a passable climate. Eventually we get to the end of the campaign and go into occupation duty. Then the dependents arrive. This unit is for permanent colonial duty. We are exiles, as it were."

"I don't know how to say this delicately. We are part Jew. My mother is fully Jewish by blood. She's quiet about it. Doesn't practice the faith, but it's on her documents. How will your Major and his subordinates cope with this? Can you perhaps send instructions to be kind?"

Gunter gave Witt a strange stare and then started to slowly shake his head. Witt was panicking, expecting the worst. "Let me guess. Oberführer Schellenberg briefed you on this himself?" Witt nodded. "And of course he neglects to mention you three were chosen because, as part-Jews you wouldn't have a problem working in a unit where the bulk of the people are of Jewish blood?" Gunter saw the relief on the three faces. He knew Schellenberg's pattern by now. The man could be deliberately cruel, but mostly it was just indifference and harassed over-work. "I had already sent instructions that the two ladies were to be treated as befit your rank. I can send a pointed reminder. Now for the big issue. You came with a mountain of cash. That means you need a safe. We can order you one from Germany, but it will never arrive in time. The ports are a madhouse, and the rail lines in are almost as bad. We have, shall we say, a backchannel for emergency purchases in Naples. Anything we buy there gets shipped priority. Joey!"

In answer to Gunter's yell, a short, disheveled young man in his twenties sauntered in. His clothes were an odd mix and match of various uniform parts and generalized civilian mechanic's work clothes. All had liberal coatings of oil, grease, and dirt. The hand he put out to shake was quite strong, but he didn't go for a macho death grip. "OK. Presume I can get you types, not models. What's available in Naples will probably be Italian makes, not German. I can figure how many cubic meters of space by the amounts of currency involved. Berlin is good at giving us that sort of nuts and bolts. But what are you used to? Key lock? Tumblers? I'd suggest not going with timers. Nothing here happens on fixed schedules."

Witt had never had to order a safe before. He'd never dealt in cash, as opposed to payment orders which some other department would issue checks against. "This is completely outside my area of expertise. What would you suggest?"

Joey started talking to himself out loud. "OK. Gregor can give you 24-hour guards on overlapping shifts, so no one is just walking off with the cash. I'll pick something heavy enough to need a winch to get it into a truck. We haven't got that many spare winches and my guys aren't that stupid. Where could they run in this oven that we couldn't track them down? Me, I'd go keylocks. Double-key so it will need two keys to unlock. How does this sound? Each of you guys carries one, and Dad has the other. If someone wants to knock you on the head, they need to hit two of you. That, plus a permanent guard section, should do. We have a safe coming already for some special things the unit lugs around. Same guard detail can cover both. We can use a large tent. Front is your office. Place your sleep tent adjacent. For now you just sleep with the damned things cuffed to you. Should have you the lock box in a week, ten days tops."

With that, Gunter called in Leutnant Schmidt to get the three new guests bedded down after their long voyage. Joey stayed behind to chat with Gunter. "Now that I've seen them, I agree with you. No way we bring these three in on our special treasures. They seem like true blue patriots who will treat their rehabilitation as a gift from the God they don't believe in. In reverse, that much cash does us no good to swipe. What would we do with it here? If Berlin's shoveling in this much cash for Alexandria, it will be ten times that for Iraq. Maybe twenty times. I'm not saying we do it. Too many things we don't know yet. But give me an hour and I can get any safe open. More so one I pick. I'll just have spare keys sent. Time comes we want to leave this army … "

"I hold those keys. Not you. I like you, Joey, but that's too much temptation for someone who one of these days will get a valid US passport in the mail."

Joey smiled. He slowly shook his head. Damned right he'd be tempted. Baghdad was supposed to be a big city. Not New York big, so say Philly.   A few million in folding money would buy safe transport damned near anywhere for an enterprising fellow. Fuck! Even split a dozen ways with all the key people doing it as a gang, this was retire-for-life money. Gunter had better not fully trust him on this. Joey didn't trust himself. Then he thought about Clara and the kids. He didn't think he'd just dump her like that, but he felt better not having the chance to talk himself into something dumb. Maybe he was starting to grow up.

1650 hours Eastern Daylight Time; 2250 hours CET
29 September 1940
West Wing of the White House, 1600 Pennsylvania Avenue, Washington DC

Hoover's nasty innuendos had by now spread widely in high-level DC circles. So Harry Hopkins was resigned to knowing smiles about how he had scheduled his mistress for a long appointment. She arrived promptly, dressed in high-quality simple garments and sensible shoes. It was all smiles until they were safely behind closed doors, after which he unloaded on her without even a bit of small talk first. "You rein in your mad dog or we will! Don't bother peddling me the fiction that Bridges and that union aren't Party-controlled. After the National Guard took over the Pacific Coast ports, they have been waging guerrilla attacks on trucks, warehouses, and railroads. This ends now, or I turn Hoover loose to take the entire Party structure down."

She didn't quite cringe. She'd been expecting this disaster for days. As usual, her instructions from higher up were absurd. She was to pacify Hopkins with vague promises and sex. Neither would work on this man. This was a person one argued policy and power with. "The entire CIO will walk out in sympathy. No coal for autumn – it will sink your man at the polls."

Hopkins could see the connection. He also knew the politics better than she did. "Take them out. Half the CIO will stay with Franklin. If we have to, we'll nationalize the mines the same as we are doing with the West Coast docks. It's plain as day that this isn't a labor dispute. It's serving as support troops for a Soviet Union that sank a US freighter, that made failed torpedo attacks on three others, that's allied to Hitler. This isn't Spain in 1937."

"Do you really want Lindy and those fascists in power?"

"Do you? Does the Party? You always knew there were limits. This isn't the day for your Leninist Revolution. The New Deal is the best you'll get here and now. It's not the perfect progressive utopia, but it's all that's attainable." Hopkins was trying to retain his normal cheerful demeanor. His stomach was on fire and felt as if it would burst from the stress. This election was half or worse lost. He didn't need sectarian ambushes from the left. "I'll give you three days. That's enough time to get the ones most at risk to Mexico. After that, it's happy time for Hoover."

She cut the appointment short. Every hour would count for those most at risk. She would have to risk jail herself. This connection was precious to the COMINTERN.

0800 hours local; 0100 hours CET
30 September 1930
Paddy fields a dozen miles south of the Yangtse near Shanghai

The entire mission was a glorified show-the-flag. A company of the new Chinese army. A company from the 2nd battalion, 4th US Marines. A company from the new provisional US Marine regiment, recruited from English-speakers in Shanghai. The standard of 'English' required amounted to a vocabulary of some two hundred words, which allowed simple commands. The USMC had made do with worse. The commanding officer of 2nd battalion of the 4th had been granted the power to hand out stripes and lower officer ranks, like candy, to anyone who could make a plausible claim of prior service anywhere with anyone. Lieutenant Colonel Chesty Puller had commanded worse in both Haiti and Nicaragua.

These lands south of the river had been bypassed and then ignored by the Japanese. This left them a no-man's-land contested by partisans of both Japan and Chiang, along with bandit gangs and the odd platoon of Communists. Further away from the river were large, formed units of Chiang's army. They hadn't done much more than rice raids in years, but given guns and money they remained a threat.

The new Chinese government Washington supported had decided to assert control. Step one was show-the-flag sweeps like this. March around with flags flying and bands playing. Let the villages see you. Stop for tea. Pay for the food you take. US dollars were regarded as real money in much of China. After a few sweeps, start leaving garrisons with radios. Some of the bandits and partisans would come over to whoever could pay and feed them. The formed units back in the hills could be left till later.

They were a mile past the last village when the sniping started. Puller had his company from the 4th up front. They went into line quickly, laying down suppressive fire. The provisionals shook out into a column to make their way across the paddy lands and chase the shooters away. This was a chance to see how the new blood could perform. Exercises were all well and good, but you only really learned when you saw them under fire. He kept the Chinese company back. On this march, they were there to observe how it was done.

0430 hours local; 0330 hours CET
30 September 1940
Ambush position 300 meters in advance of the Italian lines

The sand fleas were most annoying. More so as Greta had to stay still and let them bite. This Di Salo volunteers for ambush patrols. He even borrows Gregor's Magyar company to rotate with his men. Klaus asks to be allowed to bring a company of his own. He's never done ambushes and wants to learn. The Italian's stuck-up slut accompanies him, so of course Greta and her girls must go with Klaus.

Greta was not even really sure she could accurately aim her weapon. She had never even range-fired further out than 30 meters. None of that mattered. Naiomi and the other girls had been well trained back in Romania. If Greta was to pretend to be their commander, she must also be there to maintain that fiction.

The Italian division's line was more a set of battalion strong points than a fully connected trench line. Every night there were raids and probes from the British. Gunter said that these 'British' were in fact Palestinian Jews. Strange, she becomes a Zionist by trying to kill them.

So far it's been five hours of uncomfortable boredom. Suddenly she feels one of the girls tap her shoulder and point. Greta squints and can sort of make out dark shapes. They look more like night spirits than young men. As she was instructed before they set out, she waits for the men to open fire. This takes almost ten minutes. There must be a logic to why they let the 'enemy' sneak around, crossing in front of them from left to right. Then suddenly machine-guns are firing and flares are shot up in the air. She expends half a clip from her machine pistol so as to be seen doing something. She's pretty sure she is firing in the right direction, but presumes all she is accomplishing is making violent noise.

The Italian has led a party in close. There's a short time with grenades flying in all directions, then the firing stops. People are screaming "Cease-fire!" in German, Italian, and Yiddish. She hears some boy screaming for his mother in Magyar. She gets up and her ladies follow her. They find the poor wounded lad. He's badly gut-shot. He doesn't weigh much and looks about fifteen. No one thinks he has a chance, but four of the girls each take a limb and start carrying him back to the aid station. His Magyar didn't sound Transylvanian, but with that much pain and shock, she isn't sure. It's so easy to die in war. The thought doesn't make her happy. Her duty to her remaining family demands this of her. Doesn't mean she has to pretend to herself that this is what a nice Jewish girl was raised to be.

The Spanish *puta* is having a gay time of it all. She is yelling at the five prisoners in abysmal Yiddish. To Greta's ears it's more German, cut with some Slavic language and badly chopped up. Greta feels bad for the five guys they captured. Risking their lives in someone else's war. Probably think they are defending their families, same as she does. War is strange.

1200 hours local; 1100 CET
30 September 1940
SS GHQ Ploiesti, Romania

The trial had gone quickly. The 'jurors' Schellenberg's staff had picked were clear on what was expected of them. When the Reichsführer arranges to have a man charged with 'usurpation of command authority', the conclusion was obvious without the need for formal instruction on how to vote. Gruppenführer Paul Scharfe, the chief judge of the whole SS establishment, had kept things moving at a rapid pace. He was a strict legalist. He had also presided over a prior trial of Fegelein, where the weasel had barely avoided conviction on corruption charges.

The three military observers from the services had been somewhat startled that the charge had been usurpation and not murder. Obersturmbannführer Karl Siegel, Schellenberg's chief henchman for 'affairs in the South', had refused to explain further. Had told them that all would be explained to their superiors in Berlin. Just see what happened, and report up their chains of command.

Siegel had commanded the firing squad himself. The dim-witted piece of pig shit that had somehow become an SS field officer, Fegelein, had completely disgraced himself. He had wept and wailed like a toddler while being dragged to the place of execution. Had both pissed and shat himself. Was vomiting so badly he was choking on it as he was being tied to the post. Siegel had stopped the proceedings for some minutes while the guard sergeant bent him over and beat him till he cleared his airways through both drooling and projectile vomiting. The swine was not going to be allowed to cheat the executioner.

There had been a small change in normal firing squad proceedings. Unknown to the participants, they all had live rounds. The poor state of training of Fegelein's troops could be seen in that despite this, he was only hit twice, once in the gut and the other in a quite superficial graze to his cheek. Siegel walked up to finish him off. The lowlife was screaming in agony, alternately for the God he never believed in and for his mother. Siegel propped the head up with his left hand, looked the convicted idiot in the eye and told him to convey the Reichsführer's best wishes to Himmler when they met in

Hell. Siegel then emptied his pistol into the man's head until he was clearly dead. Pity that his uniform would need a serious cleaning from the blood and brain matter. That was wasteful but necessary. His bosses in Berlin wanted a certain set of images to be seen, to be passed along the service grapevine. Command authority would not be usurped without consequences. Policy was made in Berlin.

1600 hours CET
30 September 1940
A large brewery near the American Danzig enclave

Heydrich's liaison man for this enclave operation had been an 'adult beverage executive' during Prohibition in Milwaukee, before his quick relocation to the Reich mere hours ahead of an arrest warrant for an unfortunate incident involving multiple corpses. His formal liaison duties normally didn't take much time, so he had looked to opportunities. He had made a few connections in the proper offices, leading to his acquiring at nominal cost a large brewery that had been Aryanized in 1939 and sat idle ever since.

An active port means large numbers of sailors, stevedores, warehousemen, truckers, river boat crews, and other working men with powerful thirsts. The people he had worked with in Milwaukee and Chicago had connections with other Italian entrepreneurs in Brooklyn who had arranged for cargoes of hops, barley, and other key ingredients to somehow find their way into relief shipments. The payment for these in dollars and precious metals made a fair number of ship's officers somewhat wealthier. Indeed, the quality of his product was such that some ships were buying from him in barrel lots for 'return voyage provisions'. The brewery owner was no fool. The US since Prohibition had limited most legal beer to glorified donkey piss. A fair number of his barrels would find their way past customs. These same Italians would then make a further profit both wholesaling and retailing the product.

All of this in turn meant that the various American organizations he did liaison with often found it more convivial to meet at his place of business. They would bring good coffee and swap for beer. It was a nice sideline for all concerned. This was especially true of the Marines who formed the guard force for the enclave. Their barracks were in theory dry. In practice …

This day he was meeting with Marine Colonel Hermele, the commandant and nominal battalion commander. The so-called battalion had the strength of a regiment, but not its firepower. It had no artillery and few crew-served weapons. Indeed, many of its local recruits had only shotguns or pistols. They used their riot sticks as the main weapon in keeping order. Hermele had a small problem. The two of them were working on a solution. "Washington wants to use me as a recruiting station. Some joker added up the payroll and decided we have surplus men. Wants them for China service."

"No problem, as far as that goes. We just tattoo your globe and anchor on everyone who leaves. They ever show up fighting us, we shoot them. Use them to fight whoever you want. Just not us or our allies."

Hermele was sure enough humanitarians and legalists in Washington would have kittens at this. He was equally sure that it was always easier to beg forgiveness than get permission. If Willkie won, the US wasn't intervening in Europe. If FDR got re-elected, let whoever was USMC Commandant deal with the mess. The Corps needed warm bodies in China now. A force he would get to lead into combat if he agreed to this. "How about this? I can't agree to that. So you just make the tattoos and give me a copy of the edict on Berlin stationary. State Department will squeal, and we let someone else fight over it?"

"You are halfway there. You take the working-age men, you also take their families. If they are orphans, we assign families. Otherwise we get stuck with the useless eaters. Someday their kin may get tired of feeding them."

"Immigration laws. We can't."

"Of course you can. You are shipping these to Shanghai. You ship the parents, the wife, the widowed grandma, whatever, with them. US law doesn't apply in China. Easy for them to pay the upkeep on their kin at Chinese prices. Since you alerted me on this a few days ago, I made a run to Berlin. Big boss says he'll let you send recruiting officers into the Polish POW camps. Take as many as will come. Berlin will be happy to be rid of them. We're already letting the French do this. They don't want to be Germans, so let them be Poles in Africa or China. Gets them out of our hair."

The Marine colonel knew he was stretching the limits of his authority. He didn't care. It would work, and Washington could argue the details after the fact. Agreeing got him out of this career dead end. His new command would take the unit flag of 2nd Battalion, 6th Marines. The residual enclave guards could be 4th Battalion or Provisional Battalion. For all he cared, his successor could call them the Danzig Guards. He was going to be a China Marine and lead troops in combat.

2200 Hours Gibraltar time and CET
30 September 1930
RAF HQ, Gibraltar

The day's French air raids had been mostly ineffectual, but there was still smoke over the harbor when the flying boat landed at dusk. The French were apparently seriously annoyed. General Arthur Harris could sympathize. So was he.

That twit Dowding had disbanded Bomber Command, and the War Cabinet had backed him. Slackers, all of them! The proper answer to the London fire raid was to come back at Berlin or at least the Ruhr. You keep pounding to victory. The Empire was richer and could afford the strain longer. Sad about that silly French art museum, but omelets and eggs …

He, perhaps the leading bomber-man left in the RAF after Portal was sacked, had now been sent into exile himself. His former residence in Rhodesia had led to the halfbrights now running RAF posting him as GOC RAF Kenya. There were under fifty planes in all of East Africa, none of them modern. He was lucky they hadn't sent him to China, where there was essentially nothing. There had been promises of reinforcements. Harris would believe it when he saw it. The bombers made redundant by this truce would go to West Africa. It was closer and this balls-up Montgomery, whoever he was, had caused some disaster that had London's grandees fixated. They had lost an entire colony, Gambia. Harris doubted half of them had heard of Gambia before the French seized it, and was equally sure none could find it on a map without help. God save poor England from this gang of fools and shop stewards.

1000 hours CET
1 October 1940
Ministère de la Défense Nationale (Ministry of Defense), Vichy

Since July the various hotels of the spa town of Vichy had been the home of the French government. One of these hotels was the home of the Ministry of Defense, and so the home of General Georges Blanchard, the State Secretary of War. The last few months had been a whirlwind of change. The Fall of France, the death of Hitler and the rise of Göring ... or was it Heydrich. Vichy was divided on who ruled Germany. What was obvious was that Reichsführer Heydrich was the only one paying attention to France.

For himself, command in the disaster of the Low Countries and North Eastern France earlier this year, and then retirement. Then life took another turn as a French-German history group had been formed to write a history of the 1940 campaign. Many had been dubious of the effort, but the Germans had provided access to their own records in turn. Several sessions had been held where German and French commanders had been interviewed, and the reports compared. The process was still ongoing; the work could go on for years. One of the results of those meetings was this converted hotel room, and his occupation of it instead of General Huntziger. The former State Secretary of War had come off very poorly in the campaign review, while his own reputation was rehabilitated. Huntziger's ineptitude at Sedan could no longer be hidden by friends in the higher circles of the French Army. Huntziger was now in South East Asia as colonial official in one of the more mountainous regions of poor, landlocked Laos. All thanks to the mystery man in the black and silver of the SS, Heydrich. The history group had been his creation, one of several creations and projects.

Reports from Berlin made clear that all acknowledged Göring as Führer, but nearly all ministerial orders came by way of Heydrich. Perhaps it was best to think of Heydrich as a modern-day Richelieu, an able, ruthless but loyal minister. Richelieu the Red Eminence versus Heydrich the Black Excellency. One such ministerial missive was now on his desk. As part of what was being termed the Europa Project, the Germans desired a French army in the east to keep watch against the Soviets. General Corap and his Ninth Army has been resurrected as a beginning of this program. Besides the request, the Germans were offering help with modernizing the French Army.

Blanchard looked out the window of his suite on to the streets of Vichy. It was France, but it wasn't where he belonged, it wasn't where the French government belonged. It wasn't Paris. For now, France was prostrate ... but things could change. The missive was the latest sign from Berlin of a desire for closer ties with France; perhaps what they said of a cooperation might actually be true. Still, Blanchard was under no illusions; Germany would be on top. But there was no need to allow Italy to maintain its current place as number two. Indeed, French troops now garrisoned the Louvre, Versailles, and two arrondissements in Paris, as well as the buildings that housed a ministry. The French flag flew from the Eiffel Tower. Bordeaux was again a French city, with their German overlords departed.

A quick memo was drafted for the Marshal to review and no doubt approve. Blanchard chuckled to himself. More likely the approval would be by Petain's staff. The old man was the symbol of the New France, but at his age did less and less of the work. Rumor had it that he opposed the rapprochement with Germany, but had been overruled by Weygand and Darlan for the key military services. Thank God there were a few realists left. France would accept the German offer of help to reform the French Army. Besides, what choice did they or France have? The British were by now France's enemy, stealing her Empire. Month by month, America's backing of the British was made more evident. France's only road to its rightful place was via this new European Community.

0900 hours Eastern Daylight Time, 1500 hours CET
1 October 1940
Oval Office, White House, Washington DC

FDR had a problem. He hated to be forced to decisions he didn't like. His entire style of management was very loose, broad comments by himself, while pitting subordinates against each other. These strategies had cost him his near-to-irreplaceable political tactician, former Postmaster General Farley. That had devolved those responsibilities onto his truly irreplaceable alter ego, Harry Hopkins. Now Dear Harry was telling him unpalatable truths and refusing to be put off by grand, flowery effusions of sentiment.

"Franklin, you are on track to lose this election." Hopkins' normal style was not this confrontational, but the situation was that dire. "Do you really want Willkie as President?"

Of course Franklin didn't want to lose. He also did not want to make the decision he was being pushed into. He was the prime mover. Others didn't manipulate him. "Harry, I've overworked you. I'll get you help. It's not that bad. I'm still loved by most Americans. We saved them in 1933, and they know it."

With barely more than a month to go until the election, there just wasn't time for Franklin's usual games and moods. "Then you want to lose. I've got a road to a chance at victory. If you think you can skate through on charisma, I'll always back you; but I won't keep working myself to death. We can say I have taken leave for health reasons. I'll check into a hospital and sit out the campaign. Your way won't work. Not after the Roosevelt Depression two years ago. Not after Dear Guru. We need the city machines going all-out for you. That means Morgenthau goes at Treasury. No more civic crusade prosecutions like he did to Pendergast in Kansas City. That means you don't find another high-minded fool like Wallace for VP. I need Truman – "

"That clown? He was Pendergast's puppet Senator. He barely won the primary for reelection in a three-way race – "

"He's personally honest, and I can prove it to the press. Same way you do business with the machines but don't take a dime. He's down-the-line New Deal, even if the college-boy lefties will look down on him as a hick. The big part is that he was Pendergast's man. He knows how to get down and dirty on patronage and construction contracts. He's your proof of good faith to the bosses. You tell me – why on Earth should Frank Hague and the rest of the Jersey bosses go all out for you, just so Morgenthau can send them to prison?"

"Henry Morgenthau is one of my oldest and dearest friends."

"Yes. He is. And he had your approval to prosecute Pendergast. Now do you want to be a loyal friend, or President? Make Morgenthau ambassador to Britain. He can view it as a step up if you spend some of your bottomless charm telling him that expedient lie. He's no bureaucrat. We'll take a hit from the Chicago *Trib*. They'll see it as proof you'll declare war after the election. Their readers won't vote for you anyway. You've even lost the soft Isolationists. Midwest is a disaster. Truman can whistle-stop across the states we have a prayer of carrying outside Dixie. He was Over There in the last war. Artillery officer. Combat veteran. When he tells small-town people that you won't send their boys to die in foreign wars, they might just believe him."

The dispute took up most of the day. Roosevelt gave in the way he usually did. Grudgingly. Yet there was a part of him that was proud of Hopkins for standing up to the pounding.

1800 hours CET
1 October 1940
Prinz-Albrecht- Straße, Berlin

In theory it was just a social engagement with an old acquaintance. Admiral Canaris, head of Abwehr, requested his presence at a small reunion for coffee and biscuits. The nice Standartenführer who had delivered the invitation had been polite, but ever so uninformative as to who would be at the reunion. He had suggested civilian dress instead of uniform. The Mercedes limousine outside and the minder's rank hinted at this being more than a social occasion, so Alistare-Smythe had dressed up for it, as if he were calling on a Cabinet Minister at Whitehall.

The guess had been good, but the reality was a trifle more exalted. His friend the admiral had invited his riding companion, the ex-junior naval officer Heydrich. The topic of discussion was the 1922 Committee. The Abwehr's sources had tagged it as the key player behind the ascension of Bevin to the office of Prime Minister. Alistare-Smythe got to spend three hours educating one of the heads of Germany on British political practices. The final question took Alistare-Smythe up to the line of what he regarded as treason. Heydrich point-blank asked for names and proper forms of address, for the sending of letters direct from his office to the Committee via the Spanish Embassy in London. Alistare-Smythe made clear that he advised against this, but provided the needed names and which address would suffice.

2000 hours local; 1900 hours CET
1 October 1940
Finance administrative tent, Strauss Brigade HQ in rear of Italian lines, Alamein

The family team of Witt and sons was still settling into their new situation when they received two high-ranking visitors, Oberstleutnant's Gregor and Ivan. The Witts found the casual use of first names within the officer corps of this Brigade strange. The Witts were adapting, attempting to fit in, but it seemed most strange, almost Bolshevik in its enforced lack of proper social distance.

The two Oberstleutnant's wanted to discuss the setup of the paymaster section, something the Witts were as yet unprepared to actually accomplish. They were still awaiting their in-transit support staff. Gregor had prepped Ivan with what he felt was needed, but preferred the aristocratic ex-White officer do most of the talking. Gregor was still getting accustomed to this whole concept of himself as a field officer.

"Yes. We know nothing happens till your backup people arrive. What we want to do is make sure what you set up fits our needs. You see, we don't want our men paid yet." The Witts looked at Ivan most strangely. "Think it through. If you give them money, what on Earth will they do with it here except gamble and buy bootleg liquor? Both of those are major disciplinary problems."

Gregor felt confident enough to insert himself now with the wisdom of Feldwebel's. "You'll also have theft issues, or at least claims of theft. The different companies came from different places and services. They have no reason to trust each other that way. There will be fights, then reprisals." As an ex-Feldwebel he'd seen this pattern before.

The father did the talking. He felt he was threading his way through a minefield in the dark while partially blindfolded. "So we do what?"

Ivan was back to speaking for both. "Set up allotments for the family men. A lot of our guys have wives, kids, mothers waiting back in the Bari camp. Hell, you do. There's got to be forms so your wife can draw a part of your monthly for her own expenses. For the rest we hold the money till we take Alexandria. A big city has places for troops to spend money. Cat houses, bars, restaurants, shops. Once we are settled in, you do a paycall for each company before they get their first leave tickets. The money will help them blow off steam before we march on Palestine. Then it's the same procedure, until we take Haifa."

Sort-of-Major Witt was curious. "How do you know it's Palestine?" When he had served in the Great War all his unit had to go on were rumors, which were always wrong.

"We know. It's common knowledge among us. Hell, the British probably know. Issue is what they can do about it."

The three Witts of course agreed to everything. Mother and grandmother would need money more than they did. What a way to run a war. Troops who actually knew what they were doing. Also some fixed place where the family could be reunited. Maybe they had a chance at a real life again.

1000 hours CET
2 October 1940
Villa Recalcati, Varese, Italy

The audience was so quiet that other than the speaker's voice, you could have heard a pin drop. The room was filled to capacity with 48 of the top people in the Italian military, the relevant ministries, and the major defense contractors. The speaker was an extremely angry Italo Balbo.
"Comrades, our Italy was nurtured by Il Duce for greatness. It was for a New Roman Empire that we broke the back of the Marxist chaos to create the virile Italy of today. Our victories in Ethiopia and Spain were only prequels to the true March of Italy's Glory. We have taken Malta. Egypt is next. A new empire in Africa and the Near East will follow. Britain's day has passed. Germany is in the ascent, and Il Duce far-sightedly linked us to that new hegemon.

"At my doing, Fascist Italy recognized that the future of war, of conquest, was military aviation. Yet for the great air assault on London, Italy's contribution was minimal. Our glorious air forces could only field biplanes for this first European air armada. The prestige of the regime and dynasty, the destiny of the Italian people, need Italian-designed and -built aircraft at the forefront of the future battles to come in Africa and the Middle East. Failure is not an option. Prince Umberto and I demand new efforts worthy of the New Rome. Il Duce is watching us all, awaiting further proofs of the fruits of Italian genius.

"We must all share the pride of the designers of our gun trucks. The German general Rommel, the victor of the desert battle, sings the praises of this mighty and revolutionary Italian creation. We must have better models with a more powerful gun. We must produce enough so that the Germans and French will beg to carry Italian arms.

'Great days lie ahead. Before the year is over, our boots shall march in triumph through the streets of Cairo where the great Italian Napoleon once rode. Egypt will be ours, as it was in the times of the Caesars. We live in glorious times. Italy demands that we here prove worthy of the trust the Party and nation have placed in you."

The audience sat in rapt attention, each man thinking to himself of how he could avoid responsibility for the inevitable failures to measure up to this level of grandeur. Italy had brilliant designers – but the machinery to translate those designs into a sound industrial program wasn't there. The new German-enforced cartels were beginning to make a dent in the entrenched administrative and industrial interests that operated as a block against ever getting anything done. Marshal Balbo did not seem to be in a mood to take excuses. Examples would be made ... and each man was determined that the poisoned chalice would pass to another.

1300 hours CET
2 October 1940
War Ministry, Berlin, Germany

Relations between Minister Beck, administrative head of the Army, and Generaloberst Halder, its operational head, had been trending poorly for weeks; but today's discussion was a new low point. Beck had chosen to make the charge 'usurpation of command authority' a line of battle he was prepared to stake his position on. He wanted it changed to murder, and simply refused to see another point of view. "Göring is already hopeless. Now you as well are toadying to that little shit Heydrich. What on Earth did we overthrow the Old Regime for? These gangsters do whatever they please, overturning law and established custom." Beck was not as emotionally agitated as usual, but was even more dogmatically hostile to any view except his own.

"We recovered operational independence. We have been given a proper technocratic administrative structure for day-to-day governance. We are seeing the results every week, in more production of better weapons. We are moving towards clear, attainable strategic objectives. The production wasted on the Navy has mostly ended. The Air Force is firmly committed to an Army support role. National morale is high, thanks to both decent living standards and Führer Göring's endless round of public events. The Gauleiters have been firmly put in their place. Yet all I hear from you is endless rants about Heydrich. Yes, he's an unpleasant fellow. Yes, in our world a failed Leutnant discharged for immorality would never rise to such a position. He's kept the Party and its militias under quite firm control. He didn't let the atrocity go unpunished. Yet here you are, ranting about what charge the drunken sot of an SS was executed for. Two years ago you would have been outraged that the entire thing was hushed up."

"A proper regime would call this murder, and punish the murder! This wasn't an antipartisan operation or the heat of battle. He lined up civilians and shot them as inconvenient!"
"Yes. He did. We did the same with Himmler, Goebbels, and a few thousand others."

"Not the same at all! Our officers acted under orders!"

"Orders that were deliberately left vague. The key targets were listed, and their entourages were more generally described."

"That's operational discretion. Saddle orders. How could they possibly know precisely who was with the main targets? Know who in the designated buildings would resist?"

Halder wearily shook his head. He knew for a fact that in the cases of both the Propaganda Ministry, and Party headquarters in Berlin, no quarter had been offered. The assigned officers chose to just gun down everyone. Why? No one ever bothered to ask them. He knew for a certain fact, that Heydrich's further purges were mostly factional settling of scores within the SS and Party — coupled with subordinates being handed quotas to kill from particular headquarters or administrative groupings. Beck was beginning to get so tiresome that Halder was starting to have thoughts about doing a deal with Heydrich and Göring to replace the old man. Retire him on grounds of health or whatever. "So, we have an impasse. Heydrich is offering a general meeting to discuss this, as well as Jewish policy and Army-Party relations, at Wannsee. It will be Saturday the 12th. To keep discussion frank, he is sending his #2 Schellenberg. He proposes we do the same."

Beck thought fast. "Who is Göring sending?"

"Does it matter? Whatever flunky he sends will prepare a memo the Reichsmarschall won't read anyway. If we agree, he'll tag along. Most policy bores him. He focuses on the ceremonial, the chief of state duties. At least he's diligent about that."

It took another hour and change worth of acrimony to deal with the other major issue, the Spanish volunteers. The Franco regime was sticking to rigid neutrality, with Germany's blessings. Spain was wrecked, profoundly bankrupt. If it entered the war it would need vast aid — food, industrial goods, petroleum, coal, arms — and couldn't do much with them while the British seized its remaining colonies. Yet Franco wanted to show favor. Hence the offer of a Spanish division of volunteers. Technically, these were Falange Party militants being offered on a party-to-party basis to the German National Socialists. However, the division was too big by Wehrmacht standards. It was a WW1 square division instead of modern triangular. The troops mostly had prior combat experience, but the Army didn't see the silly civil war in Spain as a real war from which experience would produce useful cadres. Beck was adamant that he didn't want these Latin clowns. So the Heer solution was to hand the mess to Heydrich with orders to use these Spanish in one of the Party militias. However, equipping this unit was not to come from the Army's quotas on production.

2200 hours British Double Summer and CET
2 October 1940
Administrative offices of the War Cabinet Secretariat, Westminster, London

What a difference a few days make. London's blackout was over. Blackout rules were now only in force within ten miles of the southern and eastern coasts of Britain. The public found the idea of no bombers, no blackouts, to be positively wonderful. Crowds were about in the streets, celebrating. They cheered Bevin, the royal family, and anyone in uniform they saw. The world might still be at war, but Britain itself felt again safe. News reports had German planes breaking off attacks on ships as they came within sight of land. The few European high altitude reconnaissance planes were regarded as a laughable nuisance.

The royals and the PM had toured the burned-out areas of the East End, the battered ports in the South. Rebuilding had already begun. What was going up wasn't pretty, but this was wartime, and needs must.

Kim Philby had had a long chat with his control officer. He found the orders peculiar in the extreme. In the reorganization after Bevin's accession to power, Philby had gotten himself posted to the War Cabinet Secretariat. With bombing ended, this bureaucracy was reclaiming real above-ground office space. Philby had what amounted to unlimited access to the entire paper flow to and from the actual rulers of the British Empire. His control told him this was priceless. Which meant that Philby should stop thinking of himself as an active asset. He must do nothing that risked betraying who he was. So when asked for advice, think like a good liberal Tory. Give the answer that most benefited the Empire, not what he thought might aid Stalin.

The example control had used, was this armored brigade at sea headed for Egypt. With the war in Africa expanding, the War Cabinet was split on whether to divert it to Nigeria or perhaps Kenya. Philby had been tasked with two others to provide a memo outlining the options. He was now being told to consider a purely British point of view, not what might benefit the Worker's State.

The other order was to break now and permanently with his entire Cambridge circle. He was now too precious an asset to take any risks of cross-contamination from their activities. If quizzed by security officers, Moscow Center wanted Philby to have correspondence, witnesses, and the like showing an open and permanent breach. He was instructed to find personal reasons, different in each case. Philby must position himself as a reform Tory, one who might also be employed should Labor take power in its own right. As such he could have some visible sympathy for the working class, but none for the Soviet Union or British Communism. He was advised to pattern himself on Bevin, a man with whom the Soviets had repeatedly failed to establish ties.

The chief cause of this 'promotion', which in fact is what this all amounted to, was the information Philby had passed along on the MAUD Committee. This British project for a superbomb was of major interest to the NKVD. Philby was enjoined from seeking more data. Expendable assets would be risked on the penetration. Philby's job was to pass along only such information on this and other technology projects as came his way in the normal course of his work day. Philby was not even to stand in the way of the new British plan to sell this information to the Americans. Just push for as high a price as possible.

1400 hours Pacific Daylight Time; 2300 hours CET
2 October, 1940
St. Francis Hotel, San Francisco, California

It was a luxury hotel, but definitely getting on in years. For today, it was also the headquarters of the US Presidency. FDR had finally been made to see that his reelection would take nonstop campaigning until election day in early November. So needed government decisions came to the prospective third-term President.

Led by Admiral James O. Richardson, a small delegation of US Naval officers had made a presentation on the need of naval air stations to supplement FDR's new China policies. The proposal was for the acquisition of basing rights in Korea near Pusan, on an island called Okinawa, and, in China, on the Shantung peninsula and near Shanghai. This would allow both the proper anti-submarine patrols, and a more generalized search and rescue service for the East China Sea. Mentioned, but downplayed, was the probability that the Japanese would find such concepts unacceptable as regards Korea and Okinawa. Richardson kept the backup plan, to do all the patrols out of Shantung, in his vest pocket. He had found that presenting the political people with alternatives muddied the decision-making process. Plenty of time to show them Plan B if the Japanese rejected Plan A. The Japanese were phobic about foreign military on their soil. They were also at this moment desperate. The only way to find out how desperate, was to make the approach.

Franklin was at his pontificating best, responding in high-flown generalities and blowing off attempts to deal with specifics. It was not working this time. He could normally do his affable-oracle act for hours. He was starting to show his age; and more important, the effects of his various infirmities. He was experiencing a spectrum of maladies that his doctors linked to heart problems, stress, and smoking. FDR could blow the medicos off, but could no longer get his physical body to always keep up with his unconquerable spirit. In exasperation he turned on Richardson and his confederates. "Gentlemen, please remember that you do work for me. I do not wish to deal with this on the level of detail you are pushing for." He felt another twinge in his chest as he made his point. This angered him. He hated being boxed in by subordinates. He despised being betrayed by his body. Had since the polio; and refused to accept that aging applied to him.

The others stayed silent as Richardson spoke for them. The admiral was a consummate professional. "Yes Mr. President, we work for you. That is the design our Founders decreed, and we officers heartily concur in civil supremacy. More so in the case of your China policy than over your new war instructions for the Western Atlantic." Richardson ignored the President's angry look, and quietly continued to make his case. "The patrol zone in the Atlantic is a personal policy of yours. You are commander-in-chief. At least for now. You stand for election in five weeks. You may still be president next year. You may not. We serve the office of the president, not the occupant. Your China war policy is supported by your opponent Mr. Willkie, by the leadership of both Houses of Congress, by a large bulk of the most important elements of our national press, by our two most widely read national magazines. So it represents a national policy, in senses that your Atlantic policy doesn't – or at least doesn't yet."

Roosevelt could not contain himself. "How dare you, sir! I can have you relieved." His nostrils flared, but his breath was at the edge of ragged. Were they seriously threatening him?

Richardson was unaffected by the display of authority, by the obvious assertion of dominance. "Mr. President, you can relieve us at any time. You don't need cause. You need not give reasons. Feel free to do so. But until you do, we will fulfill our oaths to the Constitution. Which requires us to, in private, give you our best professional advice. You seem to be taking my recitation of constitutional norms and political realities as a threat to your office and person. It is neither. Thank God our military are not political actors. Closest we came was McClellan and Lincoln. Pray God such idiocy will never happen again. We senior officers look to the political branch for our marching orders. By normal standards, we have clear, firm marching orders on China; we do not on the Western Atlantic patrol zone. If we misunderstand the constitutional, legal, and political realities, please enlighten us. These are not our areas of specialty. This is the best advice of staff we have with such knowledge. I'm sorry you saw my comment adversely. All I meant to do was explain the situation as your senior naval people see it." Richardson had not been placating. He had been clearly subordinate.

The President managed to get his personable, populist mask back up. "What would make you Navy boys calmer about the Atlantic mission?"

Richardson was glad of the opening. "A joint resolution from Congress. Gets them on the record. Inhibits their usual pattern of pouncing on a policy, and the service carrying it out, at the first setback or casualty." He saw FDR's face start to cloud. "It doesn't even take enemy action, Mr. President. The North Atlantic is a storm-filled sea in winter, and winter is coming. One extra large wave washes six draftees overboard to their deaths, and Congress will get goaded by the press into questioning why they weren't consulted. It's a political matter, therefore your sole decision. But you did ask … "

Roosevelt filed the idea away. It wasn't a bad one, but he didn't need this debate during an election campaign. Better for a lame-duck session of Congress after the votes were counted. He'd be stronger then. He motioned Richardson to continue. Best to hear all the Navy's quibbles now, and dismiss them once and for all.

The admiral had waited patiently while his political master worked out the obvious in his head. FDR was actually more transparent than he realized, at least to skillful players of bureaucratic games. "You have dictated two quasi-wars." Roosevelt shot him a look. "It's the wording used for our first naval war against the French back in John Adams' only term. It's a way to say limited, undeclared conflict. These policies put us at war with the two most heavily armed nations in the world, Nazi Germany and Soviet Russia. You have made quasi-allies of the British Empire, the Empire of Japan, and a Japanese puppet regime of questionable actual sovereignty in Shanghai." FDR gave Richardson a smile, saying he now understood the jargon. Quasi-allies. No formal alliance, but joint action against joint enemies for the present and near future. FDR had committed the US to the survival of the Chinese Christians, and the safeguarding of the British Isles from the Nazis. He nodded at Richardson, who went on again, "The legalities and morality of this I leave to the press, Congress and the patricians over at the State Department. The foreign service seems to obsessively concern itself with legalities and a more generalized cosmopolitan moralism. The only time we in the Navy see them get practical, is when financial and banking issues are at stake. Why you care which of three supposed Chinese governments rule is not the Navy's concern. Why Japan invaded China or the Soviets set out to conquer Manchuria is again not of concern to the Navy. What matters is that you wish us to protect the East China Sea. For this we need more than ships. We need landbased four-engine planes to use for reconnaissance and anti-submarine patrol. The US has two such planes in production, the B-17 and the Liberator. You have given all the production of these to the British and the Air Corps. Actually, your designated subordinates have allocated more than 100% of this production. We are told to make do with lesser planes, with Catalina's and various two-engine bombers. Most of which are again allocated to the same two places. We cannot even use obsolete bombers. You already gave those away to the British for bases. Absent the tools, we cannot do the job. A job you have staked your prestige on. Do you wish the job done or not, Mr. President?"

Roosevelt lost his temper at this point. He flared. He shrieked. He tore the assembled officers new anal passages. He relieved Richardson on the spot. Told him to report to Shanghai to take charge of the river gunboat squadron. Richardson saluted, did a perfect about-face, and left. He had done his job. When this mess blew up in the President's face, the Navy would not take the fall. There were too many witnesses in the room. Everything in Washington leaked to the press. In the meantime, let Kimmel, his obvious successor, try to square circles over ends and means. FDR's two forward deployments were disasters waiting to happen.

0500 hours local; 0400 hours CET

3 October 1940
HQ Mason's brigade, now in what was originally 7th Division frontage at north end of the lines

Dawn would soon be breaking. Mason's staff was running around trying desperately to get people and equipment under overhead cover before the daily air attacks began. Major movements could only be done at night, and even then losses were taken from artillery fires preregistered during daylight on key movement nodes.

Given this, 8th Army staff's incessant regroupings made no sense. Two world wars now where the headquarters wallahs at division and higher were gangs of twits that seemed like prefects at a third-rate public school. The division frameworks were left in place. Division headquarters, the artillery, the depots, the support services, were all in the three sectors parceled out when the line was formed. The line ran 7th – 6th – 8th from north to south. However, no division had any of its original brigades. Some brigades had seen battalions swapped out. In a few cases companies had been swapped out of battalions. Idiots! These three formations were divisions by courtesy. All this to and fro just made the unit cohesion even more imaginary, the training standards ever lower. It also made the squads and platoons who would do the actual fighting even more sleep-deprived, and with ever less idea of the fine detail of the ground they would be fighting over.

London was sending updates several times a week, but the core message remained the same. The Hun was building up to a major push the end of the month. There would be a full army offensive backed by a thousand tanks and more than a thousand fighting planes. Britain had under a hundred fighting vehicles available, and more than half of those were armored cars. Just about all were rebuilds with nothing like full proper function. Even with weekly reinforcements, air strength rarely rose to two dozen planes. The army was short of artillery, crew-served weapons, and mines. The so-called plan amounted once again to dying in place, because a retreat was politically inexpedient.

Mason was shamelessly milking his connections and Guards status to minimize the ill effects on his brigade. Fleming's companion brigade seemed to be relying on manipulations centering on their most peculiar officer, Money-Penny. Mason had made use of the man's services a few times. He was a gentleman in the formal sense, but very much of a demimonde rouge agent in Mason's opinion. And yet … and yet he was damned effective. His latest coup was assembling for Fleming a small mechanized reserve of three Matilda's, two cruiser tanks, half a dozen mixed types of armored cars, and three dozen Bren gun carriers. Officially it was a repair shop, and supposedly none of these vehicles functioned properly. When they sortied with the Jewish raiding parties, it was described as road testing of incomplete repairs. The man and his confederates seemed to have no scruples. But damn, Mason could use such a reserve himself.

0900 local time; 0500 CET
3 October 1940
Ashkhabad, Turkmen SSR

To civilized Chinese eyes the city was not impressive. The entire region had little to recommend it. It was an arid wasteland, with agriculture around the few water sources. It was easy to see it as a place of dishonorable exile.

General Lin Biao chose to take a different point of view. His new Soviet masters had plentifully supplied him with weapons. He had some real artillery pieces. He had a few light tanks and a number of armored cars. His four divisions, two each of Chinese infantry and Central Asian cavalry, had more mortars and machine-guns than a Japanese division, more even that a British one. He had seen the documents. He had more than sufficient ammunition, food, fodder, and other stores. He had a good number of trucks, and extremely plentiful horses and mules. His Asian Army of Liberation had more than eighty thousand men. The Afghans he would face in Herat had nothing that could stand against him.

This was a far cry from having to stand up to the massive forces of Chiang and the Japanese. He would march the 700 kilometers to Herat easily enough. All but the last few kilometers were on Soviet territory, making this an administrative exercise instead of combat. Indeed, he had been given to believe that the Afghans had been subverted, been persuaded to switch sides.

This he didn't believe, as the source was his political officer and former boss, Mao. The man was a nasty political infighter, but never especially useful in the field. Lin's march began today. He expected to take Herat in two weeks. Lin was determined to make a success of his new Soviet career even if he was yoked to Mao in the process. Let Zhu De deal with the more miserable terrain to the East, slogging over mountains towards Kabul.

1200 hours CET
3 October 1940
SS-HA, Prinz-Albrecht-Straße, Berlin, Germany

The Waffen SS was a relatively small component of the party-state composite structure that was the SS and the Interior Ministry. The party-state distinction was fading under Reichsführer Heydrich, but it still had some legal and bureaucratic significance. Thus, the Waffen SS was both one of the National Socialist Party's three militias, and an armed force of Greater Germany.

The SS-HA served as both War Ministry and General Staff of the SS. It didn't exercise operational authority over Waffen SS units in the field … yet. For now, the only field Division was Hausser's Reich Division in Egypt. Division? Brigadeführer Gottlob Berger stifled a laugh. The 'Division' was an overstrength Corps in size. Berger and Sturmbannbuehrer Franz Riedwig had been keeping the SS-HA going since the removal of Himmler. The new Reichsführer had far greater duties than playing bureaucratic politics within the SS and Interior Ministry. Once Himmler's loyalists were purged, many offices were running under temporary heads and similar makeshifts. At some point someone would get the SS-HA position officially and formally. Until then, these two had been jointly tasked.

Riedwig concerned himself more with personnel matters, especially recruitment. "Thankfully Hausser's losses so far have been few, mostly wastage from endemic local diseases. The two former Divisions, the Police Division in Paris and the Deathshead in Warsaw, have only operational wastage in their field security roles. Traffic accidents, mostly, plus the occasional clash with partisans. Dietrich's LAH had even fewer losses, although new men had to be found to upgrade it from a large Regiment into a small Division." Riedwig, himself a Swiss German, had long advocated making the Waffen SS a multinational force of Aryans rather than a purely German institution.

"Yes, so you can forward the men you have to Hausser." Berger paused for a minute to recall something. "Hausser and whoever this Brigadier Strauss is. Why on Earth does he have an SS Battalion that needs rebuilding?"

Now Riedwig had to shuffle some papers on his desk. "LAH sent him a Battalion. The Battalion made a botch out of it, and they are trying to blame us. Schellenberg was quite nasty about it. He's going to stick us with part of the blame for not catching their errors."

Berger wearily shook his head. Another Dietrich fuckup. The man was brave and loyal, but a dunce on organizational issues. What's worse, he refused to surround himself with competent staff. He wanted old comrades from the early days. "So we steal the men for the new unit from the HJ and the Camp Guards?" The Army rationed the SS on both recruits and equipment. It was easy to subvert the recruiting limits. The SS simply took HJ's under the Army's recruitment age, Volksdeutsche and Aryans wishing to Germanize themselves. The equipment was the real problem. There was not enough allocated to see to Hausser's needs, much less to properly outfit Dietrich's new showcase Führer Guards unit. And now he'd been handed this Spanish volunteer unit the Army didn't want. "Where do we steal the equipment? Skoda?"

"Let me handle that. This Eichmann's Palestine Camp Complex is making a lot of people rich and solving a lot of production issues for different cartels. One hand washes the other. I can do small-quantity deals. Everyone and his cousin wants a new SS workshop to ease their production backlogs. I can jump people on the queue."

"So what do we do with this oversize Spanish Division? How did it become Waffen SS?" Berger had no problem with the Waffen SS taking non-Aryans. He was not an advocate of this in the manner of Riedwig. He was just someone who focused on the tasks that needed doing, rather than a twisted knot of ideological humbug.

"Army rejected them for sending an extra Regiment and passing it off as a square Division. Army wants cookie-cutter Divisions … "

Berger couldn't help laughing. "Look at their mobilization waves. They have dozens of special organizational models, and then modify almost ad hoc. What would the problem have been of one more?"

"Beck allows himself and his class to have dozens of weird variants on Division structure. They insist the foreign units they deal with all follow an ideal, rulebook pattern. It's a matter of class prerogative. They make unbreakable rules, and then allot themselves leave to make exceptions. Only gentlemen of the proper class with the proper staff stripe can be organizationally creative." Riegwig paused for a moment, weighing whether to utter an impolitic truth out loud, "Plus they would be against free beer if it came from the Reichsführer. I'm married into the class, and the older ones cannot get past his being run out of the Navy over personal impropriety."

"But your father-in-law … " Berger mentally answered his own question. Generals could do things that a cashiered Leutnant could not. Riedwig's father-in-law, ex-Defense Minister General von Blomberg, was allowed to keep his wife with a tainted past of pornography and perhaps prostitution. He had merely been forcibly retired. Only the now-dead Admiral Raeder had tried to demand more, pushing the man to kill himself. Perhaps that was the key with the generals. They knew Raeder was a fanatic on these issues, and just hated Heydrich for his low rank of Leutnant.

Berger allowed himself a small sigh. Back to business. "I have no problem with Spanish as SS. They may be Latins, but at least they are white Christians. Franco claims that their better classes are German-descended, from Visigoths and Vandals. An amusing fable ,but no more fantasy than many of the Volksdeutsche who are only German by culture and language. It's not as if the Spanish are polluting us with Arabs or Colored. These are white men, many of good family and many others combat veterans. My problem is basing them in Germany proper. Soldiers spend their off duty time trying to bed bar maids and shopgirls. This is a law of the universe. The Spanish are a mix of combat veterans and eager university Fascists from the Falange's youth movement. Virile young men from these backgrounds would screw anything with a pulse. In reverse, these young Latins would seem exotic and enticing to enough silly German girls to make trouble. The Race Laws did not expressly forbid this, but local opinion would demand the Party *do something.*"

Riedwig thought of a quick solution. "There's an SS force in Romania. We don't bring the Spanish to Germany in the first place. Ploiesti could always use more guards. The Romanians would appreciate more protectors from the Soviets. The Romanian theory is that they were Latins, not Slavs. So virile Latin young men could chase Latin bar maids. Problem solved."

The larger problem was equipment. The oversize division had already been converted into a Corps by edict from Heydrich. It was all well and good to proclaim that these would be Panzergrenadier Divisions. Berger had no vehicles to spare to make another Panzergrenadier Brigade, much less a Corps … yet. What he did have was German infantry kit, 'borrowed' from two of the demobilized Army divisions. For now these would be Jäger divisions. The men would need proper German training in storm tactics, mission orders, and the rest. When trucks became available they could be upgraded to motorized infantry. When the new cartels reached full production in a year or so, he would find the armored vehicles for the final transformation to Panzergrenadier status. Now all that remained was to meet with this Spanish general Yagüe to explain matters. Hopefully the man would be sensible. He certainly came with a fine combat record.

The two SS generals managed to waste an hour on the Spanish, who were an enjoyable problem with reasonable solutions. They then got back to the real problem, which involved yet again shorting Dietrich's new Guards unit for the needs of the combat theater. Dietrich would complain to Nebe, who would call another conference with Heydrich, and they would lose two days finding some face-saving compromise. The implied threat would be Führer Göring's displeasure. The two Waffen SS generals were fairly certain that Göring neither noticed nor cared. Bureaucratic infighting was the bane of every large organization.

1800 hours local; 1700 hours CET
3 October 1940
Former Senior Officer's Mess, former British base at Mersa Matruh

The field officers meeting for Hausser's oversize division was catered by staff from Strauss's brigade. As various command staffs discovered that the NL brigade had professional chefs, their services were made use of. The spread was a mix of hot rolls with a variety of eastern flavors, and quite traditional central European pastries. The nominal cost of this was some swaps between the various supply officers. The SS Fast Regiment had liberated the camp, including vast quantities of what in Europe were luxuries, such as coffee, tea, and sugar.

Gruppenführer Hausser had near a Corps's worth of troops, but far less than that of people with field-officer rank. At this stage of the war his officers were mostly both young for their command level as compared to the Army, and held ranks less than would be normal for Battalion and higher posts. The service as a whole was young, hungry, and eager. It fit the Party, which was in many ways somewhat of a youth movement.

"*Kameraden*, for the next stage of the war in this theater, we have been allocated the main mission for the Panzer Army. How we conduct ourselves will in large measure determine the fate of our service. The Waffen SS has one combat force left, ourselves. The Reichsführer is testing whether we are worthy of his patronage. If we prove ourselves to be the Aryan warriors we believe ourselves to be, I have his promise that this Division will be expanded to Army size, to be a full Panzer Army. The last battle was the Army's chance to shine. Rommel had the lead. Now it is our turn to outdo him, to show the Army what a true elite force can accomplish. Who is with me on this? For our race, our party, our Führer, VICTORY!"

The room came to its feet cheering. It was not just careerism. The men here saw themselves as a true warrior elite, with the Party's ideology giving them a faith to fight for, as the Teutonic Knights had had before them.

....

Mary Collins let the men strut. Her job was to provide a bit of food and plentiful beverages. She'd brought two bartenders, but this wasn't a hard-drinking crowd the way a British officers' mess would have been. These Nazis took war more seriously than the British officers her man had served under. So it was coffee and tea mostly.

She'd been more concerned with a dustup involving a newly-arrived pastry chef. He'd come to camp in a draft from Bari, with airs of having been second pastry chef at what he asserted had been the third-best hotel in Bucharest. Mary wouldn't have know the best hotel in Bucharest from the fourth-worst. Indeed, she couldn't have found Bucharest on a map or told you what country it was in. She knew nations by where the British had garrisons, which did not include the Balkans.

None of that mattered. She was head cook because of her connection to Frau Steiner. The middle-aged fool of a Bucharest cook refused to understand the logic. He ignored her orders, did as he wished, and tried to assert his superior status with command. He was a man with credentials. She was a mere woman, and an Asiatic to boot.

That had lasted under twenty minutes. She sent her son for Frau Greta. Greta heard the fool out, laughed in his face, and told him that, as he refused to be a cook, she had other work for him. The man had a problem accepting that a teenage girl was an important officer. He had that ancient male disease of 'don't you know who I am?' Greta had stuck a pistol in his ribs and frog-marched the fool to Hauptsturmführer Peiper.

The cook had discovered that instead of a disobedient cook, he was now a flamethrower operator. A small consignment of these had arrived. The current thought was to use them from the sidecars of motorcycles. So someone would have to strap a tank of easily-ignited flamespray on his back, and ride out on a motorcycle to battle while the British hurled hot metal at him.

Two days of field exercises and labor details had in turn produced a most contrite pastry chef. He got on his knees before Mary, begging for his old posting back. She let him sweat the night before grudgingly saying yes. She'd neglected to mention that Peiper regarded the fool as useless as a combat fighter. He'd also soured on the entire concept. Now he had Joey and Paul trying to find a way to fire the flame liquid from inside his French cavalry tanks. Meanwhile the chef's pastries were being gobbled up by the SS officers, so maybe he was at least half as good as his brags and boasts.

0200 hours CET
4 October 1940
Ravensbrück KL, Germany

She was stuck on an overnight shift again. The corrupt bitches who were her superiors could find nothing wrong with her work, so they punished her via undesirable shifts and duties. Frauke Peters had joined the female guards corps, the Aufseherinnen, as a means to do her patriotic duty to Party and Reich. She had been an avid Party member all through her time in the BDM. The Reich was at war. As a woman she couldn't pick up a rifle, but by serving as a guard, she could free a man to do so.

Frauke had excelled in her training at the camp. She had also earned a bad reputation among the supervisors who trained her. They called her a 110% girl. In theory that meant someone so dedicated to the Party that they did 110% of what was required. What they really meant was that she was a fanatic and a prude. The staff running Ravensbrück were mostly motivated by sensual pleasures and petty corruption. There were two special attached facilities where luxuries and money seemed to effortlessly flow. Exactly how was some sort of state secret, but a section of the male staff and some special prisoners were allowed girlfriends among the female guards and the more willing prisoners. There were parties every night. They also had servants among the Bible Girls in the Camp. Those weren't available for sex, but were docile house staff, seeing to cleaning, cooking, and the rest.

The new girls such as Frauke were expected to go along with the libertine behavior. The camp joke was that BDM wasn't the League of German Girls, but rather the League of SS Mattresses. The trainees who refused to take part were at least expected to walk small, keep silent, and endure the scorn of the well-connected clique. Frauke refused to bend the neck. Hitler had been her God and Mein Kampf her Bible. The Führer had not been a libertine. She saw the Movement as a pure and chaste crusading order. Fraternization and loose behavior was wrong, regardless of what the rules said. She complained. She wrote letters of denunciation to higher SS command, the Kreisleiter, to anyone she could think of. This got her reprimanded by her camp superiors, and warned verbally by the corrupt to shut her mouth and avert her eyes. As if. There had to be a way out of this degenerate shit hole, and Frauke was determined to find it. Perhaps she could get herself assigned as a transport guard. Every few weeks, there was a prisoner transport by rail to someplace in Italy. Most of those being sent were loose-living girls from the special facilities, almost as if this was some sort of a reward. Perhaps if she could get more information, someone in the Party or SS hierarchy would pay her some attention.

1700 hours Eastern Daylight Time; 2300 hours CET
4 October 1940
Institute for Advanced Study, Princeton NJ

The train ride from Manhattan had made New Jersey seem to be a set of layers. The initial belt clustered near New York harbor was mostly gritty industrial towns, with a few leafy commuter suburbs. Then came the estates of the Manhattan-centered wealthy, often with horse barns and elaborate gardens. By the time Enrico Fermi debarked from the train in the college town of Princeton, he had spent most of an hour looking at little market towns surrounded by small, green, productive farms. New Jersey's official motto was the 'Garden State'. The big grain and meat producing areas were to the west beyond the mountains. Jersey grew vegetables and similar truck garden produce, for fresh delivery to the huge markets of New York and Philadelphia.

Fermi had come to this quaint college town to see Albert Einstein. Einstein was not precisely at Princeton. He was a bit too Jewish for that storied school's taste. Instead he was employed at the 'Institute for Advanced Study', which for the nonce was co-located in the Princeton Physics Department building.

Princeton was part of something called the 'Ivy League'. It was in part an athletic union, mostly for upper-class sports like rowing. It was in equal part a grouping of the most venerable American universities, all except Cornell dating from pre-colonial days. Mostly, it was where old money East Coast white Protestants (and those of the upper middle classes seeking to ape them) sent their sons. Here these young men could spend four years getting inculcated with the proper manners and making lifetime social contacts. Yet this 'Ivy League' did not include a second group of schools, such as Amherst and Williams, who would seem to fit the profile; but included Columbia, which clearly did not.

Fermi had chosen Columbia because of this. It was nestled in Manhattan's Upper West Side. By Ivy League standards it was too cosmopolitan, too Jewish, too Italian, too Marxist, too avant garde. It was everything Fermi and his Jewish wife wished to preserve of their Europe when Il Duce's race laws drove them into exile. Why Einstein had chosen to isolate himself in the exact opposite way, to Princeton, was an abiding mystery to Fermi and his set of Euro expats. But Einstein had the name known to the power brokers in the US Government. He was the man that was needed for this crisis.

After the usual pleasantries at the station, and again on reaching the Institute offices, the two men found themselves politely left alone in a well-appointed conference room. Fermi got right to the point. "I've had a visitation from Italy. It's official now. The Nazis are going for the atomic bomb."

"Might you be so kind as to humor me with details, before pronouncing the conclusion?" Einstein had already sent one letter to FDR on this matter. Advocating for a weapon injured Einstein's pacifist conscience. He needed real data, to consider involving himself again.

Fermi was already out of his chair pacing. "They tried to recruit me to come back. They are creating a new institute to study nuclear physics. It's to be at Salo up in the lake country, near the Alps. Named CERN or some such bureaucratic drivel. The recruiters made big promises on revoking the race laws where applicable. Obviously the revocation applies to Italy and Switzerland, not the German Reich. They are offering Swiss passports for those that haven't gotten US ones. So consular protection. Swore up and down that it's not a weapons program. Some idiocy about electrical power generation. But a big research institute in Italy and a second under Heisenberg in Germany. Near unlimited budgets. What else could it be except a bomb project? You saw what they did to London. Imagine an atomic bomb used instead. The only way to defend against this is to have a bomb and threaten Berlin."

"So they admit nuclear, and you intuit bomb. Why not power plants?"

"How would you justify such grand expenditures in wartime except for a bomb? Why wouldn't they just build more coal plants? Europe has enough coal. It has to be a bomb."

Einstein didn't know the economics of coal plants, coal mining, the transportation of coal. He did know Europe lacked oil to run power plants based on that. It also seemed not to have the hydroelectric possibilities of the US West. It would take discussion long into the night, but Fermi left with the great man's signature on a letter to circulate.

0800 local; 0600 CET
5 October 1940

Deaths on the Nile

Train from Palestine to Egypt

The train had arrived in Palestine packed like a sardine tin. The two Palestinian Jews had been waiting on the platform for the unloading. The ticket seller had warned them that, as almost no one was going to Egypt given the current situation, the train reversed course back almost as soon as it emptied out. They were no longer even cleaning it before the return to Egypt.

The middle-aged woman was in charge. Golda Wittson, or Meir as she preferred to be called, was a rising official in the Palestinian Jewish Labor Zionist political hierarchy. As this trip needed her to use her American passport in the manner of a magic talisman, she was temporarily back to being Wittson. She resented having this young man attached to her as an aide. The implication was that a woman needed a bodyguard of some kind. She regarded herself as quite capable on her own. She was also aware that the young man was under suspicion of collaboration during his British captivity. He had been regarded as promising before that, so this in a sense marked his first step towards possible rehabilitation. She saw no reason why she should carry that burden. She was a modern, liberated woman. What need had she of either a male protector or a political black sheep?

The railway carriage was deserted. This made quiet conversation in Hebrew fairly safe as it was unlikely the Arab conductor spoke it fluently, should he return. "Boy, I may be stuck with you but stay out of my way. You don't talk in meetings. You don't know enough and what's worse, no one knows you."

Moishe Dayan was 25, scarcely a boy. "So why have me along at all?" Dayan knew more than he would let on to this apparatchik. The stories of how the British at the top had banned Jewish escape across Iraq, and how the New Zealanders had leaked the decision while announcing they would refuse to enforce it, were spreading rapidly. The New Zealand general had Jewish friends in Palestine. Enough of his men had acquired Jewish girlfriends. Dayan was sure there was more, and was equally sure this office wallah wouldn't tell him. "Forget what Tel Aviv ordered. When we reach Egypt, let's split up. You do the political business and keep whatever deep secrets you would prefer I didn't hear. I'll try to find Wingate and our two brigades, attempt to get a realistic appraisal of the current military situation." Even if he couldn't find Wingate, there would be staff officers of his who knew Dayan from their campaigning days together in Palestine in the 30's.

Meir argued for form's sake but didn't try very hard. Explaining what had been learned from the meeting in Istanbul would be hard enough without this Haganah officer's presence. Ben Gurion believed the tale of Axis partition of Palestine. He'd sent a delegation to Rome to try to make contact with the new overlords. Meir was less sure that trusting Fascists, much less Nazis, was wise. She gave her attention to how to convey the needed decisions to the Egyptian Jewish community without quite admitting to collaboration with Britain's enemies, with people who until now were also the sworn enemies of all Jews. Dayan was content to leave her alone. He was studying the terrain along the rail line. If a political deal wasn't reached, he might be leading troops here.

1300 hours local; 1200 hours CET
5 October 1940
Kampfgruppe Jodl artillery positions to the rear of Steiner's division, southwest of Ruweisat Ridge

The artillery duel was in full-throated concert. Felix Steiner's artillery was working over the British front lines. A few British guns were replying. The British were short of field guns, and reticent on using them in daylight for fear of air attack. Jodl's second 10.5 cm Battalion was doing counter-battery. It had only recently arrived. The General was putting the Battalion through its paces to see the training level. He had been assured it was a first-rate unit. He had no trust in OKH. Too much bad blood from when he had been at OKW.

Observing Jodl's actions was his Corps Commander, von Manstein. "General Jodl, are you satisfied with this Battalion?"

Jodl chose his words carefully. "Corps Commander, it seems adequate. On par with the original one that was sent. As ammunition resupply via Mersa Matruh is more than sufficient, I can alternate them in action, allowing a workup to my standards by the time we jump off. I'm holding the 17 cm battalion in Italy, to prioritize ammunition shipments instead. The big guns are not very useful offroad, so best to leave those for Palestine. This battlefield only has one real road. It is at the wrong end of the line for our attack plan."

"What do you propose to do with your Malta regiment?" Von Manstein had been gifted with these two Battalions. He couldn't see the function of motorized machine-guns or light mortars. Jodl was the artillerist.

"I had presumed I would gift this regiment to Steiner. Other than the weapons being airtransportable, it's a marginal formation. Steiner has a grab bag of a division. This just adds to his firepower." Jodl mentally thanked God he had gotten the abysmal 50mm mortars replaced with French 60mm ones. The German 50mm was near useless. The French 60mm was quite good, and had proven so on Malta. "The attack date is still 30 October?"

"Take that date as indicative rather than firm. We won't do a final plan until later in the month. We see no reason we cannot breach this British line at any time of our choosing. Issue is what happens next. We anticipate needing a few more weeks of reinforcement." Von Manstein was mentally congratulating himself on his decision to salvage Jodl from the First Mountain Division debacle in the runup to the Malta Operation.

The British guns had ceased firing. The German howitzers had done likewise. Jodl waited for von Manstein to end his visit so the after-action critique could begin. Kampfgruppe Jodl would do its part in the coming victory.

2000 hours local; 1900 hours CET
5 October 1940
Joey's workshop in Brigade Strauss area, to the rear of Italian lines near the coastal highway

Clara's arranging a sit-down meal so the repair crews never had to leave the workshops, had evolved into a de facto second mess hall for dinners. Paul's brother Peter took his meals there. Their father Isaak did as well. So did the adopted Uncle Ivan. This led their cousin Greta to do so. Greta meant Klaus. Klaus would bring along Peiper. Mohnke was still not well enough to take part.

Mary Collins was needed running the main mess tent, but didn't want to lose the connection to her protector and future employer, Frau Steiner. So she arranged for her son Bain to help Clara's girls bring dinner over each night, then remain to 'assist'. Bain acted as server but also kept his ears open. The boy had a natural flair for languages. He hadn't known one hundred words of German when the Betar girls had recruited his family. The initial communication had been in very basic Italian and even more primitive English. By now he was functional in German and Yiddish on a street level, and developing a bit of fluidity with Magyar.

Tonight Lieutenant Colonel Di Salo chose to attend. He had warned his mistress Coxita to be on best behavior. He enjoyed her fiery personality and reveled in dominating such a strong, difficult woman. He also knew her for the prime bitch she could be with other women, especially those she regarded as socially beneath her. Her dogmatic Stalinism was real, but was an outer layer to a condescending, spoiled, middle-class princess. Still, he enjoyed showing her off as a trophy to the other officers.

The heat was stifling even this late in the day. The flies were annoying, but the officers 'table' was in a screened office area that limited the profusion of flying bugs. Besides, at this point everyone was accustomed to the pests. The actual meal was a pleasant mild curry, with pasta instead of rice. Coxita started to make a cat comment about that being an absurd combination. Before he could stifle her, the German Communist woman, this Clara, politely put his companion in her place, without even acknowledging the original comment. Instead she told Bain to thank his mother for the intelligent mixture of what was available. She put this in Communist populist terms, making it an issue of working-class adaption to the idiot capitalist war. Coxita caught her retort, and instead seconded Clara. Di Salo marked this. These female politics were worth exploring at some point. Perhaps Coxita was finally starting to grow up a bit. Preoccupied with this, he realized he was missing the male conversation, picking up something Piper was saying in midsentence.

" – doesn't quite work. The idea is right. We could have used the flame option as close defense in the engagement at the Three Crosses. But – "

Joey was clearly exasperated. "Yeah, boss, I hear you." Joey's German was neither especially grammatical nor really fluent, but he was able by now to get key points across. "It needs a better workshop and more time. I must redesign the parts, not just shove the infantry flamethrower into the – " He caught himself for a minute. He was fishing for a word. "Damn it. The things you use are not really tank or armored car. What idiot French-ass pirate designed the damned thing? Cavalry tank? What the fuck is that?"

Di Salo put up a hand to get the men's attention. "Are you trying to make a tank with a viable flame thrower as a weapon?" He paused to see the nods. "Gentleman, Italy has whole parking lots full of them. We built them. They work for trench war, but no one saw any use for them here. The range of the flame is too short by mobile battle standards. Would you like half a dozen?"

There followed a most pleasant half hour of detailed discussion on the technical aspects, after which Di Salo promised to get eight or so as soon as possible. He suggested that Brigade Commander Strauss be enlisted to make the request through German channels as well. These Germans had found Di Salo a few real tanks. Hospitality should flow both ways. Besides, the Tenente Colonello was a patriot. It would be good propaganda for German troops to be seen using Italian weapons.

0300 hours Pacific Daylight Time; 1100 CET
6 October 1940
A diner in Bakersfield, California

It had taken days to get here. With the Communist Party outlawed, Hoover's FBI had had a field day rounding up Communist officials and big name sympathizers. The wide net had angered many leftist supporters of the New Deal, pleased many devoted followers of Lindbergh (who would never vote for

FDR anyway) … and totally failed to bag Harry Bridges, the head of the dockworkers and the ringleader of the guerrilla attacks on trucks and railways bringing goods to the West Coast ports. This in turn brought escalating pressures on the Special Agent in Charge of the Bureau's LA field office to produce results or be transferred to North Dakota.

This malign possible fate in turn led to a senior minion of the LA office dressing down from the normal Hoover G-Man uniform. Some places, you didn't wear a business suit and snappy fedora. Utilizing a movie-business intermediary, a meeting had been arranged with a particular Trotskyite man of the demimonde. The man was not precisely a criminal or a full-time revolutionary. He was a man of shadows, with a revolutionary past and particular sympathies. "Bridges. What is your boss offering?"

"I'm authorized to go ten thousand dollars. It can be cash."

The Trotskyite laughed. It was a harsh, bitter laugh. This was a man who had seen prisons of the Czar, the commissars, and the state of California. Perhaps others. The FBI file on him was hazy and full of guesswork. Indeed, the name on it probably wasn't the name he was born with. "Keep your money. Three men. Two are doing Federal time, and the third is a guest of this state." He scribbled out a list on a stray piece of paper and pushed it across. "This gets you Bridges. You get the three to El Paso. One calls me. I take you to wherever Bridges is then. You bag him and call El Paso. Your guy there walks my three over the bridge to Mexico, gives them $100 each to get them to Mexico City."

The FBI man knew the Boss wouldn't like the price but would back his play. "Why wait? I'll give you five people. Released for health reasons. Any charge that isn't carrying a death sentence. But I need him today."

The middle-aged ex-revolutionary – or maybe not so "ex" – gave a weary half-smile and looked to the movie guy, a second-rank producer and immigrant from Central Europe. "So, landsman, will you guarantee that this G-Man delivers? Him I cannot kill. Too much blowback. You have a life to lose. A wife, an ex-wife, a mistress. Several children. An aged aunt you brought over with you. Houses. A small movie studio. Should I go on?" The movie guy was getting paler and paler. He was starting to look like a corpse. "Doesn't matter if your G-Man kills me, jails me. People know who I was taking this meeting with. You know the circles I move in. This isn't some Hays Code movie. It will be bloody, messy. The Feds cannot protect you forever, and we are patient. We survived the Czar. Enough of us are surviving that swine Stalin and his Nazi lap dogs. On your life, on the lives of everyone you hold dear, do I trust this agent of Hoover Okhrana?"

The FBI official didn't wait for the terrified movie guy to stammer a reply. "The word of the Bureau is good. You want me to get the big boss out of bed early to take a phone call? Normally he'd shitcan me for a stunt like that, but he wants Bridges that badly." He watched his adversary weigh the words, shrug, and relax. "Just to satisfy a curiosity, why are you ratting Bridges out?"

"Because this isn't about the class struggle. It's about him being Stalin's whore. That Georgian murdered Lenin's revolution and is now buggering its rotting corpse. Real Communism died when Trotsky was exiled. The wheels of history often require tactical accommodation. Stalin and some of the other Old Bolsheviks informed for money. Stalin robbed banks and fenced loot as well. History will absolve them of that. The Party needed funds, and the moment for revolution was not then ripe. Tactical accommodation. The true sins came later. Revolution in one country, subordinating Leninism to Great Russian imperialism, gutting the Party into a gang of sycophants. You and I, we will never be friends – but right now we have a common enemy." He took back his list of three names and added two more.

Four hours later, Bridges and his two top lieutenants were shot down while resisting arrest in a nondescript house a few miles from where the original meeting had taken place. It had been decided that a trial would just have given the Stalinists a platform to wage a propaganda war on the United States. There was nothing in writing to that effect. The important orders all came by courier from headquarters. Verbal orders left no trail.

0900 local time; 0700 CET
6 October 1940
Main port, Kuwait

British Brigadier William Slim gave a disgusted shake of his head, surveying this dump of a small boat harbor at which the RN was attempting to land his division. Tenth Indian Division was a slapped-together force, dispatched to meet the oncoming crisis in Iraq. "We were supposed to land in Basra, gentlemen." He was talking to his chief engineering officer, the commander of the lead brigade, and the RN commander of this ad hoc convoy. "The Iraqi Army chose not to allow us to use Basra. London, Delhi, and Cairo among them proved incapable of reaching a decision on whether to initiate hostilities at this exact moment over this precise provocation. So here we are in a port mostly suited for pearl fishing and trade with Bombay. Tell me how bad this mess is, please?"

The engineer was an expert in civil construction. Cantonments, barracks, roads and the like. However, the basic mechanics of getting equipment off ships was sort of within his realm. "We can unload a good bit of kit. Give it a week and Bombay can deliver a few medium cranes to get the heavy trucks and field guns offloaded. Meantime I can build the docks to set them up on. It will mean keeping ships in harbor past plan." He turned and looked at the RN officer.

The Persian Gulf and Arabian Sea were a backwater to navy engaged in a worldwide war. The officer in charge was an overage commodore recalled to active service. His actual naval force was two armed merchant cruisers and a few home-brew gunboats whipped up in Bombay. These were good enough to deter piracy, but not much else. Serious engagements with the enemy were not anticipated in these waters. The twin expected dangers were local pirates and the Sunni officers' cabal in Iraq, the Golden Square. "Nothing else for it. It will slow down your division's deployment, but needs must. Bombay port is in chaos anyway. Congress riots. Sabotage from Bose's chaps. Muslim mobilization for the Afghan intervention. Indeed I've got a new signal here. Your division commander is off to Khandahar to lead a force of Muslim League National Guards and tribal Mujahideen. So you've been bumped from staff brigadier to divisional command."

The three men shook their heads at the unfolding escalating chaos, and sent a mess attendant for a bottle of Scotland's finest and three cups to toast the promotion. On the dock the troops continued to debark and march inland to hasty camps. The war had come to Kuwait. All three military men trusted the British resident agent to smooth this over with the dynasty.

1400 hours CET
6 October 1940
Camp Complex HQ, Palestine Camp Group, near Cracow, General Government

Another day, another distasteful task. Prinz-Albrecht-Straße had delegated the task of explaining the camp system to the would-be Ukrainian Führer Stepan Bandera. Berlin had said the man was important. Therefore Commandant Eichmann took the meeting himself. Bandera's Abwehr minder was a mere Major. The visit didn't rate parting with the real coffee Eichmann now had a stock of that, thanks to his Jewish officers. The charity shipments from their US cousins included real coffee, American cigarettes, sugar, chocolate, and other luxuries no longer readily available in blockaded Europe. Some days Eichmann felt guilty that the Yids were trying to bribe him. Most of the time he simply regarded these extras as his due as their ruler. He was sure Berlin had been informed of his good fortune. As no reprimand was sent, he presumed they at least tacitly approved.

The Ukrainian had seemed ill at ease during the tour and the follow-on presentations. Now that the three were alone in Eichmann's office, the Commandant awaited hearing what this Slav's problem was.

Bandera seemed both quite intelligent *and* a fanatic for his cause. Tact was apparently not one of his virtues. "You've shown me how Germany handles Jews. Why should Ukrainians be treated this way? And why are you treating the damned Hebrews so well? When Ukraine is independent we want ours gone, not put into workshops and left with their own arms." Bandera relaxed slightly. It seemed clear he wanted to get this out, and was relieved that the two Germans had not immediately exploded.

The Abwehr officer started to answer, but Eichmann cut in over him. "I personally despise the Jews. I'd be more comfortable exterminating them. Policy is made at a higher level. I am a loyal servant of my state and blood. I will competently execute that policy. What is in store for Ukrainians? Ask your minder. Ask Berlin. But ask yourself this. For now we are allied with Stalin. The vast bulk of your people are under his yoke. For those who can escape, how would camps like this oppress them? The Yids have work, food, and reasonable living conditions. On a day-to-day level they mostly govern themselves. When the war ends and their production is no longer needed, they will be transported to places where they are welcome. All very efficient."

Before Bandera could reply, the Abwehr man finally got his words in. "We are arming whole Battalions of your followers. We are providing refuge to as many of yours as can escape from Stalin. How do workshops retard your cause?" The Abwehr regarded a Soviet war as inevitable, and saw Bandera as a useful tool.

"Jews are natural town dwellers. Ukrainians are a people who should farm their own land, run they own factories and mines. Not do piecework for German cartels." Bandera feared this temporary setup would be made permanent. Being cut off from blood and soil was a major part of what made the Hebrews unnatural.

The Abwehr man had experience dealing with this man's paranoias. "Stalin let how many of yours starve? We welcome you, but don't have spare land to give you. How do you propose your influx, assuming you can get any real numbers past Stalin's border guards, will earn their bread? You fear this is their fate forever. Only if Stalin is capable of keeping his word to the Reich. Is he? Is he a man of honor?"

The discussion ran in circles until well into the evening. The following day Camp Ukraine #1 was staked out, beginning the process.

0700 hours CET
7 October 1940
Café Wanda, German encampment at Bari

The café and brothel ran twenty-four-hours a day, seven days a week. That said, the peak traffic times were late night and weekends. The troops in transit were normally kept at least nominally busy during daylight hours. Military philosophy tended to treat idle soldiers as trouble waiting to happen. Inventive Feldwebels can always find excuses for work parties. That said, the café was on base – so men off duty didn't need a leave pass. They just needed a few hours to their own time … unless their Feldwebel or Officer restricted them to company area. Reward and punishment.

By now, there was an overworked finance staff to count the take, check inventories, and similar. Wanda being Wanda, she always did her own checks on both, usually just before a light breakfast and going to sleep for the day. Her man Adolph had adopted her schedule. She was putting the cash into the safe when she yet-again asked him the obvious question. "Gunter's a general. Gregor's an Oberstleutnant. Are you sure you don't mind getting stuck at Major back here in Bari?"

Adolph shot her a cynical look. "Trying to get rid of me again? I've had my fill of being shot at. Of sleeping under open skies in mud and ditches, riddled with lice and drinking water out of shell holes. We have our own shack. I don't need a mansion. I need walls, a floor, windows with screens, and a mattress with you beside me; plus a couple of rooms for the kids to sleep so they aren't underfoot. I could live the rest of my life this way with you. We have cooked meals of real food, not rations. I have you next to me when I go to sleep, not a bunch of hairy men. Between their snores and their farts … "

Wanda was happy with the answer. She kept asking because she knew her man had been competitive with Gregor and Gunter for all the years she knew the three of them. "What about my idea with Gretchen, for a setup directly with Gunter in Africa?" The steady supply of new girls from Germany made this feasible.

Adolph pondered, as he usually did when this came up. "We never exactly told Gunter about all this. Do I fly over and explain? What if he keeps me there?" Adolph trusted his old friend Gunter, but was wary that Gunter's exalted new rank may have gone to his head. A General? This was an age of wonders.

"If we send Gretchen over with the unit's share of the profits, he'll work it all out. Next time you get a demand from the port authorities for warm bodies to fill out a loading, send Gretchen. Add a dozen girls and a vodka inventory, and he's in business."

"Add a couple of doctors. We have more than we need, and clean girls is how we sell this to the bosses."

The conversation was then interrupted by little Oriana bringing in the manifest from a liquor delivery, to get checked in for payment. The child had proven to be an apt apprentice to Wanda. She was still too small to be a madame. That role needed physical heft as well as knowledge. But she'd learned the mechanics of the business. She was also by now an accomplished photographer. Many soldiers paid her for portrait shots to send home. Seeing business opportunities in everyday life was part of Wanda's training curriculum. Oriana had heard more than they thought. If there was going to be a detachment of entertainment troops to rejoin her old mates from Tuscany, she was going, whether Wanda approved or not. She had snuck away to here, after all.

1500 hours local; 1400 hours CET
7 October 1940
Brigade Strauss headquarters in rear of Italian XXI Corps positions at the north end of the Alamein lines

The outdoor press conference featured a joint Propaganda Company of Germans and Italians, here to publicize the heroes of the desert battle. Major Klaus Steiner was the main object of attention. The propaganda experts found an 18-year-old field-grade hero fascinating. He wasn't the sort of fake they would have dreamed up. He was short, looked younger than his age, and had an adolescent voice, a bit high and squeaky, with the occasional stutter or stammer. His looks were at best average. He seemed more than a bit of an everyman. Yet he was a battlefield victor in Romania, Hungary, Malta, and now in the African desert.

"Did you really offer to let any man afraid of the fighting, have a note to be released with honor?"

Klaus tried to look the questioner in the eye, but he wasn't very good at that sort of contrived body language. He was just himself, a boy learning how to be a man. He had a dab of schooling but it did not include training in public speaking. It also meant analyzing himself, something he was new at. "Yes." He paused trying to make combat clear to people who hadn't been there. "We were in an advance position." He paused again, mentally visualizing both the terrain and the map. "We'd been tasked with holding our position as long as possible." He paused again, replaying in his mind the situation. "We'd been slowly giving ground to vastly superior forces. We were taking losses. Dead, maimed, equipment. The officers sent out by the Luftwaffe and artillery to aid us as spotters felt the position was too dangerous. They were older than I am. Experienced professionals, experts. It wasn't my job to waste their lives, their skills. But my seniors had given me the job of maintaining this observation position for as long as possible. I judged it possible." He gave a laugh. What a changed world where he could have an opinion worth adults taking the time to consider. "We fight out here for our nation and race. I was taught in the HJ to trust that the superiors placed over me knew what they were doing, that they would spend our blood wisely. I was going to perform my mission as long as I was physically able. I knew enough of my men would follow me. They had on Malta. So whoever felt staying to be unwise, could leave. We'd just perform the mission without them, same as if they had been killed in action." He stopped again, hoping he had made sense at least to Gunter, if not to these high-ranking professionals from a world in Berlin he could barely comprehend existed. "It's how battle is. All you see is your little piece."

"So it's about your personal glory?"

Klaus slowly shook his head. He was failing to be clear. He would have to try to find a way to be clearer, to make sense. "No one sets out to be a hero." He still found the idea of himself as a hero laughable. "You set out to be a patriot. NL is a new service. I've never been through formal recruit training. Learned on the job, sort of like being an apprentice. I was schooled well in HJ and then by Brigadier Strauss. I was recruited by him during the Loyalty Parade in Berlin. That officer is a hero. I just follow behind him and try to keep learning." He looked to Gunter hopefully, wishing he would step in and take charge.

"But aren't you afraid? You could be killed."

Klaus wearily shook his head. "Everyone in a war zone can be killed. You just get used to it. I can be killed standing here if a British plane drops a bomb on my head. I could get run over by a truck tomorrow. So a bit of fear, yes, but mostly it's fear I'll be unworthy of the positions entrusted to me. The only time I was truly terrified was in my glider over Malta. First time I'd ever had to do night navigation. Took a deep breath and just did the best I could. It worked."

"How did you like working with the Italian Arditi?"

"Excellent lads. Brave, eager, wonderful comrades. I've no idea how they ended up with us instead of with their own officers." Klaus shook his head, smiling wistfully. "War is like that. Amazing chaos. You learn to cope. Their officer found us on Malta. He was one of the heroes of the defense of Luqa. The British may had been poorly led, but they were quite brave. Kept attacking. Can't say I think much of their officers. They seem to waste the courage of their men."

The press questioning went on for a bit, after which Klaus posed for photos – including several with Greta. The final question for him was, what were his plans with his girl friend? "No time for personal plans. We are on campaign. When that's over, I'll have to see about formalizing what we have. My poor Greta is an orphan. Her family died during the Romanian campaign. But her uncles and cousins are officers in the Brigade. I think they approve of me."

Gunter was amazed that Klaus the Clueless had performed so well. He ended the session before the lad said something shallow and teen-age. The reporters looked content, and so did their Propaganda Ministry minders. He got hit with one final question about serving in combat with women. "It just sort of happened in Romania. A local Volksdeutsche Militia had both sexes. They amalgamated with my NL unit. The entire NL is still somewhat experimental. Berlin will decide if this test case gets expanded. Ask at the Ministry."

2000 hours Eastern Daylight Time, 7 October 1940
0200 hours CET, 8 October, 1940
Polo Grounds, Harlem, New York City

The press section perked up when Lindy deviated from his usual script. For the working press, covering touring politicians was mostly boring. With minor variations of wording, it was the same speech two or three times a day, seven days a week. The press pool was there in case the candidate was assassinated, or stripped naked to dance to the music of the spheres, or … or anything but minor wording differences on 'the speech'. Lindy was attacking the US Navy. "The uniformed hacks and traitors Franklin Roosevelt has put in charge of our brave fighting sailors, have again chosen to sabotage the defense of our Republic! Off Hawaii during the Japanese visit, there was a mutual demonstration of naval gunnery and torpedo exercises. Our torpedoes failed completely. The Japanese demonstrated a completely new torpedo technology. It was a brilliant success against the target ships. What did our fool admirals do? They rejected the Japanese offer to license this new technology for US production. They want to waste your hard-earned tax dollars on weapons they know won't work. We need submarines and torpedo bombers for continental defense. When Britain falls, we must be prepared to defend this hemisphere against the tyrants of Europe. We have the bravest men and the best factories. We must use those factories to equip our forces with the best weapons. The Democrat party cares nothing for defending this nation. With our ships under attack in the Western Pacific, they move ever more of our fleet to aid the British. Why? Because FDR will do in 1941 what Wilson did in 1917. Run as a peace candidate, and then manufacture a cause for war. A war we will enter unprepared, to serve the goals of British Imperialism and a cosmopolitan elite of mostly Jewish bankers. We need new admirals and a new administration, whose goals are America First, Last, Always!"

0700 hours local; 0600 hours CET
8 October 1940

Afrika Korps Headquarters, behind Italian XXth Corps lines at the southern end of the Alamein position

It was already hot. Whoever decided to have a war here had not considered the local climate. Then again, Leutnant von Kleist-Konitz's uncle had spent four years of the Great War in the East, then run a Freikorps there afterwards. Fighting Czarists, various types of Reds, and peasant bandits at the end. Five miserable winters before he came home in the spring of 1919. Uncle Uwe would have loved this place. No ice, no snow, no bottomless mud, no summer swamps. No freezing winds out of Siberia. A few Bedouin instead of the multiple flavors of Eastern partisans. No, even with the heat, bugs, sand and dust, Uncle Uwe would prefer here. Ernst von Kleist-Konitz would rather be fighting in France, or even the Balkans. But the war was here. He had wanted more combat, more active duty. This was what Germany had in October of 1940.

The Junker Leutnant had been working his network of family connections, trying to get a combat assignment instead of being with this absurd Militia unit. He had no wish to be either deputy Ia to some absurd half-Jew, or a spy for his distant cousin General von Manstein's headquarters, which was what a liaison officer amounted to. All the attempts had gotten the Oberleutnant so far was an invitation for coffee with Corps Commander von Manstein. This did not look promising.

"Please be seated, Leutnant." Ernst thought this was perhaps not so dire. Von Manstein was acting like a family friend, not an annoyed senior officer. "I thought we might save much time with a little chat."

Ernst sat down but maintained the position of attention from his waist up. Cousin or not, this was a Corps Commander whose wishes he was attempting to evade. "Yes sir."

Von Manstein let his B*ursche* serve them both some of the abysmal Ersatz coffee, which apparently was all his headquarters had. Ernst had gotten spoiled on the captured British stocks *his* unit's mess had. "These attempts to evade your posting. I've let you amuse yourself so you could discover the futility of it. You are mine till I choose to give you up. OKH has no pull here. Neither does the War Ministry. OKW is headed by my deputy, General Busse. This is an OKW theater of operations. You are completely in my power."

Ernst had been schooled since his boyhood in suppressing his emotions. His face stayed blank. There were tells, to someone who knew him well. Cousin von Manstein didn't. "As you command, Herr General Corps Commander."

Von Manstein nodded at the mandated, expected answer. "It's not so bad." He passed a folder across to the young man. He gave him a minute to skim it. "Yes. Promotion to Hauptmann. Iron Cross First Class. Letter of commendation." The general gave the entire situation another minute to sink in. "You were in a combat unit. You were the only professional officer there. The unit performed well. Of course, we would arrange for much of the credit to go to you. Our class is the arms-bearers. Now, tell me about this Strauss as a Brigadier?"

The Leutnant was still working hard at keeping the shock and pride out of his voice. "He's better than you'd expect. He's clearly over his head above the Company level, but he knows that. He relies a great deal on Oberstleutnants Gorlov and Schwabe. Both have Battalion command experience. Gorlov has Brigade command experience as well. Oberstleutnant Sommer, the new Ia, seems to be settling in well. He has the staff training to keep the headquarters functional. The Brigade staff is a bunch of civilians, but they have mercantile experience running organizations." Ernst paused for breath, waited to see if the General wanted to interrupt. He didn't. "You'd expect Strauss to be a Rommel-type of Storm Trooper. Yet unlike General Rommel, Strauss pays attention to logistics and administration. I think the key is his service with the Iron Division as an intelligence officer. He makes sure he knows the ground he's fighting on, where friendly and enemy units are. So yes, he was up front leading advance raiding forces. But his headquarter knew where he was and what was expected of them. His actions fed the overall mission. It was not just a personal quest for glory. If you think of Strauss and the three Oberstleutnant's as a team, it's functional."

Von Manstein sat there quietly, sipping the vile beverage and taking it all in. Made polite small talk about mutual acquaintances and relatives for five minutes, then sent the new Hauptmann on his way. This Strauss might prove to be of use.

1200 hours local; 1100 hours CET
8 October 1940
Brigade area, rear of Italian XXI Corps lines, northern end of Alamein positions

Mail call was a haphazard event. Most of the unit's mail came by pouch outside the normal military mails. The senior person in each new draft from Bari brought the sack of letters and parcels. This avoided the censor's office. Given the deceptions on Aryan status and general unusual nature of much of Brigade Strauss, that was probably all for the best.

Greta saw Klaus open an official-looking envelope and sadly shake his head. Anything about her man was part of her duties. Motioning her girls to hang back, she trotted over to him. Cloud cover took some of the edge off the stifling heat. Plus she was getting acclimated by now. "Klaus. Something bad from home?"

Her voice brought his focus back to here and now. "Just something silly. I signed up for the NL a few weeks short of school graduation. Seems that my Handelsschule got word of their graduate being a bit famous. The letter says they waived the last few weeks of the course and have awarded me my graduate certificate. I suppose it will help when I go looking for a job after demobilization." He laughed a bit. "We all should live that long! And the war has to eventually end. But for the war, I'd have spent the summer making the rounds trying to secure a job." He laughed again. He was visualizing putting "Battalion Commander" on his application. His kind usually were company clerks.

"Handelsschule?"

"It's a trade school, in this case for clericals. My folks were from the wear-a-tie-to-work class. Barely lower middle class. Both proud of it, and, at the same time, terrified of falling off that shelf back to the blue-collar world of their parents. Their great hope for me was a government job. Failing that, some big corporation like Krupp." Klaus ruefully shook his head again. The military were as big an institution as some government ministry, and bigger than Krupp. Yet somehow he didn't expect them to see it that way. His enlistment in the NL had been a tremendous disappointment to them. The few letters from 'home' had made that abundantly clear. Then they stopped answering, so he stopped writing. If an Iron Cross First Class and a promotion to Major didn't please them, nothing he did would.

Greta hesitated. She shouldn't be pushing him, but she was 18 and curious. "Oil fields need clerks and administrators. Will you be staying on at Kirkuk with us?"

"Do you want me to?"

She grabbed him behind his head and proceeded to say yes with her lips and tongue, ignoring the wolf-whistles and catcalls from the passers-by. When Klaus eventually came up for air, he had a big smile on his face. She was ready for another round, but he stammered something about needing to check in with Oberstleutnant Sommer. She blew him a big kiss and shook her hips a little at him. He loped off with a huge smile on his face. She motioned for Naiomi and the girls. When they joined her, the girlpack set off to find Uncle Isaac. This was important. Greta knew she needed to report in.

1230 hours local; 1130 hours CET
8 October 1940
Brigade HQ in rear of Italian XXI Corps

Klaus had briskly run to this meeting, trying to make up for lost time. He hated being late, the more so as he'd learned that the military version of 'on time' was fifteen minutes early. He started to stammer out an excuse, but Gunter waved him to silence. Gunter, Ivan Gorlov, Sommer, Peiper, and Di Salo were all there. There was one empty chair. Klaus could do that sort of fast math, and sat in the obvious place. Mary's foster son Abdul served him his coffee and withdrew back into the corner, squatting down on his heels to await any further needs of the clan lords, as he thought of them.

The Brigadier didn't seem angry at Klaus's late arrival. Then again, Gunter normally tended to a very even disposition. He never had to worry about physical dominance in any situation. That gave him the ability to be the alpha in the room, without any need for the usual macho stunts. "Klaus, Jochen, John, this meeting is to bring you three up to speed. We are reorganizing the unit. Kampfgruppe One will be Ivan's. Your three battalions. The fast troops. Kampfgruppe Two will be Isaak with the guns, and enough infantry as fusiliers for support. Kampfgruppe Three will be Gregor and Joey with the repair contingent and the administrative tail. The three of you have all worked together on these patrols you've been doing. We'll want to run some full exercises, so you get used to working together mounted. Ivan's had brigade command experience. Granted it was Russia a generation ago, but still … " Gunter let the sentence hang. He was looking around to see if any of the three being brought in had questions. All looked determined, not lost or upset.

After the pause had hung there long enough to be a de facto answer, Sommer took over. "I'll be detailing von Kleist-Konitz to you with an advance staff section. He desperately wants combat. Your group will be under the hammer enough even for an eager beaver like him. Of course, this all begs the question of what higher command wants us to do besides sit here, while the battle gets fought at the south end of the line."

Sommer looked over at his Brigade commander expectantly. There were obviously things he hadn't been told, either in Berlin or since his arrival. Schmidt/Smith was relaying messages that were commander's-eyes-only. Gunter gave him a level look. "Yes, I know things you don't. But parts of it are obvious. We have been made guardians of the financial warchest for rebuilding Alexandria. We are also being gifted with the naval experts who will supervise that. Neither makes sense unless we are also being tasked to that city. Now whether we are expected to seize it, or just follow behind as garrison … let's just say we are a bit small to storm a city that big … *if* it needs storming. Per Abwehr, the British don't have a combat garrison there. A lot of administrative and service troops, a good bit of police of various kinds, and some AAA guns. None of which matter without infantry. City fighting takes infantry. That sort of action is groundpounder hell. Now, presume that our foes don't detach some infantry to fall back there when the main line collapses. A fast group might just grab it before anything can be done. That's the best I can do for now."

The Ia did not look pacified, but he also didn't press the issue. Neither did Di Salo, although his face said he thought he was being given a snow job. He just asked, "Is that what you want the flame tanks for? I've been asking around. It's a good excuse to get you a dozen. We have them in theater, but no one sees any use for them. Can I swap a few rebuilt British trucks to get them?"

Gunter nodded yes, and the meeting wound down from there. He asked Klaus and Ivan to stay behind and sent everyone else on their way. "Get used to this. We will all be dancing around what we are doing in Alexandria. We have to fence the damned birds without our colleagues being any the wiser." Gunter thought Abdul's German wasn't good enough to follow what he said. He didn't want to run the risk of arousing suspicion of the others by sending the Arab out.

Di Salo had figured out that there was private business among the old Malta hands. Until it interfered with his Battalion, he simply didn't care. Peiper failed to twig. He was floating on air over having his status as a Battalion commander confirmed, even if his force at the moment was too weak to be a proper Battalion. Sommer knew there were layers he was excluded from. For now he was content to bide his time. He was still settling into his role in the unit. This was far too great a professional opportunity to ruin by being overly aggressive at this point. There was time enough later to get within the commander's inner circle as befitted the Ia.

Abdul waited till he was dismissed. His German was still quite basic. But his ears were young, and like many illiterates he had a memory trained to remember large chunks of spoken words. He would ask his new mother Mary what 'damned birds' were.

1900 hours local; 1800 hours CET
8 October 1940
Repairs bays, Brigade Strauss, rear of Italian XXI Corps lines

Normally Joey and Paul took light snacks instead of a big sit-down dinner. Their work schedule maximized daylight work hours. So it was a big breakfast before dawn, a good sized midday meal, a very light dinner; and a bit of finger food with a good stiff drink when they knocked off work, to aid in sleep and digestion. Plenty of coffee and snack packs throughout the day whenever there was a break. The work they did required both massive physical effort and deep thought. Today they had been converting three dysfunctional Matilda tanks into two workable ones. Obvious holes in the armor would just get welded patches which wouldn't really hold up to a proper AT round. However, they would run smoothly until knocked out. There was enough main gun ammo for at least one engagement, and essentially-unlimited machine-gun rounds. The British had thoughtfully used a copy of a Czech weapon based on the standard German rifle cartridge.

An hour ago Paul's brother Peter had pulled him away for something. Now Clara was telling Joey that he should assign tasks for the rest of the night, then come with her. They needed to change for a party. A party? In the Western Desert?

"Yes, dear. Major Steiner just got his school diploma in the mail. They waived his missing time because of his fine war record. Something about his example being an inspiration for everyone still in school there. Local HJ chapter's been renamed after him as well. The little Nazis are being indoctrinated to be worthy of the example of Klaus Steiner, Aryan superman." Her brittle laugh showed what she thought of THAT.

"So who is throwing a party?"

"His woman. Her Betar girls. His cook. Greta's family. Peiper will be there. Some Betar commissar named Begin. Di Salo and his whore. These are people whose good opinion will matter. The kids have a set of your civvies all cleaned and pressed for you. A fresh outfit for me. We do a quick spongebath to get the sweat off. You shave. I'll do a quick braiding for my hair. This is not some formal thing. But we will have a drink, toast him, and mingle."

"Huh?" Joey was not tracking Why did this social bovine feces matter to a guy like him? He was in with the big boss Gunter. Wasn't that enough?

Clara could read her man's mind. Then again, away from mechanical things, it was a fairly shallow river. "Yes, the Brigadier will be the big boss. He knows nothing of running an oil field. Greta's family knows oil fields. You want part of that work. People give work to their friends. I'll see to Greta. You just share a drink with the men and smile a bit."

Joey started to flare. He hated being bossed this way. She gave him a good hard kiss and a quite intimate stroke on his ass. He smiled in spite of himself. If she saw to these things, he didn't have to. He could talk welds and shock absorbers and stuff that mattered. So this was what marriage was like? His old man may have been right, damn him. It was high time to be thinking about a wife, only this Wanda had already found one for him. He'd have to ask her if she was willing to have kids herself. If he was going to become a captain of industry in Kirkuk, he'd want a few sons, to get a good one, worthy to inherit. He was laughing while he shaved. Maybe growing up wasn't so bad after all?

0200 hours CET
9 October, 1940
Café Wanda, Bari, Italy

The train had been the usual wartime chaos. More time spent on sidings or waiting in stations, than actual travel. The mother-in-law / daughter-in-law pair of Helena Witt and Kerstin Witt arrived at Bari exhausted, bewildered, and more than a bit terrified. Their menfolk had been conscripted by the heads of the SS for something strange in the African war. Their house was skillfully packed for storage by strangers. Ultimately for shipment to a new home somewhere at some time. Or perhaps this was all a polite cover for confiscation of their possessions? They themselves were shipped south with a Gestapo woman for a minder.

The cantonment area was vast and seemingly without coherent design. Yet their driver seemed to navigate the maze without incident. As the European air war was over, the camp was not under blackout. However, it lacked proper street lights, paved roads, or any form of visible traffic control. Vehicles were few, but drove on whichever side of the road suited the driver's whim. This had resulted in a few near-collisions. Now they had arrived at a well-lit two-story building. It appeared to be some sort of tavern, but the sounds of music and raucous partying suggested that perhaps it was a cabaret.

Once inside the two Frauen changed their judgment. It was obvious that this was a brothel. There were too many partially-clad young women for it to be anything else. So this was to be their fate? At their ages? How sad. A burly Major in SA uniform signed papers with the Gestapo lady, acknowledging the receipt of two Berlin women. He took the policewoman up to the bar to give her a drink on the house, calling out over his shoulder, "Oriana, take these two back to the office. Aunt Wanda and Frau Rachel are waiting for them."

The girlchild leading them seemed too young to be a working whore. She also wasn't dressed for it. After a few twists and turns through the building, which seemed to have been constructed in stages with no central plan, the ladies entered a brightly lit office. A robust young woman sat behind a big desk. She had a well-worn face and the arms of a manual laborer. There was a large safe behind her and file cabinets. A more mature lady was in an armchair. This one was clad in simple attire more suitable for a provincial bourgeois household, than a military cathouse.

The well-muscled young lady stood up, stuck her hand out to shake, and announced, "I'm Wanda. Glad you arrived safely. This is Frau Cohen. She will be getting you settled in."

"Cohen?" Kerstin Witt was doing the talking for her mortified mother-in-law.

"I go by Schwabe as well. Everyone here knows who the Jews are. Berlin simply seems to prefer we don't advertise it. That may change when we reach Palestine, but for now … "

"Palestine? You are Zionists?"

"No, dear. Refugees from Romania and Hungary. The locals there want no Jews, and are somewhat more violent about it than the Germans are."

More violent? The two Witts did not know what to make of this. "I presume, Frau Cohen Schwabe, that you are the madam. I'm not quite sure what's expected of us at our ages. I mean, we are scarcely blushing virgins, but … "

Wanda started to chuckle. It turned to raucous laughter as she had to struggle not to fall out of her chair. "Expected of you? Good Lord. What did they tell you you were being sent to?"

"A camp where we would be staying for some length of time."

Frau Rachel shook her head. "Ladies. A MILITARY camp. Not a prison camp. The building you are in houses the main unit offices, but it's a business we run, not the core of our existence. Mostly we are just families quartered here while our men are off at war. Your husband and sons are in Africa, with my husband and two of my three sons."

Each Witt woman gave a sigh of relief. "Then what is expected of us?"

Rachel explained, "For tonight, my daughters are arranging a temporary room for you. The parlor of our small house. We are building you two a simple dwelling, but need a few more days to complete it. Herr Witt has arranged for you two to draw a monthly stipend from his pay. This will take a week to set up, but I can advance you funds in the meantime. Take tomorrow to catch up on your sleep and begin to get accustomed to your new life. Day after, I'll meet you at the mess hall for breakfast, then take you around to get acquainted with the other ladies of note. Beyond that, if you have skills or hobbies please let us know. Some ladies teach. We have crafts workshops, card games, and lecture series held by the many here with educational credentials. You are on an enforced Italian vacation. The weather will be a mite warm by Berlin standards, but the food is decent in the cafeteria. With money, more variety can be had from the local markets. We send groups to shop a few times a week. Are either of you observant?"

Now the older woman spoke. "My daughter-in-law is Aryan. I'm the Jewess. We both worship Lutheran. Not every Sunday, but enough not to attract comment."

Wanda was now in her element. "Military have Lutheran, Evangelical, and Catholic chapels. I'll get you a guide for your first few trips. It's a healthy walk from here. A bit over a kilometer."

The Witt women were starting to relax. They were completely caught off guard by Wanda's next question. "Your men are in finance. Either of you have any experience in bookkeeping or money handling?"

Kerstin shook her head no, but mother-in-law Helena timidly said, "Yes. Before I was married, and as war work during the Kaiser's war. I also helped my husband. Before he died, he ran a small accounting business out of our flat. Why?"

"We have multiple businesses we run here. A lot of cash. I'm really needed in management, but I haven't got enough trustworthy people to do the accounts, the daily deposits and the rest. Your son and grandsons come highly recommended via both the Reichsführer's office in Berlin, and Brigade headquarters in Africa. Once you are settled in, would you consider a job?"

"You mean with the girls here?"

"Them. The bar. We also make whiskey and have workshops that make other things. Nothing you have to worry about in a legal sense. We are – shall we say – licensed by Berlin. The army administration of the cantonment is aware of this. No hiding, no police raids. Just business. Receipts, expenses, payroll. Same as any city shop."

The elder Frau smiled for the first time. Said she was sure she could teach her daughter-in-law. Within days, both women, settled into their tiny two-room house, were ensconced in camp life as if they had always been here. They had friends, jobs, and a place in society. They sent messages via pouch to their men. Now their only worry was that war would rob them of their guys.

1100 hours local; 1000 hours CET
9 October 1940
Gunter's Office, Brigade HQ, to the rear of Italian XXI Corps and the east of Bagush camp

Isaak knew he was in deep trouble as soon as he walked into the office. A midday summons, without a heads-up as to why, was unusual. The office having no one else there, not even a runner, was more so but still not a guarantee of disaster. The bottle of scotch on the desk was the proof, the veritable kiss of death. Gunter disliked this whiskey. He kept a bottle for important occasions only because he'd been told it was high status among real officers and important people in general. This bottle and two glasses was not a good sign.

Isaac liked Gunter … as far as that went. He was a decent boss. For a Nazi, he wasn't a rabid Jew-hater. He seemed almost indifferent to the 'Jewish Question' … or indeed to any of the usual Nazi racial phobias. That said, he was still the Nazi Party's voice here. Any non-Aryan was only a whim away from death or torture.

Isaak took the shot glass offered him. He sat in the seat the Brigadier indicated. He sipped the whisky after Gunter started drinking. He waited. There was nothing in particular Isaak had to feel guilt about, but … he was content to let the former SA officer start the conversation in his own good time …

"It's about Greta and Klaus."

What had the girl done now? She'd already gotten her parents and siblings killed. Was she about to send the rest of the family to their graves? "What has my niece done, or not done?" Isaak didn't flinch. This was Gunter's show.

The big man saw that he was not getting through. Isaak was never deliberately obtuse, or even evasive. Part of what made him such a pleasure to deal with. None of the usual bullshit games. "So the story about his propaganda interview hasn't made the rounds yet?" He watched Isaak's face very carefully. Gunter could read tells on most people. Isaak was not especially good at blank-face. The man didn't have a clue. "He told the German nation that when the campaign is over, he will have to ask

Greta's family for her hand. That he thinks they approve of him, but …"

Isaak got very still. He was consciously working on controlling his breathing, the actions of his limbs, everything. "What are Berlin's wishes on this? What are yours?"

"No response from Berlin yet. Mine are simple. I'm not an idiot." He again looked at the Jewish professional man before him for any sign that he had a clue. Nothing. "I know your family threw her at him." Now we could see Isaak getting flustered. It was small things, but it showed. Good. Meant he wasn't losing his touch. "It's not a criticism. If I'd wanted to break it up, I would have. I didn't. Boy was initially a mascot to me, a good luck charm on two legs. Even when the propaganda Dachshunds invented a fight with a fantasy Soviet partisan commissar, it was small change." He stopped to see if Isaak was following.

"And then came Luqa."

"And then came Luqa. He made my career. To an extent, he did the same for Rommel and Ramcke. I'm told Reichsführer Heydrich profited from it. And then your niece by accident makes him a Major." He saw Isaak start to panic further. "I believe it was an accident. She isn't a very good liar, and she's clueless on how the game of promotion and favors works. He gets bumped up to Battalion and he shines. No training, but he seems to be a natural in battle. Some people are. War's funny that way." He could see Isaak nodding a bit. The man was a veteran. Four years of real war. "So I've got to know now. Is she serious about him? Is your family?"

Isaak took a very deep breath. He was choosing his words quite carefully. Their lives rode on this turn of the dice. "Does she have a choice? Do we?"

"Good question. No easy answers. Berlin may warn us all off of this. The paperwork charade, about you all being Aryans, may be too tricky for them. Or they may be so locked into it by prior propaganda that it's easier to just keep them both far away from Germany. If tales spread from Iraq … so, they spread. There are always tales of dark, forbidden things happening in faraway places. Most people laugh at such minor gossip, but it has no force. How many laughed at stories that Hitler was part Jew? Heydrich? That Göring was a drug addict who wore women's clothes? There is always dirt out there. Some true. Some exaggerated. Some pure shit. Way of the world."

"Yes, we ordered her to be his mistress in Romania. We presumed he would find a woman. Most people in his position would have done so. He seemed to like her. Better our niece than a stranger. You saw a lucky charm. We saw the officer in charge of the airport, which is where we were. And we were wise to make the connection, as the new commander at Ploiesti wanted no Jews. We'd have been back at the mercy of the Iron Guards. No one envisioned the unit or Malta."

"And then Luqa. So here we are. He just got his diploma. Postwar he has the training to be a clerk, to train as an administrator. You'll take him into the family business?"

Isaak started to chuckle. It rose to near hysterical laughter. Gunter was looking at him strangely. "Take him?" Isaak drew some deep breaths, getting his laughter under control. "Would we take an Aryan to be our administrative head and deal with German officialdom? A decorated field officer who was a national hero? Think of it from our point of view, and answer your own question."

Gunter had never considered this from that side of the desk. He played with it in his head. He couldn't find a drawback from the Schwabe family point of view. "And your niece will go along with this?"

"She has terrible guilt about her family. She'll do it. It's not a love match, but she's fond of the boy, ready to find a husband, and very much enjoys his adoration. Her whole upbringing was geared to wife and mother, not to grand flights of romantic folly. I'll confirm it for you if you choose, but I already know the answer. We have been warning her that in the end, blood will tell. To not throw an emotional scene when he's ready to move on. She accepts that, but it distresses her. What about Berlin?"

"I'll make the decision of when to directly ask Berlin. In the meantime, you have twenty-four hours. If she wants out as soon as the fighting is over, I can keep him from formally asking. But when the break comes, she lets him down easily. That I insist on. Worth your lives if she doesn't." Gunter waited till he was sure the threat registered. "If not, I'll bring him by tomorrow night for a formal discussion. I'll expect both uncles and both cousins to be there. I'll bring a bottle of good French brandy, not this bitter English swill."

Gunter put out his huge hand and shook Isaak's vigorously. Damn, but in a way Klaus felt like kin to him right now.

1400 hours local; 1300 hours CET
9 October 1940
A small French coffee shop a bit away from the docks, in a neighborhood where the police patrol in threesomes, Alexandria

The Territorial Army colonel definitely did not feel safe arriving here. It was only three blocks from the somewhat better district, but in the manner of port-cities back to the days of the pharaohs, the back alleys ran downhill fast in terms of public order. The man was a bit past middle age and feeling his years. He'd always been a trifle shady, but since arriving in Egypt he had danced ever further into the darkness. Some bills were now coming due. He was being tailed by four large brutes to a meeting he was terrified to take, and scared spitless to duck.

He saw the man he was supposed to meet in the back. Lieutenant Commander James Money-Penny was a strikingly handsome young man, beginning a slow approach to middle age but still youthful. Money-Penny and the colonel served different nasty pashas in the Alexandria demimonde … until now.

Now the naval officer was beckoning the colonel towards his table. Was it towards a new future or towards his doom?

"I didn't tell you to kill her!"

"You also didn't tell me not to. You seem to think the Raj has much more time here than I do. We are gone by New Year's. Maybe sooner. I see you have the telegram." It lay on the table before them, even though the colonel hadn't mentioned what it said. "She's dead, and you are conveniently a continent away. Means you can marry at once. Which I suggest you do."

This was not the colonel's first dance into the shadows. He had parlayed his Great War service and medals into a match far over his head. He'd used the connections of his highborn wild-child slut of a wife to establish himself on the fringes of the City. Huge pots of liquid funds attract expediters of things where it is best not to leave a paper trail. He hadn't been the dirtiest, but 'clean' was so far in the past as to be memories of another lifetime.

He'd kept up his service connection via the Territorial Army. When the noose started tightening on one set of transactions the Inland Revenue Board was chasing, he'd fled to active service. He'd hoped for someplace further away, but in 1938 his choices were Cairo and Jerusalem. He'd had his fill of Sheenies in the City, and chose Cairo.

The investigation had died before it scooped him up. His estranged wife made sure she reminded him that this was due to her family's influence. She hadn't followed him to Cairo. She was content to continue her affairs and escapades without him. However, her debts did manage the journey to Egypt. Her family sopped up most but felt he could shoulder part of the load. On a colonel's salary quite impossible. So he had acquired other sources of income. One of those patrons had interests in conflict with Money-Penny's.

"You thought you were selling your guy out for proof for a divorce. Wouldn't have worked. Her family had too much on you. They didn't want any more of a scandal than her life had already been for them, back to seducing the chauffeur when she was ten."

"And the police will *accept* this as not being murder?"

"Of course not. She was killed in bed with another woman and a Colored rent boy. Very messy. The place was ransacked. Jewels and furs were stolen. Her family has arranged things. All three died from an unexploded bomb from that last German raid. So sad. You have your connections. I have mine." Money-Penny pulled a sheaf of documents out. The colonel started signing without reading. Arrest warrants. Search warrants. Orders for administrative confiscation of goods. If either the colonel's patron or the colonel were to fall ... well, a man had to look out for himself. Way of the world.

"About that new posting you hinted at ... "

Money-Penny showed him the papers but refused to hand them over. "Your posting to Malaya. Aide to a Sultan whose resident officer is an old associate of mine. Travel orders for yourself, your new bride, new family and retainers."

"How the deuce am I supposed to arrange travel in — "

"Here's the name of your ship. You and the in-laws get cabins. They are basic, but needs must. The rest get hammocks in crew space. You want better than crew slops, you pay off the captain to let your in-laws' cook staff do the honors for the trip, then pay out of your own pocket to stock the larder. Oh, and as a bit of an extra sweet, the customs people are going to be a tad sleepy and negligent if you come aboard on the overnight. Shift supervisor is a mate of mine. His family sailed for Ceylon two weeks back. You get the transfer and transit orders after we raid Yasir Pasha's villa — "

"About that, old boy." The colonel passed across the combination for the wall safe. Money-Penny looked expectantly. "Yes, I do expect to get paid extra for this, and more for what follows. You want to be at the villa yourself, and only with men you trust. You'll want big fellows like the four you had trail me here. The Big Guy's got this huge desk. Battleship steel, he claims. Not hardened like that, but big and heavy. There's a rug under it. Move the desk and roll up the carpet. Floor safe. A big one. Extends down into the floor below. There's a broom closet with a false back." The colonel slid across another combination. "This one your pasha doesn't know about." The colonel put up a hand. "Let's not squabble. You'll see what's there and pay me a just amount. Wedding is tomorrow evening. Just send a man by with a gift envelope. One gentleman to another. And thanks about Malaya. My little bride is a tad dusky for Singapore, but at a Rajah's court in Malaya, she's Christian enough for a man who will never go home to England. My ex-in-laws aren't stupid. They may have hated the bitch, but she was blood. Once home, I am sure some frightful but unfortunate accident would befall me. I'm for the Empire, especially its backwaters."

The colonel arose from the table and strolled out. Money-Penny gave a sign and the four large thugs fell in behind him, his escort back to officer's country. The colonel was humming "Land of Hope and Glory", as befit a Tory squire.

2300 hours local; 2200 hours CET
9 October 1940
Tents of the Schwabe family, Brigade bivouac, rear of Italian XXI corps lines

Greta was puzzled at the late-night summons. Her cousin Peter had fetched her for a 'family meeting'. When Greta's girls tried to follow her, Peter had shook his head no. Several would have contested the matter. Peter was too big for a physical confrontation, but an MP-38 is a respecter of neither size nor muscular strength. Greta waved them off. Peter was her cousin … sort of, but close enough that she simply ruled out putting a bullet through him. Besides, as 'Frau Steiner' she was untouchable to her family. Klaus was out on night maneuvers but … but he'd be back, and no one was going to harm his princess. His possessiveness gave her a feeling of safety.

Uncles Isaac and Ivan were waiting for her, along with Cousin Paul. The Schwabes had three adjacent tents, made into one big canvas structure. One small tent each for the two older and two younger men to sleep, and then a large tent as sort of living room. Greta was ushered into the big tent. There were two kerosene lamps, five mismatched chairs and a small table.

She seated herself at the indicated chair. Her Uncle Isaac as patriarch took charge. He offered her a glass of brandy. She waved it off. "Sorry, Uncle. I don't like drinking and Klaus doesn't like me drunk. We tried that once and swore off it. A little wine, sure. Maybe beer when we are someplace civilized, but the hard stuff isn't for us. We are simple people that way."

Isaac and Ivan looked at her carefully. The four men poured themselves double shots of the brandy. Paul found a semi-sweet Italian wine for her. They kept studying her, with Greta getting more and more uncomfortable. "What did I do now?"

Uncle Ivan did the talking this time. "Might you have forgotten to tell us something? A propaganda interview? Klaus telling the world he's going to ask us for your hand?"

"Oh. That."

Isaac cut in. "Yes. That! Anything about your man goes to me. Our lives ride on this."

Greta got offended. "You told me multiple times not to take his romantic gushing seriously, that in the end blood would tell."

"Gunter came to me. It's serious. Are you?"

Greta tried for petulant. What she managed was teen confusion. "You tell me I have no choice. I do what I am told. How do I have a choice now?"

"You may not. Berlin still hasn't given its opinion. If they don't interfere, what would you choose?"

Greta looked around the four male faces, trying to gauge the mood. "What do you want from me? You said 'give him what he wants'. I have. You said I'd be mistreated and I was to bear it. A woman's fate and all that. He's not that way. He sees it as love. It's probably infatuation and teen lust. I just enjoy his company. It's fun to be the Greta he thinks I am. Who wouldn't want to be thought beautiful and captivating?" She saw the four faces start to cloud. "Don't worry. My Betar girls keep my head from swelling. But he and I talk about after. That would be Iraq. He jokes that he'll ask you for a clerk's job as my dowry. Now that he has his diploma, he might actually be of use to you that way." She tossed her hair, awaiting them all calling her a stupid child or even a whore.

Her uncle tried for eye contact. She was avoiding it. "Yes or no? Do you want to be his wife?"

"If I have a choice, sure. He sometimes teases me, about going back to Germany and finding some blonde Amazon from the BDM. It's just teasing. He has taken the Romeo and Juliet propaganda to heart. He wants the fairytale ending. He knows it has to be Iraq. No way our fictional Aryan papers hold up in Germany." She weighed having to admit later that she'd held more back, and decided that blurting it all out would save her grief in the long run. "Means I'll have to convert. Mary the Cook found out somehow that he's Catholic. He says his family never took it seriously, but the girls feel me belonging to his Church will be safer for the children. If they are baptized, if we go to church on a few big holidays, we seem Aryan enough." She paused for breath. No one was saying anything. No one except Klaus and her girls ever took her this seriously. What on Earth was happening? "So do I get my dowry? Does Klaus get his job?"

Everyone started smiling, drinking, wishing her well. Greta was glad that they didn't press her. She had been Klaus's whore. Everyone knew. What decent man would have her now? It was Klaus or spinsterhood.

0400 hours local; 0300 hours CET
10 October 1940
Former Officer's Club, Bagsuh Camp

The exercise had ended roughly two hours ago. Klaus had maneuvered his battalion against Jochen's. The umpire had been Lieutenant Colonel Di Salo. Lothar Engels had brought a party of officers and senior NCO's from his new unit to observe and learn. Now they were doing the after-action critique. Di Salo was mostly criticizing Jochen's failures at night navigation. Klaus had tried tutoring him, but the SS officer seemed to have no intrinsic feel for it. Di Salo was now ready to discuss Klaus's unit. "Your SA armored car company did quite well. Where did you learn that trick of using them as your base of fire to maneuver around?"

"Just things I picked up on the last round of fighting. Our friend Lothar here trained them well. They can keep up with my wagons and motorcycles. They have better armor and heavier weapons. It just made sense to me to use them as the firepower we maneuver around." Klaus started stuttering here, fishing for a word. "Over something. Overwatch! If it goes wrong, they cover my lighter troops while we scoot back out of harm's way. Our job is spotting where the enemy is. There are heavier units to run him over. Tanks. Field artillery. That was how Rommel handled his boys and our main force when he knocked back that Western Desert whatever." Klaus was tired, and it showed.

One of Lothar's junior officers asked Klaus where he'd done his officer training. Did the NL have a regular training establishment or ... Klaus cut him off, wearily shaking his head. "Ours was the first NL unit committed to combat. Our core comes from the Ploiesti airfield garrison and a Militia that mobilized to fight with Rommel. We then went in as a glider unit during the Malta operation." Klaus stopped. He was blinking, straining to remember something. "Oh and there was a skirmish in Hungary when we were in transit. I've learned by doing. Hauptsturmführer Peiper has been giving me lessons. So have several other experienced officers. But mostly I learned in battle. Maybe when the campaign ends someone will send me for training and I'll discover why I've been doing it wrong the whole time."

The after-action went on. Klaus kept expecting harangues from Lothar and his band. He presumed they were SA. Most of the Afrika Division combat cadres were. Instead they just kept staring at him.

He was too young to comprehend that the looks were awe. In his own mind he remained Klaus, a rear rank HJ who at 17 was rated as having no leadership potential whatsoever.

1500 hours local; 1400 hours CET
10 October 1940
King David Hotel, Jerusalem, British Mandate of Palestine

There was an outdoor terrace bar that senior command had come to regard as their watering hole. General O'Connor, nominal G-O-C 9th Army, had hit on it as a place for senior staff conferences. His Army had three nominal corps. One was still working up in Australia with its first battalion in transit, nominally to Basra. The Iraqi Army was blocking Basra. So a new destination would have to be chosen, after which London and Canberra would squabble and the decision would be countermanded. It was a battalion of fairly raw recruits without much beyond WW1 rifles, so beyond symbolism it really didn't matter. Most of the corps was even less well prepared.

The Indian III Corps was supposed to be in Basra. Good luck with that. One division was trying to unload in Kuwait after being warned off Basra at gunpoint. The second division and the corps troops were still back at Bombay, waiting for someplace to be shipped to.

That left II New Zealand Corps, whose commander, Major General Freyberg, was here sipping a gin and tonic. Of course, the corps had one functional division, 2nd New Zealand, which Freyberg continued to command under a second hat. That left the fugitive Polish Carpathian Brigade and O'Connor's own old 7th Armored Division.

"Gentlemen." O'Connor focused on Freyberg. The Poles had sent a staff colonel. They were miffed … again. They had signed up to fight the Germans. Had qualms about fighting Italy as the Italians weren't at war with Poland, a state that no longer existed beyond an exile government in London and refugee military units like this brigade. Raised in Syria from Polish refugees and overseas Poles. Armed by the French, then expelled by them when Vichy dropped out of the war. Now fit to be tied, because London had shipped a brigade of them off to fight the French in Africa — as if they were mercenaries or colonials. The Pole would take notes and do jack-all without coded consultations with his London 'government'.

He gave a smile to his fellow designated scapegoat from the Western Desert, Major General Creagh. There was a little flag pin in London saying 7th Armored was here. It was. Or its division headquarters, its three brigade headquarters, and a few administrative elements, were. "Let us begin. The Iraqis have finally shown their hand. Warned us off at Basra. Ordered the RAF out of both bases. Besieged them so that any such retreat will be made disarmed, trusting to their good intentions. We can presume further moves will follow against British investments and persons. Delhi, Cairo, and London are dithering. I shall not. The issue, as ever, is whether I command any of you; or am I just your paymaster and rations clerk?" There, he had finally said it, finally put the poisoned fruit out for all to see.

The Jewish Agency representative, Moshe Sharett, was head of their pseudo-government's Political Department. "That depends. Your original plan was to abandon us all to the good intentions of the Nazis. If only Germans were coming we'd all want to leave — and have no trouble doing our share of the fighting to open a line of retreat. The Italians?" The Jew was choosing his words carefully. "Let us say some of us trust no one on that side; and some who are fools will fight for you here, but not run away to India. So which of your generals do we fight under?"

"Your split merits a simple answer. Those who leave probably go with the Poles … " O'Connor looked at the Polish officer, who glared at him but made no immediate reply. "Go send your coded messages. Either you are soldiers, or refugees."

"Poland is not at war with Iraq."

"Fine, you are refugees. General Freyberg, the first task of your division will be disarming the Poles."

"We'll fight."

"So you threaten war with Britain, but not Italy or Iraq?"

"What are you offering?"

"Right now I am feeding and paying you. I'm feeding your dependents as well. For what? You want a war against Germany on the Rhine. Sorry, but that war's lost. I'd gladly ship you off to Egypt and make you Wavell's problem, but as of last week you refused to go. So you take the Jews that want to leave. Probably some Arabs and Christians as well. You'll be renamed the Carpathian Division. Consider that a deception to mask the sudden increase in ration strength. When you get to India you can shed the extra people and go back to your fine principles. Now off with you. I've got real men to talk to about real things."

The Pole slammed down his glass and walked off to start the boring process of trying to get his London government to see reason. "The New Zealand Corps will march. Send a brigade at once, and the rest as you can. You'll get the Trans-Jordan Legion to bulk things up. You relieve RAF Habbaiya and await further orders." Freyberg started to speak, but O'Connor wanted to get it all out first. He motioned *stop* with his hand. "Yes, you can take all the local friends you want. You've got enough trucks. Yes, I know you have to clear it with home government. Ask them this: How do they propose to get you home, except through Iraq? Egypt will be gone in a few months." O'Connor saw the shocked faces. Pity he no longer cared. Flushing his career and command was the least of his problems. "The pause in the fighting now, it is pure logistics. Once the buildup is done, that line will collapse in a few weeks. Thin red line of heroes is great for the newsreels. In the grownup world it's artillery, tanks, and planes. The other side has them and we don't. It's just that simple."

The Jewish Agency man had a question. "What are our people who wish to stay to do?"

"Liaison with Major General Creagh here. You have soldiers or at least would-be soldiers. He has a set of command staffs and no troops. Consider yourselves married. The bigger issue is when do you mobilize. We all need the civilian economy here to function as long as possible so let's hold off on that. Sinai should protect us for a week or two. It's big enough. There aren't that many passes." O'Connor was asserting calmly what he personally believed to be bunkum. Birkenhead Drill. He had tens of thousands of British and Empire nationals to get out, and no safe route.

2000 hours local; 1900 hours CET
10 October 1940
Schwabe tents, Brigade Strauss area

Gunter had let Klaus sleep in after his night exercise. He got him up for a light supper, going over what was to happen tonight. Klaus seemed eager, and appeared to be quite happy that Greta's family had tentatively already given their approval. He repeatedly thanked Gunter for seeing to all this as, he admitted, he had not a clue as to how this all was done. His parents hadn't thought to train him in such yet. That was for later in their minds. He would get his diploma, a first job, a term in the Army, and then start a career. Marriage was for late 20's if successful, or early 30's more normally.

The story should have been closely guarded. It wasn't. Klaus got well-wishes from virtually everyone he met. Mary Collins had taken charge of getting the least filthy uniform for each man as clean as possible, pressed and presentable. Their best boots were shined to a gleam by her children.

His Greta seemed like a fairy princess to Klaus. Her Betar girls had washed her head to toe, provided her with clean civilian clothes borrowed from various girls' packs, and elaborately done her hair. There was no lipstick or makeup. No one had thought to bring any. Then again, Klaus was clueless. Besides, the Party youth movement encouraged the clean country-girl look. He stood at the doorway, swaying back and forth in delighted shock. Gunter had to guide him in, nudge him to shake hands around.

Instead of the 'upper class' scotch, which Gunter thought tasted like a cross between hospital medicine and industrial waste, he'd brought a bottle of aged French brandy, also stolen from British stocks on Malta. Everyone had a cup to toast the couple. Klaus and Greta choked on theirs but they swallowed. Isaak did the talking for the bride's family. "We have decided that the dowry will be the position of commercial director of our firm." He paused, to see if Gunter regarded that as sufficient.

The senior member of the groom's party gave a proper smile. Klaus started stuttering. "I'd hoped for a clerk's job. I haven't a clue as to what a commercial director does, much less how to do it."

"And six months ago you didn't know what a Leutnant did, much less a Major. We will make up a manual. We will buy a few books. Greta will tutor you. And yes, you'll make a few mistakes at first. I have faith that you will learn. You will be a valuable member of the family." Klaus blushed. Greta beamed. They were a Romeo and Juliet picture in a clean, wholesome way. The Reichsführer would have relished the propaganda photos had anyone been taking any. Didn't matter. The scene could always be staged again on command. Isaak was now focusing his attention on Gunter. "I've provided our wedding gift. Now I will ask one of you." Gunter looked perplexed and a bit put out. "Yes, it's not traditional for the bride's family to make demands, especially in such a 'special' situation. Nonetheless I will do so at the risk of your anger. We have discussed this, the four of us as both Greta's male protectors and as the working higher staff of our firm. Gunter, we wish you to sponsor our Klaus for Party membership."

Gunter was starting to understand. "The Aryan face of your firm would be more useful as a Party member. There's no Kreis office to register him at. We'll have to involve the Reichsführer's staff."

Isaak shrugged. "We are all his creatures. We live or die at his whim. I'll be technical director. Our Klaus need not learn the details on what we do. We would go as a team to get contracts. He would handle the social side, the personal interactions. A decorated officer and Party member ... "

And thus it came to pass that apolitical Klaus became a National Socialist Party member.

0800 hours local; 0700 hours CET
11 October 1940
Headquarters 'Special Night Squadron' Raiding Battalion, to the rear of what had once been 7th Division lines, north end of the Alamein position

Moshe Dayan had learned patience in British captivity. He had also learned how the British colonial world actually worked. Papers meant nothing. It was all name-dropping and personal connections. He had no military uniform, no official identification, no travel passes, nothing. He also hadn't tried to evade the responsible authorities. At the first roadblock on the way to the front, he'd hopped off the truck he had bummed a ride on, and strode confidently up to the NCO in charge. Had asked that Lieutenant Colonel Wingate be notified of his arrival. Had dropped the names of several field officers he'd been acquainted with.

He'd been under loose guard, provided with tea, biscuits, and a bench to doze on, until a lieutenant colonel had been sent to fetch him. No papers. The officer didn't even sign for him. The attitude of the troops was that if a field officer knew him, he fit into the khaki machine somewhere. Germans made war bureaucratically. British treated it all as amateur make-believe from their public school days.

On the drive, after the obligatory social reminiscing, the officer let on that he had a problem that needed Moshe's help. When they arrived at the headquarters, the two met the 'problem'. A Palestinian Jewish man, or so he claimed. Had one tattoo saying BETAR, and another one with a stylized palm tree. Man had been several days in the brig and had a story, one he told better in Yiddish, which the British officer didn't speak much of. "Dayan. You Haganah?" Moshe nodded. He wasn't exactly, but this wasn't the time or place. "I've been trying to tell these British. I was in 2nd Palestine Brigade. Captured on patrol. Three guys in German uniform come around to the prisoner compound, asking after Revisionists. Well it was hot, we were all thirsty, so I join the group."

Dayan gave a raised eyebrow. The problem kept talking. "I'm not one of them. Not really. If I'm anything I'm Labor, but who needs politics? Got an uncle and a cousin who swallow their line. I've argued with them enough so I know the talking points, know a few names to drop. Besides, the commissar in charge is from Poland. Doesn't recognize half the names from Palestine that guys were saying would vouch for them." The not-BETAR guy is desperately looking back and forth, hoping someone believes him this time. "They were recruiting. Some story that Palestine gets partitioned. Nazis get the north. Haifa and the oil pipeline. Galilee. Fascists get the rest."

Moshe is translating, and the British officer butts in. "How the bloody hell does some low-level officer know these sort of state secrets?"

"Dipped in shit if I know. This Nazi unit has a couple of thousand Betar. From all sorts of places in Europe. Even some camp complex in Poland."

The British officer was finding this level of knowledge incredible. "And I suppose you know where this camp is?"

"Somewhere around Cracow. Got approaching a million people. Some SS guy named Eichmann runs the show. Big factories making all sorts of stuff." He could see he was not being believed. This terrified him. "Look, I'm not smart enough to make this all up. They've got maps lying around with the zones marked out. Italians even have a piece set aside for the Pope. To join, they tattoo this stuff on you. If you run out on them and they catch you with this, they hang you. I've seen it. Hanging some men and shooting others out of hand. Had a chance to run when the work party I was with got scattered by some British tanks on a raid. It was our guys. I could hear them talking Yiddish. I signed up to fight Nazis, not fellow Jews. Just get me out of here back to Palestine. The big attack comes at the end of the month and I don't want to be here for it." The Palestinian was on the verge of hysteria. He wasn't going to be believed, and the thought of death unmanned him.

The British lieutenant colonel led Dayan out. "Crazy story. But he doesn't appear to be insane ... and there are the tatoos."

"Who is asking? The British Army or my old friends from the night patrols?"

The Britisher got VERY interested. "One friend to another … "

"Do I get papers letting me take him back? I have people above me who will want to ask him pointed, detailed questions. He saw more than he thinks he did … "

"So it's true?"

"True enough. We've had word. Through New York and Poland. Could be lies we are being fed, but why? We simply aren't important enough."

"I've got to pass this up the chain."

"I know. Not with my name. 'Highly placed source from the old patrols.' Partition, and they expect to be in Jerusalem in a few months. I was never here. There's no paper says I was."

"Were any of you ever going to tell us?"

"Colonial Office wouldn't believe a word we say. Neither would Cairo or London. Yet here I am, looking for Lieutenant Colonel Wingate. No papers. Just a social visit. We remember our friends, and you've been friends. You are losing this war − now − but Britain has come back from worse … "

"Your people send you?"

"It's complicated. Some think I'm a traitor, turned by you some time back. There's a lot of factionalism, and this turn of events isn't helping. They sent me to Egypt and guessed what I would do, is probably the best way to put it. If the Italians find out, I'm a traitor acting on his own in violation of orders. Probably hang me. Yet here I am. That should count for something, even if we do a Quisling when the Fascists arrive. Thousands of years, our people have survived. Means keeping a foot in many camps."

"What's the exact attack date?"

"We don't have it. But less than a month, is what we were led to believe. Jerusalem and Tel Aviv for New Year's Eve. How did you people mess this war up so badly?"

The British officer just wearily shook his head. He'd make up papers to get the line-crosser back to Palestine. He'd give his general a verbal briefing. Wingate was an old friend of Wavell. Maybe he'd get through the forest of official lies and convenient part-truths. Maybe the general would. Poor Britain.

1700 hours CET
11 October 1940
Prinz-Albrecht-Straße, Berlin

The Reichsführer hated surprises. Yet here was a surprise in three leading Berlin papers, concerning his little Klaus Steiner project. Schellenberg having failed to explain how this interview had not been passed through this headquarters for pre-approval, both were now interviewing a very frightened Hauptsturmführer. The man was a recent returnee from Hausser's Division in Africa, rotated back and on light duty from some strange regional disease. The officer was on limited duty, and shaking from trying to stand at attention without using his walking stick.

"Use the stick. Still better, sit down. I need you coherent while I decide whether to have you executed for incompetence. Why was this approved without involving either of us?" The Hauptsturmführer shakily took the indicated seat. "My predecessor briefed me that I was to keep these things off your desks. That you were too busy. I have two folders of such … "

Oberführer Schellenberg cut in. "Too busy? Since when?"

"Since you brushed off the correspondence between the Major and his parents."

"I said I was too busy that day." Schellenberg caught himself. The former aide had saluted and left, but had not returned the next day, or indeed any day. There were SO many balls to juggle. "My apologies, Reichsführer. It seems the fault is mine."

Heydrich wearily shook his head. There was so much to do, and however much more he managed, all it got him was still more work. The job of really being in charge was man-killing. "Correspondence?"

"His letters to his parents. Theirs to him. Other letters from his mayor, HJ leader, relatives, his sister … "

Heydrich wanted to scream. He didn't. It didn't fit his image which he had worked so long to develop. "Where are these letters?"

"In folders in my file cabinet. We have been sitting on all this since Romania. He's stopped writing. His last letter said that he saw no reason to write when they wouldn't bother to answer. His parents send monthly requests to what they call NL Headquarters asking if he's still alive … "

"Find yourself a BDM who can type and take dictation. Boil these down to harmless pleasantries and forward them marked 'simplified by military censors'. If a specific fact is in doubt, delete it and forward a memo to my office. Is this clear?"

"*Zu Befehl*, Reichsführer. So what do I do with today's request for him to be enrolled in the Party?"

"Party? Now? Why?"

The Hauptsturmführer was now on firm ground. "Leutnant Schmidt explained that in a separate message. It's part of the betrothal. His new in-laws will make him commercial director of their firm, but feel a Party member will be better received … "

"Firm? In-laws?" Heydrich was aware the girl was a Jewess he had made an Aryan by a wave of his hand. He must have been told who her people were, but all he remembered was that her parents and siblings had been liquidated for some reason. "What do they do?"

"Oil-field specialists of some sort. Two uncles, two male cousins in Africa, a third in Italy. There's also an aunt and four female cousins back at the Bari cantonment, along with most of the people from their firm and the similar ones."

Heydrich was almost afraid to ask. This diseased combat veteran seemed to be the only one who actually knew anything. Which meant his predecessor, now en route to Hausser's replacement battalion, had known these things all along. "How many oil-field specialists do we have at Bari?"

"My figures are probably out of date, Reichsführer. More keep being sent from Romania all the time. Standartenführer Ohlendorf keeps purging more undesirables from his work force. Slavs, Jews, Roma, foreigners of all sorts. We have several thousand at least. Then there are the ones from Hungary, where … "

"Hungary?"

"This Brigadier Strauss had an encounter with the Arrow Cross, and left a garrison which keeps accumulating refugees fleeing the chaos. A few were oil-field workers. One wrote back from Bari and now they are appearing in mass lots, begging transport to Bari so they can work in the new oil fields."

"The new oil fields? Didn't anyone tell these people that Iraq was a state secret?" Heydrich answered his own question as he asked it. He turned his attention back to Schellenberg. "Standartenführer Ohlendorf is still making excuses for the falloff in production at Ploiesti?" The

Oberführer nodded. "And all that time, he is purging his work force of non-Aryans who sit eating rations in Italy instead of getting oil out of the ground? Send a plane for the man. He is on my schedule for tomorrow." Heydrich turned back to the by-now totally terrified Hauptsturmführer. "From now on, ANYTHING concerning that unit is to be presented in writing to the Oberführer's secretary, preferably on the day it is received. Start numbering and dating these. Keep a log book and get signed receipts. You are not in trouble. You seem to be the only person in this building actually doing his job. Your predecessor will get some interesting annotations to his personnel file for failing to do his. Dismissed!"

The sick officer was out of his chair almost instantly. He saluted both superiors, and fled as fast as he could hobble. Heydrich turned on the desk voicebox and alerted his aide at the desk right outside his office, "Close the door. Hold all calls unless it's the Führer or Soviet ambassador."

"Soviet ambassador?" Schellenberg needed to be in the loop on whatever concerned his patron.

"They will declare war, and it will be at an inconvenient moment. Now back to fixing this mess. Ohlendorf is out for the oil fields. Find one of Speer's technocrats. Get with the transport office. The cousin-in-law back in Italy is to lead a special train of technicians back to Romania. Give him blanket authority to recruit. Jews, blacks, baboons, it doesn't matter. The oil flows. Have Eichmann canvas his camps for technicians. This is a national priority. Now these in-laws are hereby real Aryans. Your shop up at Ravensbrück. You get every one of them full certificates back to the 15th century. Make it all from towns in Poland and Romania, behind Soviet lines. That way no one can do a trip to the records office and embarrass us. Final question: did anyone prime this boy with his answers? He seems very polished for an 18-year-old."

Schellenberg thought quickly. "I'm sure Strauss held his hand and prettied it up, but my man Schmidt says the boy was taught polite adult speech as part of his school course. He wanted to be a ministry or cartel clerk. Being well-spoken is necessary in such situations. He cannot do fancy rhetoric, but his everyday speech is a bit above his age and class."

Heydrich was ignoring Schellenberg, staring out the window. He was thinking of months of lost oil production, and Stalin's show trials against Wreckers. Perhaps he would ask Beria for details of how to organize such. It was a most pleasant set of thoughts.

1100 hours CET
12 October 1940
Villa Mineux, Am Grossen Wannsee, Greater Berlin

The SS-owned villa was packed with representatives of the various ministries, Reich protectorates, and party organs. The conference on the Jewish Question was supposed to have been at the level of deputies and assistants. At the proverbial last minute, the two Army generals had announced they would attend themselves. This forced Reichsführer Heydrich to do the same. Normally Führer Göring avoided such visible displays of his formal powers. Which of his two females had persuaded him otherwise was unknown. But he had just arrived to the event.

As the invitation had clearly said 0700 hours, he was late. He had missed Eichmann's multi-hour presentation followed by round-robin bickering and turf defenses from the other bureaucracies. The Führer ambled in, thereby momentarily stopping a pissing match between the Finance Ministry and the General Government on the allocation of funds for barge repairs on the Vistula. The 'highest leader' was visibly hung over from a diplomatic gala the previous evening. He was surrounded by an entourage of fawning flunkies. When he motioned for the discussion to resume, both officials tried to talk at once. Embarrassed, they both stopped, thereby giving the man from the Transportation Ministry a chance to assert his organization's point of view. This in turn prompted near simultaneous objections from Organization Todt and the Party's Labor Front.

Göring's flunkies were too busy laughing at some witticism of his to notice. Generaloberst and War Minister Beck was not. He had had enough. "Quiet! All lesser minions out! The four of us will have a meeting, and then you staff people can go back to your children's playground antics."

Beck was mortified that the assembled officials all looking to Heydrich for their cues. The Reichsführer just nodded and waved them out. Without a word, they gathered binders, briefing papers, and aides, filing out in a disorganized gaggle. Göring's flunkies remained with him. Beck glared at the useless fools. Göring gave him a withering look and laughed at him. "I am still Führer. I'll keep who I wish here. If you don't like that you can leave, and we'll inform you of what was decided."

"You rule by our leave."

"That was June. This is now. Order the Berlin garrison to arrest us all, and see where it leads. You have a plan to upgrade the Gross Deutschland Regiment into a division. So far it's a four-battalion regiment out in the suburbs with a fifth battalion doing honorary guard duty downtown. When was the last time you went to the officer's mess and did a dinner? Had drinks with them?"

"I am Generaloberst! The Army obeys commands!"

"Issue the order and find out. I dare you." Göring no longer looked bored. This contest brought out his fighting spirit. He had spent four months building personal loyalties. He was the monarch the power holders knew. Heydrich had been a genius with this. Göring was prepared to admit this to himself.

Generaloberst Halder saw this heading places he did not wish to go. "Gentlemen. Please. Manners. Our committee rules the Reich. We are here to discuss Jewish policy. Reichsführer, why are we bombarded with trivia?"

Heydrich's smile was sardonic. "Because this was supposed to be a working meeting of lower-echelon people to coordinate action across vast competing bureaucracies – most of whom have some connection with Jewish policy, but none of whom really understand it."

"So what is that policy they don't understand?"

"The one I negotiated with you two the night of the coup. Yes, coup. It's just the four of us here. Let us call things what they really are." Heydrich ignored Göring's pets. They didn't matter. If necessary he could liquidate them all.   "You two were squeamish about the Party's policy towards the Jews. Which is funny, because we really didn't have one. We didn't have a firm policy towards anything. We had a self-contradictory electoral program, which we abolished when we shot Röhm at the Army's insistence and gave up on the Second Revolution. Everything after that was bureaucratic gamesmanship and a push for rearmament." He looked around the table to see if anyone was following him. No. Heydrich had a didactic side. He worked on controlling it, but apparently his colleagues needed him to state the obvious. "We are ruling Germany today because our late Führer had an obsession with faddish vegetarian diets. Couldn't digest the stuff. Endless problems with flatulence and intestinal pain. That led to quack doctors, drugs of dubious provenance, and various homeopathic poisons. Some combination of which killed him. Exit Adolph and enter us." They were nodding a bit. Just needed to be led along. "Now Adolph hated the Jews. So did enough Germans for it be electorally useful. No firm policy. Expel them from society. Beatings for some, a little time in camps for others.

Steal their money and property, then get miffed when no other nation would take in impoverished Jews. Even with that, we'd dumped a good many of our original ones. Except the victories kept giving us more, especially in Poland. These didn't need to be made impoverished. They mostly already were. We could just have shot them all. The Army objected, and the killings stopped after a few months."

Beck exploded again. "The German state is not a bunch of gangsters! Mass murder ruins discipline."

"As you will. So we have millions of them. Whom you don't want machine-gunned. I got their rich American kinsmen to feed them. Think of the food as a tax on Hollywood movie tickets, on Wall Street plunderings. Our state is making a profit on the ghettoes and camps. However, why should we let these millions sit there eating when we can work them?"

Halder was frankly curious. "Why work them there? We have factories in the Reich that need labor."

"Think it through. Our people never liked Jews. Even the ones who tolerated assimilated German Jews, despised the Yiddish-speaking Eastern Jews. What will the social and political effect be if we push masses of these Yids into German cities? We will estrange our Party members and the masses. So I did it in reverse. We have enough German labor, if it's all forced into war production. The Gauleiters fought closing down German civilian production. Standard of living. Connections. Enough small businessmen being Party members. So those small operators now move their production of table lamps and ten thousand other civilian soft goods to Eichmann's Palestine workshops. The SS earns a profit on the labor. The German workers who no longer make children's stockings and lip gloss, can be the second shift at Krupp or the third at Porsche. The very religious Jews, the elders, the orphans, the recalcitrant we dump on the Italians. They are more socialist, less racist than we are. They seem to get some work out of enough of them. For the rest of them ... think of the surplus Jews, clergy, and gypsies they take as Italy's price of Empire. The last war cost them endless casualties fighting Austria. Over a million dead, however you do the math. Compared to those oceans of blood, taking in a few million useless mouths who can be harvest labor is cheaper. Everyone wins."

Beck returned to the issue that had enraged him. "Why shoot an officer over 'command authority'? IT WAS MURDER!"

"It was murder because command authority was usurped. What if we change our minds and give an order to liquidate a ghetto? All the ghettoes? How does a field officer respond to those orders, once we have treated this time as murder? They raise questions. They insist on courts, on verification. No. We want them to obey. If the order is to transport Jews, follow the order. If the order is to slaughter a thousand Jews and then butcher the bodies as food for hogs to feed Germany, obey."

"That is gross! Hideous! No decent man could obey that order!" Beck was near beside himself.

"No decent Army officer. My SS will obey. They will not question. We are a revolutionary regime in a war of national survival. There are no limits. The stakes are victory or death. When Stalin attacks, we either win or we all go to the wall. So do our families down to third cousins twice removed. Are you really that unworldly? When YOUR KIND sent Lenin by that sealed train, you unleashed Hell on Earth. You did that for a transitory tactical advantage. Russia collapsed a few months earlier than otherwise, and you gentlemen still managed to lose the war anyway by dragging in the Americans. Which we will not do this time. There is no possible American provocation such that I will rise to their bait. You have all stated conditions on this committee. Meet one of mine. No war with America, unless they motivate themselves to declare it on us."

Beck started screaming about how Heydrich worked for them, not with them. Göring shouted him down. "Shut up! I'm calling for a vote. All those in favor of Heydrich's Jewish policy." Three hands went up. "All in favor of Heydrich's American policy." Three hands went up. "Meeting adjourned!" Göring got up without shaking hands, and walked out to his stretch-limousine, trailed by his silent, pensive flunkies. They had seen more than was safe, and worried about their life expectancy.

2300 hours CET
12 October, 1940
Heydrich's Office, Prinz-Albrecht-Straße, Berlin

Standartenführer Ohlendorf had known he was in trouble when the plane arrived with the peremptory summons back to Berlin. He had spent the flight and the long hours after arrival marshaling his defense. It centered on one key instruction, which he was now about to repeat back to his judges, Reichsführer Heydrich and Oberführer Schellenberg. This was not a formal court. It was a trial. Ohlendorf was on trial for his life. "Sirs, when I was sent to the oil fields, my prime directive was their security. I take over from that overpromoted SA idiot Strauss, and he tries to downplay his incompetence. He passes off an attack on the facilities as a demonstration by otherwise friendly local elements, the Iron Guard. That was obviously absurd on its face. Leutnant Steiner doesn't get the Iron Cross for stopping a riot and preventing a lynching. So anyone connected to Strauss was suspect in my eyes. This is confirmed a few days later when the real story is broadcast from Berlin. It was a major Red partisan assault. Everyone working there who denies this must be in league with hostile elements. Even those of nominal German blood must have acquired foreign loyalties. The Soviets are only a few days march away. The partisan remnants are likely hiding in the immediate vicinity of my facilities, awaiting the order to strike. So I've brought in fresh personnel. Broken any possible ties to the saboteurs and Communists. I know this has led to some production falloff, but it's transitory. Give me another three or four months, and my new people will be exceeding quotas." There. He'd gotten it all out. Why were they looking at him this way? Was he the designated goat in some larger internal SS power play?

"Please wait outside. I must confer with the Oberführer for a few minutes." Ohlendorf gave a proper salute and marched himself back to the waiting room, carefully closing the door behind him while reviewing whether he was really as prepared for death as he liked to pretend he was. Heydrich saw him go and turned to Schellenberg. "So my alter ego, how do we find some excuse for his dismissal that doesn't shine a light on the entire mess?"

"It's really simple, Reichsführer. Never explain. Tell him he seems not suited for oil fields. That he will be given a chance to redeem himself in the manner that Müller has with the General Government."

"Italy. Send him to Obergruppenführer Wolff. Wolff can show him around Rome and then take him to someplace in the north. Have Standartenfueher Ohlendorf head an Italo-German industrial council to coordinate production."

"Where? Milan? Turin?"

"Verona. That English playwright did a famous work on that one. It must have some culture, which will make our visiting industrial people happy. In reverse, a smaller city will welcome the added business from conferences and offices."

0600 hours local and CET

13 October 1940
Skies over Kano, British Northern Nigeria

At twelve hundred meters the air was bracingly cold as the French parachutists jumped out the door of the Potez 540 and hit the silk. The heat would come as they floated down towards the dusty plains around the city. In the low to mid 20's so close to dawn, rising to the mid to high 30's by early afternoon.

Sous Lieutenant Marcel Bigeard had been first out of his plane. Officers led the way. It was how the Germans had trained them during their abbreviated cycle. It was how French elite units behaved even without Boche instructors. The newly minted Sixth Colonial Parachute Battalion saw itself as an elite unit, and was about to demonstrate this to a wider world.

That said, there were only enough planes to drop two companies of the battalion today. Three hundred men to take a medium-sized city with a garrison of unknown size. The French had surprise, and the British at best had a garrison of colonial police. That contingent had supposedly mostly been sent to Kenya. After the campaign in France, Bigeard did not have a high opinion of French intelligence analysis. Right now he just reveled in the feeling of power that came with landing from the air like gods.

1500 hours local; 1400 hours CET
13 October 1940
Port of Monrovia, Liberia

Pursuant to a US declaration of protectorate status for the Republic of Liberia, the destroyer USS *Hatfield* landed a small party of Fleet Marines and sailors who paraded through the streets to the US embassy. From Washington, General George Marshal announced that a provisional brigade consisting of the US 24th and 25th Infantry Regiments, two historic Buffalo Soldier units, would be sent as shipping became available. The Navy Department announced that mixed battalions of US Marines and locally trained forces from Haiti, the Dominican Republic, Nicaragua, Panama, and Cuba would do likewise. The US consulates in those nations were besieged by volunteers as word spread that the men would be paid as if they were US forces, rather than at prevailing local wages.

0800 hours Eastern Daylight Time; 1400 hours CET
14 October 1940
Oval Office, White House, Washington DC

FDR was briefly back in town. Supposedly to sign legislation. In fact to rest up after a medical incident on the campaign trail. His personal physician had assured everyone in the President's political family that it hadn't actually been a heart attack. It was just an 'incident'. An 'incident' of extreme chest pain and loss of consciousness. The traveling staff had hushed this up. The official excuse was food poisoning.

Franklin didn't take orders well. Bed rest had been brushed aside. Hopkins had him on a light schedule of glad-handing from his desk. That left time for the two to chat. Hopkins was using that time to bring the legal chief executive up to date on what the acting President had been doing in his absence.

"Why did we do this thing in Liberia?"

"Because Willkie was about to demand it. Without Negro votes you will lose New York and New Jersey."

"What about Illinois?" Roosevelt knew Chicago had a huge Bronze Town.

Hopkins wearily shook his head. "Franklin, Illinois is gone. I've got Truman whistle-stopping down by Cairo, to hide our hand. Maybe we can save a few House seats. Maybe the Republicans will waste money seriously campaigning there. I keep telling you, this is going to be as close as Wilson in 1916." Wilson had been FDR's patron to higher office. He went to sleep on election night defeated, and woke up reelected as California had switched sides while the East Coast slept. The newspapers had had endless fun lambasting the Republican 'President -elect' who in fact wasn't elected anything. "You are living in a dream world and your wife, while an excellent campaigner, is adding to the fantasy. By all means keep her beating the drum on the left. It minimizes your losses there. The election will be decided in the center. By the people who don't like Nazis but don't want war. By people who hate the Republicans for Hoover's Depression, but whose fingers are still burned by yours. The NAACP and the Negro press got it in their heads that this new Franco-British war menaced the last independent African state. Forget that 98% of their readers couldn't find Liberia on a map. It became a symbol of white men screwing Colored men. The whole 'nation of freed slaves' myth. So we send a few black soldiers, establish an air base, and keep those votes."

Franklin grumbled a bit, then went on to his real peeve. "Truman. Yes, yes, the little bankrupt haberdasher can campaign in cow towns. But I had him to dinner one night in St. Louis. He's a provincial boor. He's Babbitt come to life. Couldn't you find me a Truman with an Ivy League education, who can converse like a gentleman?"

"You found Wallace. He would have sunk you."

"Yes, but wasn't there a better compromise?"

"Had you given us two years to canvas, probably. You danced on whether you were running at all. Made a game out of it. Then committed at the last second and threw Wallace at us. Even then it would have worked, had that little fairy Hoover just kept his mouth shut."

"Can't we just fire him?"

Hopkins felt as weary as FDR looked, only his ailments were in the gut, not heart. His felt like the molten core of the planet. "You know you can. And you know what it will cost. He has enough dirt to make you wish you really had retired with one of your lady friends to write detective novels. If you want to be really modern, you can have him killed. Frank Hague has the right gangster connections. I'm sure a few others do as well. Of course, whoever we give the job to will then be a bigger threat. Plus we don't know who he's hidden copies of the worst stuff with. All it takes is one set of copies reaching the *Chicago Tribune*. They will publish every word without fact checking a thing. You are stuck with the odious little toad." Hopkins was ready to die for the ideals of Progress. Why did Franklin have to make it so hard?

Hopkins' digestive tract was saved by an aide announcing the next appointment. Joe Kennedy, come to kiss the ring and try to get some plum assignment for one of his sons.

1300 hours Eastern Daylight Time; 1900 hours CET
14 October 1940

Executive Office Building, Washington DC

It had once housed the departments of War, Navy and State. Now it had various offshoots of the ever-growing office of the President. Harry Hopkins kept a suite there for meetings that were best not on the front page of the Washington dailies. Tom Dewey was down from New York to see him. Nominally, Manhattan District Attorney Tom Dewey was in town to meet Harry Hopkins about matters connected to the campaign against the US Communist Party and its many fronts and affiliates. These were especially strong in New York City, a longstanding hotbed of radicalism based in the various immigrant communities. Their aides had prepared a press release that was both accurate and nebulous. Accurate in that the listed things had been agreed to. Nebulous because it was not what today's meeting was about.

Dewey was representative today for the established moneyed interests who in fact ran the national Republican Party. Willkie was not precisely their creature, but he had been a convenient foil against the mid-American isolationist reactionaries under Taft. Events now required cooperation that Willkie could not be seen giving less than a month before a Presidential election.

"Nice of you to see me on short notice, Harry. Kudos on getting ahead of us on Liberia, but … "

"But now we have to regularize this ad hoc mess?"

"Yes. I've made the calls. The resolutions our staffs discussed will get the majority of the Republican votes in the House and Senate. They've talked to your leadership. Joint whip counts will give comfortable margins." Dewey was his usual confident self.

Hopkins looked over the documents. Joint resolutions of both Houses retroactively approving policy in China and Liberia. The President was authorized to spend money, raise troops, and construct installations subject to a one-house veto. A second resolution proclaimed that the Atlantic and Pacific Oceans constituted the defense borders of the United States, authorizing the President to take such actions as were necessary to bar access to either body of water by forces hostile to the United States. There were three statehood bills, making Alaska, Hawaii, and Puerto Rico states on New Year's Day. Quite soon, but avoiding the chaos of interjecting them into the ongoing elections. The Virgin Islands were linked to Puerto Rico, and the various US Pacific islands out to Guam and Samoa made part of Hawaii. A quite detailed statute barred the use of selective service draftees outside the United States and its defense oceans without express prior Congressional approval. The Immigration Act of 1924 was suspended in its provisions as regards Ireland. The US Communists, Nazis, and their allies were all made illegal. Hopkins saw one thing was missing. "Tom?"

"They couldn't jam Lend-Lease through as part of this package. It's just too raw. They'll start hearings, but that one is for the lame duck session." He saw Hopkins give him a withering look. "We tried. Had bankers and brokers doing calls to key people threatening credit lines, loan rollovers, and the like. You and I are going to need a lot of mineral oil to sooth a lot of very bruised assholes. I promised magic, and this is all pretty magical."

Hopkins outright laughed at him. "You are running an interventionist liberal stooge who is pretending to be a braindead isolationist to get elected. You want as much of this done before he takes office as possible. That's why you threw me the bone on the Irish. Unlimited entry of Papist Irish helps me, not you."

Dewey was an excellent attorney and a professional negotiator. "So just between us, you are conceding that my man Willkie has this?"

"I'll tell you what I have been telling Franklin. It's too damned close to call." Hopkins took a deep breath. Dewey needed him to take the heat on this, but the reverse was true as well. All this done bipartisan wouldn't move the voters who thought the *Chicago Tribune* and its ilk had a direct line to Jesus. It *would* matter to the swing voters who would decide this election. They loved the prosperity of the war boom, but didn't want their sons dead defending the British Empire. "Can your Wall Street people deliver the British on this? If they trumpet to the London press that this is all back door intervention, it could sink us all."

Dewey wasn't stupid enough to make promises he had no power to keep. "We'll do our best. Bevin isn't exactly from the circles they move in. I've got a dozen people over on the Pan Am clipper to Dublin tomorrow. We didn't send telegrams. Remember Zimmermann's in 1917? Any telegram can be stolen, decoded. Face to face, and quiet talks over drinks. The majority in Commons is still Tory. My guys' contacts in the City of London still have a lot of power."

The meeting had fewer ending pleasantries than usual. Both men were busy. Congress was doing an emergency late-night session to debate the 'national defense emergency'. The House approved the package just before midnight by a vote of 230-200. The Senate kept talking till near dawn before voting likewise 50-46. The banner headline on the next morning's *Chicago Tribune* had one word: TREASON!

0800 hours local; 0100 hours CET

15 October 1940

100 meters in front of Aztec trenches. 2km from the Chinese Eastern RR and 150 km from the original Soviet border

They had marched three days to arrive here. The Aztecs, Spanish Republicans, and a force of German comrades. They had driven the mules carrying the machine-guns and mortars while carrying their own food and ammunition. General Kleber, one of the heroes of the Battle of Madrid against the Fascists, was leading them. The commissars had promised that they were behind the main Japanese defenses.

Sadly, that was wrong. They arrived to see a double line of Japanese trenches with pill-box strong points as far as the eye could see. The orders were to attack here. Orders could not be contradicted by facts. They had spent the night digging a pitiful support trench, emplacing their heavy weapons there. The commissars had them up before dawn. Ignoring the fierce freezing winds of this plain, at what to Alexander Ruz from the tropics was the chilly gates of Hell, they got a cold breakfast plus some bad coffee. Alexander thought these Soviet comrades had no idea of how to brew coffee. That task should have been left to Cubans, or even Mexicans.

The general attacked first with the Spanish. His NKVD minders stayed in the trench, probably to direct the mortars. Revolver in hand, screaming revolutionary slogans, Kleber ran forward at the head of his men. Half never even made it out of the trench before being blown back by Japanese automatic weapons fire. The general himself lasted a good sixty meters before getting nearly cut in half by a Japanese heavy machine-gun.

Alexander charged with the second wave, the Aztecs. They managed to get further than the Spaniards. Some of them reached a hundred and twenty meters, nearly halfway to the enemy. Alexander was waving the Cuban flag as he ran. Massed Japanese fire destroyed the flag pole, spinning him to the ground. He lay there, hiding behind a mostly dead body, panting and trying not to cry.

The German comrades came last. They came in short rushes. None got close enough to the

Japanese positions to use their grenades. A German lad went to ground beside him. He bandaged the wound Alexander hadn't realized he had. This companion had kind eyes, and held Alexander while he wept. There was nothing else to do but lie there, chatting, till darkness came and they could crawl back to their trench. The German was seventeen, almost a man. Said his name was Markus Wolf. Alexander felt the bond growing between them allowed for sharing his real name, Fidel Castro.

After dark they crawled back to the trench. Fidel had the remains of the Cuban flag. Markus had retrieved the general's revolver. New comrades had arrived. French and Jewish. The commissars said they would attack again in the morning. The two boys slept what few hours of dark remained, together under a blanket. Fidel felt secure in Markus's arms.

0800 hours local; 0600 hours CET
15 October 1940
Baghdad, Iraq

The smoke from last night's pogrom still hung heavy over the city. David Baghdadi was safe at the villa of a prominent Sunni. So was his extended family, and clients of his blood and linked business affairs. The world was in a modern age, but Mesopotamia still ran on feudal logic.

David had paid off several prominent Sunni men of business and politics, as well as a few dozen Army and police officials. There had been reliable guards on his properties. The dead, the maimed, the raped had been mostly those without protectors. Mostly Jews, but some Christians and British; even a few Sunni Arabs who had been too friendly to the crown. The royal family had escaped with its retainers to the nearby RAF base. The officers of the Golden Square ruled, with one Rashid Ali at its head.

Ruled … for now. The British had troops in Kuwait, and more coming from Palestine. Rashid Ali had tried to ally with Italy and Germany. Neither had forces currently placed to aid him. The Italian ambassador had been cordial. The German had been indifferent. This did not bode well for the new regime. Strange stories were coming out of Palestine. It was the Germans who were coming here to Iraq, not the Italians. His host had even heard rumors that the Germans were bringing some Jewish mercenaries. Something called Betar. His host wished David to have coffee with him to discuss this possible turn of events. David knew nothing, but being enigmatic in a negotiation was second nature to a mercantile family head.

1300 Hours CET
15 October 1940
Reichsluftfahrtministerium (Reich Air Ministry), Berlin

In a moment of mordant humor General Der Flieger Wilhelm Wimmer, once again Generalluftzeugmeister (Luftwaffe Director-General of Equipment), contemplated the National Socialist obsession with massive architecture. The Reichsluftfahrtministerium was the largest office building in Europe, at 2,800 rooms home to thousands of bureaucrats and their secretaries. Göring had the building erected in a mere 18 months to house his personal ministerial empire. At the time, Wimmer assumed the building was another example of an attempt to compensate for the deep-seated inferiority complex that gripped so many of the National Socialists. Today, with so much of not just

Reich but also Europa business being run out of the building, there was use for the concrete and steel monstrosity.

The right hand of Heydrich, Oberführer Schellenberg, was in the building to be briefed on Luftwaffe attempts to rationalize their production and development programs. One of the many meeting rooms was filled with Luftwaffe officers, Air and Armaments Ministries bureaucrats, and Schellenberg with his aide. General Otto Hoffmann had begun the briefing, leading off with the Luftwaffe's presentation.

Hoffmann was a Great War veteran, returned to the colors in the 1930's but too old for a flying placement. The thrust of his presentation was: currently, Germany was building seventeen major types of aircraft and a bewildering array of sub-types. Observation aircraft, single- and twin-engine fighters, bombers, attack aircraft ... the list went on and on. The SS man had attended enough of these meetings to no longer be surprised at the lack of focus in war production and development.

Hoffmann completed his summation, then looked meaningfully at Wimmer. His superior rose to speak. "Gentlemen, currently we are building three different twin-engine bombers, the Ju-88, He-111, and we have just started building the Do-217. The General-feldmarschall wants this reduced to one as soon as practical." Wimmer leaned forward, locking eyes with several of the men in the room.

The men the Generalluftzeugmeister took under his gaze knew why they were the subject of his attention. There had been rumors for several weeks that this directive was coming. The various aircraft firms had been using their contacts to try to get details on it, so they could take action to make sure their design was kept. Which was exactly why Wimmer wanted this discussion to not degenerate into a pissing contest between the oversized egos of firm directors. Not that their voices wouldn't be heard; their contacts in the Luftwaffe or Air Ministry, the men in this room who acted as the go-between's for government and industry, would see to that.

The debate that followed centered on the strong and weak points of the different designs. The Do-217 could carry the heaviest internal bomb load; the He-111 was well-established; and the Ju-88 was a jack-of-all-trades. A glaring negative of the Heinkel workhorse, was that the He-111 design dated from 1933 and was showing its age, while the Ju-88 and Do-217 were much newer designs with the promise of further performance improvements down the line. Up until the new government was established, the military had favored specialized designs; this meant more models, and intentionally gave each manufacturer at least a small piece of the production pie. The new order of the day, however, was to now ruthlessly rationalize production by cutting down to just one design.

With the debate clearly going the way of the general-purpose Ju-88, the man with connections to Dornier made a last plea: "Nothing else being produced that can carry a major bomb load, has the range that the 217 does."

"Until the Heinkel-177 enters service, that is," the Luftwaffe officer overseeing the heavy bomber design sniped at the Air Ministry man.

"If they stop bursting into flames." At first glance the 177 appeared to be a twin-engine design, but in reality it was four - each wing had a single engine pod, the pod comprising two individual engines. Several of the test flights had ended with engines overheating, fires, and two prototypes lost so far to crashes.

Schellenberg had been content to let the discussion ramble, but felt it was time to assert his boss's interests. "You are all asking the wrong questions. What is the tradeoff in materials use and labor inputs between the two bombers? Both are constraints. Europa has fixed manpower and raw materials. Using more on one plane means less for other things. What is the ease of maintenance? What matters is a plane that can fly each day – rather than how many are produced. How easy is each plane to fly? I'm told you lose near as many planes to operational accidents as to combat. Start learning to think in these terms. If you cannot, reflect that we have executions at least weekly in Berlin. You will all answer for results, or lack thereof, with your lives should it come to that. The Reich is a revolutionary regime and we live in extraordinary times."

General Wimmer cleared his throat, and the bickering ended. "That's an excellent point. The Reich needs the He-177 to be fielded successfully; and so we will put additional eyes on its issues, by getting other manufacturers involved. The Do-217 will stay in production until a suitable replacement is ready, and we will phase out the He-111 after its current orders. Next item: fighters."

Current production was just the Bf-109; after combat experience so far, only a very brave or very foolish man considered the Bf-110 a serious candidate as a dog-fighter.

"Between reports on fighting in the Mediterranean, and directives from supreme command, a longer-ranged fighter is required. Even ferry flights from Italy to North Africa are difficult, with Tripoli the only possible destination as Benghazi is out of range."

Several of the men leaned forward; there were rumors on the range requirements the Air Ministry was thinking about.

"A specification for a new fighter is to be issued - 1,500 KM range and at least 700 KM/H max speed. Other details will follow."

The room was silent other than the secretaries taking notes for their principals. The range and speed being asked for were well beyond the performance capabilities of any current single-engine fighter. Only the Me-210 twin-engine fighter-bomber came close to those performance requirements; it was by all accounts a flying coffin, and that was without the enemy shooting at it. Wimmer wanted a great deal out of German industry

Schellenberg made a mental note to look into this requirement; the slack-jawed silence that had greeted it was concerning. Heydrich had made clear that war with the Soviets was coming. The East meant vast distances, extremes of weather, and primitive airfields as the battle line moved further towards the Volga and then the Urals. That said, quantity had a quality all its own. Germany had a sadly deserved reputation of going for cutting-edge, hand-crafted designs instead of mass producing good enough weapons in sufficient quantities.

"Will this impact the Fw-190 project?" a voice along the table asked. Kurt Tank, the brilliant engineer at Focke-Wulf, had put a great deal of effort into the radial-powered fighter expected to enter service sometime next year.

"No, this will be a new specification moving forward, and not a replacement for current projects.

"Next item: There is a renewed request from the army for better ground support. General Hoffmann, please review the current state of affairs."

There were but two dedicated ground-attack designs - the principal one was the Ju-87 dive bomber, which was very effective and terribly short-ranged. The second was the Hs-123 bi-plane, a dive bomber; it had served very well and was rugged, but it was also even shorter-ranged than the Ju-87. Just about every other bomber and fighter had been forced to fill in at need for the army support role. The Bf-110, unable to face front-line fighters, was commonly tasked with ground attack.

"General-feldmarschall Richthofen wanted to know about the possibility of restarting production of the Hs-123; they are very cheap, and can operate from the most primitive of airfields."

A nameless bureaucrat frowned. "I am sorry, General Wimmer, but Henschel broke down the tooling a few months ago. The plans still exist, but … "

Wimmer shrugged. "But time would be needed to set up all new tooling, I understand. No more 123's. Now what about Henschel's new project, the 129?"

The same bureaucrat smiled at drawing attention to the twin-engine ground-attack aircraft under development. It was heavily armored, with a steel bathtub around the nose and cockpit. Armed with light bombs, 20mm cannons, and machine-guns, the Henschel was intended to fly into the face of enemy anti-aircraft fire to strafe targets with high precision. The bad news was that the design had come in overweight and underpowered, resulting in very poor performance characteristics.

The Generalluftzeugmeister began a debate on whether the Hs-129 program should be terminated altogether, and a ground-attack version of the Ju-88 produced instead. The ensuing debate was the most ferocious of the meeting, and quickly led to promises being made that the Ju-87's range could be extended, and a ground-attack version of the Fw-190 could be produced. The argument against the special-purpose Henschel design, was that generalist designs like the Ju-88 and Fw-190 would better meet the production-rationalization dictates.

Schellenberg heard this all through, thinking to himself how sad it was that no one focused on why producing something that worked *now* was better than trying to make workable some other marginally-better but currently ineffective plane. Researching for the next advance in aviation was all well and good, but that was a luxury compared to planes that could be ordered today, in squadron service in a year, and coming off the production lines in quantity to absorb large wartime losses in 1942. None of these fools seemed able to face up to the existing world situation. The British war would be over in a year at most. The core of the peace terms had already been generally accepted. The British were stalling in Lisbon. All that he and his master could guess, was that they were praying for American intervention once Roosevelt had been reelected.

The little matter of each aircraft's performance issues was hammered at again and again.

There was hope that access to higher-performance French Gnome-Rhône radials, as opposed to the German inline Argus As-410, would help solve the performance issues.

Schellenberg made a note to see that this hope was made a reality. Production should now be European. Yet no one here thought that way. He recalled the legend of Sisyphus. Without the Reichsführer, Germany would likely have lost this war already.

What resolved the debate was that the Henschel aircraft had much greater range than any of the single-engine designs, and far better protection than any conversion of the Ju-88 would have. The army needed ground support aircraft. Wimmer, like Schellenberg, was party to the view that the Reich expected trouble from the Soviets — and they had a huge army, with tens of thousands of vehicles and tanks.

"Very well. The points are all settled — for now, upgrades to the Ju-87, and further prototype ground-attack versions of the Fw-190 and Ju-88, are all approved. The Hs-129 can continue forward." The Generalluftzeugmeister turned to another sheet.

"Now, the next item is setting up an agenda for meeting with key French aircraft industry figures. Be aware that a similar meeting with the Italians will of course follow. So my French associates, if you wish to be involved in that phase of the cartel, please have a delegation ready to attend in about two weeks time. We will coordinate this through your Air Ministry. Don't worry about how the small nations fit in. Coordination will be with the three European powers. The small nations will just be given orders by the new cartel management." He could see that the Europa Cartel program for joint production of designs garnered little real interest from the conference participants. *Fools*. They were cutting themselves out of the market, and were too egotistical to realize it. He concluded. "A meeting is to be held in three weeks time. I want reports on our needs, and projections on what we can hope for from France." No wonder France had lost their war in six weeks. They were unworthy heirs of their fathers from the Kaiserwar.

The meeting continued on for some time.

1900 hours Central Daylight Time, 15 October 1940
0200 hours CET, 16 October, 1940
Press conference before Lindbergh's next speech, this time in St. Louis

Lindy looked around the press gaggle. Sought out the *Chicago Tribune*'s guy, and recognized him for the first question. "Why is Willkie backing this new treason from Roosevelt and his interventionist gang?"

"Same reason I am. It's common sense." He saw the heads of the press people come up. Lindy breaking with the *Tribune* was news. "Forget how much you hate Franklin, Hopkins and his whole crowd. The deal is continental defense, and no draftees dying for British imperialism. Some of the details are not to my liking. Omelets and eggs. Nothing comes out of Congress without at least a hundred members playing with the fine points just to show they can, that they have enough power to add that clause or move this comma. This is how representative democracy works." He looked over and called on the man from the *Detroit Free Press*, ignoring the *Tribune* guy's screams on follow-up.

"So what don't you like?"

"Too much executive discretion. The limits of aid to the British aren't airtight enough. I also disagree with Mr. Willkie on Liberia. It puts the American flag down in the midst of a war zone between two colonial powers. It's a transparent appeal to the Negro press. I think our Negro citizens aren't so lacking in patriotism as to need this sort of pandering." He then called on the gentleman from the *Associated Negro Press*.

"So the descendants of freed slaves are unworthy of protection, but white Irish Catholics are welcome here?"

"Your words on Liberia, sir, not mine. I referenced a war zone. I am opposed to US servicemen dying on foreign soil. I have not been asked if I would oppose these sons and daughters of America returning to our shores. Then again, given our racial structure, why would they wish to? You campaign against Jim Crow. That is your cause and Mr. Willkie's, not mine. I will support Willkie where his views coincide with mine. Neither of us has married the other. I wish your race no harm, but my people are white, as is my nation. I accept that your ancestors were brought here against their will. It was a mistake; but how long must America suffer for that error?"

Over dozens of shouted questions, Lucky Lindy brought the session to an end. He had made his points. Indeed, the Irish point, which mattered greatly to the followers of Father Coughlin, had been made for him by the Negro journalist.

0900 hours local; 0800 hours CET
16 October 1940
Headquarters area, Brigade Strauss, in the rear of Italian XXI Corps lines

The overnight flight from Bari had been bumpy. Obersturmbannführer Siegel showed his exhaustion. He was burning the candle at both ends with a blowtorch. He was also an Obersturmbannführer now, with the possibilities of further advancement. He could sleep when he was old and retired.

Brigadier Strauss had the necessary people in attendance. Bride, groom, bride's family including uncle-by-adoption Ivan. Gregor was guarding the event with a Magyar company, and firm instructions not to interrupt for anyone whose first name wasn't General. Siegel handed out the new family trees with the Aryan certificates. "Memorize these. Guard them with your lives."

Isaak was diffident about it, but had to ask the obvious questions. "My wife? My daughters? My other son?"

"Delivered yesterday in Bari. They were instructed to mention all this to no one. They were always Aryans. Most all of what I did at that long family meeting, to prep your son Luke to lead his return convoy to Romania."

"Romania?" Isaak was frightened and trying not to show it. "What did he do wrong?"

"The reverse. Berlin has retroactively decided that purging the oil fields was not the wisest decision they ever made. So your Luke will lead a large group of oil and technical workers back."

Peter snorted. "Ah, shit!"

It was the SS officer's turn to looked worried. "What's the problem?"

"My brother is a science guy. He hasn't the hands-on experience running the work crews. That was my job." He looked at Siegel expectantly. The answer seemed obvious.

"Sorry. I cannot send you all back. Your brother was as much of a risk as I could take. Berlin's orders, and yes, it's about the new family heritages. You are all too well known there."

Peter grabbed a writing tablet off Strauss's desk. He handed pages to his father, brother Paul, and Uncle Ivan. "Everyone, start writing every name Luke should hire for this." While Siegel watched with eyes growing ever wider, the four men started writing, calling out names of people and companies, which functions each was best at. Forty minutes later they had a full plan for who to put in charge of what, with Luke back to what he was best at, interfacing with the highly educated foreign petroleum specialists. When it was done, Peter handed a full plan for manning the oil fields to the bemused Obersturmbannführer. "Be prepared for us robbing this structure blind when we get Iraq's oil. May I suggest overmanning? – so everyone of importance has a second, an apprentice. That way you get two functional producing fields, not two disasters for you to sort out. Oh, do you need who among the Romanian officials has to be paid off to make this all work?" The SS officer just nodded, thinking of how good this would look in Berlin. Ten minutes later he had who to pay off, how much, and which ones to just have shot because they were too inept or corrupt to stay bought.

This brought matters back to Klaus and his magic Party Card. Schellenberg had added a present for Klaus and Gunter. They were now Sturmbannführers in the SS General Reserve. Gunter was effusively thankful. Klaus thanked him as well, but seemed subdued. Siegel asked what the matter was?

"My parents. I'm sure you got my Aryan certificate from them. We are Aryan, or at least mostly are. I'm sure there's a Germanized Slav or two back a few centuries. That's the east – you speak good

German and cheer for the flag. That's Aryan enough for my parents' generation. The problem is the rest of this. Half the parents in the Reich would be proud of me. *They* still haven't gotten over me disappointing them by enlisting!"

"They are against the regime?"

"God no. That would mean having a firm opinion. They are neither for nor against the Party. Their opinion was that politics is for fools. Support whoever had power and stay out of trouble, unnoticed. All they cared about was me volunteering instead of waiting to be called up. Then there was choosing a combat branch. They had my future all worked out. Finish my degree. Get a job establishing my credentials as a clerical. On call-up, be sure those qualifications were listed so I could become a company clerk. My male relatives all served. They just tried to be where no one was shooting at them. My parents would have insisted that there was no need to be a hero. Clerks, warehousemen, and paymaster's assistants also serve the Fatherland. That the only military award that mattered was an honorable discharge."

Siegel was foreseeing problems. "So they won't be happy at reading about your marital plans?"

Klaus sadly shook his head while his new in-laws clustered around him. Peter asked the obvious question. "Would the problem be that my cousin is a Jew? Because now she isn't."

"No. Marrying into your family would be seen as wonderful by my parents. Except I was marrying the wrong girl." Klaus just kept shaking his head. Greta looked hurt. He didn't wish her pain, but couldn't lie to her. "My parents were as indifferent about race as they were about politics. Jews who spoke good German were fine with them, same as Poles who Germanized. On the Oder we had enough of both. They would curse me for an idiot, for marrying the boss's niece instead of one of his daughters. Marrying up to professionals who own a successful business they would see as smart. The sort of career move they would approve of. But the daughter's husband would rank over a mere niece's. When the next Depression comes the son-in-law gets fired last. In their lives they have seen two wars and two economic collapses. In their mind you live your life trying to protect yourself from disasters that are sure to come. And they see me as just blundering from one youthful mistake to another." He shrugged. "They have stopped writing, so I am spared their ill-wishes. Greta, at least by being the niece you are spared my mother pushing you to have a child at once so I can be the father of the first grandson and further secure my position."

Greta gently took his face in her hands and gave him a tender kiss. Her poor Klaus. How had he survived his boyhood?

1600 hours CET
16 October 1940
Fouga factory, Béziers

The factory hall had been erected in 1920 to handle the repair of rail stock; then in 1939, with the war, it was designated as a site for the construction of the Lorraine 37L, a fully-tracked vehicle to supply food, fuel, and munitions to the front. Nothing had been ready by the armistice, and little work had been done since, but that was now to change.

German engineers had several vehicle drawings on a table. Their French counterparts looked them over. One, labeled Panzerjäger I, was a Czech 4.7 cm anti-tank gun mounted on a Panzer Mark I hull. Splinter protection was provided for the gun crew. It had seen some service in France. Courtesy of the

Sons of Oran, it was known that this vehicle was in service in North Africa right now. The other vehicle was labeled *Nashorn*. Alkett in Germany was working on the vehicle now and intended it to mount the fearsome 8.8 cm flak cannon.

"What is your best anti-armor gun?"

Charts were pushed across the table comparing French 37mm, 47mm, and even the venerable 75mm first produced in 1897. Apart from the engineers stood two officers, one French and one German. The two field officers were to observe the proceedings on the exchange of information ... and each other. There was talk of alliance, cooperation; but mere months ago the two nations were bitter enemies, and there was still no formal peace.

The newer 47mm gun was better, but not hugely so. One of the German engineers had an idea: "We could change the munition on the 75mm."

A French engineer suspected he knew the answer. The Edgar Brandt company had been working on armor-piercing discarding-sabot rounds, but their key people had fled to the United Kingdom. A brief colloquy between the German and French engineers followed about the merits of the munition.

In their corner of the room the French officer suppressed a sigh and his German counterpart chuckled. Engineers tended to live in their own worlds. The idea of state secrets, and that perhaps the Germans were not to be fully trusted, didn't enter the head of the French engineers.

"While fascinating, it's a pity that your Brandt people aren't here. We have another idea in mind, high-explosive shaped warheads – or, 'High Explosive Anti-Tank'. The primary advantage is that armor penetration is the same at any effective range," a German said enthusiastically. "This munition would greatly improve the power of the 75mm at long range."

Now it was the turn of the German officer to groan. It appeared the Reich engineers could be just as clueless. After a few moments the French and German officers shared a chuckle at their mutual discomfort. Despite orders from Berlin and Vichy to cooperate, there were generations of mutual suspicion and rivalry to overcome.

With the weapon settled, the conversation turned to how to mount the weapon on the French munition tractor. Like the German designs, splinter protection would be provided for the gun crew. Best of all, only a few months would be needed to make the changes and have the weapons ready. Perhaps even sooner.

The SS minder for the meeting made careful notes. He would add to them a query as to whether to offer the 88mm multipurpose cannon.

1500 hours Eastern Daylight Time; 2100 hours CET
16 October 1940
Executive Office Building, Washington DC

Franklin wasn't well enough for an extensive schedule. So the duties of repairing the damage with the leaders in Congress, had been split between days and people. Today was the House, and tomorrow the Senate. Morning was FDR shining his light on the top people, rambling and bantering. Such bonhomie was an important social lubricant in politics.

This afternoon was when things got down and dirty. The new Speaker of the House, Sam Rayburn, had brought along his protégé and bagman, one Lyndon Baines Johnson. Mr. Sam set huge store on his personal integrity. Back to his days in the Texas legislature, he wouldn't take a dime of even the 'honest graft' of legal fees from interested parties in state business for his law firm. Instead his partners in the firm split those revenues … and saw that the right people got their cut. Money is the mother's milk of politics. With Rayburn's recent ascension to the Speaker's Chair, Johnson had done the dirty work of shaking the money tree and parceling out the cash.

Hopkins felt it should have been Farley drinking with these two powerful Texans. Franklin had ruined that with his fan dance on the third term. Whatever. Needs must. "I appreciate you gentlemen taking the time to discuss matters with me."

Rayburn was a gentleman by old time small town standards. The brash, crude Johnson was not. "You shoved ten tons of shit down our throats, and now we get to come back after election day for another helping."

Johnson was winding up for a long oration. Hopkins had neither the time nor patience. "Mr. Johnson, you did your patriotic duty yesterday. Now you are here to get paid for your labors." He could see Johnson clam his mouth shut while turning an ugly shade of purple. "You will want contracts for your friends at Brown and Root. You will want special favors for a host of people and interests through the South and West. All can be accommodated, and more easily than your crude shakedown of five-thousand-dollar checks out of Texas these past few weeks." Both Texans had gotten very quiet. The campaign money games they had played were supposed to have been secret. "I'll use crude terms because that seems to be all your protégé here understands. If you want to run with the Big Dogs, time to learn how the game is played. Lyndon here used telegrams. Hoover monitors damned near everything anyone of importance does. I can tell you the amount of each check and how you parceled it out." He paused to let that sink in. "It was pin money. Dewey's Wall Street pals proved that yesterday. When they want to, New York, Boston, and Philadelphia between them can yank the chains of every big-dollar interest in the South or West. The New Deal has changed that a bit, moved some of the power to DC. Some. Far from most. You are all economic colonies of the Eastern Moneyed Interests. This is what Franklin and I have spent the last eight years fighting against, the Economic Royalists."

Mr. Sam Rayburn was a soft-spoken but forceful man. It had brought him from the Texas legislature to the Speaker's Chair. "Yet you allied with them against us this week. And you propose to do so again."

"Against some of your idiot members, yes. Accept that politics stops at the water's edge. The world is at war and we, gentlemen, are not ready. We slept after the Great War. Starved our military. There is now a world of armed wolves out there, and we are the fattest cow waiting to be slaughtered."

"We have spent ungodly sums for defense. We just authorized limitless more money. Has it truly all been wasted?"

"No. By 1944 or 1945, we will be armed and relatively safe. Right now the giant fleet that will keep war beyond our shores is building. The first huge wave was funded in 1938. Battleships and aircraft carriers take time to design, to build, to be trained up after they are completed. The flood of warships starts in late 1943. The army would have trouble assembling a single combat division. Our Air Corps is a giant training program lacking the planes, airfields, and all the rest needed to be a world-class air force. Germany and Japan started in the early 30's. The British and French started by 1937. We are just getting rolling. We need time. In the interim, we need the British as a shield against the Germans, the Japanese as a bulwark against the Soviets."

Johnson was never the type to let others talk. "Thought you liked the Reds."

"To a degree, I do. Fellow Progressives, same as the Fascists are. Not total scum like the Nazis. 'Like' doesn't matter in the affairs of government. Bridges was a Red, probably a Communist. If not, then IWW or Anarchist. We shut him down hard. We've doing the same to the Communist Party. They waged war on the US to support Moscow."

Rayburn returned to the part that burned worst. "Why these new states? We will not be comfortable sharing our hallowed institution with the sort of *gentlemen* Hawaii and Puerto Rico will elect."

The 'sort of gentlemen' meant their color. Hopkins was aware. "Blame your Isolationist idiots, House and Senate both. They kept screaming that none of these places were US soil and we couldn't send draftees. So we are solving that. They are the United States. Philippines are not. Five more years, the Philippines are independent. We'll keep a few bases. The garrisons can all be volunteers if necessary. That's for Congress to decide. But Puerto Rico, Hawaii, Samoa, Wake, Guam will be US soil. Same as Texas."

"Come next year are we dealing with you, or whoever Willkie gives your job to?"

"Coin toss. The fools in your caucus who say punish us, what they will do is put Willkie in. You want to deal with Wall Street without us as a buffer, go right ahead. You can probably throw a few border states to Willkie. See how you like dealing with Dewey. Speaking of which, the next time you need serious campaign dollars, stop here first. I can get you all you need without involving the telegraph office. I pass the word, and the checks appear. All word of mouth."

Rayburn nodded to Johnson who produced a list. Hopkins waved the list aside. He didn't care who got the dollars. All he wanted was a total. He saved the last comments for the quite ambitious Johnson. "I know you are sniffing around lining up support for a Senate try. Tell me how much you need to start getting an organization in place."

"That's two years from now."

"And I can get you the money to have a permanent Texas machine, not just one cobbled together for each round of elections. The same big money people who twisted arms for Dewey will quietly give me funds as an insurance policy. This is where the Big Dogs run. Welcome to the pack." Hopkins' stomach was giving him such pain that he could not have stood to save his life. He suppressed any sign of it while spending two more hours arguing contracts and jobs. Needs must.

0700 hours local, 0600 hours CET

17 October 1940

Headquarters 7th Panzer Division, east of former British Bagush box base and west of Brigade Strauss HQ

The overnight flight from Berlin, with the last refueling stop outside Bari, had been choppy. Rommel's B*ursche* had been airsick multiple times. The general had a cast-iron stomach and a frontfighter's ability to sleep anywhere. In combat you slept when you could, and comfort be damned. Sleep deprivation was one of the perpetual problems in modern war. Old-fashioned battles took a day. Really big battles might take two or three. Now the fighting could run on for weeks or months with no letup for night or weather. Even the magic stay-awake pills only kept fatigue off you for a few days, after which (while still 'awake') your intelligence and reaction times both crashed. Under fire this could frequently be fatal.

The handover from von Stauffenberg and von Thoma had taken only a few minutes. They had had two days warning of his arrival. An exchange of handshakes, followed by a two-minute briefing, was all that had been required. Rommel would need a few days to have his division under firm control, but as the two other officers remained with 7ᵗʰ Panzer working for him, that shouldn't pose a problem. More so as the division was out of the line and slated as an army-level reserve for the upcoming offensive. The odds were that Rommel wouldn't alter the training schedules or administrative arrangements that had been set up in his absence.

Instead the General had arranged for Brigadier Strauss and Oberstleutnant Gorlov to meet him for coffee. Rommel did not like being in reserve. He had an idea ... "Welcome, gentlemen." He graciously returned their salutes and pointed to chairs. His Bursche saw to coffee service. Nothing elaborate, but good American stocks that were part of a large gift bundle the general had brought back from Berlin. Something about American aid and approved wastage rates. He let the two subordinates settle in and begin sipping their cups. "I wanted to thank you again for your proposal on breaching the Palestinian lines last month. I made sure the right people in Berlin knew of it, and that you were both credited for it. The Reichsführer was impressed."

Rommel was surprised to see the two exchange meaningful glances, after which Strauss as the senior spoke. "It's funny, you bringing that up. The British have been staging raids on Italian XXI Corps. The core of the units doing this are Palestinian Jews from those two brigades. Veterans of some joint anti-Arab raiding force from a few years back in Palestine. We have been providing counterattack patrols in aid of the Italians. We also have been taking prisoners. Even recruited a few. We were going to request an appointment with you." Strauss could see he had the General's undivided attention. "The raids frequently use a few British tanks and armored cars. Our maintenance unit has gathered a park of abandoned British vehicles. We've got a dozen in good working order. Not a lot of cannon ammunition, but their machine-guns use a round they borrowed from the Czechs, who borrowed it from us. Solved that problem. We've staked out the minefields. British are getting lazy on reconfiguring those. So we know a path. We've also been swiping passwords. Passed a few patrols through, testing. Yiddish-speaking troops with an officer with the right British accent have gotten kilometers into their rear and out again without much trouble, if we time it around their raids."

"You have such an officer?"

"Lieutenant Colonel Di Salo is British by schooling and prior residence. His mother's English. He was raised multilingual. His accent sounds 'officer' to British troops, the way an East Elbian Junker's accent does with ours."

"So you can breach their lines?"

"Yes, General. The problem comes afterwards. We are tasked to aid the navy in the occupation of Alexandria. If we make your penetration of the lines for you, will you allow us to take off down the road to the port? Instead of retaining us to aid you in rolling up the British front?"

"I take it you have a plan?"

"The raiding forces are platoon-to-company size. So we can push through a company using their types of AFV's, firing back towards our lines as they withdraw. As soon as they make a practicable breach, our brigade follows in a column. Your advance force arrives in a parallel column. We do this after the offensive has begun down south. This should pin their interest. Your division and the Italian Libyan Division, also in reserve here, should be enough to roll up a Division of second-line British troops and maybe a Battalion of Palestinians."

"How do you propose to handle our higher headquarters?" Rommel knew that von Manstein had a signed relief order sitting in his office. Rommel was out of excuses for arbitrary actions.

"All you are doing is following up on our action. Afrika Korps HQ gets daily reports on our patrol actions and raids. We don't treat it as a big deal, and they don't show much interest. Everyone knows we are mostly Militia, so we describe this all as 'field training'. You are just exploiting a breach we made outside your Division. Being ready in case we accomplished what we claim ... can be explained as prudence, no?"

Rommel sat there thinking, sipping his beverage. This could just work. If he started posting reaction reserves to back up the raids, but never actually used them, his staff and Afrika Korps would get accustomed to this. Victory covered a multitude of sins. Perhaps he could take Cairo, or at least bag a major British headquarters. It was worth risking his command. He was a storm officer, not a staff swine.

Chapter 9

0800 hours CET
18 October 1940
Headquarters, Grossdeutschland Regiment, Potsdam

Göring's boast on the loyalties of this unit had rankled OKH head Halder sufficiently that he had booked a surprise drop-in. He would assemble some field-grade officers for a 'chat' over coffee. Only none were present. Indeed there was no one here except an Oberleutnant and some senior Feldwebels. Halder asked the Leutnant the obvious question.

"A social gathering last night with the Führer, Generaloberst. It didn't break up until a few minutes ago. The commander called in before going home. I can summon him at once … " Leutnants are not used to having to brief Generaloberst's. Still less used to outlining the social life of their unit commander for such an exalted superior .

"Not necessary. Is this normal?"

"Some or all of us are invited to occasions with the Führer a few times a month, Herr Generaloberst." The Leutnant was clearly sweating, and working hard at not stammering. "Ourselves. The LAH. The new Herman Göring Division. The various watch battalions in Berlin. The 1st Parachute Division. In the event of an emergency, we are to be stood up as a Herman Göring Reserve Panzer Korps. I can show you the directive from OKW. Your headquarters was clearly carbon copied. Even the new SA Feldherrnhalle Brigade's advance cadre sometimes take part."

Halder tried to defuse the situation. The Leutnant was not to blame. However, some fool at OKH who had not brought this to his attention clearly merited being sent to the Norwegian Arctic with that fool Keitel. "I am sure it is all as you say, Leutnant. You have been to such a 'social gathering'?" He saw the boy nod. "Tell me about it."

"An open bar. A buffet with large servings of food. A dance band, which the Führer allows to play 'jungle music'. There are a lot of young Fräulein's from the cinema industry, the music industries, the other entertainment industries, to dance with. The Führer's wife is there. She is very gracious … "

The Leutnant was turning bright red and now starting to stutter. Halder could guess why. "Be at ease, Leutnant. I am aware that the Führer has a 'special friend' as well as a wife. An actress. White Russian refugee. Relation of the famous writer Chekov. The Führer bears unique burdens for the nation. He is allowed such things as a 'special friend', as dancing to 'Nigger music'. Kaisers before him had 'special friends', could bend social rules. It eases the otherwise crushing burden of command." He saw the puppy nodding vigorously. No sense telling Beck about any of this. The man was hopeless. He would destroy the officer caste with his attitude. The alliance of three from the Wannsee meeting was what was needed.

1100 Hours CET
18 October 1940
Ministère de l'Air (Air Ministry), Vichy, France

Deaths on the Nile

The building had actually been a primary school, before the French government had fled to the provincial spa and resort town of Vichy. All the hotels and official buildings had been taken over by the senior ministries, leaving the less important or less lucky ones to make do with buildings like this. Traces of its original use still were obvious to the discerning eye, and the "conference room" was packed tight.

The French side was headed by the French Ministre de l'Air Jean Bergeret and his major flunkies. They were supported by delegations from each of the six state-owned aircraft companies, amalgamated from the gaggle of smaller private airplane builders a few years ago.

The German side from the Reichsluftfahrtministerium was much smaller – three officers, plus two civilian experts, plus a few translators, and two BDM stenographers – whose main point apart from looks, was that they were able to take fluent shorthand in both German and French.

The leader of the German delegation, Otto Abetz, got up and cleared his throat, stopping all the whispered conversations in the room. The German ambassador was a well-known Francophile, and perhaps the happiest person in the foreign ministry over the change in direction Berlin had dictated. "Monsieur le Ministre, we thank you very much for organizing this meeting. We also thank all present for making time on their calendars and traveling here on such short notice and without knowing what this is all about." Left unsaid was that the timing bore no relation to when this had been announced as happening at the prior meeting on these subjects in Germany. Dictatorships in wartime are as subject to bureaucratic chaos as any other large organization, peace or war.

The fact that these opening remarks had been made in *French* did not pass unnoticed, even if the accent was rough. Ambassador Abetz continued in French; the grammar and style was good, if a bit old-fashioned.

"The subject is something that must interest you all very much – the future of the French aircraft industry." The slight rustling and uneasy movements and the note-taking in the room stopped – everyone was waiting for the anvil to drop.

"Let me start with what we – that is the Reichsluftfahrtministerium and the Luftwaffe – do not want to do. We do not want to dissolve the French aircraft companies. We do not want to take you all over. We do not want you to stop your development work – France has always been in the avant-garde in aeronautics, and we have no interest at all in abolishing that proud tradition."

He continued after a short look at his notes: "But there need to be some changes. Let me give an example. At this time or until very recently, continental Europe is producing roughly 50 different kinds of fighter aircraft. Fifty – and we are not counting subtypes and minor variants here. This is a tremendous waste that cannot be allowed to continue."

"So, you want to force our companies to build your aircraft, preferably minor things like trainers and liaison aircraft?"

"No, M. Dewoitine," he said, reading the name from the little identifying placards on every table.

"Or not in the way you describe. There will be a flying competition in six weeks, in which all of you will have a chance to present their best fighter-type aircraft. The standard you will be flying against for this competition will be a Bf-109 E-4 without any special modifications."

"So, there will be a German victory in this competition, with your propaganda trumpeting the superiority of your army and your pilots to the world." The minister hissed at one of his minions, and set him into motion in order to shush the belligerent Gaul.

"No. The competition will be fair, as fair as we can make it. The Messerschmitt aircraft will not take part as a competitor, only a standard to fly against. The rules for the competition will be handed over to you at the end of this meeting, and they do contain provisions for making requests for rule changes and additions. Please read them carefully." Abetz paused to be sure he had the attention of the Frenchmen in the room. "Let me outline three possibilities: One, we can dismantle all your factories. Move the tools to Germany. Much production is lost, and France ceases to be a major player in Europe's aviation future. Two, you all become contracted producers for German or Italian designs." He could see the looks of surprise and shock at the mention of Italy. The French never took the Italians seriously as equals.   "We keep your productive capacity, but you cease to be designers and developers. You lose a generation or two of hands-on knowledge, from which you will probably never recover. The best of your experts move to Germany. The rest find other fields of work. Three, we truly do European cartels as we in Germany wish. The best designs of all of Europe are produced. The French design bureaus remain at the forefront of aviation. We are offering you the best of these three choices. Never forget that the other two exist. France declared war on Germany, not the reverse. You let the British drag you into a war you were near totally unprepared for. When things got tough, the British ran away across the Channel. Now they have started a war with you to steal your Empire. We are aiding you in this struggle. We do not have to. It would be ever so easy to buy peace with the British using your colonies as coin. We have no way to occupy Senegal or Madagascar or Indochina. So they are a cheap price to us, but a valuable prize for Perfidious Albion. Show that Cartesian logic you French are famous for. What do we gain by humiliating you with a fake competition?"

Otto Abetz leaned forward and fixed on the glowering director of Dewoitine Aircraft: "The prize for the winning aircraft will be a permission to keep producing this aircraft, and to search for customers both in Europe – for example Bulgaria, Romania, Finland, Greece – and with the permission of Berlin, also selected countries outside Europe. An exceptional winner will also be considered for future Luftwaffe contracts." He paused for dramatic effect. "We have warned our German industrial leaders that if they don't mend their ways, they risk becoming mere contract makers for French designs. Certainly so in engines, and possibly in airframes as well." He paused again to watch the delighted shock spread around the room. "I also would like to point out that the invitation to this competition will also go to aircraft manufacturers of some selected other countries, like Fokker of the Netherlands, so if the French aircraft industry chooses not to participate, someone else might reap the benefits."

After a short period of agitated whispering, one of the other company directors present got up and asked: "What will happen with those companies that do not win this competition?"

"M. Bloch, they will be free to take part in the next competition for fighters … or in similar selections for other types of aircraft, like transports and bombers. You will also be free to tender proposals for new aircraft according to specifications issued by the Reichsluftfahrtministerium, the French Ministère de l'Air, or other European governments or private interests that Berlin will approve for European participation.

"Alternatively, or additionally, you will also be invited to participate in development and manufacturing of several aircraft we are currently developing, but where we are lacking capacity. Among these aircraft would be the Hs-129 battle aircraft and the He-177 heavy bomber – but we will invite you to discuss these after this meeting. However, let us be clear. You will work, or you will lose your machines and cease to exist. Those are your choices. Sitting on the productive capacity and waiting out the war is not an alternative. You try for that at your peril, both individually and as a nation."

That tidbit seemed to be of interest to at least a few of the managers, who had probably wondered how they were going to pay their workers in the near future.

"So, we will do work for the German Luftwaffe – or not at all. But will we receive enough money for our work, to keep our companies afloat? Or will we be driven deeper and deeper in debt, to be finally bought up by German aircraft builders?"

"There will be a profit. An honest, not exorbitant one, mind you, after all there is a war going on – but enough to keep you running and to support future development work. Just as we have also reined in the greed of our own companies. And if any companies want to buy each other, partner, merge – the RLM will keep an eye on such things to make sure things stay fair. Be prepared for onsite auditors both from your own government and from the European air cartel. Also for quality inspectors. Your design bureaus will also be open to visitations. There is one Europe at war with the British Empire. Hopefully not at war with Britain's American cousins; but that remains a choice mostly of the Americans, who seem to dance to a tune only they can hear."

1800 hours Eastern Daylight Time; 2400 hours CET
18 October 1940
Executive Office Building, Washington DC

This was supposed to have been a briefing for President Roosevelt and his alter ego Harry Hopkins. Hence the location. Both were still smoothing very rumpled Senate feathers over the multiple new laws rammed through. That left Navy Secretary Frank Knox taking the presentation, from a senior navy staff headed by Admiral Stark.

On one hand, it was clearly naval matters and thus within Knox's remit as service Secretary. On the other hand, Knox was an anti-New Deal Republican who had taken the post from FDR in the interests of national unity. His remit was administrative and organizational ... yet today he was taking a semi-secret operational briefing because no one else was available and the matter wouldn't keep.

The German, Italian, and French naval attaches had been over to see the proper senior professionals of the USN with an urgent proposal. The stated point was to 'avoid another Lusitania'. The 'Europeans', as they were calling themselves, wanted to avoid accidental combat with the US. They wanted the US 'patrol zone' defined, given the new US commitments to Ireland and Liberia. The idea was to restrict the Atlantic naval war to places US ships were not.

Thus for Ireland, they wanted the US to restrict US patrols and merchant shipping to the West Irish ports, leaving Dublin and the Irish Sea as war zones where Europe could fight the British. The war zone would extend south from there out to some agreed line in the ocean, a north-south marker. There would be war in the Bay of Biscay, Gibraltar, around the Iberian Atlantic island chains, and on as far south as Dakar. The war zone would end at an east-west line fixed at 20 miles south of Freetown in Sierre Leone. US shipping to the Baltic would have a protected zone in the North Sea such that all fighting would be south of an agreed line. US and Latin American trade to Iberia would be through Portugal by convoy from the USN. USN would announce when such were coming and the route. The ships would use running lights and display the US flag (or the flags of their nation, for Brazilian or other Latin American nations). The Europeans would instruct their forces to give these a wide corridor in and out.

Knox had not allowed the Europeans to brief him directly. He wanted USN input. "What happens if we say no?"

"Their hints were that they would feel it necessary to let the US public know that chances of avoiding war had been deliberately rejected, so the voters could draw their own conclusions."

Knox was afraid of this. In his civilian life he owned the *Chicago Daily News*, which had bumped heads with the *Chicago Tribune* for long enough for Knox to be all too aware of what they would do with this story. This was just the sort of interventionist stab in the back they endlessly warned against. "Admiral Stark. Can the US Navy live with these rules? Don't get bogged down in the weeds. These Nazis will bargain at the margins if they really want to avoid war with us that badly. Yes or no?"

Stark didn't need time to think. The navy had already reached its conclusions. "Damn right we can. It's insane as naval war, but makes total political sense if they really don't want war with us. This helps the British more than it does us. Which shows the Germans are either stupid or don't care. We have nothing to go by to figure out which it is, but our best guess is 'don't care'. The naval war here is about French colonies, not Italian or German. How the Nazis set this up you'll have to get State to tell us, but this amounts to an Anglo-French war. Either way Germany wins. Even if they lose all their ships, they didn't have a functional navy anyway. This keeps the war as far from our shores as possible and minimizes the risk on Ireland and Liberia. If the president will buy this, it gives us time to keep rebuilding the Fleet. What do you think, sir?"

Knox didn't like it. He was sure FDR would hate it. However, if the administration turned this offer down ... it would be Willkie taking the oath of office next January. It was a slick propaganda move. The Nazis were usually very clumsy with such things. What had changed? Knox didn't know, but he placed a call to Hopkins saying he had something that couldn't keep. Knox and his room of admirals would wait all night, if that was what it took to get one of the two senior people. When the secretary taking the note for Hopkins asked for the subject of the meeting, Knox said it was losing the election in the next 18 hours. That should force a response.

0800 hours local; 0430 CET
19 October 1940
Viceroy's residence, New Delhi, British Raj, India

The sensible morning start time of the meeting was deliberate. The Viceroy, Sir Winston Churchill, was a night owl. Meeting in the morning frequently resulted in Winston choosing to sleep in, sending a confidential secretary to stand-in for him. The Army Commander-in-Chief, Auchinleck, found that much more got done without Winston's bombastic speeches and tendency to ramble. As long as decisions stayed within the policy guidelines the Viceroy was evolving, the routine day-to-day coordination of governing a subcontinent in the midst of four small wars worked better at this sort of principal officers meeting. So it was the Army, the Muslim League, a representative for the Princes, someone from the Chamber of Commerce, and the people who stood in for what was now openly called the four pillars: the Indian military, the police, the civil service, and the railway workers. The pillars rotated who would attend each meeting. Auchinleck was not privy to how they arranged that the four always just happened to be two Hindus, a Moslem, and a Sikh. The whole point in Winston's system was getting the pillars, without whom India could not be ruled, used to seeing themselves as separate classes outside the narrow confines of caste, language, and religion. All four pillars had all three religions, and it was best that the collective representation of each was seen to include all three.

Today's agenda was focused on the Central Reserve Police Force. It had been two battalions of Crown Representative Police when Auchinleck had arrived. The name was changed, and emergency expansion begun, to contest Congress's 'Quit India' campaign. Ten more battalions had been stood up, initially staffed by military and police retirees plus their younger kin. The twin Congress rebellions, Bose's and Gandhi's, required more and more key infrastructure guarded so as to free up army and trained police for the real fighting. Untrained young men, with experienced sergeants, could guard while they learned the rest of their jobs. On the table were demands for forty more such battalions. There was no way to stretch resources that far. So this meeting was designed to seek field expedients. "Who wishes to speak first?" Auchinleck preferred collegial-style meetings.

"We can offer six more battalions of our National Guards." The Muslim League had been forming paramilitaries in the largely Muslim provinces, east as well as west. There were severe drawbacks on using these in areas with too many Hindus. So far the League had not flexed its muscles to push against this. "We can also offer more Mujahideen for the Afghan war."

"Thank you for the offer. I see them of use in Punjab and Sind, but fear adding to the tensions in Bengal or Bihar." Auchinleck saw the nods around the table. "Any help in Afghanistan will be welcome. We are going to lose Kabul." He paused, looking for shock. The table was nodding. Meant every faction's private intelligence net was still working well. The Soviets and their Afghan hirelings could be stalled, but not really stopped in advance of Khandahar and the Khyber Pass. Right now, weather was delaying the Bolsheviks more than the actual fighting. The local Afghans were tribal bandits, not an army. The few Indian Army units, bulked up with Mujahideen, were simply too badly outgunned to do more.

It took five more minutes to get small offerings from the Princely forces, railway police, and private guards from the business sector. The Sikh who this day was representing the civil service, was the only one who had a real idea. "Sir, Britain is evacuating many people from Egypt to points east. From what we have heard the same will happen in Palestine, Iraq, perhaps some other places. This includes a lot of Europeans with prior military experience. Poles, Jews, French, whatever. Why not divert more of them here? Once upon a time, the East India Company Army had what they called European regiments. They were of mixed nationality, but served the Company in the manner of purely British or Indian battalions. These would be mostly Christians, with some Jews. That removes them from our conflicts of religion, caste, and regional languages. They need sanctuary someplace. They are in no position to ask British wages. As long as we feed them and shelter their dependents … " He looked around the table. No one seemed to have a problem, except the Muslim League man.

"As we are all adults here, let us squarely face to what you are saying. If the British Arab Raj is coming to an end, the refugee flood will include Arabs, Muslim and Christian both. Why should we not make use of these as well? Those police and armies are British-trained. The ones who depart will not be local nationalists who find such officers repugnant." He saw the looks around the table. "I'm not suggesting that the Muslims serve in Hindu regions or police around the Sikh Golden Temple. We need people who can carry a revolver, a riot shield, and a baton. Why not Muslims as well?"

The Hindu Subedar-Major representing the Army took this all in. "The Army can accept that Muslim units get Muslim officers. We cannot accept that European or Christian Arab units get only Christian ones. Will the League accept limiting the higher officers in such units to Hindus and Sikhs in the name of balance? This will give all three religions immediate slots for promotion to colonel and lieutenant colonel." There were nods all around the table. A memo was quickly typed up and passed around for signatures. The formal agenda having ended, there was a break for tea, after which the real work began. This de facto national council of government ran on mutual exchange of favors. Everyone at the table had lists, and they began to dissolve into subgroups of two or three. Auchinleck was content to watch, intervening only when asked. His role was as peacemaker; and such refereeing was needed less and less, week by week. The interests represented here had discovered that having common enemies focused the mind on how much they had in common, instead of what divided them. A new India was taking shape. It was less unitary than the old Raj had been, but much less fragmented than what the British had found three centuries earlier. The Congress-dominated chaos zones in the 'cow belt' of massively Hindu provinces on the northern plains, focused the minds of every interest at this table on what the alternative was to the current arrangement.

0900 hours local; 0800 hours CET
19 October 1940
Headquarters Italian XXI Corps, north end of the Alamein position

In theory this was a meet-and-greet, a set of formalities for Lieutenant Colonel Di Salo to introduce himself to the senior Italian officer in the sector his Arditi battalion was assigned to. He was not under Generale di Corpo d'Armata Lorenzo Dalmazzo's command, but such professional networking was normal enough that neither Gunter nor General Rommel was likely to see through the excuses.

Dalmazzo had been only vaguely aware that Strauss had an Italian battalion. He was aware that Rommel had been assigned one, but that unit was still working up back in Tuscany. He had been made known of Di Salo by mutual connections. Now, after coffee service, he waited to see what this was all really about.

"Thank you for seeing me, your excellency. I have information important for your command – but it must be conveyed orally." The general was giving Di Salo his FULL attention. He found nothing unusual in the Germans not telling their Italian allies key things. "Generals Rommel and Strauss have a plan to breach the British lines."

"And you are breaching their confidence by telling me this, because?"

"Because I am an Italian patriot." This was the proper response, and Di Salo was making sure he got it on the record. "Also because we have mutual connections. This plan of theirs can make you look brilliant … if you are properly prepared. But also may make you look the inept fool if you have no awareness of what is intended. As I am involved in this operation, you would have every right to blame me, be angry with my family, the usual. I would rather we be friends. Everyone needs friends in life … " Yes, friends were how one got promotions, assignments, contracts for one's firm. Life ran on friendships, connections, exchanges of favors.

"What is required of me?" The Generale di Corpo d'Armata knew nothing came for free.

"I'll alert you when the operation is about to begin, and where. If the Germans fail, you do precisely nothing. It's their operation, and therefore the defeat is theirs. But I think there is a good chance this will succeed. I've taken several trial patrols through the British lines without incident. It's all a set of tricks, a ruse de guerre. But the British opposite us are sloppy and somewhat complacent. What you need to do is have your staff planning all done. This planning should presume that Brigade Strauss will force an operational-level breach in the British lines. Strauss plans to leave a holding force behind to remain in his current staging area. The rest of his brigade pours through in the direction of Alexandria. Rommel will enlarge the breach and then roll up the British line south of here, plus exploiting the British rear area. That will leave the British north of the breach for your corps. These troops will likely be backpedaling, trying to safeguard their rear and reestablish contact to the south. One and a half to two brigades of British troops. Not the best they have, as you are aware. Plus a battalion or so of this Palestinian raiding force."

"I take it that Army command is unaware of this?" Dalmazzo was sure Army knew nothing about it, but wanted to draw out this upstart junior officer.

"Yes, your excellency. More important is that Afrika Korps is also clueless. This violates direct orders. Strauss feels safe to do so. His brigade is some special project of Reichsführer Heydrich. Rommel will justify what he does as an exploitation of whatever Strauss does. Just the sort of operational opportunity German officers are trained to pounce on." Di Salo felt no loyalty to any of these Germans. He had his own country and his own career to see to.

"It will be obvious he was fully prepared for this surprise."

"Yes, sir. To me that's a fight among Germans. I just seek for you and Italy not to be surprised."

Dalmazzo paused, digesting this all. "And for this advance information you wish me as a future sponsor of your career." There was no questioning tone. It was an obvious statement.

Di Salo gave a small smile. "Of course, your excellency. Everyone needs friends. Spain showed me that arms was my proper profession, not finance. My battalion has sponsors at the highest level. I myself do not. It seemed foolish not to use this chance to start a relationship between us."

"And those stupid flamethrower tankettes you have been rounding up?"

"Two of the German advance guard battalion commanders have some silly plan to use them. Finding the machines made friendships with them. More important, it will be exploited from Rome as propaganda. Elite German troops using Italian equipment. The right people in Rome are aware. They are sending a movie team to film these in action. While they are here, they can of course dramatize your units and yourself." Di Salo was the junior here. He had to show the general how useful he could be.

The general sent for a bottle of scotch to toast this enterprise. His toast was, "This may be the start of a beautiful friendship." Both men understood the game and how to play it.

1900 hours local; 1800 hours CET
19 October 1940
Captain Morgan's House of Rare Treasures, Alexandria

The shop was several blocks off the main commercial district of the European quarter of Alexandria. It was just within the heavily patrolled section of the city that the police kept safe for tourists, had there been any such in wartime. With the war on, the shoppers needing personal security were mostly British rear-echelon personnel with a few days leave. The shop's trade in this period of wartime uncertainty was mostly in precious metals. Anything gold or silver sold at a premium to people afraid of paper money when Egypt could quickly change hands. It rated even more of a premium to those looking to escape down the Red Sea to safer climes.

Captain Morgan bought objects with paper currency, but wouldn't take paper for the monetary metals except at a large and growing discount. Golda Meir had been warned that this man and his shop were seedier than she was used to, but a valuable connection in Zionist circles. Captain Morgan also sold passports, travel documents, and many things of use getting Jews out of Egypt. Equally so providing Christian fronts to Jews wishing to journey to Israel, circumventing the British restrictions on new Jews in Palestine.

The proprietor had greeted her with a quite good British accent that didn't precisely jibe with his supposed Canadian identity. It wasn't Oxbridge but could definitely pass for a country squire or Midlands solicitor, at least to Golda's untrained ear. "Welcome, Mrs. Meir. I was advised of your probable arrival by several of the people you visited with in Cairo. How may I be of assistance?"

They were seated in his warehouse behind the shop. A quick scan showed an amazing variety of odd items, cartons, shipping crates, and general merchandise. She wondered where the photographic studio and art supplies were. Both were needed for document forgery. "Are you really Canadian?"

"I have papers that say I am. I have others making me an American from your own fine city of Milwaukee. You needn't know about the rest of my documents. Let us say I have proper documents to fit in with the new authorities when the Italians take the city. My history isn't what brings you here. You need papers and funds. Both can be provided in return for dollars deposited in an account I keep in Havana. My banking agent there can still get telegraph messages here. Do you have photos for those needing instant Americanization?"

"Not yet. Everyone is hesitating. They have homes, businesses, assets to liquidate. The market is down. This makes delay seem wise."

Captain Henry Morgan was a middle-aged nondescript man. Well kept brown hair, brown eyes, hornrimmed spectacles, a good manicure. The face looked pleasant. The eyes seemed hard. "Isn't it fun trying to educate fools? My smarter customers have been fleeing since Malta. The wisest left with the fall of France. Even the idiots are beginning to look for the exit now. We all have enough contacts with British forces. Your Ben Gurion may deal with generals and cabinet ministers. I know majors and lieutenant commanders, executive assistants to senior civil service and the like. The rats all know the game is up. Residential properties are going at 50 and 60 percent discounts. Commercial properties and inventories at still higher discounts. The rumor mill has Lower Egypt gone by year's end. Now, they could all be wrong ... but then why has the entire Fleet run away? Even retired navy people are gone. The port's civilian contractors have all decamped with their inventories and extended families. There's been a British fleet in the Mediterranean since the Glorious Revolution. Now there's nothing east of

Gibraltar till you reach Aden." He looked the Zionist lady over with an almost pitying expression. "The first thing we do is get you registered with the US consulate. That's your only protection if you are trapped here. The US will get its citizens out when the disaster hits."

"Are you registered?"

"That would be unwise of me. They know me as Canadian. As I said, I have other papers that should be acceptable to the Italian occupation authorities. My American papers will be later, after I pass out of the war zone. For right now, I'll probably try my luck as a subject of the Italian Crown. The dollars in Havana are an insurance policy, should I prove to be optimistic about how the occupation will go for one such as myself."

Meir wanted to show her disgust at this character. He was everything she had hated about the money-obsessed, eye-to-the-main-chance culture of America. The man would sell her papers, and likely sell the passport numbers to the Gestapo later if the price were right. She had her orders. She had worked with worse. The Egyptian Jews would panic when the British military lines started to go. At that point it would be about saving lives, and lost property be damned. It was her job to save who and what she could.

0730 hours local; 0630 hours CET
20 October 1940
8th Army Headquarters, 12 miles west of the Alamein lines

The three-man inspection commission from London had arrived back in Egypt during the overnight hours. One member of Commons each from the Tories, Labor, and National Liberals. Three men with staff experience from the Great War. Facing them were the same three British generals: Wavell as theater commander, and his two army commanders, Cunningham and O'Connor.

Wavell gave a briefing, trying to put the best possible spin on things. Cunningham went second, backing up his boss. He portrayed the situation as serious but not hopeless. Wavell pointedly did not ask O'Connor to speak. He had only invited him on direct orders from London. The wayward 9th Army commander had been instructed by Wavell to volunteer nothing, and answer direct questions as narrowly as possible. London was already having a fit over O'Connor's preemptive actions in Iraq. So O'Connor stayed seated and silent while Wavell asked the three parliamentarians if they had questions.

The Laborite solicitor replied, "Why no briefing from General O'Connor?"

The named general stayed seated and silent while Wavell replied that, as O'Connor's commander, he could answer any questions concerning 9th Army. The Tory squire outright laughed at that. "Been told to keep silent and shut up?" O'Connor sat silently with as close to a blank face as he could attempt. "I was given that honor a few times when briefing Haig during the Third Ypres debacle. My Corps Commander was ever so much better at mouthing expedient lies than we staff Johnnies were." He waited for the expected round of laughter. "I'm not a blockhead like Haig. We three have written authority from the War Cabinet which you all have seen. I want General O'Connor's report now. I want it without whatever limitations your orders from General Wavell contained. We have this tradition of parliamentary supremacy. General Wavell, do you seriously want a constitutional test? I'll be happy to send the precis of this dispute to London to get formal orders requiring specific and candid answers to all our questions. We know it's bad. If we didn't think there was a problem, why did we just go through an unpleasant air flight from Home by way of Gibraltar? How bad is it? No fudges. No polite straddles."

O'Connor now finally answered. "Would you please give me that order in writing?" As the Tory wrote out the order, O'Connor asked for another sheet of paper. He was handed the order, read it, and put it in his carry case. He then handed his own sheet to Wavell. It was his resignation as Commander of 9th Army, and a request to retire from active duty. As the five men in the room looked among each other in shock, O'Connor slumped in his seat. "Now ask your questions. I'm not going to stab these two men in the back. My career is over and I'll give you my opinions. As a retired has-been they won't mean bollocks, but ask away."

The three parliamentarians exchanged glances. The Laborite was silently chosen as the interrogator. "How bad is your army's situation?"

"Former army."

"London may have something to say about that, and right now we speak for London. Your army. Neither resignation has yet been accepted. You are a King's officer on active service. How bad is 9th Army's position?"

"Hopeless but not serious. Yet." He saw the shock and confusion. "As long as Egypt holds, I still have a supply line. I don't expect Egypt to hold for long, but it will hold long enough for me to reestablish a line of communications back to Basra. The Iraqi Army has numbers but limited combat capacity. Between 2nd New Zealand Division, and the odds and sods we are dignifying with the name 10th Indian Division, I will break the Iraqis. Indeed, some of their formations may defect back to us. The rebellion there is a clique of higher officers, not a full nationalist rising. The rank and file enlisted for steady pay and some prestige. They had more years of British command than independence. They remember us beating the Turks in Mesopotamia in the Great War. The Poles are a rolling disaster, but the Jews, when mobilized, will fight, at least for a time. Any other questions?"

"What's wrong with the Poles?"

"Legalisms. They signed up to fight the Germans, and only the Germans. They raise legal questions of Poland not being at war with Italy or Iraq. If our war with Vichy migrates to the Levant, they will surely refuse to attack Syria. These quibbles come from their London government, and had best be addressed there."

The National Liberal spoke up. "Legalisms. At a time like this?" O'Connor nodded firmly. The Liberal was a chartered accountant and had been a supply planner. "You speak of marching the New Zealanders to Iraq. Do you have the supplies to get them back?"

"Wouldn't matter. They won't come back. They have direct appeal to their government. They will fight in Iraq, because that's their ticket home. No way they will put their head back in the lion's mouth in Palestine. Palestine falls the month after Egypt does."

Wavell tried to cut in. The supply planner rudely motioned him to silence. "Why this opinion that all will be lost?"

O'Connor went on in a low monotone, "You can count. Count the forces in Egypt. Field guns, planes, tanks, armored cars. Count the weekly loss rates. Don't bother counting the reinforcements, because you have sent nothing more than a few dozen planes. Which are already lost playing pretend air force. You haven't even bothered to send fresh drafts for the infantry battalions. Units take losses every day. Minor combat, bombardments, illness, accidents. You just allow these units to waste away. Your excuses don't matter. You have sent forces to multiple places in Africa. You haven't sent them here."

"There are two Australian divisions on the way."

"There are two packets of untrained, virtually unarmed recruits on the way here. Zero field guns, zero fighting vehicles, zero planes. Merely grand promises of future American and Canadian production. Our enemy attacks in a few weeks. They will break the line. Our second-rate brigades will fall apart. They are full of recruits fit for nothing more than labor service. Our good ones will be ground down. The enemy has total air superiority. So no daylight movement of units or supply. They outnumber our good units by roughly three to one. In artillery by eight to one. In fighting vehicles by forty to one. In planes by over a hundred to one. You all went through the mill. With those sort of odds any infantry force, however brave and well led, gets ground down. Our boys are excellent battalion soldiers, and my two colleagues here are stalwart senior officers. Ten days to two weeks, either the entire 8th Army goes in the bag or gets destroyed trying to flee without air cover. You will have thrown away the last real army Britain has. It's been a month since we fell back on the Alamein lines. Where are the reinforcements that could have held it? What on Earth prompted you to start a war with France instead?"

The three again looked at each other. This time it was the Tory who got designated to speak. "Winston did Dakar, and after that it just all sort of happened. At any given point Egypt was forty to sixty days away. So it slid while the big names squabbled. Took us till now to untangle the mess at Army HQ. Dill was a disaster, but Cabinet never anticipated the morass that would be made replacing him with Lord Gort. Effectively no one had real responsibility, for far too long. The permanent staff abused this interregnum. They had their own agendas and no grip on reality." The three delegates had the decency to look as appalled as the situation warranted.

Wavell was a good trooper and loyal, but he had finally had enough. "We have been politely telling you how bad it is for a month. London has not wanted to hear us. You want the truth? Are you really ready for the truth? Can you handle the truth? Can London?" The three from London nodded, their faces grim. "Egypt, Palestine, and Iraq are lost. The correct answer is to flee up the Nile and across the Canal. Dynamite the port of Alexandria, every bridge in Egypt, the entire urban infrastructure. Burn the files of every ministry. Leave Cairo in a sea of flames and blasted buildings. Blow up the supplies we cannot take away. Accept leaving rear guards repeatedly to die behind mine fields so the rest can get away. Accept that tens of thousands of British nationals, that hundreds of thousands of Empire peoples and minorities who depended on us, will be lost. We will take major losses, but can hold again at Basra and somewhere south of Khartoum while you fools salvage what you can at a peace conference. We have been repeatedly asked to make bricks with mud and no straw. We will do the Birkenhead Drill when and as required. Australia will never forgive you for throwing their corps away. Indeed, once the line starts to go I fully expect the Australians to bolt for Sinai, pleading orders from their government." Wavell ran out of breath. He took a fresh sheet of paper and did a duplicate of O'Connor's note. "Gentlemen, which of you wants which of our commands?"

The London three sat there aghast. Asked leave to contact the War Cabinet for instructions. The three generals each separately thought the same basic thought. "About time!"

1400 hours local; 1300 hours CET
20 October 1940
Drill field adjacent to Brigade Strauss HQ, in the rear of Italian XXI Corps positions at Alamein

Coxita's harangue was into its second hour. The Catalans had arrived this morning, exhausted from their journey here by rail to Naples, sea to Sirte, and truck to the front. At every stage they were treated as a low-priority bother by the commands involved. This meant even their feeding was never assured; and lodging often meant spending days sleeping in train stations or adjacent lots, waiting for some transport officer to take pity on them. Now, right after a hearty breakfast and being assigned tents, this ex-commissar bitch was making them stand in formation through an endless lecture attempting to reconcile the Leninism of the late period Spanish Republic with the current Nazi Europa – through the ideology of old-shirt Falange syndicalist futurism and the Hitler-Stalin Pact. The ideological gymnastics would have rated gold medal had the Olympic Games included such an event. Meanwhile the two hundred or so men in the oversized company were out on their feet, swaying in the savage heat to which they had not yet become acclimated. Two had already fainted and the third was just falling to his knees as Coxita droned on, managing to equate syndicalism with Leninism, from which she segued to German state capitalism, and brushing aside the suppression of Catalonia in 1937.

Lieutenant Colonel John Di Salo had humored his mistress on this 'welcome in'. She spoke their native Catalan and had made a similar conversion … but now it was beginning to make him seem a fool to people who mattered, such as Brigadier Strauss. He strode up, took the microphone from Coxita, and bellowed out in a command voice, "DISMISSED!" He wasn't fully fluent in Catalan but knew the key words of command.

The men barked out a ragged cheer, gathered up the fallen, and retreated to their tents in exhausted, staggering steps. All they wanted was more water and then sleep. Coxita was bouncing on the balls of her feet from frustration. She felt she was just beginning to arrive at her point. She looked into her man's face to argue … and was instantly silent. She had never seen him this angry. He was an aristocrat. One trained in a very high-tone British sensibility. One did not show anger or fatigue or any similar emotion. Acting out in public was for proles.

She took his hand while he half-dragged her back to the tent they shared. She was not resisting him. She was self-absorbed, but not THAT foolish. The problem was that he was 15 centimeters taller than she was. Her legs were a bit long for her total height, but even so his stride was simply too long for her to comfortably keep up with. Usually he would adjust his pace so she could maintain position by taking her steps more quickly. This time he was moving at a brisk pace just this side of jogging. The anger may have been gone from his face, replacing by a gentleman's frozen mask, but his body language radiated hostile.

Once inside the tent he brutally spun her half around, then slapped her face. Hard. It wasn't a punch, but even open-handed the sound exploded like a cannon shell. She was knocked off her feet, breaking the fall with one hand. The hand held up her upper torso, while her lower body and legs were sprawled on the tent's wooden floor. Her nose wasn't broken, but there was blood oozing from it and her upper lip. He looked down on her and spoke, his voice soft but with a harsh, commanding tone. "If you ever humiliate me like that again, I will have you shipped back to Italy and dumped on the docks at Naples. You'll get the clothes on your back, one hundred lire, and your military ID marked 'discharged'. That's a thousand times better than where I found you, about to be raped to death by a gang of drunken Rif mercenaries."

She nodded her head meekly. Her survival walked on a knife edge. "Yes, John." Her voice came off more childish than her years. She knew no other way to sound submissive. At almost twenty years of age and 170 cm, the persona was not especially convincing. She was intellectually aware that her man had let her slide on this often in the past. Not today.

"I have humored your ideological obsessions for some time. It was absurd but ... but your beauty and other charms earned you those eccentricities. You have now gone from charmingly gauche, to making me look a fool obsessed with your sexual allure. It ends today. Old-shirt Falangism can be an amusing part of your persona. You really don't know what it means, but neither does anyone else we will meet in Egypt. For the rest, no more grand speeches on ideology. These Catalans all made their accommodations with reality. You made yours when you spread your legs for me. You adjusted further when you stayed with me in London. You could have thanked me for your escape and gone your way into the Left underground. The Republic had more than enough British sympathizers. You found luxury more appealing than proletariat austerity. This Clara woman of Hauptmann Bats. You will present yourself to her. You will be ingratiating, as much so as necessary. You will find an ideological line you can swallow to justify your conversion, your newly discovered old-shirt syndicalism. You will do this to my satisfaction or you will be on the docks of Naples looking for a new man."

Coxita meekly nodded and bowed her head. Emotionally, she would rather crawl across broken glass for three kilometers than abase herself in front of Clara, supposed Communist. That was the teenage-self speaking. John was right. She'd had her chances to leave. She had stayed. The bills were now coming due, and she would pay what she must to be an aristocrat's concubine instead of a dockside proletariat street whore.

0600 hours British Double Summer Time and CET
21 October 1940
Side conference room near the main War Cabinet meeting room, Westminster, London

The War Cabinet was suffering from information overload. The bombshell report from Cairo headed the list. It hit on top of Lord Gort informing the assembled ministers that the armored brigade en route to Egypt had been diverted to Lagos, Nigeria. The French had invaded Nigeria's Northern Region, which was now seen as lost. Somebody on one of the service staffs had diverted the convoy, in response to the pleas of the Governor-General. Somehow no one had bothered to tell the War Cabinet for three days. The tanks and crews were now ashore, wondering what to do next. The convoy with the First Infantry Division, promised as reinforcements to Montgomery in Sierre Leone, had in turn been diverted to the Gold Coast. De Gaulle, Montgomery, the Free French in Equatorial Africa, Percival in Kenya ... the list went on and on. Everyone and his cousin were demanding men, tanks, planes, supplies. There were two convoys at sea with planes. Neither had yet reached the Azores. Loading at Liverpool and the western ports was another large convoy with 50th Infantry Division, an army tank brigade, corps-level artillery, and two squadrons of Hurricane fighters. A decision must be made of where to send these. The Services must be told they could not divert convoys on their own hook, no matter how frantic the pleas from a Governor-General. The German proposal for a restricted sea war zone was also unprecedented and potentially worrisome.

On top of this, Winston had tossed a bomb on them. As part of his fiddling with India, he had put into the heads of a group of local dignitaries that Bombay had once been crown land. Passed to Britain in the 17th Century as part of the dowry of a Portuguese princess. Winston had proclaimed the city to again be British soil, apart from whatever happened to the rest of India. Wanted to hold a special election for Bombay's seat in Commons. No one had a clue of what to make of this daft proposal.

The War Cabinet had argued in circles all through the prior evening and now into the following morning. The members were falling down exhausted and had talked themselves hoarse. Prime Minister Bevin, Labor Party Leader Clement Atlee, and Rab Butler, nominally as Foreign Secretary, but in fact as representative for the 1922 Committee, had retired to a side room to try to make some sense out of what had happened.

Bevin had summoned the only War Cabinet secretariat member he trusted, Kim Philby, to take notes and prepare memoranda. The discussion had then rambled for a further hour before Philby at last took charge. "Gentlemen, may I suggest you are approaching this backwards." He had everyone's attention.

"How so?" This was from Atlee, still trying to decide how much he trusted Bevin's new protégé.

"Start with the Middle East. Wavell's full plan will split the Ministry. It has His Majesty's forces acting in a Nazi-like manner. Laying waste to whole nations under British protection. The legalists, moralists, and humanitarians will never stomach this. British public probably won't either, once they hear of it. Our newspaper-reading middle class sees affairs of state in moral terms. Plus, we would be wrecking the main prizes we have already mostly conceded to the Hun at the Peace Talks. Might well upset them. So, no scorched earth."

Mention of peace talks brought a response from the foreign secretary. "If we are agreed to give over the three, why not just let me make peace now? I can get a signed peace at Lisbon within a week in return for all three lands. I can quite possibly even get us left with the port of Basra and a small glacis around it."

Atlee shook his head savagely, more to clear it of fatigue than in anger at Butler. He disliked the man on principle, but not in this case as a matter of policy. "For the same reasons we couldn't last week or the week before. That collection of self-regarding grand men of British politics won't accept anything so raw till we lose Cairo, Jerusalem and probably Baghdad as well. The same litany over minority rights, local sovereignty, Suez Canal shares and a hundred other things that have nothing to do with world political realities. Their minds are still in the era when the world accommodated itself to British whims. Did you see their response to being baldly told that thousands of subjects of the crown, hundreds of thousands of imperial peoples and protected minorities would be abandoned to their fate? They pronounced it unthinkable, but then how did they respond to being told that the only way to do mass evacuation required putting down the inevitable local Arab risings the way the Huns put down Belgium in '14? Equally unthinkable! They cried out that some middle way must be in their opinions be found, so nothing so beastly happened to anyone. They are living in a dream world. Half the time, when listening to them natter on, I wish we had kept the air war going. Maybe, after half of Britain's cities burned to the ground, they would comprehend what modern war was." The other three were eyeing Atlee strangely. They had all thought similar things, but here he was saying it aloud.

"That's all well and good, Clem. We have to do something. They won't ever agree to anything. We must decide between us, and present them with facts they cannot reverse. I'm prepared to dig my political grave." Bevin looked around at the other two officeholders, who nodded assent. "Kim, you will draft the following orders over our signature. Wavell is relieved as Commander-in-Chief. He's to fold his headquarters into Cunningham's and return home. We need a military adviser to cabinet who can face down Gort and his brain-dead minions, most of whom were Dill's beforehand." He looked around the table. They were still with him. "The committee of three is to remain in Cairo. If precluded by time or communications constraints, they are given the authority to act on our behalf. O'Connor's resignations are rejected. Ninth Army is his. Advise him to get his supplies now while it's possible." Again he looked around the table for dissent. Atlee was uneasy. He opened and closed his mouth a few times, but no words came out. Instead it was a sound, low and throaty. Almost like a moan. Bevin was PM, but Clement had the duty as party leader to sell this pile of manure to the Labor caucus. A body that included many 'men of principle' who prided themselves on never letting worldly reality interfere with principles. "Both commanders are to begin evacuation of British nationals and, space and security situation permitting, to get out as many empire peoples and protected minorities as possible. These evacuations are voluntary, but people involved will be told of their danger … "

"Stress it's *war zone* danger," Butler put in. "Cannot risk telling the man in the street that we are pulling out quickly. The places will melt down and endanger our forces. Caution both commanders that not spooking the Arabs, so as to provoke uprisings and endanger military operations, takes precedence." The Foreign Secretary looked around the table and saw consternation. "If we don't give our lads an order of priorities, you are just playing Pilate – washing your hands of the lynch mob to come. That crowd in there will savage *them* when the blame is collectively *ours*. This is the fruit of the generation between the wars, of over-commitment and unwillingness to pay for redeeming our promises. I'm as much to blame as anyone. We three can mount the steps to the chopping block together. I think history will absolve us, but I am prepared to see my name dragged in the mud. Are you?" No one nodded; but neither did they say no.

"Demolitions?" Philby knew this part had to be made clear, one way or the other.

No one wanted to speak. There was no easy answer. Bevin finally stated the obvious, thereby taking the moral responsibility. "No demolitions except in the case of immediate military necessity. We act as though we will hold these lands forever, as if we will recover them soon if lost. So we don't blow up ports until they are in direct danger of loss. The same for putting the block ships into the Canal. We don't burn down Cairo's waterworks just to leave burdens on the new occupiers. We don't do mass killings of Arab civilians to terrorize them into submission. On the other hand, if it saves British lives, needs must. We already have revolts in Palestine and Iraq. Egypt will explode when the Line goes there."

Philby put it all together while his three superiors just sat there, drunk with fatigue. "Sirs, I'd add some words about preserving their armies as a matter of priority over loss of terrain or even well-known cities. Also that nothing be done to bring war to Holy Places like Jerusalem. Get our headquarters and supply dumps out of the Old City. Perhaps hand it over to a committee of neutral ambassadors and religious leaders as an open city?" No one contradicted him. "So we are agreed that Cunningham can evacuate Alamein at discretion as soon as he feels the safety of his forces is threatened. Eighth Army, less the Australian Corps, is to retire up the Nile."

Atlee was mildly surprised. "Why not the Australians?"

"Sudan is a dead end." Philby knew the region from his father's friends. "The Australian government will have kittens over their lads trapped there. Get as many of them as you can into Sinai. They can exit through Basra. They won't all make it that way. A good number end up trekking up the Nile, but you will show Canberra that we tried. It's good imperial diplomacy."

Atlee finally smiled. He was beginning to see what his colleague Bevin saw in this young Tory. He might be a toff, but he didn't look down his nose at Laborites. "Don't send the part on the Australians. Let that blame go to the Australian government in Canberra. That leaves how do we get that lot – ," He tossed his head back at the main room, making clear he was referencing the rest of the War Cabinet,

" – to avoid rehashing it." Atlee thought for a second. "What say we announce we have accepted Churchill's plan on Bombay as a constituency in Commons? They will be at least a week debating that absurd idea to death. Doesn't much matter what they decide. They will do fuck-all about anything else in the meantime. Gives Wavell the space he needs to do the handover, use the committee's Sunderland flying boat to get here, then huddle with us on how we handle what's left of this war." No one had the energy to argue; the discussion ended there.

1000 hours CET
21 October 1940
Heydrich's Office, Prinz-Albrecht-Straße, Berlin

"Would you please repeat that?" Schellenberg was traveling, and the boss was dealing directly with lesser minions. Lower-level folks whom he completely terrified. The one standing in front of him now was all but shaking in terror. "The main Messerschmitt factory used aluminum for ladders and now is complaining that they are short of this material? I would think lumber would be fine for civilian purposes in wartime."

The Sturmbannführer making the report had headed the audit team. He was not an experienced accountant or administrator. He merely had sufficient rank to stare down senior factory people, who had been most uncooperative until the Sturmbannführer had dialed Berlin to get the Reichsführer on the line. The Messerschmitt executives had then backed down for two hours while one of their number tried to telephone the Führer. Thankfully that august personage 'could not be disturbed'. "Reichsführer, there was both incredible waste and very poor controls on the use of materials. The ladders were for use in agriculture, vineyards."

In a deceptively calm voice Heydrich asked for clarification on what these ladders were to be used for in vineyards and why Messerschmitt was involved.

Desperate to end the report as quickly as possible, the Sturmbannführer all but stumbled over his words: "Messerschmitt has metalworking divisions involved in things other than war work. The aluminum was used for ladders that the grape plants will grow on to support them. What is needed is an SS office with direct control of strategic materials at the factory. Without day-to-day supervision, they will ignore national needs. They seem unable to grasp that the day of private business has passed."

"Who was the most insolent among the administrators?" Heydrich heard the reply and wrote it down. The name was inserted into a form ordering summary execution. The Sturmbannführer was directed to return to the factory with a mobile hanging truck. These had a large crane at the back from which a noose could be dropped and a body hauled up by the neck to swing in the breeze. This fool would hang tomorrow, and the rest would be told the crane could always return. Retrieve the ladders. Account for every gram of every strategic material. Welcome to the future.

1600 hours local; 1500 hours CET
21 October 1940
Headquarters Italo-German Panzer Army, 10 km southeast of Bagush Box

Officially this was just a liaison conference. First Libyan Division was a designated army reserve unit, but was in XXI Corps sector. The two commanders, Generals Dalmazzo and Maletti, wished to discuss with General Geloso, the Army Commander, certain hypothetical situations that could arise during the projected offensive at the other end of the line. In fact, the entire time was taken up exploring the possibilities Lieutenant Colonel Di Salo had presented.

"Let me be sure I fully comprehend." Geloso hated loose ends. He was a very precise person. "This happens with or without us." Both other generals nodded. Di Salo had made that crystal clear. "So when the Prince as Lieutenant General of the Realm, is sorting this out with Generals Halder and Beck after the fact, our fingerprints are in no way on this?"

Dalmazzo was quite firm on this. "I have my staff doing a number of hypothetical plans. They are loyal to me and would lie if I requested it, but in fact they have no idea that any of this is real. Di Salo doesn't have an exact day or place, so there is no specific detail for an investigation to uncover. At the point where Rommel's main body starts to move, my liaison officers notify my headquarters. I pull the closest applicable plan out of the files. We improvise from there. However, my strength is all up front in defensive positions. The obvious initial attack force should be 1st Libyan Division … "

"Which is not under your command. Hence this meeting, so you can both inform your staffs that I authorize the division passing to you under certain circumstances. I will provide such a written directive." Geloso paused. He wanted both his listeners to focus on what he said next. He had learned such rhetorical devices. "The plan will send the Libyans through first, but they will have their own objective. General Maletti, you are going to Cairo."

"Cairo?" Maletti had presumed he would be the main attack element of XXI Corps. "How does this aid the Corps battle?"

"It doesn't. It aids Italy. We have been promised Egypt by the Germans. It will be easier to get them to keep that promise if Cairo is occupied by Italians, if the Egyptian Royal Family passes into Italian hands. I will drop the Libyan Parachute Brigade, the one we used on Malta. You will link up with them, secure the Palace and the seat of government. The justification will be to avoid British demolitions in the city. The two units of Libyans speak Arabic. They are both experienced in putting down unrest. We want a compliant Egyptian monarchy, not a hostile Egyptian Arab Republic. Look at the mess the British have made for themselves in Iraq."

"How do you hide the preparations for the airborne operation?" Dalmazzo was puzzled. This was not going as he envisioned it.

Geloso laughed. "We don't. That's the beauty of it. Iraq is our excuse. We even ask for German aid in terms of transport planes, perhaps gliders as well. We refuse their offer of airborne units. The language issue. Ours speak Arabic. Theirs don't." He then threw a personal nod of approval to the two before him. "Nothing on paper, but the Prince and Marshal Balbo will be made aware of your contributions to the coming victory. I will leave reward of this Tenente Colonello to you, Generale Dalmazzo. His Germans must not learn of his duplicity, but do find some way to show your approval." Geloso thought to himself that if all went according to plan, he would in due course move on to higher command. This Di Salo might be someone he would bring with him. Perhaps he could continue to work miracles interacting with Germans. Geloso did not enjoy his dealings with the quite arrogant von Manstein. Perhaps a Colonello Di Salo might be a useful interface in the future?

1700 hours Central Daylight Time; 2300 hours CET
21 October 1940
17 East Monroe Street, Palmer House Hotel, Chicago

Willkie was on a roll, and he knew it. Franklin had stepped in it, tried to hedge and dodge on the 'Atlantic Zone of Peace'. Willkie took the high road while Lindbergh and Coughlin took it right down into the gutter, egged on by the *Chicago Tribune* and its pack of newspaper imitators. Now here he was at a high strategy meeting with Lindy and Dewey. It was not politic to be associated this closely with Coughlin at this stage of the campaign. Too many traditional Republican voters were anti-Papist. So instead of the fiery Canadian radio preacher, there was a nun from the Sisters of Providence of Mary-of-the Woods quietly in the corner. The order had a large mission in China, which hid this nun's association with Coughlin's political crusades. She nominally represented the Catholic missionaries. In fact she took excellent shorthand. She would handcarry the typed transcript to Coughlin on the overnight train.

Willkie had started his campaign expecting to be running against some other Democrat. The no-third-term custom was an unwritten law of US politics. Willkie actually liked and somewhat respected Roosevelt, their fights over the TVA aside. Still, that was then and this was now. Willkie had become used to luxury suites and top flight hotels in his business career. Rooms such as this were second nature to him. Plotting the last two weeks of a successful presidential run were not. "Tom, are you sure?"

Dewey shook his head wearily. Willkie was a shallow neophyte. This nomination should have been his. He was sure he could have beaten Taft at the convention, had the powers-that-be not rigged it for this silly man. The powers were prepared to let Tom Dewey run a campaign, but thought him too young and difficult to control as a candidate. "There is no such thing as 'sure' in politics until the votes are counted. We have the best pollsters and state managers money can buy. I'm sure that some are mistaken on cities. A few may be on whole states. However, mistakes flow in both directions. So while some states will be worse than we think, some will be better. The smart move is to follow the money. We are getting a flood of late contributions from interests normally in the Democratic column, such as independent oil. They are using back doors and fronts, but they make sure I know who you will have to thank when you are sworn in. None of these have abandoned Franklin. This is 'just in case' money. The top people on that side are scared." Dewey paused to see if Willkie had the political sense to follow. He wasn't at all sure the amateur could cope. "It's probably down to three states. California, New York, and New Jersey are tossups. With an honest count I'd say you'd take all three by a nose. However, honest counts in New York and New Jersey are always aspirational. Best we can probably do is limit the box-stuffing. However, Franklin needs all three to win."

"Truman's your problem." Lindbergh knew little about politics, and cared less. He did know the art of celebrity, of working crowds. "He's a combat veteran. You aren't. For the fence-sitters, his promise that he won't let their kids be sent to die in a 2nd AEF carries weight. He paints you as a rich boy who kept himself out of combat, then defended deserters." He saw Willkie's anger but ploughed on. "The truth doesn't matter. You are a rich boy from Wall Street to these folks. That sets it up for them to believe the worst of you."

Dewey cut in before Willkie could rise to his own defense. "Wendell, electoral politics has certain iron laws. Time you learned them. Once the public gets an impression of a candidate, it's near impossible to change it. The four of you have been defined. Different ones like or dislike you, Franklin, Truman. Your veep could stay home for all he matters. Outside Oregon, he's seen as a featherweight nonentity. Second rule: at this point over 90% of the voters have made up their minds. What you are doing at this point is chasing that last few percent and – far more important – affecting motivations. Leave Dixie out. They are still stuck in 1865, waiting for Saint Bobby Lee to come down from Heaven and save the Confederacy. You may win a few states on their fringe, but the core would vote Democrat for any white man. Outside of that benighted region, maybe 70% of the people will vote. Might get to 75%. Could drop below 60%. Who stays home is almost as important as who votes for you. You don't need Franklin's supporters to switch sides. You can win states if enough New Dealers decide the line at the polls looks too long. That's why this war-and-peace stuff matters so much. Even people who like Franklin, mostly don't want another war. Few of the pro-intervention folks want to have millions of infantry off in Europe or Africa dying like flies. Keep hammering Zone of Peace. Big navy and air force, but their boys don't get buried on other continents."

"And they don't trust Franklin's promises. He was a Wilson man, and they see Woodie as having lied his way into the war he was 'too proud to fight'." Lindy was passionate for the anti-Intervention cause. "I'm not with you for partisan reasons. And not because I liked Hitler or the Nazis. I respected what they were doing with their country, especially in aviation, but I would never want a Nazi state here. I'm not even advocating violence against the damned Red Hebrews. I just want them to act like real Americans. I don't care if I shame them into it, or scare them enough, just so long as it works."

His supposed allies were leaving Willkie nauseous. He was on the wrong side. And he knew it. He was a liberal, a decent man. And he'd sold his soul. The only way to buy it back required that he win. Or all he would be remembered for were the gutter speeches of Lindbergh and Coughlin, of the libelous headlines from the *Tribune*. "If Truman is the problem, why don't we pull him home. Schedule McNary to barnstorm the state, one county courthouse at a time. Throw Charlie and enough money at the state, and Harry either scurries home to give courthouse speeches or loses his home state."

Dewey sat in thought for near a minute. The other two let him. Dewey was the one with the voting numbers in his head, in his notepad. "Yes. I'd listed Missouri as tossup. Let's go for it." The nun in the corner politely cleared her throat. They had yet to address HER issue. "Yes Sister, I hear you. Guys, we each mention China in every speech from here out. Patton and Eisenhower are already there with some troops. No draftees. We stress that. Defense of Jesus and the free market. Freedom Airmen even somehow managed to get half a dozen P-26's over there with crews, while Chennault is still mucking around. His ship figures to land by month's end I hear."

The sister gave a polite thank-you. She had her agenda, separate from Coughlin's or indeed any of theirs. The missionary community would take support from Roosevelt but didn't trust him. Too many of his supporters were open in preferring the atheistic Chinese Communists. The meeting went on into campaign details that didn't interest her and she was sure would be of no interest to Coughlin. She continued to dutifully take notes. She could do that as second nature with no thought. Her thoughts were on God's will that the Chinese be converted and educated. She could care less about the 'free market'. The church's teaching on the dignity of labor did not jibe with this sort of Chamber of Commerce boosterism.

0800 hours local; 0100 hours CET
22 October 1940
Air southwest of Wuhan, China

Colonel Davis found his new rank difficult to digest. He knew how long it had taken his father to reach a similar plateau. Wartime often meant rapid promotion. Not this quick, however. Here he was commanding a theoretical air wing, when in fact all that had reached China so far were six P-26 fighters. Supposedly he had been sent to Shanghai. The head of the friendly Chinese government had other notions. The six planes had been shipped up river to Wuhan, the westernmost city his forces controlled. There was also some historical connection to a prior government he had headed. Davis found Chinese politics almost as confusing as Chinese geography.

This Christian China turned out to be a collection of sea ports, river ports, rail lines, and a few inland cities. Most of the rest could be defined as 'here be dragons'. No one exactly ruled. The villagers saluted any army that was present, and cursed them all behind their backs. To a farmer, armies were like Biblical plagues.

The funniest part of the whole thing was the enemy. They also flew P-26's as well as Soviet planes, one of which looked generally like a P-26 to his under-trained pilots. His men could fly. Fly far better than Davis could. His mechanics were also first rate. Most days they could get four of the six fighters ready for patrol. What they needed experience on, was wartime skills like shape recognition. One of Davis's pilots had dreamed up a way around the identification problem. A new paint scheme — red tails, blue wings, and white bodies. So far they hadn't shot any of their own down.

The next trick was getting in the air. The 'early warning system' was radio teams on the surrounding mountains. Those teams got to play vicious tag with Nationalist partisans and local bandits. The bandits were more aggressive, but less threatening. Once he proved he would ransom prisoners, they even stopped shooting at his men. They would just surround them and begin the negotiations. He had a liaison officer from the Shanghai government trying to convert this into a formal contract. He was willing to pay monthly protection money for his men's safety. In return the paid-off gang would fight anyone else trying to harm his guys. So far only one bandit chief had agreed. They weren't even really that expensive, compared to the cost of sending a division of troops all the way from the States to do the same thing.

Davis had scrambled with two companions twenty minutes ago. Half the time these flights were giant wastes of time. They would never see the enemy, and just return to base. This time the Nationalist were clearly looking for a fight. Six P-26's heading straight for Wuhan, grouped in three pairs at what appeared to be twelve thousand feet. Davis's group was at sixteen thousand. He had found the Nationalists rarely went that high. Probably inferior octane of their fuel.

His companions were clearly better pilots than he was. Rank couldn't change that. The older of the two led the flight. He kept them on a level heading as the enemy slowly rose to meet the red tails. When the Nationalists passed fourteen thousand feet, the first Tuskegee plane started its dive. The second followed, with Davis bringing up the rear.

There was a clear pattern to these fights. Davis had been given firm instructions. Use his speed advantage from the dive for a fast shooting pass, but keep going down. When he had dropped at least two thousand feet with no one on his tail, start the long loop back up to repeat the process. The moment he saw an opponent during this, dive again to shake them. Run away back to base if necessary. He was the worst pilot in the group. He was only in the air to gain familiarity. Most important, whatever he did, pay no attention to the other two Freedom Flyers. Davis needed all his attention on flying his plane, maintaining his navigational fix, and keeping his tail clean.

Davis thought he'd hit someone on his passthrough. He was pretty sure he hadn't been hit in reply. The controls didn't feel like his P-26 was damaged. One enemy plane peeled off after him. Davis increased the angle of his dive a bit and started turning towards home. The hostile clung to his tail but wasn't gaining on him. Probably the fuel differential. By now both planes were below five thousand feet and still descending. Davis momentarily lost his navigation lock. He aimed for the river. He could see it ahead. He knew his landmarks on it. He was down below a thousand feet and almost up to the river when he saw one of his memorized way points. A set of commercial buildings wrecked in the Japanese battle to take the city, and not yet cleared or rebuilt. The locals used pieces for projects of their own, but no one would do the public service of clearing the lot of more than they needed themselves that day.

Cutting out over the river, Davis broke left upstream. His foe hadn't gotten close enough for a real shot. Davis kept his heading. The Nationalist had a surprise waiting. Half a mile ahead, Davis flashed past a Freedom brigade outpost on a three-story flat roof. The guys there knew the color schemes. He was friendly, so what was chasing him wasn't. The hostile P-26 ran into four M-2 heavy machine-guns filling the air over the river with lead. He pulled away trailing smoke. This guy wasn't making it home. Davis went another mile and turned left to his main runway a half mile further. He made an easy landing. His guys were back twenty minutes after. Both planes were full of bullet holes. They were claiming two definites and a probable.

Davis had already gotten the Chinese liaison officer to work. He was getting the word out. The Yanks would pay for the crashed planes. Find them, guard them, and send messengers. Help the retrieval team, and on the return to Wuhan a nice pile of green US dollars was yours. If you preferred goods or food, just give a shopping list and it would be along in a week or two by river steamer. The wrecks were a great source of spare parts. The American way of war treated money as a weapon. They had it and their opponents did not. Wasn't a matter of patriotism anymore. Both sides were now Chinese.

0700 hours local; 0600 hours CET
22 October 1940
Headquarters Afrika Division, southwest of Bagush Box and in the rear of Italian XXII Corps line, Alamein position

The conference tent was a mix of service uniforms. There were Army, Waffen SS, SA, Navy, Air Force, and NL all mixed together among the battalion and regimental commanders of this thrown-together division. Lothar Engels sat there in shock. In this reorganized structure he was now a battalion commander in Kampfgruppe Germania.

General Steiner was explaining the new organization to everyone. "Forget the original table of organization. We have one complete unit, the Baltic regiment. That becomes the core of Kampfgruppe Baltic. The three Baltic battalions plus a fast battalion of armored cars, motorcycles and motorized infantry. A company each of anti-tank and antiaircraft guns. A navy-manned battery of French 75's. A company of Sturmpioniere from the navy. The Baltic infantry had seen some action in the prior battle at the salient, so the Kampfgruppe isn't all green. Kampfgruppe Germania is not so lucky. We have bits and pieces from the regiments that are supposed to make up the rest of this division. Out of this we have four ersatz battalions of motorized infantry, a further battalion each of motorized machine-guns and light mortars on loan from Kampfgruppe Jodl, a Sturmpionier company from our friends at the Palestine Camp Complex in the General Government, and a fast battalion of armored cars and motorcycles. No motorized infantry this time with the fast troops, but instead the fast battalion has an air force battery of eight-eights, again on loan from General Jodl's force. Our naval friends have provided a good signals company for each Kampfgruppe and an extra one for divisional HQ. Also Brigade Strauss has gifted us with a fine veteran officer, Sturmbannführer Engels."

Lothar acknowledged the mention by coming to full attention and giving a slight bow at his general. He was vastly proud of his promotion – and at a loss as to how it had happened. Steiner was droning on about a third Kampfgruppe, designated *Tirpitz*, built around the artillery regiment and a battalion of naval infantry, all of these troops Kriegsmarine personnel. Lothar's ruminations came to an abrupt halt as he heard Steiner mention his name again, " – Sturmbannführer Engels will now share with us his impressions on fighting the British in a mobile engagement."

Talk about being unprepared. Some fool should have warned him. He walked slowly to the front and began to speak, trying to keep a steady voice instead of once again letting his anger get the best of him. "My experience was as a company commander in a mixed fast battalion similar to what I will now be commanding. Four good companies, two fairly large, but no real maneuver training on working together. The British were brave. They attacked often and pressed the attacks longer than circumstances deserved. Their battlefield reconnaissance was poor – "

His new regimental commander interrupted him. The man had an SA uniform with an Oberführer's insignia, and seemed to be in his forties. "Poor how? Please be more specific."

"They didn't send forward scouting elements. They didn't even do reconnaissance by fire. They would send a mixed group of tanks, Bren gun carriers and sometimes motorized infantry forward until they ran into us. Half the time the infantry never left their trucks before the engagements were over. They would fight until they took real losses and just pull out. When they left, they all left. They didn't leave observers behind to plot our movements or call down artillery."

Several people in the audience laughed. One said, "So they are idiots?"

Lothar couldn't quite see who was talking. He was focusing on his Oberführer, and Steiner the divisional commander. He was also working overtime on his temper. He didn't want the old explosive Lothar to ruin things for him. "No. Their higher commanders simply don't respond well to mobile conditions. Mobile war takes fast reactions and constant focus on everyone's shifting positions. My battalion commander had this. The British field officers didn't."

Steiner was looking at him carefully. Lothar paused to let the general speak. "You respected your old commander?"

Ah. Lothar understood the problem. Someone had gossiped. Probably Steiner had sent someone around to his old company. One SA man to another, one of his Sturmführers would have told the story of the epic blowup. Told it making Lothar look better and the boy Major worse, but a new commander would be wary of why a unit had been trying to rid itself of a veteran commander before a major battle. "I didn't then. The fault was mine, sir. I'm old. He was young. He had been HJ before joining the NL. I'm an old fighter from the SA and couldn't bring myself to take an 18-year-old seriously. I've had time to reflect on my temper. It's bad. It's a fault I am working on correcting. Major Steiner taught me a lot of how to make mobile war work. Once I got over being pigheaded, the lessons were worth learning."

Now the room was paying rapt attention. Lothar was quite unused to important people taking him seriously. They never had before in his life. "Do go on, Sturmbannführer." This time the command was again from the Oberführer.

"Major Steiner always had motorcyclists out in all directions, almost as a screen. Mobile war is like war at sea that way. The terrain here doesn't give you landmarks. The sand and dust blows. You have to at all times be prepared to be attacked from any direction. You must also remember that holding terrain is meaningless. If facing a clearly superior force, give ground to preserve the integrity of your command." Lothar made sure he had General Steiner's full attention. He fixed his gaze on the general and continued. "Before you ask, this is where I had my falling out with my old commander. I was too much the brawler. Wanted my armored cars to slug it out with British tanks. I lost good men and several Panhard armored cars doing this. Afterwards, while I was on detached duty with the repair section, my Major prepared a chart for me. It showed which weapons could penetrate the frontal armor on which vehicles at which ranges. He was right. I would have done more damage to a British cruiser tank using a sledge-hammer than the small cannon I had. I'm an old dog, but he forced me to learn some new tricks. There's no going back there. I showed far too much disrespect. But I can use what I was forced to learn, to benefit this command." Lothar actually felt good admitting all this. Maybe it was never too late to grow up a bit.

His new Regimental commander wasn't buying this conversion. He seemed to be wishing he still had bullheaded Lothar the brawler. "So now the SA runs away from a fight?"

"Sir, no one said run. Our eight-eights can beat any tank in Africa. So can the 7.5 cm guns in the other Kampfgruppe. The trick is to maneuver the British into range of those. Failing that, you pull back before the tanks, while shooting up their support vehicles, the Bren gun carriers and trucks. You can then maneuver behind the tanks. Armored cars can damage a cruiser tank from the rear. It needs to be fairly close range. But the British are pugnacious. They will keep coming at you until bloodied fairly badly. So it isn't that hard to lead them to the field guns."

Lothar had to keep from laughing. After one battle that almost got him court-martialed, that should have gotten him drummed out of the SA as a mutinous fool, he was now the voice of wisdom to a Division. God help them all when the offensive started.

1400 hours CET
22 October 1940
Eichmann's office, Palestine Camp Group Complex, west of Cracow, General Government, and east of the Auschwitz camp complex

The next visitor thought he rated special treatment. Eichmann was besieged by entrepreneurs, influence peddlers, and oddball hustlers six days a week. Had he been willing to work on Sundays, it would have been seven days a week. He reserved Sunday for family life and sport. His wife understood his need for routine and diligence.

The businessman arrived promptly. He was immaculately dressed, with an expensive watch and (to Eichmann's taste) far too much personal jewelry. Even his belt and shoes were an exotic leather, some form of reptile. The petitioner was attempting to project an aura of success.

His letters of reference were equally ostentatious. A letter from Admiral Canaris testified to the gentleman's valuable work for the Abwehr in Bohemia and Poland in 1938-1939. A sheaf of letters from Party officials showcased his high connections within that bureaucracy. Eichmann had become a connoisseur of such. He noted that they were all from the General Government, the Bohemian Protectorate, and two border Gau's from the Reich itself. Nothing from the Party's national level, much less the actual Party Ministry in Berlin. Finally there were a dozen senior Wehrmacht, Waffen SS, and Police reference letters. Eichmann saw as good or better multiple times a day. Everyone wanted access to his pool of skilled labor and camp complexes.

This man had a slightly different set of unrealistic expectations. He had two major factories in Cracow. One was an enamel works making soldier's mess kits as well as kitchen supplies for the civilian market. It also had two production lines making ammunition. The other was a large printing works. He also already had his labor force, a mix of Jews and Poles. His problem was that he was housing and employing several thousand Jews outside the proper camps or ghettos. This had always been forbidden, and those rules were month by month being more aggressively enforced. "It's like this. I have a few guards. I need papers from you designating my facilities a subcamp of your Palestine complex. I would of course be properly grateful. There would be no expenses on your side. I can pay the guards out of my own receipts. They just need armbands making them official auxiliary police. I can even arrange their weapons and something that could pass as uniforms." The man looked at Eichmann expectantly. Eichmann returned a level gaze and said nothing. The man dropped four diamonds on the desk. Eichmann was no gemologist, but presumed they were of value. Eichmann still gave no response. The man sighed and added his watch to the proposed bribe.

"Put your idiot bribes back in your own pockets. I like my head where it is, firmly attached to my shoulders. My wife is also quite fond of it there." The slick operator seemed to deflate. He gave a half-smile as if to say it had been worth a try. Eichmann pounced. He pulled out a street map of Cracow. "Mark your locations. Production, warehousing, the sleeping accommodations, everything including where your guard posts would go, what street traffic would be blocked, and the like."

The man looked at Eichmann strangely but did it as bid. Eichmann looked over the map. No streetcar lines were blocked. No major truck routes were inconvenienced. Eichmann took out a red pen, adding changes to make the district more cohesive, mostly by adding eight more buildings. Buildings that had nothing of any economic or military importance. Eichmann's map of Cracow was quite detailed, and updated weekly. "You see the eight added buildings. Find some use for them. My accounting staff will see that they are seized by administrative fiat. You will be informed of their monthly rental. You will also have a one-time expense of moving whoever lives there, plus the businesses from the commercial space. For what you ask, the fee is six thousand marks a month as a guarantee against five percent of your gross receipts. You will also take a company of my guards, to whom yours will report. Your men can see to the prisoners and premises. Mine will see to the perimeter security." The man's eyes were half bugging out. Eichmann laughed at him in a scornful tone. "No bribes. My accounting staff will have full access to your records and billings departments, keys for all locked desks, office safes and the like. You will be billed for all of this monthly. You pay by check to the Palestine Camps Complex Main Administrative Fund, Dresdner Bank, Main Cracow office." Now the man was shaking his head as if to wake from a dream. "Whatever stupidity you do with your Party, Wehrmacht, and Waffen SS connections is your affair. I put you on warning, Herr Oskar Schindler, if I ever catch you offering so much as a pfennig to any of my people, it will be the last day of your talentless life. I'll shoot your wife in front of you, then hang you at the entrance to your plant. The New Germany does not tolerate corruption. My superior, Reichsführer Heydrich, executes Gauleiters. We less exalted people should take that as a warning. Now explain to me why you use Poles mixed in with your Jews?" A quite chastened Schindler spent a further half hour explaining the details of his operation. Eichmann thought to himself that if this 'businessman' couldn't find what to do with the new facilities, Eichmann could find other small operators who would be glad to sublet. He doubted Berlin would notice the extra money, but either way his hands were clean. Bribes? Was everyone an idiot these days?

0300 hours local; 0200 hours CET
23 October 1940
Observation post a few yards to the rear of British 7th Malta Division lines, Alamein position

A sit like this was boring in the extreme. Sergeant Billy Lincoln didn't care. He had been getting a bad feeling about things. Last time he had gotten these sort of feelings was March, 1918 in France with the Fifth Army. In his time on the Western Front, the Germans didn't attack. They counterattacked. Except that felt different. All sorts of little things were odd that March, and Billy wasn't a deep thinker. So he'd gotten his squad started on elementary preparations. Which had saved their lives when the hammer fell. He and some of his lads had made it back to the final British line after a hellish week.

Now he was getting the same bad feeling. It was all little things. This time everyone knew the attack was coming. But the toffs were all sure it would come on the southern half of the front. Front ran 7th Malta Division, 6th Commando Division, 8th Palestine Division. The actual brigades and battalions had been truly scrambled, but the command arrangement remained. Southern brigade of the 7th, where he was, should have been out of harm's way. The only action was patrols and raids being run by some Palestinian 'special unit'. Billy would have thought that Malta would have cured the staff idiots of special units, but it seemed they needed more lessons.

Billy prided himself on being a survivor. He'd parlayed a thirty-six-hour pass into tracking down the officer he had met on Malta, Lieutenant Commander Money-Penny. Man may have been a gentleman, but at heart he was the sort of thug Billy could relate to. Money-Penny heard him out. Told Billy to sit down. When the talk was done, Billy went back to his unit with papers transferring his squad to Money-Penny for some ill-defined special detail.

The detail amounted to monitoring these raids for Money-Penny. Who decided to view this one with Billy and two of his lads. The gentleman had brought containers of tea laced with brandy, decent meat pies and some other snacks to while away the time. Billy's lads couldn't quite understand how their long-serving pal Sergeant Billy had managed this magic, but it sure beat being in the lines living on bully beef. "Billy, is it always this sloppy?"

The lads were still surprised at how easily this gent talked to rankers. Billy was used to Money-Penny's style. Man didn't need petty things to establish his rank.   He could beat any man in the squad senseless one on one. Probably two on one, maybe three. Money-Penny was tough, strong, smart. The rank badges were just accessories for him, not what made him a superior. "Yes sir. Neither the Eyeties nor the Hun ever make raids back. So the lanes through the minefield are marked before every raid goes out, and the markers don't go down until they are all safely back. I've seen the raiders even send details back behind our front and then out again before daylight." Billy stopped at Money-Penny's knowing smirk. "Yes, sir. No trench raids. No artillery down on the retreating raiders. Fritz wants us fat and happy. Which goes against everything command is telling us ... "

"The same command that told us the airborne attack on Malta didn't matter, that the real invasion was coming by sea? That couldn't manage an orderly evacuation from the Grand Harbor? That got Western Desert Force savaged by an enemy attack several times their size? That hasn't gotten London to send dick-all as reinforcements?" Money-Penny didn't bother keeping the disgust and sarcasm out of his voice. "Your old regiment, Billy. Guess how many fresh drafts they have given to rebuild it?" Billy shrugged. He hadn't a clue as he was never went back. Been afraid they would ignore his new posting and keep him. "Four men. Men, not drafts. Two retired NCO's returned to colors, and two men who were in hospital. Four men who were already in Egypt. No one from home."

The two pro's exchanged knowing looks while the other two men huddled down trying to take this all in. Bad things were coming. Thankfully their sergeant would see to them. This officer seemed to have his head screwed on right. Damned upper class accent, but a proper bloke for all that.

1100 hours local; 1000 hours CET
23 October 1940
Finance tent, Brigade Strauss cantonment, rear of Italian XXI Corps line

"Choose one son. We need one of them for an active combat detail." Major Albert Witt was shocked to hear this. He and his boys were a detachment from the Interior Ministry, not real soldiers. Yet here was Brigadier Strauss changing the terms of this African safari. One boy was going forward to get shot at.

Witt played for time, hoping his brain would get in gear enough to protest. "One son? To do what, where? Why?”

"Brigade goes into combat after the main attack launches down south. If everything works right, Major Steiner here will lead his schnell battalion through with the Naval Detachment. They go to the port in Alexandria. That part may work, may not. It's war. If the air recon idiots are for once right, there's nothing on the hundred and twenty or so kilometers to the city except two military police roadblocks. The Division in front of us has a half-kilometer-deep battlefront with two lines of trenches and eight more kilometers of artillery and support positions. In effect a crust with no reserves."

The boy Major came in almost as soon as the commander finished speaking. To Papa Witt he looked like a schoolboy set among adults … until you noticed the officer's rank tabs and the Iron Cross First Class. Witt willed himself to ignore the youthful voice, stutters and breaks and all, to focus on the content. "Your son will be with my Battalion. A special Kampfgruppe makes the breach. Oberstleutnant Gorlov's battalion exploits the breach out through the battle and administrative areas, with the part of Lieutenant Colonel Di Salo's battalion that isn't in the break-in group. My Battalion supported by Sturmbannführer Peiper's does the dash to Alexandria. His has the Italian flame tankettes added. Your son and the Alexandria naval detachment go in as part of our force. The son is needed as a guardian of funds. A portion of the money should be up with us in case we need to start hiring quickly for the rebuilding of the port."

Witt stood there pensive. Deciding which son to risk in battle is not an easy decision. The Witts were professionals who worked in offices. Sure they did military service, but this was supposed to be administrative support work. If the one he chose died …

"I'll go, Papa." Uwe was the younger son. He'd always been more adventurous than his more dutiful older brother Arne. "Brigadier Strauss, Major Steiner, do I report someplace else now?"

"No. However, starting tomorrow you present yourself at my Battalion area after breakfast. We are putting you and the navy men through an abbreviated weapons and vehicles training course. It's all basics, but you should be able to handle your personal weapon, our standard machine-guns, drive one of our trucks, things like that." Steiner was glad he had a volunteer. This was going to be awkward enough with the navy men, most of whose officers had trouble accepting they were under the command of a teenager. Schellenberg's office had been queried via Leutnant Smith for how much money to send with the spearhead. Klaus wasn't sure he liked the plan. He was quite sure his opinion didn't matter. This trick by Gunter and the Italian Oberstleutnant either worked or it didn't. Steiner's troubles only started if it did. Then it was dash down a highway, burst through the two roadblocks, and take one of the largest ports in the region. What could possibly go wrong?

2000 hours local; 1900 hours CET
23 October 1940
Klaus and Greta's tent, Brigade Strauss Cantonment

This would be their last night together. Gunter had told Klaus he would be kept up all of the next night to transition him to being fully awake at night, sleeping during the daylight. The always optimistic Gunter admitted to the inner circle that this plan they had proposed to Rommel required more than a bit of luck to pull off. Klaus accepted the risks as just being part of war. Greta found it harder to quietly smile at her husband-to-be taking risks even Gunter felt where near insane. Greta wasn't sure if she exactly loved Klaus. Her views of what love was ran to romantic movies and whispered girlish conversations with her peers back home in Romania. Something long on bright sunshine, raging hormonal rushes of utter joy, and chirping birds. Greta was aware that this was a childish view. She was a woman now, as her family never stopped reminding her. Her Betar girls also gave her more practical advise.

Yes, she was no longer the silly virgin she had been back at the Ploiesti airport. The man she had given her maidenhead to had actually pledged to marry her, which was not how the stories about fallen women ran. She was to be a wife and mother … or perhaps mother and then wife, given how often they had sex. She liked Klaus well enough. She was happy around him, and happier still at how he treated her. She just had this nagging feeling that love was something more, something she had never experienced and perhaps never would. Still, he was her protector and he was about to risk his life in battle again. She was hiding her fear … and apparently doing a poor job of it.

"Greta, what's the matter?" Klaus was a clueless teenager – but then, most males find female moodiness mystifying.

Greta wanted to tell Klaus that nothing was the matter. She tried and failed. Instead she started sobbing and couldn't stop. "I'm sorry, I'm sorry, I'm sorry … "

 "Sorry for what, darling?"

She had to get words out. The sobs didn't stop but she began to whisper. "I'm afraid for you in the coming battle. This plan sounds insane. Repainted vehicles. Di Salo's English accent. It seems something out of an adventure movie."

Klaus held her tight, stroking her face. "Yes, darling. Gunter's part, Joey's, Di Salo's. The crews of the tanks and the armored cars. The boys on the vehicle tops pretending to be returning raiders. Even the first follow-on company. Maybe Uncle Ivan's battalion clearing out the immediate rear. Thousand things that could go wrong. By the time Peiper and I pass through its' worked or it hasn't. We drive down a paved highway, shoot up two roadblocks and go on into the city. One of the mechanics Joey recruited on Malta will be with me. He lived in Alexandria for half a dozen years. So I won't even get lost finding the port. Won't be any fighting there. British will have blown it up and been long gone." He caught himself calling Ivan Uncle. Mentally, Klaus shrugged. Betrothed was close enough. Besides, her people had all said he was family now.

She struggled to get words out. "Just be careful! I love you and want you to come back!" There. If she kept saying it maybe she would finally feel it. She then did what she usually did when at a loss with Klaus. She fucked his brains out.

As they finally drifted off to sleep, she decided she would ask Mary Collins. Mary had been a soldier's woman. Maybe she would know about all this. Mary had been younger than Greta when sold to her soldier.

0600 hours local and CET
24 October 1940
Cleared field southwest of Garua, Cameroun (once German Kameroun and currently under nominal Gaullist control)

They could hear the transport planes just as dawn was breaking.

"Now would be the right time, Feldwebel." The middle-aged Major had been a Hauptmann here in the Kaiser's War. Recalled by the Abwehr, he had spent years in what he believed was an absurd waste of time, assembling a small team of prior Africa hands and suitable younger men as a contingency should Germany's interests again turn to its old colonies.

The Feldwebel had been more than happy to have forgotten Africa. Civilian life had been much more appealing in the 1920's than Africa's relentless sun, endemic diseases, and endless variety of nasty insect life. Then came the Depression. When the nice man from the Abwehr looked him up, he'd jumped at it. Steady pay and the possibility of a pension was the lure. And now he was back in the African savanna. At least it wasn't the jungle. That horror was well to the south. He fired off the signal rocket. His squad of Schutztruppe veterans clustered around him. This kind of flare gun was new to them. They learned better by watching than lectures in the pidgin German creole they barely remembered from their military youth.

The four young HJ glider pilots were far from expert. After the transports cut them loose, they just lined up on the quite broad field and landed. This landing didn't need any special talents. The field was clean and clear enough. No one was shooting at them and there was precious little wind. They had volunteered, hoping to be heroes like the HJ's who had flown with the Reich's hero, Steiner, when Luqa was seized in the Malta operation. They hoped for similar glory. They also saw marching around this colonial land as much more fun than the Heer recruit barracks that would otherwise be their fate. On the ground, they helped the African porters unload the cargo. That done, they were now Gefreiters in this unit. Perhaps they might even get a chance at an encounter with bare-breasted jungle women. It had been stressed to them that the Race Laws did not apply to Africa.

At the edges of the landing field, a middle-aged man kept watch. He had been a professional hunter and safari operator before he had prudently returned to Europe in 1938. Everyone had expected war over the Sudetenland. Germans in French or British Africa would be interned. Back in Europe he found the winters even worse than his memories. The Abwehr recruiter had no problem signing him up. His duty would be as a scout and food provider via his hunting skills. Anyone who can track lion can easily track men.

At his side was a young man in his late teens. The Abwehr recruiter was quite understanding that the man with useful African skills might wish to take along a protégé. Such relationships had been common in the SA and Party before the Blood Purge. They were now frowned upon, but that was for Europe. What happened in Africa … This Thomas from Finland seemed a muscular, healthy Aryan specimen. The hunter would of course educate his 'companion' in the bush skills that formed his CV. Thomas seemed to be of a somewhat artistic temperament. Right now he was sketching muscular African boys recruited as porters.

By noon the commander had formed up the column. He debated burning the gliders, but decided against it. His mission was distraction and presence. The Free French were supposedly short of men. Let them find the gliders and give chase. He would be many kilometers away, showing the German flag and recruiting. If pressed he could fall back on the new French conquests across the river in Nigeria.

1200 hours local; 1100 hours CET
24 October 1940
Army General Headquarters Middle East (GHQ-ME), Grey Pillars (House), "Number Ten" Sharia Tolombat (aka Tolombat St. 10), Garden City, Cairo

The briefing was supposed to have been at 0730 hours. Many things were no longer happening on schedule these days. The staff colonel assigned to this task had just spent ten minutes apologizing before General Cunningham cut him off. "Jack, I accept that you will be amending these numbers for days, that the updates will cascade. Just give me what you've got and let's stop dancing. As soon as dusk gets the enemy air to return to base, I've got to scoot back to the battle HQ. I'm juggling two headquarters, and will be till we are out of Egypt."

"About that, sir. I will assign a military police company to escort you. Please bring it back along with an army one. The roads have gotten that bad. Lone British vehicles are seen as targets."

That one brought the rolling disaster home to General Cunningham. "Do we have an Iraq?"

"Not quite yet. We've got maybe a third of the Egyptian army confined to barracks because of officers we don't trust."

"What about the King and court?"

"King's content to wait for his Italian friends. Court? Some already left for India and points East. Some have vanished back to their estates to ride it out. The rest think they have enough Italian connections. The official evacuation was the straw that broke the camel's back. Rumor had us leaving for almost two months, but now it's out in the open. We have churches sacked, Europeans waylaid, even military being sniped at. The police and bureaucracy are melting. We have had to promise to evacuate thousands, and give priority to their families now. Between those families and the British community, there's jack-all we can do for the other Europeans, the Empire peoples, the minorities." If the boss wanted the unvarnished truth, the colonel would get it all on the table. "As is, we've needed cooperation from the enemy. They aren't attacking the rail lines or the bridges. Probably want to be sure they are there to be used by them. I simply must have more troops or it will all implode."

Cunningham had been aware this was coming. He'd rather just have evacuated the Alamein position and made a run for it. The ambassador, Sir Miles Lampson, would not have it. By a two to one margin, the committee of three backed him. Civilian evacuation first, then the Army. Lovely in theory. If London's super spy was right, the offensive wasn't due till at least the 30th. "My battle staff expected as much. Here's what we can give you. We have six near-worthless brigades. The rebuilds from Malta. The local recruits aren't really soldiers, but they can wave bayonets at rioters. Five of them are in positions north of the attack anyway. So here's what we can send. The least bad of the six brigades, Fleming's. A battalion each from the other five. It will be their worst, but … " Cunningham paused, trying to keep his disgust out of his voice. This was all so wretchedly stupid, but needs must. "We can get these to you over the next two nights. Just men and rifles. The machine-guns will have to stay. Third night we'll send a company from each of the remaining battalions. Add in some odds and sods, and that's 14 more companies."

"Sir, does this mean more families we have to get out?"

"If you don't make at least a pretense of it, half of them will desert. It's the same problem you have with the police. They are still with us to get their people out, and because they are too tainted by serving us to live long once the Muslim Brotherhood and the Nationalists are free to settle scores."

"And I send these families up the Nile?"

"That's policy, and we both know it's bunkum. Everyone who can will try for Palestine. Tell the officers on the Suez Bridge, at Mitla Pass, at the other Sinai traffic checkpoints, to just let anyone through. O'Connor's staff will scream. Too bad. Up the Nile will only happen when it all falls apart, and the fleeing mob will latch onto any army unit they see for protection."

The problem of getting the endless administrative and service detachments in Cairo and the Canal Zone to exit Egypt, was left to lesser staff officers. This should have been done months ago; but again, higher civilian authority had worried about imperial prestige. It was a pity that prestige had not resulted in a larger garrison with real artillery and air support. Empires are expensive, and the London government was run by accountants more concerned with maintaining sterling's value in gold.

2000 hours local; 1900 hours CET
24 October 1940
Open space behind repair area, Brigade Strauss, rear of Italian XXI Corps position

Clara Fischer had run out of excuses to avoid the Italian officer's Spanish whore. Now the bitch was going on at endless length, trying to ideologically justify her concubinage. "Just shut up, you idiot bourgeois slut. None of that matters."

Coxita stopped in midflight of convoluted rhetoric. Had she fallen so low as to be addressed like this ... "How dare you! You've opened your legs the same way I have!" She was shaking with a mix of rage and fear. John had warned her about the limits of his infatuation. The thought of being stranded on the docks of Naples was terrifying.

"Yes. I have. I just don't dance around it. Stop using ideology to justify your life. You aren't even working-class, you spoiled little princess." There. She had said it instead of biting her tongue.

"Class origins can be put aside for Party members, for the vanguard. Marx, Engels, Lenin were all revolutionary saints and none of them ever held a job where they sweated." She'd been assured that Leninism allowed for an intellectual, revolutionary vanguard. "I was a loyal Party member, a member of the local Cheka. I served at the front for almost two years as a Company Commissar. Those credentials supersede my birth!"

Clara laughed in the dumb little twat's face. " 'Justification by works.' My, my. Five hundred years later, and we are arguing Luther versus Rome. It doesn't matter. You have your reasons. I have mine. Our supposed world leader Stalin had his when he licked Hitler's ass and divided Poland with him. Forget why you got here. You are here. Why are you staying? If your precious Revolution matters to you so much, pick up a gun and attack this unit. You'll die a martyr to the World Revolution." Clara gave a sarcastic laugh at the silly little girl's visible terror.

"I don't want to die!"

"Neither do I. When the Nazis came into power, some comrades went underground to continue the struggle. Some fled abroad to do so. Neither accomplished anything. Seven years later the Nazis still rule, and all the opposition does is silly pinpricks. The rest of us stayed behind and ate shit from the Brownshirts and the Gestapo. I was reduced from student teacher to *Putzfrau*. I'd still be scrubbing floors on my knees if an old neighbor of mine hadn't had the Gestapo recruit me for Joey. You'll meet Wanda some day. Bootlegger turned brothel owner, but as working-class as they come. The ideologues like you would probably call her lumpen proletariat. Silly category, but a lot of what you Party intellectuals do is absurd."

Coxita actually was silent for three minutes, digesting all this. "So I must abandon the ideology I learned?"

Clara wearily shook her head. "Tell yourself any pretty stories you want. Just shut up about it. If you are here talking to me, your officer is getting as sick of it as the rest of us. Treat him well. Treat the rest of us with respect and some signs of sisterhood. We all have our reasons for being here. Why doesn't matter. Here we are. After we are in Alexandria, at least if you leave, you'll be in a civilized city. It's sort of half-European, or so I'm told. There has to be a student, Bohemian district where you could wait tables or serve drinks. It's what pretty girls down on their luck do. It's less money than streetwalking but I doubt you have the personal fortitude to be an outright whore. First time you pulled attitude, the John would beat you bloody. Plus there's the whole problem of pimps." The thought of Miss Precious dealing with a pimp made Clara smirk again.

"Absurd?" Now Coxita was actually curious.

"The big words, the rhetorical gymnastics, none of it matters. Take Communism as it was supposed to be. A world of Workers where no one starves, everyone has a roof over their heads. Equality, brotherhood, no more bosses. The state vanishes and people are just good because they should be. It's a dream, but it's my dream."

This wasn't ideology. This was low-church religion. Coxita decided to see where it led. "So what do I do?"

"Accept that you are human. You are young and pretty. Being a rich aristocrat's mistress beats scrubbing floors or walking a street corner in a slum. I don't begrudge what you did. I despise how you treat the rest of us. You want to be a Communist? Show some class solidarity. Treat Mary like she's a social equal. Have a kind word for slow-witted Hans. Stop looking down your nose at silly Greta. Especially Greta. Her protectors matter to your man. He'll dump you if you interfere in those relationships."

Coxita bowed her head and submitted. Inside she was seething, but more so she was terrified. She could take the rage out on the enemy, especially prisoners.

The world just wasn't supposed to be this way. The feeling reminded her of how she felt after the defeat at the Ebro. So many had died in their tracks across the Ebro. Her unit had fought hard but pulled back in good order. The 45th International Division didn't do suicide last stands. That was for others. She had heard later the same had happened in the nasty winter retreat to the French frontier. The COMINTERN had use for many of the cadres she had served with. Herself, she had been cut off in Barcelona. John had saved her from a savage gang-rape by a pack of Moroccan mercenaries out of their minds on hashish, cheap wine, and blood lust. She had never thought a human being could be so frightened as she had been at that moment.

She forgot the prisoners she had condemned to death while a Chekist. To her that was different. They were class enemies. She just knew now that she must learn to pretend to be the creature this Clara described. Pretty and pleasant. Coxita decided to think of it as a mission. She was being sent as a spy into enemy lines. Coxita thanked the older woman, and left to practice her new role.

Clara was just happy to see the idiot's back. She would again warn her sisters in the unit to be wary of this viper.

0500 hours local; 0400 hours CET
25 October 1940
I Australian Corps HQ, center/rear of Alamein lines

General Blamey had convened his three division commanders. They had executed his movement orders tonight, but wanted to know why they were suddenly clearing out their rear areas of service and support troops, of the sick, indeed of some of their reserve ammunition stocks. "Thank you for rapid work. Sorry for leaving you in the dark. Things have come up, things that cannot be written down. Look around the room. Familiarize yourself with the staff officers here. They will be bringing you orders. Orders that you will send your own staff out to verbally execute." The three division commanders looked up expectantly. "Cairo has started the pull-out. I've got my own connections there. We are not being left behind covering a British skedaddle."

The three divisional generals looked at each other, aghast. Major General Iven 'Mister Chips' Mackay somehow emerged as the spokesman. "I won't push you for how you get the information, sir. But what are our orders? You had officers doing inspections of the infantry companies – pronouncing as 'sick', men with infected bug bites, with bleeding callouses on their hands from digging. Two days ago they would have been on report for shirking had they shown up at sick call."

"I have no authority to ship out healthy men. So we are taking an aggressive and expansive view of 'sick'. The cannons and the crew-served weapons have to stay. It's a thin line between prudence and mutiny. But, before our German friends start the party, the infantry will be down to a thin line of supports for the other weapons. Egypt is falling apart behind us. Cunningham needs an armed company for escort to travel from here to Cairo. Every train to Palestine is overfilled." Blamey paused for breath. This was why Australia had insisted on a separate corps. "We are saving as many Australians as we can. Across Suez, up through Sinai and out eventually at Basra. 'Mister Chips', you get the rearguard when it all goes to Hell. You may get stuck going up the Nile. We are not being slaughtered by the British because they cannot make up their minds whether to fight in Egypt or not. It's a good position, but where are the planes, the cannons?"

1200 hours CET
25 October 1940
Parachute Forces HQ, Gerbini Aerodrome Complex, Sicily

Generalleutnant Ramcke was getting awfully tired of insane orders from Berlin. He had Oberst Maurice and Major Schmidt in his office trying to find a way to fulfill the latest flight of lunacy.

"Remember that reorganization you both assured me was impossible to make happen in the needed time frame?" Both nodded warily. After Malta, neither had a kilogram of faith that any staff officer in Berlin could find the ground after being tripped. "We are starting from scratch again."

Schmidt was a Major via rocket promotion. He had gone from aide to the General, to Regimental command in three months. His specialty was as a headquarters weasel. "What do they want now, sir?" Making Berlin happy was Schmidt's route to being Oberst Schmidt, Knight's Cross holder.

"The Suez operation has been redefined. Lack of transport aircraft, ranges from airfields to drop zone, shortages of gliders, the usual friction of war. We currently have four parachute infantry Battalions and four heavy weapons battalions, two of them parachute trained. We are now to reconfigure this into two parachute and two glider battalions. They are to take a bridge from both sides at once. Berlin asserts we can drop adjacent to the ends of the bridge, but admits the actual detailed air reconnaissance on the terrain hasn't been done. So we must be prepared to fight tanks and artillery, but may have to carry the glider-dropped weapons multiple kilometers." Ramcke paused for breath. He needed to weigh how baldly to say what came next. Oh hell, he was never going to win a prize for polite, diplomatic statements. His superiors could either accept this in him, or relieve him. "It gets better. What recon *has* been able to determine, is that the bridge and its African side approaches are usually packed with vehicle convoys. Packed 24 hours of every day. So surprise in any real sense is impossible."

"Your choices are not enough infantry to take the bridge, or not enough firepower to hold it. To say nothing of not enough ammunition for a prolonged battle if we do take the bridge." Oberst Hans Maurice was a sardonic veteran of four years as a Kaiserwar artillery commander, and years after as a Freikorps officer. He expected the worst and simply coped. His attitude mixed insubordinate words and energetic results. "I've got more experience at the sharp end than you both. Two parachute battalions where you pull an infantry company out of each and replace with a machine-gun company. That gives you the firepower to overrun the initial defenders. My two-battalion regiment of heavier weapons on gliders. You accept that if firepower cannot hold the counterattackers off, we just get overrun. It's a risk – but all solutions are."

Schmidt added a point. "Can we get a second drop in the afternoon, perhaps? Just ammunition for the heavy weapons."

Ramcke thought through the plan Maurice proposed. The man had more line experience than he did and seemed not to have a grudge at Ramcke's higher rank. "I can live with this. We drop as two Kampfgruppen. One Battalion of each type on each side of the Canal. Hans, you and Aloisb take the African side. I set down in Asia. Dawn drop. So take off in the dark … "

They would spend a day refining details. They had only four days before they were staged forward to Fuka in Egypt. Someday they hoped to be allowed to do a properly planned battle. The two older men each separately were grateful that at least so far the battles hadn't been Kaiserwar-level bloodbaths.

1900 hours Pacific Daylight Time; 25 October, 1940
0400 hours CET; 26 October, 1940
Bakersfield County Court House, Bakersfield, California

It was hot on the podium. Usually the oppressive heat of the region broke in October. This week was an Indian Summer throwback. It was still over 90 degrees this late in the day. The day before the temperature had briefly passed the 100-degree mark. Harry Truman was on a barnstorming tour of California's small and medium towns. He wasn't a crowd-pleaser in the likes of Los Angeles or San Francisco. Bakersfield, with its large population of transplanted Okies and other Southerners, was his kind of audience. "Fellow Patriots, Franklin Roosevelt saved you from the Depression. The Economic Royalists bankrolling Willkie, Lindbergh and that bastard Coughlin busted the nation out in 1929. They were content to let you all starve as long as they stayed fat and happy. Now they are screaming, 'Franklin's going to send your sons to die in Europe' I served in Europe in the last war. I'm a combat veteran, unlike that weasel Willkie who only showed up in France after the shooting stopped. We Democrats passed a law that no draftee would serve abroad. We stand by that law. We need arms for continental defense. The world's gone crazy and we've got to keep this wonderful country of ours safe. But no new AEF and no new Republican Depression. Let's keep everyone working. We need more New Deal, not more Wall Street high-handed theft. Willkie is a Wall Street guy. He's not one of us! Thank you and God Bless America."

The crowd cheered. There had been a good turnout. There always was in smaller cities happy to be noticed. Truman knew Roosevelt couldn't win without California.

1000 hours local; 0900 hours CET
26 October 1940
British Embassy, Cairo

The pall of smoke over the city was bad and worsening by the hour. Virtually every military and civilian installation was burning documents in barrels. Some were burning them in vast piles, loosely held in place by concrete riot barriers. Warehouses were smoldering where the looters had used arson when repulsed from pillaging. Shops in the European districts had been both looted and torched. So were some mansions of the various elites, European and Arab. A dozen churches were gutted wrecks. The streets were littered with bodies where the newly-trucked-in army units had put down riot with massed fire. The Egyptian police and troops had more often used riot stick and bayonet.

"This cannot go on much longer." The British Ambassador, Sir Miles Lampson, was in high dudgeon. The three-man committee from London, and a staff officer from what used to be Wavell's staff, were attempting to pacify him. General Wavell was safely in London by this time. General Cunningham claimed that pressing military necessity compelled him to stay at 8th Army battle headquarters. Lampson had spent five minutes previous to this deriding that excuse as pure cowardice. "The Egyptian King had me in for morning coffee. Wants to know what we are still doing here? He knows we have given him away at the peace talks. He's offering to get us a truce so we can leave in a civilized manner. Anyone got a good reason for why I don't tell him yes?"

"Because London won't back you on it, which means we won't. Absent our consent … " The Tory paused to gesture at his colleagues. "The Army won't obey you."

The staff officer nodded at the evident truth. "Besides, why would the enemy give us a truce?"

Lampson wondered if the army picked their stupidest men for staff school? "Because why fight for something you can get with a month's pause? We've given the place away. Same with Palestine and most of Iraq. London didn't see fit to tell me, but the King was kind enough to show me the maps, to indicate what was still at issue, all of it. He has his own issues he's asked the Italians to address for him at Lisbon. His London funds, his suzerainty over all the Sudan, his protectorship as he sees it over the Palestinian Arabs … "

"Since when did he give a damn about Palestine?" This from the Laborite solicitor, whose party was the home of most British Zionists.

"Oh, since late yesterday when he was deprived of the pleasure of three of his mistresses, each of whom his guards proved unable to convey to the Palace through the street chaos." Lampson had emptied his voice of the sarcasm he felt. It seemed to go over the heads of the others, and so wasn't worth the bother. "Pray tell me we have an actual battle plan. Some stroke of genius worthy of Wellington or Marlborough. Even of Allenby. From where I sit, this is going to be Malta repeated, just with more troops. Fight till you can justify running away."

The National Liberal man had actually been a pretty good staff officer in France and Flanders back the last go-around. He knew all too well the limits imposed by troop levels and terrain: "The 8th Army men are reasonably well dug in and will give a good account of themselves. Good troops in prepared

positions can do that … for a few days. Reality is, not enough guns, planes, tanks. West Africa got the reinforcements you needed. It will take two months to cure this, and we don't have two months. So the plan is to fight enough to get our support elements out, then leave a rear guard behind to cover an overnight pullback. Each day we stand and each night we pull back. In 1914 we did this from Mons, in Flanders, to the Gates of Paris. Yes, that was before tanks or planes. All Eighth can do is the best they can do. Finest traditions and all that. The Big Names from the 30's will spend their twilight years blaming each other in the London press. 'Thin Red Line of Heroes When The Drums Begin to Roll.' "
He paused both for breath, and in sheer frustration. "You think this is the first time a British diplomat was caught out? Happened twice in Afghanistan. But for Blucher's Prussians, would have happened in Brussels June of 1815. Before the news of the victory reached the city, there was worse chaos than what you had last night. Read Thackeray – *Vanity Fair*. Every empire gets caught out every so often, gets kicked in the teeth," he stated to Lampson.

The staff officer asked the obvious: "I can get you three more brigades of second-raters like you had out on the street last night. At that point the cupboard is bare. Do you want them? There are also a few brigades of Egyptians from Mersa Matruh that are up in Alexandria. No one ever gave them orders to go anywhere else." The staff officer's questions were interrupted by renewed firing. Volley fire, and not far distant. Single rifle shots that were probably snipers. An explosion that was probably dynamite. The ambassador just slumped in his chair and nodded shakily. Cunningham's forces would be weakened further so Cairo might hold a few days more.

1900 hours local; 1800 hours CET
26 October 1940
Space behind the main repair bays, Brigade Strauss cantonment, behind Italian XXI Corps lines

Clara and Joey had been walking on eggshells with each other since breakfast. Mary Collins had brought the family's morning meal over herself. While Abdul, Bain, and her other children handed around the food and beverages, she had taken the time to go over some details of a farewell party being put together for the inner circle before the big offensive kicked off. She had started addressing Clara as Frau Bats the day after Greta's formal announcement with Klaus. Clara hadn't quite known what to do with this. This time Joey heard. He had shot her a look, so she was clear he had caught it. But he hadn't said a word about it, hadn't allowed her a chance to explain it away. She had spent the working day looking for a right time.

This day was even more chaotically busy than usual. Joey, Paul, her brother Carl, all the guys were in constant motion trying to get every repair done before the fighting began. They were also going over the vehicles for the break-in from top to bottom. Motor vehicles were not designed for offroad movement on this type of terrain. Yet lives rode on them all working for a few key hours on a day coming soon, a day that would only be known when it happened. They had to wait for the main offensive, and then a raid of enough size for them to impersonate it.

Clara simply didn't want the tension to follow them back to the family area. It would upset the children. So the moment she saw her brother finishing a job, she substituted him for Joey, dragging her man off here. "I want to apologize about this morning. Mary doesn't really understand about us. I haven't the English to explain. I've tried in German, but hers has gaps. She tries but isn't seeing it. I'll talk to her again."

Joey gave her another hard look. He wasn't quite buying what she was saying. Or maybe he was trying to find the German to say what he needed. "Clara, I know we aren't Klaus and Greta. I'm not a silly kid like Klaus, and you know the world a lot better than Greta. We didn't do the couples dance to get here. Wanda picks you and you arrive." He paused to see if she was following. She seemed following his words but not his meaning. "Look, you never said what you wanted out of this. You interested in making this more than a wartime shack-up?"

Clara did not shock easily. She was flabbergasted. She also wasn't sure of his grasp of German on family matters, as opposed to engine rebuilds. "Are you asking me to marry you?"

"I'm trying to discuss it. You interested?"

"Discuss?"

"I never thought about getting married. I never thought about joining the army or moving to Iraq or opening a business at where ever in Hell Kirkuk is. Thought I was going to catch a boat to Los Angeles, get a job working on cars with a cousin out there. But here we are. It's all sort of happening. Question is, does this end at the oil fields, or you want to make this permanent?"

"Do I have a choice? The Gestapo sent me here … "

"Babe, you want separate tents and we just work together, say the word. I like what we have, waking up next to you in the morning, all the rest, including your kids. But I've never strong-armed a doll and I'm not starting now. I know a lot of guys see an old lady as a punching bag. I wasn't raised to that. If my old man had tried that on my mother, she would have slit his throat while he slept. He was the man of the house. No squabbles with her on that. She didn't take with a man beating on her. She brought my sisters up the same way. Then again, I doubt any husband of theirs would be that stupid. My brothers and I would knock them into next week, a sister of mine turned up with a shiner."

Clara took that all in. "If I were to become your wife, what changes?"

"Kids. Do you want kids? 'Cause I do. I'll need a few sons, to get one who will be right for taking over the business."

"So no daughters?"

"Nah. They're fine, and if that's all we get then it'll be a son-in-law I teach the trade to. Metalwork is a guy thing. You want to teach your girls a bit like you have us doing, sure. They can learn enough to earn a living. Bossing the shop needs muscle, and so does running a crew of grease-monkeys."

Clara was still mentally coping with children. She had presumed when she got pregnant by Joey, she'd just find one of the unit doctors to take care of things. The guy wanted children? Did she? She never had considered it. Single motherhood was just too hard when you are poor. "Grease monkey?" She knew Joey translated literally from his American English. What did an ape covered in lubricant have to do with …

"Mechanic. You get covered in grease and oil. So it became a name for this type of worker." Damn, he was tripping up on language and getting off the point.

"If I say yes to children, how many do you want?"

"You still never told me how old you are. My Mom told us guys that asking for more than a child every other year wasn't right, that you gals needed time to heal between pregnancies. She would laugh at the Irish ladies that dropped one a year. You tell me how many work for you – is the every other year right, or is that just some Neapolitan folklore? I also know the whole have-kids thing gets tricky after a lady gets past her mid 30's, or is that more old wives' tales?"

Clara was now being very careful with her words. This had gotten very serious. "So I have a say in how many total and how much time in between and the rest? Your mother really brought you up that way?"

"Most of the ladies in the neighborhood thought my Mom was a crazy one. She was raised by her aunts in the Old Country 'cause her Mom died young. The stories about her father were fairy tales designed to shut kids up. I put the pieces together. Grandma got herself knocked up by some guy who dumped her. It happens."

Clara had seen it happen to enough neighbors and friends. Story was probably older than the Bible. "What happens to the children I have now?"

"They stay till they get married, go off on their own. They want to stay forever, we give them jobs. But blood is blood. I want my own blood to leave the business I'm going to build. My Dad needed four boys to find the one who would inherit. My two older brothers, one has the balls without the brains, the other had the brains but next to no balls. Me? In some ways I'm the family disgrace. Dropped out of school young and went to work for strangers. Palled around with gangsters. Interested in nothing outside of work but partying. Only good part was, I wasn't a bum. Worked all my life and damned good at what I did. Never saw myself as a boss and neither did my old man. The joke was I'd die a bachelor with one hand on a bottle and the other around some joy girl."

"Yet now you talk of marriage, children, setting up a business."

"Since Gunter and I hooked up, things changed. Maybe it's the war. Maybe it's finally being away from my family, the old neighborhood, all the people that to them I was just a brash kid. Gunter recruited a man. Then you came along. The whole idea scared me. But I found I liked it, liked you. No movie romance BS like Klaus babbles about Greta. We fit together well and I don't just mean in bed. That's great and all but there's more to life than making the bedsprings bounce. I sit there having coffee in the morning with you and the kids. It feels right. Like something I've been waiting for all my life but never knew where to look for it."

"So why didn't you bring this all up before?"

"There's a war here, Babe. I go on this little adventure with Di Salo, Gunter, and Smitty. We are the ones who can sound right in English. Isaak sounds all wrong. I know he's a Hebe, but it comes out not sounding English or American. Di Salo sounds high-class Brit and we sound American. There's enough American Yids in the Palestine forces, so it may sell … or it may not, and we all get real dead. Didn't seem fair to hit you with this until our fighting was over." He looked at her expectantly, vulnerable in a way she had never seen him be.

She took his face tenderly in her hands and half whispered to him, "We will discuss this in Alexandria. You deserve a serious answer to your very serious proposal. I'll take the war risk. I like you well enough. It's the matter of children I must ponder." Good God, what on Earth was happening here. Clara had not been this unsteady on her feet since her first questioning session by the local Gestapo. She gave him a big kiss and then led him back to the repair bays. Damned right she needed to think. This was the rest of her life she was suddenly having to decide. What a crazy war.

0300 hours local; 27 October, 1940
1300 hours Eastern daylight time; 1900 hours CET; 26 October, 1940
East China Sea

USS *Langley* was not able to do flight operations. Not only had half her flight deck been removed when she was converted to a seaplane tender a few years before, she had now been demoted to an aircraft transport.

But even if she would have had her full flight deck, she would not have been able to do flight ops - both hangar and flight deck had been crammed to the gills with airplanes. The loading crews had taken a few days extra time and managed to shoehorn four more planes on board her than her usual 36, by taking a few parts off some selected aircraft – *Langley* now carried a full squadron of 24 P-40 fighters plus a few spare birds and two light transport planes. Then they went and slipped between the tied down machines, boxes and crates of spare parts and tools that they had not been able to cram in the store-rooms or the airwing quarters.

All the fuel tanks and ammo lockers had also been filled to the brim – enough gas and bullets to fight until the next transport came in. The flight crews and mechanics and other staff necessary to get a squadron flying and fighting had been put on board the SS *Maui*, a mixed cargo and passenger ship chartered for the occasion, together with more spare parts, ammo, and gasoline.

Unloading her would be like solving a Japanese puzzle, and take just as long as loading took, but this was supposed to be an administrative move under peacetime conditions, not a war-time transport.

The USN had nevertheless taken precautions to protect the small, precious convoy. A *Clemson*-class destroyer, USS *Reuben James,* had been assigned as an escort; and all ships had strict orders to sail with all lights lit and to always illuminate huge US flags painted on their sides, while they cruised at a leisurely twelve knots across the Pacific, the speed being determined by the slowest ship, the *Langley*. The supposed pirate subs, which everyone knew were Soviet, were to be left in no doubt of whether these were US ships. A flag the US Communists had sworn to the FDR administration, made them off limits.

Two more days to Shanghai – the convoy was gliding along on a calm sea under a star-bright night sky, roughly halfway between the Japanese islands Okinawa and Tanegashima. The midnight position message had been sent to both the IJN and USN headquarters, and they had received a message to expect a Mavis – an IJN long range reconnaissance flying boat – in the morning for a check up.

The twin explosions on the carrier woke the soldiers in their bunks on the SS *Maui* out of their dreams – those still on deck trying to catch a bit of fresh air, could see two columns of water and spray rising over the stricken *Langley* half a mile ahead and slightly to the left of their ship.

For a few seconds nothing else happened, then the alarm klaxons on both the *Reuben James* and *Maui* drowned the hissing sound of the collapsing water pillars. The *Reuben James* quickly doused all lights and started to accelerate, angling to right, towards were they assumed the hidden enemy to be. A few seconds later the first of a series of quick secondary explosions started to shatter the *Langley* completely.

The SS *Maui* had put her rudder hard over and started a crash turn to the left – perhaps the panic reaction of the watch officer in order to get out of the line of any other torpedoes potentially moving towards them. The action was almost successful, as one survivor later reported a single torpedo passing behind the ship – but the second torpedo caught the *Maui*'s stern, wrecking screw and rudder and starting a fire in the aft hold.

The *Reuben James* started to crisscross, firing occasional burst from its quick-firing guns and star shells from its main guns, trying to find what they had first thought to be an attack by a small surface ship like a motor torpedo boat, but could not find anything. Slowing down to reconfigure for subhunting and to give her hydrophones a chance to hear anything but the sound of water rushing by her own hull, she turned out to be doubly unlucky; not only had she failed to protect her charges, she had also blundered into a position right behind the retreating submarine, which promptly fired both stern tubes at her, scoring one more hit. That torpedo broke the destroyer's back. It took a quick V position, with bow and stern both out of the water as the cracked center split and went to the bottom. There would be no survivors. *Langley* lost more than 70% of her complement. Many of those that hit the water did so as floaters in life jackets rather than passengers in ship's boats or inflatable rafts. The evacuation of the *Maui* was a near-total cluster-fuck. Too many passengers, darkness from both the hour and immediately losing electric power for the lights, and a civilian crew that ran for their own lives, passengers be damned. There would be repercussions on this later, with their unions defending the crew and blaming the mostly dead officers. Dead because they had put rescue over their own survival.

The IJN Mavis had been scrambled after the SOS messages arrived and quickly found the site, aided by the smoke plume of the still fiercely burning *Maui*, surrounded by a gaggle of raft and life boats. Several Japanese ships, both civilian and military, were not far behind.

Colonel Chennault was faulted in the early reports for abandoning his men to save himself. It took almost a week for the truth to come out. He'd been knocked unconscious in the initial torpedo strike. He'd been carried to the deck and then over the side into a life raft by others. There were multiple surviving witnesses. Sadly, many people believed the original story, and judged his future actions accordingly.

0100 hours CET
27 October 1940
Dockside, Bari, Italy

The port was in its usual chaos. As this was Frauke Peters' first visit to a wartime port, she had no guide to what was normal. The idiot German naval Leutnant she had reported to, said it was this way every time they loaded. Claimed it had been worse before the air war stopped, thus ending the blackout.

Frauke knew she was in Italy to punish her. When she had first volunteered for prisoner transfer duty, she had been rejected. She had never asked again, so this could only be punishment. She had been detailed with two other girls from the guard corps to take a prison transfer convoy to the Bari encampment. It was a strange mix. It started with the usual 'wayward girls' from Ravensbrück, but at a stop in Berlin a group of middle-aged ladies with children appeared. These all had luggage and decent clothing, although more the fashions of years back. One police lady from the Berlin *Ordnungspolizei* saw them to Frauke's superior on this trip. The new contingent was signed for, after which the Orpo lady left.

These new arrivals were strange. They spoke in low tones but with cultured accents. They were absolutely no trouble on the trip south. The little strumpets from the camp, on the other hand, constantly tested boundaries. Even chained together to inhibit their attempts at escape or more general delinquency, they would howl out ribald suggestions to every civilian within range. Their lusts for alcohol, sex, and general mischief were bottomless. Frauke knew how to discipline the little brats. Her superior ordered Frauke to stand down. Claimed some order from on high prohibited showing physical discipline in these surroundings.

The arrival at the encampment had proven to Frauke just how degenerate the entire Ravensbrück administration was. The other two guards had travel orders back. Her superior produced an order transferring Frauke to this camp brothel. Frauke had signed up to help the war effort, but not by disciplining silly young whores. What was worse, the lady in charge, this supposedly German Pole Wanda, didn't even need her for that. The rebellious young ladies mostly managed to fit into a structure built around alcohol and promiscuity. Four just ran away and no one chased them. The general attitude was that it was a waste of time. Sadly, the world was never short of poor girls who turned tricks to survive. All wartime did was create more desperation and poverty, hence more whores.

Frauke had no wish to help run a whorehouse. Or a cabaret. Or a bootleg liquor still. Or any of the other illegal things these swine were doing. Except somehow this was all authorized. Major Adolph had given her a camp map, with the military police and camp administration clearly marked. In a bored voice told Frauke to go report them. See what good it did. This was a project of the Reichsführer's. The same as the Jewish women she had brought down from Berlin, were another of Heydrich's programs.

Her new superiors did not try to get her to participate in their sexual frolics. Frauke was shocked to discover that this was the reverse of Ravensbrück. That was a supposedly strict-regime camp with attached workshops, whose administration acted like the worst of degenerate Weimar Berlin. Here was a set of businesses centered on sex and alcohol, but the administration lived quiet lives. There were couples like the two top bosses, but no wild living. Frauke knew something was off but couldn't quite fathom what or why.

While she had no use for what they were doing, they had no particular use for her. As long as Frauke left everyone alone to do their jobs and live their lives, they were content to feed and house her.

With nothing much to do, Frauke was bored out of her mind. There were many thousands of German soldiers here. but the only responses she got from them were sexual. It was Ravensbrück all over again, except the young soldiers had better bodies but no disciplinary power over her. Enter Satan's spawn, as Frauke had come to call the child photographer named Oriana. The girl had tried to befriend Frauke. When rebuffed, she had proven her demonic origins. "Why did you join the guard corps? To be able to fight like a man?"

"Go away, silly child. Only men get to be soldiers and defend the Reich with guns."

The child had laughed at her. "Our Betar girls in Africa are armed warriors. Helped take Malta, Beat up a British army a few weeks back. Sometime the next month or so they are off to battle again, to finish conquering Egypt. I can get you papers to go there. I know who you have to see to join the fighters. I'm going on the next shipment. I'll just add you to the travel orders."

How the child got the Major to sign the orders was a mystery to Frauke. The supposed convoy to Egypt was Gretchen, the madame-to-be, leading a party with a dozen experienced girls, three doctors, and a nurse. Somehow there magically appeared a second set of orders for Frauke as guard over Oriana, a Roma whore named Dika, her pimp-musician boyfriend Stepan, and two other Roma girls. Frauke thought the three Roma young ladies seemed absurdly young but they were subhuman, so … Frauke was prepared to let a thousand absurd things happen if it got her a chance to show everyone that she could fight better than any man. One Hundred Ten percent better. Maybe more.

Which brought Frauke to this dock, and the naval Leutnant saying that the ship they were designated to travel on was overfilled. He promised to get them on another in a few days. The loading process was extremely haphazard. When naval command had requested more people from Major Adolph's contingent, they thought there was extra space. Someone had forgotten to allow for something or other. Senior officers were screaming at each other about it. Doubtless they would scream at each other about some other administrative mishap cn whatever ship Frauke got them out on. Oriana had brought cases of photographic equipment. Gretchen had case-lots of bootleg whiskey. Frauke was sure the Leutnant would find room. Frauke was blonde, blue-eyed, and eye-poppingly good-looking. Flirtation was not a game she enjoyed playing. It did not mean she didn't know how to bat her eyes and thrust out her chest to make stupid men do what she wished. Ever since she started having breasts at twelve, the world had treated her Dresden China doll good looks as some sort of magic.

0800 hours Eastern Daylight Time; 1400 hours CET
27 October 1940
Waldorf-Astoria Hotel, Manhattan

The story of the disaster in the East China Sea had spread in bits and pieces all through the night. The story had missed the regular morning dailies, but all the big city papers were doing extra editions. The *Chicago Tribune*'s headline had been WAR! The arch-Isolationists were now baying for war against the Soviet Union.

Harry Hopkins had flown up during the early morning hours with CNO Admiral Stark and Commandant of the Coast Guard Russell Waesche. The public was clueless as to the details of what had happened, but early reports were of a rally-round-the-flag feeling typical of Americans in a crisis. In the heat of a presidential campaign, Hopkins felt that before a week was out the blame game would start. The China policy itself had no serious enemies. A large minority was vocally in favor, and no one except the pro-Soviet left was opposed. NYC's leftish daily, *PM*, was under siege by a mob of 'patriots'. Most newsstands saw the bundles of today's *PM* burned by belligerent crowds. Normally an afternoon paper, they had released a morning special edition calling for calm and deliberate thought. This was not what most people wanted to hear.

Hopkins was determined to be proactive. His designated sacrifice was Stark, and the issue was the corvettes. He let FDR take the lead. "Admiral Stark, how many *Flower*-class corvette contracts have been let?"

Stark had slow-walked this vessel. The Navy did not like being forced to use a foreign design. Indeed, they thought the whole concept of barely oceanic-capable small ships was an absurdity. "Mr. President, we are still studying the issue. We hope to have a more useful design for the fleet sometime next year. Our concept is the destroyer escort, a larger ship capable of sailing stormy seas far from port, and with enough weapons to be worth building. Surely letting contracts in October for ships we won't need next May, is not a wise use of funds. More so, these little sitting-duck gunboats will cause needless deaths from both storm and battle."

"Admiral, were you given a direct order by your commander-in-chief, or not?"

"Yes, but … "

"But nothing. As the Navy refuses orders, I will give this mission to the Coast Guard."

Stark flared. The Coasties were a joke, not a second navy the way the Marines were a second army.

"It's our mission, Mr. President. The Coasties chase bootleggers and rescue stranded fishing boats."

"A mission you refused to do. Kept your destroyers for battle fleet service. What battle is it fighting this week? The only fighting was in the Far Pacific, and your one destroyer failed. Brave men died because you only sent one ship." FDR saw Harry's game. Stark would be the goat. FDR could have ordered more destroyers to shepherd *Langley*. He could have followed up on the corvettes. Now all that mattered was to be seen as decisive before the *Tribune*, Willkie, Lindbergh, and Coughlin made Roosevelt the villain. "Commandant, your service will find yards to order seventy-five corvettes by Friday, November 1st. You will have that list by the close of business on that day for my assistant Mr. Hopkins to review. You will also present a plan for the manpower needed, including increases to your shore establishment and aviation branches. The manpower will come out of the Selective Service quotas for a navy that does not know how to take orders or do its job!"

Before the Commandant could answer, Stark was on his feet. His face was brick red with the cords on his neck bulging like overstretched ropes. "Sir! This is an insult to my service and to the brave crews of the two lost ships who died as heroes. You cannot let your political needs come over the real defense needs of our fleet!" He had committed career suicide but it had to be said.

FDR smiled inside to himself. He had gotten the reaction he wanted and it hadn't even taken much baiting. He kept his outer face grave, as befitted a President doing his duty. "Admiral Stark, you are relieved. You will return to Washington by train, clean out your desk, and await further orders."

After spending five more minutes blowing smoke up the Coast Guard Commandant's ass, FDR sent him and Harry Hopkins back to Washington by the same plane that had taken them to Floyd Bennet Field from Washington. The man he wanted was Steve Early, his press secretary. It was vital that the Roosevelt version of the blowup with the navy be fed to the *New York Times*, the national newsmagazines, and the wire services before Stark got back to leak the other version.

0800 hours local; 0700 hours CET
28 October 1940
RN temporary HQ, Suez, Egypt

The smell of explosives blanketed the air, even here at the south end of the Canal. Explosives from demolitions. Destruction carried out contrary to the ambassador's express orders. Sir Miles Lampson had been informed overnight by frantic Egyptian and British officials, but no one could locate the RN senior captain in charge. The roads were no longer safe enough for a drive in the dark. Lampson and the committee of three had left Cairo at dawn. It took a battalion of Fleming's newly arrived brigade to get them through. The snipers and ad hoc roadblocks were not a serious impediment to a battalion. A platoon might well have been overwhelmed.

The captain had been there to meet them. He had apparently been expecting such an encounter. He was a middle-aged RN veteran. Clearly not command track if he had been assigned these tasks, but a competent professional for all that. "I don't care what an ambassador or three members of Commons have to say. I have written orders from Commander Mediterranean Fleet, with a covering letter from the Admiralty. The block ships and destruction of all naval and Suez Canal Company facilities were at my discretion, when the combat situation warranted it. We were taking sniper fire. The army had clearly lost control of the situation. My orders made the priority, 100% certainty that the Canal was properly blocked, and that no facilities be left that could in any way aid the foe in clearing this waterway. Mission accomplished."

Lampson was livid. His response was long on vituperation and threats. The RN officer actually laughed in his face. This was the cue for the Laborite to speak up. "May I see those orders?" After reading them he went on: "What would have dissuaded you?"

"Written orders by proper channels from the Admiralty."

"Not from the PM or the War Cabinet?"

"Chain of command, sir. They would tell the Admiralty, which would have sent new orders by teleprinter. The Ambassador forgets himself. Thinks he's still Viceroy." The captain gave a bitter laugh. He could see his future. "That's the defense I'll use at my court-martial. My career is done. I'll see if I can save my pension by the court verdict. Either way, my tombstone will read, 'He did his duty'. There's more to the senior service than ship command, gentlemen. Those of us put on the administrative track still have our duty to do. I'm fifth-generation RN. When I meet my ancestors in heaven, I can look them in the eye. I didn't sully the name."

The three overruled the Ambassador and ended the meeting. On the drive back to Cairo, they debated the message to London one word at a time. By tomorrow there would be such a message through each of the service commands, giving the ambassador and themselves the old viceregal powers of command back. Nothing outside the Alamein battle zone was to be destroyed without direct written permission.

1300 hours local; 1200 hours CET
28 October 1940
Fuka forward air base, Egypt

What had until recently been a British forward air base was rapidly being converted into an air transport hub. Engineering troops from both nations and multiple services worked round the clock adding runways and buildings. Had the British possessed a functional bomber force in Egypt this could have been a prime target – as, after dark, giant searchlights lit up the work areas. Tenente Vincenzo Pentangeli took it all in. He was filled with national pride. His Libyan Parachute Brigade had arrived this morning. He'd been told a German airborne brigade would arrive tomorrow. The two allies really were going to conquer Egypt. The Nile would be Italian , as it had been in the time of the Caesars.

2000 hours local; 1900 hours CET
28 October 1940
Space behind the main cook tent, Brigade Strauss Cantonment to the rear of Italian XXI Corps positions

Mary Collins was surprised to see Mr. Joey. These days his meals were brought to him. He never was at the cook tent anymore. Except now he was. He wanted to talk to her. In private. This seemed bad. What had she or her family done?

"Business first. Abdulah or whatever his name is and Bain are now part of Major Steiner's Battalion. They will be our first force into Alexandria. He will need someone who speaks Arabic and someone who speaks English. He got a Maltese, one of my guys, for directions but my guy hasn't much German and German is all Klaus speaks. He learned a bit of French in school but it doesn't seem to have stuck well. Anyway, Klaus and the Maltese guy communicate enough for driving directions but not much more. Bain seems to have a flair for languages and Abbub can make himself understood on simple stuff in pidgin German." Joey stopped, swearing a bit to himself. "None of us can keep his name straight so for now he's Private Abe. Tell him. Klaus will be careful with them … "

Mary had been a soldier's lady since shortly after her first lunar cycle. "Sir, my boys understand about battle. They signed up with the unit when I did. They will do us proud as they did at Three Crosses." She thought to herself that she would task Bain to find a moneychanger in Alexandria, one with contacts to home. She could send her family money again. There were rumors of chaos there. "Is there something more, sir?" He didn't need privacy to take the boys over into combat status.

Joey was hesitant. No language problem. The lady spoke English. But the whole Clara situation left him uneasy, and he was not used to the feeling. He was a take-charge kind of guy. "It's about Clara. You calling her 'Frau Bats'."

Mary was mystified. "Sir, what I did was simple courtesy, what I would expect to call an officer's lady." Mary had never dealt at length with officer's wives. Their mistresses, bibis, she sometimes knew; but the social rules of the Indian Army did not seem to apply to these strange Europeans.

Joey rolled his eyes. "Yes. I know that. You know that. She's still coming to terms with whether we are permanent or just for a while. So for now it's Fräulein Clara. She promised me an answer in Alexandria. She tells me and I'll tell you. But if it happens, not *Frau*. It would be Mrs. or Signora Battaglia. I'd say Mrs., but I have to ask her which she prefers. You ladies get fussy about that stuff." Joey could see the discomfort and fear on Mary's face. "No one's mad at you. It's just … complicated. That's a good word. Complicated. She and I never thought we were the marrying kind and here we are discussing how many kids we are going to have. War changes people I guess."

Mary could agree with that and just kept nodding till the officer left. Officers were a different species in her worldview.

0900 hours local; 0100 CET
29 October 1940
45th International Division cantonment, 2 kilometers behind current front lines in Manchuria

The front commander was inspecting the 45th this morning. Fidel held the unit's Red Flag banner next to Markus, who by now was a battalion commissar. Fidel was so proud of his special friend. The original Aztec force had been reinforced with successive waves of international comrades. It was by now a Tower of Babel, with over two dozen languages spoken. These were grouped into companies and battalions who at least vaguely understood each other's speech.

The big general, whose name Castro thought was Koniev, was praising the 45th for its valiant attacks. Fidel was glad someone important had noticed them, but from what he saw all that the successive Aztecs and Internationals had accomplished was dying. Every attack failed. Even the new unit designation, dead General Kleber's old unit number from the Spanish War, was just a pretty story. The 'division' had nothing but infantry, machine-guns, and mortars. Only real Soviets were trusted with artillery or tanks. Or so Markus told him, and Markus was right about everything.

Fidel looked forward to some quiet time with Markus. They needed to get deloused first. After that, the unit had been promised three days to sleep before they went back in the line to be heroes of the revolution.

0500 hours local; 0400 hours CET
29 October 1940
Money-Penny's patron Gisht Ari Pasha's mansion (now mostly deserted), Alexandria

It would be dawn shortly. The mansion was mostly deserted. The fine furniture, rugs, and other valuables were gone, replaced by second-hand cheap objects sufficient for the Pasha, his immediate business staff, a large garrison of Money-Penny's Villains, and a skeleton staff of servants sufficient to keep the house running and food available. The rest of the Villains were at the yacht harbor, holding down the Pasha's luxury yacht and Money-Penny's two acquisitions, a decommissioned WW1 torpedo boat and a small coastal passenger liner. All three ships were openly armed with heavy Vickers machine-guns and 40mm Bofors autocannons. A noticeable amount of money had been spent getting both the weapons and paperwork authorizing the weapons on what, to the naked eye, were civilian ships. The papers alleged that all three ships were requisitioned for some special-operations unit of the RN, commanded by a Lieutenant Commander James Money-Penny.

James was now arguing yet again with his patron over the stupidity of everyone still being in Alexandria, instead of already departed for Beirut. "They have pulled two divisions off the line to keep order in Lower Egypt, including my nominal brigade. RAF has already started redeploying back to Upper Egypt. A few of the planes are still here, but the road convoys of spare parts, administrative personnel, and reserve fuel stocks left before dawn yesterday. The line will collapse with one good push. Why are you cutting this down to the last minute?"

Normally the demi-monde figure to whom Money-Penny had sold his services wouldn't bother to answer. This time he did. "Because the moment we drive out of this compound to the yacht basin, my organization here falls apart. Once gone, it would take decades to reconstruct. This syndicate is a thing of great value. Several of my lieutenants wish to purchase it. They are trying to find a sum that pleases me. A different grouping will just try to seize it when I run. I would prefer to sell, obviously. That way I could still exercise certain influences from Beirut. I see myself as too young to retire completely. Forget the money. I would die of boredom."

"You would be alive to be bored. I cannot guarantee enough warning. The yacht basin is empty except for our three vessels."

"What would life be without risk?" The pasha decided it was time. "You have rejected my proposals that you desert the British colors and stay with me in Beirut. Pity. However, I have another proposal for you. Where will you go at the end? Your brigade hopes to escape over the Canal and from there to Palestine. Which will be lost, as will Iraq. Then what?"

James saw no purpose in saying he would go where he was ordered. The Boss didn't think that way. "India, or still further east. There's a world at war and fortunes to be made." That answer would satisfy the Egyptian.

"As I thought. When you set up someplace else, send word to me via the hawala network. If I am no longer in Beirut, the network will find me. You are a most useful man. We can find business to do. Empires come and go. Money and commerce remain, whatever the nominal laws are."

Money-Penny filed that away. He had never been Six, but he was known to them. The elder Fleming brother never bothered to deny his connections to that shadow world. Britain could use connections to a man who likely would be powerful in the new Middle East. MI-6 would not question Money-Penny making a profit on these things. They were adults in such matters, whatever the prickly scruples of their nominal masters in government. The British electorate favored such secular saints with refined morals. Pity, the world didn't work that way.

1400 hours local; 1300 hours CET
29 October 1940
KG Germania jump off positions, Italian XXIII Corps sector of Alamein lines

The plan was for Lothar's KG to pass through the Italian 233rd Legion of the 1st Blackshirt Division after the breach of the British lines. Lothar's fast battalion, augmented by the Betar Engineer Company, was to be the KG's spearhead.

Lothar had been 'gifted' with the Betar troops because the Oberführer commanding the KG refused to have anything to do with a Jew formation. The SA officer was of Baltic German descent. He would have had no problem commanding Balts had he been given that KG. He saw that as part of the natural order of the universe. Jews to him belonged on the other side, waving a red flag.

He had already branded Lothar as a coward. He now added Jew-lover and race traitor. Lothar's falling out with Major Steiner was set aside, because at the conference he had praised him. Klaus's pure German ancestry vanished because he had commanded Hebrews. Lothar laughed to himself at what the Baltic German Oberführer would have felt about Greta. Probably accepted the fantasy that she was Volksdeutsche, because Berlin had decreed it.

The Italian general commanding the corps the Blackshirts were in, was an old colonial and Spanish War veteran nicknamed "Electric Whiskers". He had been ecstatic when told Lothar had engineering troops. This led to today's meeting between Electric Whiskers, the division commander, the Oberst commanding the Legion, Lothar, and the engineering officer, a former Major in the Kaiser's service who had then served the Poles against the Reds. The Italian Obserst, called a Consul for some reason, had a major problem breaching the British mine fields, and saw these engineers as the answer to his prayers. "The British have mined and wired this entire front, then gone and done the same company strongpoint by company strongpoint. There's little artillery and no real depth to the position, but that leaves the damned mines. Our entire corps lacks enough engineering assets. Major, how good are your lads?"

The major was missing one arm at the elbow, and two fingers on the remaining hand. "Rough as a unit. Not enough training time. Fairly good individually. I screened the new intakes for people with pioneer experience. Problem is that it's from all over. I've got Kaiser veterans, Freikorps guys, ex-Polish Army, ex-Ukrainians, ex's from the three Baltic armies, ex-Czechs, ex- Red Army. I even have half a dozen who fought for the French in the last war. So yes, they can clear mines, but as they speak two dozen languages and know a dozen or more different techniques … "He paused to survey the others. He was proud of his men, but knew their limits. " … they will get you lanes. The lanes will be imperfect. Warn your men that odds say there will be one or two mines they have missed. So it's fast lanes, but they will take losses."

The division general was curious, "Fast?"

"As I said, these are veterans. I've divided them into squads based more on similarity of Yiddish dialects than anything else. Galicians and Lithuanians can barely understand each other. Think of a company with random speakers of every Latin language from Church Latin to Romanian. They can sort of all understand each other if they are speaking slowly in the mess hall. Under fire on a battlefield, not so much. Exercises we ran up in Poland on the minefields at the Auschwitz Camp complex, we could manage 100 meters or so an hour."

"Auschwitz?" Lothar was now confused. "I thought you people were out of the Palestine camps?"

"We are. Our Palestine camps are really a mix of barracks and workshops. We have a little wire as boundary markers, but no minefields or electrified wire. Our camp complex is a low-rise blob of new construction that starts at the west fringes of Cracow and growing west. Auschwitz is to our northwest, west, and spilling southeast. There are maybe 30 kilometers separating our fringes. By New Year's I doubt we will be five kilometers apart. Auschwitz is a strict regime camp for disciplinary problems, mostly Poles. Commandant there was more than happy to leave mine laying to our training program. His men kept injuring themselves." The major paused. He knew he was stepping out of line, but he also knew his craft. His wounds were from artillery fire, not mistakes with explosives. "How flexible is everyone on plan alterations?" He looked around but no one said anything, which he took as approval. "Let my lads get started tonight. We won't put the flags up till the Big Push starts. We've got little markers, look like stones, we can use for now. But the more mines we get up early, the faster we can cut through at H-Hour." No one disagreed. Some things higher command didn't need to know.

1400 hours local; 1300 hours CET
29 October 1940
Street in front of Barclay's Bank military branch, Cairo

The line stretched for two blocks and kept growing. It seemed that every British officer and attached civilian high potentate in Lower Egypt suddenly wished their money in banknotes on their person. Commander Ian Fleming had a battalion under his personal command keeping order and providing perimeter security. His brother Peter had a second battalion escorting parties of paid-off officers back to their offices and bringing new parties to the line. To keep the bank supplied with pound notes, a third battalion had spent the day convoying in more funds from outlying branches. In several cases the money transfers had been too late. Mobs of Egyptian 'patriots' led by Muslim Brotherhood and Wafd Party agitators had stormed the banks, stripping the cash drawers. In one case they had paused to dynamite the vault before torching the building. The others were just blazing wrecks. When the ashes cooled someone could try to recover funds from the vaults. The fire brigade, like other Egyptian services, had refused to intervene.

Ian's attempt to juggle the mess was now interrupted by the arrival of the Tory member of the London triumvirate, escorted by an understrength company from 1st Battalion, 9th Gurkha Rifles. The short Nepalese fellows were down to 50 or so effectives. But a third of these had Bren guns. Fleming had heard the massed fire they had used to force their way in, while they were still blocks away. The Tory member of Commons seemed none the worse for wear. "Hullo, Fleming. Situation here under control?"

Fleming was an inveterate networker. He had already sized up all three men and found social connections they had in common. "For now. There won't be a functional bank left in this city by dawn tomorrow, unless we are prepared to leave a company garrisoning each one. What is higher command playing at? How is 8th Army to fight a battle with this mess in its rear?"

"Jolly good question. London seems not to have an answer. PM wants to do a preemptive withdrawal. War Cabinet is dithering. Something about a seat in Commons for Bombay. Protocol questions about Nazi letters to the 1922 Committee. Giant row about Nazi proposals on restrictions of naval war. Some dustup with the London Polish government. Been told there is talk in Commons of naming Bevin Lord Protector, and just letting him actually do something without a cabinet."

"Lord Protector? Ernie Bevin as Cromwell the Third? Not sure he's the man for it. Too decent. Issue at hand is simpler. Does London want order restored here? It would take mass murder. Has Britain the stomach for a hundred thousand dead colonials?"

"No. Come war's end there will be harsh words from the usual suspects, on whether what is happening now was too severe. It's just hard to get sensible British opinion to accept that many things have no middle course that avoids unpleasantness." He saw a disgusted look on Fleming's face. "Not to worry. There will be a crown proclamation of general amnesty sometime next month, covering anything and everything. So we are just talking the usual clucking in the London press, 'concerned citizens'; et cetera. No, I'm here on something more mundane. Message we just decoded. When this all falls apart, you are to retreat through Sinai. I'm to accompany you. We'll be London's eyes for Palestine and Iraq. My two associates will go up the Nile." Fleming was again looking at him peculiarly. "Your friends from 54 Broadway said you were a cautious one. Said to tell you 5 clubs, redoubled and not vulnerable."

Fleming relaxed. It was a one-time code from SIS, what others called MI-6. A disastrous bridge hand that Fleming had both misbid and misplayed. The sort of code that only makes sense to the people involved. "Keep your Gurkhas with you," he said in clipped tones. "Indeed, latch onto whatever stray bits you can. We are frozen in this city for now. Need an order or a complete collapse to cut loose. Then it's going to be a replay of the retreat from Kabul in '42. We are going to need vehicles, machine-guns, and lots of ammunition. There's also the question of Empire civilians. We simply won't be able to save everyone. Too many civilians, with our fighting men spread too thin. The civvies will get mixed into the retreating columns, reducing military effectiveness to near zero, you mark my words."

"Not to worry. I'll resign my seat in Commons when this mess is over. I'm the designated goat. I've got a nephew who can stand at the by-election, keep the seat in the family as it were. RAF fighter pilot, made ace in the fighting this year. Invalided out after being shot down defending London. You need two legs to fly. Only need one and a walker to campaign. He's a good lad. A bit of a Red Tory from where I sit, but the young are always radical." The discussion was broken by sniper fire. Took the Gurkhas a few minutes to put the three fools out of action. Fleming noted with pride that they made no attempt to avoid hitting 'civilians'. There weren't any at this point. Just targets.

2100 hours Eastern daylight Time; 1500 hours CET
29 October 1940
Shibe Park, Philadelphia, Pennsylvania

The crowd went crazy as Willkie hit the stage. He was the last speaker at a three-hour rally for the entire Republican ticket from President down to the state legislature. Willkie found the lesser office seekers to be peas in a pod at this point. After similar rallies in over twenty states, the lower rungs of the ticket seemed stamped out by a machine – thirty- to forty-something, WASP, clean cut, usually blond, of athletic build, and definitely fraternity men at college. They were mostly all married, with equally photogenic wives and parents. Assemble them all for a photo and it could be a stand-in for a fraternal order like the Elks or the local Chamber of Commerce. Still, they saw to the basics. They were all against FDR's re-imposition of Wilson's old Daylight Savings Time scheme, and in favor of God, personal hygiene, and a healthy outdoorsy life.

"My fellow Americans, I stand before you in this time of peril. With the nation on the brink of war, Franklin Roosevelt has gutted the top ranks of our Navy, our first line of continental defense. Admirals Stark and Richardson have been sacked to cover errors of Roosevelt and his clique of radicals." This whole line of argument was transparently stupid. A week ago the entire Republican Party had been baying that these same admirals were traitors and dunces, over the torpedo scandal. Lindy refused to be seen as a fool in public parroting this partisan tripe; so by default, declaiming it was Willkie's job. He did it but refused to dwell on it. There was only so much partisan bile he could spew, and still retain a glimmer of self-respect. "The same set of lefties are keeping Congress from passing the Lend-Lease Act to send desperately needed assistance to our Japanese allies. The noble Japanese who so quickly responded to the perfidious Soviet attack on our heroic Navy in Far Eastern waters." The same Lend-Lease Act that a week ago Republican Isolationists had refused to act on, pushing the consideration back to the post-election Lame Duck session. "These internal enemies of everything decent in our God-blessed land, who were balking at declaring war on the Soviet swine who torpedoed our ships. Who try to insist on accepting the fiend Stalin's transparent lies that this was all the work of pirate submarines. Pirates? Who could believe such childish … "

The shots came from three directions. It all happened so quickly that Willkie couldn't even react. One round creased his cheek. At least one more hit one of the interchangeable men on the podium behind him. The man keeled over as if poleaxed. There were screams from the audience. "Kill the Kike bastards!" Sounds of thuds, of bones breaking, of a crowd in a frenzy. Someone ran up to Willkie, trying to wipe the blood off his face. The presidential candidate waved the man aside. "This is what we face. Ungodly followers of an alien regime in Moscow. Who is with me to reclaim this great land of ours? Who will lift the banner if I fall? I am prepared to give my life for my country. Who else stands beside us?" None of this was in the prepared speech. It was what the moment demanded. Willkie would prefer a more cerebral politics. The age demanded a rhetoric of blood and passion!

0700 hours local; 0100 hours CET
30 October 1940
Docks of Batavia, Java, formerly Netherlands East Indies; now under Japanese 'protection'

The troops of the Japanese 38th Infantry Division were lined up on the dock preparing to embark. Their equipment and vehicles had been loaded during the preceding 48 hours. Waiting to see them off was an honor guard from the newly-formed Indonesian-Japanese Joint Force Local Defense Division, as well as military bands from the Indonesian and Netherland East Indies armies. At the podium, the provisional president of the Indonesian Republic, Sukarno, gave a send-off in quite cultured Japanese. "Noble elder brothers, we wish you success in your defense of the Son of Heaven, of the Japanese Empire and of the Greater East Asia co-Prosperity Sphere. Your Indonesian younger brothers will maintain order in your absence. Our oil, tin, lumber, rubber, rice, and fish will continue to flow to the Home Islands to sustain the Children of the Sun Goddess in their struggle against the godless Bolshevik barbarians and their International and Chinese lackeys. Victory to Japan! Ten Thousand Years of Glory to the Emperor!" And for all ten thousand a quasi-independent Indonesia which, with Japanese and British help, would rid itself of the cancerous chokehold of Holland. Sukarno was proud he had come so far in a few short months.

0300 hours local; 0200 hours CET
30 October 1940
Minefields in front of 1st Blackshirt Division

Lothar Engels had no experience being a battalion commander. He'd been a hands-on working man all his life. In his Kaiser Army, Freikorps, and SA days he had made Feldwebel several times. And lost his stripes each one of them, due to his temper; until late 1932 when he'd gotten them back for the last time. He'd risen to Company command based on three quick promotions, between the Führer coming to power and the Blood Purge, as the SA had swelled with 'Spring Violets', the eager new adherents who had joined Party and SA in the heady first spring months of victory. His armored car company command was more a matter of no one in the Hessian SA wanting the post, when the NL was opening up so many more interesting possibilities.

By all rights, working through British minefields by dim moonlight should have been left to his new pioneer company. Lothar didn't know how to deactivate mines. But he was an immensely strong man who could carry tools forward, drag deactivated mines back. This let him observe. He prided himself on his dexterity. If he watched long enough, he was sure he would learn. This would be a good skill to have on a battlefield, as this stupid war showed no sign of ending – no matter what the damned Kikes had told him.

So he was upfront with the one-armed pioneer officer when the voice came out of the dark. "Don't shoot!" The German was clear. It was followed with something in Italian. Probably the same thing. *What the fuck*?

Lothar rose on one knee with his MP-38 pointed where he thought the sound came from. "Show yourself! Stand up and let me see your hands!" A man rose from twenty meters away with his hands empty and over his head. He stood quite still. "Forward to me, now!"

"I'll have to weave a bit, sir. I need to walk around where the mines are." The man took slow, mincing steps. He kept pausing to reorient himself. Finally he arrived. By now half a dozen Betar had clustered around. Before Lothar could do anything, one grabbed the enemy's arms and another did an expert pat-down. Called out that he was a police veteran from Vilnus, in clumsy but clear German. Announced the man was clean except for a sheaf of papers.

"Careful with those, good sirs. They are the maps for the minefields."

Lothar grabbed the man by the shirt front. "You're a deserter. Why?"

"This sector was built for three brigades. We have two understrength battalions covering it. We're Jews from Palestine. We signed up to fight the Nazis. To fight beside the British. Not to die for the damned Limeys while they run away. Flee with most of our trucks and heavy weapons, with all of our artillery and reserve ammunition." Man paused for breath. He was sweating, probably from fear. "Rumor has it there were Jewish troops fighting with you Germans. My guys and I talked it over. I speak German and Italian. Said I'd take the chance and go forward. If I heard Yiddish, the story was true. Can we join you?"

"They all want to switch sides?"

"It's complicated. Some would rather be prisoners if they can be captives of the Italians. One of us did a year in Dachau back in '34. One of the other guys did six months in Buchenwald after Kristallnacht. No one we know was sent to an Italian camp for being a Jew. They may not like us, but the dislike is less violent. Have we a deal?"

"Deal for what?"

"Some of us you enlist. The rest go into an Italian prisoner cage. I'll walk you into our strongpoint. The maps for the rest of the minefields on this brigade sector are there. We've talked to some of the others. One bunker to our right and two to our left are in. You make a breach that big, and whoever won't surrender will just drive away. Why should you have   to die here? Why should we?"

Lothar now had to make a decision as a field officer, his first. He went forward with a squad while sending back three runners to the Italian consul whose sector this was. A fourth runner was detailed to his number 2 at the battalion to bring the vehicles forward. You don't let chances like this go to waste.

0600 hours local; 0500 hours CET
30 October 1940
Formerly British bunker, now being used as Lothar's headquarters

Dawn was up. There were marked lanes in the minefields. Lothar's battalion was through the minefields and fanning out in the rear of the Palestinian positions to the south. Many surrendered. Many others fled after brief skirmishes.

Lothar would have liked to have been dealing with this. Instead he had been gifted with a visit from the SA Oberführer commanding the Kampfgruppe. The man saw everything Lothar had done, as stemming from his cowardly soul. In the Oberführer's eyes, a true SA man would have rejected offers of surrender, refused enlisting the turncoats, and bulled his way through the positions like proper storm troopers. The Oberführer was demanding that Lothar's men be pulled back and 'brought under proper discipline' while his own Battalions took over the combat mission from the cowards, queers, and Kikes. Lothar had point-blank refused, his temper once again getting the best of him. The two had been shrieking at each other for several minutes, with Lothar daring his superior to fight him man to man, unless the Oberführer wished to prove he was one of Röhm's old butt-boys. The two were all but pawing the ground like two bulls in a field.

"Do go on." Lothar and the Oberführer looked up and froze. Their Division commander, Felix Steiner, had arrived for a visit — accompanied by the Italian corps commander, Electric Whiskers. "No wonder the SS has eclipsed the SA. When this is over I suggest you two get a room in a Cairo hotel. You can beat each other senseless, with the winner getting to use the loser like a woman. Oh wait, we have to take Cairo first. Defeat the British. I seem to recall something about that. Idiots! You, Oberführer Idiot, remain silent at the position of attention. You, very recently promoted and thus easily reversible Sturmbannführer Engels, please give a report. Simple words, and nothing about your homoerotic dispute with your superior."

Lothar did so, quickly and without moving a muscle that was not involved in speech. The Italian general was shaking his head sadly. Steiner asked Lothar, "So, by accident you have destroyed weeks of planning? Instead of the multi-day combat we planned for, we have been handed the south end of the British line at no cost and days ahead of schedule?" Lothar allowed himself a brief nod. "Thank you for being honest enough not to claim any special credit for yourself. So unusual these days. Every success has ten thousand fathers. Next time, however, when you send a Gefreiten back to the divisional quartermaster company with a requisition for 110 uniform blouses and trousers, a note explaining that you had taken on new recruits might have been helpful. Our quartermaster had heard of SA proclivities in sexual matters, and presumed that over one hundred of your enlisted men had destroyed their full uniforms in such amorous wrestling.”

“Sir, one hundred ten was a guess. I can certify ninety-three, but my superior insisted on my presence here instead of letting me exercise proper supervision of my companies. I know more have been enlisted since then. We also have over three hundred prisoners that I know of, so probably over four hundred in total. I need to turn them over to proper Italian authorities.”

“Italian?”

“They distrust the treatment they will receive at German hands. A number have been prior guests of ours at Dachau et cetera. They would rather not fight at all, but if that means being guests of our camp system, every one of them prefers fighting under our colors instead. Sir, if you don’t trust them, we could always gift these Jews back to my old brigade, Strauss’s.”

“So you let prisoners dictate to you, Engels?” Steiner had a smirk on his face as he said this.

“Herr Division General, policy is that all prisoners be turned over to Italy in this theater. The Führer mandated decent treatment by the laws of war until then.”

“Ah, so you do remember policy? Perhaps there is hope for you yet.” Steiner’s tone did not indicate that he saw any such hope, even if his words conceded that possibility.

“Italy will be happy to find employment for these men.” The Italian General knew enough German to follow. “This many men make a small labor Battalion. There is always work in the rear. Roads, buildings ... ”

Steiner had heard enough. “Oberführer, you will have to live without your boyfriend. He and his two units are no longer a part of your command. Dismissed!”

Lothar remained at attention. He was fairly sure the general was not done with him. Steiner wasn’t. “Yes, you have ruined higher planning.” Steiner gave a little laugh, almost as though he was stifling himself. “These British minefields will have to be rendered harmless, with the deactivated mines gathered for our own use. Stay here for forty minutes or so till I can get supply officers up from Corps and Army to mark the routes they need cleared. Your one-armed Jewish pioneer officer used to be a soldier of the Kaiser. Means he can speak passable German. You are Reichsdeutsche and clearly know our tongue. I have a draft of seven hundred HJ’s. They were to replace the battlefield casualties I now won’t have. You two will teach them mine clearance during this new operation.” Steiner could see a puzzled look on Lothar’s face. The man simply wasn’t all that good at blank face. “Sturmbannführer, when we plan a battle we submit an allowance for casualties. These seven hundred were to replace my losses in the combat you just arranged for our Division to avoid. Oh, and congratulations on not beating that fool Oberführer senseless. I’m told he’s competent as a Company-grade infantry officer. I can clearly see he’s a dunce beyond that.” Steiner paused as a smirk came across his face. “Your Pioneer Company is now a Pioneer Battalion. The combined unit is now its own KG, reporting directly to me. Needs a name. KG Haber. A Jew who served Kaiser and Reich well. You’ve been labeled Jew-lover, and the slur will stick. Best you earn it.” Steiner walked away shaking his head, laughing very softly. Lothar just stood there. He had wanted to learn the techniques of Pioneering. Now he was a Pioneer officer. What a war!

1400 hours local; 1300 hours CET
30 October 1940
Headquarters 8th Army, behind Alam-el-Halfa Ridge

The staff officers tried to put a brave face on things. G.O.C. Cunningham wasn't having it. "Whose brilliant idea was all this?"

His chief of staff had not exactly come up with the idea. However, he had done nothing to block it. So it was, by normal protocol, his responsibility. "Sir, there was a logic to this. The Palestinians were the most expendable of the combat battalions we have. The rebuilds of the battalions off Malta won't really fight. Everyone knows it. It's why we have allowed so many to be pulled off the line for rear-area security. The Palestinians have fought. We just took the two with the least favorable battle reports from the prior skirmishes, and creamed out the most usable men. All they had to do was force a serious German offensive. We'd have gotten them out of harm's way the first night after Jerry's Big Push."

Cunningham worked hard at keeping his temper. He failed. "You regarded them as expendable – and made sure they knew it, when you creamed off the Anglo Hebrews. The ones originally from the UK, US, the Commonwealth. You took all their artillery and their supply reserves. You put squads and platoons in company strongpoints. You never precisely told them how long they had to hold. You didn't even leave proper British officers in command. And you are surprised that one unit ran up the white flag? They don't trust us. You knew that, and validated their worst fears."

"Sir, should we have left two British battalions to do this?"

"Damn it, yes. Get this through your heads! This won't be the last rearguard we drop off to buy us time between here and Khartoum. Rearguards only work if they are actually motivated to die to buy the rest time. The Jews would have done that to protect their own in Palestine. Here? I'm not that stupid for you to sell me this story. Get it through your heads! This is the last field army the Empire has left, outside the Home Islands. You will not be allowed to throw it away flattering your social prejudices. I don't care who wouldn't let a Hebrew into their London Club. I am indifferent to how many of you feel, after a prior tour of service in Palestine, that the Arabs were given a raw deal having Europe's Jewish Problem dumped on them. Round up what is left of those two battalions. Send them on to Cairo Command as security units. They for sure won't stand in battle line again anytime soon. Post them to Fleming's Brigade. He's got enough odds and sods. Be sure the armored car brigade is properly screening the vacated sector. Anyone who cannot faithfully do this, can be apply to be relieved. You can all be returned to regimental service if you so desire. My staff will show some brains, if I have to replace every one of you three times over. Dismissed!"

2000 hours local; 1900 hours CET
30 October 1940
Headquarters Italo-German Panzer Army, in the rear of what till this morning had been XXIII Corps lines

The meeting room was overcrowded with staff officers and couriers. The one fan was fighting a losing battle against late-day heat and the humidity produced by too many primates packed into a space with quite poor air circulation. In theory this was a meeting of the army commander and the three corps commanders involved in the current offensive. Then the fourth corps commander was added as a gesture of politeness. The subject was attempting to salvage a battle plan ruined by unexpected premature success.

The Panzer-Armee operations officer was just finishing the latest update on lanes through the former British positions. Most of Steiner's Afrika Division and the first of Messe's XX Corps were through. They were somewhat marking time, for fear of coming up on the prepared British positions on the east-west ridges piecemeal. That could open these two forces up to a British counterattack before the rest of the Army could arrive. "So we are now three days ahead of schedule?" German Corps Commander von Manstein was not as pedantic as the national stereotype would tend towards. But he did like precision. "Had we ever finally agreed on what the scheduled start date was?"

His Army commander General Geloso conceded this. "We generally knew it was to be within the next fortnight, probably within the next four days. We never had firm agreement on how long breaking this section of the front would take. Every Corps supply chief was waiting for one or two more shiploads of supposedly crucial supplies before we began. Logistics people – they are necessary, but never fully satisfied."

"So now what?" Manstein's mentality was geared to operational matters. He had staff people for the rest. He was not oblivious to supply and administration in the manner of a Rommel. He had been such a staff officer, solving such problems for his commanders. That was what proper staffs did. He chose good staff officers, men with family histories and strong service records. They would let him know the limits within which he would orchestrate his battle. Similarly he had faith in his two Divisional Generals for this battle, Hausser and Steiner. Forget the silly uniforms they wore. Both were good Reichswehr officers with decent records – although not the absolute best, which were men of his own class. He actually trusted both better than that prima donna Rommel.

Geloso rapped out dispositions to each Corps: "XX Corps will advance into position Division by Division, with General Steiner shielding Messe's eastward flank. Steiner will go into line when Hausser comes up to take over flank protection. General Jodl's artillery will follow in support of the two German divisions of your Afrika Korps. XXIII Corps will follow last, assuming flank guard. This KG Haber will work with XXIII Corps until no longer needed, at which time it will return to its parent Division unless otherwise directed by yourself as Corps Commander. The French brigade is Army reserve." Geloso saw the French general pretending to be Kellermann, start to rise in protest. "Don't have this argument with me. I received a request from Vichy to minimize your losses, in light of France's new African War with Britain. You remain a reserve force until I am in receipt of a countermanding order from your government. If I were they, I would save you for the pursuit up the Nile, after which you could march on Chad from Khartoum." Geloso paused to be sure he had everyone's full attention. "Let the staff people bicker over times and phase lines tonight. We will meet again tomorrow – say, 1000 hours – to review their proposals. General Dalmazzo, please remain behind for some administrative matters. I want to be certain these British raids on your front don't disrupt the main battle plans."

After the rest filed out, Geloso asked his own staff and the XXI Corps staffers to leave so the discussions could be 'frank and open'. They left, thinking Dalmazzo was about to get a dressing-down. The two Generals shared a glass of brandy and then got to the point. "You still think this Di Salo can be trusted?"

"Sir, we risk nothing finding out. All my staff has done is a series of hypothetical plans. In theory, they are preparing contingencies on the British attempting to exit the trap we are setting by attacking west through our lines. They think my hypothetical is absurd, but it's all routine planning. I think Di Salo is sincere. The skirmishes keep happening. Rommel is rotating fast groups as support for these skirmish forces. If Brigade Strauss breaches the line, I will send you the code words 'Julius Caesar'. If Rommel follows through, 'Mark Antony'. If my general offensive follows, 'Ptolemy Cleopatra'. First Libyan Division will drive hard for Cairo. May they count on airborne support?"

"Two Battalions the first full day after the breakthrough occurs. If the Germans do a proper investigation, they will find that these forces were on alert for a Cairo mission but no one knew what day. I will not have notified Rome until after this all happens … or doesn't. I do worry about leaks. Once this all happens … " Geloso caught himself. Best be cautious. "If this all happens, I will send a senior officer to the Marshal and the Prince. There will be enough glory to go around."

0530 hours local; 0430 hours CET
31 October 1940
Cantonment of the Palestinian raiding force, 1 mile to the rear of 7th Division lines, north end of Alamein position

It would be dawn in less than an hour. The small convoy of trucks from the south had been hopelessly lost. Ordinarily, Sergeant Billy would have left them to founder. His long service history in the Great War and then the interwar Territorials had long taught him that no good deed goes unpunished, so volunteer for nothing. Now that he was working for Mr. James it was different. Any time he wanted to get he and his lads out of something, he had written orders from some Major General excusing them because of some top secret posting. He'd been pressed on precisely what an NCO with a dozen or so lesser rankers knew, that a major or colonel could not. Mr. James had schooled Billy well. The correct response was to say, 'call my officers' – Mr James who was almost impossible to locate, and the general had a staff that would never bring him to the phone. Billy was not even sure the general really existed. Didn't matter. A major general trumped anyone screaming at him.

The truck convoy was full of English-speaking Hebes, creamed off from some operation down south in 8th Division sector. An operation that had lost that entire stretch of front, per what Billy picked up. Once he had offered his services as guide to the raiders camp, the major in charge had gleefully taken Billy and a few of his lads on. Billy had been given space in the cab of the lead truck while three of his new hires, as it were, followed on motorcycles. Billy had other handy pieces of paper allowing him to impress men for his 'special mission'. He'd gathered up half a dozen youngsters who wanted out of the trenches, and claimed familiarity with motor bikes. Mr. James had somehow conjured up the vehicles, a collection of prewar models from a score of nations. He and Billy used these to send couriers back and forth to Gisht Ari Pasha's mansion in Alexandria, which was Mr. James's current headquarters.

Billy's job was information. The exasperated staff major in command wasn't about to give him any. So Billy bided his time, until everyone piled out at the raider's domicile. He went fishing by ear, listening for British accents among the new men, especially those old enough to have been through the mill under Haig. Hit paydirt with his fourth try. Man had been a sergeant-major in that war. Manchester Regiment. Different battalion than Billy's, but it made a start at a connection. Billy had good English fags and a few bottles of a decent beer from Alexandria. House brew from some dive called the Spitfire, down near the docks. Mr. James sent it back by the caseload. It was currency, up where Billy operated.

"We was pulled out of our units by some staff twit. It was like they wanted to be sure the lads left behind knew they were being written off. Seems some of them ran up the white flag before the damned Nazis could even attack. What did the staff idiots expect? Two battalions holding a front built for four brigades. Battalions creamed out for their best men, especially officers and NCO's. Half the ones I left behind in my company would have started walking home to Palestine as soon as it got dark."

"When you move there?"

"Good question. Went as a tourist in 1923. It was a dump. I went home after six weeks. Decided I'd rather be a stinking Kike in Birmingham and still able to sit at my favorite pub where they knew me as a decent bloke who had been through the mill with them in Flanders, who worked down the road where half the regulars did. Then came the Crash. Made redundant. Had an insane Zionist second cousin. He found me a job in Palestine. I came over as British, not as a Jewish settler. Place I worked had a contract fixing trucks for the army and the Palestine Police. Special Branch knew I was a Jew by blood but I never made a big deal, so they didn't." Billy could read between the lines. Man had been a low-level informer. "Loyal to king and country I was. Then Winston had two brigades of Jewish Palestinians stood up. Nice man from army recruiting came around. Had my army records from the Last War. 'Suggested' I volunteer. I allowed myself to be pushed, and here I am. Detailed off to some idiot collection of Haganah zealots for suicide trench raids. I caught a piece of it when the trucks were being boarded. London's pushing for raids to show 'offensive spirit', or some such rubbish. The damned gentlemen want a body count. They make me go out on one of these, I'm showing the white flag myself first chance I get. Half the lads with me will do the same. Raids to do what? We spent four years the last time proving that raids don't accomplish shit beyond running up the death toll."

"Haganah?"

"Marxist militia the Labor Zionists run. Think Independent Labor back home. Not quite Bolshie, but cozy up to them. Not my type. All my kind want is British peace and quiet. If that means no new immigration, so be it. I'll let them claim I'm Church of England if it keeps the stupid ragheads happy. I was listed C of E when I enlisted in '14 after the news of Mons. My recruiting sergeant refused to hear answers beyond a few Low Church sects and C of E. Not that it mattered. All the chaplains were C of E and church parade was compulsory in my battalion. When we went in south of Arras in '18, I'd have taken blessing from any sky pilot, even a head-hunter with a bone in his nose. Those damned storm troops were tough. Lost half my company in a hour, to gain maybe 40 yards. Damn. I'm too old for this cack!"

Billy let the conversation wind down, and five minutes later he had his motorcycle lad ready with the message for Mr. James; and a priority pass, signed by the Major General, to get his lad through the road-blocks. The return courier would come back with packs of these a dozen at a time, that only needed Billy entering a name and date. Billy could get used to military service this way. Mr. James let him avoid almost all of the petty bullshit. Billy was much less than certain if everything Mr. James did was on the square, but as an NCO all he needed to shield himself was written orders.

Chapter 10

0700 hours Eastern Daylight Time; 1300 CET
31 October 1940
Clinton Correctional Facility, Dannemora, NY

Nominally this was the prison cell of a long-term felon. In fact, Mr. Charles Luciano ran the prison, and his cell could have passed for a luxury hotel suite. He normally didn't take visitors this early in the day, but this was an emergency. Frank Costello, his front man managing his interests while he was in prison, had arrived with an intriguing but bizarre proposition.

"Frankie, you know I ain't a snitch. So how can I get a pardon for snitching without snitching?" Luciano was not a man given to making loud threats like Hollywood movie gangsters. He didn't have to. At his word, men died. Even men in police custody.

"Charlie, the only guy you are ratting is Tom Dewey. You get to explain under oath how he stitched you up, how there was no way you did what those bitches said you did. A man at your level simply doesn't touch street money." Costello was known as a clean-hands gangster. He never touched weapons or dealt in violence. He was the link between the rackets, legit business, and the political machines. "That's all smoke anyway. Roosevelt is in trouble politically. Needs our help getting out the vote in the City, in Jersey, in a few other places. They gave me quotas by precinct. I can deliver. Gonna cost a bit but nothing we can't handle. You get a New York State pardon for all criminal acts up to the day you testify. Federal one too for the tax beef. You pay a fine and they call the taxes Kosher. You don't have to answer questions about anyone other than yourself. Those parts are lock. If Roosevelt wins, we get you a private citizenship bill. That's gonna cost, but I can make the numbers work. With a war coming, we can make this all back in three or four months. A year tops. Oh, and we got to keep the docks clean for wartime. No wildcat strikes and other shit like happened with Bridges out West. They want we should take over those locals out West, keep the Reds in line. That's the excuse for the citizenship. Patriotic support for national defense or some such malarkey."

Charlie had a nickname of Lucky. Things just broke his way. Survived a murder attempt that left him for dead. Other things. "So I do this and by Christmas I'm back in Manhattan running things?"

"They want you should stay out of the papers same as I do, but yeah. You are Boss of Bosses. Everyone comes to your suite and kisses the ring. Big wartime boom in the port like the First War. We make money grabbing with both hands even without making the military boys upset. We can milk it nine ways from Sunday. City full of soldiers shipping out, and seamen in port spending, means you can sell them dames, gambling, fast times. Mayor LaGuardia will be the pain in the ass he always is. That, the Feds say we gotta live with."

"And my mouthpiece says this is on the square?"

"Charlie, would I bring it to you otherwise? We'll have to bang a few heads with dummies who hear snitch and draw the wrong conclusions. Brownsville Boys are history, but Albert's lined up a new second squadron that is better at keeping their heads down. Do the work just fine, but no flashy hangout like the old Midnight Rose setup. Enough cutouts so your hands never get dirty. Boss, you are out of legal appeals without this. You'll die in here. Say you'll do it. I belong under you, not pretending to be top dog."

It took a bit more discussion, but the political deal was made before day's end. Costello used the warden's phone to call Harry Hopkins in Washington to say yes.

2330 hours local; 2230 hours CET
31 October 1940
Headquarters meeting room, Brigade Strauss cantonment, rear of Italian XXI Corps lines

There was a continuous crash of artillery from the south. Had been going on all day, with the volume rising hour by hour. Some of this was undoubtedly more fire. The shiploads of shells were getting expended. More of the added noise was the artillery battle creeping north towards XXI Corps. Still not there yet, but definitely closer.

The *Kapitän zur See* was commander of Naval Group Alexandria. This was a mixed set of explosives experts, port administrators, engineers, and logisticians whose job it would be to deal with the port once the ground forces had captured it. They would defuse the remaining explosive charges, prepare a plan for rebuilding, send to Europe for what had to be made there, and mobilize local resources of men and supplies for what could be done at once. His problem was with the plan to get his command to the port. He had spent three hours listening to the brigade battle plan and liking none of it. Every time he started to object, Brigadier Strauss had sat him down. Well, the ground forces idiots were finished. It was finally his turn. "This is all completely unsuitable. My mission has the highest priority in Berlin. Yet you are assigning two youngsters to break into a great city. Two Battalions for a city the size of Alexandria. Our actual escort is a green Company commanded by a young girl who was until recently a cook. I protest!"

Gunter Strauss gave the Kapitän a withering look. He had experience in battle in three wars by now. These naval clowns only knew about sailing their toys around in bathtubs. "Let me say this in words simple enough for you naval gentlemen. We have one unit that can make the breach. You will note I say can, not will. Success will mostly come down to luck. Now presume our trick works. This still leaves exploiting or widening the breach till we have an operational-level breakthrough. Again, without this, no one goes anywhere. These two measures will get my best subordinate commanders and most of our firepower. It will also leave these units disorganized. Ground war is different than naval that way. Your ships just stay in action. We have to pass through fresh units to maintain the momentum. I have allocated two Battalions with some of our faster vehicles. The commanders are young but experienced … "

"Surely the Corps Commander can give you more units and more experienced field officers."

"Yes. He could. However, what he will *do* is shut us down. Getting you to Alexandria is a priority for this Brigade. Corps has other priorities. If they are officially informed of this adventure, they will forbid it. You will then have no chance of reaching Alexandria before the British demolish everything. Now you think your pull with Berlin is so vast … Smitty, take down the Kapitän's objections and send it priority to Berlin. Leutnant Schmidt is our communications liaison with Prinz-Albrecht-Straße. Maybe the Reichsführer or OKW will agree with you. Are you willing to risk your career finding out? I am. How's your nerve?"

The Kapitän was sputtering with fury. "Yes. I will send the message, and I will include your criminal negligence in assigning a female cook to convoy us."

"Smitty, be sure to include that he objected to adding a pair of combat-tested Leutnants, Schwabe and Saxon, over the command of a Company whose Hauptmann has no prior combat experience in this war. The ladies were both blooded at Luqa and Three Crosses. Tell me Kapitän, what land battles have you fought in? Were you and yours in one of the Naval Infantry Freikorps?"

"She was a COOK!"

"Yes, Leutnant Schwabe was a cook. She was also an armed officer in the lead wave at Luqa. Helped take the airport buildings. At Three Crosses her platoon was instrumental in the repulse of a professional British Battalion. In the army we do multiple things. Cook, fire weapons, command fighters. At the southwest strongpoint engagement, we had a short platoon of machine-gunners commanded by a female language teacher and a large Zug commanded by an automotive engineer. That's why you have an escort. I'm sure you are all very brave and expert in your specialties. So are the lady Leutnants. Schwabe is the best we have left after the other slots are filled. Schwabe also had combat experience in Hungary. Saxon in Hungary and in Romania against the Soviets. We don't tell you how to repair harbors or take ocean cruises. Allow us to see to ground actions, at least till we see if the Reichsführer and OKW agree with you." Gunter paused to smirk. "Which I quite doubt. We are a special unit that the Reichsführer was instrumental in forming. I am willing to bet my career that he respects my professional judgment."

When the teletype came back the next morning, Berlin backed up Gunter on every point. It was signed Reichsführer Heydrich, but as usual came from the desk of Oberführer Schellenberg. A very chastened Kapitän had learned his place in the universe.

0900 hours local time; 0100 hours CET
1 September, 1940
Theater headquarters in the bombed-out remains of Harbin, Manchuria

Memorandum from Field Marshal Yamashita to the Imperial War Ministry, Tokyo:

You have asked for my views on the progress of the campaign. I will endeavor to keep them brief in the hopes that these problems will be acted on, instead of endlessly debated.

1. Tell the idiots in the two Air Services to stop prattling about the air battle. They may fight that as they choose as long as we get army-support attacks as well. They keep saying 'yes' and failing to do this. The priority targets are the rail lines, bridges the rail lines run over, marshaling yards, artillery ammunition depots and equipment parks. Unless they actually do this, we will be driven out of Manchuria within six months.

1. The new units you are sending are fine. In future please leave the officers home unless they are willing to obey orders. We do not care about Bushido Spirit, Samurai honor and similar childishness. We need men to bravely die in place, delaying the Soviet advance. Sergeants seem able to grasp this. Lieutenants and Captains do not.

2. Stop giving me encouraging messages about supplies that will not materialize. One cannot plan a battle this way. We need artillery, especially high-muzzle-velocity guns 76mm and above. We need automatic weapons. We need ammunition, mines and explosives. We mix these with liberal expenditures of blood to buy time.

3. Yes, we need horse-mounted units to guard the flanks of the railways and the rear areas.

We do not need idiots with katanas and dreams of feudal glory. These are to be mounted rifle units with some light support weapons. Their opponents will be Chinese partisan units similarly equipped. Our Manchus, Chinese, Mongols and White Russians seem able to grasp this. Why are our Japanese reinforcements incapable of adapting to this?

    4. Qiqihar will be encircled by year end. Harbin may be as well. I need a corps to garrison Qiqihar and a small army to garrison Harbin. Please send older reservists as they will all be lost as the Soviets eventually take both cities. Younger men are better for field service and should be preserved for defending positions along the two rail lines.

0800 hours local; 0700 hours CET
1 November 1940
Fleming's position protecting the Barclay's Military Bank Branch, Cairo

It had been another night of chaos and death. Blue Shirts from the Wafd Party, Green Shirts from Young Egypt organization, the masked al-Tanzim al-Khass of the Muslim Brotherhood, all had been out in force; but the mass of fighters and looters were ordinary Egyptians in an ecstatic frenzy of romantic nationalist zeal and Muslim religious frenzy. They were asserting control over their city, their nation. They were killing the hated foreigners. And, of course, there was the lure of loot. All of Lower Egypt was unsafe. Even almost-European-in-feeling Alexandria had seen flashes of the new order struggling to be born.

Ian Fleming had maintained his perimeter. His men had dynamited burning buildings to create a firebreak. He had personally led sorties to rescue British, Europeans, Christians, Jews, and Egyptians compromised by their service to the rapidly imploding British regime. There had been no help from that idiot Lampson. Just a barrage of inane directives, orders that contradicted each other, missives without any offer of reinforcements. The fool couldn't even get the fire brigade to keep the spreading flames out of clearly native Egyptian quarters of the city. The Raj was over.

Now he could hear Bren-gun fire from the South. Probably meant British forces. He led out a sortie by a mixed force of his own commandos and the Indian Army men the Tory committee member had hoovered up. By now going on half of 8th Army was out of the lines on security duties. Long past time to get the rest in retreat towards the next battlefields in Sudan and Palestine. The new arrivals proved to be Prince of Wales Own 4th Ghurka Rifles, the lead battalion from 5th Indian Division. Fleming thought it so typical to be shoving a new division into the furnace instead of building a blocking position in Upper Egypt. He found the temporary brigade commander up with the battalion column. "Good to see you, Colonel Fletcher. Where's the rest of your brigade?"

"Strung out over two days march south of here. There's a solid traffic flood going south. RAF, Army, British civilians and god only knows what. How many retired military and colonial service are in this damned country, anyway?"

"No one kept proper lists. No accounting for Sikhs, Hindus, Hong Kong Chinese, or any of a hundred races who can claim protection of flag and crown. Anyway, new orders: You'll take over for me here. Have your other two battalions hold in place, keeping the road south somewhat passable."

The lieutenant colonel was a very temporary brigade commander. His general, Slim, had been pulled out for some silliness up in the Persian Gulf. The new Indian Army Commander Auchinleck was being slow in forwarding a replacement. Besides, Fletcher had orders from the British ambassador to get everyone to Cairo *tout suite*. "Commander Fleming, is it? I have a sheaf of orders telling me … "

"Telling you a load of balderdash. Follow me. I've got a representative of the War Cabinet up ahead with written credentials giving him authority. Lampson's for the sack before the next week is out. Be a pity to have you join him."

1900 hours local; 1800 hours CET
1 November 1940
Brigade Strauss Headquarters, rear of Italian XXI Corps lines

Hauptmann Ernst von Kleist-Konitz was having coffee at his makeshift desk when the agitated Korvettenkapitän found him. The man was an obscure relation by marriage to his mother's clan, some of whom had done navy service instead of staying in the Heer or the civil service as proper Junkers had for centuries. When the naval contingent had arrived, Ernst had seen the name, asked the obvious genealogical questions, and, on being proven correct as to the distant but real relationship, had expended half a bottle of decent brandy welcoming in this distant sort of cousin. Now the man was back, obviously looking to presume on acquaintance. For what? Ernst was too well bred to say that, so he just looked up. Let the other man state his business.

The navy officer was desperate. His commander's complaints to Berlin had been rudely brushed aside by Heydrich's office, OKW, and the Naval General Staff. The Kapitän zur See had remembered the family connection, and detailed the underling to beg. "Is there nothing you can do to get this silly cook-girl replaced?"

"Nothing I could do; and what's more, I won't. I'm going along and think she is an excellent choice."

The navy officer was speechless. In a trembling voice he asked, "Please explain."

"Steiner is the obvious choice. Boy is a natural at combat leadership. Therefore, Leutnant Schwabe is necessary for you." Did these people truly know nothing of how this unit worked?

"What does Schwabe have to do with Steiner?"

"She sleeps in his bedroll. They are betrothed." Seeing the shock on the naval officer's face, Ernst put down his coffee cup. "Steiner is the best this Brigade has at mobile warfare. But he has this little problem. He was promoted out of the ranks. No officer training beyond reading a few manuals in his quite limited spare time. He thus has this natural tendency towards tunnel vision. You tell him exactly what you want to happen, what you want the result to be, not how to do it. He will then execute the mission. So he's been told his mission is to reach the port of Alexandria. If you cannot keep up, he'll just leave you behind. After all, your Kapitän is a superior officer and surely knows how to follow him."

"In a ship, certainly. On land in a battle … ?"

"Yes. This is obvious to you, to me, and to Brigadier Strauss. Steiner is Strauss's protégé. He knows the lad's faults. One of which is believing all people with higher ranks are demigods. So Strauss gives you the one person on this planet Steiner will never misplace or abandon. She won't have a clue as to what to say or when to say it. That's Saxon, who was trained as a paramilitary officer, trained quite well. Saxon is the brain, Schwabe is the voice. Together they keep you chained to our spearhead." Ernst had to work hard not to laugh. The looks on the face of the relative were priceless in a comic opera sort of way. "Oh, and never call her the cook."

"He gets insulted?"

"No! It may motivate her to try to cook for us. No one is sure if she can boil water without burning it. Why do you think that Saxon hired an experienced cook on Malta? Schwabe's purpose in life is to be there for Steiner. She's been assigned as his mistress since Romania."

"Assigned?"

"Ask me when we are in Alexandria and I'll regale you with the whole silly story. But you are buying dinner and drinks. I have a list of suitable restaurants sent by my mother from when some relative of ours worked in the German commercial consulate a few years back. Oh, and please dissuade your Kapitän from bothering General von Manstein at DAK. His staff has strict orders not to put you through."

"Why?"

"You don't know your family tree that well. We are all related. I'm his liaison here, as well as Assistant Ia of the Brigade. Corps General von Manstein knows enough to know that he officially has no wish to know about an operation he would have to disallow that probably happens tonight." The naval officer needed a minute to puzzle through the implications of this. "Yes, yes. If it fails badly his hands are clean. If somehow Steiner pulls another magic show like he did at Luqa and again on the Barrel Road, I'm along as von Manstein's official representative to see that enough credit in Berlin stays with the family. I'm not in the chain of command. But I'll be in the same vehicle with the two Fräuleins. Saxon has already discussed with me whether I will consent to provide helpful suggestions. So reassure your superior, there will be a well-trained Wehrmacht officer overseeing this little dash. Neither Strauss nor I think there is really much chance of this actually reaching Alexandria, much less the docks. But there's Steiner's luck. When Napoleon considered promoting a man he'd ask around if the man was lucky. Luck was shorthand for the people who somehow excel in the chaos of battle. Steiner is such a man. In Napoleon's day, he'd have been a Marshal of France before he had to shave every day."

"But what if he fails? Badly fails?"

"Then most of us die. It's war. His Battalion. Your Company-sized detachment and attached escort Company. Piper's oversized amalgamated Battalion … "

"Amalgamated?"

"Peiper was a Company commander when he arrived. He was a success, and his force is being upgraded to Battalion size. Another SS officer, Mohnke, had his Battalion almost destroyed. His few survivors, plus the ones sent to start the rebuild, will be with Peiper when we go in. Means Peiper has an amalgam of two Battalions-to-be. You use what you have when the battle starts. Total force is under three thousand men. That's spare change, the way higher commands count cost. The probable loss is worth the long-odds gamble that Steiner pulls off another miracle."

"Yet you are going along … "

"I volunteered for this theater to stay in combat. I am supposed to be at home healing my wounds and dodging my mother's attempts to get me married off. If this works, I hope to jump to Major and get my Knight's Cross. I'll be the youngest field officer in our branch of the family, since one who served Dem Alte Fritz. We advance the Reich, and our own careers. Isn't that how war works for our class?"

When the naval officer got done sputtering at this preposterous situation, he trotted off to appraise his commander of the realities. Life was not as it first seemed.

2100 hours local; 2000 hours CET
1 November, 1940
Just behind lines of Mason's Brigade, 7th Division Sector

The Hebe from Birmingham had been spot-on. Sergeant Billy and half a dozen of his boys watched the nightly raid passing the lines, heading west. They were led by three Matilda tanks and included a cruiser and a half dozen armored cars. Trotting behind them were a hundred or so Poor Bloody Infantry, the PBI. Nothing ever changes. The 'gentlemen' way back give vague orders that division 'interprets' for brigade as sending men to their deaths because … it tended to get fuzzy there. To maintain their fighting edge. To harass the enemy. Mostly to be seen to be doing something, anything more than sitting in trenches consuming rations while waiting for the next 'Big Push' with its miles-long casualty lists and paltry gains.

Billy had his ear to the ground. Brigade command had as little faith in these raids as he did. Hence the flare-pistol code. Billy and his boys had half a dozen by now, all with the proper red flares. Mr. James had given him handy requisition slips signed by another two-star general. Billy wished in retrospect he had found an officer like Mr. James in the last war.

2200 hours local; 2100 hours CET
1 November 1940
Di Salo battalion staging area, rear of XXI Corps lines

It was on for tonight. The ambush KG and the penetration KG had both already mustered and moved out. Capomanipolo Pio Ronconi was in charge of the Catalan company. He had been detailed here and given a promotion to officer rank because he actually spoke that obscure tongue.

Lieutenant Colonel Di Salo was off leading the penetration force. It was a pity he had left his whore behind. Coxita was trying to encourage the Company in the manner she had while fighting for the demonic Reds who had killed Ronconi's mother. Every man in this unit claimed he had been conscripted by the Spanish Republic against his will. The only honest Red was his commander's tart. Ronconi didn't care if he led all these swine to their deaths. What mattered was the success of the mission. God's Holy Kingdom in Jerusalem was to be recreated.

....

Coxita had taken the German comrade's instruction to heart. She spent her time explaining the mission to these men in simple terms. Many claimed to have served on the Ebro with her, others on the Aragon front. So she explained using actual operations as references. They would follow behind the spearhead, clearing out the British rear areas. They would then be resupplied and fall in at the back of the column, marching towards a big city like Barcelona. Their job was flank protection. If they hit serious opposition, there was a Panzer Division available in support.

2330 hours local; 2230 hours CET
1 November 1940
Sortie point for this night's Palestinian Raid; Mason's Brigade Sector; 7th Division Sector

There was precious little moonlight through the thick cloud cover. There was a holiday of light some kilometers to the south and west. Artillery duels, illumination rounds, the occasional massive flash as an ammunition dump cooked off. That reminded Gunter of the old days in the Kaiserwar. Riga and Michael. God, was he ever young and clueless back then. Twenty-three years seemed like a hundred to him now. He had memories of that callow lad, but found it hard to relate to that boy really being him.

Gunter was half out of the turret of a British Rolls Royce Armored Car. The design looked like a Kaiserwar antique to Gunter, but Joey had assured him this one was mechanically sound. The welded repairs to prior combat damage wouldn't stand up to much of a pounding. That shouldn't matter. The plan didn't call for much combat. This would all be a fancy trick. The complex stratagem had seemed workable when Gunter and his confederates had pitched it to Rommel. Driving into the British lines now, with his life on the line, the risks suddenly seemed insane. The pressing need to reach Alexandria before the main German forces so as to have privacy to deal with the fence about the bejeweled golden birds now seemed to be childish greed to Gunter. The dead don't need extra profits to spend.

....

Sergeant Billy was watching the approaching vehicles and dismounted squaddies. Something didn't ring true. There was an extra Matilda and two extra armored cars. The slapped-on welded plates over combat holes were in different positions on these vehicles than on the ones that gone out. The PBI was moving too crisply to be the very slapdash Palestinians. The hand signals seemed off. Billy had a tip-of-the-tongue feeling that he had, somewhere, seen troops that crossed ground that way with those signals. It would come to him. Oh, and one of the Matilda's had fired off two rounds behind them, as though to retard pursuit. There never was pursuit, and the tanks had never done that before. Billy and his guys watched every patrol. Mr. James always wanted details. Said it didn't matter what seemed important. Just get him details. Officers did that sort of deep thinking, Billy supposed.

Meantime, from his perch to the rear he could see the green-as-grass British second lieutenant, with his baker's dozen of semi-trained Egyptians, coming up to talk to the officer in the lead Matilda.

....

Di Salo was surprised at how few British were guarding the gap in the minefield, waiting for the returning raiders. No one had asked him for the days-old password he had hoped would still work. Instead they had let his Matilda and Joey's drive up, had let his accompanying Betar infantry swarm through, plant better markers in the minefield, and prepare for the next step in the dance.

The British officer wandered over. He seemed puzzled about something. Called out, "What unit?"

Di Salo answered, "Palestine brigade."

The boy lieutenant heard his voice tones. Public school, Oxbridge, City of London. Accent that said highborn superior. The young gentleman snapped to attention. His men saw him do so and did the same. They weren't trained enough to manage the position of attention particularly well. The young man was puzzled by the situation. This was not the same patrol he had seen out, but this was clearly a British officer. The lieutenant had attended a minor public school, Ewell Castle. He hoped to find a social bond to ask his questions of this obvious social superior. "May I ask where you did your schooling, sir?"

"Eton. But I learned my English from my British mother and a British governess." Di Salo let a wolfish smile come across his face. "And Italian from my father and most of my family!" Di Salo let off a burst of fire from his MP-38. "Hands up! On your knees, all of you!"

Most of the men dropped to their knees before raising their hands, but regardless of the sequence all complied with both … except the silly boy officer. Instead he fumbled for his flare pistol. He dropped it, bent quickly to retrieve it, and collapsed, having been shot multiple times. Gunter, Joey, and half a dozen infantrymen had all responded to the motion by firing their weapons. The flare gun dropped from the lieutenant's dead fingers. The fool had died a hero, but had not accomplished his task.

....

Billy remembered where he had seen this infantry drill. German storm troopers in Picardy back in '18. Shit! He saw the Germans round up the remaining 'British'. The line was breached. They fired off flares, four blue ones marking the position for the followup waves. Billy motioned to the young men he was with to start fading back. When they reached their motorcycles, Billy would do his duty and warn the rest of Mason's brigade. But only when he was back enough not to draw accurate fire. Two minutes wouldn't matter in the larger scheme of things, but could be worth his life. The red flares would attract fire.

Then Billy froze for a second. He saw red flares rising from the south. Then from the north. Then all over the position. It wasn't a down-the-line assault. He'd have heard combat noises. These panicky half-trained baboons couldn't even remember the color code on the flares. Blue, red, it hadn't mattered to them. They saw a flare and shot off their own. Billy hopped into the sidecar on the motorbike and let himself be driven off towards Alexandria. This was shaping up as a worse load of bollocks than Malta.

0120 hours local; 0020 hours CET
2 November 1940
Forward assembly area KG Steiner, formerly sector of Mason's Brigade, British 7th Division

It was time. Uncle Ivan had cleaned out the administrative zone so fast and so completely that he had even overrun the first British traffic control roadblock some 12 kilometers beyond where the KG currently was. He shook Jochen Peiper's hand as they wished each other well. Peiper was the lead until the second British road block was reached. The British moved these every day. The Elders told him this was to make it more difficult for drivers to turn inland and avoid the demand for papers. Peiper's quasi-Battalion had more firepower than Klaus's, especially the formerly Italian flame Panzers. Klaus would follow with Greta's Navy Detachment bringing up the rear. Already, important German and Italian staff officers were consulting their watches and muttering. They wanted access to the breach. Klaus could see Italian and German engineering troops widening the mine-free zone. The small pathway Gunter had made would take days for two fresh divisions to pass through. Not his problem. It was time to MARCH!

0130 hours local; 0030 hours CET
2 November 1940
Brigade rally point, Mason's Brigade, 10 miles to the rear of his original lines, slightly south-by-southwest of Mason's original Brigade HQ

The trucks had been coming in by one's and two's ever since the first warning flares had started going off. Mason found many of the stories laughable. He'd been through the mill too often last time, to take tales of last survivors and overwhelming odds that seriously. Each vehicle load of ralliers had only seen one small piece of the puzzle; and like most men in combat, were abysmal observers.

He'd whittled the numbers down to something believable for his report to 8th Army HQ. It was a three-division assault, two German and one Italian. He refined the reports to what he'd seen in France and Flanders 1914-1918 and again in 1940. The absence of artillery prep was unusual, but the storm troops had engineering and armored fighting vehicle support. Engineers were standard for them in both wars. The fighting vehicles were the norm in 1940. It was a sort of variant on Fifth Army sector in 1918. Using these templates, the breathless reports of his rallying survivors could be hammered into something coherent to pass up the chain of command. The Germans had a battle drill, and the Italians seemed to have learned it. One of Haig's 1918 armies could have beaten it back same as they had done several times in '18, before the glorious advance that was the Hundred Days.

Army HQ was, as usual, clueless. So Mason just told them he was moving his brigade remnant back to First Australian Corps headquarters. He'd fought beside them several times in the last war. Crack troops. They'd find some use for his 'brigade'. It was more like a battalion at this point. He'd send the men here with his number 2. He'd stay in place himself for a bit to see if anyone else was coming. God what an utter, complete load of bollocks. Even an inept shell of a division should have held longer than this. Haig's men had known how to fight.

0140 hours local; 0040 CET
2 November 1940
Downtown Cairo, Egypt

Anwar Sadat could hear the sounds of combat from the area around the British Embassy. Nasser had insisted on leading that attack, and Sadat had deferred to him. Taking the Embassy would be glorious. It also was not going to happen. There were at least two battalions defending the place. All attacks by mobs and militia would accomplish, was a pile of dead Egyptians for a building the occupiers would vacate tomorrow or the next day. The verdict of history was visible. Every office the British or their lackeys occupied, had mammoth burn-barrels sending sparks flying into the night sky.

Sadat was seizing the key places needed to keep the city functioning. He had already taken the main power plant, the water works, and the other key utilities. He'd been repulsed at the Misr Station, Cairo's main railroad station, and at the telephone exchange. He had led those two probes himself. Each time he had broken off once real resistance was met. Taking installations reduced to ruins, was not the optimal solution. Better to screen each position and try to seize them as the enemy pulled out. The demolitions would only come at the very end, when most of the British were already in their vehicles fighting their way out. In the meantime he was marching on the radio studio. If he could seize that, the Egyptian Islamic Republic could be proclaimed.

0200 hours local; 0100 hours CET
2 November 1940
Gisht Ari Pasha's Villa, Alexandria, Egypt

Sergeant Billy had phoned ahead from the roadblock. It had cost a carton of cigarettes to jump the line and use the telephone. Seventh Division was gone. Which meant the Alamein line was gone. The enemy would be in Alexandria by day's end. The Pasha still refused to be rushed. He was upstairs having tea with a clique of lieutenants who had purchased his operations. Everything else was packed on the trucks, and ready to be off to the yacht basin.

In the meantime, Money-Penny would pretend he was still a serving officer. He had rung up the harbor defense office. Name-dropping his two fictitious commanding generals had gotten him the senior man on the overnight shift. Pity the dullard was a blockhead. "Captain, I accept that you won't wake your admiral on a mere lieutenant commander's word. Send a party down the road to confirm my report. The line is gone and German motorized troops are on the march for Alexandria. It's time for final demolitions."

"Listen here, Lieutenant Commander whoever-you-are. My orders from the Admiralty are, no demolitions without express orders from the Ambassador in Cairo. I tried ringing them up after your last call. Telephone exchange is under attack. So is the embassy. Eighth Army headquarters denies that the line has gone. They say battle in progress. So go spread your defeatism somewhere else. My admiral will have words for your general tomorrow. If I were you I would get those three ships of yours out of my yacht basin before that happens, as you are likely to be before a court-martial for panic-mongering if they can still find you here."

Money-Penny put the phone down. He had tried. Malta all over again. When would these clods ever learn?

0245 hours local; 0145 hours CET
2 November 1940
Italo-German Panzer Army Headquarters, behind the lines of Italian XXIII Corps

The two Generals sat quietly facing each other, each waiting for the other to speak first. The entire battle plan had just blown up. Somehow Rommel's Division and Italian XXI Corps were on the march. Brigade Strauss might have done an operation on their own hook. They were Berlin's pets, and moved to a music only they could hear. Four divisions plus Corps troops … do not go into action without anyone at higher headquarters having an advance warning.

The staring contest could have lasted forever. What broke it was a communications officer with updates from Claus von Stauffenberg for von Manstein. Geloso looked at the German and politely said, "Shall we share our knowledge and plan our battle?"

Von Manstein relaxed slightly. "Yes, I had warnings. Multiple. I have an 'observer' in the Strauss Brigade. Nominally he is assistant Ia." He saw Geloso's wary look. "Yes, a brigade with such a large operations department. Most unusual, but so is everything about Strauss's formation. Strauss and his officers know he's mine. As nothing was said about it, I presume the Reichsführer did not object. My man rated the plan as possible but risky. The failure seems to be at our level. Air reconnaissance and signals intercept seem to have missed out their 7th Division being drawn down to a shell of itself. The attack was on a Company's frontage, and the entire Brigade collapsed. The other Brigade and the rest of the division are attempting flight. Your Corps seems to have pocketed them. Shall we now discuss your Libyan Division? That is set to follow in Rommel's wake, and seems bound for the British deep rear."

"For Cairo. The city is in chaos. Their king has approached ours about rescuing the city. There will be an airborne drop after dawn. So where do we send Rommel?"

Von Manstein considered an honest answer, which was to send the deceitful prima donna to the devil. Wouldn't do. Rommel's luck was still with him. "Deep rear of 8th Army behind the positions of Australian First Corps. If he can either take out their artillery or force it to flee … " Out of a further hour's discussions, a new battle plan began to form.

0320 hours local; 0220 hours CET
2 November 1940
Vicinity of second British Roadblock on coast road to Alexandria, 2 kilometers west of El-Hamam
Egypt

His infantry had dismounted 300 meters from the contact point. They were maneuvering well by platoons to find the flanks. Sturmbannführer Jochen Peiper was maneuvering his 'armored forces'. Ten AMC-35's, six Italian flame tanks, one repaired British Rolls Royce Armored Car, and five Kübelwagen with mounted ZB-53 machine-guns.

The British roadblock had been designed for traffic control. The only prepared positions seemed to be some slit trenches (whose near-random positioning made clear that their purpose was someplace to seek shelter during air raids), and a headquarters shack that by now was in flames.

Visibility was poor. Moon was close to setting, and mostly hidden by cloud cover and smoke from the combat. The defenders seemed to have been in Company strength. Peiper guessed a Platoon of whatever the British called their chain-dogs, backed by a pair of infantry Platoons. They were well provided with machine-guns and seemed to have a few antitank rifles. Two burning trucks and a damaged AMC-35 testified to those. No enemy mortars or artillery engaged. Peiper had a mortar section, but was using them for illumination rounds.

Jochen was maneuvering his vehicles carefully. He had already left six AMC's and three flametanks behind with mechanical issues. Alexandria was still over a hundred kilometers away. In his mind, preserving his strength mattered more than a bit of wasted time. So he lined up his machine-gun carriers and AMC's, using them as a base of fire. He then spent five minutes beating down the British till the return fire essentially stopped. He doubted he had hit many enemy soldiers, but they were kissing the bottom of their trenches to stay alive. He continued the machine-gun barrage as he sent two flame tanks forward, one each to approximately where the ends of the fairly linear British position seemed to be.

Some British officer must have had a trench periscope … or been especially brave. An antitank rifle fired at the flame tankette to the right. First round missed. Second knocked out a track. The crew sensibly bailed out before their immobilized vehicle turned into a torch and fried them.

Second one got to within 10 meters of the first slit trench and belched fire. The horrid screams that followed showed it was on target. Screams and disgusting smell of fried human. Peiper had smelled such in France along the Aa Canal. French or British troops, or even Belgian civilians. In that chaos one would never know.

Suddenly there were white flags showing from the British position. 'Flags' was a generous statement. White undershirts, a white napkin, and God knows what else. Peiper was immediately on the radio telling his units to cease firing. Let his infantry clean up the British position. A few dozen enemy would run away to the rear. It was the way of such things. Men with rifles and little water, were not enough of a danger to waste much time on.

Suddenly he saw road movement. A German column led by Panhard armored cars was advancing. Advancing at speed straight through the wooden traffic control arm, knocking it flying. He clicked to the frequency he and Klaus had agreed to keep open for communication between them. "Klaus, what are you doing?"

"Going on to Alexandria."

"Klaus, give me half an hour and we can go as a unit."

"Half an hour is fifteen or twenty kilometers we can be down the road. We both know the British will try to destroy the harbor. The faster we arrive, the better the chance we interrupt the process and save some of the facilities."

"Klaus, let's contact Gunter."

"You contact him. I have a radio. He can always order me to halt in place till you catch up."

Klaus knew he was pushing the limits of his authority. In his mind this was what proper commanders did. The only General he really knew was Rommel. Who led from the front and overran every halt line. Greta's family had accepted him as her husband-to-be. Time to be a hero and prove worthy of the honor. Wasn't this what should be expected of a Commercial Director who was also a Party member and SS officer? Klaus had spent years in school and the HJ, being indoctrinated in Aryan superiority and leadership by willpower. More had stuck than his instructors had realized. The boy Major was trying to live up to multiple heroic images – the State's, the Party's, and of course his princess Greta who was now an official Aryan.

0330 hours local; 0230 CET
2 November 1940
Headquarters I Australian Corps, rear left of main British positions on Ruweisat Ridge

The Australians were nonplussed by the arrival of Mason's bedraggled 'last survivors'. General Blamey insisted on a briefing. Mason himself was in some of the last vehicles. After a quick review, Blamey had rung up Eighth Army headquarters. Cunningham was 'too busy' to come to the phone. Instead, a staff colonel was arguing with the two commanders over the open line. "Good God Mason, you are a Guards officer. Enough of that rubbish. A British division does not come apart this way. Get a hold of yourself, go back and restore the line."

Mason had by now no illusions that he had a career to salvage. "Relieve me if you choose, but no. Fuck no! Seventh was at best a courtesy division. You have been milking it for days for security detachments in the rear. So what we had was a shell. Fritz seems to have gotten wind of your troop movements. They made a push and it imploded. The bulk of those men never signed up to fight, and for sure we never took the time to train them to. You never gave us the heavy weapons or artillery to be a real division. I'm sure you had your reasons. Doesn't matter. It's gone. Eighth Division collapsed yesterday. Get your Army out while you still have one. I watched the Frenchies slow-walk their responses this spring. Cost them the war."

"The general will be informed in good time. I'll ring up Seventh Division HQ to restore your front. In the meantime. I am giving you a direct order!"

"Sod off, you inept clown! Use the remaining hours of darkness to move."

Mason slammed down the phone. Blamey put down his more slowly. He turned to Mason. "What do you suggest, colonel?"

"Get your corps out of here. Give me a battalion of guns to back up what's left of my lads. We'll fight it out here, buying you as much time as we can. I served with you folks on the Somme in '16 and again in '18. You are top notch, or at least your fathers were."

Blamey beamed. "I was there for those battles. Some day when this is all over we should have drinks and compare stories."

Mason sadly shook his head. "I'm for the grave or the cages before the sun sets. I'll try to get your guns out at the end, but no guarantees. They are the only thing I'll have to keep the Jerry tanks from overrunning my lads. Half of mine are the sort of untrained newbies I told the staff idiot about. They are only here because they latched onto a real captain or sergeant. Best I can give you is a hard fight from fixed positions. I wish … " Mason's voice trailed off.

Blamey understood. The rot, the slapdash expedients, the half-measures, it was all coming due for payment. All this Guards officer could provide was a version of the Birkenhead Drill. Reminded Blamey of some of the good British officers he had soldiered with in the Last War. Needs must. Thank God he'd had his staff doing plans for a quick skedaddle.   He turned to his staff and barked out, "Variant three. Implement NOW!"

0340 hours local; 0240 hours CET
2 November 1940
Breakthrough sector of what had once been Mason's brigade

General Rommel was screaming at Gunter. Again. Gunter had been put on traffic control duty by an icily angry General von Manstein. The corps commander had been nastier than anyone Gunter had ever seen, but had neither raised his voice nor cursed. Gunter's unauthorized operation had made a grand traffic control mess. Gunter's own Brigade, Rommel's division, three Italian Divisions, and Italian Corps troops were all trying to crowd through an opening made by a Company to allow successive Battalions to traverse. Von Stauffenberg's fast group from Rommel's Division had gone through before von Manstein's radio dressing-down. To Rommel this obviously meant his entire Division must follow in support. Follow immediately as top priority.

Rommel was a Divisional commander. Von Manstein was a Corps commander. Von Manstein had decreed that the Italians came first, starting with the 1st Libyan Division. Rommel could sit there until the Italians announced that they were done. Then his Division could move, with the remainder of Brigade Strauss.

One of Gunter's radio clerks came running up with something 'urgent'. Rommel had a fit at being interrupted while yet again explaining that his order must be obeyed regardless of what the Corps Commander had decreed. Before the clerk could get out more than Peiper and Steiner, Gunter yelled at him, "**NOT NOW!** Find Oberstleutnant Gorlov. Have him take his Battalion up to Sturmbannführer Peiper and Major Steiner to sort out whatever the problem is. And **NEVER** interrupt a General officer like this again."

Rommel went back to his tirade about his higher rank than Gunter's. Gunter kept directing snarled traffic while repeating over and over the respective ranks of Rommel and von Manstein. The clerk was left to try to find someone who knew where on Earth Oberstleutnant Gorlov, or even his Battalion, was? That Battalion had dropped off the radio nets near to an hour ago.

0400 hours local; 0300 hours CET

2 November 1940
British Embassy, Cairo, Egypt

The phone call was from Eighth Army Headquarters. Ambassador Lampson was not liking what he was hearing from General Cunningham. "What do you mean, the position has collapsed? Four hours ago your staff was assuring mine that today's fighting had gone rather well."

"It had, Ambassador. Our line was taking attacks from the main enemy forces. We were punished by their artillery and air, but within expected parameters. Their infantry had only made minor lodgements and those were contained. Since midnight, a secondary attack has collapsed Seventh Division. I've got two armored divisions loose in our rear. The Australian Corps has begun pulling out, citing instructions from their home government."

"What instructions? The Australian Government assured us their men would fight. I'll have the Foreign Office wire Canberra at once to get this reversed."

"Between the two of us, Ambassador, I think the Australian General, Blamey, is inventing these instructions. Presume the Foreign Office contacts his government and gets a cable back. Then they send one to you and you call me. Then we get Blamey on the line. Six hours from now, if we are lucky. More likely 18 to 24 hours. Without the Australians in the line, the rest of the Army is pocketed and lost. It's over. By all means, start the process to fry General Blamey. However, I am beginning to pull the rest of the army out of the line. I cannot give you orders, but I strongly urge you to evacuate the embassy and start south before dawn."

"How could that division have collapsed?"

"You knew our three line divisions were glorified militia mixed with rebuilds of shattered units from Malta. So at best they were an obstacle to a serious attack. Then came your riots. We robbed 7th and 8th to provide your security units."

"You assured me it was safe to do so."

"Please re-read my memos that I sent after each round of troop movements. It was all a calculated risk based in good part on the Axis plans London sent us being accurate. Eighth was dead anyway, so making it weaker shouldn't have mattered. Seventh wasn't to be attacked, so thinning that out shouldn't have mattered. Eighth was a staff failure here. You've been copied on the report to the War Cabinet. Seventh was bad intelligence. The big thing remains this African war. They have gotten the reinforcements we needed. London made priority decisions, and we were not a priority. I hope that when Montgomery takes Dakar, the Cabinet will not repent of their decisions. That's for the future. By dawn all of Cairo will know that the army is in retreat. If you don't get yourself and your people out of Cairo, you may all be lost."

"But there's no way to get all the remaining civilians out by dawn."

"Sir, there are going to be massacres of Empire civilians. Some of my service and support people will get destroyed by air attack. More will be lost from partisan ambushes. Fortunes of war. It's over."

Lampson was furious. "My last cable to the Cabinet will hold you personally responsible for this debacle."

Cunningham's voice showed just how weary he was. "I serve at the pleasure of the Government. They can have my head anytime they choose. Until then, I will preserve the last army that Britain possesses. I'll be lucky to get half my men and a quarter of my firepower back to Upper Egypt. So be it. Now you must excuse me. This was a courtesy call, not me asking for permission. There is work to do.

Dawn is in a bit less than two hours."

The line went dead. Lampson allowed himself five minutes of vivid cursing before giving orders to evacuate the city. He thought to himself that he was going to be remembered for the worst cock-up in the history of the Empire. Why the lure of Dakar and a few lesser French African cities had kept the Cabinet in a lost war was beyond him. Then again, why promise Poland to fight, when Britain couldn't and France wouldn't?

0420 hours local; 0320 hours CET
2 November 1940
Royal Navy Headquarters, Alexandria, Egypt

The captain was sure that whoever this fool Lieutenant Commander Money-Penny was, the man was a poltroon. Rear areas were always full of such self-important types. Nonetheless, the captain had been chosen for this assignment because of a long history of painstaking attention to detail. So he was phoning around. The police were reporting disturbances in the city. A liaison officer reported that the Egyptian army units in the city – including what had once been the large garrison in the Western Desert – were forming up to pull back to Cairo. The liaison officer said he'd be motoring to RN Headquarters with a small vehicle convoy. They 'no longer felt safe' around the Egyptians.

The port area was sealed, but crowds were forming. Indians, Chinese, Jews, Greeks, Maltese, anti-fascist refugees, Egyptians known for their British sympathies … the street telegraph was saying, run to the last British positions in the city for protection. This didn't look good. He tried the Embassy again. The Cairo telephone exchange told him the Embassy was no longer answering, but they would try to find him someone in authority. In the meantime the usual Egyptian port workers – the tea ladies, the shoe-shine boys, the office help – either had not turned up or in many cases were suddenly sick and needed to get home. This was so not looking good. He resolved to wake his admiral early.

0445 hours local; 0345 CET
2 November 1940
Di Salo's Battalion, 3 kilometers east of the original lines of Mason's brigade

In theory the battalion was guarding the breach point against British counterattacks. Once the initial defenders had been cleared out, there had been no British response at all. Most unusual. Lieutenant Colonel John Di Salo, his company commanders, and Coxita were clustered having a tea break when the communications runner found them. He was looking for Oberstleutnant Ivan Gorlov or, failing finding him personally, one of his units. All had dropped off the comm net and seemed to have vanished.

Coxita was trying to prove herself useful. She was still quite frightened of being dumped in Naples or Alexandria. "Lieutenant Colonel Di Salo." She was being formal here in public, instead of asserting her rights to use familiar terms of address. "Let me take the Catalan company forward. We don't have any heavy vehicles to slow us down. We can find our two spearhead battalions and report back on whatever the problem is."

John was liking this new Coxita. Let her be subordinate in public … and feisty in his bed.

"Capomanipolo Pio Ronconi, do you feel qualified to lead such an expedition?"

Pio Ronconi was not about to plead lack of capacity, leaving his unit to be led by his commander's concubine. "I can do this. There is no need for the young lady … "

"She is my eyes and ears, as well as a combat veteran. Coxita, you are not in command. You will observe for me. Now off, both of you. This is excellent Ceylonese tea and it's getting cold."

0520 hours local; 0420 CET
2 November 1940
RN HQ Alexandria, Egypt

The admiral was not accustomed to being on duty in the predawn chill. However, he was much more decisive than his night-shift captain. He issued quick, clear orders. The crowds in front of the gates were admitted, and escorted under guard to some of the many empty warehouses. When the Mediterranean Fleet had left, any and every spare part and other useful supply had been taken along. There hadn't been shipping space or time for everything, and time was of the essence. As is, the warships were crammed to the point where fighting would have been difficult. Merchant ships were impressed for the rest. The only stores still plentiful were food and fuel of various types. The British Empire had both in abundance. No need to haul away extra, and thus abandon things that needed manufacture or personnel with skills.

In reverse, word was passed to the locals still on base. Anyone who wanted to run, do so now or get sealed in. A few sent for their families. The rest made their apologies and fled.

The admiral had no more success finding the ambassador than the captain had. The best they could reach was a Commander Fleming. The man claimed he was in command of a brigade of naval commandos. Alleged that the evacuation of Cairo was in progress. Absurd. Surely someone would have notified Alexandria had such a thing occurred.

0600 hours local; 0500 hours CET
2 November 1940
AAA position at the edge of Alexandria, Egypt

Bain Collins was thrilled to be a real soldier like his Dad had been. Different army, but that didn't matter to the young man. His father was Irish, his mother Bengali. The British Raj in India was neither of their nation. Soldiers in Bain's view enlisted with an army and were true to their oath. So he saw nothing unpatriotic in being a German soldier. Soldier was a trade, not a patriotic calling. He was only a recruit now, but if he stayed in for the full thirty years perhaps he could make Corporal or maybe Sergeant.

Now he was on a motorcycle with his foster brother Abduhl, who was now to be called Abe in the army, manning the machine-gun in the sidecar. Major Steiner had allowed Bain to be with the motorcycle vanguard. He and Abe had 'language skills'. Bain didn't see how languages had anything to do with fighting, but that was why the Major was an important officer. They KNEW things.

Up ahead Bain could see a clump of men lounging at the side of the road. Most probably British soldiers, from the color of their clothing. Abe started to get his Bren gun ready but Bain told him, "Hold your fire, I'm going to try something."

Bain waved at the Britishers as he brought his bike to a stop. "What unit?"

"74th City of Glasgow Ack Ack. You?" The British soldier answering was a lance corporal. Looked to be in his thirties, so probably a Territorial unit. Bain had been brought up to look down on these as 'weekend soldiers'. He kept the learned disdain out of his voice. "Falcons of Malta. My Major will be up in a few minutes. Needs a word with your officer."

The Territorials had never heard of a unit named 'Falcons of Malta', but knew a lot of temporary units had been evacuated from that fortress before it had fallen. This Bain had a voice that was Army ranker born and bred. So one guy asked, "What unit were you born into?"

"Third Bengal Light Cavalry. Born in Meerut Cantonment."

Territorials don't know Indian Army units, and thus missed the joke. They fetched their major just as Klaus came up with the main force of Panhards and Kübelwagen. Bain had Abe fire a burst in the air, and called out, "Hands up. You are now prisoners of the German Nibelungen Legion." There were curses, and a few men at the back ran off. Abdul gunned two down with his Bren gun and the rest stopped running. Everyone got their hands up. Klaus flagged down the lead touring car with Greta, Naiomi, von Kleist, and the two senior navy officers. "Any of yours have gunnery training?" Klaus saw a nod. "Leave two behind. I'm leaving two platoons. See if you can man these weapons or disable them. Either would do." Klaus got back in his vehicle. He tried Peiper and Gunter again. No luck. Probably out of range. Off he went, leading the column to the port with Bain in the lead.

0615 hours local; 0515 hours CET
2 November 1940
4 kilometers north north east of initial breakthrough point, former British 7th Division Sector

The damned Matilda tanks were slow. Almost slower than a walking man. Ivan Gorlov had two of the slow-moving tanks, plus two Companies of his initial Battalion, plus the 20mm AAA battery, operating in support of the Italians pocketing the rest of the British north of the penetration. This hadn't been part of the plan, but the Italians needed his two AFV's and extra firepower. The British weren't fighting very hard. He'd already detailed his other two Companies to prisoner guard duty. The Italian General he was working with kept promising that in a little while the Italian POW guard detachments would catch up and take these off their hands. "In a little while" seemed a flexible term to Italians – meaning 'in the future but definitely not now'.

He'd switched his radio to the Italian net to coordinate. Ivan didn't exactly speak Italian; but he could sort of follow the gist of any Romance language after so many years in Romania, plus his own aristocrat's French.

Gunter wasn't likely to miss him, but just in case he'd sent three messengers with updates on where he was, what he was doing. Right now what he was doing was sitting in place while some German Naval Commando unit escorted a large column of prisoners past. He'd have to ask Gunter about these. Brandenburg Regiment. Fought in British uniform. He'd shared a brandy with their Major. Man had a thick Berlin accent and had served in Denikin's army after his Freikorps had been disbanded in Kiev during the postwar German retreat. He'd even fought near Ivan at a couple of engagements.

....

Lieutenant Colonel Orde Wingate was in the back of a truck pretending to be wounded. When a dozen of his Palestinians came to him with this absurd scheme, he'd been half of a mind to just laugh it off. But it was this or go into the bag. The sixty or so German and Austrian Jews were the ones at risk, pretending to be these commando chaps. The originators had all been officers or police. Swore they could play at being themselves, only without circumcision.

0640 hours local; 0540 CET
2 November 1940
3,000 meters over the El Alamein battlefield

Hauptmann Bruno Dilley had his squadron of Ju-87 Stukas in a holding pattern south of what, by his briefing maps, had been the British positions. The briefing had been chaotic. The south and north sectors of the British lines had vanished. No one was sure if the friendly forces were current on their recognition markings. The color of the day was supposed to be red. Red flares, red panels, big red X's on the top of AFV's. So far Bruno had seen red … and green, blue, yellow, and white. The forward air controllers were trying to sort the mess out. There were thousands of vehicles in motion below. This in turn produced rising clouds of sand and dust. Bruno was giving it twenty minutes. If no one came up with a coherent answer, he was falling back on what had been working for the last few weeks. With the RAF essentially absent from the battlefield, friendly units did not shoot at planes in the sky. So anyone firing at his planes from what appeared to be a fixed position, was the enemy.

0700 hours local; 0600 hours CET
2 November 1940
City of Glasgow AAA position

Peiper's thirty minutes had proven to be a tad optimistic, as such things often were in wartime. He saw a roadblock with a dozen stopped British vehicles. When he halted to start deploying to take it out, he saw two of the road block party waving him ahead. The mystery was resolved when observation through field glasses showed they were in German uniform. Before Peiper could deal with this new situation, he was in receipt of a frantic radio message from Di Salo's idiot woman. She was engaged with the rearguard of a large British force that was in transit towards him.

……….

 Coxita was on best behavior. She didn't tell Pio Ronconi more than once that he was moving the Company far too slowly. He was in command. She was an 'observer'. So she was the one who saw the dust behind them. Some unit was closing in on them. Someone who hadn't radioed ahead to alert them. She tried to get the nominal Company Commander to pull the Company into a defensive position 'just in case'. His answer was, "I'm in command."

"Yes sir." She dropped her vehicle back to the rear of the column and faced it so the machine-gun's pintle mount could be brought to bear on the lead vehicles … which observed her redeployment and fired on her. She returned fire, joined after a minute by her rear-most platoon. The British column swerved inland and looped around the Catalans, firing wildly. It was a noisy two minutes, then the enemy was gone … up the road towards Peiper and Steiner. Coxita decided to risk John's ire. This was serious. She alerted Peiper. She couldn't raise Steiner but she was able to get her man, who said he'd notify Strauss. The next time she and John were alone she would try to politely suggest that this

Roman 'Black Nobleman' needed a bit more training. The Black Papal aristocracy did not have a great military reputation, and in Coxita's opinion this boy was living down to it.

> 0720 hours local; 0620 CET
> 2 November 1940
> 2 miles south of Cairo municipal limits, on the main road to Sudan

The last sniper round had shattered the rear window of the Rolls, and wounded the embassy clerk sitting beside him. Sir Miles Lampson was livid with rage. "How the fuck did it get this bad this fast?"

The National Liberal Cabinet representative beside him on the other side of the rearmost row of seats was long past cosseting the ambassador, whom he regarded as a blind fool, even if one with nominal viceregal powers. "Because you dithered too long. You. Your class. The London government. Respectable London opinion back to the Versailles Conference at the end of the last war. Empire is not just a pleasant inheritance from the Victorians. It has real costs. If we were not prepared to pay them, we would have been far better off giving Egypt and Palestine independence, and been done with it." From outside came the sounds of Bren-gun fire hammering the sniper's probable location. There were mounds of dead people in the streets. Combatants? Rioters? Civilians? Subjects of the Crown? The time for distinguishing among those had long passed. Buildings were burning. People were begging for rides at the side of the road, offering up infants and small children with pleading eyes. Others shuffled along on the verge beside the vehicles, pushing everything from hand-carts to baby prams. Every motor vehicle was stuffed with far too many people, far too much baggage. The column lurched along at under ten miles an hour, with frequent halts for no reason that anyone could see. It was a catastrophe of Biblical proportions. "What the fuck did you expect to happen when it all imploded?"

Lampson felt wounded to the core of his being. "Independence? Without guarantees on the Canal? On minority rights? It's just not that simple. Withdrawing is a complex process."

"Actually, it isn't. Your complex process requires we have the strength to continue our imperium. Two divisions and a fantasy air force are enough strength to hold down the King of Egypt. It is not enough to hold Egypt against hostile powers. A small army in Egypt needs a neutral or friendly Italy. Which we had, till we pissed it away over Ethiopia and the League. Italy safeguarded Austria in 1934. Stood with the West at Stresa. The reward was supposed to be Ethiopia. Which neither Western government was willing to say in public. So they supported the League in public and did the noble thing … and here we are." The parliamentarian forebore mentioning Britain undercutting everything – doing a naval treaty with Hitler, without even alerting its two 'allies' first. It was sure to occur to Italy that if everyone was doing their own deals with Hitler, being the last one to negotiate was a poor bargaining position. He shook his head as the limousine continued to inch past the pathetic flood of terrified humanity. "I saw refugee columns like this in the West before Dunkirk. Expect to see the same all the way to Khartoum, possibly to Nairobi."

Lampson returned to fuming. The wounded clerk sank rapidly into unconsciousness, and thus was not available to keep reminding Lampson that he must order key facilities to be blown up. The last phone calls from the embassy had been blocked. The rebels by then held the telephone exchange. The plan was to find a military radio unit. All thoughts of that plan died when the wounded man was given a morphine shot. Lampson was far too angry to remember on his own.

0745 hours local; 0645 CET
2 November 1940
Peiper's roadblock, road to Alexandria

This had been a Betar position, but now it was his. Peiper's SS/NL battalion made up most of the men and even more of the firepower. Of course, that wasn't counting the two British 3.7 inch Quick Fire antiaircraft cannons that the Betar had manhandled into position to fire on the road. It was sort of like the ever-useful German eight-eight. The crews had a few minutes training by the two naval officers. The guns themselves had neither high explosive nor armor-piercing rounds. No one had a clue as to what an AAA shell would do to a vehicle.

When what was probably the British column appeared, Peiper ordered the naval officers to fire. They bore-sighted each gun against the moving column of trucks, and let fly. One round missed completely and just whizzed away into the distance. The other hit a truck in the engine compartment. No detonation, so either the fusing was improperly done or didn't work on contact. The truck slewed to a stop, a few hundred meters from the roadblock. Men poured out. The other trucks reversed, picking up the stranded men. Peiper had not even ordered his machine-guns to fire yet, and already the engagement was over.

0800 hours local; 0700 hours CET
2 November 1940
Alexandria Harbor

Really smart, successful people often think they know everything. James Money-Penny had spent this morning having that problem with his Pasha. The final sale agreement for his criminal syndicate had been paid for in bullion. Gold, silver, even some platinum. Which had to be counted or weighed and then driven to the yacht basin. Through a city already fraying at the edges of riot. Yes, he had enough armed men along to deal with each blockage. But time had been lost.

Arriving at the three ships triggered a loading problem. In addition to the large quantity of bullion, all quite heavy, another large group of people had been added at the last minute as part of the negotiation, all with luggage. The Pasha had not seen the problem. There was more than enough space on the three ships. The problem was the weight of the bullion. That much extra weight on the yacht meant redistributing other freight and people to the other two ships. The Boss had needed a careful lecture from the yacht's captain on center of gravity – and what ignoring it meant to a ship at sea. All the valuables were going to be on the yacht where Money-Penny could personally be on board with the Pasha to guarantee delivery to Beirut. The Boss wasn't stupid. He was pig-ignorant on matters nautical, and more time was lost. Time while the situation continued to deteriorate. Now there appeared to be a riot over on the RN section of the port.

....

The admiral had heard intermittent firing in the city for some time. Sounded like Bren guns in his opinion, so it must be the military keeping order. Suddenly he saw mobs of people surging past him, racing in terror.

....

Klaus Steiner's Maltese guide turned out to actually know the city streets at least as well as he claimed. Perhaps he hadn't taken the best route. Klaus would need a map and some time later to check. The next time he had to take a city, he wanted maps of his own.

His unit had been using gunfire to clear the streets. He had said to fire over the heads of the swirling crowds. Some of his men obeyed. Some just fired straight at any concentration of people. His unit's passage was marked by piles and drifts of dead, and screaming wounded. Klaus knew how poorly trained they all were at city fighting, and decided he would not discipline them later for this. War was a chaotic affair.

The big mob in front of the naval dock gates fled past the traffic barrier as his column came into view, shooting as they went. Most of the guards ran away. The rest dropped their weapons and raised their hands. The Führer had mandated proper treatment of British captives. Klaus detached a platoon to guard the prisoners and open the gate.

With the gate open the Battalion followed behind him. Klaus was amazed to see no destruction. How had the British not begun demolitions? Up ahead he saw Bain motioning to him. The young man had raced ahead with his motorcycle to a knot of men in Royal Navy blue. Arriving, Klaus saw that most were officers and several seemed senior. Using Bain as a translator, he introduced himself. "I'm Major Klaus Steiner, Falcons of Malta Battalion. Please order your men to assemble in an orderly fashion. Our Führer has mandated correct treatment for all British prisoners."

The two senior British officers handed over their sidearms. The admiral was just fuming and glaring. The number two spoke for him. "I'm the Admiral's second-in-command at the moment. We have thousands of civilians. What is their fate to be?" He looked hopefully at Klaus.

"Simple situation, sir. If you will certify these civilians as under the protection of the British flag and arrange for them to be assembled, I will treat them as prisoners of war. We were instructed to take the concept of British forces in a broad setting. If they worked for you or are in some way loyal to you, it's as if they were British, no?"

"But what happens to them?"

"A few days where we will jointly need to set up some sort of feeding service, and then they will be taken back to Italy."

"Some might be anti-fascists. How will those be treated?"

"Sir, I'm just a Major. So I am going to make a suggestion and rely on you to carry it out. A base this big must have warehouses full of old uniforms and the like. Just get some sort of uniform on the ones in danger, swear them to your national service. Men, women, oldsters, whatever. A uniform top or a cap or something, and a British officer along to tell the Italians that they are military and … " Klaus let his voice trail off. On Malta he had not seen the Italians question who was and wasn't military. "The retired husband of my cook put his British uniform jacket back on, and got swept up on Malta. The Italians may eventually decide retired means civilian, but the odds say the war will be over by then, and then everyone goes home."

Just then, another column of vehicles arrived. Greta, von Kleist-Konitz, and the naval contingent. The navy personnel went running madly up and down the docks, cutting wires to the explosive charges. They could not understand why these had not been set off. Greta was more practical. Marched herself up to Klaus and said, "Darling, get the locations of the food warehouses. Best we secure those at once."

Klaus detailed Bain to the task. He had another bit of work in mind. He saw a lovely mast on top of a building. A mast with wires dangling from it. Probably running to a radio. He sent men to trace the wires, secure the communications equipment, and get back in contact with Gunter.

....

Money-Penny heard the firing getting closer and closer to the main port . The intact port that British authorities had refused to destroy because of a mash of imperial pride and bureaucratic stubbornness. He sadly shook his head. This was dozens of times worse than Malta.

0830 hours local; 0730 hours CET
2 November 1940
Field Headquarters, Brigade Strauss; 5 km east of original penetration point

Gunter was finally off traffic direction duties. He had a radio call from Corps Command. They had intercepted a message from Alexandria in the clear, in which Major Steiner was claiming the capture of the port intact and over seven thousand prisoners. Before Gunter could reply, one of the radio clerks shoved a flimsy into his hand saying just that. When Gunter acknowledged this message, he was ordered by the staff officer he was talking to to stay on the line. The next voice he heard was his Corps Commander, von Manstein. "This is the same young man who took the Luqa airfield for you at Malta?"
"Yes, Herr General."
"What were his orders, precisely."
"He and Sturmbannführer Peiper were to take their two Schnell Battalions up the road until they encountered real resistance and then report in. Real resistance must have been farther east than we envisioned. We got a garbled message about difficulties but could not get them back for details. The Battalion I wanted to send to assess the situation has proven impossible to locate. One of my other Battalion commanders on his own initiative sent a company forward that claims contact with Peiper. Also claims a large British Battalion in the area."
Von Manstein left Gunter hanging on the line. Gunter stood waiting at the position of attention. He might now have the rank of Brigadier. In his mind, Gunter was still a Feldwebel and von Manstein was a General of the Panzer Troops. When a superior wanted to think, you let him. Rank hath its privileges. "My staff will find someone else for traffic duty. You are to take as many of your units as you can find right now and motor to Alexandria. Any unit that needs ten minutes to prepare, is to be left behind to follow when they can. If this young man did half of what he is claiming, I need a superior officer on the spot. You will arrive at Alexandria, or radio with good reason why the road is blocked. You will check in with this headquarters every quarter-hour. Any questions?"
"No Herr General Corps Commander. I would advise you instructing General Rommel to forward to my column a radio detachment with better equipment than we have, so I can be sure of having enough range to reach you. I also request permission to leave my headquarters here to forward any messages they receive while I am in transit."
"Approved. Von Manstein out."
Gunter began issuing orders. As he did so Ivan Gorlov appeared. Before Ivan could get an explanation out for where he had been, Gunter instructed him to leave the ever-so-slow Matildas at this headquarters and move out with him to Alexandria. Gunter did violate the order in one small detail. He had the vehicles refueled first. As fast as they were topped off, they would depart. He himself left with a small detachment of Betar in fully-fueled vehicles of various types. What had Klaus gotten them all into this time?

0900 hours local; 0800 hours CET
2 November 1940
Gateway to the Royal Naval / Western Harbor, Alexandria, Egypt

Bain had come to fetch Hauptmann von Kleist-Konitz. There was an Egyptian that Bain felt the Wehrmacht officer should deal with. Von Kleist-Konitz had no idea why this boy pretending to be a soldier wished him to handle whatever trivial matter was involved, but on the other hand, he wasn't doing much of anything else. All around him naval and NL people were busily turning what at dawn had been a long-famous British base, into a new center of the Reich's expanded power.

Waiting for him at the gate was a man in an unfamiliar uniform. Bain made the introductions. The Egyptian had very little German. Von Kleist-Konitz had no Arabic. Both turned out to speak passable French. The man put out his hand to shake and introduced himself, "Chief Inspector Jabar Isa Gaafar, Special Branch, Alexandria Police. As the city is now in your hands, I thought it best to report here for instructions – my prior ones from our former British masters no longer seemed expedient to enforce. The young man tells me you are related to the German Supreme Commander."

Things were starting to come into focus. How the cook's son knew of his relationship to von Manstein could be explored another time. Brigadier Strauss seemed strangely adept at recruiting these sort of useful people. For now he gave the Egyptian a thorough once-over. The man was dressed as a proper European would be. The coloring was a little dark, but one could find worse in the Balkans or Iberia. "Yes. He's my cousin. Our families have been intermarried since the time of your Fatimid Dynasty." Ernst had a vague notion of how far back the family trees went, and an equally vague notion of the Fatimids as being the time of the early Crusades. He'd been forced to study history, but had little real interest in non-military events; and only a slightly greater concern for the dim recesses of his family tree. "I'm his personal representative here. This city will be a German Military Zone for the duration of this war, and perhaps afterwards as well."

"The city, but not the rest of Egypt?"

"The rest of Egypt and the Canal are to be an Italian matter. I believe your King has been in contact with them." Ernst had heard a rumor to that effect. "So I gather you wish your old job back? Perhaps a promotion as well?"

The Egyptian smiled cynically. He had no problem being seen as an opportunist, as that was in fact what he was. "Obviously, Excellency. This is a time of transition. Someone gains, someone loses. I prefer to advance myself."

"I think we understand each other. What is wished is civic calm. Mobilize what forces you have connections with. I really don't care if they were police yesterday. Everyone has cousins and nephews in need of employment. Create some sort of armband for the new recruits, and let us know here what the armband symbol is. What we wish is no looting, and proper traffic control. There are large German forces in transit. Perhaps some Italians as well. Post signs marking the route here." He looked around to find Bain waiting. "Gefreiter Collins. You will take a platoon of your motorcyclists and accompany our friend here. You will oversee the signs being emplaced. You can use telephones to report on the streets remaining peaceable. You can also find any major warehouses, British military or civilian, and see them placed under guard until Leutnant Schwabe can arrive to start doing inventories." Ernst turned back to his new Egyptian subordinate. "Compared to the British, you will find that we Germans have little use for formal law in times such as these. What matters is order and efficiency. So you are free to use force – including deadly force – but I will hold you personally responsible for results, especially violence or molestation towards civilized European residents. This includes British and others of their Imperial subjects. Our Führer wishes this to be a gentleman's war, at least as regards whites. You know who your native criminal elements are. Tell the smart ones, that looting now will deprive them of the opportunities to sell liquor, women, and night life to half a million young servicemen who will be passing through here with money burning a hole in their pockets. For the rest, just round up the usual suspects. You don't need proof or formal charges. Arrest them all and keep them under guard. Kill any who resist. Take family members hostage, as needed. Any questions?"

The Egyptian just bowed and walked back to his car. Bain started barking orders, and two dozen motorcyclists all formed up behind him. Each bike had a side car with a passenger with an automatic weapon. The Egyptian car drove off, with the group led by Bain trailing. Von Kleist-Konitz walked back to the dock headquarters, whistling an old country dance tune from the backwoods of Pomerania where one of the family estates was. Time to find the female troops, and get them started on occupying the warehouses.

0930 hours local; 0830 CET
2 November 1940
What is now Peiper's roadblock.

As they stayed in radio contact, Peiper was not surprised by Coxita's arrival. Pio Ronconi was nominally in charge, but it was clear Peiper regarded the Italian Oberstleutnant's woman as a colleague on a level above that of the Roman officer.

Jochen Peiper was not quite sure how to address Coxita. 'The Oberstleutnant's mistress' as a title seemed disrespectful, but what was she? Coxita read his face. She was actually fairly good at social cues, when she was paying attention to anything beyond her own ideological psychodrama. "My military rank was Company Commissar, which neither Fascism nor National Socialism has a congruent version of. So, for today, what say I am Command Observer Arcau LaTorre? Oberstleutnant Di Salo sent me forward as his personal observer, in part because as a native of Barcelona I am fluent in Catalan. Capomanipolo Pio Ronconi is in command of our Company. Now, how may we be of assistance?"

Peiper relaxed. Pio Ronconi stayed silent, content to let Coxita take the lead as long as his rank was clearly respected. Coxita just stood there politely looking at Peiper until he remembered he was supposed to reply. "Major Steiner has taken the port – or so he says. Hauptmann von Kleist-Konitz has mobilized a native police force who supposedly are putting up signs to mark our route to join Steiner's Battalion. Brigadier Strauss is en route with the bulk of the Brigade."

"Did the Brigadier give any specific orders?" Coxita saw she would have to gently prod the SS officer.

"Not precisely. He asked if we were in a position to reinforce Major Steiner. I was trying to explain about the need to maintain the roadblock, about prisoners to guard … and he said he was getting a message from higher command he had to take. That was twenty minutes ago. Haven't heard from him since."

"Have you heard from Major Steiner?"

"Yes. He says he has his situation well in hand. Also that Gefreiter Collins would be waiting for us with a motorcycle detachment as we entered the city limits."

Coxita looked back and forth between the two men. The answers seemed obvious … but while she was a veteran, in their eyes she was a woman, whose only use was flat on her back. "What if Capomanipolo Pio Ronconi were left here to man the roadblock? You have a pair of cannons. He has a full-strength Company of veterans. That should be enough to man a roadblock and guard a Company's worth of prisoners." Pio Ronconi nodded his acceptance. It was a simple task with clear limits. It was well within the capabilities of his formal training and limited experience. "Major Steiner seems to have left a detachment of Betar. Some are gun crews, from what I see. I'll take command of the rest and accompany you to Collins." She caught Peiper's weird look at the mention of the Gefreiter. As if he knew the name should make sense but couldn't quite place how he was to remember a mere corporal. "Sturmbannführer, the Gefreiter is the cook's son. The one who served as a translator for you when you captured the two Boers and the Arab boy out in the desert."

"Him? He was scarcely a lad."

"He's in his early teens and seems to have been given a bit of rank. I'm sure Major Steiner has a good reason for what he did. However, there are things we need to do. We should secure the telephone exchange and the radio station. If possible, the telegraph office as well. I'm sure Hauptmann von Kleist-Konitz has his new police well in hand, but even a platoon of real soldiers at each key location will help secure our control of the city." Peiper gave her a look. She read the implied question. "The Republican Army I served in did have a few successful advances. This is how we were trained. I've left off the police headquarters, the main jail, and other things because we don't have enough men yet."

Peiper shook his head. The airhead concubine might have some skills outside the bedroom. And perhaps that was why a veteran field officer brought a bedmate on campaign … beyond the obvious. Jochen was a trained officer, but his course had not included these lessons.

1015 hours local; 0915 hours CET
2 November 1940
Mason's new brigade position on Ruweisat Ridge; on what at dusk last night, had been the west end of the Australian Corps frontage

Two Italian CV-35's were burning. Four more were backpedaling fast. Colonel Garth Mason had in a sense demoted himself back to company command. He led his counterattack force in person. With a scratch unit such as this, it was the only way. He was down to the professionals and the very best-motivated of the new recruits. The force had never trained as a unit. Men needed such training to trust each other in combat. The other way was the old-fashioned follow the leader instinct of warriors. He was the known face of command.

The last Italian attack had been a most near-run thing. The assault troops were damned good and their artillery support quite professional. They had overrun two strongpoints and only been halted by the Australian 25-pounder guns firing over open sights. The guns had also put paid to the quite pathetic Italian tanks. The crews were brave and well trained. Good men with garbage equipment. The professional side of Mason's mind felt sorry for them. People in offices a continent away made bad decisions and sent good troops to their deaths. Had happened enough times to his army through the centuries. The RN got full appropriations and the army was told to make do, for budgetary reasons.

Mason had two bullet holes in his uniform and three shrapnel creases from grenades. They didn't bother him. He'd bled for King and country before. Meantime he got his wounded to the rear and tried to find a way to cover the restored line while leaving himself at least 60 staunch men for the next counterattack. The Italians were relentless. They would be back.

....

Major General Iven 'Mr. Chips' Mackay was up with his 2/4th Infantry Battalion. Observers had seen Mason's position on the verge of collapse, and triggered the designated response force. Mr. Chips had come along to get a sense of who this Mason was and how much he should rely on the man's 'brigade'. So far he was liking what he saw of the man, but could not say the same about the unit. "Hello there, Mason. Good work, getting your line back."

Mason was a combat veteran from the First War. He neither came to attention nor saluted. Both attracted snipers. "Thank you, sir. Position goes, with the next real attack. My brigade arrived here at battalion strength. I've since picked up two companies of odds and sods from the remains of 6th and 7th Divisions. Say it should be a five-company force. Except I've lost a bit over half of them so far. I've got a six-company front of seventy- or eighty-man companies, and my counterattack reserve is down to fifty or sixty men. What's left are good men. They'll die game. But beyond automatic weapons and a few Boys antitank rifles, all we have for firepower are the 25-pounders you loaned me. They are fighting hard, but we have been getting brigade-size attacks. As fast as we bloody one, the Italians just regroup and send in the next. Get your division out now, sir."

"Sadly, that's not happening till near dusk. Orders." Mason nodded at what Mackay said. He'd given similar orders as a staff officer in the last war. Mackay went on. "I'm giving you this battalion. So you now have a real counterattack reserve."

"Sir, you are condemning good men to death or the prisoner cages."

"Needs must. My orders are to buy time for the rest of the corps to get away. When the order comes, there will be trucks for your lads as well."

"We'll be gone by then. Nice having met you, sir. A small favor?" Mason reached into his tunic and took out a letter marked for his solicitor. "Could you pass this along to some officer you feel has a good chance of posting this in Palestine? Nothing to worry about in terms of the censors. Just telling my man to send along letters he has on file to my heirs and a few special friends." Mason was mostly thinking of one special friend who had given him the best years of her young life. She'd get the cottage and money anyway, but also deserved the personal last declaration of feelings, of love. It had started as an 'arrangement', but damn if he hadn't come to actually care for her, about her. She'd certainly cared more about him than his ever-so-proper wife ever had. That lady seemed to feel that delivering two healthy male heirs had fulfilled her contract. She had wanted a separate life. Golf, hounds, her gardens, her friends. No hint of scandal, and she would show up well-dressed for official functions, but beyond that his presence was neither needed nor wished for. She was born of a military family and had no wish for a version of her mother's life. Mason had frequently asked her why had she married a career officer? Her answer was family tradition. But this was the modern age and she would no longer be strangled by such conventions.

Mackay nodded. He wasn't sure anyone from his headquarters was making it out, but saying this would be a comfort to a brave officer doing his duty in a tight spot. He only hoped when his time came, he could face the end showing as good a front.

1030 hours local; 0930 hours CET
2 November 1940
Route between Alamein and Cairo

The First Libyan Division was attempting to traverse the 280 kilometers between their jump-off point and their target, the Egyptian capital of Cairo. General Pietro Maletti was with his advance guard group roughly halfway to the target. His main body and administrative services were in three disjointed packets strung out over 90 kilometers of bad road behind him. Depending on how one chose to view the situation, he was blocking an Australian Corps, or it was overrunning his small division. The last two hours had been endless rolling skirmishes. He was getting somewhat the better of these as he had set up his guns into battery, while the Australians mostly did not choose to dismount from their trucks. Instead they swerved around his men, punching holes where they could, to continue their progress east.

Maletti was sure they were Australians, because he had captured over a hundred of them. He was fairly sure the Australians were bound for Suez because there was nothing else to the east. Headquarters had offered to send Rommel to his relief. Maletti had expressed the opinion that the Germans' 7th Panzer Division was of better use pocketing the main British army to his south. He also wished to keep Rommel away from Cairo. Taking that city was to be a prize for Italy alone.

1000 hours CET
2 November 1940
Reichschancellery, Berlin

The conference of Gauleiters was supposed to have been chaired by the Führer. Göring had sent a flunky with a 'deeply regret' note. Few of the Gauleiters were surprised. Most had been up till near dawn partying with the Führer, which was why many of the chairs were occupied by the Deputy Gauleiters. Even exhausted and hung over, these had to actually show up. In this Reich, there were privileges by rank in these situations.

The Reichsführer would have preferred a proper meeting at a conference table instead of addressing this assembly from a podium. However, the public fiction that Göring was Führer needed to be maintained. The fat fool actually did a lot of useful work. Göring liked to lecture from a podium. so the room had been set up that way.

Heydrich was partway through a speech on labor reallocations and why these would be enforced, when he saw Schellenberg exit to the rear. One of the Oberführer's minions must have had something that couldn't keep. Heydrich would ask afterwards what was so important. Schellenberg rarely overstepped his bounds.

Now Schellenberg was back, walking briskly up to the microphone. He leaned into it and said, "Gentlemen, excellent news. The NL has won a great victory in Africa. I must steal the Reichsführer away for a few minutes for urgent matters of state."

Heydrich let the Oberführer guide him behind the curtain at the rear of the podium. "What was so important that it couldn't keep?"

"Steiner has taken Alexandria."

"This is ahead of schedule and outside the plans we were given. What degree of damage?"

"Intact."

"Impossible. No one could be that careless."

"Confirmed through OKM, by the naval experts with him. Everything was wired but the order for some reason was never given. It could be that Steiner arrived with his Battalion unexpectedly. He overran his orders from Brigadier Strauss. He has the entire city. They have even recruited a native police force to assist them. The problem as ever is the Italians. OKM has diverted every transport ship they control, to unload in Alexandria. The Italians refuse to do the same, pending the arrival of confirmation from their troops in Egypt. None of whom are within one hundred kilometers of the city. I need to book a direct call to their rulers and then pull you to the phone once it is about to go through. General Wolff or myself will not have the same effect as your voice. Have I your permission to do this? Supplies landed at Alexandria do not need trucking from Libya. The trucks in Libya will be needed to move enough supplies and support troops to Egypt to begin the Palestine campaign."

Heydrich did not shock easily. Intact! The boy Major had delivered this gift. The propaganda would be incalculable. "Steiner gets his next promotion and the Knight's Cross. See that the other Brigade officers get suitable rewards. Yes, yes, go place the call." He could see Schellenberg waiting to say something else. "And ... ?"

"My colored antiaircraft shells. The ones that make big bright clouds in the sky like fireworks. I have enough for a thousand-gun salute in Berlin and a few dozen cities. Today is Saturday. We have the Gauleiter order public celebrations in their main cities today, tomorrow, and Monday. Make Monday a paid holiday. The employers will grumble, but who cares. Another huge victory and no lengthy list of German casualties. General von Manstein's headquarters is doing a count, but the best guess is under two hundred actual German dead, wounded, missing."

"Under two hundred? The public will be delirious. The Kaiser's fool generals spent blood like a drunk spends his paycheck on Saturday night." Heydrich was already thinking of second- and third-order implications. He reminded himself that the Oberführer was waiting for an answer. "Yes, yes. A thousand balls of colored light for a victory. I'll go tell the Gauleiters. You get the call set up with Rome."

1140 hours CET
2 November 1940
Comando Supremo delle Forze Armate, Palazzo Vidoni-Caffarelli, Corso Vittorio Emanuele II, Rome, Italy

Prince Umberto was glad to escape the phone call from Berlin. His colleague in rule, Marshal Balbo, was in transit between Genoa and Verona, so the Prince had been forced to endure the dressing-down himself. Heydrich was polite, but left no doubt that he was giving orders, not having a discussion. Umberto was left to 'discipline' his navy. A service that had proven inept at basic staff work. A simple teleprinter message to Italo-German Panzer Army headquarters in Egypt, had produced a confirmation of the Alexandria situation.

The report was from some irregular Ardeti unit that the Prince had a recollection of retroactively authorizing after Malta. The unit had an observer forward. The commander was en route to Alexandria with his Italian battalion. The logic of moving all supplies for the Egyptian campaign directly to Egypt was obvious. His naval command had best not give him backtalk on any of this.

1300 hours local; 1200 CET
2 November 1940
Northeast of I Australian Corps engagement with 1st Libyan Division

He could hear firing to his southwest, but none to his north on any quadrant of north. To Orde Wingate, this told the entire story. The German force at the roadblock he'd detoured around was not just an isolated spearhead. Alexandria was lost, and 8th Army was in hasty retreat. He'd left the collapsing 7th Division with eight hundred plus men, almost all of them his Palestinians, the successors to his Night Squads from the Arab Rebellion. His following had climbed to over twelve hundred men by the time he came up on the cannon-armed roadblock on the coast road, having gathered up strays along the way. And now he had somewhat over 1600 people, including troops from every Dominion as well as the Mother Country, civilians from every major area in the Empire including everything from aged retirees to infants, and a variety of civilian vehicles interspersed with his army trucks and cars. His destination was Suez. He'd try for the bridge or, failing that, the railroad ferry. The key was to keep driving through the night. He'd requisition any fuel he found. Broken vehicles would be abandoned. Blackout rules on night movement would be ignored. This gamble might well fail, but anything else was a surefire disaster. He wished he was as ruthless as a German. They would have shoved the civilians and hangers-on to the side to die, preserving the core fighting unit. He might be eccentric by the rigid standards of the British Army, but he was still a gentleman. English gentlemen did not abandon the inconvenient. If such scruples were lost, what was England fighting for? Surely this war was about something more than a sordid scramble for dominion over Arabs?

1315 hours local; 1215 hours CET
2 November, 1940
Captain Morgan's House of Rare Treasures, Alexandria, Egypt

Greta's force of Betar and newly recruited Arab auxiliary police had sealed both the building and the block. Greta led a mixed squad through the front door. Two frightened store security people led her into the back where 'Captain' Morgan sat behind a desk covered with the usual business-office piles of paper. This was her Cousin Hymie? The Arab police had provided an address for a Canadian Captain Morgan in the mercantile trade. This apparently was it.
Some dumpy woman was in a chair by the side. His wife? His bookkeeper? She was both too old and too ugly to be his mistress, at least to Greta's untrained eye. Her idea of a rich man's mistress, was an exotic beauty such as Coxita.

One of her Arabs knew English and got the man to identify himself. Greta spoke to him in Magyar, which she was fairly sure no one other than her Betar girls spoke. "You were Hymie in Transylvania? I'm your cousin. Please come with us."

Morgan was not an easy man to discomfit. He answered in the same language, "I'll need ten minutes to see to my staff. Can you post guards here? The situation is – shall we say – precarious." He was frantically trying to place who on Earth the girl was. How had he a 'cousin' in German uniform with officer's tabs?

Greta couldn't read his face but could easily guess his thought processes. "Israel Levi's daughter. The Cluj branch of the family. I'm here with the Ploiesti branch of the family. Isaac Cohen and his people. We're all in the German Army now. My General has need of your professional skills. We have acquired certain items and need to discuss valuation and sale."

The 'Captain' fought to keep a smile off his face. This was business. A German General wanted him on a business matter. He had never hoped for a connection this good to fall into his lap. "What is your General's command?"

"We have a Brigade that for now is the Alexandria garrison. I don't know if he is formally Commandant, but as we created a police force and the Reichsführer's headquarters approved, it sort of amounts to the same thing."

"Reichsführer?" Morgan's head was spinning. How highly placed was this little girl cousin?

"Our unit is a direct report to him. You can say he is my General's patron."

"And this matter he needs guidance on … "

"Shall we say expensive antiquities we acquired on Malta."

Loot. They had loot they wanted fenced. The new masters accepted his criminal connections and found them useful. Maybe there was a God. Morgan could think of no other way to account for this sort of wild luck. Morgan asked if the Palestinian woman Meir could accompany him? (He mostly didn't want to leave her free to explore his premises.)

Golda was quite confused. She asked him in Yiddish, "What is going on?"

Greta replied in the same language. "This city is now in German hands. You are being taken to my General. I don't know who you are, but we have need of Captain Morgan."

Golda followed the group out the door, completely confused. Morgan had said Italian connections. Why was he now linked to the Nazis?

Greta left Naiomi in charge with two composite platoons of Betar, new Arab police, and the mixed-nationality security people of Morgan's who were now de facto part of the Occupation. Naiomi passed around armbands for Morgan's guards. None refused them, even the nominal Britishers. In times of transition, official status was a coveted prize.

Greta had everyone driven back to the docks. The streets were mostly fairly quiet. The NL and their new Arab minions had responded to disorder and looting with machine-gun and rifle fire. Order swiftly followed. Greta made a note to tell the new police to collect the bodies. She was still too new at this to tell them to get ID's so a proper list of the dead could be made. Learning on the job left knowledge gaps like that.

1345 hours local; 1245 hours CET

2 November 1940

Western outskirts of Alexandria, Egypt

Gunter arrived here with most of Di Salo's Battalion and a composite Battalion from the rest of the Brigade. The rest of his forces were strung out over 100 kilometers of road back to the original line of departure. He was met by Hauptmann von Kleist-Konitz, Gefreiter Collins, and this new Egyptian police recruit, Commissioner Jabar Isa Gaafar. There were big signs up saying 'this way to the port' in German and Italian. The streets were calm, but there was a smell of recent small-arms fire and some scattered bodies, none in uniform. Bain Collins saw the General looking. "Rioters and looters, sir. We have kept the streets clear by fire."

Gunter was surprised that the cook's young boy was now a Gefreiter. He'd ask Klaus later about it. Klaus usually had reasons for what he did. "The Führer mandated proper treatment, Gefreiter."

"That was for British service people in particular, and white people in general, sir. Colonial peoples not in British service sometimes need a firm hand, per Hauptmann von Kleist-Konitz and Major Steiner, sir."

The Egyptian put out his hand to introduce himself. After the handshake he tried to find a common language with the city's new ruler and was surprised to discover that it was English. This German spoke English with an American accent. A lower class one to boot. Interesting. "If I may be permitted, Your Excellency, Egypt is currently in a state of armed revolt. The religious fanatics of the Muslim Brotherhood, local nationalists, factions from the Egyptian Army, and the usual disorderly elements in the lower classes. They are attacking white people, government buildings, Christian churches; looting stores and warehouses. Under Hauptmann von Kleist-Konitz's command, my men are restoring order. To do this, examples must be made. Only thing these types understand. Give me twelve more hours plus continued permission to take trustworthy men into the new order police, and the city will again be calm."

"You are recruiting?"

"I was given permission. Not all the former police are to be trusted."

Gunter smiled cynically. "Not all of them recognize your authority." He was pleased to see the Egyptian nod. The man may have been an opportunist, but apparently not a fool. "You give the rest of them notice. Twenty-four hours to bend the knee or quit the city. Tell them no squabbling about rank. You are in command, and decide who keeps their former ranks and pay … as long as we find you useful."

He turned back to von Kleist-Konitz. "Where are Peiper, and Di Salo's woman?"

Von Kleist chuckled. Everyone tripped over what to call the officers' concubines. "Command Observer Arcau LaTorre suggested to the Sturmbannführer that the best use of his battalion was occupying the main airport complex at Grebe. He's there doing an inventory on the fuel tanks, which like the harbor were not destroyed in the retreat. Luftwaffe wants to move up a bunch of Ju-52's for some projected air drop at Suez in a few days. The message traffic got too technical for us very quickly. Something about load factors, ranges, fuel usage and the like. There are also over twenty German and Italian planes diverted there today because of mechanical issues. The Command Observer has occupied several key installations with her Betar. I haven't a clue where she got the Betar from. She herself seems to be at the telephone exchange monitoring long-distance calls. She speaks enough languages to do most, and the rest she is just refusing to put through."

" 'Command Observer' ?" Coxita's rank was mistress, as far as Gunter was concerned.

Von Kleist-Konitz went from chuckling to outright laughter. "Her former rank, as in before her association with Oberstleutnant Di Salo, was Company Commissar. She sensibly decided that was perhaps not suitable in this army. I always thought she was purely decorative, but it seems she is actually a veteran. Also worked on a Cheka tribunal, or so she's claiming today. Might I suggest we just make her a Hauptmann? It's less bother. Major Steiner's woman is a Leutnant, after all. Di Salo's is a veteran, while Steiner's is as untrained as he is."

Di Salo came up himself just in time to hear his name mentioned. When the story of Coxita's day was related to him, he sighed, joined the laughter, and agreed she could be a Hauptmann. Instead of reflecting poorly on him, this day she had done him proud. Women! An abiding mystery to any male.

....

Gefreiter Bain was beside himself with pride at achieving his father's rank. Father had been a Sergeant multiple times, including very briefly right before retirement. He'd rarely held it for long, even in wartime. Father claimed conspiracies among the senior NCO's ruined his career. Mother more sensibly saw it as resulting from too strong a taste for drink and bar room brawls. This was an opinion she never expressed in front of her husband. He beat her often enough after each loss of rank.

Being allowed to report directly to the General was the high point of Bain's young life. Perhaps, unlike Father, he could be a long-serving Sergeant when he retired in thirty or forty years. Perhaps he could dream of making Sergeant-Major.   Bain was hazy on what German retirement age was. He would ask Mother if when his new rank insignia were sewed onto his uniform blouse, he could send Father a picture with a note. There had to be some way of finding out what internment camp his father was posted to in Italy.

1400 hours local; 1300 hours CET
2 November 1940
Joint Italo-German Panzer Army Headquarters

Generals Carlo Geloso and Erich von Manstein stood in front of the situation map, watching their carefully constructed battle-plan dissolve in smoke. Two British divisions had vanished. A third had come apart. The bulk of the British Army was in flight, but a hard crust remained behind in the fortified east-west positions.

Complicating matters, the new battle had to be fought with conflicting national goals in mind. When this was over it was the Italians who were to be chasing the British into Upper Egypt and occupying Cairo. The Germans were to cross Suez into Sinai with some Italian support. Yet Hausser's SS division was best placed to chase the British east and then south, and Rommel was best placed to support 1st Libyan's march on Cairo.

Geloso decided to treat this as a staff school exercise. "General von Manstein, I propose the following. Your Germans will liquidate the original British position. General Rommel is not, under any circumstances, to send any troops towards Cairo. I must insist on this for reasons of Italian prestige. Your Brigade Strauss has taken Alexandria with only a single Italian battalion in support." Geloso thought to himself that Di Salo's battalion was Italian by courtesy. It was a mélange of Italians, Italian Jews, foreign Jews, Magyars, and Catalans. Propaganda would stress the word *Italian*, and Di Salo himself was presentable enough. Young, handsome, a Spanish veteran, an aristocrat. Use him in the pictures, and the home public would presume the battalion had a thousand young Italian men of good family along as volunteer Arditi.

Von Manstein spent a few minutes studying the map before replying. "As general principle, yes. A small change. I suggest splitting off Hausser's Schnell Regiment as a flank guard against raids by British light forces. Where will your Italians go?"

"This needs to be kept simple or the traffic control issues will produce chaos. XX Corps will be the pursuit force. It will be followed by XXIII Corps which will either support XX or occupy Cairo, depending on what the British do. XXI Corps will advance to Cairo and remain there until relieved by either XXIII Corps or fresh forces. I have cabled Rome for their intentions on a garrison force for Egypt. They could bring up 5th Army from Libya or fresh divisions from home, or make such a good deal with the Egyptian king that a large garrison is not needed. Absent instructions, my first duty is to secure and safeguard Lower Egypt. As is, I've ordered a parachute force into Cairo for daybreak tomorrow. The Libyans should arrive during the day to support them."

Von Manstein looked over the map again. "I see the logic of doing your movement orders by Corps. Untangling our units is going to be a monumental traffic control problem. I request that your transportation officers keep mine up to date, so we will know when to move our units out without interfering with your movements; including administration and supply truck columns. As for Rommel … " Von Manstein let his voice fade out while he considered how to phrase this. "I plan on flying to his advance headquarters myself. This is an order best delivered in person. General Rommel is a trifle high-strung." Both generals got a bit of laughter out of that understatement. One of von Manstein's junior staff officers left to order the Storch prepped. The other staff people of both nationalities gathered in knots to discuss how to implement the new plan. The bosses had done the big picture. Now fifty or so staff experts had to do the delicate brushstrokes. This would be a traffic control nightmare. Thank God for total air superiority.

1500 hours local; 1400 hours CET
2 November 1940
RN Naval Dock Headquarters / now Headquarters Steiner's *Falcons of Malta* Battalion

The slow drive to the docks had been enlightening for Gunter. There were Arabs with armbands at every major intersection on the route. Some looked quite disreputable, but in all they certainly looked tough enough. They were armed with a motley array of shotguns, pistols, clubs, and the odd hunting rifle. They threw off sloppy salutes, but clearly seemed to know who the new rulers were. There were broken shop windows, but already shopkeepers were out sweeping away glass and boarding up windows. Parties of 'Police' were gathering up bodies … and finishing off the remaining wounded. Gunter looked over to his new Police Commissioner at the first such scene.

"Best to dispose of them, sir. We will need their flats for refugee housing."

Gunter was a bit unsure he was following that. "What do dead people have to do with refugees?"

"Dead people do not need their flats. The refugees coming in from the countryside will need housing. So we start with the flats of those who died in rebellion. Evict the surviving family members, and house the newcomers. If we run out of room, we take the housing of those wounded in the street disturbances. These newly arrived people may have formerly been loyalists of the British, and before that of the Dynasty. If you house them, and give them work, they will quickly decide they are loyal to you. The various rebels only offer them rape, torture, and death. It is easy for you to make a better offer. Similarly, those you displace must either earn your trust or end up in prison camps. This whole country is overpopulated anyway."

"How will this rebellion impact the city?"

"I've posted guards on the main roads to give warning via telephone or messenger. So major raids into the city are unlikely. However, a portion of the city's food supply came in from these areas. Perishables especially."

"Would you suggest we sent armed units out to gather up these foodstuffs?" This had been the pattern for Gunter's units in the Baltic. You lived by plunder in the manner of bygone ages.

"If your command can supply motorized Companies, I can supply Alexandrine support elements in requisitioned autos and trucks to do the translating and conduct the searches." Commissioner Gaafar again saw Gunter's cynical look. "Yes sir, there will be a certain amount of score settling, and some low-level looting where country villas of the rich are involved. Both will happen either way. Better the fruits of these 'salvage missions' are returned to your city."

Gunter spent the rest of the drive pondering. On reaching Klaus's Battalion he gave the hero Major orders to do a sweep tomorrow. Battalion strength. Gunter had seen how fast a Company could be swarmed by partisans and irregulars. Commissioner Gaafar said his nephew would be at the base area gates at dawn with a thousand Arab 'volunteers'. Gunter dismissed the Commissioner. The signals traffic from Berlin and von Manstein needed his attention. These were not messages for Klaus to answer on his own. Klaus might be the hero of the day, but he was not yet mature enough to deal with higher commands.

1400 hours CET
2 November 1940
Stato Maggiore Regia Marina, Palazzo Marina, Lungotevere delle Navi 4, Rome, Italy
(Navy General Staff – Royal Italian Navy Headquarters, embankments of the River Tiber)

Every gate guard across the world has the same sort of orders. Among these orders there is one, sometimes in the official orders book, or most definitely among the unofficial ones: if there is a surprise inspection or just a high ranking officer arriving, make sure the officer of the day gets a warning!

The guards in the main entrance of Palazzo Marina, in the shadow of the two huge Austrian battleship anchors taken as trophies in the last war, followed their orders – having a German army staff officer arriving, demanding immediate access to the maritime logistics planning offices, and carrying sufficient clearance documents, was unusual enough for them to let him pass, supplying a guide who would take the officer to his destination on a circuitous route of the huge building, while they would call ahead with the necessary warning.

The naval Leutnant greeting Oberst Otto Wöhler at the entrance of the RTSO Office (the Transports Office or "Ufficio rifornimenti, traffico e spedizioni Oltremare") rooms shunted the exalted visitor to a side office to be plied with – now increasingly scarce – good Italian coffee and snacks, while he was looking for his commanding officer.

It took only a few minutes before the newly-minted head of the Transports Office, Generale di Divisione (Navy Specialist and Technical Corps) Ubaldo Diciotti entered the room. Introductions were made and Oberst Wöhler found that Diciotti's English was as good as the intelligence files on him had said. After having sent the junior officers out of the room on some errand, the Italian naval officer turned towards Wöhler and asked: "Herr Oberst, what can I do for you?"

Wöhler had not been entirely happy with the instructions that had sent him here: "Herr Admiral, I am here on a somewhat delicate mission."

"You have been sent here to light a fire under our lazy Italian butts for not having immediately given out a general order to all supply ships to change course to Alexandria some hours ago."

Oberst Wöhler was a bit taken aback by receiving this succinct description of his orders, from the person to whom he was supposed to give them.

Generale di Divisione Diciotti smiled and continued calmly: "And we are not going to do that."

Wöhler throttled his heated response in the last second. He had been expecting Mediterranean histrionics from the Tuscan-born flag officer; and hearing the refusal in such a final, calm, almost Hanseatic tone, was not in his mental plan of how this conversation should have run.

The one-star flag officer got up: "There are reasons, Herr Oberst. Come." Chuckling, he opened the door, leading the way. "And, by the way: I am not an admiral, my rank is that of a Generalmajor, same rank as in the German Army. Our navy uses a different rank system for navy officers of specialist corps who are not in the ship command track, to distinguish us from naval line officers who use the traditional ranks. For them, the equivalent-rank would be Contrammiraglio – (Rear Admiral (l.h.) - RDML). Not a few of my equivalent-rank Vessel Officer colleagues, those correctly known as admirals, would snort or even take offense at such lack of fine professional distinction."

A few doors further on they both entered a large hall – one wall held a large map of the Mediterranean Sea, with well-marked harbors and shipping lanes plus a good number of little flag markers. The other walls were, with the obvious exception of doors and windows, covered with blackboards carrying lots of notes.

The floor of the hall held, parallel to its long axis, in addition to a few writing desks three rows of tables, the center row being more sparsely laden than the tables to either side of the hall – they bore signs with names of harbors, both in Italy and on the African coast. The center row had signs with "6 hours, 12 hours, 18 hours" and so on.

On the tables were many clipboards, with ship names, origin, and destination prominent on the uppermost page, plus a stack of documents underneath the top page, and a number of wooden clothes pegs, painted in many bright colors, clamped to the sides of the clipboard.

The white-haired senior officer stopped in front of the situation map.

"First of all – yes, we received the so-called request to send all supply ships to Alexandria the first time it was sent, a bit after ten o'clock this morning. We did not ignore it as your colleagues seem to assume, but immediately asked them for some necessary information, which we have not yet received. But more about that in a moment. All the follow-up copies and amplifications of the first request have been filed properly, and Supermarina Operations Staff has been duly notified to be ready for a probable set of route change orders for ships at sea or still at docks." The Italian paused.

"The first thing I need to explain is that there is no discernible difference in the arrival time in Alexandria between a reroute order given two or three hours ago, now, or in six hours. Even giving the order tomorrow would not change arrival times that much."

General Diciotti reached up to the map and drew his hand from the south of Italy roughly south-east to the North African coast. "Making a slight turn to the left to Alexandria now or a bit later, does not change the overall distance very much." He demonstrated that fact on the map using his outstretched fingers as a pair of compasses.

"We are not operating aircraft doing hundreds of kilometers per hour, where a short delay can make huge changes in position. We are not even operating railroad trains or trucks that move fifty or sixty kilometers per hour on average – we operate cargo ships, and these ships are slow. The average cargo ship I have has an effective speed of ten or eleven knots – twenty kilometers per hour. Remember Napoleon: *"ordre et contre-ordre égale désordre"*. So we can afford the time to do it right on the first attempt."

Oberst Wöhler answered that by translating that into German: "Order plus counter order, equals disorder. An old proverb, but nevertheless true."

While the older naval flag officer had delivered the first part of his quiet and polite diatribe, work had been silently going on the room behind them – junior officers had taken some of the clipboards from the tables to make entries in the documents on them, leaving chits as placeholders behind them or moving them from one table to another, marking the progress of individual ships this way.

"One of the most important things to know is that Alexandria is a good bit further away than the harbors we originally intended – at least 400 kilometers. This means that the ships will eat into the fuel they need to return to Italy, and unless I can get firm confirmation from the German troops occupying the harbor that all three fuel types are available in Alexandria in sufficient amounts, this in turn means I risk having ships marooned in Egypt, unable to return for their next load of supplies."

"Three types of fuel?"

"Yes – coal for the older ships, bunker oil, and finally diesel oil for the most modern ones. We have been requesting updates on fuel state and projected range from all ships, so that we can decide which ones we can send to Alexandria if there is not sufficient fuel available for all."

The Generalmajor intercepted one of the working officers and took the clipboard he was carrying – showing Oberst Wöhler the entries for current position, fuel type, and remaining range, and a notice saying: "Alex capable - *yes*" on the top sheet.

"So that is one of the information requests you made to our offices? What are the others?"

"We also asked about the general state of harbor facilities – although we gather from the propaganda broadcasts they are intact – and if the harbor-entrance mine-fields have been deactivated or the safe entrance lane is known and marked. Without all this information, we would just be poking around in a fog and risking valuable ships. "

The German officer answered: "I see that you are making all necessary preparations for the change in orders, and I will try to get you all this information as quickly as possible the moment I return to headquarters."

Chapter 11

1530 hours local; 1430 hours CET
2 November 1940
Rommel's 7th Panzer Division field headquarters, 7 km southeast of the original break-through point

Erwin Rommel resented being told, not asked, to present himself at this headquarters. Told by a superior who carried in his pocket, as it were, a signed order relieving him. What truly galled him was that his little plot with Strauss had *worked*. The British front had collapsed, for which he had been punished! Seventh Panzer Division was left to move last. Precious hours were being lost. Now his superior had flown north to either chastise or relieve him. The Army was truly ruled by clowns.

Erich von Manstein knew that dealing with this General would be 'interesting'. He had been warned on being given this assignment, that General Rommel was a headstrong individual, a pet of the late Führer. After the obligatory handshake, von Manstein asked that the space be cleared for a 'command conference'. Rommel's staff officers and lesser headquarters people quickly made a large space. It was not safe to be nearby when the great and mighty quarreled.

"So, General Rommel, shall we review what you did in error?"

Rommel was prepared to be relieved. He was not about to bend the knee. "It worked. The risk was minor. At worst Strauss would have lost a couple of Battalions; and his so-called Brigade is a joke cobbled together for propaganda purposes after Malta."

"Yes, it did work. Pity the rest of our forces were not in proper position to fully exploit it. Something that perhaps could have been avoided had you bothered alerting my headquarters." Left unsaid was that both von Manstein's cousin von Kleist-Konitz, and his observer at Rommel's headquarters von Stauffenberg, had passed the details along. Von Manstein had ignored it, treating the plan as something out of a Hollywood cowboy movie. No need for Rommel to be aware of this. "Start learning to think. You are now a General officer, not a field officer in the mountain Jägers." Von Manstein paused to let that register. Had he been socially familiar with this Rommel, he would have added a Gallic shrug. "You were a good mountain Jäger. You wrote an adequate infantry tactics manual. You might have gotten divisional command only via the late Führer's patronage. He's dead. The new Führer takes no notice of Heer promotions and placements. That is the Reichsführer's domain." Von Manstein paused for this to register with Rommel. "That's all in the past. We are both among the elite that was the Reichswehr's officer corps. Those four thousand officers were not chosen by caste or service branch connections. General von Seeckt selected the best of the best, from an army of millions. We both made the grade. It is time for you to align yourself to being one of the senior members of this band of brothers."

Rommel did not have a Junker's iron sense of control. "Reichsführer Heydrich and not Generaloberst's Beck and Halder?"

Now von Manstein had a decision to make. He had led Rommel here. But the conversation had not yet crossed the Rubicon. For all this Swabian officer was difficult, he was also quite talented if properly harnessed. "Think. You are capable of it." He paused to be sure he had the Divisional General's total attention. "The Reichsführer has created a parallel army here in the South. We report to OKW, not

OKH or the Defense Ministry. A parallel army that is winning victories while the real army sits as a garrison force in the East. Promotions come from combat commands. For the ground forces, the only combat commands are here in Egypt. And you are the ONLY Heer General commanding the army's only contribution to this war. General Hausser was Reichswehr but is now Waffen SS. General Steiner was also Reichswehr but is now also Waffen SS. His division is a dog's breakfast, but very little of it is army. His artillery is navy, of all things. General Ramcke has been many things but currently is Luftwaffe. That leaves Strauss, an SA officer now in the NL, whatever that service evolves into. So if the Heer is to institutionally profit from this campaign, it needs you and your Division. Would you like to be on track for Corps command? This is what the Heer as a service needs, for you to be the success you are capable of being, for your Division to be seen as best in theater."

"Why me?"

"The Reichsführer initially chose you. However, I could have relieved you in Berlin. I didn't. For all your faults, you are an excellent commander of mobile troops. I look to take you to the next level, the one Guderian and von Kleist are on." Manstein paused to be sure Rommel was following him, grasping the implied opportunities of accepting him as a patron. "The Afrika Korps will be the source of all victories for the next six to ten months. You have the only Heer Division. Another won't be sent unless we run into major difficulties, which I don't see myself as allowing to happen. We will defeat British 9th Army with minimal Italian support."

"Ninth?"

"They have a separate headquarters for Palestine and Iraq. General O'Connor, the man you defeated in the desert battle. If Abwehr is to be believed, a Division each of New Zealanders and Poles, plus an Indian Corps. Three Divisions of professionals and one of their Dominion Sturm Divisions from the last war. Our edge will be air, tanks, and artillery. Plus we are Germans. War is a trade we have always excelled at."

"So what must I do to merit this promotion instead of getting replaced?" Rommel was finding it hard to see von Manstein as a potential friend.

"Stop pretending you are commanding your own private force fighting its own private war. You must allow yourself to fit into a campaign plan. When you deviate, your staff must keep mine abreast of the evolving situation. After we win, I'll be creating a new Panzerarmee as an OKW reserve force. You, Hausser, and Steiner will each get Corps commands. From an Army point of view I need to avoid the elite shock troops of the regime all being from these silly party Militias. The SS, SA, and NL must in time be reintegrated into the Army's structure."

"How so?"

"The same way the Bavarian and Wurttemberger armies were after the French War. When you went to war in 1914, you were both part of the Wurttemberg state army and XIII Corps of the national army. The Saxons were XII Corps. The Bavarians had an entire army, 6th. Yet officer careers saw postings between those and the rest of the army. Over time during the Kaiserwar, the differences between those state forces became largely notional. They all took replacements from elsewhere and sent cadres to form new national units. We can do the same with these Militias if … if we can establish that this campaign isn't being won despite the Heer. So Strauss's victory here and at Alexandria will have been done as though it were under your overall command. The reports must always stress that victory comes from our officer corps. Here in Africa, that's you and myself."

"Alexandria?" Rommel felt he was missing something here.

Von Manstein smiled and slowly shook his head. "So you haven't heard? One of Brigadier Strauss's Battalions took the entire port intact. Berlin is beside itself with joy. You and I are going to fly up there to congratulate Strauss, and to receive his report. After all, we are his commanders. His victory is our victory. We will send messages from there to Berlin making sure the Reichsführer associates our names with the success. We'll probably spend the night. I'll drop you off back here tomorrow on the way to corps headquarters. Meantime, have Oberst von Thoma send a reinforcement column to the city. A Company of motorized infantry plus detachments from your military police Company and signals Battalion. We will review your plan of campaign this evening, but in broad strokes you proceed north of Cairo to the Canal. Take a bridge or await bridging materials as the case may be. You will be the Corps spearhead into Sinai. In the meantime, Oberst von Stauffenberg will take your vanguard and help finish off the British rear guard. My Corps headquarters will have the coordinates of his objective for him. How long do you need to get ready?"

Offered such a career enhancement, Rommel sent his bursche to make him an overnight bag. His destiny beckoned him.

1600 hours local; 1500 hours CET
2 November 1940
Kampfgruppe Jodl gun positions in the rear of Steiner's Division

Lothar Engels still had all his Jewish deserters, even the ones who were now supposed to be under Italian command. He had been serving with Kampfgruppe Jodl's guns. His Palestinians, HJ, and the Pioneers had been unloading artillery ammunition while his Schnell troops provided a security element against British raiders. Engels hadn't seen any such British, but signals traffic had small British raiding parties out and about. Now the tide of battle was turning, and he was trying to find out when to stop unloading shells and instead reload the trucks so the guns could redeploy. He had a group of reloaded trucks sitting there because of a prior change in orders. Of course he would need to find enough of the trucks to reload the rest of the munitions if or when requested. After unloading, they had mostly returned to the rear for more supplies. Making this traffic pattern work was done by staff people above Lothar's rank.

Now, out of nowhere, the missing Italian commander, a Militia Tenente Colonello named Bruno Pieri, had appeared. The man supposedly spoke Yiddish. Lothar would take his word for it. He said words Lothar didn't understand, and the Jews obeyed. This Pieri also spoke passable German. "Now that I have my 'Battalion', have you orders for them?"

Lothar was perplexed. "I've been minding them pending your arrival. I have not a clue where Italian higher command wants them."

Pieri gave a shrug and said a bunch of words in Italian harshly. Lothar presumed he was cursing. Having vented, Pieri said, "Have you a problem if I stay with your people pending my command getting me proper orders?" Now it was Lothar's turn to shrug. Pieri sent his driver off to find an Italian headquarters. "So we are servicing German heavy artillery?"

"No one exactly told us anything else to do. My Division seems to have forgotten us. The guns arrived in the vicinity. There was a queue of trucks they were struggling to unload. I went over and volunteered our services. One of General Jodl's staff officers agreed that it made sense." As Lothar finished explaining, a runner came from the artillery commanders. The orders had changed again. Now the guns were to stay put while two Italian corps were pulled out of the line and sent east behind them. Lothar and Bruno got the men to work unloading the reloaded trucks, and rearranging the already-unloaded shells to fit some new scheme. Just the typical chaos of a war zone.

1800 hours local; 1700 hours CET
2 November 1940
Mason's positions at the west end of what had been 6th Australian Division's lines

It was over. Mason had burned through his own rump force and the first Australian battalion. 'Mr Chips' had gifted him with a second Australian battalion, plus an emergency force made up of stray remnants of British and Palestinian troops that had fled into the Australian lines for protection. Sixth Australian Division had started pulling out two hours ago.

Now what Mason had left was two company-size battlegroups and a lone field gun, spread between two blockhouses and the connecting trench. He'd called his few officers and senior NCO's together ten minutes ago during a lull between German attacks. Said it was over – so anyone who wanted to head east on his own, do so. Seventy or so had. The rest were too weary, often from wounds. Mason himself had taken a round through his shoulder, and shrapnel had clipped both his legs. At his order, everyone ceased firing. There were a dozen or so white flags he had them wave. Well, white or near-white cloth nailed onto sticks. In the gathering dark maybe the Germans would see this from their illumination rounds.

Two of his Palestinians were Viennese Jews. Using crudely made megaphones from different ends of the line, both started screaming out, "We surrender!" A German patrol came forward and started gathering them all in. The Nazis behaved as if they were civilized. Even sent medical personnel to aid in gathering in the wounded.

Mason realized as he was being processed that he'd been so exhausted that he had forgotten to order that the gun's breechblock be destroyed, that the machine-guns be rendered unfit for use. He shook his head. He'd known better, once upon a time. As a Guards officer he should have been able to at least manage that. He resolved to put himself on report when the war was over. Then laughed at himself.

He'd been escorted to see the German commander, a Brigadier named von Stauffenberg. As was often true for people of a certain class, they could both communicate in French. The German congratulated Mason on his day's work. "Damned good defense you put up. As one professional to another I'm impressed. When the war's over, perhaps we could compare notes. There might well be an article about this for our service journals." The German got a sad expression. "I'm sorry for what is now about to happen. You are on a list. If you have personal items in your position, please advise us so we may retrieve them. The Reichsführer-SS has ordered you be sent to Berlin."

Mason was in shock. What on Earth had he done? "This is against the rules of war."

"My hands are tied. You are to be billeted with someone named Colonel Kevin Duffy and a Brigadier Edward Alistare-Smythe. My order alleges you should know Colonel Duffy."

"Of course I know the man. What has this got to do with Berlin and the head of the SS?"

"I'm sure all will be explained in due course. For now I am to forward you to the Luftwaffe for transportation. So about those personal items … "

1900 hours local; 1800 hours CET
2 November 1940
Cecil Hotel, Alexandria, Egypt

There was an SS Company from Peiper's Battalion doing security for the entire block the hotel was on. The Alexandria Special Branch had rifle-armed agents on every floor and at key places throughout the building. Peiper also had an SS Platoon sealing off the corridor the two Generals were given rooms on. Rommel was in his room being served a fine meal by room service. Von Manstein was having dinner separately in his suite with his younger cousin, the former Hauptmann von Kleist-Konitz. The young man was in shock. These were the rewards he had dreamed of, but never fully expected. The General found this amusing.

"Yes, making Major roughly a month after being promoted to Hauptmann is unusual. So is being the only professional Heer officer with the formation that captured one of the great ports of the world intact. There will also be a Knight's Cross for you and a definite mention in Wehrmachtbericht. The Reichsführer is in quite a good mood at the news. Medals and promotions will shower upon Brigade Strauss. Speaking of which, it has been decided that the Brigade should have a Panzer Battalion. It will be your command. It may not arrive in time for Palestine, but you will be a combat Battalion Commander for Iraq with a notation on your personnel file to fast-track you for Regimental Command on redeployment back to the Reich."

Von Manstein let the young man bask in the joy for the next course, before adding the unwelcome part of the news. As the youngest Major in the family in decades, perhaps in over a century, he was now a MUCH hotter commodity on the marriage market. The new Major's mother would undoubtedly be contacting Frau von Manstein to help screen the prospective mates. The general doubted it had taken an entire hour before someone at OKW who had seen the signals traffic on the promotion and other rewards, had alerted his family's female relations that such a good prospective husband was available. Twenty-three-year-old Oberleutnants were common in the military aristocracy. Twenty-three-year-old Majors about to command their own Panzer Battalion and with a theater commander as a patron, were as rare as hen's teeth. Von Manstein could visualize phone calls from Berlin to everywhere from Alsace to East Prussia to Tyrol. Within the month he expected the Major to receive a book of photos with blood lines in the manner of a horse farm offering brood mares. In the meantime, he himself had also risen in status. Time to do some family business of his own.

He had a relative Ernst von Manstein, a former Heer officer and convert to Judaism. The conversion had wrecked his Heer career, and since the coming to power of the Nazis it had put his life at risk. Time to cash some favor points with Schellenberg to get protection for the cousin, his wife, and if possible the community he was part of. NL rank wasn't Heer rank, but still it was something of value. A suitable position could be found for the man and his people in Palestine or Iraq. People who would know who their patron was in Berlin, and act accordingly.

1930 hours local; 1830 hours CET
2 November 1940

Cecil Hotel, Alexandria, Egypt

Brigadier Gunter Strauss had sensibly taken a suite for himself on a different floor than the two visiting Generals. He would be staying in Alexandria for an extended period. He needed a home from which to conduct his affairs beyond the prying eyes of the officers of the German naval contingent. This was luxury beyond anything he had ever experienced, but being a General was something new to him.

His other need was to avoid excess attention from his nominal subordinates in the Alexandria police. He had given Lieutenant Colonel Di Salo his own suite on this floor, plus security duty for the floor. He doubted many prying eyes or ears spoke Catalan. Thus, it was two Platoons of these who were billeted on the floor to provide security.

How silly Greta had had the sense to find this wayward relative of hers, 'Captain Morgan', was beyond Gunter's ken. Perhaps the girl actually paid attention to more of what happened around her than he had presumed. Until now he had had her pegged as an immature provincial whose function was keeping Klaus Steiner happy. He had written off her seizure of large quantities of luxury foods on Malta as probably being done at the suggestion of some of her Betar girl friends.

When Gunter had shown Morgan pictures of the falcons, the response was upsetting. "You are too late to fence them here."

"Why?"

"The people with movable wealth have either already fled, or used all of it to buy up distressed assets. Everyone is cash-poor, and will be for some time. That's the way it is when cities change hands. Had I been offered these for sale two or three months ago, you could have made a killing on them. Now? Not a chance." Morgan saw Gunter's crestfallen face. "Excellency, I want to be of assistance. I wish you for a patron, with myself as your client. I see you have made arrangements with the former Chief Inspector Special Branch Gaafar ... "

"How do you know that!"

"I saw which men were on duty downstairs when Leutnant Schwabe brought me here. A man in my profession ... " Morgan paused so both men could give a quiet laugh as to what the former Transylvanian Jew's profession really was. "A man such as myself knows senior police on a first name basis, knows the factions within the force. You made a good choice with Gaafar. Perhaps not the best, but good."

Gunter was getting interested in a hurry. This man knew things of value to him beyond the falcons and their sale, or so it seemed. "How so?"

"He's smart, efficient, but greedy. Not a man to be fully trusted to keep a bargain – to not shop information to both sides of the street, as it were. May I make a few useful introductions to Your Excellency? The Alexandrine demimonde has many major players who would love to make the acquaintance of the new Commandant. Several might serve as useful counterweights to Gaafar. He's going to interrogate me. My presence here will be reported. I would like to be able to say I have relatives in your headquarters family, that I am now your client. Gaafar's police will be more useful to you if they are aware that there are independent eyes watching them. Checks and balances. It is how the illicit world works best. You balance me against him. You use several others I will introduce to you, to watch us both. That way your share of this commerce will be properly computed."

My share?"

"We politely call such money 'street taxes'. Your military needs order. It needs the vices of your servicemen catered to. It needs to minimize thefts from the port, from your warehouses. Complementarily, much of the commerce of this city is in foreign hands. French, Italians, Armenians, Maltese, Greeks, Jews … a hundred nationalities. Alexandria is neither Europe nor Egypt. It is something special and unique. Your Excellency has already acquired loot. There is so much more that can be done."

"Until someone reports me to Berlin."

"So arrange that the proper people in Berlin get their share. That is your affair. Now about these historic objects of art. I cannot do decent research on their provenance. I would need to communicate with London, Oxford, Cambridge, Paris, and scores of other places. Even if wartime did not limit such communications, the researches would be noticed. An owner might emerge. Transactions such as this are best done in the shadows." Morgan paused to see that Gunter was working through what he said. "Better to create a backstory. I have quite discreet people I can use here. We create several such 'histories', each with 'supporting documentation'. You use whichever serves best when you find a suitable market to place these for sale. For now I would suggest Jerusalem; or, if you have time, India."

This was all happening too fast for Gunter. He wished he had Wanda present. This was far more her world than his. Gunter had been muscle for gangsters but had never really been one himself. Besides, bootleg beer was not the sort of massive high-end corruption he had stumbled into. "What would these services cost? Why Jerusalem?"

"Cost? For you I would do this gratis. You are my patron. The cost is making clear to Gaafar that I am yours. Myself, my people, my goods, my business affairs are not to be meddled with by him or his minions. Jerusalem? Because there are large foreign communities of religious people there with fixed assets such as real estate. As these Americans and others exit the region, they will need to dispose of their assets. Jeweled golden birds are easier to transport, even if the authentication papers may not survive close scrutiny. If you have the time this will be more true of India. The new Viceroy Churchill has confirmed independence. There are many rich people from various minorities or expatriate communities who will need mobile wealth to emigrate. Exactly what independent India will look like is still unknown. That the new rulers will be some mix of Hindus and Muslims is now certain. India is a mosaic of languages, nationalities, and religions. It was a geographic expression that the British seem to have made into a state, but not yet a nation. But Excellency, that's all for the future. Have you more immediate needs? Perhaps a young lady to pass the night? Speak your needs and I will see to them. Nothing shocks or surprises me. I am at your command."

The two men spent the evening over an excellent dinner with fine wines and brandies discussing the future. Gunter preferred to sleep alone. There would be other nights to see to those amusements. He needed a clear head to think how much was Berlin to be told.

....

Morgan chose to spend the night at the hotel as well. He knew as soon as he was dropped off at his place of business, Jabar Isa Gaafar would come calling. He would need a clear head for that discussion. Also, hopefully his 'cousin' Greta in uniform.

0200 hours local, 3 November, 1940
1900 hours CET, 2 November, 1940
Chosin Reservoir, Japanese-occupied northern Korea

The ten-day hunt was at an end. By now permanent Second Lieutenant Takagi had been in action against various partisan and small airborne forces for almost two months. This particular operation was designed to chase down the arch-bandit threat Kim Il Sung. The final fight had been a forty-hour running gun battle, culminating in this final encounter on the northern heights above Toktung Pass. The dead body showed Soviet rank badges. The captured documents indicated the deceased was a senior officer. The problem was that this was the third Kim Il Sung whom Takagi had killed personally, and the fifth claimed so far in the campaign. Was Kim a cover name for whoever was senior in this bandit army? Takagi was too tired to care. He had the dead stripped of weapons, shoes, and anything else useful, and began the long trek back to the nearest Imperial garrison. Let older, wiser, and higher-ranking heads untangle the mess. The winter winds were blowing. All the lieutenant and his men wanted was shelter and sleep. This was hours away, even once they marched back to the trucks which were hopefully still waiting. Often those were summoned elsewhere when the chase ran this long. War could be Hell; and the rumors from the Manchurian front spoke only of valiant last stands.

2200 hours CET
2 November 1940
Schellenberg's office, SS HQ, Prinz-Albrecht-Straße, Berlin, Germany

"And that was when you returned to headquarters, Oberst?"
"After some additional discussion and more explanations on how things work for this kind of logistics work, yes. Back at headquarters I found your orders and the clearance to use the daily courier flight to Berlin."
Schellenberg looked up from the papers on his desk at Wöhler, seated in a comfortable chair. He asked: "What was your impression about the whole operation? Serious? Effective?"
"I got the impression they were very serious. Actually, the whole operation felt almost un-Italian – everyone was quiet and concentrated, no shouting, no running around. In fact, I noticed they had removed all telephones and similar things into smaller side offices, so that the main hall was kept quiet, perhaps even serene or contemplative. I have done my share of inspections during my career; and you get a bit of a feel for who is just going through the motions to look busy and who is really working, and these Italian officers were really working. Also, Generalmajor Ubaldo Diciotti gave me good explanations of his operations, everything very well thought out and logical."
"So why are the Italians still refusing to fully follow our commands?" asked Schellenberg, clearly annoyed.
"I am sorry, sir, but I do not understand."
"You did hear that some ships have been sent to Alexandria, before you flew from Rome?"
"Yes, Oberführer – I heard that at the airport. I gathered that those would be the ships that had enough coal or oil to return from Alexandria without refueling."
"A second batch of ships was later ordered to Alexandria – while you were in the air – after the information the Italians had requested had arrived from Alexandria. But there is a third batch, a rather sizable one, of ships that still have not received any order to go to Alexandria."
Oberst Wöhler nodded: "Yes. This was one of the things the Italian flag-officer explained to me. There are ships that need to go Libya or Tunisia. Let me give one example: both our Italian Allies and us

have huge numbers of troops and heaps of material in these two countries – troops and material that need to go to Egypt. But in order to do that they will need trucks and fuel – so it makes sense to deliver these trucks and the fuel to Tunisia or Libya. The same is also true for critical spare parts, for example."

Schellenberg took a sheet of paper from his desk and seemed to read through it, tapping his pencil on one line: "The *Conte Rosso* is a troop transport on her way to Tripoli and has not changed course – she surely is not carrying fuel or spare parts."

"A troop transport? The Italians mentioned that some ships might have to take on additional water or food before they go on to Alexandria – perhaps this is one of those."

Schellenberg looked up from his desk: "I see. It seems that the devil is – - as usual – in the details. Thank you very much, Herr Oberst. Take tomorrow on leave and surprise your wife – I will arrange for a leave pass and a return flight to Rome for the day after tomorrow."

Oberst Wöhler understood this as dismissal, rose and saluted : "Thank you, Oberführer." As he turned away, he stopped and lifted one finger: "Ah, I almost forgot, just one more thing. Generalmajor Diciotti said he is going to need more ships, and fuel for them, and asks if we could help him there."

"More ships?"

"Yes, the ships will be at sea about two more days now. This means they can make fewer deliveries in a given period, so he will need more of them."

0300 hours local; 0200 hours CET
3 November 1940
20 kilometers east-southeast of the Alam el Halfa ridge, which was the eastern end of British 8th Army's last position

This was not warfare as Klingenberg knew it. He was twenty kilometers beyond his assigned patrol line, because his forward units from his Schnell Regiment of SS reported extremely large vehicle convoys driving with lights on in the distance. The entire British Army seemed to be exiting in a massive flood. His Panzer II's had been swarmed with British soldiers hopping off trucks to engage. He had more prisoners than he knew what to do with, had taken noticeable losses, and only wished he had access to corps- and army-level artillery. This was the target package of a lifetime. Instead he kept getting increasingly stern orders to disengage and let Messe's XX Corps handle this. A Corps whose arrival time was left in the indefinite future. Klingenberg hoped this made sense to higher command, because it sure didn't to him.

0715 hours local; 0515 CET
3 November 1940
Mitla Pass, Sinai, Egypt

The road through the pass was more a track than a highway. The van of Commander Ian Fleming's brigade was just exiting the pass but the tail had yet to enter. With the sun up, they were helpless if attacked from the air. He'd made the decision to risk this, trusting that the retreating 8th Army would be a more interesting target. He'd left Cairo with a brigade of his own, and a temporary battalion based on the parliamentarian's Gurkhas. Along for the ride had been maybe ten thousand Empire and other civilians in whatever vehicles they had, plus whatever space could be found on his military trucks for desperate people. By now he'd picked up at least twice that many more. Some were military or had been or were military dependents. Most were just people with cars, trucks, motorcyles, or in at least one case an agricultural tractor towing what could have been a trailer for hauling produce, in this case stuffed with people.

If everything worked just right this excuse for a gypsy caravan had just about enough gasoline to reach someplace civilized in Palestine. He loaded every vehicle and every container his men could find with gasoline. The civilians had had their household goods ruthlessly stripped off to make room for gasoline, water, and more people. Fleming was sure this order had not been perfectly applied. Some fool who had bribed a corporal to be allowed to keep hauling his refrigerator or heavy luggage would have his auto break down on march, then stand by the road sobbing when no one would rescue him even though he had three cute children and an even cuter puppy. He already had observed one retired Indian Army officer with an Egyptian girl young enough to be his granddaughter, and a pet baboon of all things. The officer at least had the brains to have the rest of his vehicle loaded with gasoline, water, and a conspicuous hunting rifle. He was towing a trailer with the young lady's family and two good hunting dogs.

Fleming hadn't a clue if the authorities in Palestine were ready to handle this. Not his problem. His troops, or as many as he could assemble by the time the road march ended somewhere near Jerusalem, were bound for Iraq. He had a representative from the War Cabinet with him whose authority was quite sweeping. What's better, he had paperwork on Cairo Embassy stationery confirming all this. The flight from Egypt was going to be remembered in the manner of Napoleon's from Moscow.

0800 hours local; 0700 hours CET
3 November 1940
Skies over Cairo, Egypt

Primo Tenente Enrico Cirillo had led his men out of the SM 81 Bat at fifteen hundred meters. The drop zone was the Gezira Golf Course, the most famous in all of Cairo. The skies were clear and blue with no appreciable cloud cover. There was neither flak nor enemy fighters to contest the action. Supposedly, Egyptian liaison personnel awaited them at the clubhouse.

The operational briefing was a trifle strange. The British had supposedly abandoned the city, but pockets of them might remain. The Egyptian military and police were asserted to be friendly, based on negotiations between the two crowns, but some units were alleged to be part of a national uprising led by nationalists and religious fanatics. Resistance could be answered by gunfire, but the airborne units were to be guided by the supposed Royalist liaison personnel on who was and was not 'friendly'. The First Libyan Division was near, but its precise position was not exactly known owing to an engagement with a large Australian corps that was also near but supposedly retreating north of the city towards the Canal. Most peculiar in all points.

Peculiar, but also mostly the problem of senior officers. After Malta, Cirillo had told himself he would next visit Egypt as a conqueror, to recreate the New Roman Empire the Duce had foretold. Here he was with his fine airborne company, returning to land first taken for Rome by Julius Caesar. And it was glorious.

....

Floating in the air over the equestrian facilities at Heliopolis, Tenente Vincenzo Pentangeli was enjoying the view of the city of Cairo to his west. He came slowly down to a gentle landing. As if this was all a training jump, his battalion formed up fairly quickly. The Egyptian liaison people materialized as if by magic from some djin out of the Tales of the Arabian Nights. These Egyptians were army officers with complexions and bearing showing their European ancestry. Egypt might be an Arab country, but it was ruled by people who looked and acted white, were civilized. This wasn't another Ethiopia.

Pentangeli found his English useful to communicate with these people. Most spoke some English, although of course every one of the senior people on both sides spoke French. His Egyptian counterpart seemed curious about Vincenzo's American accent. They chatted about New York City, which the Egyptian only knew from films but hoped some day to visit, as the unit marched into the city. Some people cheered. Most were indifferent. Pentangeli noticed a lot of damage from riot and what was probably street fighting. Now that this was an Italian land, hopefully everything could be repaired in short order. The briefing had stressed that the two crowns were now friends.

1100 hours local; 0900 hours CET
3 November 1940
Elhovo, Bulgaria

His staff officers were still well to the rear, getting the horses and men of his oversize SS Cavalry Brigade off the trains. Standartenführer Fritz Freitag had gone ahead with a small party to survey his new posting. The town was a nothing Balkan market town in the shadow of Mount Sakar, itself in the midst of supposedly decent wine country. Freitag had better things to worry about than the local vintages. He took his new Waffen SS career seriously, more so than his predecessor the late fool Fegelein had taken his own SS duties. That idiot had been executed for not following simple orders, for usurping command prerogative. Freitag would follow Berlin's policy to the letter. Berlin wanted him to make a combat force, not complain about the rustic scenery.

The Reichsführer had renamed his 2nd SS Cavalry Regiment as 1st SS Cavalry Brigade. Freitag was to locally recruit to flesh out this formation, after which he was to keep recruiting up to division strength. The Main SS Office had ruled that any Bulgar whose family had served beside a German or Austrian unit in the Kaiserwar was Class 5 Volksdeutsche. So were the Bulgarian Thracian refugees from the Balkan Wars and after. These were now alleged to have Gothic blood from the great Goth victory at Adrianople, which was just over the Turkish border.

The excuses were for the racial theorists. His division-to-be, the *Maria Theresa*, was in Thrace in case of a Soviet attempt at the Turkish Straits. His job was to assert German interests if and when. Until then, he would teach his nominal Volksdeutsche enough German to answer commands. The Kaiser's officers had done this with African savages. It should prove possible with half-civilized Balkan bandits.

1200 hours British double summer time and CET
3 November 1940
A posh flat in London's West End

Kim Philby's new control officer was an aristocratic Belgian lady a few years his senior. She was the third wife of a much older and quite wealthy British duke. When she agreed in her early twenties to marry a man already in his eighties, certain freedoms were allowed her. He would supply her with this flat and a modest allowance to 'have a private life'. In return she was to be discreet. No scandals in the tabloids, no wild behavior in nightclubs, nothing that would reflect poorly on the duke's social prestige. The duke's needs were seen to, physically and socially. She was beautiful, spoke half a dozen languages fluently, and could make polite conversation on virtually any topic. She had a proper title, suitable at a stretch to marry a duke, but neither family money nor lands. She would have as readily consented to be the old man's mistress as his wife. He preferred 'wife' so as to scandalize his still-living siblings.

Taking Philby as a lover would fit her agreed freedoms. Only Moscow Centre was aware that the lady had been a dedicated COMINTERN agent back to her late teens. If Leninism can be thought of as a secular religion, she was a most zealous convert.

Kim's schedule respected neither clock nor calendar. The War Cabinet often worked days that ran over 24 hours, and the breaks came on random days, not weekends per se. This was not Tory 1938 when everyone of importance took weekends in the country, summered on the continent, and generally worked at a languid pace out of Regency times. He had rung up her social secretary when cabinet had quit working an hour before dawn. The secretary had arranged this timing. Everything was kept very loose and casual, as if this truly were an affair.

They were half naked in case interrupted. She was ready to physically play the part of sexual partner. Kim could not see why it was worth the bother to take the pretense that far. Half-naked covered the security services breaking in. If the flat were bugged, there was no way to hide what was happening – beyond the Duke using his influence to claim harmless gossiping instead of espionage. It wasn't that Philby didn't find her attractive. The problem was always too much to pass along, and too little time to do it. Sex would waste at least ten minutes.

"The latest excuse to not make peace is that the public wouldn't understand."

"Moscow wants the war to continue. Do you advocate for this?"

"My orders were to give honest advice from a Red Tory point of view. That advice is to quit before we lose more. Doesn't matter what I say. This gang of clowns couldn't make a decision on what to order for dinner. Winston was decisive. Whatever his other faults, he could reach a decision and ram it through."

"Yet you supported his overthrow."

"Because almost all his decisions were wrong. All he saw was the big picture, the broad panorama. The Nazis were Evil. Yes, they are. Britain's historic policy is to oppose one ruler uniting the continent. Yes, it was; and in a perfect world still would be. However, after twenty years of avoiding arming like a major power, we simply don't have the strength to face Germany one on one, much less fight this new-forming European Community. The priority was always the gold standard. However painful, those are the facts. The sad facts that prompted the 1922 Committee to turn on him."

"So what changed with these rebels?"

"The Germans queered the deal. No more air war over Britain. No more Battle of the Atlantic threatening us with starvation and ruin. To most of the public, it doesn't feel as if the Home Country is at war. All that's left is a squalid little set of campaigns for empire. England is no longer at risk. We have lost most of an army and half of Egypt these past few days. But we took two ports from the French in West Africa. Montgomery is promising some grand victory in the interior sometime soon if he gets reinforcements. Wavell and Gort say that given a few months they may be able to restore our position in Nigeria. The Americans are dangling credits sometime towards year-end, some absurd contrivance they are calling Lend-Lease, whatever that turns out to be after their Congress gets done rewriting it. So it's easy to drift, waiting to see what turns up." Philby gave a morbid chuckle. "What will turn up is, we lose tens of thousands of more men plus Palestine and the rest of Egypt. Oh, and a bit more ground to the Red Army in Afghanistan."

The duchess showed keen interest in the forces of proletariat goodness rescuing more of Afghanistan from feudal reaction. She peppered Kim with questions, elicited details. It was a pity he wouldn't fuck, but duty before pleasure. The English were so strange about sex to a sophisticated continental.

1600 hours local; 1500 hours CET
3 November 1940
The remains of a village 30 kilometers southeast of Alexandria

It was raining. Klaus had been told by Moustafa, the new police supremo's nephew, that the rains normally didn't start till December. Moustafa led twelve hundred 'auxiliary police'. Gunter had used a different word, *Hiwi's*. Helpers. Klaus lacked the worldly experience of Gunter, especially from his days with the Freikorps in Latvia, wherever in the Baltic that was. To Klaus's untrained eyes the auxiliaries looked like a street gang with looted British rifles. The rifles didn't frighten Klaus. His men had machine-guns.

The local church was gutted. The street around it was littered with bodies. Many had been beheaded or disemboweled. The females often had their breasts cut off as well. Klaus had done the subtraction before Moustafa called his attention to it. The dead included males of all ages but no nubile females. The 'Liberation Army' must have taken the young women as part of their loot, along with the contents of pillaged houses and shops. Supposedly some of these 'patriots' were nationalists, some religious, and some just opportunistic bandits. Klaus did not find the distinction interesting. Anyone taken in arms, he shot. Anyone running, he shot. Anyone resisting, he shot. Those who bowed before his authority, whether armed or otherwise, he organized into convoys. These he sent back to the city, escorted by a few of his vehicles and a few dozen Hiwi's. The refugees got to carry the food his combined force was plundering. He was aware the Hiwi's were also stealing moveable wealth, what little remained. Klaus was indifferent to that, but insisted his men get an equal share.

"Moustafa, we will need a place to encamp for the night. Where would you suggest?"

"Excellency, surely we are to return to the city?" Moustafa was a man of twenty-five. He knew he had to pretend to be commanded by this German child in an officer's uniform, but staying out was absurd. "We can leave the city again tomorrow."

"We will lose too much time coming and going. We were sent for food, and what we have mostly done is gather more people to eat what food we have." Klaus thought the entire expedition absurd. Long before the warehouses were empty, ships could bring more food from Europe. But Gunter had commanded this. So it must be about showing German might to these rebel Egyptians.

Moustafa shrugged. The resignation of the colonial to the stupidity of the supposed masters. He pointed the column towards a market town. Even through the rain, the smoke of its ruin was easy to see on the horizon of the flat Nile Delta.

1900 hours local; 1800 hours CET
3 November 1940
Makeshift airstrip near Nile River, Upper Egypt

The day's retreat had been a blur. Ambassador Lampson had been spared the ceaseless air attacks. Those were directed at the main 8th Army units further north on the roads, as these endlessly retreating columns headed upriver along both banks of the mighty Nile. Now London had added a further indignity. The army Lysander aircraft had been sent for him from Khartoum. He was to return via this two-seater tiny plane to someplace where he could catch a flying boat home. Exactly where was left vague. Khartoum? Mombasa? Lagos? In any case, he was to abandon his wife and senior staff to the horrors of this journey so London could have the benefit of his wisdom. How stupid did they think he was? Officially, he remained His Britannic Majesty's Ambassador to Egypt and Sudan, in practice he was to be the designated goat. Let them try. He knew where enough bodies were buried to take dozens of them down with him. The Lysander bounced down the dirt airstrip and was airborne. Lampson willed himself to sleep. He would need all his wits about him in London. If he was to lose his honor, be denied any chance at Privy Council or peerage, he wanted to slaughter as many high-ranking Tories as he could in the process.

1800 hours Eastern Daylight Time; 2400 hours CET
3 November 1940
Executive Office Building, Washington DC

The large cloth carpetbag had lain all day on Harry Hopkins's desk awaiting this meeting. As a piece of luggage it was decades out of fashion. Why this particular type of container had been chosen seemed a mystery. Hopkins had too many other things on his plate to satisfy his idle curiosity on this. The election was in two days, and his man Roosevelt seemed likely to lose. He needed to thread a needle in a few key states. Hence the bag and this meeting with the vainglorious Lyndon Johnson.

Johnson looked even more shifty-eyed than usual this day. "The election's going badly. Roosevelt is fading. I've got a new list of House members who urgently need 'walking around money' to get out the vote." He started to hand the list to Hopkins, who waved it away. "You said come to you. These are good, loyal New Dealers. We will need them in the new Congress."

Hopkins gave a wan smile. "More than half of these have been voting with the biparty opposition coalition since 1938." He didn't need to read the paper to guess most of the names. He saw Johnson start to retort, and waved him to silence. "A good number of them are in Midwestern districts where nothing short of divine intervention could save them. Doesn't matter." Hopkins gave a sigh. He still had enough decency to find what was about to happen unpleasant. "Open the bag." He waited while Johnson opened the bag and almost recoiled in shock. "One hundred and fifty thousand dollars. You had asked for eighty-five. So you can be a hero to even the hopeless members, in case they win back their seats in 1942. You can afford to send people on overnight express trains or rent airplanes to deliver before Election Day."

"This much cash, there's a price. What is it?"

"Lame-duck session you are personally going to logroll a private citizenship act. There are always members with such requests. You will bundle them all together and add one more name, a Charles Luciano of Manhattan."

"The gangster?"

"The gangster. Don't look so shocked. You do Klan business where you need to, to turn out votes. Up North these people can deliver votes in the tens of thousands. They are the party's only chance to carry New York and New Jersey. You can hide your hand by getting someone who wasn't reelected to propose the name. But this is your personal responsibility. There's enough extra in the bag to buy some friends in the Senate. If there's anything left over, keep it. If this fails for any reason, you will not live out next year."

Johnson looked Roosevelt's man over. He'd never figured Hopkins for a hard man. He was an affable do-gooder. An educated man with poor health. Johnson had dealt with hard men in Texas, especially in the little colonias down in the Rio Grande Valley. They ran their village or county like feudal lords. "Just like that?"

"Just like that. You, your wife. I won't know who or when, but these people don't accept excuses. This money can make you a big man in both houses. When you get your Senate seat you'll already have friends. Do this man's business and mine, and there can be more bags like this. Cash. No telegrams for Hoover to put copies of in a file. Cash. Think of it this way. This man and the city bosses allied to him are really no different than your friends at Brown & Root, in the oil industry, with the big cattle spreads. They need favors. He needs favors. This man sells liquor, women, and gambling. Don't tell me Texas has never seen those sins."

Johnson laughed in spite of himself. Hopkins was right. One more name in a list of a thousand or two, would sail through by acclamation in a lame-duck session. He could find a sure loser who would take the petty scandal as the price of Lyndon, and by implication Rayburn, owing him a big favor. Politics ran on favors and cash.

0630 hours local; 0530 hours CET
4 November 1940
Brigade Strauss cantonment

Breakfast had been at dawn, almost forty minutes ago. Clara Fischer had sent Joey and her brother Carl on ahead to the work area, alleging unspecified 'chores' she needed to do. As soon as the parade of people left she had run for a trash can to puke up breakfast. If she was a fool she would try to kid herself that it was food poisoning or some local endemic illness. A local fever sounded good. She'd use that excuse with Joey. This strange wilderness sickened many of the Europeans now there to make war. Bug bites, miasmas, strange variants on common European diseases. That was why travelers often got intestinal problems. The locals would be mostly immune to what was common in a place.

She knew better. She had had this disease before. She was pregnant. She could feel the subtle signs in her body besides the morning sickness. Child was no longer a theoretical question. Unless she aborted it, she was having Joey's child. She'd been pregnant before and had never thought twice about keeping it. Yet she was thinking of doing so now. Shit!

1000 hours local; 0900 hours CET
4 November 1940
Headquarters Italian XX Corps, 15 km south of the former British positions on Alam Hafyla ridge

Generale di Corpo d'Armata – Lieutenant General / Corps General – Giovanni Messe had just finished giving a briefing on the overnight fighting to his commander, General Carlo Geloso. His corps had taken many prisoners and vast numbers of much-needed British trucks, but the main body of British Eighth Army had gotten away clean. The air force was claiming that they were hammering the retreating columns. Neither army general had much faith in the boasts of pilots.

"You have done well." Geloso paused to let Messe absorb the praise. "Now I am going to give you instructions you will not like." He let Messe compose himself. "You will temper your pursuit. I am less concerned with the possibility of a great victory, than of you risking a great reverse."

"Do you doubt my competence, sir?"

"My reservations are as follows. Our equipment is obsolete. Our current battlefield predominance is based on air and artillery superiority. Firepower. Neither of those can be rushed forward. The air units will have to be staged to Cairo. Then staged to new bases ever further up the Nile as you advance. Your supply will have to come from Alexandria. An entire new supply line must be organized on a north-south basis after Egypt is pacified. Organized while at the same time Germany goes due east 90 degrees away from you. So, win what tactical victories you can, but do not risk serious reversals. It's a bit over two thousand kilometers from Cairo to Khartoum. It's another sixteen hundred kilometers to Juba in Sudan's south. The British have gone into a bottomless bag. Our risk is you getting ahead of your supplies and support while the British finally send reinforcements from home. If you advance twenty kilometers a day you are talking six months to Juba. Six months of slogging through rear guards and stragglers, of having to rebuild roads after British demolitions. Of having to replace your worn-out vehicles and men with fresh ones. The chance to pocket their entire army was lost when they ran away too quickly. Italy never planned for such a long campaign. Our Germans friends will help at the margin but their real desire is east, not south."

Messe stared at the map taking this all in. Napoleon's deployment from Paris to Moscow was only twenty-nine hundred kilometers. This was going to be a true operational challenge.

1000 hours CET
4 November 1940
Office of Oberführer Schellenberg, Prinz-Albrecht-Straße, Berlin, Germany

The Oberführer's administrative secretary was a young Hauptsturmführer with a legal degree from a provincial university. His school's faculty had been so decimated by Nazi purges that it was only kept going with forced transfers of professors from other, better institutions. The Nazis had renamed the school in Halle-Wittenberg for Martin Luther, but the unofficial nickname was 'Vorkuta', a camp in the Soviet GULAG. The Hauptsturmführer had been an exemplary Nazi through his student days, using that as entrée to an SS career.

The file on the Brigade Strauss safes had entries from NL Leutnant Schmidt, the Witt family of finance officials, the head of the German Army depot at the Naples docks, the finance officials in Italy who had made the payment. Brigade Strauss had ordered two large safes. One was for the cash sent with the Witts. A prudent action. The other was for … ? No one precisely knew, but it had been ordered within weeks of their arrival in Libya. The inference was that Strauss and his brigands had acquired bulky, valuable loot, probably during the Malta operation.

The annotation from the Oberführer ordered monitoring to continue on the safe and on unusual expenditures by Brigadier Strauss or his senior officers. It also said the Reichsführer was aware of this situation. The secretary put the file in his locked drawer. Data this sensitive should be away from random prying eyes. Advancement would come from anticipating the wishes of Schellenberg.

1200 hours local; 1100 hours CET
4 November 1940
Former Cohen Company offices, now Aryanized as Schwabe & Sons, Ploiesti

The new district police commissioner, Florin Prezan, was enjoying a late morning coffee with his new patrons, Luke Schwabe and Dieter Baring. The Romanian had known Schwabe and his family under the name of Cohen. For a three-rank rise in his position, Florin was prepared to believe the young man had been transformed by magic djin or German forest trolls. To him, whether a man's phallus was cut or not mattered not at all. The sexual organ that interested him was the vagina, and in the dark they all looked the same. He worked for the German Baring, a deputy of the German economic Supremo Speer. The Romanian government had made that crystal-clear. Give the German whatever he wanted. Yet what the German wanted was quiet and order. Nothing nasty, nothing that hurt Romania. Whatever the idiot Iron Guard thought, these Germans were all that stood between Romania and the traditional Russian enemy. An enemy that had recently stolen one province and a large part of another.

Florin worked for Herr Facility Director Baring, but Herr Schwabe had chosen him for his position. What was given could be taken away. "Excellencies, how may I be of service?"

Baring was content to let Schwabe do the talking. "Two issues but they are linked. We have returned many of the original workers from Italy. The Iron Guard will not be happy at Jews and other foreigners living and working here. More are coming as this facility expands. You will need a unit of reliable men to police the residential and shopping district, to keep out the Iron Guard. Do you need a formal directive from the Ministry in Bucharest, or will an order from Herr Director be sufficient?"

"If the note from Herr Director is on letterhead and with his official titles, that will be quite sufficient. However, may I contact Herr Director's administrative secretary on addresses in the capital to carbon copy? We will want multiple places to be on formal notice. I would also like a liaison officer appointed from the German garrison. The Iron Guard is prone to armed riot. It would be nice to know there is an alarm company or two tasked to support my constables in the event of a large-scale disturbance. There are rumors those fools will attempt a coup against Marshal Antonescu. The liaison officer could also be kept aware by myself on such intelligence about disturbances, so the facilities can stay secure."

Baring nodded, and Luke went on. "We now have a large garrison of Aryans and a large workforce of foreigners. They are both mostly young men. Young men need similar diversions: liquor, women, gambling. They also tend to get into fights when celebrating at these facilities. We don't need the trouble. I propose that two new red-light districts be created. One will be for the Aryans. The other will be for our oil workers. Send two officers to my old transit camp at Bari to see how to properly arrange these things. But separate places, and wired off so local toughs don't interfere."

Florin smiled. He was thinking of who he would contact and what the kickbacks would be like. "You are aware that you are giving my police a license to get somewhat wealthy?"

Luke nodded. "Yes. It will be a most desirable job. It will also be immune from Romanian military conscription. We will get a note from Berlin to your General Staff on this. You in turn will have certain duties. The girls will be clean. Medically inspected daily. The whiskey will be neither watered nor diluted with industrial additives. The games of chance will be honest. Drunk soldiers or working men will not be rolled for their wallets. You will personally be responsible for this. Failure means you will be executed and your successor charged with the cleanup. In turn you will have the power of life and death over the business people you bring in for these concessions. Clean, orderly, efficient from our point of view means a license to get moderately rich for you and your men. Did you ever wonder why my family chose you and cleared out the ranks above you?" Florin thought he knew but let the ex-Jew continue. "The others were either too greedy to stay bought or too lazy to do what was promised. You always needed little fees and gifts, but your word was good. Let it continue to be so."

Florin assured the Excellencies of this. His wife had already seen the pattern and beaten him with words on what he must do. Obey, and keep hiring relatives who would be properly grateful. This was a chance working police seldom got; and the big prize never comes twice in the lottery of life.

1400 hours local; 1300 hours CET
4 November 1940
British Army traffic control point south of Gaza, Palestine

The major was being difficult. Sergeant Billy Lincoln replied with the proper sort of barely subordinate mulish intransigence. "Sir, you have seen my orders. Signed by a major general. You have called the colonel I am ordered to report to in Haifa to confirm that my orders are valid."

"The colonel, yes. No one seems able to locate this major general. My general claims not to have heard of him."

"Not being a gentleman such as yourself, I have no way of knowing when generals become real. My officer, Lieutenant Commander Money-Penny, hands me the orders, sir." Billy knew the general was probably fake. So what?

"That's just it, sergeant. You are mixing naval and army ranks. Simply won't do. Has to be wrong!" The man was losing patience.

"Sir, please consult your records on 8th Army. There was a 6th Commando Division that included Fleming's Brigade of Naval Commandos. I was permanently detailed to that unit on Malta from the Manchester Regiment. Check army records. It's all there." Billy was sure his officer had papers covering everything, and all in their proper folders. Mr. James was a wizard that way.

The major had already confirmed the unit. He merely objected to its existence. The argument had backed up traffic for 20 minutes. A colonel appeared from one of the stalled vehicles. On being told the story, he looked at Billy's papers himself. "Sergeant, do you personally know this general?"

Billy was at the proper position of attention. He was an old sweat and knew this game. "Sir, of course not, sir. Generals don't talk to my kind. Lieutenant Commander Money-Penny and Commander Fleming deal with exalted beings such as generals. I just follow orders, and my detail follows my orders.

If I'm not to go to where I am ordered, may I please call the colonel in Haifa, wherever that is, to tell him I have been denied passage?" Billy knew exactly where Haifa was. He had had mates with Allenby in the last war and they'd swapped stories. Billy was also amazed that the colonel was real. Then again, all anyone knew for sure was that a voice on the phone said he was that colonel and the major's command admitted such a colonel existed.

Mulish won. The major was forced to let Billy's trucks and motorcycles pass. Billy thought the major to be a fool. He never even got everyone out of the vehicles to verify by headcount that it matched the transit orders. Which it didn't. Billy had excuses for that but never had to deploy them. There was a guide he was supposed to meet in Ashkelon who was supposed to have updated papers and a route map that avoided army roadblocks. Mr. James was a good officer to work for.

1500 hours local; 1400 hours CET
4 November 1940
Headquarters 7th Panzer Division, 3 kilometers east of the British prior main line of resistance

There was no such rank as Brigadier. Wilhelm Ritter von Thoma was adamant on this. Yes, the SA and SS had the rank of Oberführer. Yes, the NL seemed now to have such a rank. Heer did not, and von Thoma simply would not accept that for the army there was now such a de facto rank between Oberst and Generalmajor. Which in a way was funny, as his colleague von Stauffenberg had been a Brigadier for well over a month.

Now von Thoma had been promoted by Corps Commander von Manstein to this rank. So von Thoma would have to use this absurdity on official correspondence, to answer to it. Why should a rank from this stupid militia, the NL, matter in the real armed service of the German state? Brigadier or Oberst, von Thoma was yet again de facto commander of 7th Panzer Division. His division commander, Rommel, had returned from his overnight trip with von Manstein in an excellent mood. Von Thoma had confirmed that the initial force von Manstein had ordered to Alexandria, a reinforced Company, had in fact reached the city and passed under the command of Brigadier Strauss. Again this absurd rank! but then Brigade Strauss was an absurd unit, a creature of the Reichsführer's whimsy.

Rommel had promptly formed a two-battalion Kampfgruppe to use the coastal road to Alexandria and 'exploit opportunities'. Rommel was always overrunning his stop lines and going beyond his orders. However, he had clearly been somewhat changed by the evening with his Corps Commander. Von Thoma had been ordered to notify von Manstein's headquarters of the battle group being sent. Any additional orders from Afrika Korps to Kampfgruppe Rommel were to be forwarded via Brigade Strauss. Rommel gave his command intention as reconnaissance for a route for the bulk of the division once Italian XXI Corps had cleared the area, allowing the recovery of Kampfgruppe von Stauffenberg. A practicable route was needed from the present positions to the Suez Canal that did not interfere with Italian supply routes. Erwin Rommel actually caring about the administrative chaos one of his rear-area raids cost, was a miracle. Perhaps the great Panzer General was finally growing up to his status as a senior commander instead of thinking of himself as leading a force of Jägers.

2200 hours local; 2100 hours CET
4 November 1940

Advance Headquarters, Afrika Division, 12 kilometers south of the British east-west former positions

Lothar knew the summons could herald no good for him. He spent the hour and change of the drive mulling what he could be accused of this time. His driver spent the time trying to work his way past a series of traffic control checkpoints. The Italo-German Panzer Army was in motion. In excess of ten thousand vehicles were trying to drive in different directions through the same 30 kilometer east-west by 20 kilometer north-south box. The chaindogs and their Italian equivalents were not willing to easily make exceptions for a mere Sturmbannführer, even one answering a summons from a Brigade-führer commanding a Division.

On arrival, Steiner's staff sent Lothar right in to see the General, interrupting a staff briefing. Steiner cleared the room and motioned Lothar to sit down. Now Lothar was sweating. This seemed serious. Whose necktie had he stepped on?

Steiner clearly could read Lothar's body language and generalized funk. "Yes, it's that bad. The Oberführer you quarreled with has been an active little gossip. You have been branded an aggressive arse-bandit who tried to rape him. Oh yes, and also a Jew-lover, possibly part Jew yourself. You've also lost your nerve in combat. Clearly not a man decent Aryan SA officers can serve beside."

Lothar's never very-well controlled temper flared. "That's bullshit, sir, and you know it. Let's see him say half of that to my face. I'll rip his head off and piss down his neck. Piss with my quite uncut Aryan piece of Hessian sausage. The man never wanted me in the first place."

"Correct. Never wanted you, or your Jew pioneers who wrecked this fool's chances to command an assault on the British positions." Steiner shook his head, his expression somewhat sad beyond the exhaustion of two days with almost no sleep commanding a Division whose general orders kept changing to cope with a cascading series of unexpected British actions. "He's a decent Regimental commander. He seems able to make a workable unit out of the odds and sods he was given. No, I need him and I need the other SA officers he has enlisted in his vendetta; so you must go."

"Go? Where?"

"Alexandria. I will send you with your original Battalion, the Jews and the HJ's. No one wants to serve with the Yids. The original Führer would not approve, or some such."

"What's wrong with the HJ's? They are good German lads and well-indoctrinated in Nazi sentiments."

"Supposedly you have violated all their arses and they are now girly-men. For this campaign, I just don't have the time to purge all my combat cadres and put the division through a new training cycle. You fight with the army you have, not the one you wish you had. Alexandria is ours. Your old nemesis and my sort-of namesake Klaus Steiner took the port. DAK is beefing up the garrison. If you cannot make a home there, contact Jodl's Kampfgruppe. You impressed two of his staff Obersts with your support work."

Lothar stood, drew himself up to a perfect position of attention, snapped his right arm forward and shouted, "Heil Göring!". He then did an about-face to exit. The larger staff room he walked out into was filled with smirking SA officers and somewhat ashamed-seeming Heer ones. Lothar was aware that the support services for the Division were the remaining higher cadres of a demobilized Heer division. His fellow SA officers were now his enemy. That made the Heer men his sort of friends. He walked up to a Heer Oberst and asked for movement orders making getting him back to his unit through this mess a priority, and a similar priority for his unit movement north to Alexandria.

The old Lothar would have spent the two hours in a crawling stop-and-go back to his Kampfgruppe ranting and raving. He now recognized that as pointless. Done was done. Time to see to the future.

2300 hours Eastern Standard Time; 4 November 1940
0600 CET; 5 November, 1940
Pelham Bay Park, Bronx, New York City

Normally Harry Hopkins functioned as a behind-the-scenes operative. He was Cardinal Richelieu to FDR's Louis XIII. However, he still had a working relationship with the Communist conduit everyone thought was his mistress. It was probably her relationship with him that had kept her off Hoover's arrest lists. Her immunity made her a natural front person for the remaining underground elements of the Party to begin to reconstruct an above-ground political presence. This was named the World Peace League. Its official mission was to end the quasi-war between the US and USSR in the Western and Northern Pacific.

The World Peace League still could mobilize enough sympathizers and fellow travelers for a mass rally here in the park. FDR had desperate need of these votes. So Harry and the First Lady were both featured speakers. This insured that Hoover and the New York Police Department's Red Squad would not raid the meeting. The Secret Service and the uniformed services of the police in turn kept the usual gangs of paid Irish toughs from turning the rally into a riot. It was all intricate pieces to a puzzle.

The famed Negro singer Paul Robeson was on stage doing a series of 'Freedom Songs'. The First Lady was surrounded by working press and fervent admirers. That left Hopkins free to converse with *his* lady fair. "You do realize that this peace you claim to seek would need the first steps to come from Moscow? That they would have to admit their crimes, beg forgiveness, walk humbly for a bit ... but this shadow-boxing war helps no one."

She hadn't the authority to change Soviet policy, nor was she foolish enough to attempt to defend it. Her Leninism didn't make her blind to Stalin's faults. "What are Franklin's real chances?"

"Too close to be sure. I see it as down to three big states. Bad part is we need all three. Willkie only needs one. I've got Truman barnstorming California these last days even if it means conceding Missouri. Franklin's doing the same, upstate New York. Buffalo, Syracuse, Rochester, Utica, Albany. The more we cut the Republican margin north of the Bronx, the better the chance that the City will save us."

"You are in bed with some abysmal characters here. Machine bosses, gangsters, reactionary elements ... "

"So you prefer the Economic Royalists back in power?"

The debate wound down, unresolved. The music section of the program ended and Mrs. Roosevelt began a long uplifting speech. Hopefully it would motivate these radical political enthusiasts to vote for a mainstream party. FDR would need every one of these, plus their family, neighbors and casual acquaintances. New York was balanced on a razor's edge and the election was tomorrow.

0800 hours local; 0700 hours CET
5 November 1940
Mitla Pass, Sinai

There was no traffic checkpoint at the west entrance to the pass. The flood of vehicles moving east ran on hour after hour, day and night. Instead there was a British company and a Palestinian one monitoring the traffic and ready to serve as a joint outpost when the enemy arrived. Right now they were eating choking dust from the passing vehicles while fighting boredom.

The British company was created by five officers from 7th Armored Division, sent down from Beersheba where the nominal divisional cantonment was. They fleshed the unit out with stragglers pulled off vehicles passing through. Most of these recruits were unwilling, and a fair number deserted the moment there wasn't an officer watching them. They would just jump on a passing truck. Sometimes it worked. Often it provoked fistfights, stalled traffic, and a deserter apprehended. It being impossible to send 70% of a company to the nonexistent guardhouse, the officers were reduced to keeping lists and threatening courts-martial some nebulous time in the future. Most deserters would prefer a guard house slot in Iraq or India to facing the Germans again. So company strength fluctuated between 150 and 200, of which forty or so were minimally reliable.

Captain Moshe Dayan led the Palestinian force, a company of the new Palmach militia. These were Labor or other left party youngsters, often out of the agricultural settlements. Nominal minimum recruiting age was 17, but Dayan had chosen not to push beyond the enlistment papers although he knew of multiple younger recruits. One was 14 to his quite certain knowledge. He knew the young man's older brother, also his uncle. The political restriction made sense when the enemy was using Betar Revisionists. This made the Irgun untrustworthy and cast doubts on the General Zionists.

Dayan was passing the time chatting with the British captain in charge. The subject, as ever, was weapons. "Sir, why not give my men the heavy weapons? Mine won't run. Most of yours will."

The British captain had been briefed that this Jew was a friend of the Empire. He was willing to accept that higher command thought of him that way. Right now he saw the Jewish captain as a goading, nagging pain in his arse. "I have orders on how well we equip you. Take it up with higher command." The 'alliance' between the British Empire and these Jews was a marriage of convenience, not true love.

Dayan was back to being trusted by Ben Gurion and Haganah. Marginally. The defector from the Betar had been most useful. As Moshe had suspected, the man knew more than he thought he did. It was all in bits and pieces of camp gossip, chance sights and the like. Under skilled interrogation, he was peeled like a ripe fruit. It mostly validated what the Jewish Agency had been told by the Revisionist envoys in Istanbul and separately by the Italian Foreign office in Rome when Ben Gurion had sent envoys of his own. However, in such delicate situations the devil was often in the details. This deserter had seen up close on a day-to-day basis how deeply Betar, and therefore the Irgun, were tied in with the Nazis. This working relationship made the talk of a Revisionist state out of Haifa all too real. The information had bought the man a ticket out through Iraq. He was probably better than halfway to Basra by now. Mapai was preparing for this eventuality. They presumed Hatzohar was doing the same under the surface of their supposed coordination of all Jewish parties within the Jewish Agency and World Zionist Movement. "At least let us train on the weapons so they will be properly used when the time comes. The Germans are coming. Not quickly, but they are coming. Your superiors have been made aware. The enemy are boasting Jerusalem for New Year's Eve."

The British captain had been well briefed. Part of the briefing was admitting nothing to this Jew. Orde Wingate and his clique might trust these Hebrews. The bulk of the British regular army did not.

There were thousands of Jews fighting for the Nazis. The ones fighting for Britain had mostly deserted, and the rest didn't fight worth a damn. Jews simply weren't a martial people. That said, training wasn't surrender of the weapons. "Dry-fire exercises only. And Jerusalem is an open city under the Papal Nuncio. Our forces have left there."

"That's the Old City. That still leaves the Jewish New City." A council of religious leaders and neutral ambassadors was running the Open City. They had even created a militia to keep the Arab Higher Committee partisans and Irgun in check. The US was sending food, arms, and supplies supporting this. Dayan knew this and was sure the British officer was similarly informed. Both also knew that British officers and officials were billeting their families in this 'safe zone', which violated the spirit if not the letter of the agreements. "Shall we draw up a roster? We have little else to do for now but watch this modern version of my namesake Moses leading the people out of Egypt." Watch, choke, and sweat. Better all of those than facing the Panzer divisions that were coming.

0900 hours local; 0800 hours CET
5 November 1940
Grebe Aerodrome near Alexandria (former RN Air station)

Generalleutnant Ramcke was fuming. He had cut his force for the proposed Suez operation, the one that was to take the bridge at Ferdan, to four battalions from the eight-battalion division he had so carefully created out of the wreckage left from the Maltese debacle. The excuse had been lack of Ju-52's and gliders. Now his four-battalion Kampfgruppe had been redeployed forward to Grebe Aerodrome outside Alexandria by truck. This meant he could have brought all eight Battalions and sent the other four forward from Alexandria to Suez by truck.

There was no way he was going to get his missing units and their equipment from Sicily in time for Suez. He'd been told that he could rely on General Rommel arriving with a relief force. Ramcke had worked with Rommel in the run-up to Malta and then in the fighting on the island. Depending on Rommel to follow orders was the act of an idiot. Ramcke was simply not that naïve.

Now salvation was at hand. His colleague from Luqa, Gunter Strauss, had his enlarged Brigade in garrison at Alexandria. A quick phone call had resulted in Strauss motoring out to meet him here on the airstrip. "Good to see you, Gunter. Congratulations on your promotion." Ramcke then launched into a description of his problem.

Strauss took it in quickly. "So you need an armed escort force for your supply column? How many trucks?"

"That's the problem. I don't have the trucks or the men to drive them. I am dependent on my supposed service for a second drop that they refuse to promise they can make."

"Sir, we know each other from Luqa. In a sense we made each other's careers there. I understand comradeship. If I find the trucks and drivers, how many truckloads?"

The ever-prepared Major Schmidt of the Hal Far truce fame had numbers. Gunter looked them over. "How do you feel about Arabs?" Ramcke and Schmidt looked blankly at him. "We've recruited a bunch of auxiliary police. Hiwi's, in fact. Enough of them can drive and there are enough trucks, military and civilian, we have seized here. I'd say a two-battalion Kampfgruppe should do. Do you remember my Leutnant from Luqa? Klaus Steiner." Ramcke nodded warily. He remembered a short youth who had somehow jumped to Major. Plucky. No real military training. "He's an Oberstleutnant with a Knight's Cross now. His Battalion and a companion Waffen SS Battalion he's gotten used to working with. I'll steal a Company or two from another unit to bulk the force up. They have field guns and light armor. Will that do, sir?"

Ramcke would have preferred a more experienced officer leading the KG. Ramcke would have preferred they be his own well-trained but missing Battalions. Life in wartime is about what you will settle for. It's a matter of making do and getting the job done. Ramcke shook Strauss's hand, thanked him, and promised a 36-hour advance warning order. He figured he would need at least that long to get his own men ready.

1700 hours local; 1100 hours CET
5 November 1940
Philippine Brigade positions; northeast of Nanking, China

Ike could hear the guns of Admiral Richardson's combined Yangtse Squadron and Asiatic Fleet firing from the river. The six 6" guns of the light cruiser *Marblehead* could easily reach ten miles inland, and the Communist New Fourth Army was trying the river route again. Ike had taken most of his brigade out to meet them. He had his four-battalion Philippine Regiment and two battalions of the American-cadred Christian Chinese 'Warriors of God' Regiment arrayed in good field positions. Mines, wire, bunkers, machine-guns, and mortars. In support he had three 75mm-artillery battalions manned by Freedom Brigaders, with security screening from a Provisional Marine Battalion and a battalion based on cadres of the Old China Hand Regular Army 15th Regiment.

The Communists had probed on a succession of compass headings for weeks. Right now they were coming from the east. They lacked the strength to take the city, but refused to stop trying these spoiling attacks. There would be probes until full dark, after which they would infiltrate his lines with sappers and grenade-armed light infantry. Come morning, Ike would clear his rear with the two battalions currently screening the artillery. It was a dance of death. Both sides were green and had over-expanded their forces. Too many green newbies and too few competent cadres. As a result, they did these actions to blood half-trained units as part of a tactical finishing school.

When the units learned enough to be really useful, they'd be stripped of cadres to form still more units. The verdant farm fields the Reds were advancing across stank of night soil fertilizer. His artillery would chew up half the crops, and the mines both sides left behind would render the rest too expensive in blood to harvest. That was a problem for the Reds, who lived on food from the peasants. The food that fed Ike's troops, that fed the large Chinese garrison of the city, that fed the growing horde of refugees that clustered within the city walls, was grown in Iowa and Texas, not along the banks of the Yangtse.

Ike laughed to himself. His career had been under a cloud since World War 1 because he had never held a combat command. His war had been stateside, training and logistics. That problem was gone. He was commanding men in action. He even had a war wound. A team of Communist assassins had penetrated his headquarters two weeks ago. In the close-in fighting, Ike took a round through his shoulder and grenade shrapnel in his knee. He was reduced to using a walking stick, but he'd made the front page of the stateside papers when George Patton had pinned his Bronze Star on.

His Chinese-American driver maneuvered the Bantam BRC Pilot Model around the potholes while heading in the general direction of Philippine Regiment Headquarters. The army had shipped a few dozen hasty prototypes of the Bantam to China. The damned little four-wheel-drive reconnaissance cars were worth their weight in diamonds. Most Chinese roads were geared to oxcarts. The Bantams could cope. His staff had found a factory in Shanghai that could cobble together a version. It only needed the four-wheel drive train shipped from stateside.

The regiment commander, Colonel Ridgway, was waiting for Ike. It was the usual argument. "Ike, why do we have to sit here like lumps? Let me pitch into these dumb fucks. I know the training limits of my Filipinos, but the Commies are no better."

"So you chase them five miles. Darkness comes. Then what? Their sappers, their light troops can maneuver in the dark in platoons. Can you? The Japanese tried it your way and got their heads handed to them more times than not. We fight using firepower and fixed positions. Just like Petain's French taught us in the last war. Let them break their teeth again."

"Ike, you don't win wars defending."

"We don't win this war at all. That's the job of the Chinese we are backing. Our job is to keep them from losing until they can train up a big enough army to do the job."

"Never going to happen. You don't win wars by defense."

"Public back home didn't sign up for millions of Americans in China. Limited war to safeguard Jesus and Capitalism. I got you this command. Only active combat the army has. You do the job my way, or the next guy will. Congress didn't sign up for piles of US dead to conquer some Chinese town they cannot find on a map, a town that more likely than not we stop garrisoning in a month to go put out another fire caused by Japan pulling more divisions out for Manchuria." Ike knew that Ridgway knew better. He felt the man's frustration. He was not about to give in to it. If hell-for-leather George Patton could command a limited war, then so could safe, sensible Dwight Eisenhower.

0900 hours Eastern Standard Time; 1500 hours CET
5 November 1940
Ruppert Stadium, Newark, New Jersey

The rally at the the baseball stadium was in its second hour. Election day had dawned crisp but cold on the East Coast. The professional politicians agreed that it was good voting weather. Franklin Roosevelt hoped so. The pace of this campaign was killing him. He would never admit it to Harry Hopkins or the rest of the key people, but the chest pains were recurring. Damn, but reliable Harry had been right. This election was going to be a slog, not the triumphant crusade of 1936. FDR was used to being the charismatic center of the room. He might have brighter people in orbit around him, but they only functioned through his destiny-driven hold on mass opinion. Franklin had overcome polio and the Depression by strength of character, by his belief in his near-divine grace. This campaign was different. Was the public not responding because his body was failing? Or was the Third Term Rule an accurate reflection that after eight years, the public seeks change for change's sake?

There were two more of these mass rallies today, one in Times Square in Manhattan and the other in downtown Brooklyn near the Long Island Railroad terminus. Huge crowds would line the motorcade routes between the three events. Franklin could keep his personal speeches short. There were enough hacks eager to get their twenty minutes at the podium. He mostly had to wave, smile, and look jaunty. He also had to not keel over from the explosions in his chest, or let the public see how light-headed and disoriented he really was.

Tonight he'd take the returns at his Hyde Park estate. He would have to show himself a bit to the lesser staff people, but if he told Harry or Eleanor a toned-down version of the truth they would shield him, let him rest. He had to live through the next four years. He would not be remembered in history as the man who made that provincial boor Truman president.

2000 hours local; 1900 hours CET

5 November 1940

German transport vessel in the Eastern Mediterranean

The ship was bobbing like a cork in a spring flood, while also rolling like a ball bearing on wet grass. From the time they had cleared the placid water of Bari's harbor, near to all the passengers had been puking their guts out, getting more miserable by the hour. It was now the fourth day of what had been promised to be a two-and-a-half-day voyage to Libya. Only, they were not going to Libya any longer. They had been diverted to Egypt, to Alexandria to be precise.

The only passengers not feeding the fish with their last few day's meals were Frauke Peters and that little witch Oriana Fallaci. Frauke felt her superiority was due to pure Aryan bloodlines, that the German whores and doctors were infected with Jew or Slav blood. Oriana's strong constitution must be a Gothic ancestor somewhere in her family tree, or perhaps a more recent German traveler.

The crew coped with the deranged motions of the ship. They called it 'having their sea legs'. Frauke accepted that one could become habituated to anything. The three Roma whores were proving that. Once the crew realized they had working girls on board, lines started forming to buy their services. The German ladies of the night refused. In between barfs, all they wanted to do was huddle together and share their misery.

The three Roma girls showed their subhumanity. They could keep their legs spread and their hips pumping even while turning their heads to the side to puke into buckets that Oriana held for them. It was pure animal rutting instinct. Oriana also had somehow acquired the training to do the 'short arm' inspection of the customer's organs before the money changed hands.

Frauke's job was taking the money of those that passed the test, while administering beat-downs with a lead-core wooden club to fools who refused to take no for an answer. She had the strength to hit them hard enough to get past their rage and lust. She had the training not to damage them too badly. Besides, after having been forced into exile because she would not accommodate herself to unbridled male lusts at the Camp, this was delicious revenge on anything with a phallus.

2300 hours local; 2200 hours CET

5 November 1940

Partially damaged villa 50 kilometers east-southeast of Alexandria city limits

The villa had once been an elegant Victorian-era residence, the center of a complex of buildings that were the heart of a large agricultural estate. Half the windows were gone. The walls were pockmarked by bullet strikes. Some of the lesser buildings, starting with the stables, showed fire or smoke damage.

The siege of the complex by rebels had been broken by the arrival of Klaus with the augmented Falcons of Malta Battalion. This meeting engagement had chased off the enemy, but scarcely killed them all. As soon as the Germans pulled out, they would be back, attacking the hasty militia of Christians and farm workers thrown together by the lady of the house and two elderly retainers. One had been a Sergeant in the Sudanese Rifles and the other in a Bengali Regiment. The three had organized a makeshift defense with hunting rifles, shotguns, Molotov cocktails, and dynamite. After the first two rushes had been fought off, it had devolved into sniping and small raids.

The lady of the estate knew she needed a permanent garrison to survive. She had no wish to be a mostly-penniless refugee in the city, which was what the quite young German commander kept suggesting she do. Over the lavish welcome dinner she had her cooks prepare for the officers, she had pressed her case. He seemed to ignore her French, English, and Italian, answering in German through a boy aide, probably an officer cadet, who spoke to her in English. Logic and sentiment had failed. That left a woman's obvious weapon.

Once he had gone to bed, she had arranged her hair and makeup to best advantage while changing into a bedtime outfit that left nothing to the imagination. At 41 she might be too old for him, although many men preferred an experienced mature woman whose bedroom skills would add to their pleasures, to the nubile bodies of maidens. In case his tastes ran more to youth, she also prepared her fourteen-year-old daughter and nineteen-year-old niece. Her daughter was quite terrified, as this would be her first time. Her minx of a niece had been all but throwing herself at the man over dinner. She wanted the thrill of bagging an important man her aunt could not.

She didn't bother to knock on his door. She just entered, one young woman on each arm. Surely language wasn't needed for this. The message was obvious in any language. What was a hero's pleasure? One? Two? All three?

....

Klaus had been sleeping lightly. The whole dinner had felt *off* to him. He had tried to be polite, but the silly woman wasn't taking no for an answer. He saw how a garrison benefited her. He did not see how Gunter would find gain for Germany in a Platoon of Betar on an estate in the Nile Delta. He was also annoyed about her presumption that everyone of his rank spoke conversational French. Perhaps professional officers did. His trade school had taught French as part of the curriculum. His spoken French was good enough to say 'the boss was running late', and ask for beverage orders. He was a bit better with written French. Given his grammar book, a dictionary, and a book of verb conjugations, Klaus could send a business letter in stilted schoolboy French. Business letters have rigid forms and a fairly limited vocabulary. Klaus could write about delivery dates, payment terms, and technical specifications. He lacked the vocabulary, spoken or written, for sex. Yet sex was obviously what was being offered here. Klaus had no fantasy as to his charming personality or movie star good looks. This was a simple attempt to buy with sex what had been denied over dinner.

Klaus sat up, slid back into his uniform trousers, held up his right hand and clearly said "Non!"

The three ladies paused, more than a bit confused. This was not any of the expected male reactions. Neither was what Klaus bellowed next. "Bain!!!"

The young Gefreiter came running. He was less shocked than Klaus had been at what was occurring. His mother had been a concubine, and known girls in the cantonments who were little better than tarts. Bain had grown up on such gossip. Under Klaus's direction, he sent off the two younger females and told the lady of the house to wrap Klaus's blanket around herself. Having done so, she was instructed to sit in the arm chair. Klaus stayed seated on the bed.

"Madam, you will not get what you want by what you are offering. I am recently betrothed. My beloved more than sees to those needs. In any event, I am a patriotic German officer. I reject the garrison because I see no way that it serves German interests. It serves your personal interests, but that is not our concern."

The woman was finding the idea that field officers were faithful, hard to grasp. She was the daughter, granddaughter, and wife of such men from the British, Egyptian, French, and Ottoman services. "Is this because my husband is a serving British officer?"

Klaus had guessed as much but been too polite to ask. "Our Führer has mandated proper treatment of the British. So far you have done nothing to be our enemy. As of last week the British ruled Egypt. What does Germany gain keeping this estate alive with a garrison? I can easily spare the Platoon, which is all you would need. What is the benefit?"

The lady had to think fast. She had come expecting sex, focused on what delights she could offer and what his tastes might be. He certainly hadn't given any clues over dinner. "With two Platoons, so one could be out patrolling, you would have an island of stability to reclaim this district of the Delta. If you leave a radio as well, we could notify you of major concentrations of enemy forces. In addition, proof by this strong point you were here to stay, will cause many people to gravitate to your side. The rebels are a minority exploiting British weakness. The vast bulk of the people will defer to whoever seems to be the strong horse in this fight."

Klaus pondered for a moment. "With this island, how much produce could you gather? We are especially interested in fruits, vegetables, and dairy products."

She was nonplussed. "Why do you care?"

"These need refrigeration and thus are harder to ship by sea than grains, potatoes, cheeses, and canned meats. We have a city and an army to feed. Food from here means more space for ammunition and spare parts for our war machinery."

"Why didn't you tell us this over dinner?"

"You didn't ask. I'm not a supply or transport officer. I only know these things in generalities. This is what my general seeks. Can your estate and your militia be of use? If so, I can radio my General about the garrison."

"And this matters to you more than the sex?"

Klaus slowly shook his head. "I'm just a provincial German, not a sophisticate like you seem to be. To me marriage is between two people and for life. If my parents were more adventurous than that, they certainly didn't show it to me or my siblings. However, I am curious about one thing – I could have taken the sex and still said no in the morning."

"You knew the implied transaction. A gentleman would honor it."

"A gentleman. How did you know I was such?"

"Civilized nations do not promote ordinary people from lesser families to field grade."

"Our National Socialist Germany promotes based on accomplishments. I have gone from Leutnant to Oberstleutnant based on field victories." Klaus left off starting as a Gefreiter and how that was a step up from his HJ rank. "My General speaks English. Tomorrow morning I will get him on the radio and let you two discuss things."

At last the lady smiled. She pointed towards the bed. Klaus again shook his head no. She offered the two younger women, at which point Klaus sent them all back to their rooms. Said they could discuss the situation over breakfast and then call the general. Klaus went back to sleep. Bain filed the story away. He would tell his mother … who would tell Frau Greta. The Oberstleutnant's lady was to be their employer after the end of the war. Best to show they were loyal to her. Klaus had never considered any of this, but he was in many ways quite young.

0400 hours local; 0300 hours CET
6 November 1940
Gezira Country Club, Cairo, Egypt

The clubhouse dining room was standing room only and packed as badly as a commuter-hour bus on Cairo's busy streets. Lieutenant Gamal Abdel Nasser was into the third hour of one of his interminable speeches. The multifactioned central committee for the New Egypt was mostly sitting spellbound before the flood of words. Nasser was a known orator whose flights of rhetorical fantasy were legendary among the many activists.

Lieutenant Anwar Sadat was not one of those hypnotized by the tsunami of florid phrases. Reduced to action points, Gamal was proposing a Sarajevo. There was to be a victory parade by the Royal Egyptian and Royal Fascist Italian military to celebrate the liberation of Egypt from the yoke of British colonialism. Nasser would kill the notables participating.

Sadat preferred facts to visions of glory. Upper Egypt was still firmly in British hands, as was Sinai. Large parts of Lower Egypt still had retreating British forces. The new Italian overlords were offering a worse situation for nominally independent Egypt than what the British had conceded in 1936. It would take a long and painful further struggle to drive out the Italians and marginalize the monarchy. A struggle whose time was in the future. For now, the republican elements were too weak and the oppressors too strong.

Nasser conceded this in part but then proposed a blood deed. He would lead a team of assassins to kill both kings and the Italian dictator during the parade. Sadat thought Nasser more than somewhat credulous in believing the rumors that the two Italians would be present. Either way, killing the slothful, playboy Egyptian king risked the accession to the throne of some competent relative of his. The lines of succession were theoretical, and likely to be set aside in favor of the first aristocrat to seize the opportunity. All of this presuming that Nasser's gun and bomb squad actually killed their intended victims. The history of the politics of such deeds were. many tries and few real successes. Even Sarajevo had been a ridiculously accidental success.

Sadat didn't know everyone here at the joint meeting. Too many factions – from Muslim Brotherhood, through the various political parties, to security-service men supposedly turned patriot. Supposedly. Sadat presumed the room had at least twenty paid informers and probably twice as many who sold information to the palace on a freelance basis. Sadat was tempted to do so himself. Nasser would fail. Probably die as well. Selling him out would give Sadat some cover for the years of plotting to come. Sadat thought long-term, unlike the overly emotional Nasser.

0800 hours Eastern Standard Time; 1400 hours CET
6 November 1940
"Springwood", FDR's Hyde Park estate, Dutchess County, New York

Harry Hopkins had let Franklin sleep as long as he dared. The man had looked like death slightly warmed over when he put in an appearance in the staff room for a drink, after arriving by motorcade from a very active day campaigning. Hopkins himself had been up all night, living on nerves, Italian espresso coffee, and five-minute catnaps. The election results had been as bad as he had feared. Hopkins had handled as much as he could. Now FDR had to be involved.

Franklin could read the exhaustion in his number two's face. "How bad?"

"You've probably lost the popular vote. We have three states still out. California, New York, and New Jersey. You've got a six-thousand-vote edge in California with a bit over 90% of the vote counted. Truman's out there at state party headquarters. The boys think it will hold, based on which precincts are still out. That there's still enough old Bryan populists in the mountains and Okies in the Central Valley to make up for what's still coming in from LA. Your problems are New York and New Jersey."

FDR was thinking fast. "How much is still out?"

"Wrong question. We've been counting you in, but the number we have to beat keeps growing. Dewey's directed the remaining Republican rural areas in both states to stop reporting until we finish. So we stopped. The fraud is getting too obvious. Jersey City and the Bronx already have more votes in than residents. If either campaign takes this to court, we are both looking at a disaster. The public could lose all faith in elections." He saw Franklin's face start to cloud. The man hated being pushed, and he had never in his life been pushed like this. "I've got Dewey and Willkie coming up here this afternoon. We are going to have to make a grand bargain with them, run a joint administration."

"How dare you! No one gave you that authority!"

"Fine. I quit. I'll get a message to them somehow that the deal's off. Dewey will go into court to get an honest count in Manhattan, the Bronx, Brooklyn, Newark and the rest. You'll lose both states." Hopkins bent over, white as a ghost, clutching his middle. He grabbed for a trashcan and puked up near-pure bile. He staggered back into a chair, still clutching the trashcan. "Truman and I got you to the edge of a third term. Do what you want from here. I'm getting driven down to Manhattan and checking myself into Columbia Presbyterian. I was prepared to die for you, for the March of Progress. If that's not good enough, let me die with some dignity and without all this round-the-clock stress." Hopkins took a swig of water and spat into the trashcan to get some of the foul taste out of his mouth. He tried to stand up. He swayed and had to grab the desk but stayed on his feet. Swaying as if on a ship in a stormy sea, he lurched for the door.

Franklin was beside himself with anger ... and with naked terror at facing this disaster alone. He knew deep down it was he who had driven the indispensable Farley away. He simply couldn't make do without Harry as well. Eleanor's clique had their heads in the clouds ... and frequently up their asses. "Harry. Sit down. Your country needs you. So do I." Roosevelt almost choked getting the next words out. "I'm sorry. I know you have done your best for me, for the country, for the ideals we share. What can we salvage?"

Hopkins stopped, started to turn to answer, and lost his feet, followed by consciousness. Franklin called for help. Two Secret Service agents rushed in. They got Hopkins into a chair and then sent for a doctor. The President scarcely looked better than the half-dead, barely-breathing Hopkins.

It took ten minutes to get Hopkins reasonably awake and functional. He was in a comfortable armchair with his feet on an ottoman. The doctor had given both men mild sedatives and cautioned them against further stress. Everyone knew the outline of the political situation and thus how silly such an injunction was.

"How bad will the deal be?" Franklin simply couldn't be left to face this on his own. If it remained Harry's deal, then at some future point – when his position was better – he could ease out Harry, and escape the blame before the gods of history.

"Dewey gets the Treasury Department. Willkie gets an expanded Commerce Department. Some Republican lawyer named Dulles gets Secretary of State. We keep on the two TR progressives we have at War and Navy. Dewey and Willkie get half the patronage appointments, and a veto on the legislative program. Lindy gets a new job as coordinator of aviation production. Secretary of the Air Force or some such. They break with Coughlin and the *Chicago Tribune* and endorse the election results, because in the current world crisis the country cannot afford taking a disputed election to the courts. If this blows up the Republican Party, we back them in the fight to own the name, the ballot line. It may be trench warfare state by state on this. The *Trib* and Taft's people will shriek treason from the rafters. We all sign some statement agreeing to some bipartisan blue-ribbon commission to review our electoral system and study some unnamed reforms that neither party will support two years from now when they issue a 600-page report no one beyond some college professors will read.   Truman gets to head some joint committee from both Houses on fraud, waste, and abuse of defense spending. He's a stickler on this stuff. He'll let patronage slide, but unapproved chiseling will be prosecuted. If you run for a fourth term, it's to be a joint ticket with Dewey as VP. They have no clue of how sick you are." Hopkins sank back into the chair, his head lolling to one side. He was barely conscious, and a spent force.

Roosevelt let his man rest. The deal could have been worse. There was no rollback of the New Deal. At worst, it was a pause in Reform. He was still president, and no grand bargain had constitutional force. Let the Royalists overreach, and he could recover his political magic in the 1942 midterm elections. Intervention was dead as a serious possibility, but the Germans for some reason seemed uninterested in conquering Britain. After the Fall of France, the military had told FDR to expect the UK to fall in six weeks. Instead, what followed was a colonial war that in many ways was not of great interest to the US. FDR worked at recovering his poise. He would need to project an aura of strength when his enemies arrived this afternoon. His destiny demanded it.

Afterword

This book is where our war veers away from World War Two as most readers know it. This section is where I explain why.

Britain: The British memory of World War Two runs Dunkirk, Battle of Britain, Battle of the Atlantic, El Alamein, D-Day, Final Victory. Britain stands alone against the full might of Hitler and wins, ending the war as one of the three superpowers. This historical memory has stayed with the English through sixty years since 1945, and was on prominent display during the Brexit Campaign. (You will note I segued from 'British' to 'English', but that's another discussion outside the purview of this book. The Celtic fringes have somewhat moved on, while much of English opinion is still rooted in historical memory of the last great victory of the British Empire).

Swept away from this view are defeats, an endless parade of defeats. Norway, Dakar, Greece, Crete, multiple times against Rommel, Malaya, Hong Kong, Singapore, the South China Sea, the East Indies, Burma, in the Atlantic into 1943, the slaughter of Bomber Command over Central Europe's skies, the Arctic convoys. And also, Britain ended the war bankrupt.

The war effort was sustained by bottomless US money and production, and the willingness of the Soviets to bleed endlessly as long as they killed some Germans in the process. From mid-1943 onwards, the British were forced to disband roughly a division a month to provide enough replacements to keep the rest fighting. The fiction of Britain as a superpower collapsed once Lend-Lease ended. The world preserved the courtesy of British power in numerous summit meetings and the British permanent seat on the UN Security Council. In fact the world was bipolar till 1991, US vs Soviet. The US then got its unipolar decade, after which we quickly evolved to our current bipolar Sino-American world order. Even the emerging potential European superpower is a Franco-German construct. The British never seriously committed to it. Nostalgia for 1945 was too great.

There is the one great exception. O'Connor's Western Desert Force and its victories over the hapless Italians. Those were quite real, but the context got lost over the decades. Britain went to war in 1939 with one of the world's great fleets, the beginnings of a world-class air force ... and an army that had been starved of money and prestige since Haig's Army Group had been demobilized in 1919. What ground strength Britain had, came back from Dunkirk with its tail between its legs and without its equipment. The machines could be recreated. By the autumn of 1940, the British were outproducing Germany in planes and tanks. By early 1941, those machines and a few brave men had beaten back the Blitz and begun to recreate a modern army. An Army that had victories in the Desert thanks to O'Connor's mostly professional Western Desert Force. Left unspoken (and perhaps not fully understood by the British government) was that they had beaten an Italy whose half-assed Army in Libya lacked the trucks, tanks, and supplies to fight a modern mechanized war. The commanders had no faith in Il Duce's grand schemes. They marched into the desert, entrenched, and sat there. O'Connor was able to pick off the strong points one by one. Churchill bullied the Cabinet to reinforce these victories with the only two functional armored divisions Britain had in the Home Islands, and a flood of planes, artillery, and the rest of the instruments of war.

This reinforced British Army then got its head handed to it repeatedly by a small German Afrika Korps and a revived Italian Army. The British whisk this all away by making Rommel into superman.

The story they sell openly was that Rommel was another Napoleon. He would have beaten anyone just as badly. He just happened to be fighting the British. False. Rommel was a good mobile division commander, in over his head at corps and then army-level command. He learned the craft of higher command, but it took Second Alamein to complete his schooling. Virtually any other Panzer general would have done at least 70% as well. The 70% was because one of Rommel's great virtues was maxing out on the German pattern of fast operational tempo. The British never managed to get the hang of fighting war at the German pace. To use the *observe, orient, decide, act* maxim from fighter combat as a template, the Germans just ran rings around them. By the time the British reacted to anything, the Germans had moved a few cycles further; so the British were always responding to an outdated concept of the true situation.

The British down to the end of the war never managed to really coordinate combined arms on a German level. They never even managed to reach the competences of Haig's troops in the Hundred Days of 1918. When they won, it was by numbers and firepower. In this book they lack both. The necessary quantities of tanks, planes, artillery pieces are in Britain. The war is in Egypt. They simply have no way to win, or even to reinforce quickly enough. Churchill had the better part of a year between Dunkirk and Rommel to start a large enough sustained river of equipment and trained divisions. In this ATL Britain has 90 days. London does not see this, and vetoes running away from the huge concentration of strength that is the Italo-German Panzer Army and attached massive air fleet.

Manchuria/China: I see Stalin as a Leninist True Believer at the Macro-Strategic level. World history is to him a living force dictated by class warfare, etc. It is at the operational level that I see him as essentially an opportunist. In OTL he stays fixated on Europe because Churchill fights Hitler to a draw in the Battle of Britain. So to Stalin, Germany seems weak enough to bully. Here, Germany goes from victory in France to victory in the South. In the meantime Zhukov and others have inflicted defeats on Japan in Mongolia and along the Manchurian frontiers. So the opportunity is to expand on these victories. This is also what is behind Stalin leaking key intelligence to the British. He wants to keep Britain in the war until after victory in China.

US Election: In our history, Willkie only turns to a rabid anti-intervention campaign in the last six weeks of the electoral struggle. This converted an easy FDR win into a harder-fought one. I am telescoping this via starting the America First Committee's major push earlier. Its strength was quite real, but because it ran its main public campaign between elections, it never had the bite it could have. The US public was anti-Nazi, but even more against another army of millions sent to die on foreign soil. They felt they had been tricked into World War One and were determined not to be suckers again. Because of this change in timing, I have Willkie, Lindy, and Coughlin coordinating. This ATL has the necessary synchronicity.

Brigade Strauss: Keep reminding yourself that this is a small force, not the main German war effort. Even in terms of the Afrika Korps, the NL Brigade is a minor add-on. Klaus just has the knack of being in the right place at the right time. On its surface, the fall of a major port intact is absurd. As absurd as the same thing happening at Singapore in 1942 and Antwerp in 1944. Antwerp is truly illuminating. A Germany being relentlessly hammered in the East, West, South, and over the skies of Germany does not destroy the occupied ports of Western Europe because it would look bad, would injure Germany's prestige, would mean admitting that the days when Germany could threaten Britain with invasion were gone, never to return. In other words, for absurd reasons. Even when the Normandy front collapsed and the Anglo armies were racing across Western Europe, the German commander of Antwerp awaits a formal order from Berlin that never comes. Oops.

What comes next: The next volume, *Jerusalem of Gold*, takes the war to Palestine and Sudan. To the merry band we now add Frauke, a lady on a mission of vengeance against everyone who never took her seriously.

Dramatis Personae

Historic (all death dates are OTL).

Abetz, Otto (1903-1958): Early Nazi from Strasser/left wing of the Party. Ambassador to Vichy and an ardent Francophile. In OTL he lost power as his patron von Ribbentrop did so and as any real prospect of Vichy alliance with Nazi Germany receded. In this ATL his authority remains because Vichy and Germany do become de facto allies, although never friends.

Adenauer, Konrad (1876-1967): Catholic politician under Weimar. Anti-Nazi but geeked a bit to minimize his situation, regain his civil service pension. Jailed for a time by the Nazis, but every time he was in trouble some friend from the old days minimized his sufferings or got him off. The Nazis knew he was oppositional and part of an opposition circle, but these Catholic groups never went operational. They were content to be prepared for the inevitable defeat. Organized Germany's post-war Catholic/conservative party the Christian Democrats / Christian Socials [in Bavaria]. He and Ludwig Erhard oversaw Germany's rehabilitation as West Germany/German Federal Republic, and the postwar economic miracle. Always had a bit of a blind spot postwar for people who had served Hitler, as long as they did not espouse postwar Neo-Nazi politics.

Atlee, Clement (1883-1967): Middle class reform type, who a generation earlier would have been a radical member of the Liberal Party. WW1 veteran with multiple war wounds. Rose slowly in the Labor leadership because he was hard-working, quite competent, and avoided the sort of ideological and factional fighting that characterized the party. As postwar prime minister he vastly expanded the British welfare state. Personally into simple living, he never understood how unpopular rationing and endless controls could be for the average voter.

Auchinleck, Claude (1884-1981): Indian Army officer, one of the few who commanded British forces other than Indian Army troops. Next to Slim, the best operational field commander the British produced in WW2. Relieved from Middle East command after the Gazala-to-First-Alamein campaign, when he insisted that 8th Army needed rest, reorganization, and reinforcements before launching a counteroffensive. Replaced by Montgomery, who took more time and more reinforcements than Auchinleck had asked for. But Montgomery was from the British, not Indian, Army. Auchinleck was sacrificed because of institutional rivalry between the two. This in turn made him a convenient scapegoat for the institutional failures of the British Army - especially as regards combined arms, handling of armored troops, and the inability of British corps and divisional commanders to manage their subordinate units. They were forever too slow to respond, and never able to coordinate their actions. Both were fatal defects when fighting Germans. Was commander of the Indian Army through the postwar partition crisis. He was the only important British official not in the tank for Nehru and Congress. Nicknamed 'the Auk'.

Balbo, Italo (1896-–1940): WW1 veteran. One of the founders of Italian Fascism. One of the creators of the Italian air force as a major service. Governor General of Libya, 1933. Did not support either the anti-Jewish laws or the Nazi alliance. Killed by Italian AAA while trying to land at Tobruk, 1940.

Bandera, Stepan (1909-1959): Ukrainian nationalist leader. Worked with the Nazis, who also imprisoned him. Postwar worked with the CIA. Co-founder of the Ukrainian Nationalist Organization OUN. Helped raise paramilitaries who worked with the Germans 1941-1943 before fighting everyone

(Soviets, Germans, Poles) afterwards and continuing after the end of the war under the UPA banner. The postwar campaign was funded and armed by the CIA, although the British MI-6 claim credit for the relaunch. Hated Poles, Jews, Russians, and Communists. His troops killed large numbers of all of them. A fanatic nationalist and an unpleasant person to anyone who opposed him, but charismatic and quite competent.

Beck, Ludwig (1880–1945): served as a staff officer, Western Front WW1. Backed the Nazis in the early 30's but never joined the Party. Fired as head of Army General Staff 1938 over his opposition to Hitler's military adventurism. Part of many anti-Nazi plots, including 1944 Bomb Plot where he was slated to be chief of state. Executed when the coup failed. Beck was smart and capable, but incredibly narrow-minded. As with many in his generation and class, he regarded the Nazis as gutter-trash. Was enraged when Hitler did not let himself be "guided" by the better sort of experts such as himself. Widely revered among the old Army officer corps, which is why I make him part of the junta. Beck's name would swing the old Reichswehr officers to the new regime. He never understood how his kind lost control of Hitler, and will be equally mystified over losing control of Heydrich.

Begin, Menachem (1913-1992): Betar from age 16. Graduated in law, University of Warsaw 1935. By 1939 had been head of Betar first in Czechoslovakia and then Poland. Fled with other cadres to Vilna ahead of the advancing Nazis. The return to Poland is ATL. In OTL he stays in Vilna, is arrested by KGB, does time in GULAG and then is released as part of Anders' Army. Exits Soviet Union through Persia to Palestine, where he is allowed by Polish command to exit the Free Polish forces to work fulltime with Irgun. Brilliant orator and hardline Revisionist Zionist. Extremely intelligent.

Beresford-Peirse, Noel (1887-1953): Military family. Artillery. Commanded 4th Indian Division to victory over the Italians. Commanded Western Desert Force/XII Corps against Rommel's first offensive. Sacked for mistakes of both subordinates and superiors. Spent the rest of his career in rear-area assignments. Competent but not especially skillful.

Bergonzoli, Annibale 'Electric Whiskers' (1884-1973): Successful Italian commander in Ethiopia. Less so in Spain, but one of the few not sacked for failure. Commanded a corps in North Africa. Captured by the Australians. The failure was not his fault. In this book the Italians have enough trucks plus enough German armor and air strength to win. In OTL they were sent as lambs to the slaughter by an inept Mussolini regime.

Beria, Lavrentiy (1899–1953): Old Bolshevik with a slightly checkered political past during the Civil War years. From Georgia, but not exactly Georgian (similar to Stalin in that respect). Number 2 at NKVD in 1938, then in charge a few months after. Effectively Stalin's Number 2 in WW2. Stalin told FDR at Yalta that Beria was "his Himmler". Compared to Himmler, Beria was smarter and far more competent. Might have been the most competent of Stalin's henchmen.

Bevin, Ernest (1881-1951): Major figure in the British trades union movement, who segues to being a Labor cabinet minister. The historic Bevin had an interest in foreign affairs and was postwar foreign minister. Mildly anti-Semitic and quite anti-Communist. A realist on the Empire and more so on both US and European relations.

Bigeard, Marcel (1916-2010): Commando sergeant 1940 campaign. Escapes to Africa. Given para training and sent back to head resistance unit. Gains nickname of Bruno (his radio callsign). Stays in postwar army Indochina and Algeria. One of the paratroop mafia that did the heavy fighting, and are featured in Larteguy's novels. Didn't take part in the putsches and plots that marked the end of the Algeria adventure. Stayed in the Army and retired as a Lieutenant General. Postwar was defender of the *harkis*, Algerian Muslims in French service. Broke with de Gaulle over this. Also at the center of the endless debates on torture during the Algerian Campaign. Bigeard defended the technique but denied ever doing it himself.

Bormann, Martin (1900–1945): Served in late 1918, but never saw action. In Freikorps. Did a prison stretch for an assassination. Joins the Nazis in 1927. Founded the Nazi Socialist Motor Corps when driving or fixing autos were relatively rare skill sets. Rose in the Party bureaucracy based on financial and administrative competence, plus a natural skill at currying favor. Became Number 2 to Hitler's Number 2, Hess. Assumed Hess's job, but not his title, when the idiot flew off to Scotland chasing a madcap peace plan. Used his control over access to Hitler and to the after-meeting memos to attain vast power. Mostly used this power to sabotage every other power-holder. Also sabotaged the war economy and manpower mobilization, currying favor with the Gauleiters. Last seen leaving the Bunker in one of the escape parties. Supposedly killed. Body supposedly found some decades later. Rumored to have been a Soviet agent. Rumored to have survived into the 1960's with a lavish dacha in the Moscow suburbs.

Bose, Subhas Chandra (1897-1945): Indian nationalist and radical activist. Head of Congress Party until ousted by Gandhi/Nehru in 1939. Bose escapes to Germany and forms an Indian National Army with Nazi and Japanese help. He dies in a convenient air crash at the war's end. Compared to Gandhi/Nehru he was more radical, had more ties to labor unions (and through them to COMINTERN), more strength in non-Hindi speaking Bengal and south India. Very smart, but unlucky in the foreign alliances he chose.

Bridges, Harry (1901-1990): An Australian-born seaman and socialist, Bridges came to the US in 1920. He joined the IWW and became a longshoreman. He was active in unionization and union politics from then until his death. US government repeatedly tried to expel him 1939-1942 as a Communist. They were never quite able to prove he was a formal member, although many of his associates were and he clearly followed the party line. The US Supreme Court ruled against his deportation in 1942. He was a firm anti-militarist from the Ribbentrop-Molotov Pact in 1939 to Barbarossa in 1941, after which he was a fanatic social patriot, advocating for more arms and aid to Russia. Turned against US foreign policy, once Hitler was defeated and thus US is no longer allied to the Soviet Union. Extremely able and a dedicated Soviet patriot.

Busse, Theodore (1897-1986): WW1 veteran. Reichswehr. General Staff. Staff officer to von Manstein 1940-1944. Rapid rise from commanding division, to corps, to army, last year and a half of the war. Commanded Ninth Army at Berlin. Postwar was West Germany's civil defense chief and a military historian. Generally well regarded, but not a flamboyant personality. His unit appears in the movie "Downfall", although not with the prominence of Steiner's.

Chekhova, Olga (1897–1980): Actress. Related to Chekhov by marriage. White Russian "refugee". Probably Soviet agent. Star in Berlin cinema. Probable mistress of Goebbels. Friendly socially with Hitler. Postwar she worked in East Germany then moved to Munich.

Chennault, Claire Lee (1890-1958): US Army Air Corps officer turned mercenary in China. Created with FDR's help the supposedly independent Flying Tigers who segued back to US service after Pearl Harbor. So did he. Tight with Chiang Kai-shek, and an airpower fanatic. Much better at PR than actual military leadership.

Chiang Ching-Kuo (1910-1988): Son of long-serving Chinese, then Taiwanese President for life/autocrat Chiang Kai-shek. Sent to Moscow for higher education 1925. A hostage after his father breaks with the Chinese left in 1927. Started out as a Trotskyite, but turned Stalinist prudently when Trotsky fell from favor. Sent back to China with Belorussian Communist wife in 1937. Not in favor because of decade in Moscow. Also because in Chinese terms a leftist, and a hard-ass on vice and corruption. Promoted on Taiwan to head of secret police. Ascended in stages to President for life (1978) after father's death in 1975. Created the vibrant Taiwanese economy and began the steps that turned Taiwan into a parliamentary democracy. Very bright and hard working, overcame amazing handicaps to come as far as he did.

Chiang Kai-shek (1889-1975): Military cadet who became one of the leaders of the KMT under Sun Yat-sen. Formed a cadre of loyalists based on a military academy he ran. At various times was a man of the left, right, and nationalist center. Ideology wasn't his thing. Neither was military command. He was very good at the sort of factional politics that allowed the KMT to run much of China and dominate the remaining warlords. Made extermination of the Communists, whom he failed to either co-opt or marginalize, a major feature of his rule. Ran them out of China proper into the fringes in Yan'an. This is turn triggered the Japanese to preempt and start the Sino-Japanese War of 1937-1945. Chiang avoids defeat but becomes what amounts to a regional warlord in the west (Chunking) with only a nominal hold on most of the local and provincial Nationalist forces. Kept in the war after Pearl Harbor by US money and equipment. Fails to master inflation or corruption postwar, leading his early successes against the Communists to dissipate into a near-total defeat. Flees to Taiwan with his remnant forces. Saved there by the start of the Korean War, which leads Truman to decide Chiang's regime might again be a worthwhile ally. USN sent to police Taiwan Straits, and Chiang's regime gets large-scale US aid. His fortes were factional politics and personal rectitude. Was not an especially great ruler or general.

Churchill, Winston (1874-1965): Winston is an iconic figure in the US for a handful of speeches, the Battle of Britain, and as a symbol of Britain standing up to Hitler. Part of the British victory myth version of WW2. Only period experts tend to remember his difficult personal habits (alcoholic, kept insane hours, made military decisions based on emotion rather than logic, etc.) or the long string of defeats 1940-1942. He essentially bankrupted the UK hoping something would turn up. USSR and then US entered the war (thanks far more to Hitler than Churchill) and the three Allied powers bludgeoned Nazi Germany to death. This series deals far more with the real man, warts and all, rather than the mythic figure of Their Finest Hour etc.

Ciano (Count), Gian (1903–1944): From a wealthy family. Bomber pilot in Ethiopian War. Mussolini's son-in-law. Cultivated a playboy's lifestyle. May have been lover/customer of Duchess of Windsor while in diplomatic service in Shanghai. Turned on Mussolini, 1943. Executed by Mussolini (at request of Nazis), 1944.

Cirillo, Enrico (1909 -): He's a real officer from the Libyan paratroop order of battle. The limited data we found for him gives him an accounting degree in 1926, parachute training in 1938, and the Bronze Medal for Military Valor in August 1941 for gallantry in the desert war. Retires in 1959 as a lieutenant colonel for medical reasons. Still alive in Rome as far as our researches show.

Corap, Andre (1878-1953): French professional officer. Did his line service with colonial units, his staff duties with Petain and Foch. Commanded the 9th Army in 1940. Made the goat for mistakes by others, chiefly Huntziger and Gamelin.

Costello, Frank (1891-1973): Born Francesco Castiglia in Calabria. Known as 'The Prime Minister of the Underworld'. Costello was a clean-hands type of gangster. He hired out the violence. His specialty was the intersection of the criminal enterprises, legitimate business, the 'Tammany Hall' Manhattan Democratic machine, and the police. Costello spread the bribes and greased the wheels for the bootlegging and gambling. When Luciano went to prison, Costello was his nominal heir (in practice, he just followed Luciano's orders from prison). Chased out of the top Manhattan job by more violent types in the 1950's but kept his money, his life and some of his income streams. Very bright, very affable, but lacked the ruthless quest for power more typical of Mafia bosses.

Coughlin, Charles (1891-1979): Canadian-born Roman Catholic priest. He was an extremely effective broadcaster and political writer. He hated Communism, capitalism (especially banking/finance), and internationalism. His political views were in the Catholic corporatist tradition. He clearly expressed sympathy for fascism and Nazism. He blamed the Jews for both international finance / the Depression, and Communism (like many in the period he saw Bolshevism as a Jewish plot against Christianity). His anti-banking views led to attacks on global finance which was based in Manhattan (Jewish and Anglophile) and the City of London. This led to a large following among Irish-Americans whose loathing for the British went back to the Potato Famine. In OTL he was in the process of being silenced by a combination of FDR and his bishop at the time. I have obviously chosen a somewhat different life path for the man.

Cunningham, Alan (1887-1983): Brother of the dead admiral from book 1. Fairly standard career OTL leading to his appointment as GOC East Africa. He defeated the Italians in Somalia and Ethiopia, leading to command of the 8th Army in Egypt. Sacked by his superior Auchinleck when he wanted to break off the Crusader Offensive. Had secondary and staff appointments for balance of WW2 and postwar. He was the one who took down the British flag at Haifa when Israel became independent. In this ATL he is moved to Egypt before the East African campaign, but his realism will let him do good service. Adequate field commander at best, but his strength was an unwillingness to risk severe losses or serious reverses.

Cunningham, Andrew (1883–1963): WW1 veteran. Commander Mediterranean Fleet, 1939. Beat his fleet half to death covering the British force on Crete and then in the evacuation when resistance collapsed. Disobeyed direct orders from Churchill and the Admiralty not to risk his capital ships, refused to leave the Army to its fate: "It takes His Majesty's Government three years to build a battle cruiser. It takes three hundred years to build a tradition. We are going in." First Sea Lord, October 1943. Oversaw naval demobilization and then retired, 1946.

Darlan, Francois (1881-1942): From an old naval officer corps family. Commanded artillery battery at Verdun. Rapid rise through ranks to supreme naval command by 1939. Wanted to continue the war in 1940 and threatened to lead the fleet out to fight beside the British in the runup to the French surrender. Promised Churchill that the French fleet would never be used against Britain. Never forgave the British for the attack on the French Fleet at Oran, and swung to a policy of collaboration with the Germans. By an accident of history, Darlan was in Algiers when the Americans landed in November, 1942. He reached a deal with Eisenhower, swinging the French Maghreb, West Africa, and all overseas French naval vessels to the Allies. French ships in Toulon were scuttled at his orders. Assassinated soon after by a royalist dupe in an Anglo-Gaullist plot. Very talented but quite self-impressed.

Davis, Benjamin O. Sr. (1880-1970): African-American. Managed to reach the rank of brigadier general in the Jim Crow pre-WW2 US Army. Eased out of combat command and used in variety of PR and advisory roles in WW2. He will have a somewhat different fate in this ATL. Extremely good service politician.

Davis, Benjamin O. Jr. (1912-2002): Son of first US Army African-American general. Founded and commanded the legendary Tuskegee Airmen in WW2. This unit broke the color line for US air service. Went on to be first African-American general in US Air Force.

de Gaulle, Charles (1890-1970): From the minor provincial aristocracy. From youth had intellectual pretensions. Hero in WW1 and then POW. Protégé of Petain's for most of the interwar period. Wrote a controversial book advocating a professional armored force in place of France's traditional conscript armies. Given a scratch division in the first part of the 1940 campaign, and performed better than he had any right to. Was rewarded with a minor cabinet post that he leveraged into creating the Free French movement. There have always been rumors that this was Petain's idea, as it gave France a foot in the British camp if the tide of war changed. Ungrateful to his Anglo-Saxon benefactors and near impossible to work with. Bungled his first try at politics post-WW2. Gets a second chance in 1958 when put into office by a parachute officers coup over the Algerian War. Backstabs his original backers, abandons Algeria, and manages to survive two further coup attempts and multiple tries to assassinate him. Created the current French 5th Republic as an elective monarchy. Survives the rebellions of 1968 but resigns in a huff in 1969 when his will is thwarted on relatively minor issues. Very tall, very brave, very arrogant, and in many ways destiny's darling.

de Lattre de Tassigny, Jean (1889–1952): WW1 veteran. Youngest divisional commander, Battle of France, highly successful. Vichy until Germans overrun the "Free Zone". Heads Free French 1st Army ETO 1944–1945. Moderately successful. Allowed his troops to loot and rape in several German cities at war's last days. Probably guilty of a massacre of French SS prisoners. Brilliant command in Indochina cut short by his untimely death. A protégé of Weygand. In this series, uses nom de guerre of François Kellermann, a general of the Napoleonic Era.

Deng Xiaoping (1904-1997): Moscow-trained cadre. In Moscow he also befriended Chiang's son. Maoist in the struggle with the Stalinists during and after Long March. Survived the Cultural Revolution to create the modern Chinese superpower out of that abyss.

Dewey, Thomas (1902-1971): Very able attorney and administrator. No charisma. He was derisively named 'the little man on the wedding cake' during his losing Presidential run in 1948. Was the front man for Eisenhower's successful theft of the 1952 Republican nomination from Taft. Dewey continued to be a behind-the-scenes organizer of the old money and Wall Street eastern progressive wing of the Republican party under Nelson Rockefeller. Dewey's initial fame came as a crusading district attorney in Manhattan fighting organized crime. He was a complete weasel and his most successful case, the conviction of Lucky Luciano, was based on perjured testimony and doctored evidence. His other big cases were cleaner but none was clean. He was an end-justifies-the-means type, and felt that the decent people owed neither due process nor any real justice to those he regarded as the enemies of society.

Dietl, Eduard (1890–1944): WW1 veteran. Freikorps veteran. Early Nazi. Hero of Narvik in 1940 campaign. In OTL, led 20th Mountain Army in the Arctic against the Soviets. Died in an air crash, 1944. Capable divisional commander. His army command was unsuccessful - whether that was due to his faults, or being given small resources to accomplish huge things across amazingly poor terrain, can be debated.

Dietrich, Sepp (1892–1966): WW1 veteran. Joins Nazis, 1928. Protégé of Hitler. Head of his SS bodyguards, LAH. Key role in Blood Purge. Inept commander of LAH (which grows from a regiment to brigade to division), France, Greece, Russia. Learned on the job. Good commander at corps/army level, Normandy and Ardennes. Often blamed for failures of his army in Ardennes, although the main problem was poor higher plan and abysmal road net.

Dill, John (1881-1944): Not the brightest light in the heavens, but ended up as Chief of Imperial General Staff after a fairly undistinguished career. He was charitably viewed as obstructionist and unimaginative in that office. Given a further promotion and sent to DC when the Combined Chiefs of Staff were created in 1942. Proved to be the only British senior general able to avoid condescending to the Americans, with the result that he got on well with Marshall and his team. Died of aplastic anemia.

Dilley, Bruno (1913-1968): Excellent pilot and officer.

Doenitz, Karl (1891–1980): WW1 veteran. Created Nazi U-boat service after Versailles limits were put aside by Hitler. Created the Wolfpack tactics. Head of Navy after Raeder. A Hitler groupie more than a Nazi. Fanatic anti-Communist and anti-Semite (with the usual caveat of protecting a few part-Jews who were senior naval officers). Hitler makes him head of state after his suicide. Acquiesces in the final surrender. Convicted at Nürnberg, in part for using the same U-boat tactics USN did in the Pacific. As rigid a martinet as Raeder.

Dolmazzo, Lorenzo (1886-1959): Italian Corps Commander in North Africa, and Corps /Army Commander in the Balkans. Negotiated collaboration agreements with Croat and Albanian nationalists. Competent.

Donator, Lev Mikhaylovich (1903-1941): Soviet cavalry general at divisional and corps level during 1941 campaign. One of the few successful Soviet commanders in that kidney-stone-of-a-year's campaign.

Eden, Anthony (1897-1977): One of the early architects of Appeasement before turning against it. A perpetual candidate for Prime Minister, he finally got the job and then lost it over Suez, one of the worst inept bungles in British history. He's one of those bright young men who doesn't age well and never quite makes the grade. Also somewhat contemptuous of Italians.

Eichmann, Otto Adolf (1906–1962): Oil salesman who joins Austrian Nazis and SS in 1932. Joins German SD in 1934. Made head of 'Jewish Department' (probably because he spoke Yiddish). Works at various emigration schemes, including helping terrorize Austrian Jews into fleeing in 1938 after reunion with Germany. Helps create ghettos in Poland. When Final Solution is implemented in 1942, he becomes a transportation bureaucrat, especially for the liquidation of Hungary's Jews in 1944. Goes back to Austria at war's end. Emigrates to Argentina 1950. Kidnapped from there by Israelis in 1960. Tried in Jerusalem and executed 1962. Originally post-trial opinion pegged him as a mere clerk, a faceless minion. Recent findings of his papers from Argentina show him as far more hardcore.

Eicke, Theodor (1892–1943): WW1 veteran. Failed policeman who became a security guard at I.G. Farben. Joined Nazis and SA, 1928. Joined SS, 1930. Forced to flee to Italy, 1932, over a bomb plot. Insane asylum, 1933, over internal Nazi politics (he fell afoul of a Gauleiter). Himmler pulled him out of mental hospital to be replacement commandant of Dachau. Converts the camp from sloppy SA model to the SS strict regime we all know. In Blood Purge, personally liquidates Röhm. Head of Camp Administration, thereafter. Forms corps of camp guards.   Recruits a division out of them when the war starts. Heads the division. Inept commander, frequent massacres of prisoners and civilians. KIA, 1943. Fanatic anti-Semite and anti-Bolshevik. Not a stable personality, but not the lunatic portrayed postwar.

Eisenhower, Dwight 'Ike' David (1890-1969): Career Army officer. Scary bright but a natural diplomat so he hid it well. Pro-level athlete in his youth. Workaholic. Rocketed from mid-level staff officer to Supreme Command (TORCH, Sicily, Salerno, D-Day, ETO), in good part from the diplomatic skills. He was the only senior US general who could disguise his loathing for the British (who loathed pretty much all the Americans and made no effort to hide it, especially Monty). Never managed to deal with de Gaulle, but that prickly personality fought with almost everyone. Not an especially good operational commander, but that could be due to overstretch - the inter-Allied and US Army politics were in themselves a full time job.   In OTL spent most of 1942-1945 looking over his shoulder for fear he'd be sacked. His paranoia was quite justified. This series will show Ike progressing via a more standard promotion route, which will emphasize some aspects of his personality that OTL did not bring out. For a start, Patton will loyally support him so there will be no great fear of being sacked. Plus he actually gets to learn the operational craft instead of getting parachuted into a supreme commander slot.

Fallaci, Oriana (1929–2006): From a family of political resisters. Served in the partisans, WW2. Famous journalist, first of the left but turned anti-Islamist late in life. The Oriana character in the book is loosely based on her. VERY loosely.

Farley, James (1888-1976): Farley was a wheeler-dealer politician from New York City who became FDR's political fixer for his first two terms. FDR was noted for his casual cruelty to his subordinates. As part of FDR's coy cat and mouse game about a third term, Roosevelt had dangled the possibility of Farley being his anointed successor in 1940. FDR then snatched away the prize and refused to do the personal handholding needed to pacify this very important minion.

Fegelein, Hermann (1906-1945): Former cavalryman and Bavarian state policeman. Run out of police for stealing exam questions/answers. Early Nazi and SS man. Father ran a riding school and Hermann was a skilled rider. The skills had limits; he failed to qualify for the Berlin Olympics. Toady of Himmler's. Given command of an SS cavalry regiment for the Polish Campaign. Involved with massacres, mostly of Polish elites. Court-martialed for theft and fraud. Himmler quashed proceedings. Broke the race laws, but again protected by Himmler from Heydrich. Barbarossa saw the regiment upped to brigade strength and again used as an anti-partisan/ethnic cleansing force. Committed to combat, Fegelein proved to be inept. He got results, burned his unit out and got himself wounded. He would do the same with new units 1942 and 1943. Married Eva Braun's sister and sucked up to Bormann as well as Himmler. Fegelein was shot near the end in Berlin for desertion. He was an alcoholic and a thief with no officer training, but he was socially adept and good at ingratiating himself with superiors. In this ATL he lacks Himmler to protect him and dies sooner.

Fleming, Ian (1908–1964): Eton. Left Sandhurst after one year, due to VD. Failed foreign service exam. Worked in journalism and finance. Made a naval intelligence officer, 1939, purely due to family connections. Was involved with spies, commandos, Enigma. Postwar journalist who wrote a series of spy novels about a man named James Bond.

Fleming, Peter (1907–1971): Older brother of Ian. Successful British adventurer, journalist, and travel writer. In WW2 was reserve officer, Grenadier Guards. Served in Norway, Greece, China, Far East/South Asia. Involved with commandos, guerrillas (included preparations for guerrillas in UK in the event of German invasion), spies and various classified intelligence operations. Literary executor for his brother.

Ford, Gerald (1913–2006): 40th President of the US. In OTL, was in Yale Law School in 1940 where he helped found what became the America First Committee. The trip to Europe and work on the Hoover Relief Agency is quite fictional, but fit his views and those of his associates.

Frank, Hans (1900-1946): Old Party comrade and Hitler's personal attorney. Made Governor General of the General Government (the part of occupied Poland not formally annexed to the Reich). Frank was somewhat inept, preoccupied with factional infighting, and fairly corrupt. Convicted and hanged at Nuremberg. He is executed in 1940 in this ATL for corruption and because Heydrich doesn't like him.

Freitag, Fritz (1894-1945): Police officer in Polish campaign who transferred to Waffen SS. Did staff work and line command at regimental, brigade, and divisional level. Did both combat and anti-partisan work. Committed suicide while in US custody.

Gandhi, Mohandas K. (1897-1945): Trained attorney, Indian nationalist agitator, and prize kook.   His weird mix of non-violence, rejection of large scale production of any sort (he seemed to prefer going back to village artisans), vegetarianism, and weird asexual lifestyles fascinated progressive Westerners and the Indian rural classes. They also drove Nehru and the other professionals in the Congress Party near insane.

Geloso, Carlo (1879-1957): Staff officer WW1. Joins Fascists early in postwar. Division commander in Ethiopia. Commands an army against the Greeks. Falls out with Germans over their heavy-handed anti-partisan tactics. POW 1943-1945 first of Nazis and then Soviets. Not linked with Salo Republic. Smart planner, but not good at the factional politics of OTL's Fascist regime.

Godwin-Austin, Alfred (1889-1963): British general officer commanding in Somaliland during the 1940 Italian invasion,. Godwin-Austin prioritized getting his outnumbered troops away cleanly from overwhelming Italian forces. Churchill felt that this was a coward's way out; wanted a major battle and a casualty count to show determination. Commanded a division in East Africa and a corps in the Western Desert. Did well with both, but resigned after a command quarrel with his army commander. Churchill kept him from ever getting a field command again. In this ATL his OTL commander from East Africa, Cunningham, brings him to Egypt where he will be his usual prickly but competent self.

Goebbels, Joseph (1897-1945): No war service, due to physical disability (short leg /club foot). Short and fairly ugly. Compulsive womanizer. University graduate and failed author/journalist. Successful as professional Nazi Party official and propagandist. Good public speaker. Bureaucratic empire-builder and fanatic Hitler loyalist. Commits suicide with Hitler in the Bunker 1945.

Goerdeler, Carl (1884-1945): a monarchist and conservative beloved to the circles around General Beck that kept trying to kill Hitler. He was chancellor-designate had the Bomb Plot worked. When caught gave the Gestapo every name he could think of without even being subject to torture. He was in many ways all too typical of the 'resistance circles' who mostly lived in their own self-referential world where somehow the Kaiser would return and the madness would end. But for Stauffenberg and a small group of more active officers, they would never have gotten past muttering to each other about the gangster government.

Göring, Hermann (1893–1946): WW1 ace pilot with legendary Flying Circus. Early Nazi. Hero at Feldherrnhalle when Adolph ducked and covered. Wounded there. Became a morphine addict while a fugitive (had to keep constantly on the move instead of getting wounds properly treated). First wife was a Swedish aristocrat, the second a Berlin film star. In many ways was the "respectable" face of the Nazis during their rise to power. Founded Luftwaffe. Good bureaucratic empire-builder, but disliked doing the actual work. Libertine, art collector, cross-dresser, probably bisexual. Loved speeches, dressing up, and the accoutrements of wealth and power. Nickname: Fat Hermann.

Guderian, Heinz (1888–1954): WW1 veteran. Freikorps. Iron Division. Reichswehr. Helped found the Panzer troops. A favorite of Hitler until late 1941. Sacked for retreating against orders. Held staff positions of high title, but little power 1943–1945. Sacked before the end after a fight with Hitler. Helped organize the Bundeswehr post-WW2. Intelligent, but did not follow orders or play well with others, both characteristics he shared with Rommel.

Haber, Fritz (1868-1934): German Jewish Nobel Prize winner. His Haber-Bosch process was the key to German ability to continue manufacturing artificial fertilizer and high explosives during WW1 despite the British blockade on Chilean nitrates. Father of gas warfare. German patriot. Fled Nazis 1933 and died shortly thereafter.

Halder, Franz (1884–1972): Staff and then General Staff officer, WW1. Head of OKH 1938–1942. Half-hearted involvement in the early anti-Hitler plots, but bowed out before the 1944 Bomb Plot. Arrested anyway, but not executed. Worked postwar as historian for US Army. Capable. One of the few higher Army officers to take any interest in the Mediterranean Theater.

Halifax, Lord [given name is Edward Wood] (1881-1959): Very tall, very aristocratic, quite rich but a bit of a miser. One of the architects of Appeasement. Refused to be Prime Minister after Chamberlain, thus paving the way for Churchill. Headed the faction in the 1940 Cabinet and Tory Party which wanted to negotiate a peace with Hitler after Dunkirk. Served loyally through WW2 and after as a major Conservative Party figure.

Harris, Arthur (1892-1984): Head of RAF Bomber Command 1942-1946. Known to the London Press as Bomber Harris and to his subordinates as Butcher Harris. He was a strategic bombing fanatic who responded to the failures of his campaigns with a mixture of bluster and lies. All his raids managed to accomplish was strategic attrition on Germany via production and manpower diverted to AAA guns and night fighters. As his planes couldn't hit a target much smaller than a metropolitan area, he invented a strategy of burning down cities which somehow was going to cut into German production by destroying the workers' housing. Opposed having his planes tasked to Army support (Normandy), or to actual economic targets such as oil production or transportation. His Rhodesian connection comes from having emigrated there from Britain at age 17. His air crews sustained casualties worse than the assault waves in Haig's less successful WW1 offensives.

Hausser, Paul (1880–1972): WW1 veteran, general staff on Eastern Front. Retired Reichswehr, 1932, with rank of Lieutenant General. Joined Stahlhelm, and from there SA, and then Waffen SS. Helped create Waffen SS. Rose from division command in France, 1940, to corps, then army and finally army group. Best operational commander the Waffen SS produced. Worked for US Army historical division under Halder postwar. Nickname: Uncle Paul.

Hess, Rudolph (1894–1987): Hitler's Secretary and Deputy Führer. In OTL, flies to Scotland, 1941, as part of an insane peace plan. Bisexual or homosexual, accounts vary. May have been Hitler's lover, but then the same is alleged about Speer. Supposedly Bormann was the biological father of Hess's children. Nickname: Fräulein Anna.

Heydrich, Reinhard (1904–1942): Junior naval officer expelled for "dishonorable conduct" (broke an engagement with one girl to court and marry another). This left him in 1931 with a Nazi bride-to-be and no job. Her connections got him a job interview with Himmler. Rose rapidly in the SS from a combination of raw intelligence and extreme competence. Founded the intelligence arm of the Nazi Party, the SD, in 1931. Head of the Gestapo in 1934 and all of Party and state security agencies by 1936. Consolidates this in a meta-agency, RSHA, in 1939. Accused several times of having Jewish blood, a taint he never quite shook. In OTL, wounded in 1942 by Czech assassins in the pay of the British (they would say they were resistance fighters and Free Czechs, but assassin is descriptive; saying the Nazis were evil does not make using killers in civilian clothes into a wartime attack instead of an assassination). Died in hospital, quite possibly on orders of Himmler to his doctors, who were sent by Himmler to take charge of the case. Himmler was believed to be terrified of him. Virtually all the higher Nazis were afraid of him as well, as he had blackmail files on them all. Ruthless, amoral ... and the only competent bureaucrat among the higher Nazis. Hence my use of him in this series. Highest historic rank: Obergruppenführer and General of Police. In this ATL he is Reichsführer-SS and Deputy Chancellor, so far. Nicknames: The Blond Beast; The Man with the Iron Heart.

Himmler, Heinrich (1900–1945): Did officer training in WW1, but no active service. Involved with SA and Nazi Party. Failed chicken farmer who became a fulltime Party official. Lapsed Catholic who dived headfirst into occult, Nordic magic, and similar outre circles. Founded SS. Good bureaucratic empire-builder but poor administrator. Threw up after watching a mass execution. Betrayed Hitler in 1945 in absurd scheme to have the West make him head of a German government. Committed suicide when captured by the British.

Hindenburg (von), Paul (1847–1934): Half of the governing duo in WW1 with Ludendorff after major victories in the East. President of the German Republic, 1925–1934. A reactionary even by the standards of his social class and age, he was mostly a figurehead in the key years of the early 1930's.

Ho Chi Minh / Nguyen Ai Quc (1890-1969): No one is really sure how much of his 'past' is true - or even if it is the same person for all the times. As with Kim Il Sung, the party names were often identities of convenience swapped out among operatives. However, someone answering to these names created the Viet Minh post-WW2 and led the party/regime that fought first the French and then the Americans to stalemate.

Hopkins, Harry (1890–1946): Social worker. Active in various relief projects during the New Deal. One of the voices to the left of FDR within the administration, but not as extreme as Henry Wallace or Eleanor Roosevelt. By 1940, de facto number 2 to FDR, replacing Farley. Headed Lend-Lease. Also, FDR's frequent emissary to Stalin. Pro-Soviet, but it is uncertain whether he was a sympathizer or an active agent.

Horthy, Miklos (1868–1957): Austro-Hungarian admiral, WW1. With French help, formed "National Army" in 1919 to oppose Red regime in Budapest. Led two-year "White Terror" after Reds expelled by Romanian invasion. Although a reactionary, Horthy himself was never a radical right fanatic. Instead, he had an uneasy alliance with them, which ended in him reining in their pogroms. He became regent of the Hungarian Kingdom, whose "king" was barred by the Allies from returning. The radicals formed an ever-shifting grouping of small splinter oppositional parties divided mostly on personalities. Horthy had some sympathy for Fascist Italy, but none for Nazi Germany. He bowed to the inevitable after 1940, but was at best a halfhearted ally. When the war turned against Hitler, he tried (and failed) to change sides twice. A prisoner of the Nazis, he was sheltered by the Americans from extradition and execution postwar.

Hoover, John Edgar (1895-1972): created the FBI as we know it today out of a prior weak Federal police agency. A brilliant bureaucratic in-fighter. Also a slimy weasel even by DC standards. Compulsive collector of dirt on important people. Extreme publicity hound. Alleged to be transvestite, gay, and/or asexual. Which, if any, he was, really doesn't matter in terms of this ATL.

Huntziger, Charles (1880-1941): World War I service in Middle East and Balkans. Commander French 2nd Army at Sedan 1940. His long list of errors lost France the war. This was hidden at the time by higher commanders who thought well of him. In this ATL the German after-action reports make reality clear to Weygand and France's higher commanders.

Jinnah, Mohammed Ali (1876-1948): Attorney and labor leader. Was with Congress before opting for Muslim separatism. Played the politics of the run-up to independence/partition better than Nehru, although the British Viceroy Mountbatten was totally on Nehru's side. Father of modern Pakistan.

Skilled and smart but not as slick as he thought he was. Was not very good at accepting the inherent power disparities between the two communities.

Juin, Alphonse Pierre (1888-1967): Career officer. Family were rankers, not officers. Born in Algeria and always regarded it as part of France. Spoke Arabic. Did excellent service with 15th Motorized Division in the spring campaign. At Darlan's orders, negotiated the armistice with US forces after the TORCH landings. Commanded French Corps in Italy where it essentially won 4th Casino. Never able to control mass rapes by his Moroccans in Italy or Southern France. Chief of Staff after liberation of Paris. Opposed conduct of Indochina War, refused command twice. Served as an early NATO commander. Loyal to de Gaulle despite Algerian betrayal. Excellent field commander, good administrator.

Kaltenbrunner, Ernst (1903–1946): Austrian. Law degree. Childhood friend of Eichmann. Joined Nazis in 1930, SS in 1931. Party leader by 1934. Headed security services in Austria after reunification with Germany. Succeeded Heydrich as head of RSHA. Convicted at Nürnberg and executed.

Keitel, Wilhelm [Nickname *LaKeitel* – pun on German *Lakai*, *"Lackey"*] (1882–1946): WW1 veteran. Artillery officer. Helped organize Freikorps postwar. Staff officer in Reichswehr. Ran OKW from beginning to end. Sentenced and hanged at Nürnberg. Total toady to Hitler, and a cypher in terms of the actual war.

Keller, Alfred (1882–1974): Kesselring's number 2 in the 1940 Western Campaign. In this series, he is the hero of first Budapest and then Malta.

Kesselring, Albert (1885–1960): Artillery officer, WW1 (both fronts). General staff, 1917. Involuntary transfer to Air Force, 1933 (Air Force and Waffen SS both stole officers from the Army). Commanded air fleets in Poland, the West, Blitz, Barbarossa, and Mediterranean. Commanded army group in Italian campaign, 1943–1945. Successful with both service forces. VERY fond of luxury accommodations and food. Optimist, good people-person to equals and superiors, but often high-handed with subordinates. Art lover.

King, Martin Luther Jr. (1929-1968): Legendary African-American civil rights leader and martyr.   In this series he will have his call to the ministry at age 11, which is quite young but far from unheard of in black church circles. He and his father are introduced briefly in book 2 but their further adventures in China will be a plot line in the books to come.

King, Martin Luther Sr. (1899-1984): African-American civil rights leader best known for his son's legendary career. He actually was a major figure in his own right as both a churchman and part of the multi-decade crusade against Jim Crow.

Kleber, Emilio [actually Manfred Stern] (1896-1954): Born in Austrian Ukraine to a Jewish family. POW in WW1. Becomes a Bolshevik while a prisoner. Red Partisan officer during Russian Civil War. Fought in the Far East. Military academy graduate post-civil war, after which he goes to work for GRU in the US and China. Sent to Spain for its Civil War. Is given credit as savior of Madrid in 1936 where he leads XI International Brigade. Promoted to lead 45th International Division. Sacked for its failures (which in fact were due to poor training, and near insane orders from higher commanders). Recalled to Moscow in 1939, tried as a traitor (as were most of the Spanish veterans) and sent to the GULAG where he dies in 1954. In this series he is recalled to duty as "Kleber" to head a new 45th International Division where he essentially commits suicide by enemy action. He was probably not suited for higher unit command (his entire prior career being as an intelligence operative), but a military genius on the order of Napoleon couldn't have redeemed the FUBAR that was the Spanish Republic.

Klingenberg, Fritz (1912-1945): Waffen SS officer. Captured the city of Belgrade with five men. The ultimate lead-from-the-front combat hero .

Kluge (von), Günther (1882–1944): WW1 veteran, staff officer. Reichswehr. Very well-regarded among senior officer corps. Competent army and army group commander. Corrupt and a weasel. Toadied to Hitler while tolerating anti-Hitler plots by his staff. Avoided committing to Bomb Plot, but was compromised by his ties to major plotters. Committed suicide when recalled to Berlin.

Konev, Ivan Stepanovich (1897-1973): Soviet Marshal. Bolshevik from 1919. Survived the purges and the early years of WW2. Learned from his early mistakes. Better Front (Soviet army group equivalent) commander than Zhukov.

Laval, Pierre (1883-1945): Lower middle class origins. Attorney. Socialist. Married up, his wife being related by marriage to Alice Roosevelt among others. Pacifist, but honored draft notice. Discharged for bad veins. Brother KIA. Advocated peace but, although on arrest list, was spared for political reasons. Drifts to the right post-WW1. Stayed a friend of labor and of conciliation between the classes. Also got rich in this period. As Prime Minister kept the US Depression away from France for two years, then triggered a European collapse in a burst of nationalism over bailing out an Austrian bank. Driven from office for trying to appease Italy over Ethiopia. Against WW2. Drifts much further right, once out of office. Gets back in the Cabinet via Petain. Prime Minister for a time in Vichy. Supports the Nazis. Whether this is conviction, expediency, or spite within Vichy's bottomless factional disputes is still debated. Sham trial postwar, executed. He started as a man of principle, and aged into a complete weasel on the Lloyd George or FDR level. Important in this series because he acquires Heydrich's backing, and thus is immune to Petain's constant changes of mood on his subordinates.

'Leclerc', Philippe Francois Marie Leclerc de Hauteclocque (1902-1947): From the traditional military class. Rallied to de Gaulle, which socially estranged him from most of his class which stayed loyal to Vichy until the Americans landed in North Africa in late 1942. Made a legendary march across the Sahara with a small brigade to fight with the British in Egypt. Commanded the 2nd Armored Division in the West 1944-1945. Violated orders to liberate Paris. Tended to be disobedient to higher commanders, American and French alike. Liberated Strasbourg in Alsace. Often under US command, because he and the French First Army commander de Lattre de Tassigny (the one commanding the Sons of Oran in this series) disliked each other. Murdered captive French SS men from the Charlemagne Division at the end of WW2. Led the French back to Indochina postwar, but was reassigned when he argued for a political settlement. Died in an air crash in 1947. Good officer but a most difficult personality.

Lindbergh, Charles (1902-1974): Famous aviator and aviation expert. The accusations that he was pro-Nazi and an extreme anti-Semite were both false. He was, however, a Fortress America Isolationist and detested dual loyalties. The version of Lindbergh in this book compresses his public views in terms of time but in my opinion roughly describes them. He was a man on a mission.

Lloyd George, David (1863-1945): The last Liberal Prime Minister and one of Britain's great social reformers. Laid the foundations of the modern British welfare state. Extremely effective executive (Minister of Munitions in WW1 as prime example). Also one of the worst two-faced weasels in Britain's long political history. His betrayals and reversals caught up with him after he lost his post as Prime Minister in 1922. He spent the next two decades in the public eye but also the political wilderness. He reunited and then destroyed his Liberal Party. He was an ardent appeaser, but again there is the weasel problem. Most of Britain's political class believed he would have advocated anything and promised anything to anyone just for another term in high office. They were probably right. Has often been tagged as one of the two most likely candidates to be Britain's Petain had the Germans occupied the British Isles. That's probably accurate. Extremely bright and verbal, but was not to be trusted with money or around women.

Luciano, Charles 'Charlie' or 'Lucky' (1897-1962): Born Salvatore Lucania in Sicily. Family came to Manhattan when he was a young boy. Turned to crime early and worked his way up the ladder during Prohibition to Boss of all the Bosses by 1931. He created the structure of the Five Families and the National Commission, all of this enforced by the Brownsville Boys/Murder Incorporated. Framed by Dewey on a prostitution conspiracy which was absurd on its face. (A boss simply didn't do collections on his own, or any of the things Dewey manufactured evidence of. There were multiple levels of cutouts for that.) Released as part of a wartime deal for labor peace on the New York docks, and Sicilian Mafia aid for the 1943 US invasion. Deported to Havana, Cuba. Under US pressure Cuba deported him to Italy. Extremely smart and ruthless; but loyal to a small cadre of associates, some of whom were not Italian. Charlie understood that in the US, it's about money, not bloodlines.

Lusena, Umberto (1904–1944): Of Jewish descent. Father was a general. Umberto was a legionnaire with D'Annunzio. Trained paratrooper. Fought the Germans in 1943 with Royal Army and afterward with partisans. Captured, tortured, and executed.

Lutze, Victor (1890-1943): Early Hitler loyalist. Turned on Röhm. Rewarded with SA top job, and kept it as a sinecure until his death in an auto accident.

Maletti, Pietro (1880-1940): Some WW1 service but from 1917 onwards most of his career was in Libya except for good service in the Ethiopian War. OTL he was killed in the O'Connor offensive leading a mechanized force. Here he is commanding Libyans - at whose military quirks he is expert.

Manstein (von), Erich (1887–1973): From old Prussian military family, born Erich von Lewinski. Adopted by a childless relative from same class so had four parents. WW1 veteran. General Staff. Was the author of the Ardennes campaign concept in 1940, which he pushed through outside official channels. Probably best operational field commander in WW2, especially at the army group level. A military technocrat, willing to overlook the regime's crimes and be complicit in them.

Manstein (von), Ernst (1869-1944): Relative of the field marshal. Run out of the Kaiser's Army when he converted to Judaism. Active in the arts world and his city's Jewish community. Hounded by the Nazis in OTL. In this series, his relative chooses to revive his career.

Marshall, George Catlett (1880-1959): On Pershing's operations staff at AEF. Planned Meuse-Argonne offensive. VMI graduate Marshall was that rarity, a non-West Pointer who achieved high rank in the American army. Excellent military planner, especially in terms of relations with industry and Congress. His protégés were often less than stellar, starting with Leslie McNair and John C.H. Lee. He created an army on the model of Petain's 1917 French. The US won on massed artillery firepower.

Meir, Golda (1898-1978): American-born Labor Zionist apparatchik. Her US passport allowed her to be useful in diplomatic missions. Excellent at fund-raising in the US. Eventually became PM. Intelligent, diligent, but not especially effectual except at US fund-raising.

Messe, Giovanni (1883–1968): Helped create Arditi in WW1. Commanded motorized brigade in Ethiopian War. Corps commander in Greek War and Eastern Front. Took over the Italo-German Panzer Army command from Rommel in Tunisia. Served Royalist Italy after the side-switch in 1943. Nickname: The Italian Rommel (quite deserved).

Mohnke, Wilhelm (1911-2001): Joined the Party and the SS young, and shot up through the ranks. Seems to have been a True Believer but not the foaming maniac variety. Excellent combat record

Poland, the West, Normandy, Ardennes, Alsace, Berlin. Massive combat wound from Yugoslav air attack in 1941 kept him out of the Ost Front. Helped form the 12th SS HJ Division in 1943. Mohnke was one of the type that gave the Waffen SS its reputation. Excellent combat commander / leader of men, but heedless of casualties to his own unit. The mission was everything. Also kept being associated with massacres of prisoners. Managed to avoid war crimes prosecution mostly by luck. Highest formal rank was division commander. Highest posting was commander of the defense of Hitler's Bunker during the Siege of Berlin. Captured by the Soviets, and treated poorly but somehow survived the NKVD's abuse. Kept his head down after release, working various private sector jobs. In this series his 1940 massacre of British POW's in the runup to Dunkirk comes back to bite him, getting him shuttled off to Libya with a warning that the next report of dead POW's will result in summary execution.

Montgomery, Bernard Law 'Monty' (1887-1976): WW1 veteran, line and staff. Father was Bishop of Tasmania. Division commander Dunkirk Campaign. Performed well. Tasked for never-carried-out operations to invade Azores, Cape Verde Islands and Eire (which is how we get him available as a replacement for Dakar). Was a good training officer in the UK at Corps level. Clearly over his head at army and army group command. He was good at training, troop morale, and personal PR. He was ponderous in positional battles (Second Alamein, Normandy), and purely inept in mobile operations (pursuit of Rommel, Race Across France, Market Garden). His lies, evasions, and failures in clearing the Scheldt probably added months to WW2 in Europe. His rudeness and refusal to obey orders brought Ike to the brink of sacking him multiple times. The latest theory for his lack of social skills is Asperger's Syndrome. The London Press was in love with him, and this saved his job several times such as the idiot Battle of the Bulge speech where he essentially claimed he won the battle despite Ike and the Americans.

Müller, Gestapo (1900–1945?): Given name was actually Heinrich, but there were two Heinrich Müllers who were SS generals. WW1 service as spotter pilot. Bavarian political policeman until the Nazi takeover in 1933. Turned his coat and became a protégé of Heydrich's. Does not join the Nazi Party itself until 1939. Careerist and not especially brilliant, but hard working. Probable Soviet agent. Alleged to have died during the breakout from the Bunker. Also alleged to have retired to Moscow. Complete weasel.

Nasser, Gamal (1918-1970): One of the Free Officers plotters who overthrew the Egyptian monarchy 1952. Nasser was a charismatic orator, but a complete clod as a national leader. Had no judgment on policy or personnel. His mistakes and vanities made Egypt the bureaucratic basket case it still is today.

Nebe, Arthur (1894-1945): WW1 veteran. Career policeman who opportunistically joined the Nazi Party and SS in the early 30's. Headed the Kripo/Criminal Police. Involved with prewar euthanizing of "unfit" citizens. Headed Einsatzgruppe B in Belarus and Smolensk. Succeeds Heydrich as head of Interpol on Heydrich's death in 1942. Associated with the 1944 Bomb Plot against Hitler. Went into hiding after its failure. Betrayed by a mistress, he was arrested and executed in early 1945. He was competent, but a total weasel.

Nehru, Jawaharlal (1889-1964): Attorney, socialist, and the organization man who held Congress together and advanced it to power. Bright, somewhat charismatic, but always in Gandhi's shadow until the assassination. Nehru's socialist fixations and bureaucratic mindset made independent India into the shambling rubber-stamp mild kleptocracy it became. The nation is still digging out from his initial mistakes. They are also saddled with an intractable problem in Kashmir because he clung to that state despite its Muslim majority.

Nicolussi-Leck, Karl: (1917-1980) – From South Tyrol (Austrian land given to Italy at Versailles). Nazi propagandist. Joins Waffen SS 1940. In OTL ends war as Hauptmann and tank ace. Successful career in agricultural machinery post-war, first in Peron's Argentina and then back in South Tyrol. Fluent in Italian.

O'Connor, Richard (1889-1981): Born in India to a military family, but by service British Army rather than Indian Army. Good WW1 record, mostly as a signals officer. Rises steadily during interwar period to divisional command in Jerusalem just before outbreak of war. Command moved to Mersa Matruh in Egypt as core of what would become Western Desert Force. Even considering all the Italians' mistakes, ran a brilliant campaign in eastern Libya netting terrain and huge numbers of prisoners. Advance short-circuited by Churchill's Greek adventure. Captured during Rommel's counterattack, and spent two years as POW in Italy. Given corps command for D-Day. Performs decently, but sidelined and then sacked by Monty, who had no use for officers outside his clique from 8th Army and Alamein. Promoted to full general thereafter while doing garrison service in India.

Patton, George Smith Jr. (1885-1945): Professional officer, scion of an aristocratic, rich California family with Dixie roots. Cavalry, but led first US motorized force in Mexico 1916 and first tank brigade in France 1918. Good Army politician but always regarded as 'difficult'/prima donna. Different reasons than Rommel, but similar effects on superiors who had to deal with him. No strategic sense but a fine operational and tactical commander. Utterly fearless under fire. Never able to subordinate his chasing of personal glory/his destiny to wider command and national goals. Bit of a flake on reincarnation and similar. Ignored supply and administration by picking good subordinates and letting them do their jobs. In OTL almost selfdestructed his career over slapping incidents where he struck soldiers in hospital. Was sidelined at the tail end of the Tunisian Campaign over press complaints about his obsessions with Mickey Mouse regular army discipline (wearing neckties with the uniform, etc.). He was simply a 19th century mind who was never going to fit into New Deal populism. Press loved him for good copy but hated him personally as a spoiled rich kid. In this series, sending him to China gets him out of a lot of this negative feedback – everyone in the ranks volunteered for China service, and many are foreigners serving under the US flag.

Paulus, Friedrich (1890–1957): WW1 veteran. Served with Freikorps and then Reichswehr. Staff officer until he assumed command of Sixth Army for Stalingrad Campaign. Not a decisive leader or good field commander, but the blame for Stalingrad rests with Hitler's obsessions. Captured by Soviets and served as a stooge for them in their Free Germany front. Given a sinecure in new East German military. Related to the Romanian aristocracy.

Peiper, Joachim/Jochen: (1915-1976): Joined SS at 18 on advice of a family friend, army General von Reichenau. Became Himmler's adjutant 1938 after a tour with LAH. Served briefly with LAH during French campaign, then went back to Himmler's staff. Helped with administrative work in support of Einsatzgruppen. Back with LAH from October 1941 to end of war. His battalion earned the nickname 'the blowtorch battalion' for its treatment of Soviet villages. Good combat record to end of war, but repeatedly involved with massacres of prisoners, partisans, civilians. Responsible for Malmedy Massacre of US POW's during Bulge. Pieper was from the old SS school of command: overaggressive, and his own casualties be damned. Sentenced to death for Malmedy. Did eleven-plus years before release. Good career with Porsche and then as a professional translator of English military histories into German while residing under an assumed name in France. Outed by French Communist press and assassinated by 'activists'.

Percival, Arthur (1887-1966): Classic example of the Peter Principle. Excellent intelligence and staff officer who proved a disaster as a field army commander in Malaya and Singapore 1941-1942. Yes he had a difficult situation and some questionable subordinates/colleagues (RAF and RN), but he mishandled difficult situation into massive disaster. Reflect on why as author I gave him command in Kenya …

Petain, Henri Philippe Benoni Omer Joseph (1856-1951): Hero of Verdun. Savior of France after the 1917 army mutinies. Not from the traditional military aristocracy. Bachelor and womanizer into his 60's. Marries one of the girlfriends in 1920. Her family had previously rejected Petain because his family lacked social status. Fought against defense funding cutbacks and reduction of military service time during interwar period. De Gaulle was his protégé during this period before they had a falling out over a relatively petty matter. Made ambassador to Franco's Spain winter 1939. As such he avoided the blame for the Fall of France. Brought into the government to provide political cover to those seeking a separate peace, June 1940. They wanted a front man, but he outplayed them and became dictator of Vichy (Vichy politics are complex, and this is a massive simplification). Was against the British but never pro-German. The Nazis essentially kidnap him during the retreat from France in 1944. He voluntarily returns in 1945. Tried for treason and collaboration. Sentenced to death, commuted to fortress arrest. Lapses into senility in the late 1940's. He was an excellent field commander and commander-in-chief, excelling at every level from brigade to supreme command. He was also more than a bit of a pessimist and very definitely a man of the 19th century, who found the mid 20th distasteful and increasingly confusing. A poor politician and in the political sphere a poor chooser of colleagues and subordinates. Since 1945 a convenient whipping boy for France's many failures 1919-1945. He will be best remembered for twice saving France 1916-1917, and for essentially vetoing the plan to continue the war in the summer of 1940 from North Africa instead of seeking a separate peace.

Philby, Harold 'Kim' (1912–1988): One of the famous Cambridge spies. Journalist, MI-6, War Office, Special Operations Executive. Philby used his class and educational contacts to work through most major organs of British power during and after WW2. Penetrated OSS and CIA. Exposed numerous times by Soviet defectors, Philby was able to avoid arrest because no one believed someone of his class would betray Britain. British allowed him to flee to Moscow in 1963 when this pretense became untenable.

Puller, Lewis B. 'Chesty' (1898-1971): Fought in the Banana Wars of the interwar Caribbean and served as a China Marine in the Treaty Port garrisons. In WW2 and then Korea was among the most decorated Marines in US history (5 Navy Crosses and 1 Army Distinguished Service Cross plus lesser decorations). Held up as the ideal Marine, having served at every rank from corporal to divisional general.

Raeder, Erich (1876–1960): Naval officer. Rabid, narrow-minded reactionary/right-winger, but not a Nazi per se. Fanatically indoctrinated Navy in Nazi ideology, Hitler worship, and strict Lutheranism, all to avoid another set of naval mutinies as had happened in 1918. Raeder was obsessed with avoiding another such taint on the Navy's honor. Extreme believer in capital ships. Fired as head of Navy January, 1943, over failures of capital ships in the Arctic convoy battles. Resigns in May 1943 from active service. Rallies to Hitler during Bomb Plot.

Ramcke, Herman-Bernhard (Gerhard) (1889–1968): WW1 veteran. Freikorps and Whites in Baltic postwar. Reichswehr. Transferred to Air Force and assigned to 7th Air Division (the airborne force). Hero of Crete, 1941. Led an airborne (motorized) Brigade with Rommel, 1942–43. Formed and commanded 2nd Parachute Division, 1943. Commanded Fortress Brest in Brittany, France, 1944. POW with Americans when the port fell. Saved from French war-crimes prosecution 1951 by Americans. Unrepentant admirer of Third Reich, postwar.

Richardson, James Otto (1878-1974): Commanded US Fleet/Pacific Fleet in 1940. Bright but quarrelsome. OTL FDR fired him for somewhat different reasons than in this ATL.

Richthofen (von), Wolfram: Cousin of Red Baron. WW1 veteran flyer. Engineering degree postwar, then Reichswehr. Transferred to Luftwaffe. Commanded Condor Legion in Spain. Specialist in close air support. Extremely competent, but did not suffer fools well.

Ridgway, Matthew (1895-1993): Missed combat service in WW1 just like Ike. Served a term with 15th Infantry Regiment in interwar China. In OTL most noted for commanding the XVIII Airborne Corps in ETO, and the successful counteroffensive in Korea in 1951. One of the VERY few US senior officers who liked Monty. Korea showed him to be excellent at operational level warfare. His WW2 service mostly showed he was good at training up units. He was good at maintaining the sort of democratic populist demeanor that US enlisted personnel like. Was not well liked by his peers for arrogance and over-the-top womanizing.

Riefenstahl, Leni (1902–2003): Actress and film director. Hitler groupie, but apparently not an actual Party member. Propagandist for them. Her film, "Triumph of the Will", chronicling one of the Nürnberg Rallies, is a classic.

Robeson, Paul (1898-1976): African- American. Legendary singer (he was successful at everything from grand opera to pop tunes to gospel). Civil rights advocate / Stalinist. To what degree his Stalinism was a response to period white supremacy, and to what extent it was a true believer's conversion, has been debated for decades.

Rommel, Erwin (1891–1944): WW1 hero with mountain Jägers (spetsnaz-level special commandos). Won Blue Max for his actions at Caporetto. Finished the war as a staff officer. Deemed not suitable for general staff training and higher command in the Reichswehr. Wrote a well-regarded book on infantry tactics, which led to him being requested as commander of Hitler's army escort battalion. Hitler then bumped him to one-star general in US terminology, and gave him a Panzer division as a patronage appointment. Performed brilliantly in the French campaign, but repeatedly violated orders and acted more like an advanced guard commander than a divisional general. Readers should remember that the Desert Fox legend is in the future. Rommel was still, at this point, a brash storm officer promoted over his head. He still was, in OTL for his first few North African battles. It took until 1942 for him to learn how to be a higher commander. Implicated in the Bomb Plot, he was ordered to commit suicide, which he did to safeguard his wife and son.

Ronconi, Pio Alessandro (1920-2010): Born in Spain. Member of Black Roman nobility. Mother killed by Spanish Reds. Family then returned to Italy. Very bright. Knew over a dozen languages. Fought in North Africa as Italian. In Italy as Waffen SS officer. Orientalist; journalist; student of theology, fascism and occult. Moved easily postwar in both government and right radical circles. In this series his knowledge of Catalan has brought him to DiSalo's battalion.

Roosevelt, Eleanor (1884-1962): US First Lady during FDR's multiple terms. The marriage as marriage was long dead by the time he reached the White House (he was endlessly unfaithful, often with people within her social circle). Think of it as a political partnership. She was his mobile eyes and ears. Also his ambassador to the US left. She could and did stake out positions more radical than he could publicly take. Hoover's leaks painted her as both bisexual and desperate for affection. Probably true. Whether she was in this period a fellow-traveler of the Communists, a useful idiot, or an active agent, is open to question. I tend towards the fellow-traveler, but all three templates are defensible. She moderated a tad post WW,2 but that could have been tactical.

Roosevelt, Franklin Delano (1882-1945): Only man elected President four times (we changed the Constitution so it cannot happen again; or else Eisenhower, Reagan, and Obama would all have had third terms). Hereditary Democrat from the Hudson Valley. Upper Class (Groton, Harvard, Columbia Law School). Served in Wilson's administration and ran for Vice President on the Democratic ticket in 1920. Legs paralyzed in 1921 (possibly polio, but that is now contested). Political comeback began with election as Governor of New York in 1928. Elected President in 1932 on a non-ideological 'time for a change' vibe. His 'New Deal' essentially brought lukewarm social democracy to the US. Its economic effect is still debated, but politically it probably saved the US from Revolution. Economy collapses with a second Roosevelt Depression in 1938. His political power mostly collapses as well. Enough northern Catholic and Dixie Bourbon House members team up with the Republicans to form a conservative caucus that blocks further major reforms. His attempts at packing the Supreme Court and purging the Democratic Party via primaries blows up in his face. After 1938 he tends to be very careful to guard his remaining political capital in domestic affairs. Maneuvers the US into WW2 while swearing he is doing nothing of the kind. FDR was personally charming but shallow. His style of governance was in many ways quite similar to Hitler's. Both would appoint deputies with large but overlapping areas of authority, and then undercut them. FDR was serially unfaithful to his wife and his large cast of mistresses. He played his left supporters off against the middle class progressives. Readers should remember that the Democratic Party of this era ran from Leninists on the left, to the KKK on the right. It was a collection of disparate interests – Northern Catholics, the trades unions, Dixie, the emancipated Northern blacks, the Jews, most of the US left, the old Bryan populists of what we now call Flyover Country, and everyone aggrieved by the economic power of Big Finance and Big Business. He was regarded as a class traitor by the old moneyed aristocracy. He in turn despised them, using the IRS and FBI to pursue personal vendettas. He was a smarter warlord than Hitler. He made macrostrategic decisions and saw to relations with the British. Beyond that he let his service chiefs run the war. Thus he insisted on the Torch 1942 invasion of the French Maghreb but left all the operational matters to Marshall and King. He also never forgot that maintaining morale and civilian support for the war was his job. FDR had no scruples, and no respect for the truth. That said, beyond the press clique centered on the Chicago *Tribune*, who saw him as a mix of Lucifer and the Pied Piper of Hamelin, FDR was good enough at jollying the press such that they often gave him the undeserved benefit of the doubt. In short, he could charm the skin off a snake, but when you shook hands with him it was best to count your fingers afterwards. He had zero compunctions about not honoring deals he made.

Rus, Alexander / Fidel Castro (1926-2016): Bastard son of a rich planter by his house servant. Fidel was a radical, an orator, a nationalist, and a decent baseball player. He had the balls for the adventures in this ATL and was never especially smart. His success in becoming El Supremo in Cuba owed mostly to luck and timing.

Sadat, Anwar (1918-1981): Military cadet, partly of Nubian descent. Involved with many revolutionary organization including Free Officers, which he helped form with Nasser. Succeeds Nasser as President. Engineers a partly successful war in 1973 and then makes peace with Israel. Assassinated for that by Islamists. Sadat was a good plotter and bureaucrat. Lacked Nasser's charisma.

Scharfe, Paul (1876-1942): Chief legal officer of the SS. Well-respected in legal circles. Rank:

Gruppenführer in this book. In OTL he was promoted to Obergruppenführer shortly before his death in 1942 from 'natural causes'.

Schellenberg, Walter (1910–1952): Joined the SS out of university in 1929. Protégé of Heydrich and Himmler. Amoral weasel, but extremely competent. Encouraged and abetted Himmler's late war schemes to overthrow Hitler and do a separate peace with the West. The schemes were absurd. The desire for self-protection and self-promotion were characteristic of the both men. Was prosecution witness at Nürnberg. Given short sentence, which was commuted for ill health. May have had connections to British MI-6 from mid-war period.

Schenck, Ernst-Gunther (1904-1998): SS Doctor who ran a huge, highly successful herbal plantation at Dachau Camp. Saw some frontline duty, especially in besieged Berlin. Featured in the movie *Downfall*.

Schindler, Oskar (1908 - 1974): Glad-handing entrepreneur who never amounted to much as a businessman. Did good work for Abwehr 1938-1939. Parlayed that into being the Aryan front for a successful Jewish business in Cracow. Schindler glad-handed the high-ranking Nazis for contracts and protection. His Jewish managers ran the company. He was not unusual in this sort of arrangement. What was unusual was that he saved his Jews from death as the Reich imploded, by various frauds and bribes. On the order of twelve hundred Jews were saved from certain death. Postwar his business failures continued in Germany and Argentina. Honored by Israel for his wartime heroism. In this ATL he will still be fronting for competent Jews while being himself. However, this Reich is somewhat more puritan on bribery.

Seela, Max (1911-1999): Reichswehr and then Waffen SS pioneer officer. Fearless and a combat natural.

Sharett, Moshe (1894-1965): Taken to Palestine from Ukraine as a child. Career functionary in the Palestinian Jewish bureaucracy. "General Zionist", and Israel's Second Prime Minister in OTL. He was a pragmatist and incrementalist.

Slim, William (1891-1970): Best field commander the British produced in WW2. Naturally they buried him in the sideshow that was the Burma Campaign. We get him to Iraq by skipping his OTL service in East Africa.

Sommer, Peter (1907-1945?): Army officer and racially part Jewish. Chosen in this ATL because we needed a part Jew who had staff training (completed the course in April, 1940). Transferred to the Waffen SS in 1941. Unclear if he ever formally joined the SS, but served with them. Was Ia (operations officer/de facto operational commander) of 2nd SS Division. Highest rank: Oberst/Standartenführer (unclear if he was ever formally awarded the SS rank, because of blood lines). German Cross in Gold. Put in for Knight's Cross but not granted. Probably Himmler's influence. Vanishes at war's end. Dead? Changed his name?

Speer, Albert (1905–1981): Trained architect. Joined the Nazis 1931. Protégé of Hitler. Rumored to also be his lover. Armaments Minister from 1942. Guilty of war crimes in connection with slave labor, etc. Turned on the Nazis at Nürnberg Trials to save himself. It worked. Did long prison term, but saved his life. Complete weasel. Autobiography was a laughable tissue of lies. Competence level is still debated.

Stark, Harold (1880-1972): Chief of Naval Operation (CNO) from 1939. Oversaw the huge fleet construction program. Good bureaucrat, but implicated in the Pearl Harbor intelligence failures. Kicked to London in OTL, where he got on well with British and de Gaulle. Sent to command in Europe because he did not get on well with FDR.

Steiner, Felix (1896–1966): Yes, THAT Steiner. The one from the endlessly parodied *Downfall* scene. WW1 veteran. Freikorps in same geographic region as Iron Division. Reichswehr. Retired as Major, 1933. Joins Nazis, the SA, and finally the SS in 1935. Meteoric rise from battalion to divisional command (5th SS Viking Division). Excelled at division and corps level. Army command in last months of war. Good with foreign and Volksdeutsche troops and officers, which was unusual in the SS. Second best Panzer general in Waffen SS after Hausser.

Stauffenberg (von), Claus Philipp Maria Schenk Graf (1897-1944): Reichswehr. General Staff. Good service record Poland, West, Barbarossa, Tunisia. Multiple medals. Asked to join the resistance early. Joined late. Ultranationalist with strong anti-Polish and anti-Jewish feelings/statements, but found the actual Nazis crude and their level of violence against civilians repugnant. Left a semi-invalid in OTL by war wounds in Tunisia (lost eye, fingers, etc.). Aristocrat and devout Catholic. Almost managed to assassinate Hitler, and died a hero.

Sukarno [this is the name he was known by; this book chooses to skip the whole multiple spellings etc. rat hole] (1901-1970): Of Javan and Balinese descent. VERY well educated – professional certifications in civil engineering and architecture, with a successful practice of both professions before sidelined by politics. Ardent Indonesian nationalist (a choice over the regional and local nationalities most favored in his youth; Indonesia, like India, was a colonial construct of myriad prior polities of every size from kingdoms down to small villages and remote tribes). Fluent in multiple local languages and Dutch, German, English, French, Arabic and Japanese. For this ATL the Japanese is a key. Polymath with a photographic memory. Extremely skillful political operative and organizer. Was always sexually adventurous even by the standards of the interwar avant-garde; but the corrupt, dissolute playboy of his later years is a generation in the future of this book. So is the political grandiosity of the post-Bandung Conference period. In this period he is an amoral political tactician who in OTL used and allowed himself to be used by the Japanese. They got a useful pawn, and he got to establish a base of power to fight the return of the Dutch after the Japanese lost WW2 in OTL.

Takagi Masao (1917-1979): In 1940, the man we remember as Park Chung-Hee was a military cadet in Manchuria. In OTL he would go on to be first elected president and then dictator of South Korea. Here he is an assimilated Korean subject of the Japanese Emperor, who was trained as a teacher but decided he wanted to be an army officer instead.

Thoma (von), Wilhelm Josef Ritter (1891-1948): Won the Bavarian version of the Blue Max in WW1. Commanded ground component of Condor Legion in Spain. Had a Panzer division command in Russia. Transferred to Afrika Korps and captured at Alamein. British monitored his conversations with other senior officers in captivity. Von Thoma indiscreetly told them about V-1 and V-2, including test site. In this series, he has passed up a promotion to Generalmajor (1 star equivalent) to serve as Rommel's Ia. His wish (this ATL and OTL) was to command a Panzer division in combat. He sees service with Rommel as a step in that direction. Easter egg: before the series ends, he will get his wish and more.

Thomas, Georg (1890–1946): WW1 veteran. Administrator and logistics planner Reichswehr and Wehrmacht. Coup-plotter with ties to Beck's circle, but not active in 1944. Arrested and imprisoned, but avoided execution.

Todt, Fritz (1891–1942): WW1 veteran. Trained engineer. Gold badge Nazi Party Member. Built the Autobahns and West Wall fortifications. His Organization Todt , OTL, was a de facto labor service for Wehrmacht.

Truman, Harry (1884-1972): Missouri National Guard officer WW1. Nursed a hatred for West Point graduates for how they treated Guard officers in France. Failed small businessman (got caught in the postwar Depression and had those debts hanging over him for much of his life, but he did pay it all back). Held county office as a front for the quite corrupt Pendergast Machine but seems to have been personally honest. Truman was a hard-working detail man, the exact opposite of Roosevelt. He was also able to get down and dirty on patronage, public works contracts, and the rest of the swamp that was day-to-day governance, again the exact opposite of Roosevelt.

Udet, Ernst (1896–1941): WW1 ace fighter pilot. Interwar was stunt flyer, including Hollywood. Joined Nazis in 1933 when his old unit-mate Göring recruited him. Playboy who never coped well with bureaucratic life. In OTL, a suicide. Dive-bombing fanatic.

Umberto II (1904–1983): Crown Prince, son of Victor Emmanuel III. De facto head of state from 1944. Briefly King in 1946.

Victor Emmanuel III (1869-1947): King of Italy 1900–1946. Allowed Mussolini to take power. Mismanaged removing Mussolini in 1943, and Italy's switching sides the same year. Dethroned, 1946.

Wang Ming (1904-1974): One of the founders of the Chinese Communist Party, but spends more time 20's and 30's in Moscow than in China. Marginalized by Mao in intraparty disputes centered on both personalities and Mao's peasant/guerrilla-centric deviations from orthodox Stalinism.

Wavell, Archibald (1883-1950): Served in Boer War. Spent most of WW1 and after in staff positions, but managed a war wound (lost an eye) and medal for heroism. Regarded as a military intellectual, become commander Middle East 1939. Had success against the Italians (Libya, East Africa), but failed elsewhere against the Germans (Greece, Libya, Egypt). Swapped out June 1941 for Auchinleck, C-in-C India. Further failures in Burma, East Indies, Singapore. Political problems in India. It is probably unfair to blame Wavell for every failure under his command, as much was imperial overstretch plus idiotic decisions by war cabinet - starting with Churchill, who never was especially good at adjusting ends to means. In reverse. most of the original success in the Western Desert owes far more to O'Connor's operational brilliance and Italian command errors.

Weygand, Maxime (1867-1965): Foch's Chief of Staff 1918. Improperly credited with the Polish Miracle of the Vistula in 1920. Parked in Syria at outbreak of WW2 because of French cabinet politics. Recalled after Gamelin had lost the battle. Failed to coordinate the ill-fated attacks to sever Guderian's spearheads and restore the line. Did an extremely competent defense on the Aisne-Somme, but insisted the government sue for peace when these lines were breached because Weygand wanted to keep the Army intact in case the Communists rebelled. Loyal to Vichy. Advocated limited collaboration with the Germans. Arrested by the Nazis after TORCH and imprisoned for the rest of the war. Accused of collaboration postwar, but beat the charge because the Nazis had imprisoned him. He was a man of the late 19th century but a quite competent officer.

Wolf, Markus (1923-2006): Half-Jewish German Communist whose family fled to the USSR when Hitler came to power. Dedicated Soviet citizen; obtained Soviet identity documents. Worked for COMINTERN from an early age. Trained as a 'journalist', but when sent by the Soviets back to Germany at war's end, was made a nominal German again. Government official before being tasked with forming the East German foreign intelligence service in 1951. He is alleged to be the prototype for LeCarre's spymaster Karla. Wolf was extremely intelligent and efficient, but shunned the public eye. Even by shadow-world standards he was a mystery man during his active career.

Wolff, Karl (1900–1984): WW1. Freikorps. Banker and public relations man. Joined Nazis and SS,

1931. Protégé of Himmler's. Head of SS in occupied Italy. Helped arrange a surrender of Axis forces in Italy, April 1945, without Hitler's permission. Turned state's evidence at Nürnberg, but nonetheless did two small sentences for war crimes. Returned to the public relations business. Appeared to have had ties to CIA and US protection.

Yamashita Tomoyuki (1885-1946): Japanese general. Ran a brilliant campaign 1941-1942 in Malaya and Singapore. Then sidelined for two years in Japanese Army factional politics. Commanded on Luzon 1944-1945. Tried and executed as a war criminal in 1946. Trial was a travesty. The Manila war crimes were, in violation of his written orders, committed by Japanese naval troops who denied his right to give them orders. His real crime was making MacArthur look inept.

Dramatis Personae

Fictional

Alistare-Smythe, Edward (?-?): this is the unnamed brigadier from book 1 – here in book 2 we have his name and a hint at his amazing social contacts. Expect all to be revealed in due time.

Arcau LaTorre, Maria de la Conception (1920-?) 'Coxita': She grew up in a family of educated radicals in Barcelona. As a teen militant she drifted from Catalan nationalism to anarchism to left socialism/national Leninism before becoming a Communist/Stalinist [Spain had two Communist Parties, the other being a mix of Trotskyites and eclectic leftists] in the first months of the Spanish Civil War. She served in the local neighborhood Cheka before volunteering for the front as a company commissar in 1937. The defeat of the Republic was a huge shock to her ideals. Initially her relationship with di Salo was a matter of expedience. Being a Fascist officer's whore was better than violent gang rape by a pack of drunken Moroccan mercenaries. She still doesn't love him. She regards romantic love as a bourgeois fantasy. However, she's simply comfortable having a strong protector in a nasty world. He's rich and lives well. As long as she stays with him, so does she. Trilingual in Spanish, Catalan, French from family background. Fluent by now in English, Italian, Russian. Knows quite a bit of German, Yiddish, Polish, and Magyar from service alongside Internationals in Spain. She's smart, amoral, nihilistic, and quite blood-thirsty. Has some NKVD-taught skills as an interrogator. Beneath her apolitical exterior (di Salo has somewhat enforced this on her by the end of book 2) she is still an instinctive anti-capitalist. Her Stalinism is a façade but she thinks she believes in it. She partially justified her relationship with DiSalo by reminding herself that her man-god Stalin is allied with Germany and Italy against the capitalists. Nickname: Coxita. Promoted Hauptmann end of book 2.

Ari Pasha, Gisht (1895-?): Alexandrine gangster and businessman. Of Albanian and Alawite descent. Early life is unknown, as is place of birth. He is a major power in the demimonde, with interests throughout the region. He's brilliant, ruthless; but somewhat naïve about how the higher world of nations and major institutions works.

Baghdadi, David (1882-?): A patriarch of a merchant clan whose members span the globe from Capetown to Shanghai to Panama. These Sephardic Jews have survived the Persians, Ottomans, and now the British. The clan also does estate management, international money movement (around such minor problems as capital controls), and a variety of other profitable ventures.

Battaglia, Giuseppe (1915–?): Also goes by "Joey Bats" and "Brooklyn". Italian-American mechanical wizard. Not exactly Cosa Nostra, but ran in those circles.

Cohen, Isaac [Also known as Isaak Schwabe] (1896–?): Greta's uncle by marriage. Artillery officer WW1, Honvéd. Metallurgist specializing in oilfield pipes and machines. Fluent in German, Magyar, Romanian, English, Yiddish. Knows some French and Italian.

Cohen, Luke [Schwabe] (probably 1921 - ?): Third street kid brother/cousin. He's pegged as the oldest but it's a pure guess. Mother Rachel just assigned ages to the three urchins her husband brought home. Luke is the one who formally apprenticed to her engineering-graduate husband. Luke is the tech genius who interfaces with the foreign experts at Ploiesti. He's the least physically huge of the three but still a large guy with heavy muscles. Easygoing personality, but if pushed can take care of himself. Best linguist of the three, and the only one who learned how to be a weasel. Peter's approach to problems is fists and boots. Luke will work the angles. Paul will let his brothers handle it if possible.

Cohen, Paul [Schwabe] (probably 1923 - ?): Street kid and possible brother/cousin to Peter and Luke, adopted by Isaac Cohen / Isaak Schwabe and his wife. Paul was the machinist and technician. Excellent eye /hand coordination, and amazing ability to visualize mechanical constructs. He is of large size (Peter is huge and muscled like a troll). His schooling is functional rather than deep, but he's been helping in Isaac's metal shops since he was tall enough to reach a work bench. He doesn't have Joey Bats's knowledge of autos, but knows more about complex machinery than Bats. Extremely loyal to his foster family but better social skills than his two brothers. Goes by Schwabe when introduced in book 2.

Cohen, Peter (probably born 1922– ?): de facto adoptive son of Isaac and Rachel. Physically huge and extremely strong, even for his size and physique. A born survivor, extremely loyal to his adoptive family, including his brothers/cousins and de facto household members, such as Greta Levi and Ivan Gorlov. His solution to most problems is fists and boots. Gunter is first man he ever met who would probably be his equal in a fight. Hauptmann in book 2.

Cohen, Rachel (1898–?): Crazy Ruth's older and wiser sister. Greta's aunt. Also known as Rachel Schwabe.

Collins, Abdul (he is not quite sure how old he is - just past puberty, so the unit pegs him at 13): He's short and scrawny when captured. He fills out fast and starts to shoot up on a diet with a lot of protein. Uneducated, but a lively mind and a dead shot. Very happy to be a Collins. Gets formal rank of private of which he is immensely proud. Unit names him Abe, as they find Arabic names difficult.

Collins, Bain (1927-?): Bastard child of an Irish NCO and his Bengali concubine. Knows his letters (in English) and numbers. Extremely facile with languages. Anglophone. Speaks street Bengali, Punjabi, Urdu, Hindi, Italian, Arabic. Is rapidly learning German. Grew up around armies and knows how to fit in to military structures. He's got street smarts and a winsome personality. No national loyalties at all. Loyal to family, friends, unit. Makes Corporal and is insanely proud of this.

Collins, Mary [Mary the Cook] (1913-?): common-law-wife to retired British NCO. Bengali Hindu rebranded as Irish Catholic. Illiterate but intelligent. Speaks decent English, Bengali, Urdu, Hindi, Maltese/Italian, and passable Arabic. Knows 100-200 words of maybe 20 languages. Also Bengali from birth, and 'Army Hindi' from her time with her Irishman. Her 'British' cooking is British Indian when it comes to spices, but otherwise decent although not gourmet. Has three children, with the oldest being a 13-year-old son, Bain. Good with children and with military life in general. A born scrounger but not a law/rules-breaking weasel. She knows life from the bottom and is adaptable to change. Very class- and rank-conscious.

Dika: underage sex worker from Romania. Roma.

Di Salo, Lieutenant Colonel John Marco Karoly Riva (1902-?): Italian aristocratic father, rich English mother. Educated in England. Eton. Oxford. After university, successful career with maternal grandfather's financial firm in the City of London. Year of officer's training in Italy. Initial branch was cavalry, but did his service time with the new armored cars. Took the course for the Alpine corps before leaving service. Volunteered for service in Spain with Italian Expeditionary Corps because finance and the bachelor life in fashionable London was beginning to bore him. Brilliant career in Spain with both Italian and mixed forces. Returned to finance after Spanish Civil War, but again was bored. Returned to Italy just before Italy entered the war. Completely bilingual Italian/English. Also fluent in French, Spanish, German, Magyar, Serbo-Croat/Montenegrin [knows all three dialects from an upper class

POV]. Knows some Catalan, Arabic, Russian. Physically fit and quite good-looking. Somewhat vain about looks and ancestry. Not an ideological Fascist, but a man of the Right in an English sense. War booty mistress is Coxita the Commissar. Social links to the 'Spanish Mafia' (the Italian senior officers who served in Spain). His family has links to both Prince Umberto and Marshal Balbo. Also links to Serbian and Montenegrin nobility.

Duffy, Kevin (1894–?): Staff officer sent to Malta. Welsh Guards.

Engels, Lothar (1877-?): Village blacksmith in rural Hesse. WW1 and Freikorps veteran. Early Nazi but not Gold Badge. SA officer. From the Strasser wing of the party. Nasty temper, but far from stupid. A brawler in combat style, but a good leader of men. Sturmbannführer so far.

Fischer, Clara (1913- ?): Born a Communist, trained as a teacher, spent seven years as a cleaning lady while enduring police abuse for her family politics. Never been arrested; but she's been questioned, warned, and generally mistreated. Stepmother to a brood of abandoned children from party comrades in jail, on the run, or in exile abroad. She is smart and well-read for a working-class lady who made it through teacher's training. Her Communism is millennial visionary secular religion. She really never paid any attention to details of party dogma or the endless changes in the party line. Never a whore or a criminal, but her life at the bottom put her socially in with both. Wanda and Adolph were friends in a street sense despite their political disagreements. Now she's saddled with protecting her brother Carl, and a new situation with Joey Bats.

Jung, Lars (1919–?): Veteran of Norway, Rotterdam, Malta.

Gaafar, Jabar Isa (1902-?): lower middle class Alexandrine Egyptian by birth. Educated to high school level. Fluent in all the major European languages (French, English, Greek, Italian, Armenian, Spanish…sadly for him very little German or Yiddish; does know Ladino). Special branch officer whose official specialty was keeping down the various political oppositions, and who had managed to expand his brief into policing/finding accommodations with the demimonde. His excuse is that politics, crime, and illicit finance overlap badly. He is extremely bright, quite diligent, totally amoral, and a complete opportunist. He also reacted to the change in power faster than his rivals.

Gorlov, Ivan (1902–?): Officer cadet with the Whites in 1917. Evacuated from Crimea in 1920 as a lieutenant colonel. Massive combat experience in between. Washes up in Romania as a starving refugee in 1922, where he is taken in by Isaac Cohen and taught the family business. Lieutenant Colonel so far.

Gretchen (1895–?): Prostitute, and friend of Wanda.

Kleist-Konitz (von), Ernst– (1917- ?): Born of an old military family tracing its service back to Gustav Adolph of Sweden and the Margraves of Brandenburg. The family is reactionary and monarchist. Ernst is anti-Nazi, but a good patriot willing to fight Germany's wars even under gutter scum. His family is related by various combinations of blood, marriage and prior service to the von Lewinski's, von Mansteins, the von Kleists, the von Hindenburgs, and the von Stauffenbergs. Also to a fair amount of adjacent Polish military nobility. Oberleutnant with a week's active service during the French campaign as an infantry officer. Still has a limp from a wound taken during the breach of the Somme lines. Found recuperation leave boring, so he used family connections to get posted to von Manstein's German Afrika Korps headquarters as a supernumerary. Ernst is a recruiting-poster German warrior – tall, muscular, athletic, ash blond hair and blue eyes. Women swoon for him. He finds them boring. He likes machines, weapons, and physical activity. Is learning to ride a motorcycle and hoping to find a way to learn to pilot a Storch. Oberleutnant when book 2 starts, Major when it ends. Knight's Cross as well.

Levi, Greta (1922–?): Also known at various times as Cohen or Schwabe. Less socially awkward than her boyfriend, Klaus, but, if anything, even more politically clueless. She's intelligent in a teen, space-cadet way, but a faster learner. Oberleutnant.

Levi, Ruth (1902–1940): Greta's mother. Also known as "Crazy Ruth". Belligerent, argumentative, seen by her sister and daughter as a how-not-to manual for adult behavior.

Lincoln, Billy (1900–?): WW1 veteran, in one of the Pals Battalions. Old sweat, working-class.

Mason, Garth (1896–?): Staff officer sent to Malta. Coldstream Guards.

Maurice, Hans (1894–?): WW1, artillery. Freikorps. SA.

Money-Penny, James (1913–?): Harrow. One year of Cambridge. Soldier of fortune/gun for hire. Speaks over twenty languages. Excellent physical health, amazing reflexes, high intelligence, near to photographic memory, amazing social intelligence and no visible scruples.

Morgan, Henry[starts out as Hymie in pre-WW1 Hungary; a relative of the Cohens and Levi's] (1899-?): he's a smooth con man, counterfeiter, and fence. Has multiple identities and supposed nationalities. He is currently presenting himself as Captain Morgan, a Canadian veteran of the Great War.

Pentangeli, Vincenzo (1909–?): Italian reserve second lieutenant. used good connections to secure posting. Trained paratrooper. Fluent in English and German.

Peters, Frauke (1921-1940): A 110% Nazi who thinks Hitler was Jesus come to Earth. BMD and Camp Guard Corps. Fantastically good looking [Camp nickname was 'the Dresden China Doll']. Figure out of a Playboy Centerfold, ice blue eyes and corn silk blond rich lush hair with a perfect heart shaped face. Eyes are ever so slightly large for her face, making her look somewhat younger. Smart, despises being treated as a sex object. She's been hit on since she started to develop breasts and hips at 12 and is still a virgin by choice. Extremely determined and focused.   Of middle class Saxon descent.

Pieri, Bruno (1896-?): Think of this as a semi-fictional character. The last name, rank of militia lieutenant colonel, and approximate age correspond to a historic person. Everything else is fictional. We needed an officer who spoke Yiddish, and this gentleman from Trieste seemed likely to know that tongue. The real version stayed a POW after Italy switched sides. Either he was a true believer in Il Duce, or he just saw switching sides as treason.

Prezan, Florian (1897-?): Mildly corrupt, middling-efficient Romanian policeman known to the Schwabe/Cohen family. Any future volume resemblance to Captain Renault from Casablanca is purely coincidental.

Saxon, Naiomi (1915-?): Romanian Betar lieutenant. Veteran of Rommel's brief anti-Soviet campaign in Romania. Befriends Greta. Ran her female platoon well on Malta and is now a 1st Lieutenant. Operates under Greta's orders most of the time. Name is 'Saxon' because Strauss got tired of writing Schwabe every time the real name was too Jewish.

Schmidt, Alois (1919–?): Ramcke's aide. A hero of Malta. Major after Malta. Complete weasel but brave.

Scott, Reginald [Nickname 'Jutland'] (1900–1940): WW1 veteran, and commander of HMS *Thunderchild*. Not the sharpest knife in the drawer, but a decent officer.

Siegel, Karl (1910–?): University graduate, law. SS. Protégé of Schellenberg. "One of the smart ones".

Smith, John (1922 - ?): Born in Oregon of German immigrant parents. JHS dropout — this was the Depression and the family needed him to work. Knows driving, trucks, tractors, machinery. Family returned to the Fatherland in 1937 and he becomes Johann Schmidt. Siegel has taken him from the HJ for his English language skills. He speaks perfect General American English and only passable German (kitchen table back home, plus three-year immersion course when he arrived 'home'). He's just been bumped to NL Lieutenant and made Siegel's minder to Joey Bats, which to some extent means to Brigade Strauss.

Steiner, Klaus (1922–?): Socially awkward young man whom fate will make a hero. Short (his growth spurt is possibly late from restricted nutrition), squeaky voice, stutters. The classic "good kid". Highest Rank: NL Oberstleutnant, so far. Also SS Sturmbannführer. Just became a Nazi Party member in book 2.

Stephan (1920–?): ex-pimp, and worker at Wanda's bar/brothel. Dika's "boyfriend". Roma.

Strauss, Gunter (1902–?): WW1 veteran. Iron Division and other Freikorps, postwar. Early member Nazi Party and SA. Feldherrnhalle veteran. Spent most of the rest of the 20's in New York, but maintained Party membership. Active in SA 1930–1934. Sidelined after Blood Purge, but got postal job from patronage. Very tall, extremely muscular, bright. His ideals burned out after 1934 and he's in it for himself. Highest Rank: NL Brigadier, so far. Also SS Sturmbannführer.

Voss, Gregor (1900–?): Underage volunteer, WW1. Iron Division and Freikorps, postwar. Early Nazi and SA. Worked at the post office with Gunter and Adolph. Artificial foot and bad leg. A reactionary, nationalist hard-ass, but never took to Nazi ideology. He was Nazi instead of Nationalist because he's a populist who dislikes the old ruling elites. His adoptive "nephew" Hans is a 25-year-old with the mind of a 12-year-old. Gregor never married. Not gay but somewhat indifferent to women and sex.

Wanda [last name never mentioned in text, but was Duch] (1914–?): Her father was a Pole from Lodz who chose to serve Kaiser instead of Czar. Marries his Polish girlfriend at the end of the war, legitimizing the daughter he had by her, Wanda. Wanda is Polish by blood and German by rearing. Thinks of herself as German, but is proud of being known as "the Polack". Thrown out of her parents' house at 12 as incorrigible (boys, drinking, wild living). Has her oldest son, Adam, at 13. Always been on the fringes of the criminal life, but a hard worker and inveterate entrepreneur. Longtime bootlegger. Never was a sex worker and never did strongarm. Was friends with people who did both and worse. Hates most establishment figures and the Communists (a set of puritan zealots, in her opinion). Never formally a Nazi, but in the culture of the ex-Freikorps street fighters. Six children, the last two by Adolph Wrede. Through him, she's friends with Gunter Strauss. Never pretty and the years have not been kind. Medium height, massive muscles (did heavy labor much of her life), sharp wit, acid tongue. VERY loyal to her friends.

Witt, Alfred (1891-?): Half Jewish WW1 veteran and Finance Ministry official. Pushed out of government job by Aryanization laws. Survived by doing cash business as a bookkeeper. He didn't seem 'Jewish' (he was raised Lutheran), and his prices were cheap. He was also a wizard on filling out government forms. His two quarter-Jewish sons Arne (1915-?) and Uwe (1918-?) followed in his footsteps in terms of career. Not Aryanized until 1940 when they were expelled from Army service in the spring Aryanizations of the Army. Wife Kerstin (1896-?) was a full Aryan and Lutheran. Refused social pressure to divorce husband and abandon tainted sons. Mother Helen (1869 -?) was a full Jew. Her dead husband Karl (1864-1934) was Aryan and Lutheran. The family is educated, frugal, not especially religious, but the sort of middle class the successive German regimes built their civil service on back to the Great Elector of Brandenburg in the 17th Century. At this point in their lives they are loyal minions of Heydrich, because they are all too aware of how quickly and easily their resurrection could be reversed.

Wrede, Adolph (1898–?): WW1 veteran. Freikorps, but not Iron Division. Early Nazi and SA. Postal worker. A hard man whose one soft spot is his common-law wife Wanda and their children. NL Major and quite willing to plateau at that rank if it keeps him beside Wanda and out of field duty.

Glossary

1922 Committee – the organization of Tory backbenchers in the British Parliament. They work in the twilight but can unmake prime ministers.

54 Broadway – 1940 headquarters address for British MI-6/SIS. The address was often used as a shorthand way for those in the know to talk about the agency in public.

AEF – literally American Expeditionary Force. This was the American Army Group that Pershing commanded in France in 1918. After the war it became a shorthand for the entire idea of the US intervening in Europe's interminable wars. Retrospectively, the US public decided we had been swindled by a mix of tricky Europeans, the US arms merchants / merchants of death, the bankers (Wall Street and the City of London) and a US Eastern Establishment that was joined at the hip by marriage and schooling to the British upper classes. Quietly swept under the rug were US outrage at unrestricted submarine warfare, and the Zimmermann Telegram links to Mexican revanchism. There was just enough truth in each of the multiple overlapping conspiracy theories to give them political strength, more so once the Europeans repudiated their war debts. Even those people in the late 30's US sympathetic to the West/opposed to Hitler, found the idea of millions of Americans being sent to Europe to die in someone else's war over Danzig (which not one American in a hundred could find on a map) repugnant. That many of those pushing for intervention were Jews who seemed more concerned about their European kin than their American homeland, simply opened other fissures in the US body politic (the equally pro-war US Poles incited less bile because at least they were Christians and mostly weren't Reds). Contrapuntally, the most anti-intervention groups were US Irish (anything the hated English were for, they were opposed to) and the Upper Midwest (lots of Germans and Scandinavians who did not want the US fighting against their homelands; a generalized hatred of the East Coast and bankers; a regional dislike of the Roosevelt administration as being the creature of Dixie and the weird East Coast cities).

AH – alternate history

Air Marshal – term used for Air Force Field Marshals

Alliance Française– a French cultural organization dedicated to imparting French language and civilization in a broad sense to the world. Very influential in Alexandria, where French was in many ways the main language for communication between the city's many ethnic and religious communities.

AMR 35 – a French 'cavalry tank'. It was relatively fast but armed only with a machine gun. It was also mechanically cranky, as were many French designs. They were designed by committee, and often with more of an eye to budget constraints and defense industrial issues than combat utility; the French army could never make up its mind on tank doctrine, for complex institutional reasons.

Arditi – Italian shock troops from WW1. Similar to German storm troops, but more elite in the manner of the mountain Jägers Rommel served in. Many of these veterans helped form the Fascist Party postwar. In our ATL, Italy will bring them back.

Arrow Cross – Hungarian far-right political movement. The Hungarian right and far-right post-1918 was a maze of feuding small parties set beside the dominant ruling Horthyites. Arrow Cross were not as crazy as Romanian Iron Guard or Croatian Ustache, but even the local Hungarian Nazis thought they were insane. OTL, the German Nazis force them into power when Horthy tries to dump the Nazi alliance to save Hungary, 1943–1944.

Associated Negro Press - a press association of 150+ Negro papers and periodicals, based in Chicago (which in this era contested with New York's Harlem as the unofficial capital of Negro America). The Association reporters provided national and overseas coverage for the mostly locally-based member publications.

ATL – alternate time line. This book is an AH set in an ATL.

Banana Wars – between the two World Wars the US Marine Corps was used in various interventions the US carried out in Cuba, Haiti, the Dominican Republic, and Nicaragua. Duty included counter-guerrilla, trainers/cadres for native forces, nation building, and various other small-war operations. The Marines who served there provided a valuable source of knowledge on fighting in poorly developed tropical lands in the Pacific and post WW2 (China, South Korea, Philippines, Indochina).

BDM - *Bund Deutscher Mädel* – League of German Girls. Nazi Girl Scouts. Sarcastically known as 'League of SS Mattresses' for the obvious sexual reasons. Many modern readers may find period sexism crude. I have cleaned it up quite a bit but it will still seem over the top to sensitive souls.

beschissenes Schlamassel – shitty mess

Betar – paramilitary youth movement of Revisionist Zionists (short form, modern Likud). Strong in Poland, Baltic States, Romania.

Black Roman Nobility – the section of the aristocracy who sided with the Pope when the Italian state took Rome from the former Papal states.

Blood Purge – liquidation of the SA leadership and, to a lesser extent, of the radical wing of the Nazi Party in 1934. Used as a cover for more generalized score-settling by Göring, Himmler, et al.

Blue Max – Technically, Pour le Mérite. The highest award for bravery under Prussian Kings and German Kaisers. Dropped with the Weimar Republic. In this series, reinstated 1940 by Rommel and then confirmed by Göring.

Bomb Plot – the closest of the many anti-Hitler plots to come to actually killing him. Its failure put the radicals firmly in charge, and contributed to the huge German losses of people and physical capital in those last ten hellish months. July 20, 1944.

Brownsville Boys/ Murder Incorporated – this collection of Italian and Jewish killers was the enforcement arm of the Five Families after Luciano unified the gangs. Based out of Rosie "Midnight Rose" Gold's 24/7 candy store in Brooklyn, they also operated as contract killers for gangs across the US and for 'civilians' with gang connections (many people had such, as the gangs controlled many legitimate businesses including commercial garbage hauling - which meant every small business in NYC had a connection). Dewey destroyed the first version in the second half of the 30's. The former #2, Albert 'the Mad Hatter' Anastasia, recreated the operation with less visible people. The original cadre were street punks whose style of dress, poor anger control, and flamboyant lifestyle called too much police attention to themselves. The best guess is they killed several thousand people before Anastasia was assassinated in the late 1950's. By then the original cadre of killers were aging out and the young men preferred the drug trade, which paid better.

Buffalo Soldiers – the Regular US Army post-Civil War had four regiments of what are now called African Americans. In 1940 terms, Colored or Negro. The vast bulk of the officers were white in these. 24th, 25th Infantry; 9th, 10th Cavalry. In the world of Jim Crow America, the Army was a good job. So while the white regiments got the scum of the Earth mixed with newbies just off the boat (military service mixed poor wages, abysmal living conditions, and very low social status), the Buffalo Soldiers got top-notch men who usually stayed with the colors for 20-30 years (blacks were kept out of most of the better things that led whites to shun serving). The "Buffalo" name supposedly comes from the reaction of a Native American nation (accounts vary as to which) over the nappy, curly hair common to the West Africans these men were descended from.

Bursche – in a military sense an officer's batman or orderly

Castle Hill – government quarter of Budapest.

Chain Dogs – German military police. The name comes from a metal gorget they wore as a means of branch identification. Deserved reputation as "hardcore".

Chancellery Guard – fictional security force created by Heydrich and Nebe. Nebe is first head.

Chicago Tribune – the most widely read of a linked group of fanatically anti-New Deal, anti-FDR, Isolationist newspapers in the US. Best known for publishing the US Navy's secret WW2 code breaking operations after the victory at Midway in 1942. Tribune did this essentially out of spite and bile.

China Marines – US treaty garrison force interwar period, mostly in Shanghai but like the Army force in Tientsin (15th Infantry Regiment) often pulled hither and yon protecting consulates and other US interests. These two regiments were the only US source for ground combat cadres with any knowledge of East Asian culture or methods of war.

China Station – USN headquarters in Shanghai. Controlled a small squadron of ocean-going ships, the riverine boats (by treaty US and Britain were allowed armed patrol boats on China's major rivers, especially the Yangtse), the China Marine garrisons in Shanghai and Tientsin, and the most important signal intercept station the USN possessed. In OTL it was tasking against Japan almost up to Pearl. Pulled out just in time for air transport to Hawaii.

Congress of Industrial Organizations/CIO – the more radical of the two US labor federations. In OTL it would (mostly) purge the actual Communists post-WW2. As the name says, it did organization by industry rather than crafts as the more traditional American Federation of Labor did. CIO was the more politically active of the two, and tended to back FDR and squabble with him from the Left. They merge into AFL-CIO in 1950's. AFL initially dominated the politics of the Federation for the first generation, but, over time, the Federation becomes more like the CIO, and has drifted leftwards, in part due to the rising strength of government workers unions.

Control Group – Japanese Army faction that opposed the radicals of both Imperial Way/Strike North and the IJN's Strike South faction. It was more status quo and reactive. This is the group that ran things, with some brief interruptions, 1931-1945.

Counterfactuals – new term for AH's by professionals trying to remove the amateur and fiction taint from such speculations.

Falange / old shirt Falangism – interwar Spanish rightwing revolutionary party. Its doctrines were a bizarre mix of futurism, syndicalism, Italian fascism, and some unique strains of Spanish autocratic nationalism. The membership was mostly young, urban, highly educated middle-to-upper-middle-class youngsters who wanted the chic of being radicals but rebelled at the left's internationalism and hatred of the traditional higher classes. There was a second, much smaller wing, of the children of rural landlords to whom it was a chic way to defend their traditional privileges without the rigid Catholicism of the normal Spanish right. The urban wing was near exterminated at the start of the Spanish Civil War. The cities stayed loyal to the Republic, and the left chekas knew who the Falangists were. Franco then took over the dead husk of the party. Dictators of the period were supposed to have a party, and the Falange label was a banner under which to unite opportunists and careerists. However, a small wing tried to remain loyal to its revolutionary roots. These were a mix of relatives of the slaughtered original members (especially younger brothers) and Anarchist defectors to whom the revolutionary syndicalism was familiar. These were known as old shirt Falangists from the claim that they still had their tattered old blue Falange shirts from before the Civil War (and thus were distinguished from the mass of newbies who had no ideology beyond selfserving loyalty to Franco personally). Coxita was attempting to reposition herself as one of these, instead of the selfish little sellout that she is. DiSalo wasn't having it. He didn't care if she played let's-pretend. He just wanted the pretentiousness dialed radically back.

Fascist Grand Council – a mixed body of Italian state and Fascist Party officials that ran Italy under Mussolini. This was the body that voted Mussolini out in 1943.

Fascist Militia – in theory, a separate Party Militia in the manner of the SS. In practice, a reserve force for the Italian Army that also had public order duties.

Feldherrnhalle – a building in downtown Munich. Site of the ending of Hitler's Beer Hall Putsch in 1923. Having marched with Hitler on that day made one an "old fighter" in the Nazi Party, comparable to being in Napoleon's Old Guard. Gunter was, having marched behind the banner that day and stood tall under fire near Ludendorff while Adolph ran like the rabbit he was. Gregor went back that far in the Party but his physical problems kept him from marching that day.

Gau – The Nazi Party divided Germany (and later many surrounding annexed areas) into individual Gau's as the political entity immediately below the national government. The head was the Gauleiter. In OTL, many of these ran their Gau as a semi-independent fief, backed by Bormann, who controlled access to Hitler. In this ATL, Heydrich takes much firmer control.

General Government – the Nazi colonial regime imposed on Poland after the 1939 conquest. The Nazis sliced off portions of their sector of prewar Poland, and formally made them part of Germany (essentially, the 1914 borders with some "improvements"). The rump was labeled the General Government and run from Crakow, not Warsaw.

General Zionism – bourgeois nationalists and predominantly middle class, these faction of the Zionist Movement dominated the international Zionist organizations. They were capitalist, incrementalist, legalistic, and somewhat willing to work with the British. The leader was Chaim Weizmann, Israel's first President. The remains of this strand are now part of Likud.

Gestapo – GeStaPo - *Geheime Staatspolizei* (Secret State Police). Founded by Göring from the pre-Nazi Prussian political police. Had a deserved reputation for violence, even by Nazi standards.

Golden Square – cabal of Iraqi Sunni senior military officers who made and unmade governments, before leading an unsuccessful revolt against the British in OTL. In this ATL the results are a tad more extreme and chaotic.

GRU – Soviet military intelligence. From Lenin's time semi-autonomous from Cheka/NKVD. The two were bitter rivals (worse than FBI/CIA in US or MI-5/MI-6 in UK). GRU always had vastly fewer resources, but usually accomplished more, in part because they were willing to provide accurate information even when it was not what the bosses in Moscow wanted to hear. They were also less likely to rely on ideological sympathizers for agents, preferring the more normal intelligence methods of blackmail, cash, etc.

Haganah – Palestinian Jewish semi-clandestine militia. The "semi-clandestine" is because, while officially illegal, it often cooperated with the British - whose policy on this ebbed and flowed. Controlled by the Labor Party (in US terms, social democrats with a strong, more Marxist wing) it was strongest in the communal agricultural settlements but had real strength in the cities through control of the Trade Union Federation. The level of cooperation in these books is greater than OTL. In OTL London was always more worried about triggering another Arab Revolt than this series allows for. Of course, in this ATL the British position in Egypt and the Middle East is much weaker than OTL for a variety of reasons this series explores - starting with the Axis campaign beginning nearly a full year earlier and with FAR more German support.

Hatzohar – The Palestinian Revisionist Party - Revisionist Zionist organization and political party in Mandatory Palestine. Its main tenets were a willingness to respond to the Arab resistance with offensive measures, including both preemptive attacks and terrorism, plus an assertion that the proposed Jewish state should be all of the Palestine Mandate, including what is now Jordan, instead of just a portion of Palestine without Jordan. They were also more open and accepting of the need to ethnically cleanse the existing Arabs. Preempted during WW2 and after through the War of Independence, by its originally subordinate armed wing, the Irgun. When Irgun forms its own political party, Herut, post Independence, Hatzohar folds into it. With some twists and turns the reassembled party evolves into the modern Likud.

Hauptumsiedlungslager für Juden Rakowitz / Palestine #1 Jewish Relocation Center – fictional camp/ghetto adjacent to the old site of Cracow airport and adjacent "new city" suburb of Nowa Huta. Nazis clear the Poles out to make this happen. Think of it as a Jewish-run and -guarded ghetto. Eichmann is nominally in charge with a tiny SS staff, but otherwise the Jews administer the camp themselves while being fed by the Hoover Relief Agency. Initially a place to ship the Jews of the Baltic States, it will over time have added the Jews of Poland, Slovakia, Romania, Greater Germany, and the Benelux, plus many of the Hungarian Jews. It is vast and keeps growing. It's also thrown together and eclectic in the manner of many modern refugee camps, such as Goma in 1994. Rakowitz #1 is a tiny administrative facility run by Eichmann with a small SS and BDM staff. Palestine #2 and after are the ever-growing numbers of residential camps with attached light industrial workshops.

Hawala – network for money transfers in the greater Indian Ocean/Islamic world areas. Used the equivalent of letters of credit to bypass the formal banking system and thus official notice. Most transactions are done by word of mouth and physical couriers. This is how Mary Collins got money from where ever she was, to her perpetually debt-ridden family in rural Bengal.

Heer – the German Army

Hiwi – literally "helper". From Hilfswilliger - "willing helper". In terms of WW2 the "willing" part should be taken ironically. A generalized term used for locals and POW's taken into German units. Some were volunteers. Some were little better than slaves.

HJ – *Hitlerjugend* - Hitler Youth. Nazi Boy Scouts, but with more emphasis on physical fitness and basic military skills.

Home Counties – the south and southeast of England, anchored on London and the Channel Ports. It is the most historically upscale part of England, and thus of the British Empire.

Honvéd – the national guard of the Kingdom of Hungary under the Habsburgs and then Horthy. It was technically a separate military service, not part of the Army.

Hoover Relief Agency – Fictional organization used for this series. It is a copy of an actual historic relief agency that Hoover headed in WW1, which fed Belgians and French behind German lines and later expanded to postwar relief, including saving Lenin's regime from self-induced famine. OTL German policy allowed the Jews and, to a lesser extent, the Poles to starve so as to assure adequate food for

Germans. Churchill historically vetoed proposals for relief aid through the blockade in the manner of Hoover's WW1 work. In OTL, Churchill would finally relent to save the starving Greeks in 1943. Here, we have Heydrich making a diplomatic push that FDR chooses to answer. FDR's running for a third term in 1940 was a major breach of US customs. His victory was quite uncertain down to election day. So, this would pander to US citizen Poles and Jews, who would raise the money and gratefully vote for him. The British were, in fact, in no position to risk firing on US ships going to 'neutral ports' [in this case a US zone of Danzig]. The American enclave in Danzig is nominally US soil and thus neutral. In OTL British took US ships into British ports to inspect for blockade compliance. In this ATL FDR does not allow this. Disputing this, and thus risking war with the US, is something the Cabinet would have sacked Churchill over.

Imperial Way – Japanese Army faction advocating war against the Soviets.

Iron Division – a post-WW1 Freikorps that operated in the Baltic states nominally on behalf of Germany, the Whites, and, at times, the Latvian Government. It was one of a grouping of similar such collections of embittered veterans and freebooters. Sometimes combat-effective, but other times acted like a bandit gang out of the Thirty Years' War.

Iron Guard – Romanian far-right movement. Also called the Legion of the Archangel Michael and the Green Shirts. Extreme nationalists, populists, anti-capitalists, anti-Communists, anti-Semites. Used by and made use of the ruling Romanian royalists and military reactionaries. Fanatic Orthodox Christians. They were ultra-violent, emphasized action over ideas, and prone to spontaneous outbreaks against Jews and the ruling Romanian classes. Think chaotic evil with a strong emphasis on chaotic. Even other right-wingers, such as the local Nazis, thought they were unstable and violent. In OTL, Gestapo found their pogroms to be revolting overkill.

Indian National Congress – the political vehicle of Gandhi in particular and Indian nationalism in general. In theory somewhat socialist. In practice it ran the gamut from bourgeois nationalist to quite radical. In theory it was above caste, religion, and region. In practice most of the Muslims split off to form Muslim League. Congress's strength was highest in the Hindi-speaking north, but the party was resolutely secularist. In theory rigidly non-violent. In practice that was Gandhi, not Congress; and the struggle between the two paths continued down to independence day.

Jewish Agency – the Zionist parallel government during the period of the British mandate. Although the organization was big tent to the point of including Jewish philanthropic organizations with no interest in political Zionism, it was in practice controlled by what is now the Israeli Labor Party. Formal party names in Israel get tricksy. There has been an endless process of factional splits, short term coalitions and similar. Short form is that Labor covers what we now call secular liberals and socialists including some, but not all, Marxists. Revisionists were blood and soil nationalists who refused to be bound by non-violence. General Zionists were moderates and mostly in favor of some level of capitalism. The modern Likud is a fusion of the Revisionists and most of the General Zionists. Sort of. Tricksy.

Kenpeitai – police arm of the IJA; functioned both as conventional MP's, and also performed intelligence and black operations functions in the various conquered territories and satellite states (and a limited domestic internal-security role in Japan itself).

KG – Kampfgruppe. Battle group, usually combined arms. The Germans were the best of the WW2 armies at fighting as combined-arms task forces, and getting the different components to actually work together.

KMT – Kuomintang. The main successful Chinese nationalist movement of the 20th century. By Western standards its ideology was all over the lot. Governed more or less continually from mid 1920's to 1949. A party of the same name and claiming descent from it is one of the two major parties of modern Taiwan but the linkage is mostly mythic.

Kreis – county or district. The next level of political entity below Gau. The leader was a Kreisleiter.

Kripo – *Kriminalpolizei* - the national criminal police under the Himmler/Heydrich reorganizations of the 30's. In US terms, the FBI minus the counterintelligence function.

LAH – Hitler's life guards. Originally personal bodyguards, they expanded to headquarters guards, and then a hit squad for the Blood Purge. The original members were chosen for size and physique. This changed when the unit went to war in 1939. Over time, it just became an elite SS mechanized unit. Had a bad record of prisoner murders, but never got the rep for it that the 3rd SS Death's Head division did. This is the unit that perpetrated the 1944 Malmedy Massacre of US prisoners in the Bulge.

Livret militaire – French military identity papers

Luftwaffe – the German Air Force

Mapai – Ben Gurion's party circa 1940. A mix of socialists, social democrats and patronage clients. Mapai dominated the Jewish Agency and the Labor Federation. Life was easier if one were seen as a member. Evolves into the Labor Party. As noted above, such lineages in Israeli politics are tricksy. Ben Gurion's personal faction was one of the founding blocks in the original creation of Likud. Left and returned to that block for personalist and factional reasons. This Rafi faction's better known personages were Dayan and Shimon Peres.

Movement – the Nazi Party, speaking broadly to cover all its attached organizations. The Party/state overlap is confusing for many Anglophones, in part because it tended to chaotic/overlapping authority. One could be a believer in the Movement even while despising the formal Party for its petty tyrannies and bureaucratic absurdities.

Muslim Brotherhood – pan-Islamic movement founded in Egypt in 1928. Had above ground and underground components. The ideology was reactionary theocracy. The organizational structure including the above ground social and charitable network was quite modern. Their paramilitaries in Egypt were al-Tanzim al-Khass.

Muslim League / All-India Muslim League – the Muslim minority's counter to Congress. A pure democracy of all India meant that Congress rules forever based on a rural Hindi speaking Hindu block vote. Originally supposed to be the four Muslim majority provinces of India's northwest, it loses focus trying to rope in Bengal.

Nibelungen Legion – NL; new Party Militia fictionally created in this series.

Night Squads/Special Night Squads – mixed British and Palestinian Jewish counter terror organization during the 1936-1939 Arab Revolt. Protected the Kirkuk pipeline in part by preemptive night attacks on Arab villages deemed as bases for insurgents. It worked by making the villagers more scared of the Night Squads than they were of the partisans. The success frightened the British, who banished its commander Orde Wingate from Palestine, and stood down the Jews, using them only as static guards.

NKVD – Soviets went through multiple rounds of re-namings and reorganizations of their security forces back to Lenin's original Cheka. For this period, the main designation is NKVD. I avoided burdening readers with the variant sister organizations and plan to continue to do so. They will all be NKVD. For current readers, think KGB/FSB.

Nürnberg Rallies – annual Nazi national gatherings (1923–1938). In Nürnberg from 1927. Largest reached a bit under a million participants. Elaborately staged and filmed for propaganda purposes and to inspire awe among its participants.

OKH – Army (Heer) High Command

OKW – Armed Forces High Command. In 1940, still a small planning staff serving as an adjunct to Hitler's personal headquarters. In OTL, becomes a parallel OKH, handling all theaters of war other than the Eastern Front and the Replacement Army.

Ordnungspolizei – Order police. Other names Orpo and the Green Police [from the uniforms]. In 1936 Himmler unified and nationalized the various state and municipal police forces as well as firemen. In US terms included all uniformed first responders such as coast guard and air raid wardens as well. Starting with the Polish war and occupation, battalions of these were mobilized for field service {antipartian and occupation duties which in OTL came to include ethnic cleansing of Jews etc.).

OTL – our time line. History as we know it.

Panhard 178 – French armored car. The design was good enough to stay in service into the 1960's.

Pawiak Prison: Famous Warsaw men's prison taken over by Gestapo on occupation, 1939. The assault on the Warsaw Ghetto was staged from here.

Polish Blue Police – Polish police under the General Government. Completely penetrated by Home Army.

Polish Home Army – the Germans overran Poland in 1939, but the Poles set up a parallel state to preserve their authority for their supposed liberation by the West. The military branch, the Home Army, was dominant, but not outside civilian control, both within Poland and from the exile government in London.

*P*utzfrau – cleaning lady

Quit India Movement – in OTL happens in 1942. Congress turns on the British and the war. Demand immediate independence and British evacuation. In this series happens two years earlier and much more violently. With Bose waging a parallel people's-war campaign of bombs and assassinations, Nehru and the other secularist/realist Congress leaders are willing to push back more against Gandhi's utopian ideals.

Race Laws – the Nürnberg Race Laws were a series of laws designed to remove the Jews (and other undesirable-by-Nazi-criteria minorities) from German social and economic life. The specific subpart that will come up in this series are the rules on "race-mixing". Sex between Aryans and non-Aryans was banned, with punishments including possible use of the death penalty. Needless to say, the rules were more likely to be applied when the Aryan was female. From 1938, there were a parallel, but less extreme, group of laws in Italy. Italy will repudiate it in this series over time, and in OTL never enforced their Race Laws with German rigidity or enthusiasm.

Ravensbrück – Concentration Camp some 80 kilometers north of Berlin, founded to house female inmates. A hellhole late in the war in OTL. Most of the camps imploded in the period from late 1944 to war's end from a mix of lack of resources, fantastic overcrowding as inmates from camps about to be overrun were death-marched to new camps deeper in the interior, and the guard forces being increasingly from the ever-diminishing portion of the German people who were still fanatic regime supporters. At this point [1940] the inmates were mostly German women, with Poles as a secondary population. The Germans were mostly a mix of prostitutes, Jehovah's Witnesses/Bible Girls, and rebellious young girls down to tween ages (what we would today call "minors in need of supervision" rather than actual juvenile criminals). The Poles were a mix of religious orders and politicals. The Jehovah's Witnesses [and similar small Protestant pacifist sects] were political-oppositional, but completely non-violent about it - thus tending to get the best treatment when confined, as they were easy prisoners to deal with.

Razvedrota – intelligence/reconnaissance units of 1940 Red Army. A regiment would have a company of these. Somewhat elite.

Red Tory – a faction of the British Conservative (Tory) Party who advocated radical reforms. Think of them as national socialists, but without the extreme racialism or tendency to extralegal violence.

Red November – the revolts against the Kaiser and war that overthrew the monarchy and led to the German surrender. Supposedly a conspiracy of Marxists, Jews, and traitors that stabbed in the back a still-victorious Germany army and people (this is the right-wing and nationalist myth, started originally by Ludendorff). The professional naval officers felt special shame for this, as the trigger was the mutiny of the High Seas Fleet. The naval officers had planned a suicide death sortie. Their crews were not of similar mind, and a series of acts of disobedience culminated in the November 3rd, 1918 mutiny of the fleet under Communist leadership. These red sailors were a major feature of the immediate postwar chaos in Berlin and northern Germany. The naval officer corps regarded this as a matter of personal dishonor to their caste and institution. Hence they created a new navy dedicated to creating a new mythos of an ultra-loyal, ultra-nationalist Fleet. Raeder was extreme but hardly unique in these views.

Reichsführer – fancy rank invented for Himmler as supreme leader of SS and police.

Reichsmarschall – fancy rank Göring invented and got Hitler to give him, so he would out-rank Army and Air Force Field Marshals.

Reichstag – German parliament of the Weimar and Nazi eras.

Reichswehr – the interwar German army of the Weimar years.

Royal Carabinieri – Italian paramilitary service. I n US terms, they had both police and military functions. Extremely loyal to the Crown.

RSHA – *Reichssicherheitshauptamt* - Reich Main Security Office - a composite organization of all police and security forces of both the German state and Nazi Party.

SA – Original Nazi Party militia. Somewhat open question of whether they are part of the Nazi Party or allied to it. Leadership liquidated by 1934 Blood Purge. Vestigial after that, but still had hundreds of thousands of members in 1940. Blood Purge also settled their subordination to Nazi Party. Had a deserved reputation for disorderly, violent behavior. Also tended to be populist/second revolution types.

Schnell – literally fast. Mixed units of motorcyclists, autos, truck mounted forces sometimes with armored cars or tankettes but rarely have real tanks or assault guns.

SD – *Sicherheitsdienst* - Nazi Party intelligence service. Founded by Heydrich.

Second Revolution – from the beginning, the Nazis always had a radical wing that took seriously the socialist part of the Party name of "National Socialist". Pressure for a second, populist revolution was one of the causes of the 1934 Blood Purge. In OTL, this was then suppressed until after the 1944 Bomb Plot. Comes back to the forefront in the short year between that and final defeat.

Sonderverband – literally special operations unit. Think of it as an ad hoc force of battalion to regimental size.

SS – A split-off from the SA. Always subordinate to Hitler and the Party. Often higher social class/ better educated than the SA. After the Blood Purge, the main defenders of the regime.

SS House – Prinz-Albrecht-Straße. The top floor of # 8 was Himmler's (subsequently Schellenberg's) office; Heydrich SD/RSHA HQ was in the Palais itself – in the ATL, he chooses to keep his office there. With several adjacent buildings, they formed a complex in which SS, SD, Gestapo, RSHA, etc. were based.

Stalhelm – the street militia of the Weimar Era Nationalist Party. Like the SA, also an illegal reserve for Reichswehr.

Tante Ju – nickname for Junkers Ju 52/3m transport plane.

TUC/Trades Union Conference – Labor federation of England and Wales, NOT the entire UK or British Empire. Technically separate from the Labor Party.

TVA – Tennessee Valley Authority. A government agency that provided power and socioeconomic development to the Tennessee Valley. The idea was of public dams to provide cheap electricity for a backward multistate region grouped around the middle and upper Tennessee river valley. This had been a US progressive dream. It took the Great Depression to make this sort of public ownership popular enough to get the law passed and the dams funded. The TVA generated a lot of electrical power, but like most New Deal projects had a fair number of pie-in-the-sky nostrums it also unsuccessfully backed. Wendell Willkie was attorney and then chief executive of the private power company the TVA put out of business. This public fight was what led Willkie to become a Republican for the 1940 election. The TVA power plants also in OTL provided the massive power needed by the nuclear facilities at Oak Ridge. So in a sense the TVA makes the Manhattan Project successful on a time scale that mattered for the war. As is, the A-bomb barely arrived in time to prevent the invasion of Japan, which would have been a bloodbath of biblical proportions.

Volksdeutsche – Germans by race or culture, but not citizens of the German Reich. It was Nazi policy to ingather these large populations of "Germans" to the Reich. The problem was defining who was such a "German". Of most interest in this series is the Class 5 "Germanizable Elements". This was a quite flexible term, although OTL's Nazis did not in fact use much flexibility before 1944 (by which time the war was lost). Here, Heydrich takes a more expansive path.

Wafd – Egyptian bourgeois nationalist party. They desired to get the British to leave, and replace the monarchy with something more modern. They were divided on whether that should be parliamentary, or autocratic in the Italian mold. Their militant youth wing were the Blue Shirts. The other revolutionaries saw the Wafd as sellouts because they would do short term deals with the British and the throne. The Wafd, for their part, saw the Muslim Brotherhood and Young Egypt Movement as hopeless idealists unable to play the political game. There is a large element of truth in both appraisals. It took WW2 to weaken the British enough to make evicting them in one try feasible.

Walking Around Money – the US term of art for cash spread around on election day to get people to the polls. It was how the local influentials and precinct workers got paid beyond petty graft.

Wehrmacht – the German armed forces as a whole – Heer, Kriegsmarine, Luftwaffe

Wehrmachtbericht – Daily military bulletin. Getting individual mention was a high honor; equivalent to the British military's "Mentioned in dispatches."

Western Desert Force – Corps-sized British field force in Egypt west of Alexandria summer 1940. In

OTL they pull off stupendous victories against the Italian 10th Army. Here the battle goes otherwise.

World Peace League – this ATL's above-ground front for the remaining Communists, now that the party has been outlawed over the sinking of US ships starting with *Langley* and *Reuben James*.

Wrangel's White Army – White/Monarchist/Anti-Communist Army in South Russia 1919-1920. Wrangel was successor to Denekin. Ivan Gorlov served with these two and several of their predecessors.

Young Egypt Party – more radical nationalist counterpart to the Wafd. Their youth militants were the Green Shirts. Think of them as religious-tinged Egyptian pseudo-fascists. Into politics of the deed, street fighting, and assassinations. Their strength was their militancy. Their weakness was their obsession with action over organization.

9 781938 339479